MANGO HILL

MANGO HILL

PATRICIA SHAW

headline

First published in 2007
by HEADLINE PUBLISHING GROUP

1

Cataloguing in Publication Data is available from the British Library

Hardback 978 0 7553 2928 1
Trade paperback 978 0 7553 2929 8

Typeset in Bembo by Avon DataSet Ltd,
Bidford-on-Avon, Warwickshire

Printed and bound in Great Britain by
Clays Ltd, St Ives plc

Headline's policy is to use papers that are natural, renewable and recyclable
products and made from wood grown in sustainable forests. The logging
and manufacturing processes are expected to conform to the environmental
regulations of the country of origin.

HEADLINE PUBLISHING GROUP
A division of Hachette Livre UK Ltd
338 Euston Road
London NW1 3BH

www.headline.co.uk
www.hodderheadline.com

PLANT A TREE

Queensland

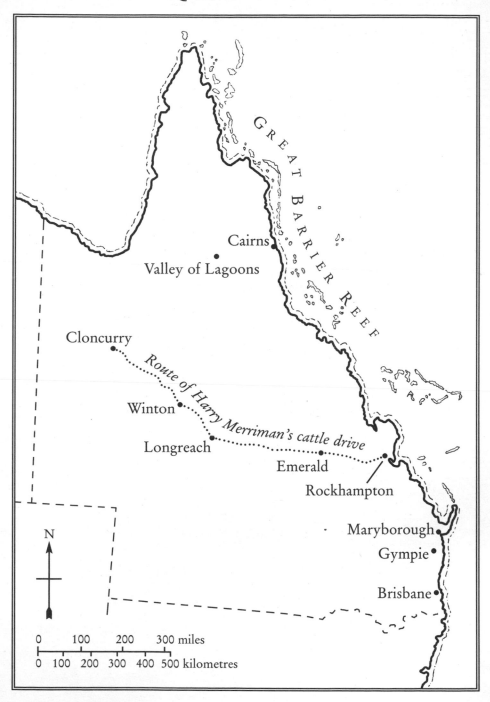

Great Barrier Reef

Cairns

Valley of Lagoons

Cloncurry

Route of Harry Merriman's cattle drive

Winton

Longreach

Emerald

Rockhampton

Maryborough

Gympie

Brisbane

N

| 0 | 100 | 200 | 300 miles |

| 0 | 100 | 200 | 300 | 400 | 500 kilometres |

PROLOGUE

1884

She was about nineteen years old, a lean, muscular woman with wiry black hair drawn back from a strong, angular face, and she had a baby in a sling across her back. She wore a ragged shirt, dusty dungarees and a fringed shawl, but no boots, the usual mismatch foisted on Aborigine women thrust into the white world.

Despite her odd appearance, she carried herself well, striding steadily towards the three horsemen with a confidence that startled them, though her voice was gentle.

She addressed Paul. 'You maybe boss man here, eh?'

He stared down at her, astonished at the serenity in her dark eyes, feeling as if he'd suddenly come upon a benign force.

'What do you want?' he stammered.

'Come find uncle in that place!' She pointed in the direction of the blacks' camp, located near the western boundary of Mango Hill Station. 'Him old fella, allasame call Guringja.'

'Hey! Look out, boss!' called Sam, reaching down for his rifle. 'Look over there!'

'Jesus wept!' blurted Noah, the other stockman.

Not more than thirty yards away from them, a huge Aborigine warrior in full ceremonial dress was standing on an elevated rocky ledge. His hair was piled high and decorated with plumes of cockatoo feathers. His coal-black face, with a bone through the nose, was striped with white paint, and tufts of black hair jutted from his jaw. His powerful body was daubed with paint as if outlining the bone structure, and he wore ankle bands of white feathers.

'Steady,' murmured Paul, looking warily at the tall spear the black man had jammed firmly in front of him as if he were throwing down a challenge. He turned to the woman. 'Who's he?'

'That my husbin,' she said proudly, her eyes glistening. 'He brung me here. For safe.'

Paul frowned. None of the blacks on this property were hostile, and they certainly did not march about got up like this fellow. Their war days were long gone.

'You go,' he said to her. 'I don't want either of you here. You don't belong with our mob. Go back to your own mob, and take him with you.' He jerked his head at the husband.

The woman drew an arc in the dust with her toe, and studied it for a few minutes as if deciding what to do.

Sam patted his rifle. 'Do you want me to show the big feller the gate, boss?'

The woman looked at Paul. 'My husbin he go way now. He bring me long walk.'

'Good. You go with him. You can't stay here.'

She seemed not to have heard him. She hitched the baby higher and began to walk up the track towards the homestead.

Paul gazed uncertainly at the husband, who was watching them, and then back at the woman.

'Whoa!' he called. 'Come on back here. I told you. You don't belong here. What mob are you?'

'Kalkadoon!' she said, head high.

'Never heard of them.'

'Yes you have,' Noah reminded him. 'They're the mob Duke talked about. They hail from the back country. Plenty trouble too. Do you reckon they're coming this way now?'

'What? An army of two? Turn it up!' Paul called after the woman: 'You come back now. You and your husband, out! Do you hear me?'

She turned and looked up at him, tears welling on to her grimy cheeks. 'He gone, boss.'

Her grief confused Paul. His horse reared suddenly, spooking the other mounts and causing them to back away, bumping into one another. As he dragged at the reins to keep his horse in check, he saw old Guringja wobbling down the track with the aid of a stout stick and his two wives.

'The big bloke's disappeared,' Sam said, pulling his mount into line. 'I'd better go and round him up.'

'He gone,' the woman insisted. She ran towards Guringja, babbling in her own language.

'What's she saying, Sadie?' Paul asked one of Guringja's wives.

Sadie shrugged. 'Doan know that talk.'

Eventually Guringja explained. 'She Kalkadoon. Her name Wiradji. My mumma Kalkadoon so she kin of me. Big trouble where she comen from so she come here for safe with babba.'

'What about her husband?' Paul asked. 'I'm not having him here.'

Guringja's eyes seemed to flatten. 'No husbin, boss.'

'Don't give me that! He's lurking over there somewhere. She knows he's here.'

'Ah! Dat no one, boss. No one.'

'She said he was her husband,' Sam growled at him. 'I heard her.'

Paul turned to Sadie. 'You saw him when you were walking down here, didn't you? You must have . . .'

She shook her head and trudged over to the woman. 'Where your husbin?'

'He gone,' Wiradji replied sadly.

'Gone where?' Paul demanded, but Guringja grabbed Sadie's arm. He whispered something to her and the men saw her dark face blanch.

'Mr Paul,' she said quietly, 'better we take her longa camp, eh?'

'Not until I know where her husband's got to! I won't have him hanging about.'

Sadie sighed and walked over to Paul. She patted his horse gently and spoke so softly he had to lean down to hear her.

'No husbin here. Him fight big war. Got killt dead. She still makin' crying time.'

'What? Bloody rubbish! He was here! We saw him!'

Sadie lowered her eyes and scratched the back of her neck, obviously anxious not to discuss this any further.

Inadvertently Paul scratched the back of his own neck, maybe for the same reason. The hairs there felt like needles, and a shudder ran through him. For a minute he was at a complete loss to decide what to do.

Noah shifted uneasily in his saddle. 'Are they trying to tell us that blackfeller wasn't there?'

'No,' Paul said. 'It's just their usual double talk.'

'Where has he gone anyway?'

'I don't know!' Paul said crankily. 'He's just gone. Let me know if you spot him again.'

He nodded to the little group of Aborigines. 'Go on then. Take her up to your camp. She looks as if she needs a good feed.'

As the three horsemen rode away, Sam laughed. 'If Noah ever sights that husband feller again, you won't see him for dust!'

'What about you?' Paul asked.

Sam shrugged. 'Me? I never saw no one.'

CHAPTER ONE

Brisbane, 1878

Intrigued by the occasion, the crowds stood stoically outside St Stephen's Cathedral on this hot and humid morning, breathing air drenched with the perfume of frangipani. Normally the buttery white blooms would have a lighter scent, more refined, but the low-set tree near the arched entrance to the cathedral had grown into a large and splendid specimen, almost vulgar in its profusion of delicate flowers. The residents of this newly acclaimed northern city were proud of the tree, along with the tall palms, flamboyant purple jacarandas and massive Moreton Bay figs that shaded their streets, despite the fact that nature in this sub-tropical location seemed a little 'too much', as genteel newcomers were wont to say behind their fans, disassociating themselves from earlier settlers who had known the district as the infamous Moreton Bay penal settlement.

Ah yes. Not the most prestigious of foundations. But when that establishment was closed down, and the site renamed Brisbane, it had begun to blossom into respectability.

The streets were regally named after English kings in one direction and queens in the other: Elizabeth – which boasted the cathedral – Charlotte, and so forth. Botanic gardens had been founded along the banks of the wide river, while proud public buildings like Parliament House and the stately museum added dignity.

The rich squatters who had arrived early enough to grasp huge tracts of land for sheep runs had always been the elite of the Australian colonies, but in Brisbane another powerful group was emerging. They were the cattlemen, pushing their herds northwards into the wild and mostly unexplored colony of Queensland.

Seafarers, watchful of the reefs that guarded the shores of this colony, estimated that the coastline ran to more than a staggering three thousand miles, and what lay beyond had been a mystery until Leichhardt, the German explorer, told of great plains well watered by a succession of fine rivers.

'A land of plenty, and plenty for all,' was the cry, and a rush was on, halted

very suddenly in its tracks by the discovery that the owners of these boun-
teous pastures were unwilling to move on, and were in fact downright savage
in their attitude to trespassers.

But the ambitious white settlers did not regard themselves as trespassers.

'There are no houses, no towns,' they said. 'No one lives here, so it's ours for
the taking.'

When it was pointed out that people did live there, Aborigine people, they
answered: 'No they don't. They're just nomads. There are no boundaries and
there aren't even any villages.'

This particular river area was the meeting place of three nations, Undangi,
Jagaro and Jukambe, and their various associated clans. To them the boundaries
of the nations were as clear as day, and the laws regarding them had to be
respected. No one in his right mind would enter another's territory without
invitation or permission. It was a very dangerous thing to do and could cause
nasty repercussions. When the white men came blundering in, the same rules
applied. There were paybacks.

But the white men kept coming, with their amazing weaponry. They were
simply 'opening up the land'.

The Aborigines had another name for these operations. They called them
war.

Not far from the cathedral, not too long ago, in front of the GPO to be
exact, the hero of the Aborigines' resistance, Dundalli, was hanged. In
retaliation, the blackfellows killed Captain Logan, the commandant of the
penal settlement, though that was not a bad thing, according to the convicts
who had suffered under his merciless reign and regarded the man as nothing
less than a vicious monster.

Then the war moved on, moved north and west with the tide of settlers and
was mostly forgotten in Brisbane, but it did come to mind for Milly Forrest,
who was in the crowd outside the cathedral with her daughter Lucy Mae.
They were here to attend the funeral service of their dear friend Dolour
Rivadavia.

An emotional woman, Milly dabbed at her eyes as she recalled Dolour's first
husband, Pace MacNamara, who'd been murdered by blacks in the far north.
That friendship went back a long way, she reflected sadly. Pace had voyaged
to the colony on the same ship as Milly and her late husband Dermott, all
three of them young and eager to start new lives.

She gave a half sob. They'd all done well too. In cattle, of all things. First as
station managers, then with their own properties. But in the beginning,
outback country life had been hard for a little English girl like Milly, who'd
not ventured beyond the outskirts of Manchester until her beloved Dermott
had swept her off her feet and brought her out to this strange world.

It was Dolour, a feisty Irishwoman, who'd taught her to stand up for herself,

Milly recalled. And it was Dolour who was there to help when she and Dermott were struggling. Poor Dermott. Only two years back, when everything was going so well for them, when they'd retired to their lovely house overlooking the river, he'd been struck down by diphtheria, and within weeks had breathed his last breath.

Milly sighed. Still getting over the shock, she told herself. And then Lucy Mae's husband, that scoundrel Bartling, had drowned in a shipwreck off Fraser Island. He was no loss, but she'd been devastated to hear that Dolour was dying of the dreaded cancer.

'Shouldn't we go in?' Lucy Mae said.

'Not yet,' Milly hissed. She wanted to wait and see who'd come; you'd miss too much sitting in the family pews at the front with your back to the congregation.

Juan Rivadavia was a leading citizen in this country these days. A cattle man from Argentina, he'd come here many years ago and immediately set about buying properties. Milly had always liked him – he was absolutely charming, no doubt about that – but she'd been surprised when Dolour had married him so soon after Pace's death.

'Who's that?' Lucy Mae asked, as a carriage pulled in and a young woman wearing a mantle of black lace instead of a hat stepped down.

'Dolour's stepdaughter, Rosa,' Milly replied, as people about her surged forward to get a better look at this darling of the society pages, where she was often referred to as 'the Spanish beauty', with airy disregard for her Argentinian parentage. 'That's her husband, Charlie Palliser. He's a famous surgeon.'

Lucy Mae signed. 'What a beautiful gown. So elegant!'

'Imported!' her mother commented as she cast her eyes over Lucy Mae's outfit. 'You could do with a new black. That dress is too loose on you. It doesn't give you any shape.'

'I've lost weight since Russ died.'

'You look better for it. We'll go shopping tomorrow.'

Milly watched Rosa Palliser pluck a frangipani bloom, take in the scent, then toss it away as she entered the cathedral with her husband.

'Typical,' she snorted.

'What is?'

'Nothing. Oh dear, here comes Juan.'

Milly watched as Rivadavia hurried up the steps, head down, acknowledging no one. He looked tired and drawn, she thought, but just as suave and handsome as ever. That Dolour, she smiled, you had to hand it to her: she married two of the nicest men in town. And the two best-looking in their day. And her just a little Irish convict girl. Few knew that, though Dolour wouldn't have cared if they did. She was her own person, thought Milly, my word she was.

There was another surge in the crowd as the Governor's carriage arrived. One of the liveried footmen sitting atop jumped down to place a footstool by the door to assist the Governor, the Marquis of Normanby, and his lady wife to step from the ornate carriage down to earth.

Someone clapped and was frowned upon by the Marchioness as they progressed up the short path. Her husband, sweat trickling from his florid face under his large plumed hat, hurried her along, but already interest had swerved to a gentleman who'd come dashing across the road.

'I told you everyone who's anyone would be here today,' Milly said, nudging her daughter as the Premier of Queensland approached, handshaking the lucky front-rowers. When he came to Milly, he stopped.

'Well, God spare me days! It's you, Mrs Forrest. What are you doing out here in the heat?'

'Um, waiting, Mr Palmer,' Milly stammered. 'It's so difficult. The crowds . . . We were just about to . . . You know my daughter Lucy Mae?'

'Yes, of course. Mrs Bartling! Now come along, ladies. I'll escort you in myself.'

Just then the MacNamaras, John Pace and Paul, arrived with their families and several friends, and they were all caught up in a muddle of sorrowful greetings at the door. Eventually they filtered into the scent-laden gloom of the cathedral, where the Premier, Sir Arthur Palmer, charged off with Lucy Mae on his arm.

Milly was rather taken aback. It was then that she saw the coffin, covered in wreaths with stands of candles on either side, and it hit her! That was Dolour! That was her friend!

She burst into tears, sobbing uncontrollably as she stumbled into the arms of a gentleman nearby. She wept even more when she recognised Duke MacNamara, Dolour's youngest son and the spitting image of his father!

The choir began to sing: 'Faith of our fathers . . .'

'Oh! I'm sorry, Duke,' Milly cried. 'Perhaps I'd better go outside. I'll just upset everyone.'

'No, Milly, it's all right. We'll help each other get through this. Would you walk down with me? I'm sure Mother would like that.'

His words almost sent her off into another paroxysm of grief, but she took a deep breath and kept control as he offered her his arm.

Turning, she saw more people hurrying into the cathedral and moving out to the side aisles, and then, just for a second, she spotted a familiar figure silhouetted against the light in the open doorway.

Milly Forrest almost tripped when the realisation of who it was came to her.

'Good Lord!' she said, leaning heavily on Duke.

'Are you all right?' he asked.

'Yes,' she said, embarrassed. These days she had what was known as an ample figure. No lightweight. 'Yes thank you, Duke.'

When they took their places she did not dare twist round to make sure. The cathedral was packed anyway. And she really didn't need to. She knew who it was. The cheek of him! Heselwood! Lord bloody Heselwood!

Streaming through a pane of stained glass, the sun seemed to be aimed deliberately into the eyes of Charlie Palliser, who was sitting in the front pew with his wife, his father and his father-in-law Juan Rivadavia. He was fretting, certain that his late mother was deliberately trying to blind him, because he couldn't escape the sharp rays no matter which was he leaned his head. Punishment, he supposed, for throwing in his lot with foreigners. There had been no logic to her fear of foreigners of any description, so she had been extremely upset when he'd broken it to her that he intended to marry the daughter of Juan Rivadavia.

'That foreigner!' she'd cried, aghast.

His father, Duncan, had mollified her somewhat by explaining that Rosa was only half a foreigner, her mother being a titled Englishwoman. It took time, and constant persuasion for the formidable Dora Palliser to receive Miss Rivadavia, though on the day in question she seated herself across the room at a safe distance from her guest. Fortunately Rosa's charm got Charlie through the nerve-wracking encounter. The best that could be said of Dora, in this situation, Charlie reflected, blinking, was that she finally agreed to endure her younger son's choice of bride.

But the problem with his mother hadn't been half as traumatic as the time he'd told his father that he had decided to study medicine at Sydney University. He was living at home then, on their head station by the Darling River, and at first Duncan hadn't understood. He was a rugged country man who'd started on the lowest peg in the cattle business, working for years as a stockman on an outback property, where all he owned was a horse and a rifle. But he'd loved the life and the everyday challenges of station work.

'I don't know where you'll find time to do that,' he'd said. 'You're sixteen now. I've been waiting for you to leave school. I want you to get out and run the Blackbutt Station. That clown of a manager is losing too many cattle in the scrub and your brother hasn't got time to sort him out. You can take some stockmen out there, get rid of him and do a muster. Find out what's going on. It's my bet the bastard's been selling them himself.'

'Do you want me to stay on there?'

'Why don't you listen? I said I want you to run it, not drift in, do a count and wander off.'

Charlie shuddered, recalling the explosion when he explained that he had already enrolled in a medical college in Sydney.

His mother had come running. 'What's all this noise about?'

'Him!' Duncan had shouted. 'And it's all your fault. Putting ideas in his head. Sending him off to that fancy school. Now look at him! Wanting to go back and learn how to be a bloody doctor. He doesn't mind the money the stations bring in, does he? But he won't lift a finger to contribute.'

She'd tried to calm him. 'I think we should consider it. Give the idea a few days. We'll think about it for a while.'

'I don't need to think about it!' Duncan roared. 'I know what's at the bottom of this and don't either of you try to deny it. He doesn't like work. Why can't he get into it like Langley does? And like I do? I've had to work hard all my life, and glad to do it, to get ahead in the world. But not him, he's a taker . . .'

'Now you know that's not true, Duncan,' she'd said. But as he listened to them arguing, Charlie knew his father was right, to a certain extent. Life on a cattle station was hard work, day in and day out. Their stations were so huge, the men had to camp out several nights a week to cover the territory. Charlie had often gone out to work with them, once his father had considered he was strong enough to handle a stock horse, and as a youngster he had enjoyed himself, but the novelty had been worn down by the heat and dust and the surprisingly cold nights in the open, as well as having to swallow greasy camp stews thrown together by men too tired to fuss about quality as long as there was enough for all.

Langley had always looked out for his younger brother, and this time he didn't let him down, arguing that Charlie had a right to please himself in what he did. But in the end it was their mother who saved the day. She talked Duncan around, and even suggested that as soon as Charlie finished the course and became a real doctor, he could come back home and help out. Her reasoning astonished Charlie. She seemed to think that medicine sat quite well with veterinary work. He didn't enlighten her, and he was amused to find that from the first day he entered medical school, she referred to him as Dr Palliser.

'Ah well.' Duncan shrugged. 'Rosa will own a string of cattle stations when Rivadavia passes on. So will you when I kick the bucket. I suppose the two of you will sell up and let all our good work go for nothing.'

'Don't start that again. You ought to be pleased. You'll have grandchildren to pick up the reins. Anyway, Rosa might be his only daughter, but he has three stepsons, and they're in the cattle business too.'

'And who might they be?'

'The MacNamaras.'

'Where from?'

'Kooramin Station and Oberon up north. And they've got other runs, I believe.'

'You don't mean Pace MacNamara's sons?'

'Yes. I think so. Juan married his widow.'

'God Almighty! So he did. Now you listen to me, Charlie. You're getting into a hornets' nest there. Pace had enemies. He crossed a few influential characters in his time. I knew him; he wasn't a bad feller, always on the hunt for land, but he pushed his luck. Went too far too soon. Rivadavia has probably told you about that.'

Charlie could see from his father's smug raised eyebrows that he'd guessed Juan had not.

'Why would he? It's not important, whatever it was.'

'Maybe not,' Duncan said. 'But you take a word from the wise: I'd give this a lot more thought. Get to know one another better. There's no rush, is there?'

'No, except I love her, and she loves me.'

Duncan reached for his pipe and began stuffing it with tobacco. 'You don't think she might be a bit hi-falutin for us?'

Charlie was stung into anger. 'What do you mean?'

'I can read. I see her in the papers. She's a high stepper, you have to grant that. Always about here and there. In our day people who had their picture in the paper were either common or criminals.'

'Oh for crying out loud! What other logs can you throw on the road? I'm going; I'll come back when you're in a better mood.'

The funeral service, a requiem mass, was interminable. The cathedral felt like a steam bath, and Charlie's stiff collar was too tight. Rosa, by his side, was fanning herself, and on his other side Duncan was probably regretting his kind decision to attend – the second time he'd graced St Stephen's with his presence.

The congregation stood, and Charlie hoped it was to depart, but more ceremony followed, and then a hearty hymn.

Rosa whispered to him: 'I'm feeling faint. I have to go outside for air.'

He clasped her hand. 'I'll come with you.'

'No, no, no. Don't fuss.'

'Are you sure you'll be all right?'

'Yes, of course.'

She kissed him on the cheek and slipped out through a side door. It occurred to Charlie that she might be pregnant, and he hummed along with the hymn, his heart full of joy.

As she stepped outside, Rosa put a hand on the cool stone wall to steady herself for a few minutes, relieved to feel her head clearing. This pain had begun earlier, when her maid had brought flowers into the breakfast room. She'd immediately begun sneezing and snuffling, and when the headache developed, Charlie had brought her a draught that had dulled it a little.

Normally she wasn't prone to headaches, but she'd worked out that acacia plants were the villains of the piece, and tried to avoid them.

She sighed and walked into the side garden, hoping there were no acacias loitering here, and along the shaded path towards the front of the cathedral. The mass was almost over now, so they'd be coming out and the tears would start all over again.

Rosa had liked Dolour, more so than Delia, her own mother, who had not been able to cope with this climate, or with station life. An English gentle-woman, she'd left Juan and returned home, taking Rosa with her. But she'd always been difficult to please, and was determined to be unhappy; her letters to Juan were a litany of complaints. Finally she'd written that she could not be expected to bring up a ten-year-old girl on her own – though Juan had seen to it that she had a lovely home in Kensington and wanted for nothing.

Rosa still suffered from bouts of anxiety that emanated from the day she heard her mother tell the housekeeper that she could no longer bear the wretched child mooning about the house.

'I'm simply not well enough,' Delia had explained. 'I'm a frail person, anyone can see that. I cannot abide noise of any sort. I'm sending her off to her father. I want you to take her.'

'Where to, madam?' the woman asked fearfully.

'To Argentina, of course!'

'Oh no, madam, I couldn't do that!' the woman shrieked. 'I'm not knowing where is such a place.'

She threw her apron over her face and dashed from the room. Rosa wished she had an apron to throw over her own face, which was glowing red with humiliation. She peered into her mother's boudoir. She had always loved it: a rainbow room of coloured satin pillows, embroidered, beaded and pleated, large and small, scattered everywhere – on the bed, the chaise, the big plump armchair, banked up high on the window seat and even thrown willy-nilly about the floor.

Delia was seated at her dressing table, her long hair brushed down over her shoulders.

'What do you want?' she called.

Rosa scowled. She was never allowed in this room, so she called back: 'I don't want to go to Argentina.'

'Of course you don't. You never want to do anything you're told.'

'I do so. How long would I have to stay there?'

Delia waved a white-gloved hand. 'I don't know. That's up to your father.'

'What if he doesn't want me either?'

'Then he'll probably send you back.' Delia yawned. 'For heaven's sake, stop nagging me. Tell that woman I'll have tea now, and a boiled egg.'

'What woman?' Often Rosa took revenge on her vague mother by pretending not to understand instructions.

'The person who just left here.'

'What person?'

'Oh, any person, you stupid girl!'

'I'll see if I can find one.'

She made no attempt to deliver the message. There was nothing wrong with her mother, the doctor had said.

'She stays in bed too much, Rosa. You should encourage her to get up and take walks or her joints will stiffen up.'

Rosa decided that problem could be easily solved.

'We'll starve her out,' she informed the cook, who took no notice at all. Nor did the housekeeper.

The plan to ship Rosa off to Argentina seemed to have been forgotten, so she continued attending St Mary's College across the square until a week after her twelfth birthday, when she came home to find her father waiting for her in the parlour.

She barely knew this softly spoken man, with his dark eyes and blinding smile, so she sat giddily on the edge of a chair, answering his polite little questions, wishing he would go away, until her mother swept in wearing the swishest grey lace dress with a short fishtail train, and a beautiful hat covered in grey georgette. She looked fantastic!

'Are you going out?' Rosa asked, incredulous. On the rare occasions when Delia did go out, she bundled herself up in coats and scarves to protect her fragile constitution.

'Yes.'

'Not just yet,' her husband said. 'Sit down, Delia.'

'I prefer to stand,' she said haughtily.

'And I want you to sit, so please do so.'

She sulked into the nearest chair, sitting upright without the assistance of cushions. Rosa wished the doctor could see her now.

'I understand you would like to come to live with me,' her father said.

Rosa sat mute, red-faced again. Had Delia lied? She wouldn't put it past her. But did her father want her? He didn't sound too enthusiastic. She frowned.

'I can't speak Spanish.'

'They speak English in the Australian colonies.'

'I thought you lived in Argentina.'

Irritated, he shook his head at Delia. 'I come from Argentina originally. We have family and property in that country. But my home is Rosario Station, north of Brisbane.'

'Rosario?' His daughter was enchanted. 'Did you name your house after me?'

'More than a house,' Delia sniffed. 'It's the size of a county. A big empty county.'

'Yes, it was named after you, Rosa. Now, your mother and I are going to tea at the Grosvenor, which I'm told is very pleasant. If you would care to join us, we could talk more.'

'The Grosvenor?' Rosa cried. 'I'd love to.'

'She can't come, she doesn't have anything to wear,' Delia said, smoothing her gloves.

'I beg your pardon?' Juan sounded displeased, and Rosa shrank back in her chair, but Delia stood.

'I told you, she doesn't have anything to wear, and she's too young.'

Her father seemed not to believe Delia. He turned to Rosa. 'Do you not have a nice summer dress and hat?'

'Not really,' she admitted.

'Then we will go to tea tomorrow.'

'We will not!' Delia cried. 'I want to go today.'

'We will go tomorrow,' he repeated. 'And I will be here first thing in the morning, Rosa, to take you shopping so that you can come with us.'

'I might not be well enough tomorrow,' Delia countered.

'Then stay home,' he said angrily. 'I am outraged that my daughter does not have a wardrobe befitting her status. And I apologise to you, Rosa, for my laxity in allowing this state of affairs to come about. Will it be convenient if I call for you at ten?'

'Yes,' she breathed, starry-eyed.

The next morning, when Juan arrived on the tick of ten, Delia stayed in bed sulking, but he was unconcerned. He took his daughter to boutiques in Bond Street, not one but several, and bought her boxes of beautiful hats and dresses, all of which were sent out to a waiting carriage.

Rosa was too shy to comment when the shopping spree spread to travelling outfits. It was obvious that Juan had already made the decision that she should return with him, but she was so overwhelmed by all this finery that she was happy to agree. Not that anyone had asked her.

That afternoon she wore a white empire-line Swiss cotton dress with pink trimming, and a light straw bonnet that to her mind looked rather plain, with just a few tiny pink roses under the brim, but the lady in the shop had said it was perfect and Juan agreed.

Delia, furious when all the purchases were delivered, frowned and said they were too old for her. Rosa wasn't sure who was right, but she didn't care; she was so happy to be taking afternoon tea at the Grosvenor along with London's fashionable elite.

Contrary to the end, Delia accused Juan of trying to steal Rosa away from her by bribing her with a ridiculous show of cheap finery.

14

'They were not cheap, Mother, believe me,' Rosa whispered.

'Be quiet, you silly girl.'

'That's enough, Delia,' her husband said softly. 'Behave yourself. You're giving a bad example to the child. It is not done to argue in public.'

'Then I shall see my solicitor,' Delia retorted. 'You can argue with him.'

Rosa saw that flash of anger in his eyes once again, and was intrigued to realise that this nice, polite man actually disliked his wife. She didn't blame him. Her mother was a real pain in the neck to live with. She wondered why he'd married her in the first place. Good looks, she supposed. People who saw Delia at her best said she was lovely-looking.

He ignored the threat of Delia's solicitor, calmly offering the tiered silver cake tray to Rosa.

'Did you hear me?' Delia insisted.

'Yes, my dear. You do as you please.'

With that, Delia seemed to slump, as if the solicitor business had been a bluff, and Rosa felt a little sorry for her.

The trunks were packed. Rosa's chaperone and tutor, a young widow, Mrs Lark Pilgrim, was installed in the house, ready to travel with them. Delia remained in her room, claiming that Lark was her husband's whore and that he was using Rosa as an excuse to travel with the woman.

The housekeeper was embarrassed. She explained to Lark that her mistress couldn't receive her because she was too upset at the prospect of her daughter's departure.

Rosa didn't know what to make of the situation. It was the first time she'd heard that word spoken, and it was such a shock she felt as if someone had boxed her ears. Then she began to wonder if it were true. Was Lark her father's lover?

Finally she asked the housekeeper, who said: 'Certainly not!'

Rosa had to steel herself for the departure date. As she'd expected, Delia was hysterical that morning, flinging herself about in her dressing gown, weeping and screaming at the front door. Though she'd seen these tantrums before, and was almost sure that her mother would be over it by teatime, Rosa cried too, feeling horribly guilty that she was so thrilled to be off on this great adventure with a father she adored.

As for Lark, once aboard she was happy and relaxed with Rosa, but though she was a very pretty woman, she was painfully shy and petrified of her employer, so that answered the question for Rosa, who had been watching them closely.

Lark took her meals in the suite she occupied with Rosa, since the only other alternative on this fine ship was second class and that wouldn't do, but she accompanied Rosa on deck, joining in games and other activities.

However, six weeks at sea is a long time. Within the first week several gentlemen were eager to make Lark's acquaintance, and they soon became suitors, at her beck and call. Rosa thought this was fun until she noticed her father was taking an interest in Lark too, though he tried to pretend he wasn't.

By the time the ship berthed in Brisbane, her father and Lark were definitely having an affair, a term she'd learned on the ship. And to her astonishment, her father took two rooms at the Victoria Hotel in Queen Street, one for her and the other for Lark and himself!

Now she walked towards the front of the cathedral and seated herself on a carved stone bench in the dappled shade of a gum tree, shaking her head at his cool disregard for convention. He'd always been like that. So sophisticated in many ways, but strict and old fashioned with his daughter. And that had caused some unholy rows over the years.

She saw a gentleman slip out of the church and stop to replace his top hat. He was tall and distinguished, impeccably dressed, with a London cut to his dark suit, yet his face was lightly weathered. She guessed he was one of her father's grazier friends.

As he passed, he raised his hat and acknowledged her. 'Mrs Palliser,' he said, and for a minute there she thought he intended to stay and speak to her, but he kept going.

She watched him walk down the steps to the street and cross over, walking tall, head held high, almost arrogantly, but then other people began exiting the cathedral and she forgot about him. Remembering Dolour again, and her own mother.

Rosa had been thirteen and living at Rosario Station when her father broke the news to her that her mother had been killed. Run down by a brewery lorry as she tried to cross a busy street in London. It was months before they could make it to London and take her favourite white roses to Delia's grave; just the two of them; and it hadn't seemed real to Rosa. It was as if her mother had simply drifted off to heaven in her vague way, leaving behind the light perfume of the roses. Delia's little memorial service had been so much better than this, Dolour's crowded, misery-driven day, with the graveside ordeal ahead of them yet. And after that the wake, which Juan had insisted was to be held at his Brisbane home, where he and Dolour had lived when they were in town, which wasn't often. Dolour preferred the bush.

Charlie came rushing to her side. 'Are you all right, darling?'

'Yes. Can we go now?'

'Oh, no. I'm a pall-bearer. As long as you're all right?'

He hurried away and Rosa sat and waited. The ugly black hearse with glass windows was also waiting. Patiently. Inevitably.

A few people came out of the church, and Rosa stood as her father led the cortège of men who carried the coffin out of the church and down the steps.

Some urchins ducked around them to get a better view of this curious procession, and were chased away by the undertaker as the coffin was loaded into place. His underling began adding flowers, and the men with Juan backed away uncertainly.

Once again Charlie was by her side.

'Thank God that's over,' she said. 'Let's go.'

'We can't. We have to support your father.'

His own father, tall and angular like his son, was standing behind him. He shrugged at Rosa, as if to say: 'Sorry. You can't get out of that.'

Rosa sighed and allowed Charlie to take her over to Juan's side on the main path, where friends, and strangers she noted, could pay their respects to the bereaved.

One by one and two by two they came to commiserate, some red-faced from the heat, some dabbing tears, making attempts to say the right thing, all telling them about Dolour, that fine woman; while the country men, wordless, just shook Juan's hand firmly and nodded to the couple supporting him.

Rosa could feel her father's agony as the line of sympathisers moved slowly towards them.

'This is barbaric,' she whispered to him. 'Come on. We must go now.'

'We can't yet,' he said, his voice strained. 'Sir Samuel . . .'

She looked up and saw the Governor and his wife, taking their time to enjoy a genial conversation with the priest near the main entrance, and it annoyed her.

'Go and tell them we're all waiting to leave,' she said to Charlie.

'I can't do that.'

'I can,' offered a voice behind her, and she watched, pleased, as her stepbrother Duke MacNamara strode over and had a quick word.

'Ah yes,' the Governor said, quickly shaking hands with the priest and hurrying his wife over to them.

The stragglers in the queue made way for the important couple, who did their commiserating and departed, allowing the priest to claim Juan's attention.

'Thank you, Duke,' Rosa said. 'It's nice to see you again. Are you still out at Kooramin?'

'Yes, but I'm going north soon.' He grinned. 'By gee, Rosa, you shine up well. But you always were good on the eye. And you're an old married lady now!'

She tapped him with her fan. 'I'm only two years older than you, remember.'

They were interrupted by Mrs Forrest, who'd come over with him.

'Yes, you must be twenty-four now, Duke,' she said. 'When are you getting married?'

'Probably never, now that Rosa's taken,' he said, turning to the girl behind

17

them. 'Can I leave your mother in your capable hands now, Lucy Mae? This has been quite an ordeal for her.'

'Of course,' she nodded.

Out of the corner of her eye Rosa saw John Pace MacNamara looking at her, and turned away quickly.

'I'm going home now,' she said to Charlie.

'We have to go to the cemetery.'

'I have to get back to the house and see to the catering,' she lied. 'I'll tell Juan you'll go with him.'

'But you have to come. You can't just . . .'

'It's all right, Charlie,' Mrs Forrest said. 'It's not really expected for women to attend the graveside after the service.'

Rosa gave the old dear a smile as she walked away, knowing that Milly had probably made that up. She could be helpful at times, when she wasn't homing in on every last bit of gossip in the colony.

John Pace saw Palliser call a hansom cab for Rosa and assist her to step up into it. Then he gave the address to the driver and went back to wait on Rivadavia, who was looking pale and confused.

The least she could have done was stand by her father, he reflected angrily, but that was Rosa, as selfish as ever. Was it too much for the most spoiled woman on God's earth to have seen Dolour to her last resting place, even if she'd only been her stepmother? Only! he thought. Dolour had loved Rosa as her own. She'd been delighted with her.

'What a lovely change it is for me,' she'd teased her sons, 'to have a dear sweet girl in my house after all you lumbering lads.'

When Dolour had married Rivadavia, he'd taken her and Rosa to visit his family in Argentina. He'd invited young Duke too, but he'd flatly refused, preferring to remain at Kooramin Station with his brothers. They were all, John Pace recalled, still uncomfortable with their mother's decision to marry again only six months after their father's death . . . his murder. And to his best friend!

Everyone had opinions on the whys and wherefores of her decision, but Dolour had never discussed it with anyone. Except of course, he supposed, Rivadavia. Some people said it was for the money. Paul, his twin brother, claimed she was paying back Pace for riding into the valley of death just to acquire more land. Which was in keeping with Dolour's Irish logic. She and their father had fought a lot, until, as Pace used to laugh: 'She asked me what I would do for love of her. And I gave her the right answer.'

John Pace himself thought it was clear that Dolour loved Rivadavia, though she never actually said so, and maybe needed him to take her away from all the sad memories.

Whatever her motive, one thing was very, very clear. Rivadavia adored Dolour. Milly Forrest said he'd always loved her, from the first day they'd met, when she was married to Pace.

A year later they were back from Argentina, living in the Spanish-style mansion with a ballroom that he'd built in the hills overlooking the city, and Dolour was glad of Rosa's company, because Juan's cattle business took him far afield. For her part, Rosa was delighted to be living in town at last, and in a house that was just made for entertaining.

John Pace remembered how Rosa's eighteenth birthday party was held in that ballroom, a glittering affair he'd never forget, because he was Rosa's escort. How he'd crowed over Paul, who'd been hoping she'd ask him!

He'd kissed her that night and realised he was giddily mad about her, taking it for granted that Rosa was to be his girl from then on. How wrong could you be? he thought angrily.

'Are you coming?' his wife called to him, and that brought him quickly back to the present, feeling even more miserable than he'd been in the church, having to sit by his mother's coffin.

'Can't you wait a minute?' he snapped. 'We're going to the cemetery in the second carriage with Paul and Laura.'

'Laura isn't coming, so there's room for us with Juan and Charlie.'

He had no wish to share a carriage with either Rivadavia or Rosa's husband.

'Eileen,' he said firmly, 'we're taking the second carriage. If you don't mind, I'd prefer to be with my own family today.'

'Oh, suit yourself!' she huffed. He'd always teased her for being a social climber, but today he wasn't amused.

'Where's Duke?' he asked.

'He wouldn't ride with Rivadavia either! He's gone in Mrs Forrest's flash carriage. Is she invited back to the house?'

'I've no idea,' he groaned, dreading his mother's burial and wondering if he could absent himself from the wake without creating havoc.

It occurred to him that from tomorrow he could please himself when it came to Rivadavia. He was no longer obliged to pander to the man for Dolour's sake. It was time to think in terms of their beloved parents, Pace and Dolour. Not of the man who was with Pace when he was murdered by savages.

Or was he? Many were the questions asked when Rivadavia returned from that expedition alone, John Pace recalled darkly.

Laura MacNamara slipped away from the crowds and walked down the street as quickly as she could without drawing attention to herself, but instead of turning right at the next corner and making for the Victoria Hotel, where most of the out-of-towners were staying, she kept walking, right down to William Street.

Her husband, a thoughtful man, had told her there was really no need for her to come out to the cemetery, since she hadn't known his mother for long, and most of the people at the funeral were strangers to her, so Laura had taken him up on the offer.

'Are you sure you don't want me with you?' she'd asked.

'Sweetheart, no. I'm just numb now. I want to spare you the rest of this.' Dolour herself couldn't abide funerals. She called them 'public hand-wringing'. The memorial mass for his father had been beautiful. There were only five mourners: his three sons, John Pace's wife Eileen, and Dolour. 'You have a rest and I'll meet you later at the Rivadavia house. Or do you want me to come back for you?'

She smiled. 'No, I'll make my own way out there. Don't worry.'

Laura's home town was Rockhampton, more than a hundred miles north of Brisbane, and her father had been a Member of Parliament. He'd died some time ago, only a couple of years after the official Parliament House was built. Now she was anxious to see this much-acclaimed building, since she hadn't had a chance until now.

As she hurried down the quiet, tree-lined street, a police inspector was walking towards her. She recognised Marcus Beresford immediately, and tried to pretend she had not, but it was too late.

'Why, it's Miss Maskey!' he said. 'How nice to see you again. What brings you to our town?'

She allowed herself to acknowledge him but would not enlighten him further. Inspector Beresford was officer-in-charge of the infamous Queensland Native Police. Her father had approved of him. Her husband hated him. With good reason.

'I'm just on my way to view the House,' she said. 'I've never seen it before.'

'It's quite stunning! Magnificently appointed inside. I should be happy to show you around.'

'No thank you. I don't have time.'

The wrought-iron gates were just ahead, and behind them stood the lovely, almost pink sandstone walls of the colony's pride and joy.

'Are you sure?'

'Excuse me,' she said, making for the gates, 'but I really must go.'

'Perhaps I could take you to tea one afternoon,' he persisted, falling into step with her.

'No thank you.'

He opened the tall gate and Laura moved quickly inside, then closed it in his face, giving him no chance to follow.

For a few minutes she hid in the lobby, signing the visitors' book and looking about until she judged that Beresford would have gone on his way, then walked out again. She had not intended to request a tour of the House; she'd only wanted to view the building and its surrounds today.

Her path took her around the building on the river side so she could see the setting as well. It was, as she'd heard, a very picturesque location, right on the bend of the river. But Beresford had spoiled it for her. It was really unfortunate that she'd had to bump into him and be reminded of the tragedies Paul had to contend with.

Laura was Paul's second wife, and she was still nervous in the presence of his family. His first wife, Jeannie, and her maid had been murdered on Oberon Station by native troopers of Beresford's company.

Most people, including Laura's own father, did not – could not, she supposed – blame Beresford. But Paul did. He claimed that the men of the Native Police were renegades in the first place, trained to kill their own people, trained for nothing else but killing, for the benefit of white settlers. He laid the blame for a great number of their heinous activities at the feet of their officer, and was fiercely critical of the very existence of these troops.

She sighed. Thank God her husband hadn't bumped into Beresford. And thank God for gloves, which hid her wedding ring and curtailed interested questions from the fellow.

'I might as well go back now,' she muttered crossly. 'I'll come here another time for a nice peaceful visit.'

She decided to walk up to the hotel, have a rest, and then take a hansom cab out to the Rivadavia house. She had the address, and the hotel porter would be able to direct the cabbie.

The house was set in a large formal garden, carefully planned so as not to restrict the views over the town and the winding river.

Laura, in need of exercise, left the cab at the gate and walked up the sloping drive. She and Paul had been in Brisbane for some weeks prior to his mother's demise, and now that Dolour had been laid to rest, they would be going home, maybe as early as tomorrow.

The white house, with its cloistered walks along each side of the front entrance, looked so cool and inviting that Laura quickened her steps. A fragrant rose garden bordered the driveway, with hundreds of flowers in full bloom, as if in tribute to the lost lady of the house. She noticed they all had a tinge of pink, obviously Dolour's choice.

Someone called to her from beyond a low hedge, and as she turned, Laura recognised Mrs Palliser.

'Helloo,' she called. 'Over here. You're the new girl, Laura, aren't you?'

'Yes. You could say that.' Laura smiled. 'And you're Mrs Palliser?'

'No need to be stuffy. I'm Rosa. How do you do?'

'Very well, thank you. Aren't they back yet?'

'No. And I'm keeping out of the way, because the housekeeper, Mrs Payne, is in charge of the catering, and the way she's performing, you'd think royalty was coming instead of family and a few friends.'

Laura nodded. 'It's a lovely house. Sad to think your father will be here all alone now.'

'He'll be all right. But I've been wondering. How are you coping with them all? I mean, it must have been hard for you to meet the family with the tragedy of Paul's first wife still ringing in their ears. I think you were brave to come down here.'

'I'm not brave. I didn't volunteer. Paul insisted. He said that it wouldn't matter when I met friends and relations of Jeannie; even in ten years' time Jeannie would still come to mind, so we had to just get on with it.'

Rosa wandered over to a shaded garden seat and invited Laura to join her. 'Would you mind staying out here for a while? No one else is here yet.'

'Oh, heavens, am I too early?'

'No, they won't be far away. Did you know Dolour?'

'Sadly I only met her a little while before she died, but she said she was happy I'd married Paul, and that was such a relief. It gave me some confidence, at least.'

Rosa nodded. 'Yes, that sounds like Dolour. I was amazed when Daddy married her, and very much put out. But she was so nice, and so sensible about everything, even my occasional tantrums, and his, I couldn't help but like her. Unfortunately, though we didn't actually fall out over my marriage to Charlie, she disapproved. Said I was too young.' She laughed. 'Then I heard her arguing with Juan. He said twenty was the right age for marriage and she rounded on him for that: "You men! You invent these myths to get your daughters off your hands!"'

Laura was shocked. 'Oh no! But she wouldn't have meant it. I mean, she wouldn't have meant anyone to take it personally!'

'Yes she did. For all I know, she could have been right about that, but she wasn't right about my being too young. Charlie and I are gloriously happy.'

Laura smiled. 'It's a good feeling, isn't it?'

'Oh, bother, here they come.'

The two women stood and watched riders turning in at the gate ahead of the first carriage.

'I'd better get up there now or Sergeant Payne'll be after my neck. Come on. Let's go.'

Laura dashed with her around a maze of paths, across the drive and up the front steps to rush across the polished floor of a lobby and on into a long parlour furnished with comfortable-looking leather chairs and sofas.

'You stay here,' Rosa said. 'I have to be doorman. Dolour wouldn't have butlers and so forth, and the maids are all out in the ballroom setting the food on the buffet now that the first guests have arrived.'

'Righto.' Laura grinned as Rosa, her new friend, rushed away. She looked about the room with its interesting portraits and coloured wall hangings and walked down to examine a jewel-encrusted cross lying in a glass case. 'Oh my!' she breathed, dazzled by the cornucopia of rubies, emeralds and pearls. 'Are they real?'

She glanced about furtively, hoping no one had heard that foolish outburst, because she knew in her heart that those jewels certainly were real. A black-clad procession was passing the open door, but she turned back to gaze at the bejewelled cross in awe, finding the sheer beauty of it almost overwhelming.

The ballroom had been converted into a carpeted drawing room, with low occasional tables placed by clusters of upholstered chairs and divans. Already older ladies and gentlemen were taking advantage of the tranquil setting to rest their weary bones.

Eileen MacNamara was surprised by this transformation. She'd been critical of the very idea of holding the gathering in a ballroom renowned for its glitz and glitter, blaming Rosa for such a faux pas.

'What does it matter?' John Pace had said. 'It's not as if it's a real Irish wake. It's to be just a gathering after the funeral, with a little food and sustenance for all. A sort of high tea, I think.'

'Who told you that?'

'The housekeeper. Yesterday, when I brought over the extra flowers. She said Mr Rivadavia didn't want speeches either. But don't the flowers look nice?'

Eileen had already noticed them. There were huge bowls of pink roses by the open side doors that led to a shaded courtyard. Overdone, she thought.

Sombre maids were drifting silently about the room, offering tea and cakes, but her husband headed for a side door.

'There's a buffet on the terrace,' he said enthusiastically. 'Let's go out there. I'm starving.'

There was also a gathering of the younger folk, Eileen noticed. She would have preferred to stay in this room, which was already filling up with important people, like the local MP, and Jasper Forsyth, president of the Queensland Cattlemen's Association, with his wife. These were the people they should be mixing with, not just hobnobbing about with friends and relations, but John Pace had charged off so she had to follow him.

Rosa, who had discarded the lace head-cover, was talking to Laura, and John Pace headed over to acknowledge his brothers before he made for the buffet.

'He's always hungry,' Eileen sighed.

'Good on the tooth,' Duke said. 'He'd eat a horse and chase the rider.' He nodded towards Laura. 'Looks like you've been deserted, Paul.'

His brother smiled. 'Yes, they seem to be getting along well.'

'Both naughty girls,' Eileen remarked. 'They dodged the last rites for Dolour at the cemetery and yet they wouldn't miss the social side of the day.'

'Is that right?' Duke asked sarcastically, and walked away.

Paul glowered at his sister-in-law. 'In actual fact, Laura didn't want to come here. I had to talk her into it.'

'Why did you do that? I thought you'd have more respect for Jeannie's family.' Eileen gazed about the now crowded courtyard. 'You must have known Jeannie's parents would be here. And her sister. I don't know how they must feel having your new wife flaunted at them.'

'That's enough, Eileen,' John Pace snapped. 'I'm sorry, Paul. She's talking through her hat.'

His twin brother turned away. 'I'd forgotten they'd be here. Truly.'

'Yes, but never mind. Don't let Eileen get to you.'

Paul shook his head. 'She doesn't.'

As he too moved off, threading through the crowds towards Laura, he reflected on his situation.

'My wife and another lady were foully murdered,' he said to himself.

After something like that happened, a person became immune to hurt. Gossipy opinions, such as those that Eileen would spout, had been flying about since he married Laura, but they hadn't touched him. He couldn't care less. And as for Laura, she was a strong-willed wench who could look after herself.

'Come to think of it,' he murmured as he approached his wife, 'Eileen had better watch her step.'

Rosa felt a slight hush in the gathering and saw her father come into the main room with Duncan Palliser, so she excused herself and hurried in to meet them.

She took Juan's arm, hugging it to her side. 'All right, are you, Daddy?'

'Yes.' He nodded to confirm that and looked about him. 'Is everything going nicely here? Enough food?'

'Oh yes. It's delicious too. Can I get you something? And you, Mr Palliser?'

'Not for me, not just yet, dear, but you could take Mr Palliser through to my study and offer him a port wine. I wanted to show him a picture of the Angus bull, Minotaur. So . . . I'll leave you in Rosa's capable hands, sir. I shall not be long.'

Rosa watched him straighten his black silk cravat, square his shoulders the way he often did as he prepared to summon that famous Latin charm, and walk towards the nearest couple, arms outstretched.

'Just a minute,' she said to Duncan as she summoned a serving maid.

'Would you make up a nice tray of eats for two gentlemen, please, and deliver it to Mr Rivadavia's study.'

'Yes, madam.' The girl bobbed.

'I can't have you two eating leftovers,' Rosa explained to her father-in-law. 'But come along now and view his darling Angus.' Her tone dropped a little then. 'He seems to be holding up quite well, doesn't he?'

'Yes, I got frowned upon by Charlie, but on the way back I thought we could have a good old talk about the cattle stations in Argentina. I've never had the chance to ask your father about them before this.'

'You did exactly the right thing. Talk cattle with him and he's immediately won over. Where's Charlie anyway?'

Duncan laughed. 'He's gone off to settle with the undertaker, who was huffy no one paid him today.'

'Oh no! How awful. I hired him and took it for granted he'd send a bill!'

'Apparently not. Cash up was the call, the minute your dad turned his back. If that happened in the bush, he'd get chucked in a creek.'

'So he should be!' she said indignantly.

'Then we shan't have him at our funerals, eh?'

Rosa hesitated a minute, then burst out laughing. 'Oh dear, I almost missed that. You are a treat, Duncan. It's such a sad day for everyone. How long do people stay on at these gatherings?'

'They'll drift off soon.'

She took him along the wide passageway to Juan's book-lined study, and Duncan looked about him, impressed. 'I'm not one for books, missy, except station journals and catalogues, but these are the best-looking office chairs I ever saw.' He sat himself down in one with a sigh of pleasure. 'Darned if this leather seat isn't as soft as a cushion. I'll have to get one for my office back home. It'd be a welcome sight for my old bones come dusk, I can tell you.'

'Then you shall have one, Duncan, I'll see to it.'

She poured his port into a small crystal glass, kissed him on the cheek for looking after her daddy and went back to their other guests.

Sometimes he wondered what Rosa saw in his Charlie. He was a handsome fellow, sure enough . . . tall and straight, with a good head of brown hair, compliments of his mother, who'd had beautiful hair. But he was a bookish type and very staid.

His sister-in-law disagreed. 'Charlie is not staid,' she'd said. 'He simply knows how to behave. He has good manners, which is rare these days.'

Of course she disliked Rosa. She claimed the girl was spoiled and flighty.

'Alice, if she's like that,' Duncan countered, 'why would she choose Charlie, him being such a sedate gentleman? Opposites attract, maybe?'

'Certainly not. She's marrying him because he asked her. Can't you see that? I'd wager he's her first serious suitor. She is beautiful; she'd frighten most young men off until they gained manly confidence. Charlie simply got in first, and she got carried away with the excitement of it all.'

He laughed. 'Is that how you came to marry your first husband, Alice?'

'Yes,' she said stonily, 'and I lived to regret it.'

Rivadavia came into the study with Charlie, who stayed long enough to take a glass of port with them, but with little interest in their enthusiasm for the bull's bloodline, he soon drifted off in search of his wife.

For Charlie, the long day was almost over. Dolour had been laid to rest. He wondered what Juan would do now, rattling about this large house on his own.

As he walked back along the wide passageway with its polished floor and red-patterned Axminster runner, he reached out and touched the cool white wall. He'd watched the builders at work on this house and thought it very strange at the time, even remarking to a carpenter that the passages were 'exceeding wide'.

'That's how he wants them, sir,' the man replied. 'Right through the house; more like hallways they are.'

And put to good use, Charlie nodded, as he passed by an ebony cabinet, and further along a carved ebony chair, more like a throne. All the artefacts displayed here were immensely interesting to him, as was the house itself. He believed that this architectural style was more in keeping with the climate than the high-set timber houses so popular in Queensland.

He found Rosa in the lobby, farewelling the last of the guests, as thunder rolled across the eastern sky.

'I hope it rains,' she said. 'It'll cool us down.'

'Bound to. It's been too hot the last few days even for this time of the year. Do you think we ought to start for home before the storm hits? It looks very black out there.'

'I don't like to leave Daddy alone tonight. Maybe we should stay over?'

'If he would like us to. By all means, my dear.'

'Yes. I'll ask him.' She turned sadly, looking around her. 'It's so quiet now, isn't it, Charlie? I keep expecting Dolour to come bouncing out of the parlour or dash past us on some mission.'

He nodded in sympathy and put an arm about her.

Mrs Forrest and Lucy Mae were in the second to last carriage to crunch down the drive and out on to leafy Sycamore Road. Milly was always careful about things like that. She never wanted it said she was the last to leave.

'You were very quiet in there,' Lucy Mae said. 'Are you missing Dolour terribly?'

'Yes, I am. Very much.' Milly sniffed.

'I'm sorry. It's hard to lose such a good friend.'

'Yes, it is.'

It was hard also, Milly pondered, to have the best bit of gossip and no one to tell it to. It would be wasted on Lucy Mae.

'I didn't see Lady Rowan-Smith there. Was she in the church?'

'No,' Lucy Mae said. 'I believe she went down to Sydney for the summer.'

'So she did.' Her mother shrugged.

'But she didn't know Dolour, did she?'

'No, but she knew Pace.'

'That's hardly a reason to attend this funeral. He's been dead for years.'

'I know that!' Milly snapped. She folded her arms and sat back on the well-upholstered seat as Lucy Mae leaned forward to close the window flaps against the oncoming rain. 'I think we'll have morning tea at the Victoria Hotel tomorrow,' she added quietly. 'Or maybe lunch.'

'Why?'

'Because the MacNamaras are all staying there, and I believe the reading of the will is taking place tomorrow at nine.'

'And?'

'And we'll see how it all turns out.'

'But Dolour hadn't much of her own, had she?'

'Not much? She still owned Kooramin Station. It's huge. Worth a mint, with land prices rising by the hour.'

'I didn't know that. I sort of imagined the station would have become incorporated in Juan's holdings.'

'Never. That was her station. She and Pace built it from scratch. She'd never let go of it.'

'Then what . . .?'

'We'll see. Tomorrow.'

As her carriage spun through streets already flooding in the cloudburst, Milly wondered what Heselwood was doing in town.

Jasin, Lord Heselwood, was late for the meeting held in the boardroom of the Cattlemen's Club on Wickham Terrace.

'Sorry,' he whispered to all, before taking the empty place at the table set for eight, and nodding at the speaker to continue.

Ronald Conrad, aged twenty-eight, elder son of the chairman of the club, was standing at the head of the table. He frowned at Heselwood and tapped a map laid out before him, anchored with an ashtray.

'As I was saying, gentlemen, we know there's excellent grazing land to this latitude, but we don't know what's beyond. Dalrymple has explored the coast up to the Eighteenth Parallel, to a place he called Cardwell, after the Secretary of State for the Colonies, a gentleman I had the honour of meeting on several occasions last year during my visit to London. Which, I may say, is a very pleasant city indeed, and the populace most accommodating to colonial visitors. Most accommodating. And as for the Secretary himself, I found him to be very much in favour of further exploration in Queensland.'

'How much is he putting up?' asked Langley Palliser, owner of Cameo Downs cattle station and veteran of two inland expeditions.

That brought a laugh from Conrad's audience.

'The very fact, gentlemen, that we have Mr Cardwell's goodwill is a welcome addition to our endeavours, and that goodwill is borne out by the presence here today of the Treasurer, Mr Gordon Porter, and his sons Hugh and Royce.'

'So,' Palliser drawled, 'how much is the government prepared to put up?'

'We're prepared to come to the party with two surveyors when we see what's on the table,' Porter said. 'But from a personal point of view, Hugh is keen to join you gentlemen, and would of course contribute to expenses on an equal basis with all other members of the expedition.'

Jasin Heselwood nodded but said nothing. He'd been wondering where the ginger-haired fellow sitting across from him fitted into this picture. On Jasin's left was Harvey Bell, a geologist, and the two on his right were Jack and Clem Batterson, from one of his own cattle stations, Montone.

When Conrad asked if he were interested in a north Queensland exploratory expedition, and if he could suggest other men he might approach, Jasin considered investing in the scheme. It was always important to stay close to the action when it came to finding new pastures. He already had three cattle stations north of Brisbane, as well as his head station, Carlton Park, but the far north climate spelled rain, precious rain, and after these last drought-ridden years, he could surely do with a slice of that territory.

'It'll be tough going,' Langley had said to him. 'I'd think twice if I were you.'

'Rubbish. I might be nearing fifty, but I'd back myself against you boys any time. Mitchell was well into his fifties when he led important expeditions.'

'Very well.' Langley shrugged.

'And I have two more starters for you. Too many explorers have come to grief. I wouldn't set foot in that country without reliable bushmen at my side. I'll be bringing two of my own station hands, and will stand accountable for their share of the initial outlay. Investors are no use if we end up like Kennedy and his party . . . very dead.'

He could have added, 'And later Pace MacNamara,' but he preferred not to mention that two-man expedition.

Now Harvey Bell peered over his spectacles. 'I understand that we are to disembark from the ship at Cardwell and strike north. According to your map, this place is the only port between Bowen and the tip of the continent, at Cape York, a coastline of more than a thousand miles. Could you tell us, Mr Conrad, what section of this coastline you have in mind for exploration?'

'Ah yes. That I can do.' Conrad jabbed a finger at the map. 'Here! We'll take the section between Cardwell and the Endeavour River. Where Captain Cook landed.'

'What?' Jasin exploded from his chair. 'Let me see!' He studied the map. 'That's hundreds of miles. It's too far.'

'Not necessarily,' Conrad replied smugly. 'We'll have a ship waiting for us at the Endeavour River.'

'Hold on,' Hugh Porter said. 'Cardwell is situated between a range of mountains and the sea. I suggest we go inland first and take a look at what's ahead of us from one of those peaks.'

'Waste of time,' his brother Royce said. 'Let's stick to the plan. We're not interested in the ranges. You don't climb a mountain to look at the next one. Our brief is the coastal terrain: to seek out pastureland and see what rivers and bays might be serviceable as ports. The government is anxious to develop ports for trade with India and the East Indies. We might even find a river like the Mississippi for cargo transport.'

'Then we'll need a goodly number of bearers.' Hugh sounded peeved at the blunt rejection of his suggestion.

'So we shall.'

Jack Batterson nudged his boss. 'Mr Conrad's going the Kennedy route. The terrain doesn't change with time. I wouldn't risk it, boss.'

Disappointed, Jasin waited out the rest of the meeting, then walked down to the public library, where he read up on the Kennedy expedition, which had taken place before he'd emigrated to this country from England.

The story shocked him. He would retreat from the Conrad syndicate, and forget about exploration for the time being.

'I wonder why Rivadavia isn't here?' Eileen whispered to John Pace, as they sat in the lawyer's office waiting for Duke, so that Hubert Bloom could read the will.

'Because she didn't leave him anything, obviously. He's got plenty, why would she?'

It suddenly occurred to John Pace that Dolour might already have done so. He hadn't seen the deeds of Kooramin for years. Dolour had taken them with her when she'd married Rivadavia. Her husband could have talked her into amalgamating their properties into one company, into *his* company, Cordoba Holdings.

But surely not! Their mother wouldn't do that to them. He and Eileen had been managing the station very successfully and settling up with Dolour at the end of each year. His heart thumping, he gazed at the spreading purple of a jacaranda tree outside the window and tried to tell himself to desist from these imaginings; that they were only bred from the misery of losing the mater. When this was over, they'd be going home. Born and bred on Kooramin Station, he had never been one for big towns: too many people, too much noise.

To pass the time, he asked Mr Bloom: 'When do you think they'll get around to calling this town a city?'

'Lord only knows, John Pace. I find it very odd that Brisbane is the capital of the colony and yet not a city.'

'I don't,' Paul said. 'It's way down the bottom corner of the colony. My home town of Rockhampton is a far better bet, halfway up the coast.'

'Rockhampton?' his brother laughed. 'Who's ever heard of the place? You can't have a capital city no one can find.'

'Don't be so sure. Hang on, look out there!'

Paul jumped up, went to the open window and gave a shrill whistle.

'Hey, Duke!' he yelled. 'Get up here! We're waiting for you!'

He turned back exasperated. 'He was over the road, chatting to some ladies. I'm sorry, Mr Bloom, he's on his way now.'

When Duke came in and pulled up a chair, the lawyer accepted his apology. Then he opened a drawer and produced a small ring case.

'As you probably know,' he said, 'Mrs Rivadavia was never much one for jewellery, though her husband did give her some expensive pieces. Those she has given to her stepdaughter Rosa. And I believe you received a ring, Eileen? And you, Laura, received the cameo brooch?'

The two women nodded.

'Yes. Dolour told me they were her favourite pieces and she wanted you to have them in memory of her. She was buried with her wedding ring, but this wedding ring was given to her by Pace. She wanted you to have it, Duke, to help you choose a wife carefully.'

He handed the box to Duke, who opened it and gazed at the small gold ring.

'Now there's no mention of anything else in the will except Kooramin,' Bloom continued. 'When I asked about other assets, she simply told me there were none.'

They all looked surprised, but no one spoke.

The lawyer opened the parchment document in front of him, read the preamble to the last will and testament of Dolour Rivadavia, then commented: 'It's a very simple will. "Being of sound mind, I, Dolour Rivadavia, hereby bequeath my property Kooramin Station to my three beloved sons, John Pace, Paul and Duke, with my blessing, upon my demise." '

He looked up with an approving smile to be met with blank stares from the three men.

'Is that all?' John Pace demanded. 'Nothing more?'

Bloom handed him the will. 'I explained that your mother had no other possessions.'

'She had money in the bank.'

'Your mother closed that account some time ago and donated the contents, quite a significant amount I believe, to charity.'

'And where do I fit in here?'

'What do you mean, John Pace?'

'Kooramin. That's my home, not theirs. Duke has a property in the Valley of Lagoons. A huge spread up north.'

Duke protested: 'Sure it's there, empty land with a thousand blackfellers camped on it. It's useless.'

John Pace rounded on his twin brother. 'What about you, Paul? You already own a good station. Oberon's one of the best, you've said so yourself many a time. You certainly don't need a share of Kooramin.'

'Calm down,' Paul said. 'We'll sort it out. Obviously the mater didn't want to differentiate between us.'

'But she bloody well has!'

'Thank you, Mr Bloom,' Duke said, stepping forward to shake the lawyer's hand. 'We'll not take up any more of your time.'

Bloom stood and saw them all out of his office, then went back to his desk. He had warned Dolour that leaving each son a third share in Kooramin Station would cause conflict. It was a huge station, marked out of virgin land by the young Pace MacNamara long before the government surveyors came in sight. Once that land was officially recognised as belonging to MacNamara, who had first claim on it, the impoverished Irishman was catapulted into the ranks of the elite squatters . . . major landholders.

Paul had been right, he reflected. She simply could not or would not differentiate between them.

'My husband', she'd said, meaning MacNamara, 'built up that station for his sons. I've done my duty and handed it to them, so that's the end of it. What happens now is their concern. They're grown men, they can work it out.'

Bloom shrugged. He'd known Dolour for years. Watched her hair turn white with the shock of MacNamara's death. Shared the surprise of her family that she'd married Rivadavia within a year of the tragedy. And come to realise that though she was a passionate woman in many respects, she wasn't given to sentimentality.

There was a knock at the door and his clerk announced that a client was waiting.

'Without an appointment?' he said, frowning.

'It's Mrs Forrest.'

The lawyer hesitated. The woman seemed to think she could bowl in and out of the office whenever she pleased. But then she was a valued client.

'Ask her to come in,' he said, arranging a welcoming smile on his whiskered face as he stood.

'Dear lady!' he beamed. 'To what do I owe this honour?'

'It's about that rascal Bartling. My daughter hasn't received a penny. What about all those properties he claimed to own? Were any of them worthwhile?'

'I'm afraid not. We checked every one of those titles carefully, but I'm sorry to say they were all forgeries, used to borrow money. It appears that Bartling was involved in many shady land deals . . .'

'That would have seen him imprisoned, had he not got himself drowned.'

Bloom nodded. His clerk brought in the Forrest file and placed it on the side of his desk.

'These are Bartling's papers,' the lawyer murmured. 'They're of no use to anyone. Do you want me to destroy them?'

'Could I have a look at them?'

'Certainly.'

Mrs Forrest took her spectacles from her large handbag and began turning the pages.

'Oh my! What a cheek! The villain claimed ownership of some well-known family properties. And look at this! He even tried to set his stamp on Carlton Park! What a hoopla that would have caused.' She laughed. 'Jasin would have had a fit!'

'Jasin who?'

'Lord Heselwood!'

'Does he still own Carlton Park? I thought he sold it when his son went to live in England.'

'No, he leased it. And his son didn't just leave, he was thrown out.'

'Ah yes,' Bloom murmured tactfully. He and his wife were always interested in titbits about the colony's elite, especially when aristocrats were involved. Now he aimed a question squarely at Mrs Forrest, fishing for an answer to the mystery that had surrounded young Heselwood's sudden departure for England. 'I heard that story', he ventured, 'but I set no store by it. Surely a young gentleman . . . what was he? Barely seventeen . . .'

'Yes.'

'Surely the young gentleman would know better than to harass a lady like Mrs MacNamara.'

'One would think he'd know better than to harass any lady!' Mrs Forrest sniffed. 'But it wasn't just harassment, it was attempted rape.'

'Good heavens!' Bloom was genuinely startled.

'Yes. It happened while her husband, Pace, was away, thank God, or there would have been hell to pay. Dolour never told anyone in the family, but Lady Heselwood got an earful.'

'She did? And no charges were laid?'

'Ha! Neither they were. Dolour told Edward's parents to get him out of the country or he would be charged.'

Bloom considered the matter. 'Difficult to prove, and a dreadful ordeal for a lady.'

Mrs Forrest laughed. 'She knew she'd lose. That was the whole point. But he'd have been taken to court for the entire world to see. And you know what people say: "No smoke without fire." She was ready to lose, up against Lord Heselwood and his might, but she warned them she'd appeal. Get their son into court again! Well, they had to give in, didn't they? Edward was bundled out of the country pretty damn quick.'

'Ah well.' Bloom shrugged, curiosity satisfied. 'These things happen. History now.'

'Indeed! And guess who I saw at Dolour's funeral? In the church?'

'Half the town,' he smiled. 'I was there.'

'Of course you were. But did you see Jasin Heselwood?'

'No. Was he there?'

'Large as life.'

'Good heavens. Why on earth . . .?'

She gathered herself up. 'Makes you wonder, doesn't it?'

'It certainly does. They must have buried the hatchet after all. Now, do you want any of these papers?'

'No.' She pushed the file back to him. 'If my son-in-law had worked as hard at being honest, he might have made something of himself.'

Hubert Bloom lunched at his club most days, and on this occasion he was on the lookout for Lord Heselwood's solicitor, Edgar Fitzwilliam, a pretentious person of whom it was said that he talked only to God and aristocracy.

Spotting his quarry reading a paper at his favourite table by the window, Hubert walked quietly by, and then, as if due to an afterthought, turned back.

'I say, Fitzwilliam. Am I correct in believing that you act for the interests of the owners of Carlton Park?'

Fitzwilliam frowned at the interruption, straightened his monocle and nodded. 'You are.'

It was more of a dismissal than a question, but Hubert pressed on.

'I was wondering if you knew there are problems with claims on that station.'

'And what does that have to do with you?'

'Not a lot, sir. Details came across my desk, that's all, but as long as you are aware . . . never mind at all. Carry on!'

With that he passed on by, heading for the exit, having decided against lunching at the club.

Let him come and find me now, he reflected coldly. I wouldn't be surprised if he doesn't yet know who the claimant R. Bartling is . . . or was . . . or where to find him.

Since none of them had residences in Brisbane, the MacNamaras retreated to Duke's hotel bedroom to discuss this problem rather than air family matters in the public arena.

Eileen took the only armchair; John Pace sat on one of the single beds, and Paul and Laura on the other. Duke preferred to stand, leaning against the wall by the tall window.

He opened the discussion. 'We have to sell Kooramin. Right?'

'We will not!' Eileen cried. 'How dare you suggest such a thing! Kooramin is our home. Our children's home.'

'Where are they now?' Laura asked.

'A maid took them to visit the Gardens.'

'I know it's your home,' Duke said to her, 'so don't carry on. We'll sell our shares to you.'

'Who says we will?' Paul growled, at the same time as John Pace loudly opposed that idea.

'Shut up, the pair of you,' Duke snapped, 'and listen to me. We've had a good run there, John Pace. It belongs to the three of us now and I want my share. I want to go out on my own.'

'You can still do that; Paul did,' John Pace argued.

'Yeah? Well he might have, scratching about on Oberon Station, living in a hut until he got enough coin to build a house. But that's not for me. Either you buy us out, or we sell the lot and take our shares.'

'I think, John Pace, you should consider raising a loan to buy us out,' Paul said quietly. 'I could do with the money now.'

Duke agreed with him. 'He's right. You don't hear Paul complaining that we reaped the benefits of living on the family station while he slogged it out up north, with no help from anyone.'

'Oh shut up!' Eileen cried. 'Since when do you care about anyone but yourself, Duke? This sympathy for Paul is sheer bloody hypocrisy. He chose to go north. No one forced him out. And I never heard you offering to go up and give him a hand.'

'Or kill yourself with work on Kooramin either,' John Pace snapped.

'All the more reason for you to get rid of me,' his younger brother drawled. 'I'm out. Find the money, John, or sell up.'

'Steady on,' Paul said, but Duke was adamant.

'You're weak. You want to sell but you haven't got the guts to say so. They've been on a good thing for years; why should we support them?'

'We'd all share the profits.'

'What bloody profits? With the drought and the way he and Eileen run the place, the mater has hardly seen a bean for years.'

'She didn't need the money,' Eileen burst out.

'What's that got to do with it?' Duke asked as he made for the bedroom door. 'You had me in a grip out there. I had to put up with you two or leave. It didn't suit me to leave, but it does now.'

The door slammed after him.

'It's still two to one,' John Pace said to his twin. 'He can't do a thing.'

Paul took Laura by the hand as he stood. 'I'm sorry, but if one wants out, it's only fair to let him go. And as I said, I really could do with the money.'

'He's right! You're weak,' Eileen wept.

'I didn't think you'd let us down like this,' John Pace said angrily. 'I always thought I could rely on you.'

'You still can. Come on down to the bar and I'll buy you a drink.'

'Go to hell!'

Eileen grabbed Paul's arm. 'If you side with Duke, we'll take you to court.'

'That would be foolish, Eileen. No one wants a court case.' Paul sighed. 'Lucky there aren't four sons, or there really would be an impasse. Two out of three wins the day.'

John Pace kicked one of Duke's riding boots out of his way. 'Don't you realise you're letting Pace down? He wouldn't want us to sell Kooramin.'

'Don't give me that! Dolour made the decision, not me. You make up your minds what you intend to do. I think buying us out is the best bet. You can raise a loan on your equity.'

Eileen appealed to Laura, who'd been careful, as a newcomer to the family, not to become involved. 'You talk to him, Laura. He'll listen to you. Surely you don't want to see us thrown off the property?'

'I'm sorry, Eileen,' Laura said. 'It's really not up to me.'

With that Paul ushered her out. 'I'll give you a couple of days,' he called back to John Pace, 'but that's all. We have to get on home.'

Jasin Heselwood was also keen to get back to his property, after wasting his time at that meeting. He'd had a private conversation with the geologist, Harvey Bell, suggesting that they take their own expedition ashore at the same spot the Kennedy expedition had left from, but find a way inland, over the mountains, instead of taking on the difficult trek north.

He did not mention that inland from Cardwell, over those very same mountains, was the famed Valley of Lagoons, and that the only land so far claimed in that picturesque district, described so well by Leichhardt, belonged to Pace MacNamara's youngest son. Jasin would give anything to get a foot in there too.

'No fear,' Harvey had said. 'Those hills are too dangerous. The blacks would pick us off the minute we raised our heads. The only way to get into that country is overland, from the south. I wouldn't mind looking into that one day.'

Jasin shuddered. He'd thought a short cut over the mountains would have been the answer. The alternative was a hard slog over more than five hundred miles through waterless country in winter and floods in the summer.

'Burke and Wills had the best-equipped expedition in the history of this colony,' he said. 'And they died out there. I think I'll wait awhile.'

Harvey nodded. 'Keep in touch, though. You're looking for grazing land; I'm after minerals. One hand can help the other.'

'By all means.'

The next person to intrude on Edgar Fitzwilliam at lunch calmly drew up a chair and called for a whisky as he sat down.

'What's that you're eating, Edgar?' he asked. 'It looks like something the cat dragged in.'

'Tripe and onions, milord. Very tasty too.'

'Good God! Now have you patched up that mistake on my title deeds?'

'It's not as easy as it seems. But I'm looking at it.'

Heselwood leaned over and tugged the lawyer's plate away. 'I didn't ask you to look at it. I said to fix it. Have you done that?'

'Not quite. My clerk's having trouble running down the owner of that claim so that we can refute it.'

'What's his name?'

'Bartling. A Mr R. Bartling. His address is simply care of Toowoomba post office.'

'And what did they say up there?'

'No idea. Rather out of my territory.'

Heselwood fumed. 'So you sit on your fat posterior eating pig swill and hoping this Bartling will come to you?'

Fitzwilliam, his fork plunged into a square of tripe, suddenly remembered something.

'A chap I know did mention the matter of discrepancies on your title. I wonder why?'

'Because civil servants can't keep their mouths shut. I wanted this sorted out before people got to hear of it. What did he want?'

'I didn't ask. He simply remarked upon the situation. Here. Not a half-hour ago.'

'Oh for Christ's sake! Who was he?'

'A lawyer, Hubert Bloom. Odd little fellow.'

'Is he still here?'

'I don't see him.'

Heselwood shoved his chair back and marched over to the reception desk.

'Bloody rude!' Edgar mumbled, and was relieved to see his client push out through the glass doors without a backward glance.

Mr Bloom saw him striding across the street, and was suddenly all of a dither. It looked as if the gentleman were actually coming in this direction. He leapt up and peered down from his first-floor office through the jacaranda blossoms, and sure enough Heselwood had disappeared! Into this very building!

He pulled on his jacket, regardless of the steamy heat of his office, jerked his waistcoat into place, combed his fingers through his beard and croaked, 'Enter!' at the first knock.

His lordship stuck his head round the door. 'Mr Bloom?'

'Yes.' The lawyer turned from his stance at the window. 'Do come in, sir. Lord Heselwood, is it?'

'Indeed. Yes. Could I have a word with you?'

'By all means. Do take a seat. Hot day, is it not?'

'Hot in here, Mr Bloom.'

'Yes, I should open a window, but the street smells get a bit high by this time of day.'

'I suppose they would. You should demand more street sweepers.'

'I suppose I should,' Bloom said, cross with himself for sounding like an echo. And to this man of all people.

'I wanted to ask you about a fellow called Bartling. Do you know where I could find him?'

'Bartling?' Though delighted at the swift result of his little fishing expedition, Bloom adopted a suitable frown. 'I'm sorry to have to inform you that Mr Bartling is no longer with us. He was lost at sea in the *Eastern Star*. Remember that ship? It was wrecked off Fraser Island some months ago.'

'Was he now? No wonder they were having trouble locating him! But tell me. You have some knowledge of the fellow causing a nuisance regarding the title deeds at Carlton Park, I'm told. How did that come about?'

'A simple matter, really. I was trying to establish the extent of Mr Bartling's estate.'

'Why?'

'There was no will.'

'And you just happened across this piece of information?'

Mr Bloom squared his shoulders. 'Certainly not. Mr Bartling appeared to own a number of properties, but careful inspection of these claims uncovered forged documents. Among them was a forgery purporting to ownership of Carlton Park.'

'What?'

'I thought you'd be pleased to know the fellow was nothing more than a shyster.'

'And all Fitzwilliam can do is run around in circles looking for a dead man. Bloody fool. Was Bartling your client?'

'No, but his widow is.'

'And she's clear that she has no claim at all on Carlton Park?'

'Oh, quite! The lady is extremely embarrassed. She wouldn't want to upset anyone. The forged documents have all been destroyed.'

'Thank God for that. It's all been a damn nuisance.' Heselwood jumped to his feet. 'Charmed to meet you, Bloom. And thank you for sorting things out here. Send your bill to Carlton Park. We might have lunch at the club next time I'm in Brisbane.'

'I'd be delighted, milord.'

When Heselwood had left, Hubert Bloom decided to reward himself. He removed his jacket, opened the windows and lit a fat cigar.

Not too many people have two of the town's leading cattlemen on their books, he gloated. Dolour brought me Rivadavia, and now Lucy Mae has delivered his lordship to my door. Well done, ladies.

CHAPTER TWO

Georgina, Lady Heselwood, was not impressed with Brisbane. She found the climate oppressive, the town dingy and unkempt, despite the addition of some grandiose buildings, and the population of country bumpkins absolutely unbearable.

Heselwood had promised her they'd be staying here for only a couple of days before traveling on to Montone Station, which he'd reopened several years ago, but it had been more than a week now, and she was still stuck in this horrible hotel. If the Royal Park Hotel was said to be the best in Brisbane, she'd hate to see the worst.

With nothing better to do, she decided to take a stroll through the Botanic Gardens across the road, though she'd walked through them so often now, the exotic trees and flowers were beginning to lose their charm.

Two women were coming towards her, their faces alight with recognition, and Georgina cringed, unable to recall their names.

'Why, Lady Heselwood!' the first woman cried, while the other hung back shyly. 'How wonderful to see you again! Are you staying a while?'

'Not really,' Georgina said, agonising over the names. 'We're on our way to Montone Station.'

'No! After all this time. Well, I'm pleased to hear it. I remember you saying you'd never go back there again, and I hoped the day would come when you'd change your mind. Sir Arthur always said it was a beautiful property.'

Sir Arthur? It dawned on Georgina that the woman was Mrs Palmer, the Premier's wife, and she almost gushed her relief.

'Yes, I loved it. I never dreamt the blacks would attack us.'

'It must have been terrifying. They say you had to ride for your lives!'

'We lost several of our people,' Georgina sighed. 'That was the worst of it. But I believe the area is secure now. No more troubles, I hope.'

'My dear Lady Heselwood, I promise you you'll be perfectly safe now. And you have some wonderful scenery out Gympie way.'

'So I believe. I'm really looking forward to that journey.'

Georgina couldn't place the other lady at all, so she judged it was time to move on before she was caught out, but Mrs Palmer had other ideas.

'Would you care to join us? We're due to meet Sir Arthur for lunch at Parliament House. I know it's a bit irregular with no notice, but we don't stand on ceremony.'

'Thank you, Mrs Palmer, it's too kind. But I have other arrangements and I must get back.'

Georgina managed to take her leave of the other lady as well, without causing offence she hoped, and followed a path around a lotus-filled lagoon, past a grove of bamboos, until she came to the orchid house. She ducked in there to while away more time admiring the lovely native varieties, before making her way reluctantly back to the hotel.

To her surprise, her husband was waiting for her, pacing impatiently about the foyer.

'Where have you been? I told you we have a luncheon appointment at one o'clock, and here you are wandering about dressed like a milkmaid.'

Georgina had forgotten the lunch, since none of his business friends interested her, but she resented his criticism. 'I am not dressed like a milkmaid!' she said angrily. 'This is the latest in summer gowns, and my hat is the best leghorn. Do not try to tell me how to dress, Heselwood. Where are we lunching anyway?'

'Well we can't eat in this place . . .'

'I'm glad we agree on something!'

'So I've booked a private room at the Pavillion.'

'Good, then I have absolutely no need to change . . .' She stopped and stared at him. 'A private room? What on earth for?'

'Because my business acquaintance prefers it that way.'

'And am I to be enlightened as to who this acquaintance might be?'

But Heselwood had rushed out to call a hansom cab, and she was hurried into it, since they were late.

'How much longer are we staying here, Jasin?' she asked fretfully.

'Tomorrow!' he said. 'We leave for Montone tomorrow! I have your coach ticket. And my stockmen have a good horse for me so that we can ride on ahead.'

'Thank God.'

Georgina was still working out which one of her travelling suits would be suitable for the coach when they arrived at the Pavillion and were ushered into a private room overlooking the gardens where a large table, beautifully presented with gleaming silver and trailing flowers, was set for three. The room was gaily decorated with coloured streamers.

Georgina gazed around her in astonishment. She saw a young gentleman standing at one side, and she turned back to Heselwood with a question on her lips, but it was left unspoken as the gentleman stepped forward.

'Hello, Mother.'

At first she simply stared at him, then, laughing and weeping at the same time, Georgina embraced the son she hadn't seen since she last visited him in London two years ago.

'What are you doing here?' she cried. 'I mean, how did you come to be here in the colony, in Brisbane? Heavens, Edward, this is such an amazing surprise.'

'Aha! It's all part of the conspiracy!' Edward said. 'I arrived in Singapore some weeks ago and telegraphed Father that I would be coming home to Sydney. He replied that I should step ashore in Brisbane instead, as you two were planning to visit Montone.'

'So tomorrow we're all going out there together,' Jasin said, motioning to the waiter to serve the chilled champagne.

'Father met the ship this morning and rushed me here, then dashed off to collect you.'

Jasin laughed. 'I called into the shipping office yesterday, to make certain his ship was on schedule, but I never trust those reports, so I was very glad to see her coming down the river, I can tell you.'

His son looked about the room with an appreciative nod.

'Everything worked out perfectly, as it always does for Father. The ship's captain would not dare upset his luncheon plans. And may I say the buffet looks absolutely splendid after the revolting food on that ship. I'm starving. Come and sit down, Mother.'

'A toast first,' Jasin called. 'To us, to our family. Together again.'

'Together again,' they echoed.

Georgina couldn't recall when she'd enjoyed herself more than on this day. Jasin was so happy to see his son home again that he could talk of nothing else but his great plans for the future. Edward was looking well, and very much like his father, though not as tall, and he was carrying a lot more weight. As a result of inactivity on those long voyages, Georgina supposed. And he has a young man's good appetite, she noticed happily, as he tucked into course after course.

'I can tell you, Father,' he said, 'I haven't seen a spread like this in years. I suppose food's cheap out here, is it?'

Jasin blinked. 'I really wouldn't know. Nothing to compare it with.'

'England's so expensive these days. I was pleased to get out. When I heard that woman was on her last legs, I booked passage the very next day.'

His mother winced. With all the excitement of his homecoming, she'd forgotten that Edward had been banished. In fact she hadn't given that aspect a thought in years, since all this time he'd been enjoying life with her brother and his family on their estate in Devon. His exile was more of a punishment for his parents than for Edward, but she'd never been able to persuade Dolour

MacNamara, as she was at the time, to that effect. Those Irishwomen could be hard.

Come to think of it, she wondered, how had Edward found out that the woman was terminally ill? It seemed quite unedifying to think he might have been waiting in Singapore for her demise. Surely not!

She listened to them talking about Montone Station. Near Gimpii, now known as Gympie. The stock. Cattle counted by the thousand. Its size. More than forty square miles. Hill country. Gold country. Heselwood bragging about his lucky country. Cattle prices still soaring. When the blacks burned the homestead to the ground, he'd been devastated. He'd have given the place away. But he'd hung on through thick and thin.

Not quite, Georgina mused. There was no thin. The gold he'd found on that property, and hidden from his creditors, had kept them on Easy Street. Then, when the prospectors came through in their thousands, and had to be fed, his cattle turned to gold.

Her mind drifted back to Edward. She supposed it must have been Heselwood who'd given him the tip-off about Dolour's illness to get him home at last. Somehow, though, it sounded a bit out of character. Heselwood could be outrageous, totally roughshod when it came to business affairs or even dealings with friend or foe, but she couldn't see him as the culprit here. He'd gone very quiet when Edward had referred to Dolour as 'that woman'.

Georgina had always known that Dolour was the real cause of the fierce animosity between Pace MacNamara and Jasin. At one stage she'd feared her husband would leave her for the Irish girl, and that fear hadn't subsided when Dolour married Pace.

'I'm really looking forward to tomorrow, Mother,' Edward said. 'Would you mind riding in the coach on your own? I'd love to ride up there with Father.'

'It's more than a hundred miles, dear! Are you up to it?'

'Of course he is,' Jasin cried. 'It'll do him good. Get some of that fat off him!'

'I'm not fat!' Edward snapped.

'You're not? It must be the mirrors in here. What do you think, Georgina? Or do you want to ride with us?'

'I'd prefer the coach, thank you. I might as well go back in style.'

As she walked out with them, Georgina thought that perhaps she should warn Edward not to be touchy about his father's comments. It wouldn't pay. Then she sighed. Why bother? He's twenty-five. He'll have to learn to deal with all manner of men if he's to live on a cattle station in this country. Coping with Heselwood will probably be good practice.

'Where is the Victoria Hotel?' Edward asked.

'In the main street, Queen Street, not far from here,' Jasin said.

'Excellent. Then I shall see you two in the morning. I have to meet some chaps from the ship. You'll look after my trunks, eh?'

He was out the door and hurrying up the street before they had time to reply. Georgina called to him, but he didn't hear her.

'He's going in the wrong direction,' she cried.

Heselwood took her arm. 'Then he'll have to turn back, won't he?'

Jasin was bitterly disappointed that he hadn't been invited to join Edward's shipboard pals at the Victoria. After all, he mused, I'm not exactly Methuselah. And I enjoy stimulating company.

'Well, that was an excellent repast, was it not?' he said, feigning merriment because he didn't want Georgina to think he was bothered by Edward's thoughtlessness. 'I think the crisp duckling was the best I've ever tasted.'

'Yes, they must have a Chinese fellow in the kitchen as well as their chef to present new flavours. That's all the rage in Sydney now. The fish was delicious too. I couldn't fault any of the courses, so,' she laughed, 'having eaten a little more than I should, I'd prefer to walk back to the hotel.'

'By all means.'

As they set off, keeping to the shaded side of the street, Georgina wanted to know if Jasin had any plans for Edward now.

'Since you knew he was coming home, you must have something in mind. It will be nice for him to come back to Carlton Park.'

'No. His future is in the north. In cattle. There are endless opportunities up here in Queensland. He can start by managing Montone.'

'Is that why we're going there? I thought it was to show me how it had progressed.'

'Both,' he grinned. 'I didn't imagine you'd resent having Edward along. Which reminds me, I got a bit carried away back there, talking about riding with him and all that. I can't allow you to travel alone in the coach. Edward can ride on ahead with Jack and Clem; they'll get him home safe and sound. I'll come with you.'

Georgina shook her head. 'I wouldn't dream of spoiling your fun. You'll enjoy that ride, I know you will. I believe you were actually looking forward to it. I'm quite capable of travelling alone, and I won't be alone anyway. There are bound to be other travellers.'

'That's what I'm worried about. God knows what types you'll have to contend with!'

'Don't fuss, Jasin. It's only two days. Cobb and Co. have a good reputation. I enquired. They have coach stops at registered inns. I'm sure I'll find it all very interesting.' She sighed. 'I still can't believe Edward's back. That was a wonderful surprise, Jasin, really wonderful. But don't you think it's a bit soon to give him authority at Montone? He doesn't know a thing about cattle.'

'He can learn. Jack Batterson will still be the overseer, and Clem is head stockman. They're old hands, they can teach him the ropes.'

'But as a manager?'

'Georgina, he'll have to learn to run a station from the top down. Jack's not good with the books; he'll gladly hand the office work over to Edward. And I'll have a quiet word with Clem to get him out and about the property as much as possible. Anyway, we'll be there for a few weeks. I'll start him off myself.'

'Oh, very well. I suppose he'll be all right.' She looked up. 'We'd better hurry, there's another downpour looming. Does it rain every day in Brisbane?'

'Often enough in the summer,' he said.

He saw her to their room in the hotel and then booked a room nearby for his son.

'Would you send a man to collect Mr Heselwood's luggage from the shipping office?' he asked the manager. 'He'll be along later.'

'Certainly, sir. Are you stepping out again now?'

'Yes.'

'Then you might need this umbrella.'

'No thanks, I'll take my chances.' Though Jasin often carried an umbrella in Sydney, he knew that up this end of the world it was considered unmanly for able-bodied men to sport one.

He made it to the Cobb and Co. office, arranged a ticket for Lady Heselwood for the following morning and gave notice that she'd be travelling with an extra trunk.

'Who else will be on that coach?' he asked the elderly clerk.

'Ah now, let me see . . . your lady wife is bound for Gympie. Also a Dr and Mrs Lombe, and two nuns.'

'Is that all?'

'Inside the coach, as long as no one else turns up, yes, I'd say so, sir. Yes. Other gentlemen ride up top.'

'And you have good drivers?'

'The very best, sir. Experienced men they are. Been with the company for years.'

'Thank you.' He handed the fellow a shilling. 'See that my wife has a seat facing the horses. And be sure it is a window seat on the right-hand side so that she has the morning sun but does not have to suffer the afternoon heat.'

The clerk beamed. 'Consider it done, your honour.'

Jasin walked out of the office into a steamy downpour, and watched as a half-dozen weary-looking stockmen rode into town, ropes and rifles slung by their saddles, swags resting on their horses' rumps and the inevitable cattle dog loping along at their heels.

The sight of them gave him a thrill of excitement. He'd been too long on his tame, well-run property of Carlton Park down there in New South Wales, retreating to their Sydney home in the summer. When he'd heard of that expedition heading north from Cardwell, he was more than interested; he saw it as a grand opportunity to escape the boredom that had assailed him of late. He needed to get back in the saddle and live a man's life again; he'd had enough of playing country squire, and had to give himself another challenge. Montone had been a challenge, a magnificent challenge, and he'd won. Now he was looking to claim land somewhere up in that top grazing country that Leichhardt had called the Valley of Lagoons.

It had been out of reach for years. It would be one heck of a challenge! But right now, just riding into the back country with his son was exciting.

He crossed the road and went in search of his two station hands.

John Pace resumed the argument the next day, nagging Paul for hours until, to keep the peace, he finally acceded to his twin's demand not to make any decision until everyone had given the matter more thought.

'Very well,' he said. 'I guess we'll work something out between us. As long as you and Eileen don't talk court cases.'

'It'll be best for everyone if things stay as they are,' John Pace said, 'except that we pay each of us a third of the profits.'

'I'll see Duke and tell him nothing's actually decided.'

He found Duke in the bar and explained the arrangement to him, but their younger brother was far from impressed.

'Isn't anyone listening to me? I've made it plain I'm not going back to Kooramin. I've been stuck out there all my life. I want to look about a bit. Make a change now.'

'Why don't you come to Oberon and work for me, then? That's a change. You haven't even seen my station, and you've never been on a sea voyage. I'll get you a ticket.'

'Where does the ship go to?'

'To Rockhampton. It's a real nice town. You'll like it. We only have a few days aboard ship and then a half-day's ride out to the station.'

Duke wasn't too sure. 'I'd thought of looking about here for a while.'

'You could always come back here. It's time you saw a bit more of Queensland.'

'Yes. I suppose so. All right, I'll come with you. Do you want a drink?'

'No. Laura's waiting for me.'

Paul would have enjoyed a drink; he'd taken a liking to the Carlton beer that they served here – imported from Melbourne – but deemed it wiser to move on before Duke changed his mind.

He might as well have stayed for the beer, because Duke was still in two minds about leaving Brisbane just yet for another country town. And there was the will. He had no patience with his brothers' wait-and-see attitude.

He contemplated three young men who were celebrating down the end of the bar. Apparently they'd arrived in Brisbane by ship from Singapore, where, according to their loud drunken complaints, drinks were a lot cheaper than in this overpriced establishment.

Duke grinned. They were annoying hell out of the bartender as well as two elderly gents who took their drinks and retreated to the veranda. Unfortunately, though, Duke couldn't stay to watch the fun; he had to see Mr Bloom.

'Will the title deeds to Kooramin have to be changed now?' he asked the lawyer.

'Oh yes, Duke, I've already applied to have that done in accordance with your mother's wishes.'

'And do you need the will any more?'

'Yes.' The lawyer blinked. 'It has to be registered.'

'Oh well, let me know when I can collect it. By the way . . . who gets to hold the deeds to Kooramin if we all own it?'

'Any one of the three of you.'

'Then it might as well be me. Mr Bloom, can I appoint you my lawyer? I mean for me only, when the will business is fixed?'

'Yes, Duke. I'd be happy to attend to your affairs.'

'Good. You can start with holding the deeds to Kooramin in my box.'

'Box?'

'Wherever you keep things.'

'Oh, I see. Yes. Do you want me to advise your brothers?'

'No need. I'll tell them. I have to rush now to catch up with them.'

He grabbed his hat, shook hands with Bloom and left.

Feeling smug about that little piece of footwork, Duke headed for the hotel to change. It would have to be a quick change, he mused, in and out as swiftly as he could, to avoid bumping into his brothers. Then he'd go off and have a drink somewhere before it was time to test the romps at the Bijou Palace. He'd heard about the Palace and couldn't wait to pay a visit, never having known such a place existed before coming to town.

Someone had told him it was a famous whorehouse, but it turned out to be much more than that.

A Pleasure House for Fine Gentlemen, announced a sign at the cloakroom door, that also warned against spitting, firearms, fighting and cheating at cards.

The crowded main hall was a blaze of colour and excitement, but Duke immediately homed in on the women, all scantily dressed and all showing off the best breasts in creation.

The country lad was dazzled. Two of the beauties took him to the bar, where they ordered drinks and kept him company until he got the hang of the place. There was a stage in one corner, where show girls were singing and dancing to the cheers of the crowd, and then, to his delight, came down to mix with the crowd.

There were billiard rooms, the girls told him, and card rooms and private dining rooms, but he was most interested in the 'other' rooms.

'Where are they?' he asked, his arms around a buxom girl in a bitty red spangled dress.

'Do you want me to show you?'

'No time like the present.'

She led him upstairs to where a woman, refusing to bargain, took three shillings from him.

'One hour with Bunny,' she said, making a note in a journal.

'Make it two,' he said, showing off, and tossing down three more shillings.

The small room was stark, compared with the rest of the house, but Bunny was accommodating.

'What do you do?' she asked him.

'I'm a grazier,' he said grandly, eyes popping.

When they emerged he told the woman it was six shillings well spent, and that made Bunny happy, but for the sheer romping fun of it he determined to try another girl the next night. Maybe two.

Just thinking about the Palace put a skip in his step, and he was hurrying through the hotel foyer when a clerk called to him.

'Mr MacNamara. A message for you. From Mrs Forrest. She was here for morning tea, one of our regulars, you know. She had hoped to see you this morning, but she must have missed you.'

Surprised, he opened the seal to find a neatly written invitation to dine with Mrs Forrest and her daughter Lucy Mae at home this very evening. At seven.

Duke was about to send a messenger declining the invitation, with the best excuse of short notice, but suddenly he remembered Lucy Mae, and grinned.

He'd been trying to think who Bunny had reminded him of.

Lucy Mae, of course. At the church. He hadn't seen her for ages, but she'd been instantly recognisable, a pretty woman who still had the curly blond hair, blue eyes and rosy cheeks that he remembered from childhood days. Though Bunny's cheeks and very red lips were painted, he admitted. Then he began to laugh, wondering what Lucy Mae would look like done up in circus spangles.

'I could go,' he said to himself. 'That's a good place to hide out from my brothers. Unless they've been invited too! Oh no!'

He turned back to the desk. 'Did my brothers receive these notes too?' he asked.

'No, sir, Mrs Forrest only left the one note. For you.'

'This works out well,' Duke told the mirror as he dressed for dinner. 'I should get to the Palace easily by ten thirty or eleven. Perfect! And I'll get a good meal as well. Mrs F was always known to give a good table.'

'Do you think he'll come?' Milly asked her daughter for the fourth time, as she fussed with the large flower arrangement in the hall.

'No, I don't. Why would he, with only a few hours' notice? I don't know what you were thinking of.'

'I simply asked him to dinner. Is that a crime? It was only an informal note. And why are you wearing your hair up like that? It looks so much prettier down.'

'Because I'm not sixteen, Mother. And curls are not fashionable these days.'

'Well go and play the piano. You play beautifully and it would be so nice for a gentleman to hear good music as he comes up the path.'

'Oh for God's sake!' Lucy Mae swept across the passage to the music room, not to play the piano as requested, but to escape her mother's nagging.

She picked up a magazine and sat at a table turning the pages, not managing to absorb anything much. The society pages reminded her of her late husband. Russ Bartling had been a very attractive man, and very amusing. He was enormously good company too, much admired in the drawing rooms. She'd been flattered, overwhelmed, when he'd asked for her hand in marriage, and had accepted eagerly. But then Mr Kent, an old friend of her late father's, whispered to her that she might 'go slow' on the wedding arrangements for a while, because it had come to his ears that her fiancé wasn't quite on the up and up. And worse, she discovered that he owed money to various tradesmen.

Foolishly she'd disregarded the warnings because she wanted to be married. To have her own home. Which never eventuated anyway . . . They'd lived in a dingy flat in Brisbane, with that house always just a few pounds away. As soon as he was paid money people owed him. As soon as he sold acres of land he owned outside Brisbane. Or his gold mine paid off.

In the end they couldn't pay the rent, and after only three years were forced to move back into this house with Milly.

Lucy Mae had hated him for that. Hated him. She'd felt nothing when that ship went down, except sadness for the four other passengers who were lost.

Now her mother was busily trying to marry her off to someone else, and Lucy Mae found her efforts horribly embarrassing. She wished she could think of some reason to leave here, somewhere to go, without having to use marriage as a ticket again.

She heard Milly shriek and took fright for a minute, thinking she'd had an accident, but her mother came rushing in, her taffeta skirts swishing on the polished floor.

'He's here! Duke! He's coming up the drive! Oh my, I knew he'd come! Such a dear boy.'

The little dinner party was pleasant, with Mrs Forrest fussing over him and Lucy Mae watching with a glint of amusement.

At first he'd thought the two ladies were still wearing mourning out of respect for his late mother, but then he remembered that Lucy Mae was a widow.

'I was so sorry to hear you lost your husband in the *Eastern Star* shipwreck, Lucy Mae. Really sorry. It must have been a terrible shock for you.'

She nodded, more of a shrug, and thanked him. He considered telling her how well she looked, but thought better of it, grateful that Mrs Forrest had sherry served to them and then insisted on showing him the additions she'd made to the house – a wide veranda overlooking a terraced garden that stretched down to the river.

'We could do with something like this at Kooramin,' he said. 'Or John Pace could. I won't be there.'

'Why, where are you going?' Mrs Forrest asked.

'Up to visit Paul's station and have a look about the countryside.'

'I don't know how people can live up there. It's hot enough here.'

'I suppose I'll find out,' he said.

'Did you mean you're not going back to Kooramin at all?' Lucy Mae asked, tucking away a wisp of hair that had fallen across her forehead.

'No. It's time I moved on. By the way, what happened to your curls?'

'Oh! She pulls them back into that bun,' her mother said. 'Ruining her hair.'

'It's not a bun, it's called a chignon, Mother. And it doesn't hurt my hair at all.'

Duke approved. 'I think it's a very smart style. Suits you, Lucy Mae.'

So does that black dress, he mused. Marriage must have been good for you. Strange to think of you as a widow now. And so very grown up.

Without breaching the rules of decorum, since they were all in mourning, Mrs Forrest managed to make it a cheerful evening by doing most of the talking, as usual, and Duke thoroughly enjoyed the array of desserts served after the main course of seasoned roast pork. Since he couldn't decide which one to choose, Lucy Mae brought him a small helping of each one, with lashings of cream.

After dinner, when they retired to the parlour, she returned to their previous conversation.

'I believe the forests in the north are very beautiful, Duke. They call them rain forests.'

'There are rain forests here too,' her mother said.

'Yes, but not to the same extent as in the north. I've seen pictures of them. They're just beautiful, with wonderful ferns and exotic flowers, and real jungle. It must be magical country.'

'Then I've got something to look forward to,' Duke grinned. 'Paul has sent me down pictures, but they're usually of prize bulls.'

'Oh no! How could he?'

Mrs Forrest jumped in. 'Why don't you play the piano for us, Lucy Mae?'

Duke saw her glare at her mother. 'Heavens, no. Duke didn't come to hear my amateur pieces.'

He had no choice. 'I'd love you to play, Lucy Mae.'

She was quite good, he agreed, but the clock struck eleven as she closed the piano, giving him the opportunity to make the break.

'You're definitely going tomorrow?' Mrs Forrest asked him as he was leaving.

'Off to sea in the good ship *Wyke Regis*.' He was sorry he'd said that – mentioning ships in Lucy Mae's presence – so he hurried his departure, but not before Lucy Mae made him promise to write and send pictures.

As he strode across town, Duke was looking forward to the delights of the Palace, deciding he might try his hand at their card tables before choosing a girl for an hour. Not two. They were expensive. And he'd look for one a bit classier than Bunny. It was a pity the private rooms were so bare and ugly, he thought. Coming from Mrs Forrest's fine house, with everything agleam, they rather put a man off.

Nevertheless, after a few drinks and a win at cards with pretty girls draped all round him, he soon forgot that a room could put him off and ran up the stairs with a lusty Italian girl who delivered him back to the bar at the close of the hour.

By that time the Palace had deteriorated from jollity to a sad picture of listless girls slumped at tables with weary customers, and a few argumentative drunks. Duke had a last rum and ginger, paid his bill and wandered out into the night.

It was raining heavily, so he pulled his top hat down on his head, turned up his collar and made for the lane beside the Palace that would allow him a short cut through to Queen Street, but as he came to the corner he heard shouts and saw a man thrown out of a side door, where he was set upon by three muggers.

'Hey!' he yelled, as the victim tried to fight them off. 'Get away from him!'

They ignored him, still bashing into the fellow as Duke ran towards them. He had no weapon and couldn't even see a stick to use, so he had no choice but to wade into the fight. And wade it was, the lane slippery with mud in the teeming rain. He was taller than the muggers, he was relieved to find, and was able to land a heavy punch, using his boots when the first one went down to exact more pain.

The free-for-all didn't last long. Apparently the muggers had their loot. One of them lunged at Duke with a knife, as another tried to pull his mate to his feet. The knife handler missed, sliding forward and tripping over the victim.

Duke caught the mugger by his coat tails, banged him against the wall and threw him, sprawling, after his mates, who were sprinting towards the other end of the lane.

'Bloody bastards,' the stranger muttered as Duke helped him up. 'Where the hell are we?'

'Outside the Palace. Are you all right?'

'I don't know. The ankle's not too good.' He tried to walk but stumbled. 'Damn nuisance. It's bloody twisted, I think.'

'Come on then, I'll help you.'

'Be obliged.'

As Duke assisted him out of the lane, he realised he'd seen this fellow before.

'Weren't you at the Victoria earlier?' he asked.

'Is that a bar?' the stranger muttered. 'If so, I was there.'

'You're new here?'

'Excuse me, I'm feeling ill,' the man replied, so Duke turned quickly and heaved him back into the lane, leaving him to steady himself against a wall as he spewed and retched and spewed again.

Muddied and sopping wet, Duke stood at the entrance to the lane. He wanted to walk away from this character, but his better nature took over and he waited until the retching ceased, then called:

'Where are you staying?'

'Not bloody sure. The Pavillion, I think.'

'That's a restaurant. Try again.'

'Ah well, let's see. Name a hotel.'

'The Victoria?'

'No, that's a bar.'

Duke figured this chap's accent could place him somewhere more expensive.

'The Royal Park Hotel, is it?'

'Jolly good. I think so. It'll do anyway. Now where might it be?'

'A few streets away. Come on.'

'Sorry, old chap, I need a hand. Damned unsteady here.'

Reluctantly Duke came back, stepping carefully, trying to avoid the vomit since there were no gutters in the lane. Unceremoniously he grabbed the stranger's arm and looped it across his own shoulder, then set off, lurching and slipping with this almost dead weight on him.

'Use your feet,' he snapped. 'I'm not your keeper!'

'The ankle's giving me hell.'

'So what! It's still there. Try to walk or I'll leave you here.'

At the next corner he saw a cab coming and had to drag his companion out on to the deserted road to hail it because of the blinding rain, which brought him abuse from the driver for frightening his horse.

'You pair of drunks, you stink,' he yelled at them as Duke pushed his companion into the cab.

'Bloody insolent fellow!' exclaimed the stranger. Duke, however, had remembered the muggers.

'Have you got any money?' he called, holding the door open.

'He better have,' the driver yelled, 'or he gets out now!'

'You pipe down,' Duke said.

As the stranger fished about in his sodden clothes, Duke turned his head away to avoid the smell of vomit that now permeated the warm cab.

'I've been robbed!' the man suddenly shouted from the dark depths of the leather interior. 'Someone's taken my money!'

'Is that so?' Duke said drily. He handed over some silver coins. 'Here you are. That'll get you to the hotel.'

'Bloody nice of you,' the stranger said. 'I must repay you. What's your name?'

'Don't worry about it. It's only a few shillings.'

'No, I must. Give me your name.'

'The name's Duke . . .' But then he had to jump aside as the cab jerked away and clattered off into the night.

Left standing in the rain, Duke took stock. He'd lost his new top hat. The first evening suit he'd ever owned was ruined.

'Ah, what the hell!' he laughed, and began to walk back towards his hotel. But he did pause under a tree to break off a stick, in case there were more muggers around.

Two hours later, as a cacophony of birdsong welcomed the dawn, Jasin marched into his son's bedroom to wake him and get this day on its feet. Once inside, the stench of the room disgusted him. Angrily he threw back the drapes and opened the windows, to find Edward still asleep, or, as he soon concluded, out cold, lying across the bed in filthy clothes.

'Wake up,' he shouted, taking a pitcher of water from the bedside table and hurling it at his son's head.

Edward, jerked from a dead sleep, struggled to sit up. 'What? Wha . . . what the hell are you doing?'

'Up and on your feet,' Jasin growled. 'We're taking your mother to the coach.'

'What time is it?' Edward muttered, flinching at the sudden glare of the morning.

'It's five o'clock. Get moving.'

'Did I sleep all day?' he asked groggily.

'It's five in the morning, you damn fool!'

Edward bent over to drag off his shoes and gave a yelp of pain.

'What's the matter with you?' his father barked.

'I got mugged, that's what! This bloody disgusting town! I'm black and blue!' He went to stand up but toppled over. 'Holy Christ! I think I've broken my ankle.'

His father yanked him up from the floor and threw a towel at him.

'You smell like a brewery. Get yourself across the passage to the bathroom and clean yourself up. When you've washed the stink off I'll have a look at you.' He stormed off, leaving his son to hobble about under his own steam.

Edward found the lack of sympathy somehow familiar, but was too intent on his injuries, plus the heavy thumping behind his eyes, to give it more thought.

He found an elderly maid in the hall, who turned out to be the housekeeper, and enlisted her help in running a bath. While he waited, still in his soggy clothes, he had her unpack his bags, find his dressing gown and put out suitable riding apparel.

The lady went about her duties happily, but his father was enraged when he returned to find Edward still soaking in the tub.

'Get out!' he yelled. 'Your mother's waiting. Why aren't you packed?'

'What's the hurry? I'm not riding in the coach.'

'Your bags are, you damn fool.'

When his mother saw him, she was concerned. 'You look dreadful, Edward. What happened to you?'

'He says he was mugged,' Jasin sneered. 'Probably by a bottle of whisky.'

'But look at his ankle. It's swollen.'

Jasin peered at it. 'So it is. Put your boots on, Edward, and lace 'em tight; that'll hold you together.'

A porter packed their bags on to a donkey cart. Edward could hardly cadge a ride on that vehicle, so he had no alternative but to hobble along to the Cobb and Co. depot, with his parents, trying to agree with Georgina, who was extolling the tingling beauty of this clear morning.

After all that rush, he discovered they were early, which didn't please him, and when they turned a corner and saw the dark red coach with its five horses standing by, he was unimpressed. On each side of the coach was a central door with a window, but the other openings had no glass, just rough leather blinds. Eight gentlemen were already sitting up top, exposed to the elements, and some ladies had taken their places inside.

Since his uncle's stables in Devon had several very presentable buggies and a carriage for formal occasions, as well as a string of good horses for riding, Edward knew nothing of public transport.

He turned to his father. 'Mother can't ride in a wretched vehicle like that.'

'Yes I can,' she said. 'I'm sure I'll quite enjoy it. Now hand me up, Jasin, and when you bring my horse into Gympie, be sure it has a side saddle.'

'You used to ride astride,' he teased.

'In the bush,' she retorted. 'And not when I'm wearing these skirts.'

As she stepped into the coach, undecided which red padded seat to take, Jasin said quickly: 'This one by the window facing front is yours.'

Georgina looked to the other ladies to confirm, and they agreed, so she smiled, offered them a cheerful good morning and was seated.

Edward limped up to view the five horses, surprised to find they were colour-matched, all bays, but still strong-looking animals.

'Five?' he queried the groom, who was giving the reins a last check.

'Yes,' the man answered enthusiastically. 'This is a good team, one of our best, and they can get up some pace.'

'But why five? It looks unbalanced.'

'That's where you're wrong, mate. Three in front, two in back as you see, and that makes for only one leader. He's the middle front feller, name of Jerome. The boss paid seventy pounds for him.'

As Edward watched, the driver came out and, with a flourish, jumped up to his seat, threading the reins through his left hand and picking up a huge whip with his right. It was at least twelve feet long!

'Rather a ferocious-looking weapon to use on a fine horse like Jerome,' Edward said tartly, but the groom took offence.

'Our drivers don't whip the horses! These animals never need the whip, they don't play up! If they did, they wouldn't be on these teams. No, sir!' He looked proudly at the driver. 'That's Teddy. He's famous. I'm gonna be a driver like him one day. Do you know, he sings to the horses as they go and they love it.'

Edward stood back, admiring the sleek animals. He could almost feel the speed of them. 'I'd love to drive a five in hand,' he said, his palms sweating at the thought, but the groom had moved off to check the large kerosene lamp above the driver's seat.

His mother seemed content to take on this journey, so Edward reached in to shake her gloved hand and wish her well before the coach door was closed. As he moved back with his father to join the small crowd that had gathered to farewell the coach, a clerk came out holding up his watch and called: 'Six o'clock, Teddy!'

'Then we're off, me beauties!' Teddy shouted, cracking the huge whip rather theatrically, Edward thought. The horses sprang away as one, gathering speed as they headed down the road, mud flying from their hooves.

'I wouldn't care to be a passenger up top there today,' Edward said. 'The box seat has a hood. The others don't.'

His father laughed. 'Not at all. They'll have the time of their lives, with hey,

54

ho, the wind and the rain! Now we have to get going, but we'll have breakfast first. What about some fried chops and eggs?'

Edward's face turned green. 'No thanks,' he muttered.

'Then you'll wait while I eat,' his father snapped.

Georgina was pleased with her decision to wear her navy travelling suit with a white blouse so that she could take the jacket off if the heat became too intense.

The seats and back rests in the coach were cushioned rather thinly, she noticed after they'd travelled a few miles, but she was agreeably surprised that the vehicle ran so smoothly, and commented on this as the four lady passengers made each other's acquaintance.

Sister Catherine, the elder nun, was a Roman Catholic, of the Sisters of Mercy order, and a seasoned coach traveller. She explained that the body of the Cobb and Co. coaches rested on leather rather than steel springs, which made for a more comfortable ride. She and her companion, Sister Jude, were on their way to open a convent school in Gympie.

'We're so excited to be given this honour,' she added. 'We can hardly wait to get there.'

Seated at the other window facing front was a Mrs Lombe. She was wearing a severe black dress with a white lace collar, and a small straw hat which she removed and placed on the rack over her head. Georgina was quick to make the most of the woman's informality by taking off her own elegant felt hat.

'That's a relief,' she smiled as her hat went up into the rack as well. 'I hope you don't mind,' she said to the nuns.

'Not at all,' Sister Catherine grinned. 'You'll forgive us if we don't follow suit.'

Georgina laughed, contemplating the nuns' starched wimples and veils.

Sister Catherine then addressed Mrs Lombe. 'I do hope your husband is all right sitting up top. There is room in here for six. We shouldn't want him to be discomforted.'

Mrs Lombe shrugged. 'My husband has taken himself off to sit on the box seat by the driver. He claims he's giving up his seat in here so that we ladies should be more comfortable, but I'm more inclined to think he's dodging having to sit and listen to women talk.'

'Did I hear someone say he is a doctor?' Sister Catherine asked.

'You probably did, but it's not correct. People make that mistake all the time. I'm a registered doctor, Sister. I intend to open a practice in Gympie. My husband is a stock and station agent.'

'Oh, I beg your pardon, Doctor,' the nun said. 'But may I congratulate you? You're the first lady doctor I've had the honour of meeting.'

'I have to apologise too,' Georgina said. 'My husband was advised that I'd be travelling with a doctor and his wife! But ladies, may I say you will all be most welcome in Gympie, I'm sure. I myself am only a visitor; I will be staying on my husband's cattle station.'

'So you know something about the area, Mrs Heselwood?' the elder nun asked.

'Not much, I'm sorry. I haven't been this way for quite a while.' Georgina shuddered, remembering that perilous ride out of the area. She was so relieved to be in this coach and not out on the road, no matter how pleasant it seemed now. She still suffered nightmares from the terror of the night when Montone was raided by blacks who fought their way into the homestead . . .

Perspiration glistened on her forehead. She began to tremble as the memory of that horror welled up again, rekindling fears she'd been trying so hard to overcome.

Sister Jude, sitting opposite, leaned over and handed her a tiny bottle of lavender water.

''Tis said to be cooling,' she whispered shyly.

Georgina looked at the kindly brown eyes of the young nun and sighed. 'Thank you, Sister.'

She took the bottle, opened the stopper and breathed the familiar fragrance.

'It really does help,' she said after a few minutes. 'I am feeling a little better now.' More from the interruption than the fragrance, she mused, but Sister Jude glowed, delighted to be able to do a good deed.

Georgina found the thunder of the horses' hooves and the pace of the coach exhilarating, though it did lurch about quite a bit. As a result, conversation was amiable but desultory, allowing them to view the changing outskirts of Brisbane Town.

Two hours later, the driver warned of the coach's approach to the first stop of the day by blowing his bugle, and they pulled into the staging post at Petrie, where grooms went swiftly to work changing the horses.

'If any of you ladies need to make use of a lavatory at any of these stops, you must do so,' the doctor said. 'If you are shy, I will accompany you. But you must not hold on. Too many ladies do this and it's so foolish.'

They all thanked her but shook their heads, and minutes later they were off again. Next stop, they were told by Mr Lombe, who had climbed down to see that nobody had fallen out, was Stony Creek. He also informed them that because of the recent rains they were travelling the 'wet' route, which was eighteen miles longer than the 'dry' one.

After Stony Creek came Naraba, for the next change of horses. Here the countryside was drier, and as they set off again the coach raised clouds of dust, which meant having to drop the leather blinds. From then on the journey seemed to become more difficult.

Georgina held her breath whenever she heard the brake grinding as they drove down steep hills and into dry gullies, and gazed transfixed, lifting her feet from the floor for fear of imminent flooding, as the vehicle rattled and swished through river crossings.

When they stopped at Banksfort House, where another team of fresh horses was rushed out, the ladies gladly climbed down to do the doctor's bidding, after which they had a quick lunch of tea, buns and cakes. Quite a few of the men, they noticed curiously, were served coffee by the pint.

They travelled on then through the spectacular Glasshouse Mountains, with the blinds rolled up once more, all surprised that they could glimpse the blue sea in the distance. They were quickly becoming accustomed to the hazards of the road. At one stage they made their way through a trackless forest, and further on rattled across the bone-shaking bed of yet another stony creek. Eventually they came to a place called Mellin Creek, and from there, as the afternoon sun began its descent, they raced on to Cobb's Camp near Woombye Village.

The women clapped with relief when they heard the triumphant bugle, and Sister Catherine noted that they were right on time entering Cobb's Camp, where they were to stay for the night.

The inn was a stone building with a wide veranda at the front, shaded by peppercorn trees. A small crowd was lined up outside to greet them. No sooner had they pulled up than several gentlemen leapt down from the roof and bolted for the bar.

Mr Lombe appeared at the coach door to 'decant the ladies', as he called that pleasant duty, and they all stepped down, not a little wobbly from the rolling motion of the coach.

'I feel as if I've been at sea for a week,' Dr Lombe said, taking her husband's arm, and then a gentleman offered his arm to Georgina.

She looked up, surprised to see Jasin.

'What are you doing here?'

'We got here this afternoon,' he said, 'so I decided we'd wait for you, in case you'd changed your mind about public transport.'

'No, no,' she said. 'I'm fine. Except I'm rather hot and thirsty. But where is Edward?'

'He's inside with Jack and Clem.'

Jasin escorted her up the steps to the veranda and on to a long cool hallway, where the innkeeper's wife, Mrs Stumpf, greeted her.

'Ah! You're here!' she cried. 'Your husband, he's been worried about you. You go on down to your room, Mrs Heselwood, and I send you down a cold drink.'

'I thought I was to share with the ladies,' Georgina said as Jasin led her to a small bedroom.

'Sorry. You'll have to share with me instead. We're staying over too. I've been talking to Mr Stumpf. They've been here for a couple of years now and they have a reputation for an excellent table. We might as well enjoy it.'

The evening meal was served on two long tables in the wide kitchen. The Heselwood party of five shared with bearded miners on their way to the goldfields. At the other table, Dr and Mr Lombe were in the company of the driver, several commercial travellers and three more miners. Georgina had hoped they'd leave room for the nuns at one of the tables, but soon realised they would prefer to dine in private, and were probably being served in their room. Nevertheless she did enquire of the serving maid, and was relieved to find that Mrs Stumpf had already accommodated the sisters.

The soup was full bodied and plentiful, and was followed by platters of pork and mutton chops, whole cooked potatoes, and jugs of rich onion gravy. The men took to the food with gusto. Even Jasin, she smiled, who was usually so fussy about meals. She supposed he was already settling into outback mode, to which he was no stranger. She herself hadn't minded roughing it at Montone when they'd first occupied that homestead, busying herself with furnishings and setting out the gardens. But she was younger then. And shocked to the core when it was burned to the ground!

The new homestead, Jasin had warned, wasn't as spacious as the original. It had begun as a small stone cottage for stockmen and had grown from there. 'Nothing fancy,' he'd said. 'Not even any curtains, since we're miles from anywhere.' Georgina had made sure she had curtain materials in her trunk.

After dinner, most of the travellers retired to their rooms, aware of another early call the next morning.

Georgina didn't sleep well. The large white mosquito net was no help to her. She could hear the little beasts buzzing during the night but couldn't make out whether they were outside or inside the net, so she lay there in a constant state of alarm. To make matters worse, her husband slept heavily, unconcerned by the blood-sucking menaces in their room.

At a quarter to five, according to her gold fob watch, a family of currawongs woke her with ear-splitting whistles and calls reminiscent of a tinpot band, so she struggled out of bed and faced the dawn, shading her tired eyes from the glare.

With time to spare, she washed, brushed her fair hair out, parted it and then rewound it into a soft bun, flat enough to allow her hat to stay in place. For a few minutes she couldn't find her hat, and then she remembered it was still in the coach.

'You're in the country now,' she laughed. 'You're allowed to forget your hat.'

Feeling better, she woke Jasin, reminding him of the early start, and walked along to the kitchen. As she peered in the door she saw that several men, including Edward, were already at breakfast. 'Good morning, Mother,' he called, leaving the table to come and greet her.

'I'm surprised to find you up so early,' she said. 'I thought I'd have to send someone to wake you.'

'No need,' he whispered. 'I didn't sleep a wink. I was relegated to a dormitory room full of smells and snores.'

She frowned a warning at him, lest someone hear him, and changed the subject. 'What are you having for breakfast?'

'The works,' he grinned. 'Chops and eggs and lamb's fry and bacon and potatoes. And a bucket of onion gravy again. No kippers, though.'

Just then Mrs Stumpf called to her: 'Come in! Come in! A beautiful morning it is, no? What you like for your breakfast, lady?'

'I really couldn't eat a big breakfast, thank you, Mrs Stumpf. I'll just have a coffee.'

'Ah, but you must have something. You have a long way to go! I find you something nice and light, eh? Maybe you like to eat out on the veranda with the other lady. It's nice and cool there in the mornings.'

She turned to Edward. 'You finish your breakfast, Mr Heselwood, before it goes cold. I look after your mother.'

Greatly relieved to have been spared the rich aroma of the men's hearty breakfasts, Georgina was ushered through to the front veranda to find Dr Lombe seated at a small table.

'Good morning, Mrs Heselwood,' the doctor said. 'Do join me. Mrs Stumpf makes excellent coffee, and look! The most superb pastries! Much better for our constitutions than all that meat the men are putting away.'

'Thank you, I will.' Georgina slid on to a high-backed bench beside Dr Lombe. 'This seat is very nice,' she added. 'I wonder where it came from? It seems sad to find it out here, exposed to the elements.'

'Yes. It has seen better days. In a church maybe. It's cedar, and beautifully carved. We're quite honoured, I think.'

A serving maid bustled out with a jug of fresh coffee and more sweet pastries, seemingly quite concerned that this was all that the ladies required for breakfast. Once convinced, however, she hurried away.

'At least we can share the view, since we're both facing out,' Dr Lombe said as she poured the coffee. 'I've been out here for a while; the sunrise was spectacular.'

'It's still lovely,' Georgina said, admiring the deep greenery of the hills set against the glittering skyline.

Just then two grooms led their coach and horses around to the wide clearing in front of the inn.

'Oh my!' Dr Lombe said. 'We've got a team of brown horses this time. But they all look very strong.'

'Indeed they do.' Georgina was enjoying an apple-filled pastry, and at the same time was fascinated by the sight of the grooms checking the harnesses and collars. 'They're very thorough,' she commented, and Dr Lombe agreed.

'I heard that Cobb and Co. go to a great deal of trouble for safety reasons,' she said, 'but I had no idea that they employed such a detailed check. Those men are testing every strap and trace.' She leaned forward to get a better view. 'Even the metals, the harness rings and so forth,' she added, astonished.

By this time several gentlemen had come out of the inn and wandered down the steps to smoke their pipes and watch all the intricate harnessing. So far there was no sign of Jasin, but Edward was out there asking questions of the grooms.

Typical of him, Georgina smiled. He'd always loved horses . . . was keenly interested in anything to do with them for that matter, especially the hunt. She remembered that he'd written to tell his parents that his uncle had allowed him to drive his four-wheeled brougham around the estate, a dangerous pastime. And apparently, as he'd told them at lunch, his latest sport was an equestrian game called polo, though he was disappointed to hear that it was not played in the colonies. Jasin had mentioned that a game of that name had recently been introduced into the colony of Victoria, but it might not be the same one.

'Isn't that your son?' Dr Lombe asked her.

Georgina looked over to see that a groom was having trouble with a horse that was rejecting its blinkers, and Edward was helping to quieten it.

'Yes,' she nodded, relieved that the horse was settling.

The men were now checking the traces, and Edward, being helpful again, climbed up into the driver's seat, holding up each of the reins in turn.

'Righto!' the groom called to him. 'They're all in order, mister. Hang on now, I'll come up and hold them traces for Teddy.'

As the groom walked towards the coach, Georgina saw a mischievous grin on Edward's face. She recognised it and thought: No, surely not!

But even as the thought flashed through her mind, Edward flipped a rein across the rump of the lead horse and it jumped forward, confused by the unfamiliar signal.

Georgina leapt from her seat, calling out: 'No! Edward! No!' But she was too late. The horses had bolted across the clearing and out on to the road, the coach rattling along behind them.

The wide hem of Georgina's long skirt had caught on the leg of their breakfast table as she was trying to extricate herself. Now it gave way and she went forward with such momentum that she tripped and fell down the steps of the veranda before anyone could reach out to her.

She heard herself scream as she fell, mortified that she should make such a spectacle of herself. Then she landed heavily in the gravel and screamed again as an intense jolt of pain coursed through her body, remaining, excruciatingly, within her as if its exit were somehow blocked.

All about her men were shouting. Georgina, fearful for Edward, tried to raise herself, but her arms were like rubber, refusing to support her. She called out to the men, needing to know what was happening; had Edward been able to control those horses?

It was Jasin who answered her. 'Yes, dear. They've got more sense than him. They pulled up of their own accord a short way down the road. Come on now, we'll help you up.'

There was another man with him, and as they began to assist her to her feet, Georgina shook her head and groaned in pain. 'No,' she whispered. 'I'm sorry, I can't . . .'

Faces were staring down, ringed around her as if she were an exhibit, and she snapped at them to move away, but it wasn't her voice, it was Dr Lombe's. Not that it mattered. Georgina was grateful for some privacy so that she could get to her feet with a little dignity.

The doctor was kneeling beside her in the dirt, and Jasin was squatting at her left side.

'Please,' she begged. 'Let me up.'

'In a sec,' Dr Lombe said. 'You've had a bad fall, Mrs Heselwood. We'll just go quietly now.'

Mrs Stumpf appeared carrying a folded blanket and dropped to the ground beside them, her chubby face full of concern.

'So lucky we are to have a doctor with us today,' she moaned, as Dr Lombe examined the patient.

'What's wrong with her?' Jasin asked, impatience in his voice. 'Couldn't you do this inside, Mrs Lombe? My wife can't be kept lying out here indefinitely.'

'She has a broken leg and maybe other injuries,' the doctor said softly. 'She will need to be carried inside. Carefully. A stretcher will have to be made.'

'My men will do that immediately. Where can we take my wife, Mrs Stumpf?'

'Into my sitting room,' the woman replied eagerly.

Georgina was trying to follow all this, but their voices seemed to fade now and again. She worried that the fall was bringing on deafness. After all, she had banged her head and it was aching fiercely. She could hear activity all around her and a swishing of wind in the gum trees high above. Then she realised that the men were carrying her inside on a stretcher. She found it almost a miracle that Mrs Stumpf should have a stretcher standing by for emergencies and made a mental note to commend her for her foresight. She was comfortable on this stretcher too, very comfortable; a better way to travel than those hard seats in the coach, with their inadequate cushions. She would recommend them to Mr Cobb as soon as possible.

Though Jasin was wary of a female doctor's opinion, he could hardly argue with the woman, who claimed it was possible that his wife had other injuries and that she should only be moved with great care.

She'd given Georgina laudanum for the pain, and covered her with the rug, while Clem and Jack constructed a makeshift stretcher from branches and canvas. Fortunately Georgina was a slight woman, so they were able to carry her safely into the sitting room, where the doctor insisted that Mrs Heselwood be placed on a firm mattress on the floor.

'You can't leave her there!' Jasin objected. 'For God's sake, woman, put her on the couch or she'll be at the mercy of all the spiders and cockroaches that tramp these floors at night. Even snakes! I won't have it, madam!'

'Mr Heselwood, in these circumstances I need the patient to remain flat. That narrow couch is too short and quite unsuitable. Kindly allow me to continue my examination.'

While he waited, the innkeeper gave Jasin a brandy and broke the news to him that Teddy, the driver, had imprisoned his son in a shed.

'I don't know what I should do about that,' Mr Stumpf moaned. 'The young man is saying it was only a joke and it is illegal to lock him up. But Teddy says he stays.'

'The driver is right,' Jasin snapped. 'Leave him there until I have time to think about him.'

'Then there's something else, milord.'

'What?'

'The coach has to leave. He's late already. Cobb coaches are never late.'

Jasin shrugged. 'Tell him to go. And thank him for waiting. My wife isn't well enough to travel today.'

'The driver is waiting for the doctor lady. Her husband says she must hurry.'

'Oh God. She can't leave. My wife needs her.'

He dashed out to the coach to confer with the driver, and then with Mr Lombe, who was adamant that Dr Lombe should board the coach immediately.

Eventually Sister Catherine intervened. 'Gentlemen, give me a few minutes while I have a word with the doctor.'

Without waiting for a response, she dashed across to the inn, rosary beads swinging from her belt, took the steps in her stride and disappeared inside.

Anxiously she beckoned to Dr Lombe. 'Will you be able to set the lady's leg?'

'I'll do my best, with whatever I can utilise, maybe some saplings and canvas strips, but I'll have to prepare her first. Surely they'll wait?'

'They will have to,' the nun said firmly. 'Sister Jude and I will assist you. I haven't had any nursing experience, but Sister Jude has. Just hold on a moment.'

Jasin was waiting outside the sitting room. 'What is happening in there, Sister?'

'The doctor intends to set your wife's leg. Sister Jude and I will assist. I am sure that if you appeal to the other passengers to support you, that coach will have to wait. Your wife is not ready, and there are three ladies who refuse to board without her,' she said with a twinkle in her eyes. 'I'm sure you can persuade the others.'

'And my wife will be able to travel?'

'Dr Lombe believes it's best if she does. She has to go into hospital as soon as possible, and Gympie is the closest. She can be put into traction there. Now, we'll make room for her and the doctor inside the coach; Sister Jude and I will be happy to sit up top.'

'Thank you, Sister. I'll want to board the coach too now. Tell Dr Lombe to leave it to me. The coach will wait!'

Sister Catherine nodded. 'Excellent. I thought we could rely on you to make them see sense. Would you mind asking Sister Jude to come in now?'

She returned to Dr Lombe. 'How's the patient?'

'Still out of it. We'll have to work quickly. Could you get Mrs Stumpf for me?'

'Yes, of course. But don't be worrying. The coach will wait.'

'Really?'

'Yes. I think we can rely on Lord Heselwood to have the last word.'

'Is he a lord? I didn't know.'

'I saw it on the manifest, but obviously neither of them insists on their title being used.'

It takes all types to make a world, she smiled to herself as she went in search of Mrs Stumpf.

'About bloody time,' Edward said, angrily brushing chaff from his clothes as Clem unlocked the shed to release him.

'Your dad's none too pleased with you,' Clem shrugged.

'It was only a lark, I only wanted to drive the rig out to the road. No harm done.'

'Tell that to your mum,' Clem spat, and strode off to the stables.

CHAPTER THREE

Paul was exasperated. 'You never know what Duke will do next!' he complained to Laura.

'Why, what's wrong?'

'He's not coming to Rockhampton with us! After I had to slip the clerk an extra two shillings to get him a ticket! The boat is packed with miners convinced there's gold in our hills.'

'Is he going back to Kooramin with John Pace and Eileen after all?'

'No. He's decided to stay on in Brisbane for a while.'

She laughed. 'What's wrong with that? He's never been up this way before. He probably just wants to look around.'

'He said he'd come up and give us a hand with the mustering. I was counting on him.'

'We can hire some stockmen in the township.'

'If we're lucky. They're all carrying picks instead of stockwhips.'

'It's no use worrying about that now. I'm looking forward to the sea voyage. I hope we have a nice cabin.'

Paul grunted, as if the chances of that were remote. 'You go down, love, I'll bring the bags. John Pace and Eileen are in the lounge waiting for us. Eileen wants us to go with them to St Stephen's before the ship sails, to say a rosary for Mum. Is that all right with you?'

'Of course.'

As she walked down the stairs, Laura felt an affinity with her husband's younger brother. She would have liked to stay on in Brisbane too, at least for a few more days, but Paul had come down to be with his mother, which had been a sad two weeks. Now he saw no reason to delay their return.

Laura did, though. The cattle station could be a lonely place at times, and Rockhampton was only a village. It would have been nice to spend some time shopping in Brisbane, and take in a visit to the theatre, which was only a few doors down the street. But then she was wise enough not to mention such outings while the brothers were in mourning.

'I'll bet Dolour wouldn't have minded if we'd managed a little enjoyment during our stay here,' she told herself, making for the lounge.

Eileen was seated, straight-backed, on the edge of a leather armchair, still in her funereal black, with her handbag plugged on her knee.

'Where's Paul?' she asked, frowning at Laura's navy costume, but digging her heels in, Laura didn't see why she should have to explain to this woman. Explain that she only had one suitable black outfit and that she'd worn it for two days. And that that was enough in this heat.

'He's coming.'

'And Duke? Where's he?'

'I have no idea.'

'There's no need for you to come to St Stephen's,' Eileen said bluntly. 'I've invited poor Jeannie's parents. They were Dolour's friends as well, you know. It could be awkward for Paul to have you there.'

Laura stared at her. 'You like to make him suffer, don't you, Eileen?'

'I do not! I'm simply mindful of people's feelings.'

Instead of taking a seat in the lounge with her sister-in-law, Laura kept walking. She strolled around the table in the middle of the room, glanced in the large gilt-edged mirror on the wall as she passed, looked out of the windows, then left the room.

She met Paul in the lobby. 'I think it's better if we don't go with them to the church.'

'Why not?'

'Because Jeannie's parents are attending.'

'Eileen's work?'

'Yes.'

'I thought so. Just ignore her. We're going.'

'I know it's important for you to farewell your mother this morning, so you go. I'll stay here.'

He took her arm and led her out on to the veranda. 'Laura, you are coming. If you don't, she's won, don't you see? You can't let her run your life.'

Laura glanced along the veranda and saw John Pace sitting in a cane armchair smoking his pipe. He was obviously waiting for the rest to assemble.

'You miss the point, Paul,' she said quietly. 'It's not a case of who wins and who doesn't win. I don't care for her attitude. If it doesn't bother you, then you go with them. I'm going for a walk.'

She stepped into Queen Street and began walking briskly with other pedestrians, fully expecting Paul to come after her. When that didn't happen, she had no choice but to keep up the pace, though she was busting to look back and see if he were following.

Quickly she turned a corner and slowed to small steps, peering in shop windows, seeing nothing, listening for his voice. Finally she stopped, using a well-stocked window as an excuse, becoming angrier as the minutes passed. He didn't have to go to the church with them! There was still plenty of time. They could go later, she and Paul. They could go together, say private prayers for his mother.

She decided to hurry on and approach the hotel from the other direction. Give the impression that she'd simply taken a turn around the block. Find him waiting for her.

Curiosity caused her to look back in case he was following, and that was a mistake! She saw them then, all three of them, John Pace, Eileen and Paul, walking along the other side of the street, headed for St Stephen's.

He had gone without her! He'd allowed Eileen to dismiss his wife as if she were not part of his family. Where they were concerned, Paul was as weak as water. And all to please his dead wife's parents.

She turned quickly and stormed into a nearby doorway, to find herself in a large emporium, this section devoted to ladies' fashions. Her mood improved as she began wandering along the aisles, amazed at the finery on display. She homed in on exquisite items that would never find their way to the wooden counters in her hometown general store, and began shopping with the help of a gentleman floorwalker, who provided her with a hand-crafted basket for her purchases. She bought elegant handkerchiefs and scarves, a delicious perfume from France, face cream, even powder, which she'd never used before, though she was too shy to accept the rouge a shopgirl was offering.

Up a flight of steps she discovered gorgeous ladies' costumes, with bustles much more flamboyant than the curve that accented her slim waistline from the rear, and she giggled, daring herself to buy one. Laura's reputation in Rockhampton had long been that of a rebel: the girl who had defied her father, a citizen of influence in the town, jilted her fiancé, and finally shocked the whole town by marrying the young widower Paul MacNamara.

'Snared him too soon after Jeannie's death,' the gossips in the pubs and the sewing circles had carped. 'What with her marble gravestone out there in the cemetery still shinin' new in the sunlight.'

Resisting temptation, Laura turned away, only to be confronted by a small blue velvet toque trimmed with tiny rosebuds. It was so pretty that she had to try it on.

Even as she purchased her hat, and saw it carefully placed in a striped hatbox, Laura couldn't imagine where she'd wear it, but for the present it was immaterial.

She was walking happily out of the store with her booty when she met Rosa Palliser. Both women were pleased to see each other again, and after an excited discussion about Laura's purchases, they headed for a nearby café.

'I can't stay long,' Laura said. 'Our ship sails this afternoon.'

'So you're doing some last-minute shopping?'

'Sort of . . . I haven't much time.'

'Then you must come down again. Stay with us. I love shopping. Not much else to do here . . .'

They ordered their coffee and the inevitable cakes, and Laura asked:

'What do you prefer to do?'

'I'd rather be out in the country. I love to ride, and see new places. But home is here.'

'So do I,' Laura said.

'Are you still at Oberon Station?'

'Yes.'

'My father has been there. He says it's a very beautiful property.'

'Has he? I didn't know that. You'll have to visit some time, and we'll explore together.'

'I'd love to.'

Their meeting ended in a rush as both realised time had slipped by too quickly.

'Now don't forget to write to me,' Laura said.

'I won't,' Rosa laughed. 'After all, we are related.'

'We are?'

'Yes, of course. Paul is my father's stepson. So that'd make you my stepsister-in-law, wouldn't it?'

Just then another joined the conversation. 'Ah, here are my two favourite ladies! What mischief are you pair up to?'

Rosa giggled, correcting him. 'You mean your two favourite sisters, Duke!'

'Sisters? Perish the thought! Come on, I'll take you both to lunch. Where's a good dining room, Rosa?'

'Thank you but I can't,' Rosa said. 'I have to meet Charlie.'

'And I've got to get back to the hotel,' Laura told him. 'Are you coming?'

'No thanks.'

'Did you go to the church this morning?'

'No. I talk to my mum on my own time.'

As she hurried down Queen Street, Laura realised that Duke wasn't surprised that she hadn't attended St Stephen's either.

There wasn't much time left. Duke wished he'd had a chance to talk to Laura, but it was too late now. He just wanted to be on his own, a few days' break from the family. He was sick of them organising him.

Anyway, he wanted to stay in touch with Bloom, not to be relying on mail. When the will was cleared, then he'd go north to placate Paul, but one thing was sure, he was never returning to Eileen's miserable company. For years he'd taken it for granted that he'd marry one day, and leave Kooramin for his own place, so he hadn't given the matter much thought. Mainly because the right girl hadn't come along. But when his mother, seriously ill, had told him she'd dearly love to see him married and settled down before she went to the Lord, he'd asked himself the question: settle down where?

Surely, when Dolour left Kooramin to her three sons, she'd known that the youngest, a single man, couldn't be expected to live and work there like a station hand for ever. She wasn't a silly woman. Far from it. Dolour always knew exactly what she was doing, but she was a closed book. She never explained herself. Never made excuses. Not even when she up and married Rivadavia.

The more he thought about it, the more Duke saw that she'd given him a way out. He would own his share of the station and could do what he liked with it. His mother had enabled him to strike out on his own by not placing any conditions on their inheritance.

It was a straight three-way split.

He would go to the church and thank her, after he'd waved them all out of Brisbane.

The wharves were thronged with people keen to farewell those fortunate enough to have acquired tickets aboard the coastal steamer *Wyke Regis*, as well as townsfolk curious to witness the exodus of local men who fancied themselves as miners.

'You'd think they were going to the North Pole instead of just up the coast to Rockhampton,' Milly Forrest said loudly, as she elbowed her way past tearful women and children clinging to men already equipped with swags and bush hats.

'That ship's going to Cairns as well,' Lucy Mae gasped as she tried to keep up with her mother. Milly, an imposing woman with a penchant for very large hats, could wade through crowds like an ocean liner, her daughter pondered, dodging small bags and boxes that waited underfoot to trip the unwary. She was always left struggling in her mother's wake. Often even apologising to placate resentment.

As soon as she spotted Paul MacNamara near the gangway, Milly made a beeline towards him, calling over her shoulder to Lucy Mae to get a move on.

That morning Lucy Mae had been surprised to be told they were going down to the wharves to 'see off' Laura and Paul.

'They're dear friends, the MacNamaras,' Milly had insisted. 'Just because their mother has died, we mustn't drop them.'

'Not going to see them off doesn't mean we're dropping them,' Lucy Mae said. 'I don't suppose this idea has anything to do with the fact that Duke is travelling with them?'

'What if it does? Someone has to look out for you, so that you don't make another mistake. I won't be around for ever, you know.'

Rather than invite that conversation again, Lucy Mae had agreed.

'Very well, but we don't need to go on board the ship. I hate that, it's always so much of a crush. We'll just go and say goodbye to them and leave.'

Her mother's shrug told her that Milly would eventually do as she pleased, but now Lucy Mae was happy to see that the steamer, looming above them, was already too crowded to cope with more visitors.

Just then the ship's hooter was sounded, and a group of young men, wearing coloured bandannas and waving a placard that read: GOLD DUST OR BUST, charged frantically past her, obviously in a panic lest they miss the boat.

Lucy Mae had the presence of mind to step quickly behind the last of them and allow them to forge a path for her right to where two officers were practically throwing disembarking visitors ashore so that the last of the passengers could mount their wobbling gangway. She had time to wish Laura and Paul a safe trip home, then turned back to find her mother giving Duke a hearty hug before he too boarded the ship.

'But I'm not a passenger, Mrs Forrest,' he was saying, trying to disentangle himself. 'I'm not going!'

Embarrassed by her mother's mistake, Lucy Mae turned to Eileen MacNamara, who was standing nearby with John Pace and their two children.

'How are you, Eileen?' she asked.

'Well enough,' Eileen replied grimly. 'Duke's not going to Rockhampton after all. He's let Paul down. And us too, for that matter.'

'How?'

'We've a long journey ahead of us to get back to Kooramin Station, as you know, Lucy Mae. But Duke's not coming back with us either. We'll just have to manage without him!'

'Eileen,' her husband said tersely, 'if Duke had gone on with Paul and Laura, we'd have had to manage without him. I told you I've engaged a rider to accompany us. Look!' He took the younger child and held her up. 'There they are, by the rails. Wave to Uncle Paul and Aunt Laura!'

Milly bounded over to join them, looking very smug and pleased with herself.

'Eileen, dear,' she cried. 'I do believe you're getting prettier every time I see you. Your red hair has never lost its colour, has it? I used to have lovely red hair once.'

'I'm hardly at the age of having it fade as yet, Mrs Forrest!'

'No, of course not. How are things at Kooramin?'

'Excellent,' Eileen said, picking up the other little girl and pointing to the ship.

'I'll lift Tess up higher so she can see better,' Duke offered.

'Don't bother!' Eileen snapped.

The ship seemed to take ages pulling away into the wide river, and Lucy

Mae wished she could leave to escape the tension between this trio, but all around her people lingered as if life depended on a last glimpse of the *Wyke Regis* chugging towards Moreton Bay. She felt it would be unseemly to turn one's back too soon. Not that the wait bothered Milly, she noticed. Her mother, chatting amiably with the MacNamaras, seemed to be totally unaware of any problem.

'I was not unaware,' she said to Lucy Mae on the way home. 'Eileen was so rude to Duke one would have to be deaf and blind not to notice. But she has always been a jumped-up little piece. Ever since she became the mistress of Kooramin, she's forgotten her dad's name. Poor old Harry. It was Dolour who got him out of the madhouse and found him a job as a yardman in a nunnery.'

'Was he insane?' Lucy Mae had a great fear of madmen, though she'd never met one.

'No, just weak in the head from too much liquor. But I don't know why Eileen was so down on Duke.'

'She wanted him to accompany them home. It takes at least two weeks to get out there, and they've got the children along.'

'No. That's not it. I'll bet it's something to do with Dolour's will. I must look out for it.'

'You can't just go and read it.'

'I don't have to go anywhere. Wills are published in newspapers.'

'I didn't know that,' Lucy Mae said, relieved her husband had died intestate so the world couldn't learn he was penniless.

'Anyway,' Milly said, as the driver turned their buggy into Brunswick Street, 'Duke is coming to the races at Eagle Farm with us tomorrow.'

'He's coming with us?'

'Yes. I invited him. He's not a member of the Brisbane Turf Club. I told him your dear father was a founding member, and that I have life membership. We can't leave him on the outer. It should be a really good day. And it's time you stopped wearing black.'

'Mother, I wish you'd stop harping on what I wear.'

'Somebody has to . . .'

At dawn, from habit, Duke was up and standing at the window of his hotel room, looking down at the deserted main street, wondering what a man was supposed to do having to wait so long for breakfast. No one seemed to move in this town until the shops opened. Then, suddenly, he remembered: they'd all gone! The ship had sailed for Rockhampton with Paul and Laura, and the other two had finally got themselves mounted up and set off for home. He was on his own at last. Free to do whatever he liked. Whatever he bloody liked!

70

Eileen was angry that he wasn't returning with them, claimed he'd reneged on them, and even John Pace had been in a bad mood. On the journey up to Brisbane, John Pace and Eileen and the two little girls had travelled in the big well-sprung buggy, and Duke had accompanied them on horseback, often riding ahead to arrange accommodation for them all, mostly at station homesteads. They'd seen some fine properties on the way, but as all three of them had agreed, few could match their own Kooramin Station in the fertile Namoi Valley. Except, maybe, the larger neighbouring station, Carlton Park, owned by Jasin Heselwood. Everyone admired Carlton Park, which was rather posh with its grand homestead, but there were problems looming for that property.

As had happened everywhere, a village had followed the early settlers like Pace and Heselwood, and now that village was a town called Narrabri, which was expanding ominously towards Carlton Park. The Heselwoods lived in Sydney these days, but the Carlton Park manager had said it was inevitable that the government would demand they subdivide. Even Lord Heselwood couldn't hold back the tide. Duke felt sorry for him. He didn't believe the government had the right to destroy the great sheep and cattle stations that had been the lifeblood of the country since day one.

He'd enjoyed the ride north from Narrabri. Eileen had been on her best behaviour when they'd stayed at the station homesteads, and they had seen some spectacular countryside on their long trek east to Tenterfield and then up over the Queensland border to Warwick and on to Brisbane. None of them had been this far from home before, so the journey was a real adventure, even though every day they worried about Dolour. She was now suffering from pneumonia and fading fast, Juan had written. All they could do was pray for the mercy of time.

There was no faster route to Brisbane than the one they'd undertaken, because they lived even further from the nearest reliable port, so buggy it had to be, and thank God Dolour had hung on long enough to see them for the last time and hug her only grandchildren.

John Pace had been upset that there'd been no mention of the grandchildren in the will, but Mr Bloom had pointed out that it had been written before his children were born.

'Probably', he'd said, 'your mother simply hadn't got around to rewriting it.'

'Fortunately,' Duke grinned now as he picked up his hat and headed downstairs.

'When can I get a newspaper?' he asked a porter.

'About an hour. Will I save one for you, sir?'

'If you like.'

Duke wandered out into the street. He watched a horse-drawn cart laden with barrels turn into the narrow lane beside the hotel, stood around for a while, and then, bored, strode down to Wharf Street, lured by the interesting ships moored in the river. He stood by the banks, fascinated by a huge five-masted schooner, wondering where it had come from, even thinking he might take passage on that ship if it were northward bound. Further along were grimy warehouses that spoiled his view of the imposing white Customs House with its domed roof, but at least by now the town was beginning to wake. More goods-laden lorries rumbled through the streets; a few pedestrians hurried by, looking up at clouds that were beginning to assemble in the sky. Duke looked up too, hoping the day would stay fine. He couldn't think of a better way to spend a Saturday than at the races with a lady like Lucy Mae on his arm, even if they were to be chaperoned by Mrs Forrest.

Hang on, though, he reminded himself. Lucy Mae was a widow! She didn't really require a chaperone. Her virginity no longer needed guarding. That added colour to his day. Considerable colour, he mused happily. Maybe with a little more attention, he could persuade Lucy Mae to be kind to him. What luck, too, that not only were all the family out of the way, but he had a very nice room in the hotel. Very private. Ideal for seduction. If he could manage to ditch her mother.

He saw a paperboy emerge from a shop and raced after him to buy a *Brisbane Courier*.

In the quiet of the hotel lounge, Duke studied every page of that paper until he came to a notice of the contents of the will of one Jeremy James Bernover. He scanned the rest of the page, but as yet there was no mention of his mother's will. When that was published, readers would know that he, Duke MacNamara, had inherited one third of the prosperous seventy-square-mile Kooramin Station. Important readers, in his mind, were bank managers. He wasn't leaving Brisbane until that information was well established in the banking world, so that he could raise a loan on his share of the estate.

With a loan he could purchase his own property wherever he liked, and still reap a third of the profits of Kooramin.

He was in high spirits when he sat down to breakfast, telling the waitress to bring him a steak and everything else Cook put with it, and a good old cup of black tea.

'Yes, sir,' she smiled, batting her long eyelashes at this handsome young bushie, who was single and, as the other girls said, very well off. They had recognised him as being of the elite squatter class. The young maids, and older ones too, saw a way to making their own fortunes when these gentlemen crossed their paths, so Mr MacNamara was offered sterling service.

'What's your name?' he asked this nice girl who had brought him extra toast and refilled his teacup without being reminded.

'Caroline,' she said shyly.

'That is a very pretty name,' he said. 'It suits you.'

'Thank you, sir. Will you be in for lunch?'

'Yes. Early, though. I'm going to the races.'

Caroline lingered. 'I love the races.'

'Yes, I do too,' he said cheerily as he stood up to leave, towering over her. 'I might see you there.'

'Not likely,' she muttered as she cleared the table. But then again, it mightn't be a bad idea to find out more about these races, and how you got in without a partner.

Duke was a little taken aback by Mrs Forrest's race-day finery. He thought her flashy gown would give the jockeys a run for their money when it came to colours; her flowery hat was almost wide enough to provide shade for her shoulders, and she had more rings than fingers. Back where he came from, the ladies didn't go in for fripperies at the races. They wore sun hats and pretty dresses, but the art was to keep cool.

He looked about as they entered the busy members' clubroom and noticed that two or three ladies could compete with Mrs Forrest in the showy stakes, so he consoled himself that he knew nothing about fashion.

Lucy Mae looked smart, he thought. Very smart. Even a little intimidating, in a slim white dress with a blue sash and a small hat with a fancy net across her forehead. He had to keep reminding himself that she was no longer the plump brat he'd once known.

At first he was rather nervous with this pair, who seemed to know everyone, but a glass at the bar settled him down, and then the races were under way and the general excitement took over. To his delight, Mrs Forrest went off to join friends and discuss the serious business of picking winners.

'I hope I'm not monopolising you, Lucy Mae,' Duke said as they strolled out to the grandstand.

'Not at all,' she said. 'Mother likes me to accompany her, but once here, she buzzes about like a March fly and I end up on my own.'

'But you'd have a lot of friends in town, wouldn't you?'

'Not really. I grew up on our station, as you know. Mother sold it when Dad died, and moved us to town, and then I got married, which was a mistake.'

He was startled by her candour. 'Your marriage was a mistake?'

'Yes. He was a rat, Duke. I don't know how I could have been so stupid.'

'You weren't known for being a dunce,' he laughed. 'A bit reckless, maybe.'

They talked for quite a while about their younger days, with Lucy Mae admitting she used to dread visiting Kooramin Station with her parents, 'because you boys were such teases!'

'That was because you looked so wrong out in the bush in a frilly dress, with your hair all frizzed up.'

'I knew that, but Mother didn't. Here she comes now.'

73

'Are you winning?' Mrs Forrest asked, bearing down on them with a dejected air. 'Mr Merriman told me about two horses that couldn't lose, and of course I believed him and thanks to his ill advice lost quite a bit of money. Really, people ought to keep their mouths shut when they don't know what they're talking about!'

'Who's Mr Merriman?' Lucy Mae enquired.

'He's here with Marcus Beresford. Do you know Marcus?' she asked Duke.

'Can't say I've had the pleasure. Is he a Brisbane chap?'

'Not exactly. He's a police officer.' Then she added rather archly: 'Inspector Marcus de la Poer Beresford!'

'That's quite a handle,' Duke said. 'Where'd he get a name like that?'

'Oh, my dear! He's royalty, don't you know? Nephew of a marquis. And a very nice chap.'

'I'm sure he is.' Duke nodded, a twinkle in his eye, which faded when Mrs Forrest said: 'Lucy Mae rides with him.'

'Not often, Mother. Not often at all. Marcus belongs to the same riding club as I do, so we're sometimes in the same group. He is an excellent rider.'

So am I, Duke said to himself, but I don't have to join a bloody club to prove it.

'He's won quite a few equestrian events,' Mrs Forrest said proudly.

'How would he go at a buckjumping event?' Duke asked, and Lucy Mae laughed.

'Don't answer him, Mother, he's teasing you.'

'Oh.' Her mother blinked. Then she turned to Duke. 'Your father was a terrible tease too. But I've been meaning to ask you, Duke. Are you still going north to Paul's station? It seemed to me that John Pace would rather have you back at Kooramin with them.'

'Yeah. They'll miss me,' he grinned. 'But they'll get along without me. When I have things sorted out here, it's off to Oberon to give big brother a hand. I can't be everywhere.'

Later in the day he was introduced to the Mr Harry Merriman who couldn't pick winners, and his friend Beresford, and to his surprise they both turned out to be very interesting men. Listening to them talk about their travels in north Queensland made Duke feel like a new chum. Everything north of the Tropic of Capricorn fascinated him.

'Merriman here', Beresford said, 'intends to settle in the Thomson River valley.'

'Where's that?' Duke asked.

'Too far west to even think about,' Beresford laughed.

'Ah.' Duke nodded, as if he could picture the place.

'It's right on the edge of civilisation,' Beresford added. 'Kalkadoon country.'

'How do you know that?' Merriman appeared surprised.

'Because the officers in our barracks were given a talk on the outback tribes recently, by a mineralogist who travels out there on safari. So, am I right?'

'Could be. There are hostile blacks, but I don't know their tribal names, or which areas they occupy.'

'Then you'd better learn. Those blacks have a bad reputation. Have you struck any trouble?'

'Some.' Merriman shrugged, turning away as if he didn't wish to discuss the matter.

'Our information is that they're a warlike mob,' Beresford persisted. 'Worse than the Irukandji tribe up on the Palmer River. And *they're* a murderous lot.'

Duke was intrigued. He wondered what trouble Merriman had run into.

'Was the Palmer River named after our premier?' Mrs Forrest asked.

Beresford nodded. 'Yes, I believe so.'

'Ah, how interesting.' She looked up as people began walking towards the track. 'Oh goodness, this must be the last race. But I won't bother with it. I'm a bit weary. I think I might go home. You two stay if you wish,' she told Lucy Mae and Duke, but to his disappointment, Lucy Mae chose not to stay.

As he walked them out to their buggy, where their driver awaited, he thought of asking Lucy Mae to dine with him, but there didn't seem to be an opportunity.

'We're off to the gala gymkhana on Saturday,' her mother called, as the driver settled into his seat. 'Lucy Mae's riding. You must come!'

'I'll be there,' he promised, more in reaction than enthusiasm.

He returned to the course and joined Beresford and Merriman at the bar.

'I was wondering,' he said to Merriman, 'is the place you're going to anywhere near the Valley of Lagoons?'

'You mean the area Leichhardt explored?'

'Yes.'

Both men laughed.

'It would be hundreds of miles south of the Valley of Lagoons,' Beresford told him. 'Not what you'd call close, my friend. Why?'

'I've got a property in that valley.'

'You have?' Merriman said. 'By Jove, I'd love to see that country one day.'

'When they clean the blacks out,' Beresford said.

'That's rather crudely put.' Merriman frowned.

'Well let's ask him. Your land, Duke. Is it a working station?'

'Not yet. Too risky. Too many blacks!'

'There you are, Merriman. It's dangerous country too. Will you be happy when we've made it safe for white folk, Duke?'

'Bloody oath, I will.'

Merriman shook his head. 'The blacks are not as bad as people make out. It's important to treat them with respect; that's the way to keep the peace.'

'My father always treated blacks with respect,' Duke said bitterly. 'He always stood up for them.'

'I'm glad to hear it.'

'Yes, I'm sure you are. But the blacks in the Valley of Lagoons murdered him. So you watch your back, mate.'

The subject of Aborigines was forgotten when Marcus won four pounds on the last race and insisted that they dine at his club, where, Duke was disappointed to discover, no ladies were permitted.

It was a boozy night, Duke recalled the next morning, that had included a lot of jolly horseplay among the club members. He had never seen grown gentlemen playing piggybacks and leapfrog before, and apparently neither had Merriman, who became irritated by the tomfoolery and called Beresford's friends 'juveniles'.

Privately Duke agreed, but he preferred to stay at the bar rather than involve himself in the ensuing uproar, except to warn Merriman as he passed by that they were heavily outnumbered, and it might be a good idea if they retreated to the Victoria Hotel, where the proprietor kept a 'cupboard' bar open for late-night drinkers.

Eventually Merriman took him up on that suggestion, and Duke was relieved that he had at least made it back to his hotel, because Merriman was a tough bushman who, he'd observed, could drink until the cows came home without turning a hair, while he himself wasn't much of a drinker at all, and was already seeing double by that time.

In the morning, not feeling the best, he decided to grow a beard to avoid the razor, and took a cold shower-bath to clear his head, because something Merriman had said interested him. Something about minerals just waiting to be picked up. Duke wondered if he meant gold, because he hadn't given up on the idea of going gold-prospecting, though both his brothers were dead against it. They argued that it was a fool's game; that very few of the thousands of men chasing the dream ever made it pay.

'They say the big syndicates find gold,' Duke had argued.

'Yes, and the shareholders are lucky to get a look-in,' John Pace had warned.

Duke was pleased to find Merriman in the dining room and be invited to join him, but when he mentioned the subject of gold, Merriman shook his head.

'Couldn't say about gold, but I've seen mineralogists poking about the hills, their packhorses laden with samples, so I'll have a look-see myself when I get back. I've bought a few books on the subject. A man has to learn a bit about it first, and that'll give me something to do when I light my lamp.'

'I suppose it would,' Duke said, not relishing the idea of reading books about rocks. 'But you say it's good cattle country?'

'Yes, wide open. I've been on a cattle drive out there, and I can't wait to get back.'

'Did you have trouble with the blacks?'

'There's trouble on both sides!'

Once again Merriman dodged the direct question, so Duke changed the subject.

'Where are you from, Harry?'

'DeLisle's Crossing. A village about fifty miles sou'-west of Brisbane. But I don't live there. I've got a place high on a hill in Rockhampton where I can put my feet up when I feel the need. That's where I met Marcus. But I'm curious. Where did you get the name Duke?'

'My father inflicted it on me. No one argued with my dad.'

'I see. I'm sorry about what happened to him.'

Duke shrugged, but Harry saw the pain in his face, and envied him. He'd always missed having a dad he cared about. Even now he couldn't bring himself to return to DeLisle's Crossing, and lately that presented a problem.

Harry had long dreamed of escaping from the misery of Merriman farm and the clutches of his callous parents, and one day determination and luck combined to rescue him. Aware that his father took out loans from the local bank, Harry, at thirteen, decided to apply for a loan of five dollars.

Looking back now he was amused by the amount of the loan, which to him at the time had seemed immense, and to his great joy, Mr Buschell, the good-natured bank manager, had approved. Wishing him well.

Harry had a feeling that Mr Buschell guessed he was running away, so he wasted no time putting his plans into action. Unfortunately his neighbour and good friend Tottie Otway came to the same conclusion and was so upset, he promised to write to her; to keep in touch.

He'd kept his word, and they'd corresponded for years, cementing the friendship into a much warmer relationship.

By the time he was twenty, Harry had repaid Mr Buschell. Not in dibs and dabs the way his father repaid his debts; instead he had a mate deliver five pounds to the gentleman, along with his thanks and a fine cigar, because he couldn't face returning to DeLisle's Crossing. Not even to see Tottie.

While he was working as a stockman at Cameo Downs he'd been surprised to receive a letter from her father George Otway. It was a kindly letter, mentioning that he was always pleased to hear news of Harry from Antonia (Tottie being only a nickname).

In his last letter, Harry had told Tottie that he would be taking a break from work in the wet season and visiting Brisbane. He'd said that he was looking forward to staying at the Victoria Hotel, because that was where he'd found his first job, as a stable boy, when he ran away. From guests in the hotel he'd learned about better-paid live-in jobs on cattle stations, so he'd soon moved on, but he'd always had a fancy to actually stay in that posh hotel.

Mr Otway was aware that he was coming south to Brisbane, and since it was 'not so far from DeLisle's Crossing', his letter contained an invitation to visit. He wrote that Harry would be most welcome to stay with the Otway family, and they were all looking forward to seeing him again.

Now Harry was in Brisbane. He'd been here nearly a week. And he still hadn't answered that letter. He'd thought about it constantly. Worried about it. Wondered if there could be more to it than there seemed.

He was twenty-two now. Tottie would be twenty. She often mentioned going to dances and seemed to have a busy social life, but she never wrote a word about suitors. He'd teased her about that. As for him, he'd had a few girlfriends, but could never bring himself to mention them to Tottie because they were unimportant.

So, he reasoned, was Mr Otway matchmaking?

He hoped not. He had a lot of time for Tottie, sure he did. But he had plans, serious plans, to head west, and that was no place for women. His experience with poor Lena had taught him that.

Then again, who do you think you are? he asked himself. Tottie Otway was a smart girl. She could do a lot better than him. The Otways were highly thought of in the community. And he was a nobody.

Which didn't alter the fact that he would not be visiting the Crossing.

He was still trying to make himself write a gentle refusal when he fancied he saw Mr Otway walk into the hotel. Thinking his eyes were playing tricks on him, he squinted against the sharp light outside to get a better look at the man. He was a mite stooped, and a lot greyer, but it was him all right.

Harry hurried across the foyer. 'Mr Otway?'

Tottie's father stood back and stared. 'Harry?'

'Yes, sir. Me, all right.'

'Good Lord. I'd never have known you. Why, you're taller than me now! But you're looking well.'

'You too, Mr Otway. Still catching fish on Sundays?'

Otway smiled. 'Oh yes. I still like my Sunday-night fish dinner.'

'And how is everyone?'

'All right,' Otway said, sounding rather vague. 'Do you reckon we could get a cup of tea somewhere around here, lad?'

'Yes. Come on into the dining room.'

The farmer hesitated. 'I don't know. It's a bit flash for me.'

'No it's not,' Harry grinned. 'They put up with me.'

When they were seated in a quiet corner of the room, Mr Otway looked so ill at ease, Harry had to push the conversation along by asking about Mrs

Otway, Tottie and her brother and enquiring about the farm until, mercifully, the waitress came and took their order.

'Now she's out of the way,' Otway said, 'I have to talk to you, Harry.'

'Yes?' Harry bet himself this would be about Tottie.

'It's about your mum and dad.'

'Ah yes,' Harry said. Unimpressed. Feeling like steel. Cold steel.

'There's been an accident.'

An accident didn't interest Harry one bit, but he couldn't say that, because Mr Otway would frown the way he used to when someone spoke out of turn.

'Your father,' Mr Otway said. 'He had a heart attack. Out in the west paddock. You mother found him. I carried him up to the house for her.'

He took out a neatly pressed handkerchief and mopped his damp forehead. 'You know, Harry, I just took a chance coming up to town. I figured you'd be here about now. Or I was going to leave a message. But I hoped I'd find you.' He sighed. 'I'm real sorry to have to tell you, Harry. But Gillie was dead when I got there. Nothing I could do for him.'

'When was this?'

'Nine days ago. Your mum arranged the funeral two days later. Your dad is buried in the cemetery behind the church.'

He blinked, and stammered: 'Harry . . . then there's your mum.'

'What about her?'

'She's gone too.'

Harry was confused. 'Gone? Where?'

Mr Otway took a deep breath. 'This'll be hard on you, Harry, but your mum . . . Grief is hard on some people. They don't give it time. You see, Hester, your mum . . . after the funeral . . . she went home and threw herself in the river. She drowned. Some farmhands saw it happen, from the other side of the river, but they couldn't get to her. She was swept away from them.'

Harry nodded. Mute.

'We buried her next to Gillie. Vicar Trenmell got special permission.'

From who? Harry wondered vaguely. And why? No family around, I suppose.

'You all right?' Mr Otway asked. 'If you want a glass of brandy I can get one for you, Harry. It dulls the shock.'

'No thanks, Mr Otway. Tea'll do for now.' He was thinking of her. That she had taken her own life the minute her husband was gone for good didn't surprise him at all.

'Typical,' he muttered. 'Bloody typical.'

Duke was becoming irritated with Bloom. The lawyer had promised to send a copy of the will over to the hotel, but it hadn't been delivered, and he was forced to rely on the newspaper, but once again it wasn't mentioned.

With nothing better to do that morning, he tramped around to Bloom's office, only to find the lawyer was in court.

'Never mind,' he told the clerk. 'I came to collect a copy of my mother's will. Would you get it for me, please?'

'Ah yes, Mr MacNamara. I'm afraid that hasn't been done just yet. We've been so busy lately. It seems everyone's needs have to be attended to with urgency, so it has been a rush to keep up.'

'I need that will urgently too!'

'You do?' The clerk blinked under his green-lined eyeshade.

'Yes, I do. I'll collect it tomorrow.'

'Tomorrow is Saturday. Shall we try for Monday?'

'It is urgent,' Duke snapped, and left.

'Of course,' Milly said to the Premier's wife, 'they were always good friends, Dolour and Jasin, despite her husband's differences with him.'

'Really? I didn't know that.' Cissie Palmer was intrigued.

'Oh yes. I wasn't surprised when I saw Jasin Heselwood at the church. I knew he'd want to pay his respects.'

'Without Lady Heselwood? He went to Mrs Rivadavia's funeral service without his wife?'

'Between you and me,' Milly whispered across the small table in the Victoria tearooms, 'I doubt Georgina knew about it. She and Dolour were definitely not friends. They had a serious falling-out some years ago. Just after Pace was killed.'

'Goodness me. What about?'

'I was never too sure,' Milly said warily. She was reminded that she'd blurted out the secret to Mr Bloom. She wished she hadn't, because Dolour had never told anyone in the family about Edward's attack upon her person. Her sons would have been outraged, and there'd have been hell to pay. There still would be.

Then again, Milly comforted herself, if a lawyer couldn't be discreet, who could you trust?

Cissie Palmer was facing the door of the tearooms. 'Isn't that one of the MacNamaras out there now?'

'Where?' Milly wheeled about.

'Yes,' she said, 'that's Duke.' She waved to him, beckoning him in, but he didn't notice her, and went on into the hotel.

'Nice-looking young man,' Cissie commented.

'Indeed he is. And very well connected. He has his eye on my Lucy Mae, you know.'

Cissie's eyebrows went up. 'Isn't it a little too soon? I mean no criticism, but Lucy Mae's still in mourning, isn't she?'

'Not really. Her husband's drowning was a dreadful shock, but I keep telling her she can't go on grieving for ever. Duke being around is quite a tonic for her; they're old friends.'

'That is fortunate then,' Cissie said without conviction. 'But Milly, I really must be getting along now. Arthur has been barnstorming the countryside, preparing for the election. I'm expecting him home this evening.'

'I can't imagine why the Premier believes he has to go out asking for votes,' Milly said gallantly. 'He doesn't need to, you know. People love him.'

'That's reassuring, Milly. I do hope you're right. He'll be dreadfully disappointed if his ministry is defeated, because he has so many excellent plans for Queensland.'

Milly Forrest hoped Premier Palmer would succeed. She was quite fond of him and his wife, and it was very pleasant being driven about in the first lady's carriage. As she settled into the soft leather seat beside her friend, she noticed a tall, elegant woman being assisted from another carriage and found her vaguely familiar. She looked to be in her thirties, fair haired, her smiling face mistily shaded by a lacy straw hat, her soft summery dress of hail-spot muslin seeming to float about her as she walked to the entrance of the hotel.

'Doesn't that lady look beautiful?' Cissie said. 'Do you know her?'

'Yes,' Milly said. 'I know her from somewhere. I just can't place her.'

Hours after she arrived home, Milly was dining with Lucy Mae when the name came to her.

'Good heavens! Guess who's back in town?'

'I don't know.'

'Lark Pilgrim!'

'Who's she?'

'She was Juan Rivadavia's fancy woman. He dumped her when he married Dolour. That was more than eight years ago, but I have to say she's carrying her age well. I met her a few times. Juan was always brazen about his women. She lived in Red Hill.'

'And did he support her?'

'Of course!'

Lucy Mae sighed. 'I wish I could find a man to support me. I'd make an excellent kept woman for a nice gentleman like Juan. Of course he'd have to be generous.'

'Don't talk rot! You'd be ruined socially.'

'I already am. Bartling managed that.'

'Stuff and nonsense. Anyway, you seem to me to be quite keen on Duke.'

'I am not!' Lucy Mae flared.

'You're not fooling me, girl. I've seen the way you look at him when he's not looking. You should give him that adoring expression when he *is* looking, if you want my advice.'

'Well I don't want your advice,' Lucy Mae said. 'He's going away shortly anyway. That'll probably be the last I'll see of him.'

'Then give him something to remember you by,' her mother murmured, and Lucy Mae flushed scarlet.

For Duke, a man who'd spent most of his waking hours in the saddle, the gymkhana wasn't very interesting. These people seemed to concentrate on obedience and novelty events, and far too many children's contests.

He saw Lucy Mae easily win her hurdles competition and complimented her, and while he had the chance he suggested they leave now, so that he could take her to lunch 'somewhere nice'.

'Oh no, I can't,' she said. 'I'm in two more events yet. I couldn't let the organisers down. It's so hard to find starters. Perhaps we could have lunch tomorrow? A picnic?'

'I love picnics!'

'Very well, I'll prepare a hamper for us.'

'And choose the spot.'

Beresford was competing too. Duke was amused that he'd come second in his hurdles event.

'How come you only got second?' he asked. 'I thought you won.'

'I should have,' Marcus growled. 'They take points off for dress as well, in this game.'

'Yours or the horse's?' Duke laughed.

'Both.'

'Is that right? I was only joking.'

'Yes, I'm getting rather bored with this. I'm withdrawing from the other events. Think I'll go sailing. I don't suppose you'd like to join me?'

'Sailing? On the river?'

'Where else? The officers stationed here have their own boathouse and sailboats down near the bridge. Are you on for it?'

'Too right I am, but be warned, I've never tried it before.'

They both took leave of Lucy Mae and Mrs Forrest, neither of whom seemed overly pleased.

'I don't believe we're too popular,' Beresford laughed.

Duke grinned. 'They'll get over it.'

They had a great time sailing a fourteen-foot yacht on the river, which was much wider, Duke reflected, when you were out there rushing along with the wind, and it was interesting to see the town from a new angle. Brisbane's Botanic Gardens, the sandstone Parliament House and many graceful houses, wreathed in greenery, lined the banks, and further along they were able to look up to the cliffs of Kangaroo Point.

'I plan to build a house up there one of these days,' Beresford said. 'Kangaroo Point has the most splendid view right across to the town.'

'I reckon it would have. Where do you live now?'

'Here and there, wherever the powers send us. I'm betting our next foray will be west, to keep an eye on the big stations out there.'

Duke scanned the shoreline. 'I was looking for Mrs Forrest's house.'

'It's further on.'

They sailed back under the bridge to the boat shed, where several of Beresford's colleagues and lady friends were gathered around a barrel of beer. Duke didn't need a second invitation to join them, and after a while Merriman arrived too.

Later that night all three of them, Duke, Marcus and Harry Merriman, by now very drunk and the very best of friends, repaired to the Palace, where the real fun began.

The next day the last thing Duke wanted to do was lift his clanging head from his pillow, so he simply stayed there gloating that Eileen could no longer bully him from his bed of rest. But he'd forgotten about the hotel housemaids, who had work to do, and at midday a severe voice asked: 'Haven't you got anything better to do than lie abed all day, Mr MacNamara? It's nigh on noon!'

'Gawd!' he shouted and leapt from the bed. 'The picnic!'

He grabbed a hansom cab to rush him down to the Forrest house, where Lucy Mae was waiting patiently with the buggy packed. There was no sign of her mother, for which he was grateful. He helped Lucy Mae up into the seat beside him.

'Ready to go?' he asked her as he flapped the reins with all the good cheer he could muster, and they were away.

They sat under the trees in the Botanic Gardens to enjoy their lunch and watch the passers-by, and after lunch they strolled along the riverbank until Duke found a more secluded spot. He placed the rug on the sharp weedy grass and they sat quietly for a while until he took Lucy Mae's hand and kissed it.

Soon she was in his arms and he was kissing her passionately. They lay back on the rug together, kissing and caressing, and he was desperate to make love to her. He called her his love and all the sweet words he could think of, and he could feel her brimming with excitement.

'You're so beautiful, Lucy Mae,' he murmured into her full breasts as his hand went to her skirts, but she stopped him.

'Not here,' she whispered. 'Not here, Duke.'

'But we must, Lucy Mae, we have to. Can't you feel what's happening between us? Don't spoil it.'

'Not here,' she moaned, and that gave him heart.

'Let's go back to my room then,' he said softly, quietly, so as not to spook her. He kissed her breasts as he buttoned her blouse for her, found her shoes and put them on her feet, and set her hair straight, teasing her now, telling her the colour in her cheeks made her look delicious. Before they walked away from that heavenly spot, he took her in his arms again and kissed her gently.

'You look so lovely today, I was proud to be walking with you. Are you happy, Lucy Mae?'

Her brown eyes looked into his. 'Yes,' she sighed. 'I am, Duke.'

But at the entrance to the hotel she balked. 'I can't do this,' she said. 'I can't just walk in with you and go up to your room. Someone might see us.'

'Who cares?'

'I care, Duke.'

'All right. I'll go on up and you follow. I'm in room fourteen, straight down the passage.'

'What if one of the hotel staff bails me up? Asks me if I'm staying in the house? I'd faint.'

'They won't.'

'Are you sure?'

'Yes, of course. I'll go in now. You only have to follow.' He put an arm around her to reassure her, gave her a small hug and walked away.

Duke strode across the lobby, walked sedately up the stairs and sprinted to his room. Leaving the door a mite ajar, he drank a glass of water from the carafe on the tiled washstand, brushed his hair and then sat on the bed to wait for her. He wondered if he should take off his boots, decided not to, went to the door, peered out, retreated to the big comfortable armchair facing the door and studied his boots. They were hand-tooled, made for town wear, a far cry from his big work boots, but they'd do for riding when he got home. Then he remembered he wasn't going home; he was heading north to Rockhampton, where he'd buy a horse and find his own way out to Oberon, Paul's station . . .

Lucy Mae had walked confidently into the lobby on her way towards that staircase, but the gentleman at the reception desk had looked up and smiled at her, so she veered into the lounge, where she sat quaking. She tried for a long time to calm herself, but when she was able to breathe evenly again, she gave more thought to the situation.

She remembered how her husband used to joke about the widow next door, saying widows were easy, which was why the woman had so many men friends, and she wondered if Duke thought she was easy too. Did he think that being a widow made her more worldly-wise about sex than single girls? More eager?

Lucy Mae blushed to her fingertips. She really cared for Duke. She was responsive to his advances and was so happy that he felt the same. He'd been so loving, she'd wanted to please him. Knowing that she could!

That revelation startled her, but it was true. She was experienced; she'd truly be able to please a bachelor like Duke. The very idea excited her.

But she couldn't go up those stairs. She could not bear to be seen going up there.

The best thing to do, she decided, was to remain here by the door until he came down to find her. And there'd be no argument. She'd simply tell him it was time she went home.

There was no argument. Duke did not come down. Her would-be lover had fallen asleep in the soft and cosy armchair.

After a while, anger made the decision for Lucy Mae. She stormed out of the hotel as the sun was setting, marched down the side lane to the stables, called on a groom to assist her and drove herself home.

'Where's Duke?' her mother called.

'I dropped him off at the hotel.'

The notice was in the paper! Will of the late Mrs Juan Rivadavia, née Callinan.

Duke didn't have to wait for a copy from Bloom now. He bought three newspapers, borrowed scissors from a housemaid and placed the clippings on his dressing table.

At ten minutes to ten o'clock, he was standing under an awning with other customers, waiting for the Queensland National Bank to open, listening to them discuss the sweeping rain that had them huddled around the doorway.

'The wet season should be over now,' one fellow commented.

'It takes its time,' a woman sighed.

Duke recalled Harry Merriman saying he wouldn't be going home until after the wet season. Up here they only spoke of two seasons, wet and dry, and he thought that was rather exotic compared with the four seasons down south.

But then the door opened and they all bustled in.

The bank manager, a portly fellow by the name of Trew, was amenable. He preferred to see a copy of the will, which Duke assured him Mr Bloom would provide, but was happy to oblige his new client.

'Why do you require this loan?' he asked.

'I'm about to purchase a property up north.'

'And where might it be?'

'I haven't decided yet. Maybe Rockhampton. Somewhere like that.'

That wasn't the answer the gentleman needed.

'I can't extend a loan to you without the title deeds, Mr MacNamara,' he said, 'but I shall provide you with a letter of credit up to a specific amount, say one hundred pounds, inasmuch as your family is in good standing in our community. Indeed, I knew Kooramin Station from my younger days as a teller before I came to Queensland. You must be very proud to be part owner of such a substantial station.'

'Yes, I am.' Duke nodded obediently. He was pleased to get his hands on a hundred pounds; it seemed like a fortune to him, since he'd never received wages, only money that Eileen handed out when he needed it. And then she was as mean as a bag of bees. She had given him six pounds to spend up here, but it was disappearing fast.

'My condolences on the death of your dear mother, Mr MacNamara. It's a terrible blow.'

'Yes,' Duke said grimly.

'And you might be kind enough to extend my condolences to your stepfather, Mr Rivadavia?' added Mr Trew silkily.

'Yes, sir. I'd better be getting along now, I suppose.'

The banker nodded. 'Keep in touch. I'll be interested to hear where you invest. By the way, are you thinking of selling your share of Kooramin, Mr MacNamara?'

'Well I don't know. Why? Are you interested?'

'I know a few gentlemen who would be.'

'Do you now? I'll keep it in mind.'

Mr Trew walked him to the door, even escorted him a few steps along the street to show him where the shipping office was located, and Duke walked tall, pleased with himself that he was no longer merely the family's station hand, but a businessman to be reckoned with.

There were no tickets left on the next steamer to Rockhampton, which was due to sail in three days, but he was advised to go down to the port and ask about, since there were many private boats leaving for the goldfields. It was still raining as he made his way along the slippery wharves, calling to seamen on the smaller boats, asking about passage to Rockhampton. Eventually the skipper on an aged schooner called *Vagabond* said he could come aboard.

Several passengers stood on the rusting deck, grinning as Duke tried to bargain over the fare.

'Ten shillen, mister,' the skipper said, 'and yez sleeps below. I don't have no fancy cabins.'

'Ten shillings?' Duke yelped. 'My brother paid less than that for a cabin on the steamer.'

'Walk then.'

'All right, I'll get my bags. When do you sail?'

'Four hours.'

Duke paid him and walked back to the hotel. He went in search of Harry Merriman to say goodbye, but found that Harry had checked out.

Disappointed, he then left a note to be delivered to Inspector Beresford at the police barracks, advising him that he was on his way to Rockhampton. He felt quite let down, departing the hotel with not a soul to bid him bon voyage, and his mood didn't improve when he remembered the state of the boat he was taking and realised there'd be nothing *bon* about this voyage.

That afternoon he was once again sailing down the Brisbane River, this time in the company of a dozen miners and a cargo of onions.

As the schooner passed Kangaroo Point, a strong wind blew up, but Duke stayed on deck, leaning on the rail, absently looking at the houses along the shoreline until, startled, he recognised the terrace of Milly Forrest's house, and the well-kept lawns that sloped down to the riverbank.

Inadvertently he pulled back. Almost ducked, for fear they might see him. As if they could, he chided himself, but he knew that guilt was at work here. He had treated Lucy Mae shabbily. In his heart he acknowledged that, though excuses did present themselves. If she hadn't reneged on the plan, he wouldn't have fallen asleep. She should have sent a porter up to fetch him and he would have taken her home.

'You're weak,' he muttered into the breeze. 'And mean.'

Apart from the fact that he did find Lucy Mae attractive, she was a friend. An old friend. She deserved better.

But did he love her? He flushed, recalling the afternoon and his thoughtless declarations of love. And worse, her response. Was Lucy Mae looking for love? Duke certainly wasn't. That was the real explanation for the sudden vanishing trick, he told himself. 'If you put all the cards in order, you'll find you just didn't want to face her.'

But what could he have said? 'I'm sorry, Lucy Mae, I got a bit carried away. I didn't really mean all that, I don't think. Also, I was a little drunk from the night before with the lads.'

And where did that leave her? High and dry. Feeling stupid for believing him. Insult to injury. A quick glance in the morning had shown him that she'd taken the buggy and driven herself home, having been deserted by her escort. Some friend! He wondered what her mother would have thought of that.

Duke leaned over the rails looking at the rushing waters, searching for a good excuse for his behaviour, but when nothing feasible came to mind, he decided he would write to her when he reached Rockhampton. It would be tricky, though; he had no doubt Milly Forrest would manage a peek at it, given half a chance. He'd write direct to Lucy Mae, apologising for having to leave Brisbane at such short notice and thanking her for the most enjoyable picnic. Regards to her mother. That sort of thing. He was no great hand at letter-writing, but he'd have a go. He supposed it was the least he could do to patch things up, the families being friends and all.

Sheet lightning flashed continously over deep grey skies, and thunder rolled and banged, trying to keep pace, heralding more rain and a sudden onslaught of grinding hail. The crew wrestled their boat in to shore, frantically hauling down the sails, while Duke dashed below to be met by a passenger who was trying to exit, too late: he vomited on Duke's new boots.

After a miserable night, the morning brought glittering sunshine and the promise of good weather ahead, so *Vagabond* set off again, the skipper in high spirits, the passengers apprehensive.

An hour or so later, they reached the mouth of the Brisbane River and headed out into the choppy waters of Moreton Bay, accompanied by some frisky dolphins. Duke was fascinated. They were skimming the water so swiftly, he was certain they were racing the schooner, and he laughed with delight as one flew out of the water, showing off.

Their vitality set the mood for him, and maybe for the ship's company too, he thought, because everything went well after that. They crossed the bay and made for the open ocean on a clear blue day, following the shoreline north.

CHAPTER FOUR

Rockhampton, to Duke's surprise, was another river town.

'Where is it?' he asked the skipper as they sailed up the Fitzroy River between dark greenery that seemed to be inhabited only by myriad screeching birds.

But he was wrong already. One of the miners nudged him.

'Look over there, son, on that patch of mud.'

'Oh Jeez!' Duke exploded. 'Will you look at that!'

He was staring at a huge crocodile, at least nineteen feet long, and as wide around the girth as a horse.

As he spoke, more men came to the rails, pointing to another beast that swished into the river with its red eyes barely visible under its ancient ironclad skull.

'They're bloody monsters!' a miner cried, and the skipper laughed.

'Yes, and they love prospectors! They race up and grab them while they're sluicing for gold in the river!' He turned to a crewman nearby. 'How many have they eaten this year?'

'Only three, but old Clarrie Stern is still missing.'

The skipper nodded. 'Take a tip, you blokes, dusk is feeding time. Never camp anywhere near their nests at night.'

'How will we know where the nests are?'

'You can smell them.'

'Smell what?'

'You don't want to know,' the skipper said cheerfully.

Though he didn't intend to be sluicing for gold, Duke vowed he wouldn't set foot anywhere near this river. He spent the rest of the voyage spotting crocodiles, shocked to see so many of the creatures dozing on the muddy banks.

When they rounded a bend and came upon the town of Rockhampton, with its neat white buildings all in a row along the front, they suddenly seemed to have stepped into the present. It was as if those prehistoric beasts and their jungle surrounds were of another age, of eras long gone, and a door had closed on them, leaving them back in time.

Greatly relieved by this return to civilisation, Duke was moved to remark to the skipper that this looked like a very nice town. 'My brother and his wife live up this way,' he added quite proudly, to underline his expectations.

'You talkin' about Rocky?' the skipper jeered, chomping on a lump of beef jerky. 'That's a good one. Behind Quay Street there, this town is about as rip-roaring as they get. When you step ashore, son, hang on to your hat; the streets are full of whores and rip-off merchants. There are more cat-houses than pubs here, and that's saying something. The local lads get to lairising with their guns and picking fights most nights, and further in, you got the opium dens and the blacks' camps.'

He gave Duke a playful punch in the chest. 'Nice place, eh? Where I come from, this town is known as Sin, Sweat and Tears!'

On that advice, Duke decided to start at the front. He took a room at a plush hotel facing the river, spared time for a decent meal and went for a walk around the crowded streets, remembering not to take offence when swaggering cowboys accompanied by blowsy women shouldered him aside.

His first impression, though, was of heat, and mud. He figured the temperature had to be around a hundred, but it was a humid heat that had sweat dripping from his face. He tried to pick his way across solid ground, but in places the prevailing mud was up to six inches deep, and often mixed with foaming droppings from passing cattle and horses. All of it impossible to avoid. He was fascinated, watching women with their skirts held high trying to negotiate a clean path, wondering why they bothered, since he'd seen several women in dungarees and sensible calf-high boots.

Fancy girls called to him from balconies overlooking the street and he waved to them in high good humour, unfazed, even impressed, that 'Rocky' was a town of sin. He decided he might stay around for a few days.

The next morning he was at the sale yards bright and early, so that he could spend an hour or so inspecting the horses. He finally decided on a chestnut thoroughbred. It was a magnificent horse, called Nelson, and Duke entered the bidding with enthusiasm. The price was creeping up into a higher bracket than had been his original intent, but he wanted the horse and stuck with it until the figure was over the fifty pounds mark. Just then a black stablehand in a red jumper caught his eye and shook his head. Duke hesitated for a few minutes and then dropped out of the bidding. Reluctantly, though, because he'd taken a liking to that horse.

A little while later the horse was passed in. No sale.

Confused, Duke approached the black lad. 'What was wrong with that horse?'

'Nelson? Nuttin' wrong with him, he a good strong feller. But not too many buyers dis day. Them fellas working tricks on you, boss. You the only one want him.'

'What?' Duke looked about him, bewildered, until he realised what had happened. The auctioneer had been pushing the price up with dummy bidders!

His face flamed. He'd nearly made a fool of himself.

'There's a good start,' he muttered, and went in search of the white-haired auctioneer with the tobacco-stained moustache.

'That horse, Nelson,' he said angrily. 'I'll give you fifteen pounds for him.'

'I'll take forty,' the auctioneer replied coolly.

'Thirty!' Duke said. 'Last offer.'

'Done! What's your name?'

'MacNamara,' Duke said as he counted notes and banged them on to the table.

Unconcerned, the fellow collected the money and entered the transaction into his ledger. Still miffed, Duke asked for a receipt.

'Nelson ain't no cup winner, mate. This here book's proof enough he's yours. MacNamara?' he added, looking up at Duke. 'Any relation to Paul MacNamara out there at Oberon Station?'

'He's my brother.'

'Well! You don't say! Pleased to meet you, Mr MacNamara. I'm Chester Newitt. He's a good bloke, is Paul. Had some terrible times but he's stout of heart. He never let up until he caught every one of them murderers. But I suppose you know all about that. You got a saddle and harness?'

'Not yet.'

'Then come with me. I'll fit you up with the best, you being Paul's brother. Buy you a drink too. We'll go into the Victory Hotel. You been there? Grand it is. No riff-raff. Town is stuffed to the guts with riff-raff.'

Duke was so pleased to have bought Nelson, and at a better price, he forgave this character for trying to dud him, and rode back to town with him to the Victory Hotel. He noticed a sign on the shop front next door: *Chester Newitt, Auctioneer, Stock and Station Agent*.

Chester was a fine host. He shouted him drinks and introduced Duke to the 'best shepherd's pie this side of the Black Stump'. They sat at a long rickety table, where Chester managed to devour his pie and order seconds while talking to other customers, to whom he presented Duke MacNamara as 'of the famous pioneer family'. Duke thought this was a bit hot, since his father was the only one in the family who could have been called a pioneer, but he figured that this man would see status as good for business.

The map that Duke had bought for himself in Brisbane simply showed the towns. Chester produced one that was far more detailed; every sheep and cattle station was named as if they were towns. And sure enough there was Oberon Station, a fair way out on the other side of the river.

'This is good grazing country,' Chester said, pointing to an area south-west of Rockhampton. 'I'm going out there tomorrow, auctioning horses and to offload some land. Not sure what's offering but it'll be interesting. You want to come along?'

'Sure,' Duke said. Oberon could wait another day.

They came to the Toombye sale yards first, and rode up to a group of angry men and women who began shouting at Chester, insisting he haul Boss Murphy out of his house.

'What the hell for?' he demanded.

'Because he's stolen fifty of our horses.'

'Hang on,' Chester cried, as others clamoured around him. 'Now one at a time!'

Their spokesman explained that most of the sellers had come fair distances and so had corralled their horses in Murphy's fenced paddocks the day before, to have them fresh for the sales. The paddocks were down near the sale yards, while their owners had been permitted to camp overnight near the homestead.

'Then last night Boss Murphy runs a barn dance for us,' the man continued, 'and folks come from far and wide. It was a good old dance too, with fiddlers and all, and plenty of rum . . .'

'And when we get up in the morning, fifty of the horses are gone!' another man screeched. 'Bloody gone! The paddock as empty as Murphy's head.'

'So how many are left for me to auction?' Chester asked, more concerned with his commission.

'Who gives a bugger?' the first man roared. 'We've got a posse out searching for them thieves, and I tell you, it'll be shoot first and ask questions afterwards if those mongrels are caught. Some blokes reckon it was a put-up job and that Murphy's in on it, so they shot holes in his roof. Now he won't come out of the house.'

'I don't blame him,' Chester said. 'No word from the posse yet?'

'Nothin'. Them bloody thieves coulda got a six-hour start.'

'Has someone gone for the police?' Chester asked, but nobody seemed to know.

'What about a black tracker?' Duke said. 'You must have a few up this way.'

'There's Jimmy Jim,' a flame-haired woman said. 'He lives here. You go and find him, Bluey.'

Bluey, her carrot-headed son, was sullen. 'How can I? My horse got stole too.'

She clouted him over the head with a hand like a club. 'Get one of Murphy's.'

'We better go up to the house,' Chester said. 'You coming, Jessie?'

'No,' the woman growled. 'I'll wait for Bluey.'

Duke was admiring the countryside, so rich and green thanks to the wet season he'd been experiencing since he'd first set foot in this state. He'd never in his life seen such heavy downpours, and was now learning to ignore both the heat and the rain like everyone else did.

As they approached the Murphy homestead, they rode past huge fruit trees that Chester informed him were mango trees. He picked a fruit and tossed it to Duke.

'Go on, eat it!' he grinned. 'It won't poison you.'

Not only did it not poison him; the taste won him over and he sucked the juicy flesh to the kernel.

'All right?' Chester asked as they dismounted at the homestead gate.

'Marvellous!' sighed Duke.

Two men with shotguns attempted to stop them, but Chester shoved them out of the way.

'We're going in. Come on, Duke.'

They marched up the path and across the veranda, as a curtain was pulled aside and a woman peeked out.

'Hang on, Chester,' she yelled.

They heard furniture being dragged aside and the door was opened by a burly Irishman with a hound dog snarling at his feet.

'Those damn fools out there,' he muttered. 'They'll kill someone if they're not careful. Did they tell you about the horses? Bloody hell, Chester, we haven't had horse-duffers out this way for years. Damned if I'll have sales on my property again.'

'Who's this?' Murphy's wife asked, peering at Duke, the stranger in their midst.

Chester introduced him as a new chum just having a look around.

'How d'you do?' she said, dismissing Duke and turning to the auctioneer.

'They're blaming us, Chester. They're claiming that Boss set this up. That he arranged to have those thieves come in while the party was going full swing and steal their horses away. Well he didn't! He didn't! He shouldn't never have given them that party! Wasting our good food on a pack of ingrates. And our rum. They better not come near the house again or we'll fill them full of shot.'

'Bluey Morton's gone off to find Jimmy Jim,' Chester told them. 'You should set him on their tracks.'

'Jimmy Jim's gone walkabout with his mates,' she sighed, 'or we'd have sent him ourselves bloody quick smart.'

She looked out of a side window. 'There's some riders coming back, I think.'

'You better get them some breakfast, Maisie,' Murphy said. 'They bin out since dawn.'

'The hell I will!'

'Get the breakfast!' he repeated, and she plunged off to the rear of the house.

'I'll go and see what's happening,' Chester said. 'You wait here, Duke.'

So Duke remained with Boss Murphy, both of them watching the riders coming across the paddocks.

'Your men with them?' Duke asked.

'Yes, three of my stockmen are coming in; that doesn't look too good.'

They stood making desultory comments to one another until Murphy, still distracted, said, 'Did you say your name was MacNamara?'

'That's right.'

'Any relation to Paul?'

'Yes. Seems everyone knows my brother.'

'Ah well. That's the way things go. He was out here last time Chester auctioned off land, some six months ago. Seems he's wantin' to quit Oberon. Fair enough, I be saying, with the sadness of the place for him.'

'He was looking to buy land?'

'Yes, but all the properties listed were too small for his needs. The thing is,' Murphy added, still watching out the window, 'he was pretty much taken with Toombye.'

'This place? Here? Your station?' Duke asked.

'He was indeed. Had a talk with me, but I wasn't much for sellin'.'

'I suppose not,' Duke said quietly. Even warily.

'Seen him again in town a while back, and he was askin' me again, but nothin' came of it. I still wasn't keen then, but Maisie, she said . . .'

Duke saw riders coming towards the rear of the homestead. Chester was with them. Murphy dashed outside and Duke followed.

The day wasn't all wasted for Chester Newitt. He sold four horses that the thieves had missed, but only one of the properties advertised in the Rockhampton paper.

None of the searchers had found any sign of the stolen horses, and the mood of everyone connected with the sales was angry and suspicious. They hung about the yard accepting as their right, mugs of tea and the stew Maisie slung on to tin plates, assisted by a shy black girl. And they waited.

It wasn't the first time Duke had encountered horse duffing; back home, though, cattle was the usual target. These thieves, he knew, could be smart, planning their escape route with care, and probably with a market already in mind. There was every possibility, too, that quite a few of these horses wouldn't have been branded yet.

He sat in the kitchen with Murphy and Chester, his stomach rumbling hungrily when he heard Maisie complain that they were nearly out of stew. But help was at hand. Murphy went to a meat safe, brought out a handful of chops and threw them on the top of the stove.

Their instant juicy sizzle cheered Duke no end.

Maisie came in, absently threw a handful of salt over the chops and turned her back to her husband, who had seated himself at the table again with his two visitors.

'What are they waiting for?' she asked him. 'They bin fed, why don't they go home?'

Chester answered: 'Some of them have lost their own mounts. Most of them have lost good money with their horses stole. Money that would have bought supplies to take home. Now they're going back to their families empty-handed. Have a heart, Maisie. Just let them digest their losses with your good stew.'

'Just so long as they don't go blaming Boss again,' she snapped. 'I heard some of them whingein' that he didn't lose any horses, and I told them that was because our horses are in the home paddock like always, and not to go makin' up lies!'

'Trouble is,' Murphy reflected, 'until they find the thieves they'll have me in their sights, now that some of them have pointed the finger.'

Duke disagreed. 'I wouldn't be worrying. It's just bad luck the horses were here, and the thieves made the most of it.'

'Sure they did,' Murphy said glumly. 'But mud sticks. Some of them blokes out there now are so shat off they'd string me up for tuppence.'

Chester decided not to wait for the police. 'We'll probably meet Sergeant Moynahan on the way home.'

Before they left, Murphy took Duke aside. 'You know, Duke, with this trouble hanging over me head, I am leaning to sell now. Any time you and your brother want to have a real inspection of Toombye, just come on out. We'll show you round. But if you're interested in buying, don't mention it to Chester, otherwise he'll want commission.'

Duke laughed, thinking they'd probably get a better price direct from Murphy anyway, without interference from Chester, who'd already shown he wasn't allergic to bumping up prices.

On the way back to Rockhampton, he and Chester fell in with a group of twenty stockmen coming in from some outback properties, and someone threw up a challenge to one and all: a race to town! The leader headed off at a breakneck pace, but his horse tired and he was gradually overtaken. The cross-country race continued until the leader hurtled down the main street of Rockhampton with Duke second and a half-dozen horsemen hard on his heels.

They hitched their horses outside a pub and strode in, many of the stockmen, on leave, slamming their pay on the counter.

Duke laughed. Stockmen were no different the country over, it seemed.

He stayed for a few drinks with them but soon left, thinking about Toombye Station.

In the morning he decided that Toombye could be worth an inspection; not only the property, but the station books. From what he'd seen, it was a beautiful place. Even Paul had liked it.

A forlorn Murphy met him as he rode up.

'Good to see a cheerful face,' he said. 'Moynahan didn't deign to turn up until this morning, and he brought along a know-it-all constable to search every acre, as if I've got fifty horses hid in me barn.'

'I suppose they have their routines. And they'd have telegraphed other areas so folk would be on the lookout.'

'It's my bet them horses are hid way out in them far hills until the police lose interest. Had I the time, I wouldn't be wasting it with routine searches, but I'm short-handed here lately, and we've gotta start mustering the cattle.'

'I thought I saw some cattle in the scrub along the road. Would they be yours?'

'Sure they are. When the river's in flood, like it is every year, we have to get them on high ground and a lot of it's scrub. Now we have to find them again. Anyway, come on up to the house and have a bite, then you can ride out with me to where the lads are working. They'll need a hand or two.'

Murphy wasn't kidding, Duke realised. He'd taken it for granted his visitor would play his part in chasing the great lumbering brutes out of the scrub.

It was a hot, humid afternoon by the time Duke and Murphy caught up with the four stockmen. They had several cattle in a temporary log enclosure, but, as they told their boss, there were plenty more of the recalcitrant brutes still out there, trying to keep out of sight.

Murphy dismounted. 'You ever been mustering before, Duke?'

'Of course I have.'

'Good.' He tossed a rope and a stockwhip up to him. 'Then give the lads a hand, will ya? I'm heading up this way.'

Duke hauled his horse about and raced at the bush in search of the roaming cattle.

'Down there to the left, mate,' a stockman called. 'I saw a big fella nosing about in there. About two hundred yards in.'

Dutifully the visitor set off after his prey, but he soon realised this bush was a far cry from the sparse home variety. The grass was waist high, hiding fallen logs, the undergrowth was damp and slimy, and even though the same tall skinny gums reached up to the sky, they had to compete with palms and thick vines that blocked the sunlight.

Fortunately Nelson didn't seem as concerned as he was, ploughing on through the rough until he saw a bullock up ahead, almost concealed in the dappled light. The horse began to tread carefully towards it, and Duke warned him, 'Careful, boy, careful,' as the sun glinted on the animal's horns.

Duke was trying to ease Nelson around behind the animal. He'd almost made it when the bullock suddenly swung about to face him, baleful eyes challenging. Duke was afraid he'd charge. There was a stillness in the scrub for that minute, suddenly broken by the shrill calls of a squadron of wild geese. Using the distraction, Duke jerked at the reins, causing Nelson to lurch sideways into the cover of a tree stump.

At the same time the bullock broke and ran, dodging back among the trees, deeper into the scrub.

Duke went after him, but Nelson was no stockhorse; he was built for speed, not for dancing in and out of the timber. A stockman came flying by to take up the chase and Duke watched, impressed, as the man's horse kept pace with the fleeing bullock, twisting and turning, manoeuvring the heavy animal closer and closer to the clearing until another rider managed to rope him.

'Well done,' Duke said to the first stockman. 'That was fancy riding!'

They shared water from a canvas bag hanging on the fence, and Duke decided he'd do a better job helping to muster the cattle as they were pushed out of the scrub.

At dusk Murphy called it a day, and they brought more than fifty head of cattle out to open grazing land about a mile from the homestead.

At ten o'clock Duke was sitting down to dinner with Boss Murphy and his wife, when she asked: 'Are you staying the night, Duke?'

'If you'll have me,' he stammered, not having considered finding his own way back to town in the dark.

'No trouble,' she said, and as the grandfather clock in the hallway of Toombye homestead struck eleven, there he was lying on a bunk on Murphy's front veranda, under a mosquito net.

These days, back at Kooramin, he had his own quarters, but now, outdoors on this warm and velvety night, he was reminded of his childhood, when all three boys slept on the veranda and he was so proud to be out there with his big brothers.

He heard the rasping voices of flying foxes returning from foraging expeditions and the familiar squeaks and cries of other night animals, and felt very much at home at Toombye, though he didn't go much on the name.

Then came the rain, solid, steady rain that went right to the heart of his quest. He was tired of the despair that droughts inflicted on graziers out Kooramin way. Tired of the constant uncertainty of floods one year followed by two or three years of drought, and the misery of watching livestock perish while they waited for the drought to break.

What wouldn't they give, back home, for annual wet seasons, and the advance notice of probable flooding? It was always a mystery to him that Kooramin managed to survive the bad years, even to thrive in good times, but the concern remained. Eyes always turned skywards. Wary.

A wallaby bounced on to the veranda seeking shelter, and Duke let it be, comforted by the company.

Sunrise gave the last of the clouds long streaks of gold before they drifted off into the distance, leaving a clear blue sky in the hands of an increasingly hot sun.

'A nice day at last!' Maisie Murphy said to Duke as she served him beefsteak and three eggs for breakfast. 'Do you want some bacon with that? I sugar-cure me own bacon.'

'I wouldn't say no to sugar-cured bacon.'

She slid three large rashers on to his plate.

'I gotta get back to the cookhouse now,' she said, making it clear that having to come up to cook for him was a pain in the neck. 'Our cook run off a couple of weeks ago, so I got to feed all them hungry mouths.'

He felt guilty detaining her, and wanted to say that he'd have been happy to have a meal with the station hands, but she dived out the door and disappeared down the steps into the yard.

A few minutes later Murphy ambled in. 'How're you going? She give you enough to eat?'

'Yes thank you. Plenty.'

'Good.' He went over to the stove, lit his pipe with a taper and sat himself down at the table.

'If you'll be wanting to see more of the property, I'll take you out meself, but not if you're just sticky-nosin'. Because we're mighty busy. You'll find there's a lull over the wet months up here, but once the weather clears, everyone has to work like hell to get everything back in shape, so you better say now where you're placed.'

Duke chewed on the bacon. And chewed. It was as tough as old boots.

'Well,' he said chomping hard. 'Well . . .' In the end he had to remove the lump of bacon from his mouth so that he could speak. 'I am interested in buying a property. I've got a part share in our family station in New South Wales where I've lived all my life, so I'm not exactly a new chum. I like the look of Toombye but I'd need to know a lot more.'

Duke thought his speech was adequate to the occasion, but Murphy countered with: 'Aye, I'll grant you that, but I can't be wasting me time on you, 'less I know you've got the spondulicks. For me and the missus to walk off Toombye we'd have to be looking at four hundred pounds. We're still a bit so-so about sellin', you see.'

'I certainly can afford to buy, if Toombye fits the bill. And if we can agree on a price,' Duke said firmly, refusing to be sucked in by Murphy's story.

'Righto then, hang on here and I'll bring you a surveyor's map, so you can see for yourself where you are.'

Duke finished his meal and took his plate over to the bench, then Murphy returned, cleared the table and laid out the map.

Toombye, he pointed out, was sixteen thousand acres; a dog's leg property that ran the gamut of wide grazing land watered by a string of lagoons, and the section already seen of heavily timbered scrub.

'From the window here', he said, 'you can see old Ironstone Mountain. That's past our boundary, but at the base is a swamp. If you ever wanted to clear that, you could get it from the council for next to nothing.

'We run about two thousand head of cattle here, so it's a good little property, easy to manage. We keep at least fifty horses, and Maisie has her porkers out there. She likes raising pigs. Good market for them, she says, but I dunno, she never tells me what she makes on them. There used to be an orchard out back, but insects got to it so we don't bother any more; we just let the mango trees and the bananas have their own way. The birds planted them . . .'

As Murphy rattled on about Toombye, and the uncle who'd pioneered the station, Duke wondered if they'd ever get out of the kitchen. But eventually the boss cleaned out his pipe and took him on a tour of the homestead area, which included the men's quarters and cookhouse, a blacksmith's shed, and the usual barns and storehouses, before sending an old blackfellow called Hector to bring up their horses.

Then they were off, Duke trying hard to subdue his enthusiasm for this superb property.

They rode across open prairie where herds of cattle grazed quietly, on to deep lagoons fringed by pandanus trees, and visited an Aborigine camp in a lightly wooded area not far from the lagoons.

'Is this a permanent camp?' Duke asked.

'Yeah. Some of the lads work as stockmen and three women work for Maisie.'

'How many blacks here altogether?'

'They come and go. Sometimes a hundred or so.'

'And they don't give you any trouble?'

'No. Some of them get a bit boozed at times, but we kick them up the bum and they shut up.'

Duke nodded and rode on. He didn't like this at all. Those blackfellows looked a wild lot to him. The only blacks on Kooramin were workers, men and women, and a few piccaninnies.

He was relieved when they came to another mustering camp, being run by the middle-aged foreman Snowy Drummond, whom Duke had met the day before. They were counting steers, and when that was completed, Duke rode over to him.

'No sign of the stolen horses?'

'Not a peep! They've vanished into bloody thin air. I can't figure it out. It's got Boss spooked with folk blaming him.'

'What did the police say?'

'What could they say?' Drummond shrugged. 'The sergeant and his offsider prowled about looking for tracks, but it was a bit late. It was teeming during the dance when the horses went missing. And it rained again last night. What tracks?'

'So what are you doing here now?'

'We've got a mob to be branded, then we'll move them to drier pastures.'

'The cattle are all in good nick from what I've seen.'

'Yes, the sales start in Rockhampton soon. It's becoming an important beef centre, which is good for business.'

'Yes, it would be,' Duke nodded. His brother suddenly came to mind. He supposed Paul would trade cattle there too. But he didn't want to think about Paul; he was too excited about this fine station.

He and Murphy had a meal at a temporary camp, then turned for home. They passed another herd of cattle watched over by two black boys on horseback, and Duke noticed a fetid smell coming from behind an unusual strip of fencing. It was built of logs but they were close together, unlike the usual two or three rails.

'Why the fence?'

'Oh, that,' Murphy said absently. 'It's a crocodile fence. The swamp's on the other side.'

Duke was startled. 'Are there crocodiles in the swamp?'

'Sure are, but they won't bother you if you don't go past the fence. The only other way in is through thick scrub, so you don't want to clear that, it doesn't pay.'

Duke wouldn't allow himself to be bothered by the presence of crocodiles; he was totally enamoured of this beautiful scenic property even though he'd only seen a part of it, and was desperate to buy it.

That night they got down to business over a bottle of rum.

'I've also got a good block of land in the Valley of Lagoons,' Duke said to Murphy. 'What about taking that as part payment?'

'Never heard of it. Where is it?'

'North. Inland from Cardwell.'

'That's almost into Cape York. Surely you jest, son! My uncle braved spears; I'm not about to start. No, cash up!'

'But four hundred's far too much to ask when half of the property is scrub or rocks.'

'No it's not. You take another look at the map. It's damn good grazing country. And I'm throwing in a thousand head of cattle. The rest you buy. I'll auction them.'

'That's another thing,' Duke said. 'What's the count? How many cattle are out there now?'

'Well, you saw plenty, but the lads are working on it. It's handy that you came along when we're mustering. We'll have most of them accounted for in a few days, Snowy reckons. Now the horses. I could sell them to you as a job lot. Or you can choose which ones you want to buy.'

Duke was nervous. The price was creeping up. He had envisaged buying a cheap property up here in little-known Queensland, so far from anywhere, but there was nothing cheap about Toombye. Then again, what sort of a place would he find on the cheap?

It occurred to him that he should hold off for a while. Get in touch with Harry Merriman and think about leasing a real swag of land from the government, at a rock-bottom price, out Cloncurry way. Beresford had said Harry would make a fortune by getting in on the ground floor. It wasn't too late to join the ranks of the rich squatters as his father and Rivadavia had done in the early days.

If only Pace had lived. He'd had such a drive, such a thirst for land. He'd have gone on and made millions given the chance.

Duke knew he had not inherited that drive.

He didn't want to have to start from scratch like Harry was doing. Like his father had done. Clearing land. Overlanding cattle. Building dams and living quarters . . .

And this was a nice little homestead. Well kept. Well settled.

In the end they shook hands on three hundred and eighty pounds. Which Duke hoped he could raise. He also planned to try to sell his land in the Valley of Lagoons, to help him meet expenses.

He couldn't sleep that night for the joy of ownership! Of independence!

Now he could take a ride out to Oberon and say hello to the folks.

'Where the hell have you been?' Paul roared. 'I told you I was coming back to get the mustering under way. You said you'd give me a hand, but what do you do? Turn up when we're just about finished.'

'Then you didn't need me after all,' Duke shrugged.

'That's not the bloody point.'

A steer cut loose from a moving mass of cattle that was being worked into mustering yards by three stockmen. Paul spun his horse away to head it off, and startled, Nelson reared, leaping aside into a stretch of thick mud and steaming manure churned up by the thousands of hooves.

As Duke gained control of the horse, he saw Paul had gone back to work, racing after tailenders on his fast little stockhorse, a black cattle dog flying along with him. He sat his horse for a while, watching the men straining in their saddles, whistling and calling to the cattle, then he rode around to a high gate where a stockman sat, concentrating on counting the cattle.

Rather than trust Murphy with the count at Toombye, Duke had employed a 'counter' in Rockhampton recommended by the obliging manager of the local branch of the Queensland Commercial Bank, and sent him out to the station. This bank manager, Sam Pattison, was younger and far more easy-going than Trew. A handsome fellow, with a thin dark moustache and straight black hair tied back with a bootlace, he wore an open-necked check shirt with dungarees and high riding boots.

Pattison sat back in his chair and smoked a cigar as Duke introduced himself, interested to hear he was Paul's brother but not much inclined to listen to his practised spiel on the collateral he held and why he needed this loan.

'How much do you need?' he asked amiably, interrupting the tale.

'Four hundred pounds?' Duke responded nervously.

'Righto. You've got that letter of credit. Give me that. And the title to the land at where? Valley of Lagoons? Never heard of it. But there's an ocean of new land turning up these days. Anyway, leave that with me. And I'll want the deeds to Toombye, of course. You can settle up with Murphy in here. Watch that old windbag, Duke. He's slippery.'

'I'm keeping a close eye on him, don't worry.'

'The cattle. Here's the name of a counter. Send him out pronto. Gents out this way have been known to push the same mob of cattle through a few times, to up the numbers.'

Duke had heard of that trick before but didn't bother to enlarge. He'd pulled off the loan. That was all that mattered.

Hanging about these busy cattle yards in this humidity was like sitting in a sweat box, so he soon turned Nelson about and made for the long tree-lined drive up to the Oberon homestead. He took the horse to the rear of the house, and rode him over to a water trough, where he removed his saddle and other belongings and handed him over to a young Aborigine boy who emerged from the stables.

'What name you?' the boy asked.

'Duke.'

The boy grinned, satisfied. 'What name this feller?'

'Nelson.'

'Ah.' He looked up. 'Missus waiting for you!'

Only then did Duke notice his sister-in-law standing by a water tank outside what appeared to be the laundry.

'Hello!' he shouted. 'How are you, Laura? You're looking a picture!'

'Yes,' she said cheerfully, looking down at her rough shirt and muddied dungarees. 'This is what the leading debutantes are wearing this season.'

'And they've never looked better,' he said, picking a tiny white blossom from a shrub as he passed and handing it to her.

She popped it behind her ear. 'Does Paul know you're here?'

'Yes, I saw him down at the yards.' He looked about him. 'You've got a nice setup here. I didn't expect your house to be quite so big. It's a real showplace, isn't it?'

'Glad you like it. Why don't you go on inside, I'm just feeding some calves.'

'Can I help?'

'No. The kettle's hot. Make yourself some tea.'

He wandered around the large house, interested in the design, which he found unusual. The wide wrap-around veranda was completely enclosed with trellis, and was furnished here and there with cane easy chairs and sofas. The main rooms seemed to be a house within a house. Most of them had French windows opening on to the veranda, with cool lace curtains floating in the doorways. It was such a serene place, compared to Murphy's plain farmhouse with its rough utility furniture, that Duke experienced a twinge of jealousy.

From the side veranda he was looking towards the river when he recognised willow trees on the bank and realised they were the willows people spoke of in hushed tones.

He shuddered and turned away, to see Laura standing behind him, barefoot.

'Everyone does that,' she said bitterly.

'Does what?'

'Shudders when they look over there. Over where Jeannie and Clara were murdered. Raped and murdered. People even come for Sunday drives out here. Paul fenced the front. Now they leave their jinkers and walk right across our property to view the horror site, and do some real shuddering.'

He reached out to her. 'Laura, you shouldn't take on so. This is such a nice house, and from what I've seen, Oberon is a real treasure. All that stuff's history. You have to forget about it.'

'Easy to say, but people won't let us. That's why we're selling up as soon as Paul can find another station. Did you make tea?'

'Not yet.' *As soon as he can find another station.* Duke felt queasy. He'd prepared himself for a blast from Paul if his brother had really wanted to buy Toombye, and been ready to counter with a brotherly 'Bad luck! I got in first!' joke. But now he was nervous. Maybe it wasn't quite that simple.

'Hang on then,' she said. 'I'll just get cleaned up, then we'll have tea on the veranda and you can tell me what you've been up to all this time. I've been betting you found a girl in Brisbane.'

Paul's irritation had diminished by the time dinner was served that night because there were other guests, the owner of an adjacent station and his manager, and they mostly talked about cattle and local difficulties, all of which kept Duke's news at bay.

In the morning they seemed to have lost interest in the reason for his late arrival. At dawn he clambered out of bed when he heard movement in the house, and joined them in the kitchen for a hurried breakfast.

'What's happening today?' he asked.

'We should have the last of the stragglers mustered by nightfall,' Paul said. 'You can ride a stockhorse. Then tomorrow I'll take sixty steers into Rockhampton to test the market. Do you want to come with me?'

No, he did not want to go into town with the well-known Paul MacNamara.

'Why? Do you need a hand?'

Paul frowned. 'You'd free a man to get on with the work here.'

'What has to be done here?'

'A million bloody things have to be done!' Paul exploded. 'You can get out there and dig bloody post-holes if you'd prefer that to going to town.'

Digging post-holes was a tough job, to be avoided whenever possible, but Duke reached for it.

'I don't mind digging post-holes,' he said coolly.

'Then you'll do just that,' his brother snapped.

'Duke just got here,' Laura said. 'I don't suppose he feels like turning around and riding back to town. Let him settle in.'

Paul stood and rounded on Duke. 'Have you finished your breakfast, or are you staying here all day?'

'I'm coming.' He gulped down hot tea and pushed the chair back. 'Thanks, Laura. I'll see you later.' Then he winked. 'If I survive.'

It occurred to Duke that he ought to grab his gear and push off before Paul came home from the Rockhampton cattle sales, but he kept on digging, and setting rough logs into place, with the help of an ancient station hand who never stopped talking about the old days when the ground was as hard as concrete and they had to chop it with an axe to even make a dent.

'You blokes have it easy now, I say,' the old-timer added. 'I used to be a contract fencer. You had to work with eyes in the back of your head or you'd collect a spear. A mate of mine got speared in the bum. Couldn't sit a horse for weeks. Went mad, he did. Thought he saw a blackfeller comin' in the door one night. Shot him. Turned out to be his missus . . .'

Duke gritted his teeth, shut down his ears and worked on.

'You don't say much, do you, son?'

Duke pretended not to hear.

Paul came in late that night with a saddlebag of gifts for Laura.

'One bottle of claret,' he said, as he unpacked. 'One box of scented soap. One tin of toffees. Two scarves sold to me by gypsies. I couldn't decide so I bought both. And fresh coffee from the Italian shop.'

She kissed him. 'Thank you, darling. Does this mean we're celebrating?'

'Yes, my love, cattle prices are on the up again. Also I picked up the mail. And look here . . .' Suddenly his eyes were flat and angry. 'Two for Duke!'

Laura reached over playfully and picked up the top letter. 'There, I knew it. A lady's handwriting.'

'The other one's interesting,' Paul said coldly.

'Oh? What?' Laura asked. But then she stopped. 'What's the matter?'

'Ask him.' Paul tossed the other letter across the table. 'It's from the Queensland Commercial Bank. And look. It doesn't have a stamp on it. And do you know why, Laura?'

She shook her head, bewildered.

'It doesn't have a stamp because while I was in the bank Sam Pattison came out to have a chat. He was full of news, and he asked me to give my brother this letter. Apparently Duke here has gone into business on his own.'

He glared at Duke. 'What's the matter? Cat got your tongue?'

'No, why should it?' Duke snapped, wishing he'd left Oberon Station that afternoon while he had the chance. 'Sure, I had dealings with the bank. Is that any of your business?'

'One would have thought so. Being family. You bought a cattle station?'

'You did?' Laura cried. 'Where? Why didn't you tell us?'

'I hadn't got around to it, that's all. It's the other side of Rockhampton.'

'Up here? That's marvellous. I was just thinking you must have bought in Brisbane, and that's what delayed you.'

'Tell me this,' Paul said. 'Where did you get the money?'

'From the bank. I got a loan.'

'On what collateral?'

'Valley of Lagoons.'

'Tell me another. Sam Pattison deals a mean hand. He wouldn't give you a penny on land in the far north.'

'Then you go and ask him if he's got the Valley of Lagoons papers in his safe.'

Paul wavered. 'You didn't put me down as a guarantor, did you?'

'No.'

'Which station is it?' Laura asked excitedly. 'We know most of them in that area.'

In that split second Duke searched about for a name. 'I'm calling it Mango Hill,' he said breathlessly. 'Yes. Mango Hill.'

The rest of it took three days. Duke wondered why he hung about for so long, knowing that the axe could fall. He supposed it was because he was enjoying his time here. The company probably. Even if Paul were still playing the know-it-all brother, Laura was fun. And anyway, the settlement date wasn't for another week. He had nowhere else to go.

Paul released him from the fencing duties and roped him into a work party to clean out and widen a flooded creek. He was going well until a new station hand joined them. The other men introduced him as Jack, explaining he'd been away for a week with a few broken ribs after a fall from the roof of a barn.

'You're the boss's brother?' the newcomer said. 'Pleased to meet you.'

They exchanged pleasantries for a few minutes and then Jack added: 'You're the one who bought Murphy's place, eh? Toombye.'

Another worker looked up. 'Is that right, Duke. You bought it?'

Duke nodded and dug his spade into the soft ground.

'Thought it had to be you. My dad saw you out there. He lost three horses to those bloody thieves.'

'Did the police catch any of them?' Duke asked.

'Not as far as I know. My dad was plenty savage with Murphy. Reckons he was in on it.'

'I don't think so. He and his wife were furious.'

The other men were anxious to hear more about the theft of so many horses and the conversation went off in that direction, but Duke didn't hold any hope that Jack's information about his purchase of Toombye would stay in this quiet neck of the woods. It would be the talk of Oberon within the hour.

That night, when Paul and a group of his stockmen rode in, Duke happened by and waited to join his brother as he turned out his horse and started up the track, lugging his saddle.

'I wanted a word with you,' he said.

'Yeah? What about?'

'The property I bought. I bought Murphy's place. Toombye.'

Paul strode ahead of him into a barn and threw down his saddle. As he emerged, he said: 'I know. Sam Pattison told me. I was wondering when you were going to spit it out. Now I'd like to know how it came about.'

'It was simple,' Duke said, relieved that there was no explosion this time. 'I met Chester Newitt when I bought Nelson and he took me out to the auction sales at Toombye.'

'Where some thieves had just taken off with fifty horses! Another bit of trivia you forgot to mention. But go on.'

'Anyway, Murphy was in a state because some of the men who'd brought horses to the sales were blaming him. So I got talking to him and he said he was going to sell up. That's when I got interested. It's a nice property.'

'And he didn't tell you that another MacNamara had been looking at buying Toombye, I don't suppose.'

'Why would he? He and his wife were barricaded in the house when we came along. The owners of those horses were shooting at them. He had better things to think about than who we were and what we were up to.'

106

'And over all your discussions and the inspections I presume you made before you bought . . .'

Duke nodded. 'I had a good look round, believe me.'

'. . . Murphy didn't mention me?'

'I don't know. He might have,' Duke stammered.

His brother swung a punch to his jaw that sent him sprawling in the mud.

'You're a bloody liar, Duke. I had my heart set on Toombye and you stole it from under my nose. If you wanted it that bad, you're bloody welcome to it. Now get your gear and take yourself back there. I don't want you here.'

Laura tried to intervene, but Paul wouldn't relent.

'I've got a bad feeling about the loan that Duke's lumbered himself with,' he said to her. 'He hasn't got much money of his own and he couldn't have bought Toombye on the strength of Valley of Lagoons. That's a joke.'

'Where else could he have got it?'

'I'm damned if I know.'

'Could you ask Pattison?'

'I suppose I could, but it's not done. He could refuse to divulge, and I wouldn't like to put him in that position. I wonder what the bugger paid for Toombye. I offered Murphy three hundred and fifty pounds all up, lock, stock and barrel.'

'He must have got more out of Duke then.'

'Impossible. Duke couldn't borrow that sort of money. Not from a bank.'

'Then who? Your stepfather? Mr Rivadavia.'

'Not a chance. Duke hates him.'

Laura headed for Duke's bedroom. 'I'm really worried about him now. He's only young. He could have got himself in too deep to cope. Let me have a word with him.'

But she was back in minutes. 'He's gone. You should go after him, Paul. Bring him back and find out what's going on.'

'No. Let him go. As soon as I have time, you and I are going hunting for a new roost, my love. At least he's done us a small favour: we're no longer hanging out waiting for Murphy to make up his mind.'

Eileen was a rare person, she maintained, in that she did not welcome the mailman's wagon trundling up the drive once a week. She couldn't understand the excitement that letters generated, since nine out of ten of them carried bills or bad news. And as for the telegrams . . .

Her husband said she was a born pessimist, but Eileen begged to differ.

'Don't expect me to open any telegrams that come to this house,' she said to him. 'I'd faint first.'

John Pace laughed. 'You'd faint? Like hell you would. You've never received a telegram! Your curiosity wouldn't let you last three seconds. You'd be tearing it open.'

Recalling that conversation, Eileen had a habit of searching the Kooramin Station mailbag carefully to weed out telegrams, which were always delivered with the mail. Today, fortunately, she found only one for the cook.

She ran through the house and thrust it at the woman, waiting breathlessly for the verdict.

'My auntie died,' Cook announced. 'Fine old lady she was too. She brought me up, she did. My mum and dad died when I was six. I'll have to go to the funeral if you can spare me for a few days, Mrs Mac.'

Eileen frowned. 'I suppose I'll have to.'

'There you are,' she said, marching back to her office, rehearsing her speech for John Pace when he came in. 'That one brought double trouble. A death for Cook and an inconvenience for us.'

That done, she sorted the rest of the mail for staff and family, placing the staff letters on the windowsill for the station manager to distribute.

Among the family mail of bills and catalogues, Eileen found a letter from Paul, and opened it with trepidation. The letter they'd received from someone up at Oberon to say his wife and servant girl had been murdered would keep her afeared of mail for the rest of her life.

This letter sounded quite cheerful to begin with. Hoping they'd had a good trip home and found everything and everyone in order. He'd had a good year on Oberon Station and was now ready to sell and move on.

Then it became very interesting. Eileen took the letter over to the window for better light.

Duke finally turned up, Paul had written. *He's been a busy boy. Bought a small cattle station south of Rockhampton. All very hush-hush for some reason, except that Rockhampton's talkers never heard of hush-hush, and the news was out before the ink was dry.*

Beats me where he found the cash, though, and he's not about to say. It's a going concern, by no means cheap. He says he put up Valley of Lagoons but that wouldn't cover a back paddock. A great mystery it is, but let's hope he flourishes.

How are the kids? . . .

Eileen stood back and stared! Duke had bought his own cattle station! A going concern? Which meant he'd bought cattle and rigs and stuff as well. And a homestead? Did he have a homestead too? Of his own? And what was it like? The questions flew about her head like Bogong moths. As fast as she batted them away, others flapped at her. Where could Duke have got that sort of money?

She hurried out of the house and looked down towards the bank of trees that sheltered the men's quarters, but all was quiet; there didn't seem to be anyone about. She was so keen to show this letter to John Pace that she considered riding out to him, but she wasn't sure where he would be working this morning.

Frustrated, she rushed out to the mailman, who had finished the lunch he always had at Kooramin, 'compliments of the management', as Eileen always remarked, to remind people of her largesse.

'Paddy,' she called, as he was ambling over to his buggy. 'Can you hang on a bit? I've an urgent letter to send.'

'Time I took to the track, missus.' He frowned to let her know who was boss. 'I got a big run these days. The work I have to do would kill a bullock.'

'I won't be long,' she countered and dived back inside.

The letter to Paul was flooded with those questions. The main one, though, underlined, was *What's Duke's address?*

When her husband finally came in, Eileen rushed at him, waving a letter.

'You'll never believe what Duke's got up to. Look at this! It's from Paul. I tell you, you won't believe this . . .'

'Give me a go,' he said. 'Can't I shake the dust off first?'

When he did read the letter, several times, John Pace was equally mystified, but he was inclined to think Paul had it wrong. In the end he said: 'Duke couldn't afford to buy a property. I reckon he's taken up a lease, that's what he's done. No doubt he'll tell us in due time. What's for dinner?'

But Eileen had no intention of letting the matter rest there. Weeks went by as she waited impatiently for a reply from Paul, fretting about him living so far away, up there in the wilds on a property she'd never seen, and never would. She hoped they'd be sensible this time and move back to New South Wales. To civilisation.

'No matter what they say,' she told her sister, Fiona, when she came to visit, 'I still maintain that's blackfeller country north of Brisbane. It'll never be anything else. I thought Paul was mad moving up there in the first place, and I was right, wasn't I? By God I was right, and I wish I wasn't.'

'But they say a lot of towns up there like Rockhampton are well developed now, Eileen, and people are making fortunes, especially with the gold rushes.'

'Rubbish. They're just a pack of grasshoppers.'

'Not from what the papers say. You ought to go up there and see for yourself. I'll come with you. We could go by ship, it'd be exciting.'

'By ship? The coastline is littered with wrecks! I wouldn't set foot on a ship!'

Fiona was disappointed. She lived with her parents on their station not two hundred miles from Kooramin, and at twenty-two and still single, she yearned to see more of the world. Only recently her father had agreed to allow her to visit the MacNamaras in Rockhampton, on condition Eileen accompanied her.

'Father said it's quite safe to go as far as Rockhampton now. He wouldn't let us go if he thought the ships were not safe.'

'Will you stop!' Eileen snapped. 'You've been nagging me for days. I'm not going up there and that's that! We could ride into Narrabri tomorrow if you like.'

'No thank you. That town's boring.'

Eileen shrugged. 'Please yourself.'

When Paul's reply did reach them, he had nothing more to offer about Duke's finances except that he had spoken to the previous owner and Duke had definitely bought the property. He was more interested in stock and feed prices, and the availability of good drovers, who seemed to be in great demand over the border. But he did have Duke's address. Simply: Mango Hill Station, via Rockhampton.

Eileen sat down and wrote to Duke immediately.

No beating about the bush here. She said she hoped he was well, and that she'd heard he'd bought a property: *but we are concerned and wish to know how you raised the money to buy that place. We don't believe for a moment that Valley of Lagoons would give you enough collateral so the truth would be helpful. We do think you should have sought Paul's advice before rushing off and buying the first place you set foot on, as you seem to have done. Please write as soon as you get this and let us know how matters stand.*

Duke's 'affectionate' sister-in-law signed herself 'most sincerely', and settled down for another long wait, but as the months went by it was obvious that they could not expect to hear from him.

'Looks like they had a real falling-out,' Eileen said. 'More than Paul's letting on to us. But he could at least try to find out.'

Her husband shrugged. 'Paul doesn't want to know, and I'm beginning to feel the same.'

'Well I'm not.'

John Pace grinned. 'All right. Just as long as you don't sit there pining for Duke to answer that letter you sent him. It was about as tactful as a nettle tree.'

'Tact is wasted on Duke,' she sniffed.

They'd almost forgotten that Hubert Bloom had been arranging the transfer of Kooramin from the estate of the late Dolour Rivadavia to the new owners until the official papers came by post, thereby reviving Eileen's dread of mail.

The papers didn't let her down. She was horrified to read that Kooramin was now owned by the three brothers in equal shares. Ever since she and John Pace had been running the station, she'd taken it for granted her husband would inherit it. Staring at the parchment pages now, she still found the reality hard to believe, and it was no consolation to her that John Pace had not harboured the same expectation.

'What happens now?' she demanded.

'I become the manager. We'll work out a salary deal, and at the end of the year we have a meeting to discuss the financial situation. We may need to reinvest profits sometimes instead of sharing.'

'And you do all the work?'

'Eileen, I've just explained to you that I get paid.'

'When does this meeting take place?'

'I don't know, come to think of it. We should have come to some arrangement when we were in Brisbane.'

'And now it's too late!'

He sighed. 'As soon as I get time I'll write up a management proposal. It's fairly straightforward. Dozens of stations are left to management. I'll send copies to Paul and to Duke.'

'Fat chance of him replying, let alone agreeing to anything.'

'He will if there's money in it. If he doesn't, we'll take it as said.'

'Good! Then we start paying ourselves wages as from now. I'll see to that. And I'm making it weekly.'

John Pace sat up with a jolt. 'Wait on. I'm the manager. I get paid. Not you. We don't pay managers' wives.'

'We do now, John Pace MacNamara! I work here too, and I want to be paid. I insist or I'm going on strike. That means you do the books, you midwife the mares, you cook for the men on their cook's day off, and you order the stores and take on my ten-hour days. I'll sack Minnie the nurse and mind the kids myself.'

She stormed out, leaving him gaping.

'Dolour,' he said, looking at the photograph of his mother on the wall, 'why did you have to sell all the rest of Dad's holdings when he died? Were you that angry with him? Why leave us to argue over one property?'

It had always been John Pace's conviction that his mother's grief was tainted with rage that her husband had got himself killed. That was her expression: 'Pace got himself killed,' she'd say.

Pace's memorial service was held only days after Rivadavia broke the news to them, without regard for people who needed to travel long distances, and Dolour had stood at the front of the church, cold and withdrawn. She barely had a word of consolation for her broken-hearted sons; that was left to Milly and Dermott Forrest.

She called in a stock and station agent and sold their other station with no notice to the management and staff, as if they were all part of a conspiracy to keep her husband from her. She then disposed of other land holdings that he'd owned. John Pace remembered Milly Forrest saying in awestruck tones: 'Good heavens, Dolour! I had no idea Pace had so much land!'

'He was a miser, that's what he was,' Dolour said angrily. 'A damned land miser. And where did it get him?'

'Ah now, dear, don't be taking on so. Pace was thinking of his family. He always wanted to see his sons well placed.'

'Oh sure he did. With no father.'

111

John Pace had heard afterwards that when Dolour announced she intended to marry Juan Rivadavia, while she was still nursing that cold grief, it was Milly Forrest who'd said to her: 'Oh yes, Dolour. That'll really pay Pace out. Now he'll be sorry!'

And Dolour had burst into tears. The first tears she'd shed, publicly, since his death.

John Pace had often wondered what had become of the money from all those sales. Not a penny of it went through Kooramin's books, or her only known bank account. At her sons' request, Bloom had made enquiries, but had come up blank. Rivadavia, a wealthy man in his own right, had no knowledge of it. No one knew. She'd simply disposed of it. Wilfully, John Pace thought.

And that was where matters stood. Only Kooramin Station remained. A legacy of trouble.

The strike only lasted a day. Eileen came up with a new scheme. She would be the manager, and engage her husband as head stockman. John Pace's reaction to that was a decisive no. But he did suggest engaging his wife as book-keeper, hoping that his brothers would accept that idea.

Mollified for the time being, Eileen's curiosity settled on Duke again. Where had he found the money?

Suddenly, as she was giving her daughters Tess and Brigit their breakfasts, a plan came to her, so she quickly handed them over to Minnie and rushed back to the office.

Jeannie's parents. Paul's late wife's parents! They'd lived in Rockhampton at one stage. Rolf Stanmore, now retired, had been a magistrate up there for some years.

Dear Rolf and Florence, she began, chewing the pen awhile before writing the usual preliminaries, and news of Tess and Brigit, who would both be going to boarding school in Sydney next year. In the centre of this epistle she managed a few lines about Duke. Did they know he had purchased a cattle property called Mango Hill in Rockhampton? *John Pace*, she continued, *is a little anxious that Duke may have got himself in over his head with a loan. But you know Duke. He won't admit he may have made a mistake.*

She rattled on about the weather and how nice it had been to see them in Brisbane after the funeral, enough to fill the second small page, and then she closed, spiriting the letter away until she could hand it to Paddy the mailman herself.

Rolf Stanmore was bored. Forced to retire after suffering two heart attacks, he missed the vitality of the courtrooms, and the characters who passed through them, finding the quiet of home life unbearable. His sharp wit and attention to detail had made him a shrewd judicial officer, much respected in the courts.

These days Rolf kept in touch with the community at large by reading newspapers and writing letters, most of which were addressed to editors and contained his forthright views on any number of subjects. He also corresponded with friends, family and acquaintances at length, treating those who failed to reply with severe lectures on bad form.

Eileen's letter landed on his desk on a particularly lean day. His wife had returned from the post office with only two letters for him. One advised that his membership fees at the country club, from which he'd resigned two years previously, were overdue, and if they were not paid within seven days, the club secretary would be forced to take steps to remove his name from the list.

'Bah!' he growled, placing it aside to be answered with caustic comment.

His Huon pine letter-opener, a gift from a former Tasmanian convict, slid effortlessly through the thin envelope and delivered him Eileen's neat pages.

Though Rolf would never forgive Paul for failing to protect his daughter, Jeannie, he had a soft spot for the rest of the MacNamaras. Their father, a handsome and charismatic Irishman, had attended his wedding to Florence. Such a long time ago, he sighed. And Pace had surprised everyone by bringing along three fiddlers to add to the occasion.

Eileen, he remembered, was very solicitous about their feelings when he and Florence had attended the formal tea after Dolour's funeral. She'd gone out of her way to see that they were comfortably seated and well served, and made an effort to screen them from the young woman who'd already taken Jeannie's place in Paul's heart. Florence had been grateful to her for her thoughtfulness.

'Now, Eileen,' Rolf said, as he settled back in the worn leather chair that had travelled with him on many magisterial adventures, 'what have you to say for yourself?'

Not a lot, he mused, as his practised eye ran down the page, except for this piece about Duke.

'I wonder what he has been up to?' Rolf asked himself, conceding that Eileen had a good point. How would a young bloke like Duke rustle up that sort of collateral? And why all the secrecy?

Rolf smelled a rat.

He gave the matter serious thought, weighing the available evidence and wondering what lurked beneath the surface.

'I think this is a matter for Tedmund Tanner,' he murmured, conjuring up a picture of a neat little fellow, disbarred years ago for a long-forgotten offence, who had gradually become indispensable to many in his subsequent role as a private detective. 'Yes, Eileen,' he added. 'Tedmund's your lad.'

And Tedmund didn't fail him.

His first response carried the information that one Duke MacNamara, who was in fact not a duke, had purchased a property called Toombye Station, a going concern, and changed the name to Mango Hill.

He had obtained a loan of four hundred pounds from the Queensland Commercial Bank in Rockhampton, approved by the manager Sam Pattison. The loan was in order, having been gained by using two properties as security: first the Valley of Lagoons; and second Kooramin Station, of which the purchaser had a third part share.

Mr Duke MacNamara also had a letter of credit for one hundred pounds from the Brisbane head office of the Queensland Commercial Bank, which he had utilised.

'Well there you are,' Rolf said to Florence. 'Duke MacNamara is spreading his wings. But it is strange that Eileen should think Duke has gotten himself in over his head. Tedmund doesn't mention any complications. And Paul is up there. He'd know if he had, and disallowed the loan.'

Florence smiled. 'She probably doesn't understand men's business arrangements, dear. I mean, I wouldn't know where to start, walking into a bank and asking them to lend me money.'

Rolf nodded. 'Ah yes. I see. I'll explain it to her then, as Tedmund told me. That will set her mind at rest.'

'You won't mention him, though!' Florence had never approved of Tedmund Tanner or his occupation.

'Entirely unnecessary, my dear.'

With winter approaching, Kooramin Station looked its best. The winds from the south brought early rains, rejuvenating the dams and billabongs and greening the dusty countryside. The frangipani that shaded the kitchen was now shedding its leaves to allow the sun to counter the chill, and the orchard was dispatching the last of the summer fruit.

In the kitchen, Eileen and Cook were busy bottling peaches and pickling small onions, the men's favourites. Eileen was also making her speciality, piccalilli, born of her grandmother's prize recipe from her genteel Raj life in India: pickles made with spices and finely chopped vegetables. She had won prizes at local shows with her piccalilli.

She was in a good mood today, much preferring winter to the hot, dry summer, and often took time to marvel at the strange weather Paul experienced up north, where the summers were wet and the winters dry. Weather that Duke would be experiencing now, she recalled angrily, putting paid to that good mood.

As if telepathy were at work, just as Duke was brought to mind, Cook looked out of the window and said: 'The mailman's coming. Across the back track there.'

Trying not to look eager, Eileen dried her hands on her large black apron and hurried into the office to collect the canvas bag with *Kooramin* stencilled on it that contained outgoing mail. She walked through the house to her bedroom, where she brushed out her hair and wound it back into its bun. While she was there, stalling, she plumped and smoothed the pillows on the bed she shared with John Pace, shook the light feather-filled eiderdown, replaced it over the counterpane, and glanced through the plain muslin curtains to make sure the mail wagon had come to a halt down at the gate. Then she picked up the bag and walked out, mistress of the house, stepping briskly down the sandy path to exchange this bag for the one containing incoming mail.

The deliberate delaying tactic she was employing was wasted on Paddy, who was too busy complaining about herds of cattle on the roads, but it gave her time to compose herself, because she felt sure there'd be a reply from Rolf Stanmore this time. Whether that was a good thing or a bad thing she couldn't begin to guess, but her instinct, as usual, sensed the worst.

In the privacy of the office, Eileen took a deep breath and emptied the contents of the bag on to the table. There were only about twenty letters, and she sorted them swiftly, pouncing on one addressed to her.

She read Rolf's response carefully, twice over, and showed it to her husband that night at dinner, taking him by surprise. He spluttered his soup, leapt up from the dinner table and read it again, standing as close as he could get to the lamp on the mantelpiece.

'Is he saying that Duke raised money on Kooramin?' His voice croaked in disbelief.

'Looks like it,' Eileen said in smug understatement.

'Four hundred pounds?'

She nodded. 'More.'

'Bloody hell! Who said he could do that? I'll knock his bloody head off, the little bastard. But wait a minute. How did Rolf get into the picture?'

'I asked him.'

'You had no right to do that, Eileen. No bloody right at all. I don't want strangers messing in our affairs.'

'Oh yes,' she sneered. 'Just sit back and do nothing while your brothers steal Kooramin from under us.'

'Brothers? What has Paul got to do with this?'

'A lot more than he's saying, I bet. Duke's been up there all this time. Paul must have known what he was up to. And if Rolf Stanmore could find out, why couldn't Paul? He's on the spot. Rolf's in Brisbane.'

John Pace was confused. 'Didn't Paul say he doesn't know how Duke got the money?'

'He could have, but it's suspicious, the both of them in the same town with two stations now, and Paul talking about buying another one.'

'When he sells Oberon.'

'Maybe . . .'

Upset, John Pace bypassed dinner. He wrote a letter full of rage to Duke, and another, only slightly less angry, to Paul.

There was no reply from either of them.

Duke tossed his letter on the fire. It was exactly the reaction he'd expected when his brothers found out about the loan, and so what?

Paul was shocked to learn the truth, but offended by his twin brother's insinuation that he was involved in Duke's machinations.

He and Laura rode into town the next day, and took a room at the comfortable Criterion Hotel. Though they did not discuss it, Laura knew that he would not leave her on the station in his absence. Their home was safe now and twenty station hands lived on the property, but Paul still bore the scars of the tragedy, so she always packed up to ride with him when he left for overnight journeys, as a matter of course.

Sam Pattison was not surprised to see the burly elder MacNamara come thumping into the bank demanding to see him immediately.

'What can I do for you, Paul?' he asked with his usual welcoming smile.

'You can come clean on the loan you gave my brother!'

'Quieten down, you'll frighten my tellers,' Sam grinned. 'They'll think you're a bank robber. You're not, are you?'

'You'll wipe that smarmy smile off your face by the time I've finished with you,' Paul threatened.

'Oh, calm down. Come into my office. Do you want a cup of tea?'

'No I don't!' Paul said, following him into the office.

'A whisky? You look more like you could do with a whisky. Now what's up?'

He slid behind his desk, opened a drawer and poured a slug of whisky from a silver flask, offering it to Paul, who refused it.

'Very well! Bottoms up, can't waste it.' He downed the whisky. 'Well, what's the problem?'

'You approved a loan to my brother Duke?'

'Yes.'

'An illegal loan,' Paul fumed.

'Hey! Whoa! What was illegal about it?'

'He used Kooramin Station as security!'

'That's right. Sit down. I'm getting a stiff neck.'

Instead of sitting, Paul placed both hands on Pattison's desk and leaned over him.

'Duke doesn't own Kooramin!' he growled.

'He owns a third of it, and I'm sure four hundred pounds is barely a bump on Kooramin's worth.'

'What are you talking about? Four hundred pounds is a lot of money in anyone's terms. Or have you become so doused in bank funds and whisky you've lost perspective?'

'That's enough, Paul. I won't have you crowding me! Sit down so we can talk this out man to man, or the conversation is over.'

Man to man? Paul thought as, reluctantly, he sank into the chair. This was like talking to a slippery fish.

'Duke only has a third share of Kooramin,' he repeated.

'I know that. You and your brother John Pace own the rest. I was under the impression it was a family decision to get him started. The MacNamaras have a good name, and I saw no reason to refuse him. He was even carrying a letter of credit from the head office of this bank in Brisbane on the strength of your good name. If I've made a mistake in allowing the loan, then let me worry.'

'You worry? You've got far more security than you need! And you gave him the loan without the approval of the other owners of the property. My brother and I were not even consulted!'

'Would you have refused it?' Sam seemed quite bewildered, but Paul saw through his innocent gaze.

'Don't try moving the cups around on me, you shifty bugger,' he said. 'You've now got a lien on our property without notifying me or John Pace. It's bloody illegal.'

They argued the case for ten minutes, but Paul couldn't seem to get ahead of this man, who kept coming back to the point that Duke had perhaps obtained the loan under false pretences, while Paul was reluctant to accuse his brother.

In the end, Pattison shrugged. 'I'm tired of this. I gave him the loan in good faith . . .'

'Good faith?' Paul snapped. 'You couldn't even spell it.'

'So . . .' Pattison continued, 'what do you want me to do about it? Have him charged with false pretences? I don't think you'd like that. Or would you rather I called in the loan? What do you want, MacNamara?'

Paul felt like upending the desk between them as he stood to leave.

'I'll think about it,' he said, desperately upset at how this interview had turned out.

'I heard from a reliable source,' Pattison said archly, 'that you were after Murphy's place yourself. Did your brother beat you to the punch?'

Paul ignored that. 'Be assured, Pattison, your head office will be made aware of this matter, so don't expect to keep that seat warm much longer.'

★　★　★

Eventually they heard the bad news from Paul, reinforcing the information forwarded to them by Rolf Stanmore. They were left stunned, unable to offer a solution. Not one that was tenable anyway, because John Pace favoured the horsewhip and Eileen was all for charging Duke with fraud.

'It all boils down to this,' John Pace said wearily. 'I'm not happy with our situation.'

'Neither am I,' said his wife. 'Duke's got us buffaloed.'

'No, it's not that. I think this is just the beginning of all sorts of ructions now that we're working for Paul and Duke.'

'We're not!' Eileen began belligerently, but then, when she thought about it, she corrected herself. 'I suppose in a way we are.'

John Pace added: 'Duke hasn't signed the contract I sent him outlining our salary and entitlements.'

'And he won't! So we ignore him.'

'Not a good idea. What if he stands up one day and says he didn't agree to the salary. He's a wild card, Eileen.'

'I'll never forgive him for doing this to us,' she sniffed into her handkerchief.

'It's not Duke,' he said, 'it's circumstances. Can I make you a cup of tea?'

'I'll get it,' she said, wandering off to the kitchen in a daze.

'No, it's not Duke,' he murmured. 'It's you, Dolour. This is your doing. You wouldn't instruct Bloom to sell Kooramin; you knew we'd object. The last thing Pace would have wanted. So you threw it to us to fight over. Aren't you satisfied yet? You're scattering his holdings to the winds. How you must have loved him, you mad Irishwoman! But I won't let you scatter Kooramin as well. It was Pace's home. I won't let you.'

When Eileen returned, he put an arm around her.

'Don't be worrying. I've made up my mind. We won't sell and we won't let them push us into a situation where we have to raise enough money to pay them both out. This property belongs to all three of us, and it stays that way.'

'How will you stop them?'

'With a shotgun if necessary! We won't let buyers near the place. I'm not about to let Dolour beat me.'

'Dolour!' she said. 'Why would she want to beat you?'

'It's complicated. I'll tell you another time. Right now I want you to write to both of them, tell them of our decision and inform them that they will follow the same procedures we had with Dolour. I remain manager, on the wage as specified. I will forward six-monthly statements with a cheque. The difference now being that we divide the cheque into three. We each have a third share in the profits.'

'Why don't I add that on no account will we even contemplate the sale of Kooramin? And that we resent any suggestion of a sale. I should also tell them . . .'

John Pace scowled. 'Tell 'em what you like. Just as long as they know the rules!'

Some time later Milly Forrest sent John Pace a clipping from a Sydney newspaper:

> Members of the Board of St Mary's Female Orphanage, Parramatta, wish to thank the person who most generously donated a substantial sum to this Establishment, and who has chosen to remain anonymous. Mindful that our Benefactor requested that said Funds be used for the education of the orphans residing in these Premises, we now advise that a Schoolhouse has been built on the Premises and daily lessons are conducted by Miss Evangeline Croft.

Milly had placed a question mark beside the public notice, and John Pace nodded.

'Entirely possible,' he said to his wife.

'Why would she do that?'

'I suppose the female factory at Parramatta was closed by then,' he said bitterly.

'The female *convict* factory! It closed years ago. What's that got to do with Dolour?'

'That's where she started off in Australia.'

'She was a *convict*?'

'Yes. Transported when she was seventeen.'

'You never told me that.'

'Oh for Christ's sake, Eileen. I have so. You just don't want to know.'

'Well you couldn't blame me for that.'

Duke received a letter from Lucy Mae, forwarded from the Rockhampton post office, enquiring after his health and situation, and he was pleased to answer that. Pleased to write and tell her: *I have my own station now, which I call Mango Hill, with two thousand head of cattle, which keep me busy, but it's prospering you'll be happy to hear.*

He grimaced at that point. Mango Hill wasn't prospering so far, nor did it still have two thousand head. He'd had to sell hundreds of cattle to keep the men paid and the bank at bay, and to raise more money he had taken a team of his men chasing brumbies. That had sounded like a good idea at the time, and they'd caught some good horses, but he had had to build taller and stronger stockyards to hold them and then break them himself, to save having to pay a breaker.

Some of the wild horses were as mean as cut snakes, so it was hard work, but his men enjoyed watching their boss skidding about in the dust at the end of a rope, day after day. He was patient with the brumbies – he had to be, with an audience – and gradually those horses taught him a thing or two about the job, what they would put up with and what they would not tolerate, which he accepted to avoid injury. In time, to his surprise, Duke found his niche. His men claimed their boss was a 'gun' breaker; an expert.

This was his first chance to tell someone about his station. He enjoyed sitting up by lamplight in his own house, with a glass of rum, so he rambled on for a few pages, finally suggesting that Lucy Mae and her mother should visit. He was sure they'd find Rockhampton an interesting town, and it would be an honour to show them his property.

'How kind of Duke to invite us,' Milly said. 'We can't refuse. He sounds so proud of his place. We will go. You call in at the shipping office today and book us a cabin. It has to be first class and a decent ship. We'll have a look at this town and visit Paul and Laura as well. I'm quite excited, aren't you?'

Nervous, more like it, Lucy Mae thought. She wasn't sure how to handle Duke.

As for the man himself, no sooner had he sent that letter off to Brisbane than he met a young woman at a christening on a neighbouring property. Her name was Beth Delaney and she lived in Rockhampton with her parents, who owned the Turf Club Hotel. By the time Lucy Mae and her mother stepped ashore in Quay Street, Rockhampton, where their friend Duke MacNamara was waiting for them, Jack Delaney had accepted him as a serious suitor for his second daughter's hand, with conditions.

'You can't be marrying Beth until I get her elder sister Carmel off me hands,' he warned. 'She don't want to be called an old maid before her time.'

That suited Duke. He hadn't marriage in mind, only seduction.

And: 'If you get her in the family way,' Delaney added, 'don't think you'll be marryin' her, because they'll be fishing you out of the river.'

That definitely didn't suit him; in fact it caused him to lose interest in Beth almost immediately, so he welcomed the ladies with open arms and took them to the Criterion Hotel, where the first people they met in the foyer were Paul and Laura MacNamara.

CHAPTER FIVE

In rugged red ranges high above Bulla Bulla, a man stepped over crumbling plates of rock at the top of a gorge and took a deep breath. He was absorbing the colour of this ancient land, from the coppery pinks and greys of the rocks under his feet to the straw-like streaks of gold down the tumbling walls of the gorge. He raised a hand to better view the earthy green of sparse forests clinging to the heat-baked hills, and then moved his gaze on to the treeless summits that surrounded him, their tawny shades at peace with the softening blue-to-pink of the massive sunset skies.

For years this man had been coming here from the coastal regions . . . over the barrier of the great dividing range, and on into the vast interior where dwell many clans, for he was a trader. He now travelled with his two sons, who were both strong and long legged like their father, teaching them the way of things, against the time when his own legs would begin to buckle.

This journey took all of the two seasons, and the waterholes at Bulla Bulla were an important centre. Here the Pitta Pitta people made the best spears and shields. Also, traders came in from the deserts further into the centre of the great land, with the prized Pituri leaves that came from trees in secret locations they would never divulge. At least this trader knew how to prepare the leaves to gain the best effect on a man's consciousness, but to comply with the law he might not pass the knowledge on to his sons until their beards began to turn grey.

These young men carried the trader's wares; anything from personal ornaments to massive broadswords, specialised nets and even grindstones, easily sold and replaced by other items in this well-populated area. But this trader also carried information, reliable information, so his arrival was greeted with great excitement.

They were not to be disappointed. On this occasion he also had a message stick bearing the date and location of a great corroboree, to be held shortly. Not only were the Pitta Pitta invited, but also the Mitakoodi and the Kalkadoon clans, a rare meeting and therefore judged to be very important, so immediately people rushed to prepare.

There would be talks and discussions among the elders, of course, but a corroboree of this magnitude could not be just business. There were special ceremonies to be observed; dances to practise; ornaments and paints to be found; and feasts to prepare.

With all this activity about him in full swing, the trader approached the elders to ask a favour.

'Your cave paintings are famous throughout the land, but few people have seen them. I was wondering if I might be permitted to behold this joy, before my sons and I begin our trek back to the shores of the great ocean.'

An elder known simply as Kapakupa, replied. 'Ladjipiri,' he said, for that was the trader's name. 'Ladjipiri, you have come far and you know many things. We are grateful to you for your assistance to us over the years. It will be an honour to escort you to the main cave this very day. To see the paintings in their full glory, it is necessary to sleep in the mountains tonight, so as to be present when sunrise floods light and changing colour into their depths.'

'I am humbled and greatly excited by this honour.'

'That pleases us,' the elder replied, 'and I'm sure you will not refuse our small request.'

'Oh–oh,' the trader murmured inside himself. 'I might have known there'd be a small request. One I cannot refuse.'

His sons were mightily impressed that he was given permission to visit the sacred cave, and delighted that the three of them had been invited to attend the corroboree, which was to be held in eight days' time. Distance travellers like Ladjipiri had little time to spare for such occasions, and for that matter, having no kin connections in strange lands, were rarely welcome. This time, however, the trader's wide experience of the world, and his occasional associations with the dreaded white men and their animals, could prove valuable.

'I cannot tell you much,' he had said. 'We keep away from their campfires whenever possible. I prefer to observe them from a distance.'

'Ah, but from the gathering of elders there will be questions. Some have not even glimpsed a shadow of them.'

At that, an old man called querulously: 'Do they have shadows? If they are white, how does a shadow fall?'

And another asked: 'Is it true that some of them have four legs?'

'No. Some ride upon a large animal with four legs.'

'You see,' the elder commented. 'Your answers will help people learn about them. People trust that you will speak truthfully.'

In the morning, before sunrise, an agile guide called Murrabung led Ladjipiri through a maze of huge boulders and down into a clearing dotted with spiky waddi trees. At the far end of the clearing they slid through a narrow gap in the rocks and, turning a corner, came to a dead end on a narrow ledge that gave a panoramic view way out to the silver-thin river on the flat country.

Ladjipiri, unhappy with heights, grabbed a tree that had managed to grow from a niche in the rock wall and hung on, while Murrabung, unconcerned that he was standing at the edge of a sheer drop, grinned and pointed to the glare of the rising sun in the east. Then he turned.

'Look!'

Still clutching the tree, the trader turned gingerly and found himself staring into the gaping maw of a wide cave.

Together they stepped into the huge and silent gallery with its low roof, their whispered, respectful voices sounding like the boom of a didgeridoo. Stepping carefully over the rubble of fallen rocks to go deeper into the cave, Ladjipiri experienced a feeling of being reduced in size. Suddenly he felt like a tiny creature, no bigger than a bee! And yet his shadow was still there. A long shadow.

Disoriented, he stumbled back towards the entrance and saw a painting on the wall of a white stick figure representing a man at a waterhole with a palm tree above it. The man was on the ground. He seemed dead. And the scene seemed real, as if a dead man were lying there in front of him. Terrified, he fled.

It took a while, but eventually Murrabung talked him into coming back into the cave.

'You came all this way. You don't want to go now. No bad spirits here. I take your hand. Try again.'

'No. Might be I am the wrong skin for here.'

'Not true. You have permission. That is enough. Now come on.'

Ladjipiri returned to the cave, looking to the wall that had held that painting, but it was gone.

'You imagine it,' Murrabung laughed. 'Give yourself a pretty good scare, eh? Now look here. This old man on the wall here, he chasing a big red kangaroo with a stick, never catch him. And this big tall spirit man with the round head, he powerful.'

Further into the cave they saw more and more paintings of people and animals and events, and sometimes even Dreamtime spirits, for Ladjipiri knew they'd been painted countless ages ago.

'Why do the paintings last so long?' he asked.

'Because the ochre paint is so fine it sinks into this special sort of rock, it doesn't sit on top. It becomes part of the rock and only weather can wear it out. No weather in here, eh?'

'Ah now. I didn't know that.'

He continued walking about admiring the old paintings and their stories until Murrabung called to him.

'Stop there. Where you are now.'

Concerned that he might be transgressing somehow, Ladjipiri came to a sudden halt.

'Now lie down.'

'Lie down?'

'Yes. On your back.'

'Why?'

'Just do it.'

He lay down and stretched out, fearing that refusing to oblige might cause offence. The dust and rubble were uncomfortable on his bare body, and he grimaced as he brushed sharp particles aside, but then suddenly he saw the painting on the roof above him.

It was a huge bird with bat wings, but it had the body of a fat reptile and a long snout with rows of sharp teeth!

The trader was awestruck, not only by the sheer size of the painting but by what it represented. As he gazed in wonder, the large yellow eyes of the bird seemed to be focused straight ahead, as if it did not wish to be interrupted in its flight.

'What is it?' he gasped.

'A Dreamtime bird. They say that bird and many other strange animals roamed this world before the water became scarce.'

Ladjipiri nodded. 'That bird could drink a waterhole dry.'

The trek back down to the camp took a half-day, but Ladjipiri was still full of wonder. It was the closest he'd ever come to finding himself in the presence of spirits, and he found the experience had entered his heart and somehow made changes. What changes he could not say, but the next morning he felt different, clearer in the head, and his eyes felt wider, as if he were able to see new things.

'What new things?' he asked himself. 'You're getting woman-like, hysterical. Better not to tell this stuff to anyone or they'll send for a kidachji man to cure you.'

The day came, and because the distance wasn't so great, the trader loaded his sons up with tall shields on which he placed tools and bags of armbands, girdles and headbands made by local women, assured of good sales at such a gathering. He himself wore his favourite display wares: shell necklaces, a bright red headband and tassels made of coloured twine that hung from a rope girdle slung about his hips.

It was a six-day march over the ranges and on to the flat country called Warrukayi, which meant emu in the Pitta Pitta language. At night, as they descended the hills, the travellers could see campfires along the banks of the big river far in the distance, far more campfires than they'd ever expected to see in one place in their lifetime. There were gasps of astonishment and awe. Many of the young, unable to contain their enthusiasm, ran on through the night to join the throng, and the trader had to be firm with his sons, who were both still in their ten-by-two years, refusing to allow them to join the rush.

While the elders of the three clans conferred, men and boys competed in games of strength and ability, children played in the river and women prepared the daily feasts. At night, various dance troupes in full paint burst into the firelight to entertain with their stories to the accompaniment of singers, didgeridoos and clapsticks, and the audiences were dazzled.

On the third day, Ladjipiri was invited to attend a meeting of the elders in a quiet place further downriver. Time to return the favour. The heat was intense, and the ground seemed to sizzle under his feet, but it didn't appear to bother these old men, fifteen of them he noted, sitting cross-legged in the red dust under the full glare of the sun.

Most of them, he was told, had seen white men travelling through their lands, often more than ten at a time. At first they were allowed to pass, even though they did not adhere to any of the rules repecting tribal boundaries, let alone the rest of the laws.

'They drink at forbidden waterholes,' one man called out angrily. 'Water is life. These waterholes are preserved for a reason. It is a crime to drink or steal that water. Why are they not punished?'

'That is why we are here,' a Mitakoodi man said. 'The white men are not only intruding on our territory, they are committing crimes day after day. Two women from our camp alone are missing and it is feared they've been stolen by whites.'

'And you sit here talking about it? A Kalkadoon man would never admit to such an outrage!' The speaker, a powerfully built man with his hair twisted into a topknot and decorated with white cockatoo feathers, was younger than the others.

'Perhaps Kalkadoon men do not know that the white men have fearsome weapons. I myself have seen and heard their gunsticks. I saw with my own eyes a kangaroo felled by one of them.'

'Kalkadoon men would not creep off and let the crime go unpunished.'

The argument was interrupted by Kapakupa. 'It is time for the trader to speak. In the matter of the stolen women, we have to decide for ourselves what action to take. But I ask: what would the white men do in the same circumstances? If we took two of their women?'

There was a buzz of interest as all eyes turned to Ladjipiri, who brushed flies from his face, cleared his throat nervously, and spoke.

'I believe the white men would fight to kill the abductors.'

'And if we stole their animals?'

'The same.' The trader was afraid to reveal that he had seen white men hang men of the Darambal tribe outside the village they called Rockhampton, for he was a Darambal man and he had fled in fright. Most of his people had left the area to escape the invaders.

A voice called to him, almost in derision: 'I have seen nine white men myself. They were kind to me. They gave me water and meat. How many have you seen?'

Ladjipiri looked about him. How to say this without upsetting them? They were so far from the white villages that they would probably only ever come across the odd few curious travellers.

'I have seen', he said quietly, 'villages with more people in them than you have at this corroboree. But that was a whole dry season's march away from here.'

Stunned silence greeted that revelation.

'You lie,' the same voice shouted at last.

There were other questions, about the white men's habits, their animals and, of course, their women. Some wanted to know where they had come from, but this he could not tell them.

'I have heard the word "invaders",' the Kalkadoon man said, as if he'd read Ladjipiri's mind. 'Do you know that word?'

The trader nodded.

'And is it used in the other nations? Among the clans?'

'Yes. They are called "the invaders" by many people, in many languages along the seashore of the land.'

'So they are not just on your shore. They have invaded at many points?'

'I believe so. My trading route is directly inland and back. So I only see some . . .' His voice trailed off.

The Kalkadoon man stood. 'An invader is an enemy. We must prepare. We must not make them welcome or accept any gifts from them, like the mealy-mouth over there. Let them know that all of this land is ours by law. We must strike a treaty, a war treaty of the Pitta Pitta and the Mitakoodi and the Kalkadoon. This great force will preserve our nations and keep our people safe.'

After a while Ladjipiri was excused, because the debate was dragging on, but he was told that an announcement would be made to all the people present on the following evening, the last night of the corroboree. He understood that the elders would have come to a decision by then, and their policy as regarded the white people would be set in place until further notice.

A spokesman from each of the clans made a pronouncement to the huge gathering, in his own language. They informed their people that they could expect some white men to be walkabout on their lands, possibly just for a look-see, since their country was very beautiful. They warned that it would not be wise to antagonise the white people in any way, since they carried new

126

and fearsome weapons. Better to avoid them when possible. Curiosity could be dangerous. Lastly, all sightings of white people and their animals were to be reported to the elders without fail.

The Kalkadoon man who had spoken so forcibly at the meeting the trader had attended was called Uluyan. Apparently this was Kalkadoon country, so he was accorded the honour of farewelling their guests and wishing them safe travel to their home campfires. As he did so, judging by the shouts of dismay from the clan leaders standing behind him, he broke with tradition by adding a few words of his own.

'You have been told the policy is peace. A wait-and-see peace. So be it. But Kalkadoon men are warriors . . .'

Shouts of support came from a large group of men and women who pushed a young man forward.

'Who is he?' the trader asked urgently.

'The Kalkadoon's son.'

He must have been about eighteen and had the firm, straight features of his parent. And the same confidence, Ladjipiri noted, as the newcomer sprang forward to stand, arms folded, beside his father, who continued:

'Kalkadoon men will strike back if attacked!'

Someone behind him protested.

He half turned and shouted: 'We will wait and see!' Then he laughed, his jaw jutting belligerently. 'This is my son. What say you, boy? Am I breaking the pact?'

'No!' the boy shouted. 'That is fair by our laws.'

Their supporters cheered, stamping their feet, but already the crowds were drifting away, and Ladjipiri went in search of his own sons to prepare to move on. They had sold all their wares, and there was nothing left to buy, so he decided to avoid the ranges and walk south-east, into the lands of the Wanamara people, where he knew he could obtain fine strong hunting boomerangs and an interesting variety for ornamental or ceremonial use.

They were travelling well on this homeward route, over rivers and creeks too shallow to bother them at this time of the year, meeting many folk who were heading for their wet-season camps.

Ten days after the corroboree they topped a rise overlooking the long reach of a river, and from that vantage point they sighted a huge cloud of dust out on the plains. Believing they were in for yet another of the hated red dust storms, which normally came from the centre of the land, they downed their burdens and took shelter among some trees.

But the dust storm was slow approaching. Too slow. So they strained their eyes to try to make out what strangeness nature was unfolding before them now, for there were many strangenesses in this back country that never failed to surprise them.

'It's the cattle animals,' his elder son called. 'A big mob. They go back as far as the eye can see. Look, Father, they are coming this way and there are horse riders with them. Where are they going?'

Ladjipiri was confounded. 'I do not know,' he admitted. 'But I do know that they trade in the cattle animals, which they keep for food. But there's no one to trade with out here.'

His other son laughed. 'I say they're lost.'

'They may be lost. They are months away from their seashore villages.'

They watched as the great herd rumbled towards them, while the riders cracked whips and rode up and down keeping the animals in order. After a while, though, the cattle became restless, making their mooing noises, and Ladjipiri was quick to tell the boys: 'They can smell water! They're thirsty.'

As if on cue, the cattle began to move faster, and then one of them broke into a lumbering gallop and the rest of the huge mob began rushing after it.

Ladjipiri and his sons had seen mobs of kangaroos trying to escape capture, but they'd never seen a rush of this size. They were on their feet, whooping with excitement as the cattle thundered towards the river, the riders frantically trying to slow them down. The horsemen were riding at breakneck pace, trying to deflect the mob, shouting, whistling, cracking whips, often disappearing in the great swirl of dust, to emerge further forward.

'They're thirsty,' the boys objected. 'Why don't those men let them drink?'

'Too many, I think,' their father explained, without averting his eyes. He didn't want to miss a second of this grand scene. 'They could trample each other.'

Sure enough, some stumbled in the mad rush and were trampled under the thunder of the hooves. The watching men could hear the screams of the animals as they went down and the moans of the wounded left behind, scattered in the settling dust.

When it was all over, when the cattle had drunk their fill and been moved on to make room for others, all was quiet again, the riders keeping watch, riding slowly, cautiously, on the outskirts of the mob.

One man rode back, dismounted from his horse and checked the wounded animals. Most seemed dead, but the flash of a knife told the watchers that he was putting the others out of their misery.

A large covered wagon pulled by two horses came into view and drew up some distance from the settling mob.

'I think they're stopping for the night now,' Ladjipiri said. 'We might as well do the same.'

When they continued their trek towards the coast, the trader was saddened to find more and more white people, with their animals and their wagons, spreading across the land like a flood. Where once he would have seen men two by two on horseback, and the occasional small troupe with the other beasts of burden, the humped-back animals, now there were families. These people were not visitors, they were settlers; or, as the Kalkadoon leader had called them, invaders.

Over the following weeks, they began to meet more and more of their own people fleeing the terrors of the white invasion, believing they would find safety on the other side of the mountains, and Ladjipiri's sons became nervous.

'No one speaks of our kin. Do you think our mother and sisters and the others are safe?'

'Yes,' replied Ladjipiri grimly when he reached the summit of the coast range and looked down at the wide green valley below, and the big river that wound between odd-shaped hills. The scene was the same as it had always been, except now there were cattle grazing in the lush valley and a house was set close to the river, which was a haven for wildfowl.

He knew where his family would be. He had told them to stay out on the coast, away from the village that was being settled inland, well upriver. There they could still hunt and fish and not be noticed, at least until he came back with the lads.

As they made their way through the foothills, though, the news was even more frightening. The white man claimed the right to kill blackfellows without mercy, if it pleased him, and not just men! Whole families! Even the most respected elders were cast aside to die in the most horrific manner. But now the Darambal people were fighting back.

'The toll of white men is growing daily,' a young friend exulted. 'We are avenging our loved ones. Killing their cattle! Burning down their dwellings! Smashing their upstart fences!'

Ladjipiri's sons were afire with excitement. They begged to be allowed to join the resistance fighters, but he forbade them to do so, reminding them that their place was with their family.

'We will find them on the shores of the bay, at the mouth of the river, if things are as bad as they seem.' He was finding so many of these shocking stories difficult to believe. 'When we get there, I will seek out the Woppa-bura people from the big island in the bay. They trade plant foods for tools and spearheads, but they are very skilful people. I have been over there. They build boats, and they make themselves strong shelters of wood and stone. They're extremely interesting. I intend to ask them to take us in.'

'You want us to be cowards, to run and hide!'

'No, we'll visit the island for a while. Until the fighting is over.'

'Until we get rid of all the whites?' his younger son asked angrily.

Ladjipiri couldn't bring himself to lie. 'Well, no. Until things cool down.'

'You mean until the whites win?'

'I will not argue any more. We will be home in four days. Your mother is expecting you. Now get some sleep.'

In the morning they were gone.

Ladjipiri grieved as he trudged on, his feet now as heavy as his heart, even though he was back at his beloved river.

He was shocked by the size of the village where rocks prevented further river traffic; it had expanded in all directions. And there were the most amazing boats and canoes in the river. He was tempted to take a small canoe, on principle, for the last leg of his journey but decided against it. There was no point in courting trouble when he could so easily build a raft strong enough to take him out to the bay.

There were tears of joy and relief when he walked up the long beach to where his people were camped. And more stories of terror.

Ladjipiri sighed. How things had changed. Once upon a time everyone would have been waiting to hear his stories of the great world out there, of the wondrous things he had seen . . . like the ancient paintings, and the strange people he had met.

The Woppa-bura elders were firm. They agreed to take only their friend the trader and his immediate family, including grandparents, across the sea to their island, explaining that they could not feed any more people because of the shortage of available meat on the island.

His wife, like Ladjipiri himself, was realistic. 'So be it,' she said, and put her arms about her daughters.

CHAPTER SIX

Harry Merriman and George Otway managed to catch the afternoon train to Ipswich but, due to heavy rains, a landslide was blocking the track further ahead, so they had to stay overnight at the Railway Hotel.

Neither of them had much to say in the train, both searching for appropriate subjects and not making much of a hand of them. Harry appreciated George's kindness in coming to break the news to him personally, and his valiant efforts to comfort him, but he wished he hadn't come to Brisbane. Hadn't found him.

They sat on the hotel veranda after dinner, smoking their pipes. Harry wanted to tell George that his compassion was misplaced. That he felt nothing for his parents. Nothing. But he couldn't say that in case it offended this good man, so he talked about his years as a stockman and his other job as a drover on a big cattle drive.

'It was a huge mob of cattle,' he said, 'moving across the land like a flood, raising a mile-wide cloud of dust, I reckon. I never saw the like. And bellowing! Complaining, you'd have to say, but we'd have to watch 'em come water. They'd rush water. Stampede.'

'I always thought there was no water out that way at all. Just desert.'

'The deserts are toward the centre,' Harry told him.

'Gracious me! I imagined you were already placed well past the centre of the country!'

Harry shook his head. 'I'll show you a map some time, George. I think I'll go up now, if it's all right with you.'

'Yes, you go on up and get a good rest. This has all been a bad shock for you. I'll have a wee nightcap in the bar.'

For Harry, sleep was another world away. He opened the bedroom windows, kicked off his boots and lay on the bed thinking of that cattle drive, where he'd worked for a boss drover, Slim Collinson, and his outfit, taking two thousand head of cattle west from Rockhampton.

When he'd left the farm at DeLisle's Crossing, he'd vowed to get as far away as possible, and in taking on the droving job, after years of working as a stockman, he'd certainly done that.

Every one of the drovers on this trek trusted Slim's uncanny sense of direction, but there was still nervous talk that they could be lost. There was a terrible sameness about this land; few memorable landmarks, just a wilderness of red soil and poky trees, with backdrops of distant hills. Nevertheless, they'd pushed the cattle over the tough unknown country for more than four hundred miles, the monotony broken only by massive flocks of birds, mobs of big red kangaroos that stopped to stare, and emus that tore past on what Harry called urgent business.

This was blackfellow country, they all knew that, but they saw few of the local residents, mainly small groups going walkabout, or watchers on high vantage points.

After months on the trail, whingeing about the bloody drive, the bloody flies, and bloody everyone and everything was the norm, but Harry still found it exciting. He woke every morning eager for the day. He'd fallen in love with this huge landscape, with its terrain so full of colour his eyes ached. Out here they were beyond beyond. They were fording rivers named by the tragic explorers Burke and Wills not so long ago, and trekking across country few white men had even glimpsed! Harry was mightily impressed.

At twenty-two, this was his first job as a drover, and all these weeks in the saddle had given him time to think. He hadn't been much of a thinker until then; a sort of plotter maybe, but a proper thinker? he mused. Not a lot.

As a lad, he used to plot against a father who'd beaten the daylights out of him from as far back as he could remember. And it wasn't that Gillie Merriman was a boozer. No, nothing like that, Harry recalled. He was just a cruel, mean bastard. His son prided himself that he wasn't afraid of him. He just wasn't stupid enough to show it. Not until he was ready.

The Merriman farm at DeLisle's Crossing was neat; well kept, folks would say. It had a dozen dairy cows, large fields of corn and potatoes, and chooks. Much the same as the others along Ballinger's Road. The timber farmhouse was like all the others, except Gillie's was hidden by an ugly tea-tree hedge.

Gillie was a Scot, a bear of a man with a grudge against the world, or so it appeared to local folk, who learned not to waste their time saying g'day to him in the street, for he wouldn't even spare them a nod. His wife, Hester, was a distant relative of the shire clerk, so that gave the Merrimans a middling place in the pecking order of the district, which was just as well, because she was known to be a sour piece of work.

But the Merrimans paid their bills and worked hard. All three of them.

Hester was a willing worker. All she needed in life was Gillie's approval, and she toiled for it, never tiring. She was a good cook and saw to it that he was well fed, no matter the hour. She milked the cows, separated the cream, and made cheeses that she sold to the storekeeper, haggling over halfpence every inch of the way. As long as her husband was out there working in the fields, Hester was with him, even clearing the land for the plough, for she was as strong with an axe as most men. She had a vegetable garden in the front of her house that was the envy of her neighbours, but they never saw so much as a carrot, so they retaliated by planting flower gardens.

The floral displays of Ballinger's Road became a delight, with their beds of roses and carnations and snapdragons and sweet williams, and buggies slowed as they passed. This began to annoy Gillie, so he erected his spoiler, the ugly tea-tree hedge that he allowed to grow as tall and skinny as it pleased.

And all the time there was the son, Harry, who'd worked alongside them since he was a little kid.

'Worked bloody hard too,' neighbours reported. And as the child grew, they also reported witnessing Gillie belting the hell out of him.

The schoolmaster at DeLisle's Crossing State School Number 438, fed up with Harry Merriman's constant absences, called him to the front of the class and took the strap to him. This was too much for his friend and neighbour, Tottie Otway, who boldly stood to defend him.

'His cranky old dad keeps him home!' she cried. 'He makes him stay home and work. And he belts him too!'

Harry never forgot that day. The shame of it.

'What did you have to do that for?' he yelled at her as they trudged home. 'I didn't ask you to do that.'

'Because it's true. And it's not fair for you to get the strap.'

'I don't care. Just leave me alone, will you? And mind your own business.'

She trailed after him, calling to him. Saying she was sorry. Tottie of the coppery hair and the pale, pale skin and the smile that shone. He wouldn't talk to her.

But Harry was growing up. Becoming more confident. He managed to do well at school, despite his family situation, as his now-sympathetic teacher explained to him privately; and he was popular with the other kids, mainly because he was the ringleader in village mischief and mayhem.

So time dragged on at DeLisle's Crossing, fifty miles from the town of Brisbane, which might as well have been London for these villagers, most of whom had never set foot in the 'bright lights', as Brisbane was termed from their perspective.

Nothing of note happened in the district until the ferry sank in a storm the day after old man DeLisle passed into the hereafter. It was said to be a portent, an omen, of bad times ahead. People strewed salt on their stoops to ward off evil, and nailed horseshoes over barn doors; and a gypsy fortune-teller out at the crossroads began coining money.

Then an elderly spinster, Margery Field, claimed she saw the ghost of old man DeLisle by the riverbank, under the oak tree that he'd planted so long ago. Others said they saw him too, and that made everyone jumpy and jittery.

Fed up with all this fuss, the Reverend Robert Trenmell, in his Sunday sermon, warned against superstitions seeping into communities and ordered a stop to all this foolishness.

Miss Field was deeply offended. She stood up in the church and said so.

'Reverend! I'll not be called foolish! I saw Mr DeLisle plain as day!' She turned to the congregation. 'A lot of you saw him too, didn't you?'

Faced with the stern eye of their pastor, no one supported her, and for a few minutes there was an uneasy silence, until a voice called:

'Yes. I saw him!'

It was Harry Merriman who stood.

Tottie, sitting across the aisle, almost choked laughing, but the Reverend Trenmell had his measure.

'Sit down, Mr Merriman,' he said wearily. 'We will now turn to verse . . .'

But now Tottie Otway was on her feet. 'I saw it too, didn't I, Harry? We both saw it . . . him.'

'Bless you, children,' Miss Field cried.

'Thank you, Miss Otway,' the reverend said to Tottie. 'Now I should like you to remain standing while Mr Merriman repeats after me this verse from the New Testament. Would you be so kind, sir?'

Harry nodded, none too enthusiastically, and Trenmell began:

'When I was a child, I spake as a child . . .'

The lad standing before him took up the verse as it continued:

'. . . I understood as a child, I thought as a child, but when I became a man, I put away childish things.'

As Harry repeated the last line, the reverend suddenly looked to him.

'And how old are you now, Mr Merriman?'

'Thirteen, sir.'

'Then think about it,' was the response, as smirks and giggles rippled amid the Sunday-best shiny suits and bonnets.

Outside, Tottie saw Gillie Merriman shove his furious bearded chin at his son. 'You wait until you get home, you bloody lout,' he snarled, and plunged on past him.

'Oh no! You're gonna get belted again,' she said to Harry, unconcerned that she would be in line for a talking-to from her parents. 'I'm sorry.'

'I don't care!' He shook his thatch of fair hair and kicked at a stone.

'What does your mother say about that? About him belting you?'

Harry was surprised by the question. He turned and looked at her. 'She says he never hits me on the head.'

He was grinning, as if this were a joke, but his blue eyes were ice.

Tottie always remembered Harry's expression that day. And Harry never forgot the occasion either.

He took the pastor's message to heart. He had to grow up. He wasn't about to stay old Gillie's unpaid farmhand and punching bag for ever. He had to figure out a way to get shot of him and not get arrested and jailed as a vagrant. Often he'd thought of running away, but somewhere along the line he'd picked up the word 'vagrant', examined it, and replaced it like a hot coal.

There had to be other ways. Plotting escape became a favourite pastime.

Then Gillie, the surly Scot, fell out with the bank manager, Mr Buschell. Shouted at him once too often, with the result that Buschell refused to do business with him. Told him to send his wife in instead, so that everyone in the bank could have some peace.

But Hestor Merriman refused.

'My mum is scared stiff of banks,' Harry told Tottie. 'She's never set foot in one. She says she can't do sums, and she won't have Buschell trying to make a fool of her.' He snorted with laughter. 'As if Mr Buschell gives folk tests at the door! Mum flapped about like a bird in a cage saying her mother never had to go into a bank, and neither will she.'

'So what happened?'

'They had to send me. I have to go into the bank and make the monthly payment on the mortgage.'

'Well I never!' Tottie said.

Harry enjoyed those visits to the bank. Mr Buschell liked to have a yarn with him, when he had time, often asking what he intended to do when he left school.

'I'll have a farm of my own,' Harry would tell him, without adding: 'As far away from here as my boots will take me.'

Harry was growing in size and in confidence. He was destined not to inherit his father's brawny, big-boned physique, rather leaning towards Hester's line, tall and slim, with firm, labour-earned muscles.

There came an evening when he was late for supper. As he was coming up the back steps, Gillie strode out and abused him for keeping his mother waiting.

'I couldn't help it,' Harry muttered. 'You wanted that corn bagged. It took a bloody long time.'

'Don't you swear at me, you loafer,' Gillie shouted. 'I could have done it in half the time.'

'Then you should have!'

Harry took the rest of the steps in his stride and went to push past his father, but Gillie brought a broom handle down on his back with such force that Harry stumbled against the wall. He spun back and grabbed the weapon as it was raised to strike him again, wrenching it from his father and hurling it across the yard. Then he stormed into the kitchen, dragged out a chair and sat down, only then realising the table had been cleared.

His mother was hanging kitchen cloths on a line over the stove.

'We ate,' she said. Then she added: 'Your father says you're too late.'

'No I'm not. I work as hard as he does. I'll have my supper.'

She turned, standing by the stove in her black dress and black apron, wispy hair dragged back from her angular face, thin lips pursed, hands clasped firmly in front of her, as if to demonstrate that the larder was locked.

'Anyway,' she said, 'you won't be going to school no more. Your father says you've been there long enough.'

'I have to stay until I'm fourteen. That's the law.'

'That law don't count with farmers.'

'We'll see about that. And I'll have my supper.'

'I told you . . .' she began.

'Does he ever beat you?' he asked casually.

'What a question! Why would he?'

'Then why do I have to put up with him?'

'Because that's the way he was brung up. You have to learn how to behave.'

Harry stood. Stood over her. 'I have. He's brought me up the same, and if you don't do as you're told, I'll do what he's taught me to do. I'll bash the stuffing out of you! Now get out of my way!'

She shrieked, pulled back in fright and ran out of the kitchen, slamming the door behind her.

Harry grinned, took a plate, ladled out a large helping of warm rabbit stew and settled himself at the table. He could hear them muttering outside. He knew his schooldays were over, which was unfortunate, but the beatings would continue. Unless he fought back, and what sort of a life would he have then?

He faced his situation fair and square, deciding that there was no point in hanging about any longer.

The next time he was in town to do the banking, he sought out Mr Buschell and asked if he could take out a loan.

'A loan?' Buschell beamed. 'How old are you, lad?'

'Fourteen,' Harry said, cribbing a year.

'My word, you're growing up, aren't you? But I'm afraid you're too young to take out a loan. The bank has rules. How much do you need?'

'Five pounds.' Harry had thought of asking for twenty, but his courage had ebbed. If you had five pounds, you couldn't be a vagrant.

'That's a lot of money for a lad. What do you need it for?'

The very question he had hoped wouldn't be asked. Harry was numb. He went to say something, changed his mind, and sat on the edge of the chair, preparing to bolt.

'I'm sure it wouldn't be for anything illegal, would it?' the manager asked, encouraging him.

'No, nothing like that.' Suddenly Harry had an idea. Clothes. He needed clothes. For the first time he saw himself through the eyes of the neatly turned-out bank people. A farm boy in patched pants and a greying shirt who didn't even own a pair of boots. Few of the boys out his way had boots, but that didn't alter the present picture.

'Clothes,' he said finally. 'I need clothes.'

'Won't your mother buy you some?' That question confirmed to Harry that Mr Buschell saw that he did need clothes, and it shook him up a bit.

Embarrassed now, he clung on to an excuse that had become a reason.

'She won't,' he said. 'They won't!'

Buschell nodded kindly, and Harry's reserve broke down. He found himself begging.

'Sir, I need five pounds. I have to get clothes so I can get a job. I have to go out and get a job now. Please. I'll write you an IOU, and I swear I'll pay it back. I promise you, Mr Buschell. Cross my heart and hope to die.'

Buschell laughed. 'We can't have you dying on us, Harry. Here . . .'

He took up a pen and wrote an IOU, stating that Harry Merriman owed H. Buschell the sum of five pounds. Then he added the date and passed it over the desk.

'Now read that, Harry, and sign it, if you please. You'll see that I am loaning you five pounds. I am giving you the loan, not the bank, and I do, of course, expect you to repay me.'

Harry couldn't believe his eyes as Mr Buschell counted out five pounds. Recalling the signs on jumbled boxes of work shirts and trousers in the local store, he realised you could buy a whole lot of clothes for five pounds. He guessed that Mr Buschell would know that too, but it didn't seem to matter to him.

'Doesn't look as if those trouser pockets would hold them for long,' he commented, as Harry signed his name with care.

Harry nodded. 'Yeah. They're pretty much wore out.'

'Then you'll need this.' Mr Buschell picked up the money and dropped it into a small drawstring pouch. 'There you are now,' he said as he handed it over. 'Your first business transaction. We'll shake on it.'

As he watched the tall, gangly lad walk quietly out of the bank, Buschell murmured: 'I wonder where you're going, Harry? But good luck to you.'

★   ★   ★

The horse. He'd already made a decision about that. Dodds was his horse. He rode him all the time. His father didn't need two. So Harry was keeping him. In which case, there was no need to go home. He had no other possessions.

But he still had the bank book. He should take it back to the bank, but couldn't risk Mr Buschell changing his mind. So he walked into the store, borrowed a pencil and wrote on a slip of paper: *Goodbye*.

That was all they deserved. Then he took one of the brown paper bags hanging on a string by the counter, shoved the bank book inside, along with his message, and handed it to Myrtle, the girl who worked in the store.

'Will you give this to my mum when she comes in?'

'Yeah. Orright.'

He was off. On his way. Planning to get some new clothes in Brisbane, where he wouldn't be recognised. He was almost skipping with happiness as he ran over towards Dodds. But there were Mrs Otway and Tottie, walking towards him!

'You're looking pleased with yourself,' called Tottie, who never missed a trick. 'What are you up to?'

'Um . . .' He didn't want to say, but he couldn't lie to them. To Tottie. 'I'm going away,' he said, almost in a whisper.

'Going away?' Tottie cried. 'Where to? You can't just go away.'

Harry was accustomed to Tottie's outbursts, but he could do without one right now. 'Yes I can. I have to go.'

'Where to?' she demanded. 'Tell me where you're going?'

Her mother sighed. Exasperated. She tried to diffuse the situation. 'We'll miss you, Harry. But you boys are growing up now . . . I wish you well, dear.'

'You're encouraging him!' Tottie screamed. 'He's not grown up at all. He's running away!'

He forgot Mrs Otway was there.

'Shut up, Tottie!' he hissed. 'And look . . . I'll be back. I'm not dropping off the ends of the earth.'

'Take me with you!' she cried suddenly. Seriously. 'I'll get a job too.'

'Tottie!' Her mother had had enough. 'For heaven's sake!'

Harry was stunned by this outburst. People were staring. He backed away and swung on to his horse, upset that Tottie was crying.

'Please don't go, Harry!' she wept.

'I'll write to you if you like,' he offered.

Her mother put an arm about her to comfort her, at the same time nodding to Harry, so he took the hint and turned the horse towards the crossroads, and soon Dodds was cantering along the sandy road that would eventually take them to Brisbane Town.

★ ★ ★

Their journey ended, Slim Collinson, the boss drover, instructed his men to make camp, because there was some work to do before they could begin the long trek home. Not that he had a home with four walls and a roof and a dunny down the back; he and his wife Lena and their eighteen-year-old son, known simply as Colly, were nomads. They went where the droving took them, crisscrossing the outback with their cook-wagon, their spare horses and their band of men. Occasionally one of their stockmen would have an unpaid black boy for an offsider, and Slim raised no objection. He could always do with an extra hand. Lena would keep a keen eye on the boy, aware that the offsider was in fact a black girl, a young lubra in shabby men's clothing, hair clipped, face shy under a stockman's floppy hat. What these men did for company, she always said, was none of her business.

'But they better treat them poor little black girls proper. We don't stand for no rough stuff.'

There was only one black girl on this drive, and she was called Jacky. At night she and her bloke camped a few hundred yards away from the others, and no one took much notice of them.

While they waited for the owner of the fledgling cattle station to arrive with his own men, Slim's men cut timber for fences to corral the horses, freeing them from the hobbles used on the trek. It was a bonus for the station owner, who would need those fences, and more, for his own mob of horses. The days were still hot under opal-blue skies, but the nights became so cold that the men set to work to build a wattle-and-daub shelter, which was appreciated as the days dragged on and there was still no sign of the owner, who Harry learned was a Mr Palliser.

Slim was worried. 'Palliser is setting this place up as an outstation. His main station, Cameo Downs, starts seventy miles north-east of here. It's a big property, already takes in a thousand or more square miles, but he wants to add on these river flats.'

'So Cameo Station is extended right to this river now?' Harry was amazed at this fellow Palliser's cheek. 'What's he want all that land for?'

'To run more cattle, bless his heart,' Lena said. 'But he should be here by this. Come on, I'll show you some of the trees they've marked. That's how Slim finds these outback blocks.'

They rode back up the stock route and Lena's sharp eye caught the blazed trees well before Harry could find them. She pointed to the ochre-coloured anthills, strange monoliths dotted about the landscape, some more than six feet high. 'You'll find markers on them too.'

'Where does this outstation end, then?' he asked.

'Well, the river's the boundary, and just over there, the purply ridge, Slim says that's where Palliser called a halt. That's his other boundary.'

Harry glanced at it. 'Who owns the other side?'

'Whoever claims it and squats on it,' she said. 'Then again,' she added quietly, jerking her head towards the ridge, 'maybe not. We'd better get back.'

Only then did Harry see the three Aborigines. They were standing on higher ground, just above them, their bodies painted so that they merged into a stand of scrappy gums.

'We'll go quietly,' Lena said as she turned her horse back towards the camp. 'Don't spook them. Let them know we don't mean them any harm. Just ride back down the track.'

Harry wondered what harm they could do to the three bearded men when both he and Lena had wandered off looking for markers without rifles. Slim and a couple of old bushies working for him were always nagging everyone to have rifles nearby at all times, mainly for snakes and other bush hazards, including wild blacks, but Harry had always felt the latter hazard to be a bit dramatic.

Ever since he'd left home he'd been in contact with blacks. As a lowly farmhand he'd shared jobs with Aboriginal boys, and as he grew older and worked as a stockman on the big stations Aborigines were there again, many of them proving to be first-rate stockmen and riders. He'd met their families, their mobs, shared grub with them and sat round their campfires. He understood they were all hard done by, and sympathised with their troubles; he'd even been invited to corroborees, enjoying all the events and the laughter. It was this attitude, of a man accustomed to the company of blackfellows, that caused him to react slowly. Maybe even with curiosity. Why not talk to them? Who were they? What clan? Most of the families he'd known were Kamilaroi. Of the Kamilaroi nation, their elders used to say.

His horse had smelled the urgency in Lena's voice; or maybe it had picked up the scent of these strange men, but when Harry jerked its head into a turn, it jumped sideways and compensated by leaping ahead to catch up and pass Lena's more disciplined animal.

Harry was able to rein it in just a few yards ahead of Lena, but as he turned to speak to her, he heard the thud. Heard it before he saw the spear that had buried itself in her back and taken her from the saddle, slowly sliding down, her face agape as if the shout she'd tried for had never been allowed the time to transform into sound.

It was Harry who shouted. Screamed! Leapt from his horse to try to catch her, with that stout spear wavering over them, and lift her to the ground and place her . . . how? On her side? He was terrified, shaking, searching for a decision. Asking her, Lena, what he should do. He'd encountered death before. Death from accidents, snake bites. He'd once pulled a drowned man from a dam, but this . . . the spear. Should he pull it out? Would it save her? Would it cause her more agony? He'd seen spears before; some of them had jagged tips. Would it tear at her as jagged fishhooks did?

Her arm moved as she rolled, trying to reach that monstrous thing embedded in her being, and she whispered: 'Help me. Get it out!'

There was blood as he placed one hand firmly on her back and took hold of the smooth spear. He could feel Lena bracing herself, see her lined face frown and the grey eyes squeeze as he tried to ease it out, a bloodied stone tip beginning to emerge, but then her body shut down. It slumped just as the spear came away intact. The frown disappeared; her face was suddenly smooth. She gave a great sigh as if relieved that that was over, and her eyes closed.

Harry threw the spear aside and tore at her shirt to press a bunched piece over the wound, talking to her about something, babbling, until he realised that Lena was still. Too still. There was no life pumping through her. She lay in the bluegrass; it brushed at her face gently, affectionately . . .

He twisted about, remembering their attackers, remembering that one of them had thrown that spear, and started shouting at them, abusing them for this shocking deed, this unnecessary, bloody, horrible thing they had done, and in a mad way, calling on them for help.

But there was no answer. No sign of them. He sat back on his haunches, watching her. Waiting. Afraid to disturb her; she looked so peaceful. Light clouds drifted towards the ridge; a goanna swaggered across the clearing and the horses shifted nervously. A butcher bird tried a few tentative notes, then filled the air with melody, its tone–perfect song reminding Harry of the flute that Tottie's mother used to play.

He shook his head. This was not the time to be thinking about Tottie; he had to see to Lena.

It seemed disrespectful to heave her on to the horse's back like a swag or a pack, so he simply took hold of the reins, and picked Lena up as best he could, to carry her himself. She was a lot heavier than he'd imagined, but he couldn't bring himself to leave her here, alone, while he went for help.

Back at the camp, Jacky heard him shouting. 'Who was that?' she asked.

No one else had heard a sound, out there in the wild open country, not even the swish of the slow–running river.

'You're hearing things,' the boss said to the little black 'boy'.

But Jacky knew. She'd heard someone screaming and it was still reverberating in her head. She set off towards that sound, bare feet skimming over the silky red soil, following it to its source as surely as tracing a ripple in a pond. As she ran, she was calling: 'Coo-ee, coo-ee,' a whip–like call that carried far in the bush, and was copied by the currawong. Or maybe the currawong came first.

Harry might have heard her. He wasn't listening; he was stumbling along with Lena, dazed. Had they chosen to do so, those two horses could have wandered off, because he'd let go of their reins, forgotten them, but under the circumstances, there being danger afoot, they chose to tag along behind him, in single file.

But then they heard Jacky, and it was Lena's horse that answered with a mournful wail, and brought her dashing through the scrub to confront the pitiful group.

'Jeez, Harry!' she cried through clenched teeth. 'What happen? Whatamatter wit Lena? Oh Cri', she dead there, Harry? She dead? What happen? Snake get her?'

He shook his head and placed Lena on the grass under a spindly tree.

'You mind her, I'll go for help,' he told Jacky, but then he remembered the attackers. They might still be about, watching. He couldn't leave this little girl out here on her own.

'Take Lena's horse,' he said. 'Go quickly. Get the boss.'

Slim was devastated by the news. When they brought her body in, he flew into a rage and led a posse of riders from the camp to hunt down the savages.

Frantically they scoured the area where the attack had taken place, racing into the foothills that led to the high ridge with its craggy wind-ravaged sides that could have provided a perfect escape route for agile climbers.

By nightfall the riders were all back at camp, hanging nervously around the cook-wagon, while Jacky served stale damper with beans and beef stew. As usual, two men then rode out to take on the night shift, patrolling the out-skirts of the mob of cattle, keeping them calm, but two more men were assigned to guard the camp in case there were more hostile Aborigines around. Harry volunteered to stand guard duty, but Tom Dunne, one of the drovers, dismissed his offer.

'You a guard! You couldn't even look after Lena!'

'Ah, turn it up, Tom,' a voice said out of the darkness.

Harry appreciated that someone had come to his defence, but it was little comfort. He was sure that many of them blamed him for the catastrophe, and why wouldn't they?

Slim stayed in the shed where his wife's body lay swathed in blankets, with his son and two of his old mates for company. They broke out a bottle of rum, and yarned through the night. At first light they emerged to get on with the business of burial.

Burdened with guilt, Harry tried to tell Slim, again, how sorry he was, but the drover put a hand on his shoulder. 'What's done is done, mate. You just thank your stars, young Harry, that you didn't go with her.'

During the sad little service by Lena's grave, in the shade of a handsome coolabah tree, a huge flock of pink and grey galahs swooped overhead, as if in salute. Slim wept as his son, Colly, spoke of the best mum a man could have, and to Harry's surprise thanked him for 'sticking with her'.

'Dingoes could have got her,' he said, 'as she lay there unprotected. Or those black bastards could have come after her themselves.'

Harry wanted to say that attacks on the woman's body hadn't entered his head. He'd been so shocked, and so sorry about what had happened to her, that he'd stayed to keep her company; he'd not wanted to leave her there in that lonely spot. But he kept those thoughts to himself because they seemed foolish now.

Afterwards Slim tried to discover what had brought on the attack. He listened to Harry's description of the three men again and said: 'Sounds like war paint, by God. But why? We've come all this way without no trouble. They've seen us, plenty of them have seen us, you can bet on that, but they've let us pass. Why now? And why only three of the buggers? And where's Palliser and his mob? That's what I want to know. He's two weeks late. I'll give him two more days because I don't want to leave Lena just yet, and then we're packing up. I'll need three volunteers to stay on and mind the herd. You'll be well armed. Any takers?'

'I'll stay,' Harry said, knowing that it would be better for all concerned if he parted company with Slim's lot.

'Me too.' Matt, another first-time drover, nodded.

Ginger Magee, an old-timer, knocked ash from his pipe. 'Someone will have to keep an eye on that raw pair, I suppose. Do we get to keep the mob if Palliser doesn't front?'

'I'll have to think what to do about that,' Slim said.

That night, however, Palliser and three stockmen rode into their camp. They were thirsty, exhausted, and caked with dust but, wisely, decided to wait until full daylight before heading for the luxury of the river, rather than encounter crocodiles, which were known to dwell in the Queensland rivers.

But dawn brought a sudden whirlwind, a howling willy-willy of such force that their shelters were smashed, the wagon overturned and equipment scattered in all directions. The wind, thick with dust, lashed at the men, who sought shelter flat on the ground to escape flying debris, hoping to God the cattle wouldn't stampede. Fortunately these animals had already experienced dust storms so they huddled together, heads down. Only one horse took fright and broke loose, bolting towards the river.

When the willy-willy tore away into the distance, all of the men stumbled down to the river to rid their eyes of grit, but their first sight of the water revealed a huge crocodile dragging at the body of the drowned horse.

It seemed to them all to be the last straw.

Palliser had a story to tell, an explanation for his delayed arrival at this prearranged location, but that could wait until later. He was still shocked to hear that Lena Collinson had been killed by blacks. He'd known Slim and Lena for years. Known them to be the most reliable drovers in the outback.

But then, life went on. He paid Slim for the job, and gave him an extra pound for good luck.

There was no need now for the volunteers to shepherd the cattle, since the owner was taking charge, but Harry approached the squatter and was accepted into his team.

Once again he was working as a stockman, this time for the famed Cameo Downs plant.

CHAPTER SEVEN

Langley Palliser had grown up on his father's station to the west of Brisbane, and was educated at Sydney Grammar. He had had all the advantages of a squire's son and, at the age of thirty, was just as ambitious as his father. Between them they opened up the vast Cameo Downs cattle station, with a plan to move stock from drought-affected areas to well-watered districts whenever necessity struck. Certainly these two diverse properties, hundreds of miles apart, were an ideal selection in terms of climate and rainfall, but Palliser Senior kept a close watch on markets offering superior prices.

At first Langley's grandfather had simply claimed and stocked pastureland beyond the boundaries of civilisation, knowing that it would be a while before the government could step in and require that these huge parcels of land, such as his claim, be registered as leasehold. This done, the next generation bought the leases and settled into their hard-won ownership of large stations.

The pioneers soon came into conflict with Aborigines, and a bloody conflict it was; harassment and attacks by black raiding parties brought swift and indiscriminate revenge until the tribal clans disintegrated and family groups sought peace.

Langley knew that he too would run into opposition from the blacks. It was expected. In a way he felt sorry for them, even though two of his uncle's men had been felled by the savages. History had shown they didn't have a chance against the white man. It was just a matter of time before the tribes died out. In the meantime, though, he hoped to run Cameo Downs with as little trouble as possible.

So there he was, standing on the veranda of his homestead with his pipe, a fine stamp of a man, with short-clipped black hair, smooth skin, blue eyes and good teeth. Langley was proud of his even teeth; he believed they were evidence of good breeding. He had married a girl who could not provide a dowry but who had very good teeth.

He insisted on addressing every new employee himself when time allowed.

'If you want to work on Cameo Downs,' he'd say, 'you'd better pay attention to what I'm telling you. I'm a God-fearing man and I don't want any trouble with the blacks. I won't have my men harassing them. First thing, leave their women alone. Second, do not shoot at blacks unless in fear of your life. Three, if you join any mad shooting parties out after blacks instead of game, I'll see you hanged. Got it?'

He became dismayed when he realised there were more blacks roaming his newly established Queensland estate than Grandpa Langley had seen in a lifetime, and they were cheekier. They marched across his land as if they owned it, pretending not to understand requests to keep away from the homestead and sheds, taking anything they fancied when backs were turned. Even when he acquired a black translator to deal with this problem, there was no improvement. However, with a mob of blacks, a hundred or so, camped two miles from the homestead, Langley was managing to keep the peace. And to maintain that peace he gave them a bullock, already butchered, every three weeks, pleased to see the broad smiles of gratitude.

Apart from a few regrettable incidents where a blackfellow was killed in a fight with a station hand, or a lubra ran off with, or was abducted by, a gang of fencers, all seemed to be under control at Cameo Downs, until there was trouble at a teamsters' depot twenty miles from his homestead.

The depot consisted of a general store, a blacksmith, and a few rough humpies for shelter, and was frequented by bullock teams hauling timber and other heavy loads, such as water tanks. There were horse-drawn lorries and sometimes Afghans with their camels, who mostly carried ore and mineral deposits sent in by the mineralogists. The teamsters came and went from all points of the compass, like the drovers, and their lives were just as tough, battling extreme weather of one sort or another across mainly trackless land, once they were this far inland.

This depot was known as Barleycorn's Retreat, for the amount of liquor consumed there, and was the venue for many memorable fights, mainly bare fisticuffs, that could last, man to man, for many execrable hours. Liquor-born brawls were also frequent occurrences, there being nary much else to do out here, passing close, as most thought, to the dead heart of the continent. The fights were soon forgotten, if ever recalled, by the protagonists, who pushed on, quarts of mean liquor causing barely a tickle in the heads of these hard men as they tramped off into the distance.

But one night there was a real, meaningful brawl. Someone had broken into the store, stolen food . . . cheese, eggs, flour and tea, already in short supply, and worst of all, the last of the alcohol. Bottles of rum and whisky.

Outrage ran amok. Blame came a good second. Fights broke out. Tents were searched. Loads overturned. The storekeeper sent for the police, who were too far away to care. Someone remembered that the Afghans had left by starlight, and horsemen went after them, returning empty-handed, tired and thirstier, at midday, to find the Retreat almost deserted.

'They've all scarpered,' the storekeeper said.

In their absence, it was declared that 'Abos' were the obvious thieves, and a posse of riders went looking for them. They found a camp at Mischief Creek, so named because a teamster had dallied there with the storekeeper's daughter, who was offended when she discovered he was after more mischief than she'd had in mind, and leapt on her horse and rode off, taking with her not only his horse but his boots as well.

There was no lightness, no mere mischief, in the minds of the wild horsemen who rode in among the people camped there by the side of the fast-running creek; some sleeping with their children nearby; some just sitting, yarning, round the warm embers of a campfire.

The onslaught of hooves took them by surprise. Some ran for cover. Others were up, wandering, groggy from sleep. Confused by the shouting. Shocked by the screams as their attackers wasted no time with questions, wielding the butts of rifles like waddies. But then blackfellows came out of the darkness with real waddies, slamming at the riders and their mounts with such force that the horses joined the screaming and men were felled. So the real business of rifles came to the fore, and the shots were fast and furious in the whirling and trampling at Mischief Creek.

Then there was silence, and the riders backed their horses away from the camp. Only one man, a bullocky, jumped down from his horse to inspect the carnage, and only because he was seeking his brother.

He found his brother crushed under the weight of his wounded horse and screamed for help. Two men dragged the dead man out, and between them they managed to load the heavy body on to the bleeding horse, and lead it away from that place.

The storekeeper reported that a lubra with a broken arm had come to his wife for help. Nine Aborigines had been killed, including three women and two children. The family had taken their dead away for burial, he said. So had the teamster.

'Everyone else bolted,' he said. 'My son has gone to report this to the police.'

That night the lubra came back to warn them, so he and his wife and daughter, and the blacksmith, hid in the bush waiting for the inevitable. The store, the blacksmith's shed and the humpies were burned to the ground by a silent, grim little group of savages.

Word of the happenings at Barleycorn's Retreat spread rapidly through the district, causing a general alert. Several teamsters decided to form a new camp and meeting place at the spot known as One Tree Hill, along a stock route that cut through Cameo Downs.

Langley Palliser had no objection to them using the stock route because it was essential for regular transport in the area, and would, before long, become a well-worn road, but he wouldn't permit them to congregate on his land. He'd had reports that there were several mobs of strange blackfellows in the area now, and that worried him, so he was signalling to the local blacks that he would not let the bad men sit down on his land.

When the teamsters, most of them innocent of the heinous crime, ignored his objection, he was not moved. He sent armed men to get rid of them, infuriating the leaders, who threatened to boycott deliveries of any sort to his homestead.

Palliser retaliated by running a herd of cattle through their camp, destroying their equipment and temporary shelters. Having dealt with them, he turned his hand to his own defences. His homestead was already fenced, but now he enclosed his sunny veranda, set loaded guns near to hand, dug an exit from the cellar, which they used as a cool room, to a covered trapdoor outside the house, for emergencies, and insisted his wife and children stay inside for the time being. No bush walks, no riding, and no swimming in the dam.

At the same time his men added security to their quarters by fencing the area, and though Palliser had ordered night patrols, they kept a watchman on the roof at night as well.

Having done their best, they resumed normal duties, paying careful attention to news of the massacre, and the fire at the Retreat, that filtered through to them via the bush telegraph; but it was difficult to sort the wheat from the chaff. Some now said that the blacks had attacked the Retreat first and the teamsters had retaliated, and what was more, only one old blackfellow was killed!

Then the lubra with the broken arm, resting in very efficient splints, was seen with some of the Cameo Downs people, and Palliser tried to talk to her, but she was too frightened to speak.

Just on sunset that evening he heard two warning shots from the rooftop guard down at the men's quarters, and hurried out to the front of his house.

He saw about ten painted men standing in a line a hundred yards or so from the fence, and recognised a couple of them as Cameo Downs blacks, but he had to respond to that signal, so he stepped forward and fired two shots in the air.

The men before him didn't flinch.

'What do you want?' he shouted, thinking then that he should have bought a loudhailer like the ones auctioneers used. That would shake up these fellows.

A skinny elder whom he didn't recognise stepped forward. 'Where dem fellas kill our people, boss?'

'Those bad people. They ran away.'

'You bring 'em back, eh?'

'I'm sorry. I wish I could. I don't know them.'

The old fellow jammed his spear into the ground. 'You find 'em, boss!' It was a clear threat. He bared his teeth (good strong teeth too, Langley thought, for an old fellow) into a snarl. 'They kill our people!'

'They're not here. What can I do?'

Someone behind the speaker interrupted him, and they seemed to forget their fierce approach as a quick discussion ensued. Obviously the elder was being briefed. He turned back to the boss.

'Police, mistah. Where your police?'

Good point, Langley mused. Where the hell are they? I haven't heard a peep from them.

He strode forward. Addressing them all through their leader.

'I am as sorrowful as you for the killings. Bad joss that. I have called for the police with their guns and they are looking for the killers, and as soon as they catch them, bang! Dead! All right?'

The elder was unsure if he could believe this.

Langley continued: 'You good men. All of you good men. I will get the police and you must tell them what happened. All right?'

After further discussion, they agreed to disperse. Only then did Langley see four of his men, mounted and armed, on the sidelines.

He felt sorry for the blackfellows as they backed off. It was painful to see such a miserable, dispirited group of would-be warriors trudging away into the night.

He did that much. He wrote a letter to the chief of police in Brisbane, requiring information about the incidents with blacks and teamsters at Mischief Creek 'which have caused much unrest and possible danger to white persons in the vicinity'. Then, already nearly two weeks late, he set off with some stockmen to collect his cattle from Slim at the prearranged long reach of the Thomson River.

As they covered the miles to the Thomson, they came across deserted blacks' camps and the corpses of several cattle that had been killed, not for food but for nuisance value. Or maybe payback. Who would know?

That night, weary men took turns to stand guard while others slept, but someone must have dozed. In the morning they found all but one of their water bottles missing.

'I reckon some station blacks have gone wild again, boss,' one of his men said to him. 'Else how would them fellers know what water bottles look like?'

'True enough.' Palliser nodded. It seemed to him that since the blacks were all steamed up over the murders at Mischief Creek, he would be better advised to drive the new herd on to his home pastures for a while. He still had plenty of feed. Outstations manned only by a couple of men could be unsafe at times like this.

When they finally made it to Slim's camp and found the drovers in a state of shock over the killing of Lena Collinson, the decision was made for him. There was plenty of time; the land was marked out as part of Cameo Downs; no point in risking lives at this stage.

'We're pulling out,' he told his men, when the drovers left. 'We'll drive this mob closer to home until I can get troopers out here to keep order.'

As soon as he was safely home, Langley Palliser wrote to the police commissioner in Brisbane, and followed this up with another letter, this time to his father, telling him that he had to pull back from the Thomson River pastures, for the time being, because of the blacks' activities.

So what about telling the new Premier of Queensland, whoever he is, that we need to have more Police stationed in the far west to protect Pastoralists and the Scientists who are already claiming that country is rich in copper and other minerals.

You keep saying the Government is strapped for Cash. Well, Copper will mint them money, but few will work out west without protection. It's hard enough for us to keep going. We need more Police Protection here. My nearest Police station is fifty miles hence and that's manned by two men. It's bloody ridiculous. Some Teamsters ran amok here and killed nine blacks. Result: Payback. And since no one has bothered to investigate the incidents, the Blacks are getting bolder.

Please impress on the Premier that if we Pastoralists pull up stumps, then the Villages that service us will collapse. It's a pity Palmer isn't still at the helm. He knows the back country and would have sent the military to keep the peace.

He thanked his father for sending up the new herd of cattle, most of which had arrived in good nick, and continued the letter with day-to-day reports on the children and station affairs, finally signing off as *Your affectionate son, Langley.* Most people called him Lang, but his mother had always insisted on Langley, and so it stayed, in the family at least.

A few days later he received a welcome letter from his brother Charlie, too soon to have heard his latest news from their father.

Langley was so proud of Charlie, who was now one of the colony's leading surgeons, and always told people that he himself was behind the door when brains were handed out, so Charlie had got his share as well.

'I'm just a bushie,' he'd say. But he and Charlie both knew that Langley loved being a bushie.

'Yeah, a big-time boss bushie,' Charlie would laugh.

His brother had nabbed Rosa Rivadavia for a wife, surprising everyone. Langley had heard she was a looker, but was stunned when he finally met her.

'She's gorgeous!' he told his own wife, who was far from impressed by his enthusiasm, so he didn't add that Rosa had beautiful teeth. Like pearls.

Charlie and Rosa were in Gympie, apparently. Charlie wrote to say that, some months ago, Lady Heselwood had suffered an accident en route to one of the Heselwood cattle stations there.

'The reopened Heselwood station, called Montone,' Langley corrected as he read.

The lady had been traveling in a Cobb & Co. coach and had fallen down some steps at a coach stop and broken her leg. A woman claiming to be a registered doctor had treated her and botched the job. So it was Dr Palliser to the rescue! Charlie's services had been requested by his lordship, the famed Jasin Heselwood himself.

Langley nodded. Charlie had all the luck. Langley would have enjoyed a conversation with Heselwood. It would be wasted on Charlie, who had no interest in the business of raising beef cattle.

At the same time, in the men's quarters, Harry Merriman was also writing a letter. This was his first chance since the cattle drive to get a letter off to Tottie, back there at DeLisle's Crossing. She'd be wondering what had become of him.

Dr Palliser was flattered to hear from Lord Heselwood, pleading for him to come to Gympie and rescue his wife from the hands of 'incompetents'.

It seemed that Lady Heselwood had broken her right leg in a fall. At the scene of the accident, a Dr Lombe had administered treatment in the form of pain relief, and had set the leg with makeshift splints. Since the accident had occurred at a coach stop, Lady Heselwood had had to continue her journey, and was installed in the coach with some difficulty, increasing her discomfort.

When they arrived at the Gympie Bush Hospital, his lordship was severely unimpressed by conditions, but his wife could not be admitted anyway as the place was already overcrowded, due to the influx of gold prospectors, so he took her to his station homestead, and Dr Lombe accompanied them. She attended the patient again, and put the leg in plaster.

Charlie had sympathised with poor Lady Heselwood, having to cope with the misery of the broken leg and the plaster in that heat.

'I mean,' he said to Rosa, 'she must be dreadfully uncomfortable. I met her some years ago. At a charity function. She's a charming woman, very gracious. I believe they have a beautiful home in Sydney.'

'So what was she doing in Gympie?'

'Inspecting the new homestead, her husband says. And now she's stuck there. She's not up to the inconvenience of another long coach trip to take her out. Anyway, when the plaster came off, her leg was putrid, which often happens, unfortunately, after weeks in a cast, but Lord Heselwood blamed Dr Lombe. Still does. And then they found that the bone hadn't knitted.'

'Oh God! How awful!'

'Then they discovered that this Dr Lombe . . . a woman, to make matters worse . . . is a quack. Heselwood should have checked. There are no female doctors registered in Australia and not likely to be. She's carting certificates

151

claiming she took her degree at some learned institute in Geneva, Switzerland.'

'Do you think that's true?'

'Not a chance. There are all sorts of imposters roaming about the country-side, especially in the goldfields. Faith healers, dentists, doctors, you name it, they're out there. Even fake surgeons, God help us!'

'What will happen to Lady Heselwood now?'

'Heselwood got rid of Lombe and is so mistrustful of doctors that he refuses to allow either of the two working at the Gympie hospital to call on his wife. Lombe's story, by the way, of travelling north to take up duties at Gympie was all lies. They'd never heard of her.'

'What a cheek!'

'End result, he wants me to go up, all expenses paid, and treat Lady Heselwood. He is so concerned, I feel it would be unkind of me to refuse.'

'Really?' Rosa said with a mischievous grin. 'It wouldn't be the title, would it? I mean, would you have agreed if that were Farmer Dan's missus?'

He frowned. 'That remark is uncalled for. I have my career to think about. A plea from someone like Heselwood is a feather in the cap for me. If I can assist the poor woman I will, and I should not have to explain myself to my wife.'

'Oh, Charlie,' she said. 'Don't take it to heart. I was only teasing.'

'Then believe me when I say that flippancy does not become you.'

He strode off to the parlour and picked up a newspaper, but Rosa followed him.

'When are you going? To this Gympie place?'

'As soon as I am able to arrange transport. I have been studying a map. I could probably board a ship to Maryborough and ride the rest of the way. I'm told it's around fifty miles or so from the river port to the Heselwood property.'

Rosa sat beside him. 'How long will you be away?'

'Goodness me! How can I say? When my patient is in no further need of me, I suppose. Why?'

'Just because,' she said archly, 'because I'll miss you.'

'Well that can't be helped, my dear. I'm sure you're quite capable of entertaining yourself while I'm away. You have plenty of friends.'

That night at dinner, Rosa announced that she intended to join the Equestrian Club.

'What for?' Charlie asked. 'I shouldn't imagine you'd want to mix with that common lot.'

'But I do. You know I love to ride, and it would be fun to have company sometimes, because you're always too busy, and so is my father . . .' she hesitated, 'these days.'

'Why? What's Juan up to?' he asked.

'Nothing much.'

He nodded. 'I'd prefer you kept away from that amateur horsey mob. They say that club is now overrun with officers from a new regiment that is arriving in town.'

'Ooh la la! That'll please the ladies,' she laughed.

Charlie frowned and motioned the maid for more gravy on his roast beef. He wondered if Rosa knew that Juan Rivadavia had taken up with his previous paramour, Mrs Pilgrim. Moved her back into the house, if you don't mind! And his wife barely cold in her grave. Those Latins . . . He glanced at his wife, a Latin herself, at her lovely olive skin and her full, sensuous lips! There was an Italian doctor working at the Brisbane infirmary. Charlie had actually heard him say that he couldn't sleep in an empty bed. And certainly there appeared to be plenty of women from the nurses' training school willing to accommodate him.

'The beef is excellent,' he said to Rosa. 'Perhaps we could take a walk after dinner.'

He'd just had a very good idea. It would seem paltry of him to forbid her to join that club, because she did enjoy riding, and it was good exercise for women, but he couldn't have that collection of tin soldiers leering at her. She didn't understand these things; that men looked at her differently from the way women did. Women admired looks, locks and loveliness, but men, to put it bluntly, admired and lusted for what was underneath.

Mature women learned this in time, but young women, like Rosa, enjoyed admiring glances from all sides. They revelled in it, competed even, and it was difficult for husbands not to show their disapproval and so be judged ill natured in society. Charlie wished his mother were still alive; she would have been able to approach this sensitive subject with her daughter-in-law. Maybe.

They walked down the street to the riverbank, where wallabies were already grazing and squabbling parrots were settling for the night, and sat on the low stone wall watching two fishermen casting lines from a small boat.

'I was thinking,' Charlie said, 'that it might be possible for you to join me on this northern excursion. What do you think?'

'I wouldn't be intruding?'

'Well, of course I'd have to check with Heselwood, to see that you are billeted with me, if not in their home. I haven't come down to details with him yet.'

She took his arm, hugging into him. 'That would be such fun, Charlie. A sea voyage, and then a good long cross-country ride. I'd love it.'

Charlie shook his head. 'Do not think of this as light-hearted fun, Rosa. There is my patient to consider, and possibly I should have to hire guards to protect us, riding through those hills. Perhaps I've been a bit hasty, come to think of it. I'm not sure you should be coming with me after all.'

'Oh no!' she cried. 'You can't renege on me, darling. You invited me, and I'm so excited to be going to sea and all that!' She threw her arms around his shoulders, kissing him on the neck and nuzzling his ears. 'Tell me you'll take me!'

'Rosa. Cease! Not in public. Cease this minute.'

He tried to release her arms but she hung on, laughing. 'No, no, no. I won't let you go, you darling thing, until you promise you'll take me. The Heselwoods won't mind. They'll be thrilled you're making the effort! And you'll cure Lady Heselwood and then we'll come home and everyone will live happily ever after!'

'Oh, very well. I'll write to them tonight.'

Lord Heselwood responded to Charlie's letter by telegraph, advising of his gratitude that Dr Palliser had heard his plea, and extending a warm welcome to Mrs Palliser as well. He also instructed them to require a first-class cabin, if possible. And to be assured that fine horses and escorts would be provided to accompany them to his station, with no regard to expense. He added that Lady Heselwood felt greatly relieved that Dr Palliser would see her.

To save her busy husband the time, Rosa volunteered to arrange passage for them to this town of Maryborough, and found a clerk in the shipping office who was exceedingly helpful. He showed her a map, and explained the route their ship would take . . . sailing up the coast from Brisbane until they came to Fraser Island, whereupon the skipper would enter Hervey Bay and, in a very short time, turn inland along the Mary River towards Maryborough.

Unfortunately, though, the earliest passage they could confirm would be on Thursday, two days hence, but it was on a coastal steamer, *Laguna*, that didn't offer first-class cabins. If she cared to wait, however, there was a large cargo ship headed that way next Sunday, and it did cater for a few passengers in fine style.

'Oh, but our journey is urgent,' Rosa persisted. 'We have to leave as soon as possible. Tell me about the *Laguna*. I presume it's seaworthy?'

'Yes, Mrs Palliser. It's in excellent condition, but there are only two cabins; the rest is steerage.'

'Are the cabins already booked?'

'Oh no. They each accommodate six persons, one for ladies, one for gentlemen.'

'I see.' Rosa pondered. 'And we could get on that ship?'

'Yes.'

'And it's only for three nights?'

'Yes. And good weather expected.'

'Thank you. I'll take two berths.'

She hurried up to Charlie's surgery on Wickham Terrace, to tell him she had managed tickets for this Thursday, and he was delighted.

'That'll work out well. Yes, we can go Thursday. What ship?'

'*Laguna*.'

'*Laguna*? I can't place her. A nice ship, did they say?'

'Oh yes, very seaworthy.'

Charlie picked up the tickets and opened the top door of his desk to place them safely inside, but then he blinked, staring at the print.

'This doesn't say first class. I hope you made it plain we're travelling first class. I think you'd better go back and check, Rosa.'

'No need. I couldn't get first class. That ship doesn't run to it. We have to share.'

'What?'

She began to explain the accommodation arrangements, but he cut her short.

'Share what?'

'A cabin. With other people. They put the women . . .'

He folded the tickets and handed them back to her. 'Rosa dear, be a good girl and take them back and ask again. There has to be first class on something; there are so many ships plying up and down this coast, it's like a two-way Derby.'

'There are berths available in first class, but not until Sunday.'

Charlie sat back. 'Then do go back and exchange those tickets for the . . . which one was it?'

'I didn't ask. I thought you wanted to go as soon as possible.'

'So I do, darling, but within reason.'

'But what about Lady Heselwood? She needs you.'

'Don't you be worrying your head. I'll look after her. She'll be all right. Listen, I'll exchange them myself.'

He stood up to kiss her and escort her past waiting patients to the front door, but Rosa was concerned.

'Would *Laguna* be so bad?' she asked. 'Lord Heselwood is hoping you'll be there as soon as possible.'

'We will be, darling, we will.'

Stepping ashore from the *Albion* in Maryborough, they were amazed at the high riverbanks. The town seemed to look down upon the wide river and its conglomeration of boats. Above them stood warehouses and customs offices, as if to emphasise that they were firmly planted on government property and excise cheats should take note.

Black-uniformed police and customs inspectors waded through the busy wharves, bailing up barrowmen and miners for their licences, searching crates of imports and chatting to newly arrived gaudy ladies.

Rosa was intrigued. This was the first time she'd encountered a real gold-mining port, a stepping-off place for the goldfields just a march away, and she felt madness in the air. It was all about: in the eyes of disembarking folk; in their shove and push to get ashore with no time to waste; and in the giddy way they surged up into the town, looking frantically about for their bearings. She had the feeling that most of them had no idea of what they were about.

A young gentleman came forward to greet them, introducing himself as Edward Heselwood.

'I'm delighted to meet you, Doctor, and you too, Mrs Palliser. I hope you had a pleasant voyage.'

'We did, thank you,' Charlie said. 'But may I ask, how is your mother?'

'Oh, bearing up, poor love. But she'll be happy to see you. A shocking thing to happen! I was appalled that my parents let themselves be duped into believing a woman was a doctor! And then to allow her to lay hands on my mother's person. Shocking! I can't imagine what my father was thinking of!'

He turned and beckoned to a tall man leaning on the gatepost at the entrance to the wharves.

'Now where's your luggage? My man will attend to it.'

Surprised, Rosa glanced at Charlie. The man ambling over to them was wearing a check shirt and dungarees, a weatherbeaten hat and riding boots that were heavily buffed at the heel, from the action of spurs. Obviously a stockman. It was hardly the done thing to refer to a stockman as 'my man'.

Charlie didn't appear to register. He wouldn't catch her eye either, making a business of pointing out their two suitcases and his medical bag for Edward's 'man' to collect, so that they could set off up the road to the town.

As Edward explained the plan, that he'd found a decent hotel for them to stay in overnight, and so on, Rosa studied his clothes, quite the finest countryman's attire she'd ever seen. Not that they were loud or overdone, she mused. No, it was just that the tweed jacket was beautifully cut, as were his white buckskin trousers and fitted riding boots. Even the flat grey felt hat, worn almost as uniform by squatters, couldn't spoil the picture.

Charlie, in his best frock coat, was talking earnestly to Edward as they proceeded along the main street, but the young man kept leaning forward to address Rosa, asking what she thought of the town, if they were walking too quickly for her, if she enjoyed riding: all sorts of questions, which Rosa recognised as an excuse to talk to her, thereby irritating her husband, who hated to be interrupted at the best of times.

She was relieved when they arrived at the hotel and walked into the foyer.

'This is rather posh, isn't it?' she smiled, taking in the red carpet, the plush drapes and gilded paintwork.

'Oh yes,' Edward laughed. 'The very best. Can't say the same for the clientele, though. Gold, like rain, is indiscriminate. It showers riches upon the weirdest people.'

As she looked around her, she realised he was right. It was eleven in the morning, but men and women in outlandish evening wear were swanning past; a man in a moth-eaten suit raised his topper to her, bowed, wished her a good morning and staggered away.

'Did you see that?' Charlie, stunned, turned to Edward. 'His hands were covered in diamond rings!'

'Yes, Doctor, and if Mrs Palliser had asked for one, he'd surely have presented it to her.'

He stepped aside to allow a long-haired beggar, crying out for alms, to dodge towards the open parlour, a porter in close pursuit.

'I think we ought to find our rooms,' Charlie said.

As arranged, Rosa and Charlie were met at the hotel stables the next morning by the stockman, who introduced himself as Clem. As it turned out, Clem was also Montone Station's overseer.

He had two fine Thoroughbred horses ready for them.

'This one's Bessie,' he said. 'You'll like her, Mrs Palliser, she rides smooth as silk. And the chestnut here, Doc, he's yours. Say hello to Omar. He can travel, this lad.'

'He's a beauty,' Charlie said, patting the horse's flanks. 'And what do you think, Rosa? Are you happy with your mount?'

'Oh yes, she seems to like me. What's happening with our luggage?'

'Clem is having both bags sent out, so that we don't have a packhorse slowing us up.'

'Oh good! We'll really have a ride, won't we?' She watched Clem strap on the saddle. 'I'm all turned around now. Which way do we go?'

'Due south, only about fifty miles. Ha! Here's Edward . . . we're on our way.'

Charlie and Rosa were stunned to find the roads into the lovely hill country cluttered with junk; all sorts of junk, from bedding to worn saddles, rags and rusting pots and pans . . . every imaginable scrap of human flotsam and jetsam. Even broken-down wagons lay askew, as if bewildered by a world turned topsy-turvy.

'What is all this?' Charlie asked.

'You have to get used to it,' Edward replied. 'It's bloody disgusting, but that's what happens when thousands upon thousands of mad gold-seekers are let loose on the land. Some came to the goldfields on horseback, some in wagons as you see, but the rest had to leg it, chucking off stuff as the miles wore them down. Or when they had no further use for things.'

'Good Lord! I had no idea.'

'A lot of them, done in and defeated, died by the roadside, I believe,' Edward said. 'A boon for the local morticians!'

'There aren't as many people on the road as I expected.'

'No. And as you see, most of them are heading back to Maryborough. It's nearly all over.'

'The rush for gold?'

'No. The gold. The alluvial gold ran out in about a year, so then they had to dig for it, but a couple of years have seen that out. If there's any more gold it's too deep. The party's over. Around here anyway, which is a good thing.'

Charlie was surprised by that comment. 'But surely you'll lose a lucrative market? I imagined butchers wouldn't be able to keep up with the demand.'

'Oh yes, I suppose there's that. I hope this ride isn't too much for Mrs Palliser?'

'I don't think so.' Charlie smiled at Rosa, who was riding ahead with Clem. 'She seems to be enjoying herself.'

'That's good. She really is a very beautiful woman, isn't she?'

Charlie nodded his appreciation, rather than have to voice a reply. He had no wish to discuss his wife with this fellow.

Rosa was disappointed in this ride. It was depressing to see so many exhausted people struggling back to Maryborough, like refugees from a sacked village. The women and children dragging along with the men looked so gaunt and worn that Rosa's heart went out to them, but there was nothing she could do to help, apart from offering a little water. Even then it was Clem who stepped in when two women ran towards her, begging for water.

'Steady on, Mrs Palliser. Don't dismount,' he called. 'I'll see to them.'

He poured water into their metal cups from his canvas water bag and bade them good day.

'A lot of these poor folk are desperate,' he said to Rosa as they rode away. 'Riders have been dragged from their horses. So you have to be a bit careful.'

At midday they rested at an inn, while Clem watered the horses. The innkeeper explained that he was closing down in a few days, due to the collapse of the goldfields, so he'd let all his staff go. He could only offer them buns and bush honey.

'If that will do?' he asked.

'It will have to do, I suppose,' Rosa said.

Charlie was unimpressed. 'Can't we go on to another place?'

Rosa was hungry. She dug into a bun while the men argued, and had the innkeeper wrap a second for her, since by then the two men were all for moving on to the next inn.

An hour later they found the next inn was closed and the water tank empty, so they set off again. Fortunately Clem had refilled all their water bottles at the last stop. It was about this time that her husband and Edward Heselwood, both in bad moods, began sniping at each other over every little thing, so she moved ahead to ride with Clem again.

A little later she heard Edward snap at Charlie: 'You're so like my father! He knows everything about everything too!'

Clem looked over at her and winked.

She giggled.

Edward rode his horse forward to keep beside her, forcing Charlie to fume in the rear.

So what with stopping and starting, eventually finding a place where Edward and Charlie could 'dine', as Rosa put it sarcastically, they arrived at their destination late at night, in teeming rain.

Rosa, fed up with the company of the two men, was so pleased when Clem pointed out the lights of Montone Station in the distance that she would have raced away towards them had he not kept her trotting carefully along the dark track.

Lord Heselwood was waiting anxiously for them. He welcomed Rosa with a broad smile.

'Mrs Palliser, I am so sorry that you have come upon us on such a night. I'll have a fine day for you tomorrow.

'Dr Palliser,' he said, in a more serious tone, 'I cannot thank you enough for your kindness in making this journey. Lady Heselwood has retired but we'll have her up and ready for you first thing in the morning.'

He led them into the house. 'Now, if you wish to retire straight away I won't be offended. The housekeeper will bring your supper to you.'

Charlie glanced at Rosa. 'Perhaps you ought to, my dear. I'll have supper with Lord Heselwood, so that I can hear more of Lady Heselwood's condition before we actually meet.'

'Yes, of course,' Rosa smiled.

'Very well,' their host said kindly.

He introduced them to Mrs Ansell, the housekeeper, a busy little woman who was just as concerned for her mistress as her employer was.

'I'm so glad you're here,' she whispered to Charlie. 'I'm real worried about her. I tried to get them to let a local doctor see that leg, but they wouldn't have it, and I don't know what to do for her.'

'Don't worry,' he said. 'We'll sort it all out in the morning.'

The Heselwood homestead did not appear to be large, by outback-station standards, but still, within a very compact floor plan, it had two public rooms and four bedrooms. Maybe, Charlie thought, this floor plan had evolved because of the station history. A night attack by a tribe of murdering savages would not lightly be forgotten. It was possible that when Heselwood designed this house, he was subconsciously looking at protective measures, even though another attack was remote. At least not by blacks.

The walls of the neat stone building were thick, and there were no verandas. Normally a veranda was regarded as obligatory for houses in this climate; they were for shade, for socialising, for a quiet time and even for spare bedrooms, but there was no sign of one here. The heavy front door, centred between four windows on either side, had iron bolts on the inside, taking Charlie back to his father's house, where the outer doors were never closed, except against dust storms. This house was built with a courtyard in the middle. Charlie had never encountered the style before.

'It's like a fort,' he commented, when morning came and they were able to view their surrounds.

Rosa disagreed. 'No it's not. The building, if not the furnishings, is sort of Spanish style, very much like my father's country house.'

'Has Lord Heselwood ever visited that house?' Charlie asked, curiously wondering if he'd copied the design.

'Oh no. He's never been there. Didn't I mention that Lord Heselwood and my father never got on?'

'What? Why?'

'I don't know. It might be a good idea not to mention Daddy while we're here.'

Charlie was mortified. He'd never have brought Rosa with him had he known that. It seemed an imposition to inflict dissension on an already harassed family.

Fortunately, Lord Heselwood himself took them both for a walk after breakfast, to show them the orchard that Lady Heselwood had begun so many years ago and that was now being restored. Their host was perfectly charming to Rosa, and so Charlie was able to start his first day at Montone without the nervous qualms that had been threatening.

While he waited to be summoned to attend Lady Heselwood, he dashed off a letter to his brother Langley.

Eventually Charlie was ushered into the bedroom to meet his patient, who was an extremely attractive woman for her age. In her fifties, he thought, and carrying the years elegantly. Her greying fair hair was lightly waved and held back from her face by ivory combs, and as she looked up to him with a sweet smile of welcome, he couldn't help but note the strain in her deep blue eyes.

She was propped in an awkward position on the bed, among a sea of lacy pillows, some to prop her up, others to support her injured leg. Even though it was heavily bandaged, Charlie could smell the leg, and his heart sank.

'Thank you so much for coming to see me, Doctor,' Lady Heselwood was saying. 'I am so grateful that you could spare the time.'

'It is my pleasure, your ladyship.'

'So what do you think, Doctor?' she asked, after he'd unwound the bandages and cleansed her swollen, infected leg. 'I want you to be open with me. No secrets with Heselwood, please. My leg, I can't put it on the ground without pain. It's out of shape, isn't it? And my big toe. Is that gangrene I'm looking at?'

He gulped. 'I'm sorry, your ladyship, yes. That's gangrene. I'll have to attend to that. And the leg . . . I'll lance some of those sores and get the skin cleared up, but I'm afraid I'll have to try to reset it.'

'What will that involve?'

'Anaesthetic again, I'm afraid. I'll have to call in one of the local doctors to assist me. Is that all right?'

'Of course. And don't let Jasin talk you out of it. He was so shocked at the treatment I had from that woman, he just didn't know who to trust. But believe me, I was taken in by her too. It never occurred to me, or to the two nuns travelling in the coach, that anyone could be so cruel as to pretend to be a doctor. To lie like that! She even administered some sort of anaesthetic, because it put me out for some time.'

Charlie shuddered. 'I'm so sorry that you've had misfortune piled upon you like this, Lady Heselwood, but we'll have you up and about in no time.'

He looked around him. It was a large room, with high ceilings and a cedar floor; the walls were white, as were the curtains and linen, the cool whiteness broken only by the black-painted iron bedhead.

'It looks like a hospital room, doesn't it?' she said. 'Jasin furnished the whole house in a hurry, to surprise me, expecting that I would add my own touches, but I don't think I'll bother. This place gives me the willies.'

'As a matter of fact, you read my mind. I was just thinking that this room would be much cleaner than the hospital rooms, from what I hear. I'm hoping the doctor will come out here, rather than having to take you in to Gympie. Would you allow us to operate in here?'

'Yes,' she said quietly. 'I would feel happier here.'

'Good. We can only try.' He took her hand. 'Now, this is the routine I propose. I'll have a quick word with your husband, then I'm coming back to lance those sores. May I call in Mrs Ansell?'

'Of course.'

'Then I'll ride into Gympie and have a word with the doctors. I'll need to make an appointment for one of them to come out here to meet you and Lord Heselwood first, and if all is agreed, we should be able to operate on your leg within a few days. All right?'

'Thank you, Dr Palliser. I appreciate everything you're trying to do.'

She rang a tiny silver bell by the bed, and Mrs Ansell's grey head popped around the door.

'Where is my husband?' Lady Heselwood asked.

'In the parlour, ma'am.'

'Take Dr Palliser to the parlour and then come back. We'll have to prepare for some little operations.'

'Very well, ma'am.'

Jasin was waiting nervously for Palliser's opinion. Last night, when they'd had a private discussion about Georgina's situation, he'd felt that the doctor had been critical of his failure to call local doctors to see his wife, although he hadn't actually said so.

'How did you find out that this so-called Dr Lombe was an imposter?' Palliser had asked.

'She stayed here at Montone. I asked her to delay reporting to the hospital for a few days so that she could remain here and care for my wife. I saw her credentials from Geneva University and they seemed in order. But then, as a matter of course, one enters into conversations with guests over a meal and what have you, and it dawned on one that the woman knew nothing about Europe.

'In case it was my imagination at work, I sent Edward to quiz her. Surreptitiously, one should add. Well he quizzed her all right! Ended up calling her a liar and creating a great row! So there I was with this hulking woman storming about my house, demanding an apology, my wife upset, and Edward glowering in the hall.

'To solve it, I had Clem ride post-haste to town and speak with the hospital authorities, who of course had never heard of Lombe. The woman's husband, who claimed to be a stock and station agent, had come to Gympie with her, so Clem sought him out and told him to collect his wife from Montone before the police did the honours.

'They both fled the district with the police hot on their tails.'

Later Palliser said: 'I still don't understand why you didn't call in local doctors.'

Jasin couldn't say why. For the life of him, he couldn't say. And his explanation to Palliser sounded limp.

'It was as I've said. What did I know of them? I'd been fooled once, and my wife had suffered severely as a result. She couldn't bear another mistake. I did visit the hospital, though, and had a few words with the superintendent, and he advised me to wait until the plaster came off. He said nothing could be done in the mean time.'

'I see.' Palliser nodded. Jasin found the nod irritating; patronising; as if he'd come upon the village idiot but had to treat him gently.

The doctor was sitting by the window. As Jasin listened to his worries about Georgina's treatment, he could see Mrs Palliser walking across the front of the house with Edward, who should have been out working.

'Excuse me, Doctor, I just remembered, Lady Heselwood has been anxious to meet your wife. I'm dreadfully sorry for the oversight. Don't you think we should ask her to come in before you begin the treatment?'

Palliser jumped up. 'Certainly. I shall go down to the room and fetch her.'

'No need. She's out there.'

Palliser twisted about, and saw her strolling with Edward. He frowned. 'I'll get her,' he said, and made for the front door.

Jasin was intrigued by the frown, guessing a jealous streak. And what husband wouldn't be jealous? he sighed, remembering the morning of Dolour's funeral. He'd seen photographs of Rivadavia's daughter in the social pages, and recognised her sitting alone outside the church, but it had taken a few seconds for him to haul up her married name.

It had stayed with him. Palliser. Mrs Palliser. Wife of the eminent surgeon.

The patient was delighted when Rosa visited her. 'Oh my!' she said. 'Aren't you lovely! And so like your father. How is he?'

'He's well, thank you, Lady Heselwood.' Rosa hesitated. 'Do you know my father?'

'Oh yes. In the early days there were great feuds.' Lady Heselwood laughed. 'Heselwood fell out with Juan, *and* with Pace MacNamara, but I never felt I had to be part of it. I liked them both. So you must give my best regards to Juan, and congratulate him on his lovely daughter. He never had any other children, did he?'

'No. But he inherited the MacNamara boys, so to speak, when he married Dolour, and I suddenly found I had three brothers. When I was young I thought they were such wretches, but now they couldn't be nicer.'

They talked for a while, and Rosa could see she was nervous, even stalling for the time when Charlie would be in to remove those bandages. The odour from them was revolting, but it didn't seem to bother Lady Heselwood, who, she reasoned, must have become immune to it. Poor thing.

Finally Rosa had to make the decision. She held Lady Heselwood's hands and kissed her on the forehead. 'Is there anything I can do for you before I go?'

'No thanks. You're a dear girl. I'm so happy to have met you. We'll have a nice chat later.'

There was a small and very bright rainbow connecting the hills that morning, and Georgina was able to see it from her bedroom window. To his mother it was beautiful, but Edward could only think of the old saying: 'A rainbow in the morning is the shepherd's warning'; and it served to increase his concern.

He'd thought it was quite mad of his father to wait until the plaster of Paris came off, even if he had been acting under advice from some bureaucrat at the hospital. As time passed by, the putrid smell from Georgina's leg was distressing her.

'Something is badly wrong,' Edward kept telling his father. 'That Lombe woman probably had no idea what she was doing, beyond mixing the powder with water and slapping it on Mother's leg. There must have been more to it. Mother said she had cuts and grazes on her leg when she fell. Did that woman clean them up first? Who knows? She wouldn't let us into the room. I wanted to go in but you forbade me!'

'I didn't want to upset your mother. She was very nervous.'

'And she had damn good reason.'

When Mrs Ansell had cut away the plaster, with Jasin's help, Georgina had fainted. For that matter, they were all in shock. Her leg was a disgusting mess, and, as was obvious to all, it was found to be askew. What was more, it was very painful without the support of that filthy plaster.

Immediately Edward had said he would ride into town and get a doctor, but Jasin wouldn't hear of it. He said Georgina had to have the best, and he would call in Palliser, Brisbane's leading surgeon. He simply refused to have 'yokels' near her.

Their correspondence took up more precious time and Edward fumed at the delay. At one stage he even confronted his father and threatened to bring out a local doctor.

'This is my house!' Jasin had shouted at him. 'I won't have them near her. Can't you see how bad she is? If she doesn't get the right treatment now, she'll lose her leg.'

'And you think no treatment is better? Where is this doctor? Didn't you say it was urgent?'

'He'll be here.'

'That's what you keep telling Mother. She won't mind seeing one of the local doctors. I've been into town and found out about them. They're both experienced country doctors, well thought of. Especially Dr Oliver.'

Jasin was livid. 'You've discussed them with your mother?'

'Of course I have. She's not stupid. If there's a hospital, there has to be doctors.'

'You keep away from her, you bloody fool. I won't have you upsetting her. Don't you think you've done enough?'

'Oh, I see, we're back to that, are we? It's all my fault.'

'If the shoe fits, wear it!'

Jasin had stormed away and they hadn't spoken since.

Not that they talked much anyway. The station work had continued, and

Edward had been exploring the property on his own when Clem was busy, finding it much larger than he'd expected. They had about thirty thousand cattle, and slaughter yards servicing the Gympie butchers as well as the freelancers operating on the widespread goldfields. He had been gradually getting to know the place, and the station hands, when Jasin had come down to the sheds and told him to try his hand at branding. Edward recalled watching the men rope and brand cattle when he was a kid, so he agreed to have a go, finding it a lot harder than he'd imagined.

There was no getting away from it: he'd been a dead loss, as one of the men had commented, on the first day, which had irritated his father, so he'd stuck at it, and it had been hellish work for a body totally unaccustomed to rough treatment. Finally he'd pulled a muscle in his back, and agony had set in. Naturally Jasin decided he was malingering.

'How do you like Montone?' Clem had asked him. 'It's a beaut little station, isn't it?'

Since Clem had answered the question himself, Edward agreed. It probably was. It would be even better when his father went home. For all his talk, Jasin had never done the stock work, like roping and branding, and week-long mustering from camps. He'd claimed cattle runs from raw bush and marked out that land as his own. Then he'd bought cattle, hired stockmen and driven the cattle over the mountains and out to Carlton Park, his first station. After that he'd used drovers to deliver cattle to new runs, and stockmen to work the stations. He was a squatter, a pastoralist, who'd chosen good land, employed experienced men, and succeeded beyond a man's wildest dreams, ending up with holdings in various areas of Queensland and New South Wales that would cover half of England. And sure, he'd become an expert cattle breeder. But he didn't have to muck in with the men!

Georgina had realised there were problems between father and son, and he'd talked to her about Jasin's attitude.

'He wants me to work as a stockman, Mother. I'm simply not cut out for it.'

'I know. But he means well. He just wants you to learn how everything works.'

'I'm quite sure he was never a stockman. I'll bet he never got his hands dirty!'

She shook her head. 'Where did you get that idea from? Your father worked hard for years and years. He would be out in the bush for months on end, and sometimes he'd come home so thin and tired I would despair. I'd have to beg him to take a few months' rest.'

Edward respected her opinion, but he rather thought she'd heard Jasin's stories of his tough pioneering days too many times.

And then the eminent surgeon arrived, with his marvellous wife in tow!

'Had I a wife who looked like that,' Edward told his mother, to make her laugh, 'I wouldn't be leaving her home either.'

One of the local doctors was called in to assist. A perfectly reasonable fellow of about fifty, with scrubbed pink skin and fluffy white sideburns. Dr Oliver shared Palliser's concern; Edward could see they were both very worried. But to his delight, Dr Oliver flatly refused to operate in the house. He insisted that they had a perfectly good operating theatre in the hospital, with excellent light and a proper surgical table at the right height.

'Also,' he added stiffly, 'Matron herself is a trained nurse; she will be assisting us.'

So it was settled.

On the morning of the operation, Jasin waited in the matron's small office, while Edward paced about a shaded area reserved for visitors' mounts. He lit a small cheroot, and wandered over to a fence that bordered the hospital grounds, to watch about fifty mounted police troopers in drab uniforms being put through their paces by an officer.

It was obvious that the police officer was not impressed by his troops, and with good reason. Though they were well over on the other side of the paddock, Edward could see they were a bumbling lot, unable to keep their horses under control, let alone form lines, and he could hear their irate sergeant roaring commands. Convinced they were the worst recruits he'd ever come across, Edward was enjoying the comic spectacle when the officer, enraged by the troops' performance, kneed his horse and cantered across the clearing straight at them, his whip flailing.

He charged at the sergeant, lashed him around the head and shoulders, and then took on the troopers, throwing his horse in among them, thumping and battering everyone who couldn't move fast enough to dodge the slash of the leather whip.

The result of course was chaos, riders scattering in all directions.

Taken by surprise, the sergeant had fallen off his horse, so he was once again the target of his superior's fury, frantically trying to remount as the officer berated him and, pointing to the troops, began yelling orders at him.

Not long after that, the officer rode out of the paddock and minutes later Edward saw him coming into the hospital grounds.

He hitched his horse next to Edward's mount, stood to admire it and then turned to him. 'I say, is this your horse? He's a beauty!'

'Yes. He is rather special, isn't he? His ancestors were Arabian, of the *Kehilan* or Thoroughbred group.'

'Ah, is that so? Yes . . . well, he's got a powerful look about him, and the big alert eyes of an Arab horse. Any more like him at home?'

'I'm afraid not. He was a gift from my parents.' Edward patted the horse fondly. 'You're a good fellow, aren't you? His name is Red Shadow, but we just call him Saul. By the way, I've been watching your troops training out there.' He grinned. 'A bit raw, what?'

'A bit raw? They're bloody hopeless. But what can you expect from blacks!'

'What blacks?'

The officer jerked his head in their direction. 'Those so-called troopers. They're the newest recruits for the Native Mounted Police, and I don't think they've ever seen a horse before.'

'You mean they're blacks? Aborigines?'

'Yes. The military is finally waking up to the fact that we have to fight fire with fire. Hence Aborigine troops to rout out renegade blacks and teach their mates to behave.'

'What a good idea.'

They discussed that concept for a while, meandering on to other subjects, until they seemed to be getting along so well that Inspector Marcus Beresford decided it was time to introduce himself, and Edward reciprocated.

'From Montone Station,' he added.

'Have you someone in the hospital?' Marcus asked.

'Yes.' Edward's face clouded. 'My mother. She had an accident. Injured her leg. They're operating.'

'Ah, sorry. I hope she'll be all right. I'm just here to collect some field bandages, and medical aids and assortments from the apothecary. If you'd care to, we could have a drink or two some time. I'm staying down there at the Gympie Hotel.'

'Thank you, I'll take you up on that,' Edward said. 'I've been feeling hemmed in at Montone, not knowing anyone significant in the town.'

Beresford hurried over to the hospital, and it wasn't long before he returned carrying a lumpy canvas bag.

'I spoke to one of the nurse girls,' he said to Edward. 'She said your mother is out of surgery and is all right. Sleeping now.'

'Oh, thank you!'

He rushed into the matron's office and found his father sitting with her, sharing morning tea. Edward was furious that Jasin hadn't bothered to let him know that the operation was over, but he remained calm, asking Matron directly about the patient.

'She's doing as best she can,' the woman replied. 'Would you like a cup of tea, Mr Heselwood?'

'No thank you, Matron. Did they reset Lady Heselwood's leg?'

'As best they could,' she said, her patronising tone irritating him.

'What exactly does that mean?'

'It means your mother has chalky bones,' Jasin told him, with a measure of resentment in his voice. 'They have reset the leg but are not sure of success, and won't be for a while.'

'Oh, we'll see, Lord Heselwood,' the matron cooed. 'We'll see. But at least we caught that gangrene before it got any worse!'

'What gangrene?' Edward cried.

'Her toe, Mr Heselwood.'

Jasin's voice was now a conduit for repressed anger. 'The big toe on your mother's right foot had to be amputated!' he said, as if Edward himself was to blame.

'I don't know how that dreadful Lombe woman can live with herself,' the matron said. 'And do you know? She hasn't been arrested! She's claiming she never said she was a doctor, and was only trying to help. The magistrate said that since she hadn't been paid, just sacked by you, Lord Heselwood, and since no money changed hands, the police in actuality had no case to . . .'

Jasin stood abruptly, and plunged out of the room.

The matron's voice trailed off. 'Oh,' she said to Edward. 'He's upset.'

'Really?' Edward snapped. 'May I see my mother?'

'I don't know if she's awake. I'll find out.'

As she moved towards the open door, he caught a whiff of the sickening smell of ether, and felt nauseated.

He clutched the matron's arm. 'I think I'm going to be sick,' he managed to say before he vomited in her doorway.

'Oh, good God!' Edward heard his father's anger at this exhibition, and saw him stride away, disgusted, before his son's stomach heaved again.

While they had him in their hospital, both of the local doctors prevailed upon the surgeon to operate on some urgent cases already awaiting treatment. Having seen Dr Palliser's swift and precise work in the operating theatre, Dr Oliver was now full of praise for the Brisbane surgeon.

'We should appreciate it if you could take over these operations,' he said. 'And the patients can consider this their lucky day!'

Charlie obliged them. He saw it not only as a duty to the patients, but as an opportunity to demonstrate new procedures to these country doctors.

'I hope you don't mind,' he explained to Lord Heselwood, 'but I'll be remaining here for the day. I'm listed for some more operations.'

'So Matron tells me,' Heselwood said. 'It's exceeding generous of you to spare them your precious time.'

'Thank you, sir. But be assured I won't neglect Lady Heselwood. I'll be popping in on her through the day.'

'When do you think I could take her home?'

'A few days. She will need a pulley, though, to keep the leg raised. According to your housekeeper, the plaster that woman applied previously was very thin, hardly more than a sheath. But this time it's stronger and heavier. Lady Heselwood couldn't possibly hold it up, even on pillows.'

'You want a pulley and brace installed in the bedroom at home?'

'Yes. If possible. Otherwise she would have to stay here.'

'I'll have Clem come in and look at the contraption. He's a very resourceful fellow. He'll know what to do. Is there anything you need? Anything I can get for you?'

'I don't think so. No, not really.'

'Then I might run along for a while. I'll come back this evening.'

Jasin was depressed. And shocked. When he first heard the bad news, he'd asked Dr Palliser if he could explain the situation to Georgina, when she was well enough, as he simply couldn't face up to her distress.

Palliser had smiled. 'I think Lady Heselwood is already very much aware of what this day would bring, but I will be chatting to her anyway.'

'But did she know her toe would be amputated?' Jasin asked anxiously.

'Oh yes, she had a pretty good idea.'

'She never said a word to me about that.'

'I suppose she didn't want to worry you. What could you have done? I'm sure she had your best interests at heart.'

As he walked out of the building, Jasin took note, for the first time, of the conditions in this hospital, and felt a little guilty that he had managed a private room for his wife when the two long dormitories were packed, and several patients were lying abed in the entrance hall.

'Perhaps,' he mused, 'I ought to help them along with another wing. There's plenty of space in the hospital grounds.'

Edward's horse had gone, which was no surprise. Jasin considered buying lunch at one of the hotels in the town, but discarded that notion when he realised he'd still have a few hours to kill before it was time to return to the hospital, so he decided to eat at home. It was only a thirty-minute ride, and he still found pleasure in this hilly countryside with its quiet valleys and grand tall gums.

At Montone he cut across country, passing the small cemetery where, years ago, he'd buried Mrs Moore, the cook, and five of his stockmen after the raid. He gave them a small salute and splashed through a shallow creek to head uphill towards the homestead.

The ride made him feel better, much better, and he was hungry now. He handed his horse over to a groom and strode towards the side of the house, thinking that perhaps he might have some cold cuts and hot buttered potato slices for lunch, with a stein of beer. He shoved the side door open, almost colliding with a woman who was exiting at the same time.

She gave a shriek and jumped back as Jasin, also caught by surprise, tried to retreat and then, seeing it was Mrs Palliser, burst into abject apologies at his clumsiness. But, he realised, not before something between them had taken his breath away, even though they had only just brushed past each other. For a second, only a second, he'd felt a magnetism in that confined space, when they were almost wedged together, facing each other, before they stumbled apart. He was startled by it. Nothing like that had ever happened to him before.

'I'm so sorry,' he managed to say to her again, then, with a desperate attempt at levity, added with a smile: 'Do continue, Mrs Palliser! Notice the door is quite ajar and there are no obstacles. I'll try not to get in your way this time.'

She blushed, stepped out of the door on to the flagged path and then turned back.

'Oh goodness, Lord Heselwood! I'm the one who should be apologising. How is Lady Heselwood?'

'Resting well, thank God,' he said. 'We're all very grateful to your husband. In fact the medical gentlemen are so impressed they've asked him to do some more operations.'

He was embarrassed now, realising that he had totally forgotten about Mrs Palliser, and by the sound of things, so had Dr Palliser. He tried to make amends.

'It was a shame we had to leave you here alone this morning,' he said. 'I do hope you weren't too bored.'

Just then Mrs Ansell came upon them. 'Oh, your lordship, I guessed you gentlemen would be home for lunch. You'll join them, won't you, Mrs Palliser? She's only had a nibble so far. I'll serve as soon as you're ready, your lordship. I've made a lovely beef and onion pie.'

Having been summoned back into the house, Mrs Palliser obeyed meekly, as her host, still holding the door, called to Mrs Ansell: 'Dr Palliser won't be in for lunch. Is Edward home yet?'

'No, sir.'

'Well,' he said to her, 'thank heavens Mrs Palliser is here, or I'd have to dine alone, and I hate having to dine alone.'

'He does too,' the housekeeper said to Mrs Palliser, whose cheeks were pink again.

Jasin, still bewildered by that incident in the doorway, wondered if she had felt the same jolt, but he wouldn't dream of asking her. She'd think he'd gone off his head; or worse, think he was some sort of lecher. Then again, she could be thinking that he was almost old enough to be her father.

He went out of his way, over luncheon, to be kind to her, but distant. Even enquiring after her father.

'He's well, thank you, Lord Heselwood. Coming to terms with Dolour's death.' She looked up suddenly, as if just remembering that she'd seen him at the funeral service. 'I didn't know you knew her,' she added.

'Ah, yes,' he murmured. 'Yes. Well, of course . . .' He hadn't meant the conversation to move in this direction. Quite glad that Georgina wasn't at the table with them. 'Everyone seemed to know everyone else in those days; we were a rather small community.' To gloss over Dolour's presence in the room, he added. 'Why, we even knew your mother! We came out on the same ship.'

'Oh, did you?' she said.

'Yes. Charming woman. Would you care for dessert?'

Since she did not wish for anything further, having enjoyed a goodly helping of Mrs Ansell's excellent pie, she thought she might retire to her room for a little while.

'I'm returning to the hospital shortly,' he told her. 'Would you care to join me?'

'I'd better not,' she said. 'Charlie will be busy. He might feel I'm intruding. But do give my best wishes to Lady Heselwood, won't you? Maybe I could visit her tomorrow.'

'By all means. Now if you need anything, just call Mrs Ansell.'

To Jasin, that luncheon had been an ordeal. He'd felt like a bumbling youth, trying to entertain a woman with a perfectly lovely face, and eyes that shone as she talked to him. Interested in everything he had to say. Totally captivating him.

He was glad to be out on the lonely road again, trying not to think about her. He'd found her a handsome young lady at first sight; an elegant woman, her dark hair rolled up into the latest chignon; but to see her with it down, sitting across the table from him, he was reminded of a painting of some beauty. He couldn't remember which painting. Not that it mattered. He was so distracted he'd hardly known what he was talking about. She must have thought him quite a fool.

Far from it. Rosa had thoroughly enjoyed his company. He was so easy to talk to. And she'd thought it was so good of him to mention Juan, rather than skirt around the subject. He'd even known Delia. She wasn't surprised that he'd found her mother charming; she could be when it suited her. But how amazing that they'd come out from England on the same ship! What a coincidence. And so nice. No one in the colony seemed to have known her mother, who hadn't liked living out here at all.

'It's full of snakes and savages,' she used to tell Rosa. 'I was terrified the whole time. I had to absolutely insist that your father return me to civilisation forthwith.'

Rosa walked across the courtyard to their room, picked up a book of poems and songs by Henry Kendall, and sat in the easy chair by the window, trying to concentrate. She was disconcerted that Charlie had chosen to remain on and work at the hospital, because she'd rather have heard the verdict on Lady Heselwood from him. Then again, she supposed he could hardly refuse to help people in need of a surgeon.

Just then she saw her host riding away with Clem, so she put down the book, and made for the door, intent on taking the walk that had been interrupted. She always loved pottering about the 'innards' of a station, investigating the horses and the cattle yards, and the blacksmith's and whatever was going on. Unlike her mother, snakes never bothered her, and this area's savages were long gone.

Edward walked into the dingy little hospital room, taken aback to find his mother sleeping and her leg, once again in plaster, suspended from the ceiling by a sort of sling. She looked so pale and wan, he wished he could pick her up and take her away from this purgatory.

There was a small table with a lamp this side of the bed, so he tiptoed around the other side and wedged himself on to a chair that could barely fit between bed and wall. Then he stared at the bandaged foot, and almost wept when he realised they'd amputated her toe.

How would she cope? he wondered miserably. She was so fastidious. And shoes? Would her shoes fit now? What happened in those circumstances?

Georgina stirred and looked at him. 'Why, Edward,' she smiled. 'How long have you been sitting there?'

'Not long, Mother.' He stood and kissed her on the forehead. 'How are you feeling?'

'A bit woozy, but I'm all right, I think.'

'Is it hurting? Your leg, I mean. It's not pulled up too high, is it? You don't look very comfortable.'

'Don't worry. I daresay I'll get used to it. All in a good cause. I have decided to take one day at a time.'

He was desperate to help. 'Do you want some tea? Or water or something? Shall I call a nurse or someone?'

'No, dear, I'll just rest awhile.'

'Oh God, did I disturb you? Do you want me to go? To let you rest?'

'Of course not. And I must say, you're looking very smart. I haven't seen that waistcoat before, have I?'

'I don't think so.' He took her hand. 'Mother, I need to talk to you. I wanted to tell you how sorry I am about all this. Your leg . . .'

She smiled. 'It can't be helped. It was just unfortunate that that wretch of a woman interfered. My internment would have been over by this.'

'No,' he said. 'I don't mean that. I mean I am so, so dreadfully sorry that I caused you to fall.'

'Darling! You didn't cause me to fall! I tripped, that's all.'

'You tripped because I was doing something stupid. I heard you call out, and I know you fell trying to stop me.'

'Please, Edward, don't say that. It's not right.'

'But it is right, and I want you to know how dreadfully sorry I am. I'll never forgive myself for being such an idiot. I know I caused you a lot of pain and embarrassment years ago, and I was hoping to make up for it this time around, and I'm making a mess of it all over again.'

'No you're not. I tripped, Edward, and that's the end of it. One can have regrets, everyone does, but it is of no benefit to wear them on your sleeve. Now I want you to say with me: what's done is done. Come on now, say it with me: what's done is done!'

He whispered the words with her, wondering if his father would ever see it that way. He remembered Jasin's rage when he heard about his son's episode with Dolour MacNamara, as she was then. It was stupid . . . yes, unforgivable, but he had been very drunk, showing off in front of two stockmen.

'I begged Dolour not to force you to leave the colony,' his mother had said, 'but she can be very hard. She wouldn't give an inch!'

'And she's right,' Jasin shouted. 'Send him to England, the useless lout! Get rid of him!'

His father hadn't even come down to the ship to see him off. Now he was blaming him for Georgina's predicament. And he was right again. Angrily Edward wondered what it must be like to be such a perfect specimen of manhood as Lord Heselwood.

Just then the great man strode in. He kissed his wife, gave his son a sour sniff, as if still inhaling vomit, and began examining the contraption, as he called it, that held her leg aloft.

'Clem's outside,' he said to Georgina. 'When you're feeling up to it, he'd like to take a look at this sling, so that we can build one at home.'

'Who's here? Clem? Why? Is he coming back to Sydney with us?'

'No!' Jasin was confused. 'No, back to Montone. You can't travel to Sydney.'

She sighed. 'I've been thinking about it ever since Dr Palliser arrived. You can take me by coach to Maryborough . . .'

'Impossible. You saw how difficult it was for you in that Cobb coach, to get this far. And embarrassing.'

Georgina didn't reply. The latter part of that journey had been frightful. She'd been in agony with the leg, and the coach might have been well sprung but the bumpy roads weren't. On top of all that, she needed to go to the lavatory not long after they'd bundled her, still rendered insensible, into that coach. She couldn't request or look forward to a lavatory stop, because they would have had to carry her out . . . She shook her head to banish any further consideration of that situation, because hours later, unable to contain it any longer, she'd been in serious bother. Thank God her husband was the only one in the coach with her. Even so, she'd whispered the problem to him.

'Wait on,' he said. 'I once heard that some of these coaches carry pots for ladies.'

He'd searched high and low without success. 'Obviously that's not true,' he'd had to say in the end.

It was quite some time before she could manage to tell him, through her tears, that she'd wet herself.

And that was what Jasin meant by embarrassment. They'd both been embarrassed. When they'd arrived at Montone, he had demanded blankets for her and insisted on carrying her inside himself, during which time Georgina was petrified he'd drop her.

'I have worked it out,' she said now, struggling for strength in her voice. 'I will need a good carriage. I want to be taken to Maryborough to board a ship. Mrs Palliser alone will sit inside with me. This time there'll be no stops. And no strangers.'

'But Georgina! You can't go by carriage. And there mightn't be a suitable ship in port.'

'You could telegraph and find out. We could be there in a day with good horses and a good driver. Like you or Clem.'

Edward listened glumly, noticing that he wasn't mentioned as a good driver. But it seemed to him that Jasin thought she was still etherised.

'Don't be worrying about that now, pet,' he said to her. 'You just rest and we'll talk about it some other time.'

She seemed to slump in the bed. 'Jasin,' she said, her voice hardly audible, 'please. I really do want to go home.'

He didn't hear her. He was already on his way out of the door.

Edward saw a tear trickle down her cheek. He walked quietly out of the room and then hurried to catch up with his father.

'You didn't hear what Mother just said,' he called. 'She wants to go home!'

'I'm taking her home. To Montane.'

'No, Father, she really wants to go home to Sydney. Can't you understand that? If she has to be confined to a room again, why can't it be in her home where she's surrounded by her own things. Not at Montone . . .'

'What's wrong with Montone?'

'There's nothing wrong with it, but for Mother it's not home. It's just a shell.'

'And how do you propose to get her home?'

'You heard. She has it all worked out.'

'The hell she has. It's impossible.'

'Oh for God's sake, can't you even try? You really upset her, marching off like that.'

Jasin stood fuming, looking along the passage at Clem, who was waiting politely, hat in hand, then back at Georgina's open door.

'She doesn't know what she's talking about!' he snapped.

'Then humour her. Go along with her.'

As his father turned on his heel, back to the hospital room, Edward walked down to explain the situation to Clem.

After a fair number of arguments with various people, Jasin found a carriage and arranged for Clem to drive Georgina and Mrs Palliser to Maryborough, while he rode in with Edward and the doctor.

He had booked two first-class cabins, one for Georgina and himself, the other for the Pallisers, who would disembark in Brisbane.

Clem was instructed to return the carriage to its owner, and Edward had the job of taking the two spare horses back to Montone from Maryborough.

'All completed with military precision,' he said sarcastically to Clem, as the ship pulled out into the river.

'Yes,' Clem grinned. 'Your mother won that round.'

It was taken for granted that Edward would remain to work on Montone Station, but once he'd brought the horses back, he saw no reason to stay. Georgina hadn't liked Montone, and neither did her son. He decided to ride into town and have a talk with Inspector Beresford.

'You're just in time to bid me farewell,' Beresford told him. 'I've been ordered to take the new recruits up north to Rockhampton.'

'What sort of a place is that?'

'A river port. Like Maryborough, but folks there are much more sociable. I've been stationed there before, and rather enjoyed the place, so I don't mind this job. But forgive me, how is your mama? I heard she'd quit the hospital already.'

'That's true. Quit the hospital and Queensland! She survived the operation, but was very distressed to have the leg in plaster again, so Father has taken her home to Sydney. They sailed a couple of days ago.'

'So you're the boss at Montone now?'

'Ah, no. We have an excellent station manager. I was contemplating going down to Sydney with them, but I wanted to see more of Queensland first.'

'Then here's your chance. Ride north with me. I'd appreciate your company. My sergeant's white, but the troopers are all blackfellows. Native Mounted Police, remember?'

'Oh yes, quite.'

Edward was unsure of this company. He hadn't planned on travelling with blackfellows who might spear a man in the back while he slept.

'Don't worry,' Beresford grinned. 'They're tame. I keep them under the thumb. By the time we get to Rockhampton, they'll be passable troopers or I'll want to know why.'

'How far is it to Rockhampton?'

'From here, about two hundred and fifty miles. Not a bad trip. I'll take them up the coast; there are some good little towns along the way with decent food.

Better than the damned inland tours I've had to do. A man could starve out there. Actually, old chap, I could string this trip out a few days to make it more enjoyable. Do a spot of fishing. Are you up for it?'

'Why not? When do we leave?'

Langley's father, Duncan Palliser, was a forthright man. Having been told by the Queensland police commissioner that new territories now being opened up by pastoralists would be afforded full support and protection by the police, he was very annoyed to hear from Langley that no such police presence had eventuated.

He took himself off to visit his old friend George Thorn, whose son George Junior had only recently managed to dislodge MacAlister and step into his shoes as premier of the colony. George, a former politician himself, was gracious in accepting Duncan's congratulations that his son had reached such high office, but by no means enthusiastic about the state of governance.

'It might work with my son, and his mates at the helm this time,' he growled, 'but they're turning out premiers like sausages and that's no good at all. The last two hardly got the seats warm before they were shown the door.'

'But that won't happen to George, surely?' Duncan said, offering encouragement.

'I hope not, but I wouldn't bet on it. He'll have to move fast to get things moving. MacAlister said complaints outweigh compliments a hundred to one on that job. Anyway, how's your boy, Langley, doing up north?'

Duncan shook his head wearily. 'I hesitate to mention how he's going now. All the graziers up there are hamstrung by a serious lack of police. Not only law and order problems, but the blacks are turning nasty.'

'They always are up that way,' George grinned. 'But if our new premier loses the support of the younger generation of graziers like your lad, he'll hit the slippery slide too.'

'I don't think they'll blame him, since he's just walked in the door.'

'Oh yes they will. They'll want results, fast.'

George walked over to a map on the wall, and stubbed his finger on it. 'Isn't that about where Langley's station is?'

'Yes,' Duncan said. 'He had cattle out as far as the Thomson River here . . .' he pointed. 'But he had to pull back. Good cattle country but too dangerous to risk men and herds yet.'

'I didn't know that. We heard settlers are going great guns, pushing west. But all is not lost, my friend. On this one the Premier can shift the blame. I'll have a word with him. I reckon a new police commissioner would be the shot. Sack this bloke, and give the new fellow the job of protecting white folk trying to go about their lawful affairs. What do you think?'

'Well I hope he can find someone who can see past the Brisbane office.'

'Better still,' George laughed, 'someone with an ultimatum tied to his tail. Get police out there or pick up your cap and go the same way as the last fellow! Only faster.'

The new police commissioner, Andrew Pedley, believed he was equal to the job. He studied the latest maps, had several meetings with his deputies, and arranged to speak at a lavish dinner to which he had invited a number of leading graziers, including the well-known Juan Rivadavia, who did not accept.

At the dinner he displayed maps setting out new police districts, north and south of the Tropic of Capricorn and reaching out to the Cloncurry River in the far west, on past the new settlement of Longreach.

Then with his deputy, and their wives, who were sisters, he sailed for Rockhampton, and checked his party into the Criterion Hotel.

The next day he inspected a parade of mounted police at the Rockhampton barracks, disappointed that they could only rally, in all, twenty-three officers and men.

'Where are the rest?' he asked crankily, and was informed by the chief inspector that he had brought in all available men from a radius of one hundred miles.

At that Pedley commandeered an office and set to work.

First he instructed his deputy to liaise with police officers to ascertain the names of thirty leading Rockhampton citizens, gentlemen only, and invite them to a dinner at the Criterion Hotel. He wished to reassure them that their back-country friends and relatives would soon have police headquarters established in several districts.

He lectured his local police on the desirability of more police presence in outlying districts, and received enthusiastic cheers. The hard-pressed men were even more enthused when the commissioner displayed maps that marked the boundaries of four new police districts, each one to be under the command of an inspector.

'I don't want this to be a slapdash operation,' he said. 'I have worked it out that each district should make a start with thirty men.'

His deputy blanched. 'How many?'

'Two sergeants and twenty-eight constables. They wouldn't be able to cope with fewer. Those districts are immense, most of them eighty by a hundred miles.'

Chief Inspector Pennington, officer in charge of the Rockhampton district, was worried. 'That's a lot of horses, sir. We couldn't afford to supply them from here.'

'You'll have the money,' the commissioner said testily. 'It won't happen tomorrow. My office will attend to the logistics.'

'It's a lot of men too,' his deputy said quietly. 'All of the colony's police stations are undermanned. I don't know where we'll get them from.'

'That's your job. Find them! Pull in more recruits.'

A dinner party was arranged for the following Saturday night. Among those attending were the police commissioner, his deputy, and Chief Inspector Pennington.

They were met by the publican, who informed them that the banquet his wife had prepared would be worthy of this important event. He showed them to their seats at the top of a long table, neatly set with the added flourish of starched linen and place cards, as the mayor arrived with his wife and several friends who were not on the invitation list, thereby creating the first mischief of the evening.

Not known for his tact, the deputy commissioner saw fit to tell the mayor that this was a gentlemen-only dinner.

'Ladies were not invited, sir,' he murmured.

The Mayor roared laughing. 'That's all right, mate. She's no lady anyway.'

Unaware that he was welcoming gentlemen who had no place at the table, the police commissioner pumped hands and congratulated all on their fine town. He also met an auctioneer by the name of Chester Newitt, and some cattle men including two fellows who came in together, Messrs Paul MacNamara and Langley Palliser.

The seating plan was chaotic as the mayor told his friends not to worry; to pull up chairs 'any old where'.

By the time the commissioner rose to speak, so much liquor had been consumed that he could hardly be heard. Then, when he asked if anyone else would like to address the company, the mayor volunteered, inviting his wife to sing a few songs. Surprisingly, she had a fine voice.

Palliser rose to speak, complimenting her on her beautiful rendition of much-loved ballads, but then aimed a few hard questions at the police commissioner, implying that his plans were all pie in the sky. Assured that they were not, he asked Chief Inspector Pennington if any of the men who had murdered a family of Aborigines at Mischief Creek two months ago had been apprehended.

'I can't say that they have been as yet, because there have been differing versions of what actually happened out there, Mr Palliser. Our investigations seem to point to attacks by blacks in the first place. They attacked the teamsters and burned down the store.'

'That is not true,' Palliser said.

'It is the information placed before me.'

'You're a liar, sir. I placed the information before you, in a letter I wrote to you myself.'

'I probably didn't receive it.'

'Then how come you answered it?'

While they were arguing, Pedley was trying to recall something about the Palliser name.

'Good God!' he whispered to his deputy. 'That's Duncan Palliser's son! Do something.'

The deputy interrupted, offering to make an appointment with Mr Palliser to take the details of the incident from him, causing Palliser to retort that he'd hardly call cold-blooded murders an incident. Then Mr Paul MacNamara had a question for the chief inspector.

'Is it true that a contingent of Native Mounted Police is to be based in Rockhampton again?'

The inspector deliberately passed this buck to the deputy with a mean smile, knowing that MacNamara and his friends had succeeded in having the troops banned from the area. 'Could you fill us in on this, sir?'

'On that matter, yes I can. A contingent of our excellent Native Police, led by Inspector Beresford, is on its way. I can guarantee that you will be able to avail yourself of their services, Chief Inspector, as soon as they arrive. I'm sure they'll be of great assistance . . .'

'Bloody hell!' MacNamara shouted at the mayor. 'You promised that pack of renegades would never be let loose in this district again.'

'Send 'em out west to one of your new districts,' Palliser added. 'They won't be so brave out there.'

Chester Newitt made his contribution to the evening: 'I reckon we oughta adjourn to the bar.'

The trio of grandly uniformed police were abandoned by their guests, giving the publican an opportunity to present the deputy with his bill. That gentleman passed it on to the local chief inspector, who stared at it in dismay.

'I can't pay this. My budget doesn't run to this sort of a booze-up.' He handed it to the police commissioner: 'Thank you, sir, it has been a very pleasant evening. By the way, the new troopers, not the Native Police, will they be mustered here in Rockhampton before heading inland?'

'Yes,' Pedley said. He was tired, and his gout was playing up. 'That's best, I'd say.'

'Then I shall have to requisition funds to purchase horses for them, I suppose? And extra rigs and supplies?'

'Yes, yes, whatever!' Pedley turned to his deputy. 'You see to that, and fix up this bill.'

CHAPTER EIGHT

Milly Forrest soon saw that there was trouble between the brothers. When they walked in the front door of the hotel and met Paul MacNamara, his face lit up with pleasure.

'Why! Mrs Forrest and Lucy Mae! What are you doing here?'

Then his jaw dropped almost to the floor, as Duke followed them.

'Ah, Duke,' he said, as if he'd swallowed a bad egg.

His wife Laura patched up the moment by welcoming all three and inviting them into the lounge for morning tea.

Milly was quick to accept, choosing to ignore whatever bug the two men had up their noses.

'Thank you. We'd love tea, Laura. We've just stepped off the boat. We've come to explore Rockhampton. Duke is taking us to visit his station but we wouldn't have left without visiting you at Oberon.' She was still talking as they seated themselves in a cluster of chairs in the lounge. 'What a lovely coincidence to bump into you here. Are you staying at the hotel?'

'Yes, but we're going home today,' Paul said. 'And how are you, Lucy Mae? Feeling better these days? We were very sorry to hear of the loss of your husband . . .'

'Oh, she's all right now,' Milly said. 'It was some time ago. Life has to go on.'

Suddenly she realised that Paul had lost his first wife, so she added: 'That's why we're travelling. I thought a sea voyage would do us both the world of good. And we had a lovely time on the ship. Did we not, Lucy Mae?'

'Yes, and we had perfect weather. The sea was like a pond.'

As the two young women compared notes on the voyage from Brisbane, Paul and Duke sat glumly waiting for tea to be served, and Milly pondered the animosity between them. She recalled Duke saying that he was going north to help Paul at Oberon, but instead he had bought his own station. That could easily have caused a row.

'Isn't it wonderful that Duke has his own station?' she said to them.

'Yes,' Paul muttered.

'Mrs Forrest and Lucy Mae are coming out to stay for a few days,' Duke announced. 'I've warned them it's not as flash as Oberon.'

'But I'm sure it's quite lovely,' Laura added.

'You haven't seen Duke's place yet?' Milly's keen ear had picked up that interesting piece of information.

'Laura hasn't had time,' Paul said quickly.

'But obviously you have,' Milly said gaily. 'And did you give it the stamp of approval?'

Duke rose from his gloom to laugh. 'Oh yes. He sure did. Paul thinks I got a real bargain.'

His brother shrugged. 'Yes.' And turned to talk to Lucy Mae.

After morning tea it was time for Paul and Laura to leave. They insisted that the two ladies find time to visit Oberon before they returned home, and Milly was happy to accept.

Milly had lived on several sheep and cattle stations, and having been shown around this green and fertile property pronounced it a gem. The homestead, though, she told him, was badly in need of sustenance. So while Duke and Lucy Mae went riding, which she hoped meant courting, Milly drew up lists of renovations in order of priority, and another list of household requirements such as furniture, linen and cutlery.

She was right, of course. The riders followed a scenic track into a rain forest section of the property, where Lucy Mae was enthralled by so many strange and exotic plants. They led the horses on through the forest to a fast-flowing creek at the base of a series of small cascades, and Lucy Mae was ecstatic. She took off her boots and stockings to paddle in the cool waters, and persuaded Duke to join her.

Later, as they sat on the grassy bank of the creek, watching little yellow-green budgerigars flitting in and out of the trees, Duke reached out to Lucy Mae and took her in his arms.

Afterwards, as they trekked out to open country, he was overwhelmed. He looked at Lucy Mae and found her calm, even light-hearted, joking about the old tree stumps and rotting branches on the forest floor that barred their exit.

He'd hoped he could make love to Lucy Mae that morning simply because the opportunity would be there. Not because he imagined it would be anything special. After all, this was only Lucy Mae, childhood friend now grown up. But something had happened in their lovemaking that Duke couldn't explain. He still hadn't come down from that experience. It was Lucy Mae who'd had to insist that it was time to go. He'd wanted to stay with her for ever. He'd made love to other girls before, other girls as well as whores, but none had affected him like this. Not one. He was mad for her.

As they rode in, there was old Milly waving to them from the back veranda, calling out that she'd cooked something special for them. Duke wished her to hell. He wanted this new Lucy Mae all to himself. In his bed. In his arms in the mornings.

By the look of Duke – moonstruck he was, Milly thought – she guessed they'd made love. She couldn't detect any difference in Lucy Mae's demeanour, but then Lucy Mae was smart enough not to let on.

That night, to tease Duke, Milly deliberately sat up talking to them until Lucy Mae went to bed, in the bedroom she was sharing with her mother. That would give him something to think about. The next night, though, she retired early with a headache and heard Lucy Mae creep in very late.

The day it rained and the roof leaked, she had the overseer up to fix it, and while he was there, to clean out the flue over the stove because it smoked far too much. She had already enquired about female help around the house and discovered that some of the women from the blacks' camp had worked for the previous owners, but Duke preferred to look after his own house and eat meals prepared for the men by the station cook, who was a Chinaman.

That information told her plenty. That this bachelor had no idea how to keep house, and more importantly that he wasn't given to seducing black gins, as did so many men in his position. There had always been black families living on Kooramin Station, she mused, but obviously Dolour and Eileen had trained him to keep his hands off their women.

She made a point of strolling down to talk to the Chinaman, a simple little fellow who had no interest in discussing cooking with her; instead he waxed on, in his sing-song voice, about the boss being the best horse breaker! 'Win good bets on our boss.'

'Horses?' she asked.

'Yeah. Boss go brumby catching. He busy alla time.'

Milly was pleased to hear that Duke took his work seriously. No wonder the station was doing so well.

'He seems very fond of you,' she commented to Lucy Mae.

'I know.'

'And what about you?'

Lucy Mae shrugged. 'I really don't know him very well. I mean, it's a bit early for serious thought.'

'Good Lord! You realise he owns a third of Kooramin as well as this station. And Valley of Lagoons. That's not bad for a young fellow.'

'And it's not everything. When are we going to visit Oberon?'

'There's no hurry.'

She wished her mother would stop harping on Duke's financial situation. It only served to remind her daughter of her disastrous marriage. But then, given what she stood to inherit one day, Lucy Mae Forrest was a far better catch than Duke MacNamara! And like any other gentleman, Duke would be well aware of that fact. Also, she hadn't forgotten the night he'd left her stranded and embarrassed in the public lounge of the Victoria Hotel.

Now he was telling her he loved her; but there seemed no romance in this relationship, no outward sign that he was fond of her; it appeared to be more of an affair, and that upset her.

Duke had read Milly's shopping and renovation lists with feigned appreciation. She was right, of course: renovations and a lot of paint would make a difference, and finery would make it a home, but he couldn't spare a penny on such things at present. This was a working homestead. It was a wife's duty to tizzy up a house if she so wished.

He dreamed of Lucy Mae as his darling, beloved wife, and fortunately she wasn't impressed by her mother's plans for his house.

'Don't let her bully you into anything,' she said. 'This is your place, Duke. Not hers.'

Relief caused him to love her more. He even managed to interpret that statement as meaning that changes to a household were not the province of a mother-in-law.

When his guests became more accustomed to their surrounds and better able to entertain themselves during the day, Duke spent more time working, coming in dutifully at dusk to find dinner prepared by Lucy Mae. Apparently Milly's enthusiasm as his cook had waned.

Since Sundays were not work days, Duke would take Lucy Mae riding, but this particular morning, with Milly ensconced on the veranda with her needlework, and the horses already saddled, one of the men called that a buggy was coming up the track.

Paul and Laura had come to visit.

Duke had no choice in front of his guests but to greet them cheerily. As Laura jumped down to give all three a hug, she turned to Lucy Mae: 'We wondered if you were still here, and since I haven't had a chance to see Duke's station, here we are!'

'We wouldn't have left without visiting you at Oberon,' Lucy Mae replied, 'but it's so nice to see you. A lovely surprise, isn't it, Duke?'

'It surely is,' he said.

'You've sold quite a few cattle, I hear,' Paul commented as he lifted a picnic basket from the buggy.

'Yes,' Duke replied, refusing to discuss his business with Paul. He pointed to the basket. 'What have you got there?'

'Laura brought some eats.'

'Eats, he says!' Laura pretended displeasure. 'I'll thank you to note we have here cooked poultry and a ham, my best pickles and a sponge cake. And over there in the bag, a hand of bananas. Home-grown.'

'Marvellous,' Milly said. 'Let's have a picnic out under the mango tree.'

'Aren't you going to ask us in?' Paul challenged his brother. 'I could do with a cup of tea.'

'Yes, of course,' Duke said, offering his arm to Laura.

'Are you cross with us?' she whispered.

Duke shrugged, as if he didn't care one way or another.

'Now stop that,' she chided. 'It was my idea. I won't have you two playing no speaks.'

In the end, they did have a pleasant day. After lunch they all strolled around the immediate working areas, stopping to chat with Duke's overseer, who was sitting outside his cottage.

'I never knew you had a brother up here,' he said to Duke, as the others moved on.

'He's over the other side of the river. At Oberon.'

The overseer whistled. 'Oberon? Of course! MacNamara! Jeez! He all right now? He went after those black bastards like the wrath of God.'

'Yes, he's all right,' Duke allowed. It seemed then that the air was clearing between them, until later, when Laura asked Milly, point blank, when she and Lucy Mae were coming to visit.

'You've been here three weeks now. It's our turn.'

'That's so sweet of you, dear, but it's up to Lucy Mae.'

Since when? Lucy Mae asked herself angrily. Milly was deliberately putting her on the spot, wanting her to choose to stay on and make Duke happy. Practically throwing her daughter at him!

They all looked at her.

'Well,' she said, 'we have had a lovely time. This property is superb, everything is so green and grand up here. And Duke has been the perfect host. But we don't want to outstay our welcome, do we, Mother?'

Duke was having trouble keeping up with this conversation. What was Lucy Mae saying? Had? Had a lovely time?

'You haven't outstayed your welcome!' he spluttered. 'You've come so far. You're welcome to stay as long as you like.'

'If you want to take the opportunity to come back with us,' Paul said, 'we can manage that. But if it's a bit sudden, Duke will bring you when you're ready.'

'Yes,' Duke agreed with his brother. 'There's no rush.'

'And by the way!' Paul suddenly remembered something. 'What's this I hear about you courting Beth Delaney? Her dad says you'll be his second son-in-law now that Carmel's engaged.'

He turned back to the others. 'Jack Delaney's got the Turf Club Hotel in town.'

'Delaney's talking through his hat,' Duke snapped.

'Ah, come on now,' Paul laughed. 'Don't be bashful. I was in the hotel last week, and Jack shouted me a glass of his best Irish whiskey on the strength of us "bein' relayted".'

'Oh do tell!' Mrs Forrest chirruped to him, her small eyes cold. 'Why haven't we met Beth?'

'Don't tease him,' Laura smiled. 'All in good time, eh, Duke?'

He ignored that, to ask if she wanted to take some mangoes. 'They're coming to the end of the crop,' he said, 'but they're still good quality.'

'I'd love some,' she said. 'I can make mango jam.'

She went out with him, holding the bucket as he climbed a ladder, handing down ripe mangoes carefully so as not to bruise them.

'Tell Paul to plant some, Laura. They take about seven years to bear fruit, I'm told, but they're worth the effort. And besides, they're attractive trees and give plenty of shade.'

In their absence Milly Forrest had come to a decision. She broke the news to Duke as soon as he walked in the door.

'I hope you won't think we're deserting you, Duke, but you're a busy man, and we can journey out to Oberon in Paul's buggy rather than put you to the trouble, so Lucy Mae's packing. It's been wonderful staying here, and so interesting.'

He was devastated, but since it was obvious that she wouldn't change her mind, he refused to allow it to show.

'I'm sorry you're going,' he said blandly. 'I've greatly enjoyed your company, Mrs Forrest, and Lucy Mae's. The house will be lonely without you.' He sighed. 'I'll have to fall back on Ah Chow's cooking. But if you'll excuse me, I might just see if Lucy Mae needs a hand.'

Duke exited the small parlour feeling as if all three sets of eyes were boring into his back.

The door was open. 'So you're packing?' he said to Lucy Mae.

'Yes. I suppose it's best to go with them while we can. It will save a lot of inconvenience.'

'I would have driven you, whenever you wanted me to.'

She was pushing shoes and slippers into the suitcase. 'I know, Duke. But we wouldn't have been staying much longer. You know that.'

'Why don't you stay? Let your mother go with them.'

'I can't do that.'

'Even if I beg you?' He shouldered into the room and took her in his arms. 'Stay. Just stay and to hell with them!'

'That's impossible. Let me go, Duke.'

He stood back. 'It's because of that Delaney rubbish, isn't it? There was nothing to it, I swear. I took her to a dance, that's all. It's typical of Paul to bring up that stuff to cause trouble.'

'What trouble?' she asked coolly. 'How would Paul know we've been having an affair? You treat me like a stranger, as if you're ashamed of knowing me.'

'An affair? Is that all it was to you? I love you and you call it an affair?'

Automatically he helped her tighten the straps on her suitcase.

'What was it then?' she asked.

'Lucy Mae,' he said quietly, 'you're sulking over Beth Delaney, that's all. If you want to punish me, then go on to Oberon, and write to me when you're feeling happier. I'll come to see you as soon as I hear from you.'

He picked up the two suitcases and took them out into the yard, where the four-seater buggy was waiting.

Dutifully he gave the ladies a hug, shook Paul's hand, listened again to Milly and Lucy Mae's profuse thanks for a lovely holiday and waved them off.

Then he strode back into the house and poured himself a rum and ginger. He was furious with Lucy Mae for deserting him. And hurt that she could do that to him so coolly. Angry with Paul for causing this rift. And angry with bloody Milly Forrest for being such a witch.

He determined never to have her here again.

Days later he received the 'bread and butter' letter from Milly, gushing over with thanks on behalf of herself and Lucy Mae. Not a word from Lucy Mae herself.

Weeks passed. And no letter. Until Laura wrote to tell him that Milly and Lucy Mae were leaving for Brisbane on the *Minerva* on the first of the month and would dearly love to see him before they sailed.

Duke was determined to oblige. He rode into Rockhampton the day before; first stop the barber, where he had his dark hair and beard trimmed. He dropped a parcel of clothes into the Chinese laundry, and then went on to buy shirts, a new pair of swish riding boots and a wide hat befitting his status as a pastoralist.

The next morning, one of Rockhampton's dazzling blue days, the raw heat of summer forgotten, he stepped out along the very smart Quay Street, with a pretty blond girl in a pink and white striped cotton dress and a perky little straw hat. Folk smiled at them as they strolled by, and Duke lifted his hat. They crossed the road and walked along the wharves to where *Minerva* was berthed, and approached the group of four waiting near the gangway.

'Good morning, everyone,' he said with a smile and a stately bow. 'May I introduce Miss Beth Delaney?'

★ ★ ★

That afternoon he borrowed a gig and took Beth driving around Rockhampton She suggested they visit her elderly aunt, who lived high on the range overlooking the town. As the gig slowed to turn into the aunt's driveway, Duke noticed the name H. Merriman burned into a timber board at the entrance to the adjoining block.

Miss Delaney's grand white house had splendid views, but Duke was more interested in her neighbour.

'H. Merriman,' he said. 'Do you know who that is, Miss Delaney?'

'Yes,' she said. 'A young chap. Nice fellow, name of Harry.'

'Is he home?'

'I don't think so, but I wish he would come back. The block is so overgrown, it's a menace.'

'Where's his house?' Beth asked. 'I can't even see a house.'

'Hidden behind all that jungle. He calls it his cottage, built it himself, but it's more of a log cabin.'

'How awful!' Beth said. 'What a cheek, to put a log cabin on this nice street!'

Duke looked at her, surprised. 'What's wrong with that?'

'Nothing,' her aunt said firmly. 'Young fellows have to start somewhere. It took all his savings to buy the block, he told me. And I said not to worry about that because he'd made a good choice. Do you know him, Mr MacNamara?'

'I think so. Fair-haired chap. A stockman, I think. I met him in Brisbane.'

'That'd be him. He's away a lot.'

Duke stared at the lush greenery. 'If that bothers you, Miss Delaney, I'll clear it. I don't think Harry would object.'

'You're very kind! I would appreciate it, because people throw rubbish on unattended blocks, and the undergrowth is a haven for rats and snakes. I've seen a roughscale and a tiger snake near that fence in the last week.'

'Then Mr Merriman should attend to it himself,' Beth snapped. 'Why should you have to do it, Duke?'

Just because I feel like it, Duke said to himself, irritated by her stance.

'It's a small block,' he said. 'It will only take a day or so.'

On the way home he realised he was looking forward to seeing Harry again. It would be good to have a mate up here. He was tiring of women and their bewildering attitudes. Except for dear old Miss Delaney, he decided, having enjoyed the afternoon in her company. She's true blue.

Mrs Otway was waiting at the little railway station with the gig to take Harry and her husband out to DeLisle's Crossing.

'Do call me Annie,' she said to Harry, as soon as she came forward to greet him. 'I'm so, so sorry about Gillie and Hester. It must have been the most awful shock for you, dear. But I'm glad you're here now. And don't forget if there's anything we can do to help, you just let us know. Isn't that right, George?'

He nodded. 'I was worried that you'd come all this way to meet the train yesterday, all for nothing.'

'No, the postmistress told me not to go. She'd heard about the landslides. I guessed they would have been cleared by today, so here I am. And it's a lovely day for a drive, isn't it?'

They climbed into the gig and spun away down the sandy road lined with tall gum trees that Harry knew so well. As kids they used to tramp nine miles from the Crossing to watch the huge steam train come puffing past and wave to their hero, the train driver, and often he'd wave back, causing great excitement to the mites below.

The big corrugated-iron cheese factory was still there, with its large open doors above eye level, where the lorries pulled up and the cheeses and boxes of butter were placed aboard, though it wasn't so big any more, and the produce outlet was a mere hole in the wall.

'Tottie's cooking dinner,' Annie told him over her shoulder, as George slapped the reins and kept the horse at an even pace. He was always a careful driver but Harry felt as if he were being extra careful today; solicitous, so as not to upset this fragile passenger sitting on the half-seat behind them.

Early this morning he'd strolled around the streets of Ipswich, brooding over the reception he was about to receive in the Crossing. People would be feeling sorry for him, for Harry Merriman, who was already feeling a hypocrite in George's company. Then he saw men emerging from their mean little houses with their lunchboxes, heading off on the long hike towards the coal mines, and that shook him. Another legacy of country town lore was a dread of the mines that had lured many young men from the Crossing and sent them back wheezing old fellows with sunken chests and clay pipes.

'It doesn't hurt to remember you've got a good life,' he chastised himself. 'You're not sad about the old people, and yet you're sounding sorry for yourself. Just get on and do what you have to do.'

George took a roundabout route through the village, to acquaint Harry with the new buildings that had sprung up since he'd left, though he felt he already knew every corner of them from Tottie's letters. This detour also made it possible for George to avoid passing the Merriman farm. They didn't stop in the village, but drove straight on to his house, where Tottie's young brother Loftus, grown tall and handsome, was waiting at the gate.

All the way up the drive to the farmhouse, Harry was nervous. What to say to Tottie? What would she think of him now that he'd been away so long? He hadn't made his fortune. He was just a stockman. A bushie. Getting a bit bandy-legged, his mates teased, from too long on horseback . . . and God!

There she was at the door, in a white blouse with puffy sleeves, and a full skirt that swirled as she twisted back to pull off her apron and reappear. She'd said in her letters that she'd grown tall, but she didn't seem so to him. Her coppery hair was longer now, he noticed, tied back in a ponytail.

He was climbing down from the gig, dropping over the high wheels, disappointed that Tottie's hair was tied back, not brushed into shining loose waves the way he'd always imagined it would be when he met her again.

Loftus was speaking to him. Telling him how sorry he was about his mum and dad. Then Tottie took a few steps forward, her hands on her hips.

'Harry Merriman!' she called. 'About time!'

He suddenly knew she was right. It *was* about time! He stood back, laughing as he threw his arms wide and Tottie Otway came running to him! In seconds she was in his arms, being swung about high and low as if she were a child, and they were both laughing until he slowed, and kissed her.

Unabashed, she grabbed his hand and ran with him around the corner of the house until they were out of sight of the family. She had only half turned back to him when he crushed her to him, kissing her long and passionately, as if to make up for lost time.

'Thank you, God,' Tottie whispered as she popped into bed that night.

God was kind after all, she supposed, but a bit hard on Gillie and Hester. Though you couldn't count Hester as His fault, since she'd drowned herself.

Tottie had prayed like mad from the minute her father had threatened to write to Harry Merriman and ask him his intentions as regarded his daughter. It was all because she refused to entertain suitors, even though one of them was a nice chap and a good dancer, and Manny Forsyth had good prospects.

'Darling,' her mother had said, 'you haven't seen Harry for nearly ten years.'

'Nine.'

'Has he once, in all those years, mentioned marriage in his letters?'

'No.'

'Or said that he loves you?'

'No.'

'Well, Tottie, you have to get on with your life. What will you do if he writes and tells you, one of these days, that he is married?'

'Then I'll be an old maid,' she grinned, 'and you'll have someone to look after you in your old age. I don't know what you're complaining about.'

Many a time Tottie had thought of telling Harry that she loved him, of writing that to him in plain English, but she was inclined to think that girls who actually said that to boys scared them off. And she didn't want to scare Harry off. God, no!

But if his parents hadn't gone to God, would he have been back in town now? She didn't think so. That letter her father had written, finally, inviting him to visit them had really upset her.

'What did you do that for?' she'd shouted at him. 'How dare you do that? Are you sure you didn't send him that stupid ultimatum you were threatening? Making a fool of me!'

'I told you I did not. I simply invited him to visit.'

'Well he hasn't answered, has he? And he won't answer now, because you're trying to push him into a corner.'

It wasn't just that, Tottie knew. Never once, in all the years, had he enquired about his parents. Not once. But she'd often mentioned them to let him know they were all right. And never once did he ever say he was coming back to this village, though she'd scrutinised his letters looking for a sign. She'd kept all his letters in neat boxes; travel talks she used to say they were, of all the strange places he'd lived and worked up north. While hers, she often pondered, could be held up as a history of DeLisle's Crossing, they were so boring. She wondered if he'd kept them, but didn't dare ask.

Then came the time when he wrote, casually, that he had a cottage in Rockhampton, and that had sent her scurrying for the battered map to search out the river town that sat tantalisingly along the Tropic of Capricorn.

Her heart sank when she located it. Sank right down to her boots. It was so far away, he might never come home. Then she didn't hear from him for ages after that, absolute ages, while she pictured him with a blank-faced bride in front of the prettiest little cottage you ever saw, with garlands of roses over the door.

But now he was home, and he had a farm right next door.

Tottie reminded herself to say a prayer for Gillie and Hester.

That first night, Harry walked across the fields to the house alone. He'd told them he'd preferred to go alone. To the place he was still unable to call home.

He was thirteen again, stepping easily over the stile, with a canvas carrybag thrown over his shoulder, cutting across to the back paddock where a nervous horse whinnied and sidled over to him, looking for company. He patted it, said a few words and moved on, vaulting the gate, pleased with himself . . . He couldn't do that before!

Come to think of it, he laughed, rattling matches in his pocket, there are a lot of things you can do now you couldn't do before, like marching into that house unafraid. You were kidding yourself that you weren't afraid of Gillie! You were scared stiff of him, from when you were a little nipper and he booted you across the kitchen, bang into that bag of apples!

George had told him that the neighbours had pitched in after Hester's funeral, taking care of the farm while they waited to locate him.

'You know,' he said sadly, 'milking the cows, feeding the horse and the rest of it.' Harry was grateful for their kindness.

'The ladies kept the house nice inside,' he'd added. 'But Annie said they only needed to dust. Your mum left the place as neat as a new pin.'

Harry had nodded. 'Yes.'

He shrugged as he lit the lamp on the kitchen table and looked about him. Then he picked up the lamp and explored the house. Nothing seemed to have changed except his room, the sleepout as it was known, tacked on the back of the house. It was now an extra pantry for shelves of preserves, and bins of pumpkins, potatoes and other vegetables that they'd never share with anyone. They'd rot first. He remembered the sour smell of rotting potatoes that he'd have to pick out of the bin.

'So,' he said. 'That's that.'

He slept on the hard couch, fully clothed. He wanted no part of this house, but knew he'd have to stay here and maintain the farm until he could find a buyer.

In the morning he found the papers he needed in the dresser drawers where they were always kept. The deeds to the farm, in Gillie's name. His bankbook, receipts, old letters, council notices, even their marriage certificate were all there. But no wills. Neither of them had left a will. Which suited their son just fine.

He stripped off his good clothes, found some old overalls hanging on a nail by the back steps, pulled them on and headed for the far paddock, where he called: 'C'mo-on, c'mo-on,' in the same old way, and the cows, though they knew him not, responded. They trundled down to the rough log cowshed to wait their turn in the bails, while Harry found a scrubbed milk bucket, exactly where he knew it would be.

His work day had begun.

At midday he saddled the horse and rode in to the Crossing, where he found a lawyer new to the town and handed over the deeds to the Merriman farm.

'My father died intestate, as far as I know,' he explained. 'You probably know that my mother subsequently passed on, but she didn't leave a note, I'm told, and I don't believe she wrote a will either. I'm the only child of that union. I want the farm registered in my name as soon as possible. Can you do that for me?'

The lawyer, by name Jules Fountain, agreed, but warned it would take some time.

'That's a bad start,' Harry said. 'You're telling me I shouldn't have any faith in your ability to do a simple job.'

'It's not that simple, sir. I mean . . . no wills . . .'

'Listen, mate, you know and I know that I could do this without a lawyer, but I haven't got the time. It's only paperwork. I want you to get started today. Is that possible?'

191

'Yes. I suppose so.'

'Good. I'll be at the farm. Let me know how you're progressing.'

Next he was to be found in the pub, having a drink with a school friend who now worked in his father's real estate office.

'I'm a customer, Robbie,' he said, after the usual condolences had been offered. 'I want you to sell the farm for me.'

Robbie was surprised. 'We thought you'd be staying now, Harry. I mean it's a good farm, that. And you could do a lot more with it, a young bloke like you.'

'Why don't you buy it then?'

'Because I'm not a farmer, mate.'

'Neither am I.'

'What are you gonna do then?'

'Run cattle. A lot of cattle. But listen, where can I get a feed? Does this pub serve meals?'

'Only six to seven on Saturday nights. I'm going home for lunch; you might as well come with me. My mum'll be pleased to see you.'

Come midday, Tottie rode over to the Merriman farm with a picnic lunch for Harry. When she realised that neither Gille's horse nor Harry was home, she sat red-faced on the back step, the basket at her feet.

Her mother had told her not to bother him so soon, but she hadn't listened. She loved Harry and he loved her, though he had not actually said so. In fact, she was rather surprised that he hadn't come for her first thing. How could he not want to be with her every minute now?

'Let him settle in,' Annie had said. 'It's a terrible thing has happened to the lad. He's got his mourning to do. And he'll surely want to go to the church and visit their graves.'

After a while Tottie worked out that she was probably right, but he could have taken her with him. For comfort. For company.

Eventually she unpacked the basket in his kitchen, and went on home armed with a reason for his absence from the farm.

'He must have gone to visit their graves.'

Later in the afternoon he did come to call, and sat in the shade of the sycamore tree talking to her about this and that: the picnic lunch, for which he thanked her, saying he was pleased to have a ready-made supper awaiting him now; and the town; and her brother Loftus, who was leaving soon to take up a position as a clerk in a lawyer's office in Ipswich.

Eventually he had to go. He kissed her, waved to her mother, who was bringing in the washing, it being Monday, and left. No arrangement to see her on the morrow, she reflected miserably, or any other day.

Next day he was in town again, she soon heard, to buy supplies and see Jules

Fountain about his father's estate. He also called on the Reverend Trenmell. But he didn't call on Tottie.

'I don't think he really cares for me at all,' she complained to her mother, who said: 'For goodness' sake, girl! Give him time to breathe! Get it through your head that men have business matters to attend to! Stop sitting whining like Little Miss Muffet and make yourself useful. The stove could do with a good scrub.'

Never in her life had Tottie felt so insecure. It was a horrible feeling to be fretting like this. Several times in the week that Harry had been back in town she'd almost burst into tears without warning, she was so emotionally fraught.

Then came Sunday.

Her father had asked him if he'd like to come to church with them, in the gig, explaining that there would be room as Loftus preferred to ride. He'd felt that the Otway family should accompany him.

'Sort of moral support,' he'd said. But Harry had declined.

'Thanks all the same, George, but don't worry about me.'

'Whatever that meant,' Tottie said peevishly, and Loftus laughed.

'She's got it bad, hasn't she? Well you better get a move on, sis. He's selling the farm.'

'Who is?' Annie Otway was startled.

'Harry, of course! He told Robbie Phelan to find him a buyer. And you know what else they're saying in town. He's never been near old Gillie's grave, or his mum's.'

'You shouldn't say things like that, Loftus,' Annie said. 'They told me in the store that he's already been to see Reverend Trenmell about them.'

'Yeah. About them. He's chasing up the death certificates, because Jules Fountain couldn't find them. Turns out Harry located them himself. Dr Bunce gave them to the reverend to fill in the church records, and forgot about them. They say Jules got a real earful from Harry about it.'

'Why?' Annie asked. 'Why does Harry need them?'

'So he can claim ownership of the farm, which is still in Gillie's name. Neither of his parents left wills, so he has to produce the death certificates and his birth certificate for the government department to prove he is who he says he is.'

'What a lot of rigmarole,' Annie said. 'Everyone knows that's Harry's farm now.'

She walked away, knowing full well that Gilbert Merriman had left a will. She'd seen it with her own eyes, in the dresser drawer in his kitchen, with a lot of other papers, when she was looking for Hester's birth certificate to give to the mortician. She hadn't found the birth certificate but she had seen that will. She couldn't have missed it. If it had been a dog it'd have bitten her.

It was in a small square envelope with the words, in Gillie's stiff and purposeful handwriting: *This here's the last will of Gilbert Merriman.*

Curiosity it was that had her pluck it out of the drawer by her fingertips, and spirit it into her pocket in case someone walked into the house and caught her with it. Once she'd made sure she was alone in the quiet house, she took it out and stared at it. Disappointed. It was sealed; dried traces of clag flaking from the back of the envelope.

But, she reminded herself, steam from a kettle would soon fix that.

What kettle? She could hardly light the stove in this house.

Minutes later Annie was walking swiftly back home. She only wanted a peep, she kept telling herself. No one need know. There was no one home. Open it while it was damp. Carefully. Read it. Then trot back, innocent as you like, and stuff it back in the drawer.

At any rate, she reasoned as she waited for her kettle to boil, she ought to look at what old Gillie'd had to say; her daughter Tottie could have a stake in this. Hadn't George gone to Brisbane to bring her boyfriend home, Gillie's son? There was every chance that stubborn Tottie would end up marrying him.

She clucked her approval as she held the envelope over the steam, which soon began to dampen the cheap paper. Quickly she transferred it to the table, laid it flat and delicately opened the flap. While she waited for it to dry, she mixed a teaspoon of flour with a few drops of water to make clag, so that she could reseal the letter.

And there it was. The date, five years ago. Gillie had written: *To who it may concern. I, Gilbert Merriman, do hereby leave this farm and all my goods and chattels to my wife, Hester Merriman.*

That was all. How boring.

'He always was a man of few words,' Annie shrugged as she folded the thin page back into the dry envelope. 'And the old villain! Not a penny to his son. Leaving her the lot!'

But now she was gone, and Harry was the son and heir. The only beneficiary.

Or was he? This will showed Gillie hadn't meant Harry to get a bean. And Hester hadn't bothered to leave a will at all. Probably of the same mind, since Harry had run away from them.

'We'll see about that,' Annie Otway said stoutly.

She hooked the small stove door open and pushed Gillie's last will and testament into the fire. It burned in seconds.

Harry did not attend church on Sunday; he was too busy trying not to be a farmer. He'd milked the cows, fed the horse and the chooks and collected the eggs. Now he was faced with an over-supply of produce, as well as a maize crop ready to be harvested.

He decided to sell the cows and give the chooks to Annie Otway, and before he left he'd sell the horse.

All of this stuff was minor, though, compared with his worry about Tottie. He was amazed that he'd taken one look at her and fallen madly in love with her. So much for the years of simple friendship. Overturned in a glance! But what to do about her? Harry knew her so well, he was very much aware that she needed him to declare his love for her. Put her heart at ease, because she had stars in her eyes for him.

Then what?

The Otways were already regarding him as their neighbour. And Tottie's future husband, he had no doubt. And their expectations were fair and sensible, except that he had his dream. To run cattle. The last thing he could ever be persuaded to do was settle down on this farm. He hated every minute living under their roof. He still slept on the couch. All their things were still here. The wardrobe with their clothes. Her linen. Boxes of combs and hairclips and collar studs. All here, waiting for someone to do something about them.

Maybe he could explain that quietly to George.

'Yes,' he muttered, 'and have George suggest that if I feel that way, I should sell. There are other good farms in the district I could buy with the money from the sale of this place.'

That was another thing. He had planned to return to Cameo Downs and work for Palliser so that he could keep a wage coming in, and stick with the Palliser outfit when they went back to the Thomson River district.

But once he sold this farm, he'd have enough to strike out there with his own cattle. More than enough. And the sooner the better; he wasn't the only one chasing great stretches of free land.

He had gone out to the barn to find a ladder so that he could block up a hole where possums were getting into the roof, feeling a little smug about the extra funds that were about to drop into his lap, when Tottie came around the side of the house. She looked a picture in her Sunday best, her straw hat lit with daisies.

Delighted to see her, Harry dropped the ladder. 'What a pleasant surprise.'

He went to kiss her, but she pulled away.

'I'm sorry, Tottie. I forgot I was in these work clothes. I don't want to get your dress dirty.'

'Are you selling the farm?' she asked angrily.

Taken aback by her tone, he stared at her. 'What?'

'I asked you a simple question. Are you selling the farm?'

'Yes,' he gulped.

'You really are? You're selling?'

He nodded. 'Yes. Come inside and we'll talk about it. Just wait until I wash my hands.'

They sat at the kitchen table, Tottie still angry, refusing to let him touch her; refusing even a glass of water.

'No, I don't want a drink of water, thank you. In fact I don't know why I'm even here. You must be busy packing up.'

He shook his head. 'Don't carry on so, Tottie. You know I wouldn't live in this house. You must know that. So why are you upset?'

'Because I need to know, that's all,' she said, a flush creeping across her cheeks. 'So you sell the farm. Then what?'

'Then we'll have to talk, won't we?'

'What about?'

'All right. Let me explain. When I sell here I'm going back to north Queensland. How do you feel about that?'

Her eyes flashed, the anger returning. 'What's it got to do with me?'

Harry sighed and leaned across the table to take her hands in his. 'Everything, Tottie dear. Because I wanted to ask you to marry me, but first you have to consider the fact that I'm not staying here.'

A smile crept into her eyes. 'Are you asking me to marry you or not, Harry Merriman?'

'Well yes, but . . .'

She pushed the chair back and stood up. 'Would you do me a favour?'

'Of course, what is it?'

'Ask the question and then we'll talk about it!'

He took her in his arms, and the question became muddled in the passion of the moment, and then the excitement that they were to be married. She stayed with him for the rest of the day, and they both laughed that there hadn't been much talking after all, when they set off at dusk to take the good news to her parents.

'I had a notion that this was on the cards,' George said when Harry asked for his daughter's hand in marriage, 'and I couldn't be more pleased. Let me congratulate you both.' He shook hands with Harry and kissed his daughter.

'My turn,' Annie said tearfully, hugging them both. 'I'm so happy, I can hardly speak.'

Tottie hoped that Harry would leave it at that for the time being, but trust him to want to bring his plans out in the open.

'So there's no misunderstanding,' he told them, 'I love Tottie, I always have, and I want her to come north with me.'

'North?' Annie cried. 'Why in heaven's name would you want to do that? We heard you're selling the farm . . .'

'Not a good time to sell,' George said.

'. . . but you can buy another one here. I mean, how lucky are you two, just a young couple, to get such a good start in life!'

Fortunately Harry kept calm while he was forced to explain his plans step by step, and no one seemed to notice that Tottie wasn't taking any part in it.

For Tottie had her own dreams. All these years she'd had to sit in this staid little village, going about the daily drudge, struggling to find something interesting to write about, while his letters were full of excitement. His was the big country life, distance counted in hundreds of miles, not fives, or even tens; his bosses didn't have ten cows, they had thousands. He spoke of bulls that weighed a ton, and steers and bullocks and wild horses, and all the various camps he knew along the tracks; and of wild weather, of hurricanes, and floods that were regarded as a blessing; and of birds by the thousands, and the colour . . . the colour!

Tottie wanted to see this world, be part of it. They called it a man's world out there but it wasn't true. She'd seen pictures of outback women; read their stories; was entranced that they led tough lives and were proud of their achievements. Pick up any newspaper and you could read about pioneer women blazing trails, with their men, across the north and the far west of the country, but Harry's letters were living proof that folk like that enjoyed the paths they'd chosen to take. Look at him! He couldn't get back there fast enough. All this talk about land grabs was only part of it . . .

'You're very quiet, miss!' her mother said, as she heard George ask Harry, her fiancé, if this plan to move north was some sort of ultimatum.

'What do you mean?' Tottie flared.

'We were saying, what if *you* would rather settle down here?' Annie told her.

'But I wouldn't rather settle down here. I want to go with Harry. I was frightened he'd sell up and leave without me.'

'You realise what sort of country Harry has in mind?' her mother reminded her. 'It's blackfellow country, for God's sake. It's dangerous!'

'I want you to be very sure,' Harry added, and Tottie was afraid that they'd persuade him to stay here in DeLisle's Crossing, and live a safe and boring life and he'd never forgive her.

'But where Harry's taking me won't be dangerous. He's got a cottage in Rockhampton. I thought we could live there. I would be safe there while he's off chasing cattle.'

In the end her plan prevailed, and Annie switched to talking about the wedding while George and Harry had a couple of whiskies to celebrate.

Later, though, Harry wasn't so sure about leaving Tottie alone for months in the Rockhampton cottage, which he now admitted was only a one-room cabin. With a view.

'What was your alternative?' she asked him. 'Did you think you could marry me and leave me here?'

'That was the problem,' he said. 'I couldn't figure out what to do.'

'Then don't worry about it, love,' she told him sweetly. 'Let's just say we'll have our base in Rockhampton. It'll be wonderful.'

The world was opening up for Tottie at last; the tall, coppery-haired girl who'd never even travelled as far as the bright lights of Brisbane.

Dr Charlie Palliser had disapproved of the whole exercise, right from the start, but these people, these aristocratic Heselwoods, had overridden his advice at every turn.

In the first place he'd allowed that Lady Georgina could be taken from hospital to the house, on the condition that a competent sling could be arranged to rest her leg, now reset. But before she had even left hospital, the fuss started about her being homesick, and wanting to return to her Sydney home overlooking the harbour.

'It's in Point Piper,' Rosa told him. 'Apparently it was originally the home of Captain Piper; a wonderful house I believe.'

That information, he recalled sourly, had no bearing on the situation that was unfolding before his eyes. Lady Heselwood wished to return home, so her husband and son had devised this preposterous plan to do just that.

'I don't believe moving our patient is in her best interests,' he'd said to them. 'She should be in traction.'

'My father can arrange that as soon as he takes her home, Doctor,' Edward Heselwood said to him, dismissing his concerns. 'And he'll call in a Sydney specialist to make certain the apparatus is correctly fitted. So don't worry, we'll take excellent care of her.'

It occurred to Charlie that young Heselwood was as anxious to get the hell away from this lonely outpost as was his mother.

'I really do believe . . .' he began, but Edward cut him short.

'Doctor. If you please, try not to be so negative; you'll worry Lady Heselwood.'

But the plan didn't work so smoothly for Edward either, since his father had decreed that he return to Montone and learn about the cattle business. Not that Charlie cared one way or another; he could only hover about on the outskirts of Heselwood's entourage until all were safely settled aboard ship.

The patient had refused to admit she was suffering any pain as she was being transported to Maryborough, though Charlie was certain that only divine intervention could have made that statement a truth.

As they sailed south, Rosa had been such a great help to Lady Heselwood that Charlie was proud of her. No personal maid could have done a better job of caring for the lady through the difficulties the patient encountered in the small cabin. She dressed the woman, bathed her, attended to her every need.

'Rosa is such a darling girl,' Lady Heselwood said to him. 'So very patient with me.'

'I'm glad she could be of assistance,' he said, relieved that they were only a few hours from docking in Brisbane and that his responsibility for the woman's well-being could be handed back to her husband.

'I don't know what I should have done without her,' Lady Heselwood continued, as she lay back on her bunk, the bulky leg raised on pillows and hidden under a blanket. 'Which is why I wanted to ask you if you could consider allowing Rosa to come on with me to Sydney. I really do need her, and she tells me she's willing to look after me for the rest of the voyage, if you have no objections.'

She put the question so sweetly, so suddenly, that Charlie was caught off guard. Caught napping, he told himself angrily, when he was unable to ferret out a viable excuse. Hindsight chastised him for not offering to find a qualified nurse to travel with her. Too late, of course.

He went in search of Rosa, who was on deck chatting to his lordship, forcing his anger to tap its toe while waiting for an opportunity to raise the matter with his wife. They were discussing the high hills surrounding Brisbane, trying to count them, and likening the town to Rome and its seven hills, which annoyed Charlie, since this pair were obviously familiar with Rome and he'd never been to Europe.

'How many hills can you name?' Rosa asked him.

'About four,' he snapped. 'I was looking for my panama hat, Rosa. Have you seen it?'

'Isn't it in the cabin?'

His aggravated sigh signalled to her that it might be a good idea for her to help him.

'Righto,' she laughed. 'I shall instigate a search for your hat. And when I find it, Charlie, you have to name five of those hills.'

They were barely in their cabin when he turned on her: 'How dare you arrange to go on to Sydney without consulting me!'

'I haven't. I had every intention of asking you if you'd mind. Georgina does need me.'

'Oh, it's Georgina now, is it? And is he Jasin?'

'Don't be silly. I don't have to wash him and do his hair. Really, Charlie, what's got into you?'

'You're the one being silly. Your patient asked me if you could accompany her to Sydney, leaving me no option, as a gentleman, but to approve, since you two had already discussed it.'

She sat on the hard bunk. 'Your hat is on the hook there.'

'So what am I supposed to do when this ship berths? Just make myself scarce?'

'If you don't want me to go with them, say so. I'll simply say it's not convenient; they wouldn't expect an explanation.'

'I see. And then Dr Palliser gets blamed for leaving his patient in the lurch?'

'Up to you,' she shrugged.

'It is not! You've left me with no choice!'

'You do have a choice, darling. Why don't you come too? We'll both go to Sydney.'

'I was not invited!' he huffed.

'You don't have to be! You're her doctor!'

'Does it occur to you that I am a busy person? I have patients waiting. I've been away too long as it is. My career doesn't seem to mean a thing to you. You're always wanting to go off somewhere. Only two months ago we spent a week at the seaside.'

'And it was heaven,' she said. 'We ought to go there every year.'

She took his arm and kissed him. 'Don't get angry with me. I'm sorry, but I really do believe Lady Georgina needs me. She isn't accustomed to such handicaps and she gets very depressed. Besides, it makes me feel useful.'

'Stop making excuses. You're going to Sydney! Very well! I'd appreciate it if you could find time to pack my bag, since I shall be disembarking alone.'

Charlie knew she was often bored, especially when he was late home. The solution was obvious. Babies! And the sooner the better. Unfortunately, though they'd been married for four years now and their sex life was satisfactory, they were still childless. He had discussed the matter with the senior medical doctor at the hospital, who was unable to offer a solution, beyond laughingly suggesting that Charlie should add stout and oysters to his daily diet.

He did not find that amusing; nor was he impressed by his father-in-law's oft-repeated questions as to when he would provide him with a grandson. As if Rivadavia could talk, Charlie mused. He was hardly a role model. He only had the one child. As far as is known, he added meanly.

It grated on Charlie that those men seemed to imply that it was his fault. He wished Rosa was more like Langley's wife, Gracie. Married six years, four kids. She was content to live out in the wilds of north Queensland, wherever her husband put down stakes. He couldn't imagine Gracie being bored.

When the ship brought them back into Brisbane, there was an excited reporter from the *Courier* waiting to interview Lord and Lady Heselwood.

'I wonder if I could have a word, your lordship,' he called as soon as Jasin stepped ashore.

'What about?'

'I believe your wife had an accident in Gympie, sir?'

'Her ladyship suffered a mishap. Yes.'

Rosa was next down the narrow gangway, with Charlie following.

As Heselwood turned to hand her on to solid ground, the reporter dashed up to her.

'Are you all right now, Lady Heselwood?'

Rosa stared. 'I beg your pardon!'

'This is not Lady Heselwood,' her husband snapped from over her shoulder. 'How dare you accost my wife?'

'Ah! Sorry!' the reporter said, unperturbed. 'You're Dr Palliser, aren't you? We heard you and your wife were aboard too. All travelling together?'

'Yes.'

'And Lady Heselwood?'

'Her ladyship is not coming ashore.'

'Why is that?'

Heselwood interrupted. 'Because it doesn't suit her.' He shook Charlie's hand, and thanked him for his wonderful care. 'And don't worry, we'll look after your wife.' He dashed back on board to escape the reporter, who picked up on that remark.

'Are you travelling on, Mrs Palliser?' he asked her quickly.

'Why yes,' Rosa said. 'Yes.'

'To Sydney?'

'Yes.'

'And you're not, Dr Palliser?'

'I don't have the time. Would you please excuse us? Good day to you.'

He pushed him away from Rosa. 'Damned impertinence! You wait here with the luggage. I'll call a hansom cab.'

She was still waiting when the reporter approached again. 'Are you staying in Brisbane after all, Mrs Palliser?'

'No. I have a few hours before sailing time to reconstruct my wardrobe,' she said cheerfully. 'My husband's calling a hansom cab.'

'Oh dear. It's race day. You may have to wait a while. Would you mind if this gentleman took a photograph of you for the paper? It's not often he finds such a beautiful subject.'

'That's true,' the photographer called as he set up his camera. 'Head high, my dear! That's right! Lovely, just lovely! If only I could depict you in colour.'

Charlie returned as the two men from the *Brisbane Courier* were walking away.

'Don't tell me you let that fellow with the camera take your photograph, Rosa!'

'Why not? It's fun. You must watch for it in the paper.'

'You seem to have no sense of propriety at times. I've told you before that it's just not done in polite circles to have your picture in a newspaper. You could take a lead from the Heselwoods on that. Believe me.'

★   ★   ★

201

Milly Forrest saw the portrait of Rosa in the *Courier* and thought she looked truly gorgeous, with her thick hair looped in a shining mass under a pretty little chapeau, but she was more interested in the article that accompanied it.

She learned that Lady Georgina Heselwood had suffered a mishap, believed to be a broken leg, and was now returning to Sydney aboard the good ship *Periclese*, accompanied by her husband and a friend, Mrs Charlie Palliser.

'Oho!' she called to Lucy Mae. 'Come and look at this.'

Lucy Mae peered over her shoulder. 'How does she get to look so good in photographs?'

'But where is Dr Palliser?' Milly brayed. 'That's a nice threesome, with Georgina laid up and Heselwood forced to endure the company of a beautiful girl like Rosa! He'll be in his element.'

'Why? Is he a flirt?'

'Yes, she'd better watch out. I didn't know she even knew the Heselwoods. Her father wouldn't have Jasin in the house.'

'Seems to me it's Dr Palliser who ought to watch out. Some men don't appreciate their wives until it's too late.'

It's the same with Duke MacNamara, Lucy Mae said to herself as she left her mother with the paper. He didn't fool me with that cheap little floozy he brought down to the ship. That was to punish me for walking out on him. He has a lot to learn. I think it's time to write to him now. He said he loved me, and I believe he does, but on his terms . . . which are not good enough.

She wandered into the garden, looking out over the wide Brisbane River.

I can't allow myself to make a mistake a second time, she reflected, finding it interesting that she'd changed her attitude of late. Where previously she'd been hell-bent on remarrying, to have her own home and family, now she was more cautious. I could love Duke, if he'd let me. I could be very happy with him. At least I know him. Russ Bartling was a stranger to me and it was hell discovering who and what he was. That was where I took the wrong path.

'And anyway,' she said to a magpie picking at the grass by her feet, 'if that turns out to have been just an affair with Duke, then that's all right too, bird. I feel freer. Happier now. It was a jolly good holiday after all.'

Lucy Mae would have been delighted to hear the latest gossip: that Beth Delaney had a new boyfriend, a captain in the Queensland Volunteer Corps, now based in Rockhampton. Duke, however, was not at all pleased about it.

When he confronted Beth, she was forthright about her change of heart.

'He treats me better than you do, Duke. He brings me presents and chocs, and he says if I marry him he'll buy me a pearl ring. I always wanted a pearl ring.'

'Ah, is that how things stand? I didn't know you could be bought for a few cheap trinkets.'

Beth's right hand flew. She slapped him hard across the face.

'And another thing,' she said, before he had a chance to recover. 'I wouldn't be walking out with you again; you're too bold for the company of a decent girl.'

He had started clearing Harry Merriman's block, tearing away at the tangled undergrowth, some of it waist-high, that would be a fire risk in the dry season, and as he worked he chewed over Beth's unfair accusations, deciding she wasn't worth worrying about.

Nevertheless, anger at being treated like that sent him slashing at the weeds and vines at such a fast rate, a corner of the block was starting to look presentable. Once he'd hacked away the thick vines that had overwhelmed tall trees, allowing more light on the lower levels, he discovered some superb tree-ferns, with their bright green crowns, and other varieties of fern he hadn't known existed, as well as palms and grevilleas and, on the forest floor, a host of delicate flowers.

Miss Delaney, hobbling along with the aid of a walking stick, came by to compliment him on his hard work. Duke was embarrassed by his sweaty appearance, and by the fact that her niece had dumped him, but she didn't seem concerned.

'Will you clear a path?' she asked.

'I think not. I don't know where he would want to place it, but once I get all this rubbish out of the way, he'll have a better chance to work out which trees he wants to keep. There are even banana trees hidden away in here, you know.'

'Yes, and thorn trees and stinging nettles!'

'I've found them,' he said ruefully. 'But it's not so bad. Some of the vines have even started overgrowing the cabin. I don't suppose you've heard anything from Harry?'

'No, I'm afraid not. Would you care for a cup of tea?'

'No thanks, Miss Delaney. I'll keep going here.'

For a while yet, he added to himself. It's damn hot work. Then I think I'll shout myself a room at the Criterion, since Delaney's hotel is out of bounds.

There was no point in looking out for Harry as yet, for the would-be cattle man was busy that day. The day of his wedding.

Harry and his beloved Tottie were married by the Reverend Trenmell in the little church at DeLisle's Crossing. His best man was Loftus Otway and the groomsman was Robbie Phelan, whose mother played the organ.

After so many years on his own, Harry almost wept at the warmth and friendship extended to him that day, when half the folk in his home town turned out to see them happily wed, and throw rice as they emerged from the church. So much so that for the first time, his determination to leave the Crossing wavered.

He looked down at Tottie, who was so beautiful in a flurry of white lace; at her trusting smile, and the tableau of two maids in blue beside her. And there, in front, were Annie and George, oozing happiness, and Mr Buschell, who'd ridden over to the Crossing especially to wish him well. And a sea of familiar faces.

He seemed to be floating in that sea, to be carried away into an orderly world, where everything was in place behind neat hedges; where farmers slept in their beds; where their women were houseproud and the kids walked to school.

At the wedding breakfast, when it came time for the groom to speak, he looked at all these people, saw how secure they were, in themselves and their futures, and wondered what he could have been thinking to toss all this away. To walk into that furnace of the far north, into such privation, such dangers that these people could not even imagine, when he didn't have to! He could stay here and . . .

'I've been thinking,' he said to them, 'what a nice place this is. And how fortunate I was to grow up here, but after I left, I missed Antonia.' He looked at her fondly and she squeezed his hand. 'Through her letters, she came to be my anchor. No matter how far I travelled, she was always there. My backstop. And when I came back and saw what a beautiful woman she'd grown into, I reckoned I'd got back just in time. Before someone took her from me.'

His audience laughed.

'That's why I've been thinking . . .' He was beginning to ramble. Stalling. Trying to tell them that he'd decided they should settle here, but the words wouldn't come out. A voice kept telling him that wedding days were not real. This gathering was not reality. DeLisle's Crossing was only an enclave, a ghetto where people knew that a child among them was being beaten, ill treated, tyrannised by sadistic parents, but did nothing. Nothing! Because they didn't want to upset their applecart of a village. Because they were cowards.

'What were you thinking?' someone called.

'You're a pack of bastards,' Harry's inner voice prompted, but he said, 'It's time to go,' and sat down before that almost forgotten rage flared again and he embarrassed his wife.

George Otway saw, only fleetingly, a hard, cold expression on Harry's face, and the determined jut of his jaw, before he dropped whatever he'd meant to say and resumed his seat at the bridal table.

It worried George. He wondered if any of them really knew who Harry Merriman was. But he was consoled by one thought. The man did love his daughter. Of that he had no doubt.

★ ★ ★

The book work, as Harry called it, was taking time. A sister of the late Hester Merriman laid claim to a share in her estate.

'I think it might be a good idea to pay her a small amount to facilitate the settling of the estate,' Harry's lawyer, Jules Fountain, suggested.

'Not one penny,' Harry growled. 'I wouldn't piss on her if she was on fire.'

Fountain was startled. 'Really, Mr Merriman! I hardly think that's called for.'

'Just so's you get the message. Not a penny.'

'We might have to go to court.'

'Then we go to court.'

The newlyweds moved into the Merriman farm, annoyed that they were not able to sell as yet. Instead they had to submit an inventory of the property and contents to the lawyers.

Eventually, though, after a harrowing six weeks, the law deemed that Gilbert Merriman had died intestate, and it was reasonable to accept that he would have left the farm and contents to his wife and only son, and not to his sister-in-law, since he was known to have had a pronounced dislike of that woman. That meant that this discussion now centred on only a half-share of the property, that belonging to Hester Merriman, since her son already owned the other half. It followed then that Hester, also dying intestate, would have left her share to her son.

His sister protested that had Hester written a will after Gilbert's death, she would never have bequeathed the farm to a son she hadn't seen or heard from in years. It was Jules Fountain who pointed out that had Hester written a will at that particular time, when she was suicidal, she could not possibly have been deemed 'of sound mind'.

The application for ownership of the Merriman estate was duly allowed to Harold Merriman, and the sale went through the following day.

At this time Harry's pal Marcus Beresford was about fifty miles south of Rockhampton, caught in a narrow gorge, under attack by rock-throwing blacks.

The Native Police recruits were sheltering in a cave with him, while their sergeant, felled by a rain of rocks, was lying beside a pleasant little stream bubbling with fish. It had seemed an ideal camping spot the previous night.

From his position among some boulders, Edward could hear Marcus roaring at his men to get out there and bring the sergeant in! Only minutes before the attack, Edward had been standing beside Sergeant Wiley as he leaned down to fill their water bottles.

'Look out!' he'd yelled, when the first rocks came crashing down, instantly racing for safety, believing this was a small landslide, but the sergeant, facing the water, had been slower off the mark.

Eventually two of the troopers scrambled out, running barefoot; no boots had been issued to them. Or guns, Edward sighed, thinking they could have been handy now. But only the two blackfellows guarding the horses had guns.

Another hail of rocks greeted the troopers, who turned tail and raced back to the cave.

Beresford appeared and began shooting at the heights, to give the impression of cover, because at that angle he wasn't likely to hit anyone. He could be heard furiously urging the men out again, but there seemed to be no takers.

Edward, hidden among a mass of boulders on the floor of the gorge, was in a better position to shoot at the attackers, but of course his firearm, one of his father's finest, was in that cave with the rest of their equipment. He saw the sergeant's arm move and was relieved that he was still alive, but now blood was seeping into the stream.

Edward rubbed his eyes. Strong yellow light from the western sun was bouncing off the tall walls above the cave to his right, but the other side of the gorge was black with shadow. He thought he saw movement there, and held his breath as his eyes fought for clarity. Someone was definitely moving in the shadows; he squinted to accustom his eyes to the darkness, certain that he could make out a moving form, possibly one of the blacks creeping forward.

Just then the form materialised, slinking into the light, and Edward gasped with relief. It was only a dog. For a few seconds he remained still, panting to gain his breath again, until he realised his mistake. He glimpsed the animal moving furtively between scattered rocks, in the direction of the sergeant. And knew the danger.

'Marcus!' he shouted. 'Dingo!' his voice clanging about, echoing as if he were inside a church bell.

The rock throwing had stopped. All was quiet. They too were watching, without pity for the helpless man by the stream.

'Dingo!' Edward shouted again.

Then a shot rang out. The dingo yelped, stumbled, and fell into the stream, its jaws gaping, but Edward wasn't watching. He had already begun his run, bolting out to grab Wiley under the armpits, and drag him back towards the cave. By the time the rock throwing recommenced, he had almost made it and only one struck him, glancing off his shoulder.

Wiley was unconscious, seriously battered by the rocks. Marcus bandaged the deep head wound but couldn't stem the bleeding.

'He's got broken ribs too,' he said, shaking his head as they examined the sergeant's badly bruised body.

One hour later, Sergeant Wiley died. Marcus entered the time and details of his death in his notebook. He went through the dead man's pockets, fishing out tobacco and a few papers, and then pulled off his boots.

'Ah,' he sighed, 'you always were a smart lad, Wiley. But it didn't help this time. Look at this, Ned . . .'

Edward had accepted that Marcus preferred to call him Ned rather than Edward, which he claimed was too much of a mouthful.

His friend had slid a knife from one of the boots. 'This ain't cutlery,' he smiled, testing the blade with his thumb. 'It's as sharp as a razor. And strong.' He tossed it to Edward. 'There you go! It's yours.'

They wrapped the body in a blanket, securing it with leather straps, and waited until nightfall, when several of the troopers were ordered to strip and patrol the area to see if any of the attackers were still about.

'That's where my blackfellows come in handy,' Marcus said morosely. 'At night, and in the buff, they can spy for me.'

'What will we do about the sergeant?' Edward asked, feeling sick to his stomach.

'We'll have to take him with us to the nearest town. For burial. We can't leave him here for the dingoes to get him. Or those two-legged animals up top. By the way, that was good of you to bring him in, poor fellow. I couldn't get these bastards out. Big bloody help they are. I'll have their hides when I get a chance.'

'I didn't think, I just ran,' Edward replied nervously. 'How can we get out of here?'

'My men believe the blacks have gone. They say it was just bad luck that they stumbled on us.'

Bad luck? Edward was in shock, his insides gaping like the jaws of that dingo out there. Marcus and the troopers were all so matter-of-fact about this business and a man was lying dead in front of them. Killed. As if this were an everyday experience. The thought of dingoes tearing at Wiley's body turned his stomach and he gulped hard to control rising bile, yet over to the side of the shallow cave some troopers were huddled together, arguing. Finally one of them called to Marcus:

'Hey, boss!'

'Don't call me boss! How many times do I have to tell you? You call me sir!'

Edward shook his head at Sergeant Wiley, as if to apologise for the fact that they'd forgotten about him.

'What do you want?' Marcus was buttoning up his uniform jacket.

'Them boots, sir. Him sergeant won't be needin' them no more, eh?'

Marcus looked at the bundle. At Wiley. And then nodded. 'Yes. You might as well.' He threw them over and the trooper caught them one by one, grinning as if he'd just been given a gold brick.

The inspector stood at the entrance to the cave and peered out at the darkness. 'Damn bad luck losing Wiley,' he murmured. 'Damn bad luck.'

The gorge was so quiet now that the waters of the stream seemed unduly loud. A bird screeched and Edward, his nerves taut, jumped. He was thinking that this might be more bad management than bad luck.

'I didn't know there were any wild blacks around this area,' he croaked, his throat as dry as stone.

'Ah yes.' Marcus yawned. 'A few of them. Just renegades. Too stupid to lie down.'

The troopers slipped back into the cave to assure the inspector that the hostile blacks had disappeared and the horses were safe.

As streaks of light began to appear on the horizon, they rode away from the gorge, firearms ready in case the blacks were lying in wait, but there was no more trouble. It was a slow journey, with one of their number, a black tracker called Abraham, leading the way until they were into open country again.

Finally, Abraham guided them into a sleepy village called Plenty. Only then could Edward release his grip on the rifle that hadn't left his hand since they exited the gorge.

Marcus dismounted outside a police station hardly bigger than a sentry box, and found a bell hanging by the door. He rang it heartily and suddenly doors flew open and agitated people stumbled into the street. The local policeman ran down from the timber cottage behind his stationhouse pulling a uniform jacket over his night shirt and calling out, 'Where?'

'Where what?' Marcus asked him.

'You rang the fire bell!'

'Oh! Sorry! I have a dead comrade here, sir, and I need your assistance.'

When the situation was explained to him, the constable took over without fuss, calmly and quietly. Edward began to realise that these men were trained to view death from a different platform, and felt rather a fool for having an attack of the vapours. He hoped that Marcus hadn't noticed.

The policeman's wife invited him to sit in her parlour with a cup of tea while he waited for the inspector to resume the journey.

'Where have you come from?' she asked kindly.

'Gympie.'

'Oh, that's a long way. And are you travelling with those blackfellows?'

'Yes. Raw recruits. They were rather confused at first, about the uniforms and the care of the horses, but they seem to be settling in to the job.'

She nodded. 'Just the same, sir, I wouldn't be trusting them.'

The two Englishmen, both, by chance, of aristocratic lineage, had bonded well on that journey, and Edward was feeling a little lost as he left Marcus and his troopers at the Rockhampton police barracks.

He found a stable for his horse, Saul, reflecting on how well the Thoroughbred had handled the long journey, and enquired about nearby accommodation.

The groom gave his considered advice.

'The Colonial Boarding House, across the road, is clean and she keeps a good table. You might get in there.'

Edward was surprised to be offered boarding house accommodation, but then he realised he must appear to be the worse for wear by this time, with a stubble of beard and clothes that would need a Chinese laundryman to beat the dust out of them.

'What name, mister?' the groom called as he slid the saddle from Saul's back.

Edward hesitated. He'd been warned by Marcus to keep low-key when it came to their heritage. Marcus himself had made the mistake of signing his full name of Marcus de la Poer Beresford for some years until he realised it was creating antagonism among friends and foe alike.

'Why?' Edward had asked.

'Because half the population are British convicts and descendants thereof, and the "tyrants", as they are inclined to call authority, hail from the British Establishment . . . to wit, people like us.'

'I don't see how that should affect me.'

'Oh, it's just a massive case of birds of a feather, old chap. But I have to say that thousands of our compatriots were treated badly in the prisons and that could have added to the great divide of them and us.'

'Convicts who deserved what they got?'

'There are some who are not so sure about that now,' Beresford had murmured.

'Your name, mister?' the groom repeated.

'Ah . . . Ned. Ned Heselwood.'

'And this is your horse, is it?' There was suspicion in his voice.

You can't win, Edward thought crankily. If I'm upper class they're agin me; if I'm a poor traveller with a good horse, I'm a thief.

'It is,' he said firmly. 'His name is Saul. You take good care of him.'

He made a better impression on the bustling landlady, even though he walked in her front door looking just as scruffy, with a saddle pack slung over his shoulder.

'Come on in,' she said, observing him as he stepped into her hallway. 'I've got a real nice room you can have. In the front here. Two and sixpence a week with meals. I like to see a gent what's got the manners to wipe his feet on the mat before he comes in.'

She ushered him into an undoubtedly clean room that featured bare boards, a double bed, white cotton cover turned back to reveal well-rubbed sheets, a cane chair and a cane dresser.

It occurred to Edward, now Ned, that had there been a speck of dust it would have been disposed of instantly.

She walked over to stroke a lamp on the dresser. 'This here's a kerosene lamp,' she said proudly. 'You ever seen one of them before?'

Ned blinked, finding it difficult now to recall when kerosene was first used for lamps. Years back anyway.

'I think so,' he said, presuming that he'd stepped back in time, once he'd neared the rim of civilisation.

'Breakfast at seven,' his landlady said. She yanked back the window drapes and the hard sunlight hit him like the blare of a trumpet. 'Front doors locked at ten; there's some hard cases hangin' round this town, I tell you. But if you're late, the back door's always open. You all right now?'

Ned was more than all right. He couldn't wait for her to leave so that he could close those drapes and stretch out on that bed to rest his weary bones. He could hardly believe that he was still on his feet after the attack in the gorge, riding for hours, watching Beresford attending to business in the town of Plenty, and then being told to mount up again for a full day's ride over rough country.

As soon as he'd ushered her out, he stumped over to sit on the bed and drag at his boots. He was so tired it was hard work to get them off, but he managed to drop them on the floor before the soft bed claimed him.

CHAPTER NINE

From a narrow ridge hidden by shrubs, the rock throwers watched daylight begin to creep from behind the hills to send the night animals sliding and scurrying back to their nests. They heard a distant hoo-hoo of a kookaburra just before the majestic songbirds took over, determined to wake everyone to a glittering day – a day worth their truest notes, their best riffs and cadences.

Parrots flashed past them at a dazzling pace, diving into blossom-laden trees to spend the early morn sipping honey and chattering tipsily as they clambered through the rich foliage.

Down below, rock wallabies skipped like dancers across boulders and ledges, stopping to observe the world as they chewed on sweet grass shoots, and lizards emerged to find warm spots, prepearing to laze in the sun.

Gudala glanced at his brother, and at his spear, as a wild pig nudged and snorted at a nardoo, a clover fern, but Banggu shook his head. More important was the wait; they had to see what they had accomplished, besides harassing soldiers. A whole mob of them! A daring attack. Or so it could be said, though this was not their original aim when Banggu led his four-man party to the crest of the gorge. He'd simply wanted to show his young friends the spectacular view from the heights and then make their way down to the gorge, which was so narrow it was an ideal site to ensnare a pig.

But once they reached the plateau, it had been more interesting, and more challenging, to venture to the rim of the gorge and peer into its depths.

It had been Gudala who'd pulled back in shock.

'Are they soldiers?' he cried. 'Down there! I think they're soldiers! Fine place you pick to catch pigs, Banggu! A bullet, more like it. Come on, let's get out of here.'

Curiosity held sway, though. They crept forward and lay flat, edging right to the rim to observe the enemies making camp. Stuff everywhere.

Banggu was frustrated and angry. He felt he'd lost face with his new friends from the island the white men called Keppel. Everything was going wrong lately.

He and Gudala had run off from their father Ladjipiri back in the far country, and had been permitted to hunt with the Pitta Pitta men. They'd stayed for two seasons, and Banggu had enjoyed every minute with these gentle folk, exploring new country, learning their language and most of all finding a woman to love, the most beautiful woman in the world, of the proud and handsome Kalkadoon people. He'd seen her at a corroboree, sitting with her mother.

Kalkadoon. There was the problem. Their skin laws were strict and he was an outsider. He had spoken to the elders of both clans about his problem and they'd given him little hope, since other suitors had to be heard, including Uluyan, a popular young warrior.

That had sent Banggu into a panic. Though the girl, Nyandjara, was young, it was said she had a mind of her own and would make her own choice. How this came about he had been unable to discover, since, as yet, he'd not been permitted to speak with her.

Uluyan was the son of a clan hero, who was pressing for war with the white men. He wanted them eradicated before they got too numerous in blackfellow territory.

'How powerful are these white men after all?' Uluyan had asked, roaring at mobs of people in imitation of his father. 'That three men carrying only spears can frighten them off?'

This appeared to be true. Three men from the north, said to be from the fierce Irukandji tribe, were passing through when they came upon the great mob of cattle that Banggu and Gudala had seen when they were travelling with their father, the trader Ladjipiri.

Angered by this outrage, one of the north men raised a spear and felled a horse rider, who turned out to be a woman. Then the Irukandji men sought out the Pitta Pitta elders, who had granted them safe passage through their land in the first place, and apologised in case they had broken any laws. Since there were no laws applying to the white trespassers, there was no problem. In gratitude, they presented the elders with huge horns taken from the head of a dead he-cattle, a gift that was much prized. It was lashed to a tree by the river that Banggu now knew to be the Thomson River.

Not long after the killing of the white woman, to everyone's amazement, the horse riders took their cattle, every one of them, and went back east. They retreated! Men with guns retreated!

A kidachji man was called upon to explain this mystery, so he put on his emu-feather slippers and examined the landscape, battered by a multitude of hooves. He pointed to the remains of snakes and lizards and wombats and other crushed creatures, and said their spirits had joined forces to exact revenge upon the trespassers and their cattle animals by decreeing death to the white woman, and sending an evil spirit to live in that reach of the river and frighten them away.

All of this added fuel to Uluyan's fiery speeches.

'Now is the time!' he shouted. 'We should kill every one of the trespassers the first time their covered feet tread our lands!'

But then the Pitta Pitta people, to whom he spoke that day, were timid people.

Dreaming of his love, back in that wild, astonishing country, Banggu almost missed the boss soldier leading his men out of the gorge, but then they all came streaming out, riding the worn foot track under a line of trees, and there it was! This was what they'd waited to see. The man they'd felled had died! They had actually killed one of the soldiers with rocks, and a white soldier at that! It was easily seen he was dead: the body bundle was lashed to a horse's back with ropes linked under its belly.

As soon as the soldiers were out of sight, the four young men leapt about in glee. This was a great accomplishment! It would be spoken of round the campfires for years. But who had thrown the rock that knocked the soldier down in the first place? Before they'd all rained more rocks on him to keep him down.

'It was me,' Gudala said. 'I got him!'

'You're nearly blind,' the others laughed. 'You couldn't hit a kangaroo if it was standing on your big toe.'

'I saw the soldiers first, didn't I?'

In the end Banggu agreed that Gudala could claim to have struck the first blow. He felt sorry for his brother because he'd caught the dreaded eye blight while they were hunting with the Pitta Pitta people. At first his eyes were sore with grit, for it was dusty country out there, but then they began to weep, and pus formed in the corners. He became upset and moody, blaming his brother for talking him into leaving their green homeland for these hard hills, and demanding they return home.

The women bathed Gudala's eyes with soothing lotions but could not find a cure.

'He wants to go home,' they said. 'You should take him home while you can. This eye sickness will send him blind in time. Don't leave it too late for him to go home to his mammy.'

Faced with the expectation that this was the least he could do for his brother, Banggu was forced to leave, even before he had had a chance to declare his love for the beautiful Nyandjara. Two men volunteered to show them the shortest routes to take that would lead them into better-known country.

'I don't know why you are so heartsick over that girl,' Gudala complained as the weeks passed. 'You didn't have a chance against Uluyan. He's a big fellow already; he'll soon have the body of a warrior and no woman will be able to resist him.'

'You know nothing about love or you wouldn't say such foolishness. Love is carried in the heart; I have my love for her right here in my heart and it warms my spirit. Even if I never see her again, the love will remain.'

'What if Uluyan has just as much love for her in his heart?' Gudala scoffed.

'Sometimes I wonder why I am making this sacrifice for you, you whining bag of wind. I ought to let you go the rest of the way on your own.'

But he had persevered. They'd found their way home to their mother and she'd wept with joy at their sudden appearance on the island. Even though Ladjipiri was stern with them for running away from him, they saw the soft happiness in his eyes and were glad. It was good to be home.

'What about that pig?' Gudala called to him now. 'The soldiers have gone! We can get it now. They make good eating.'

He was right. Between them they could hunt that pig into the gorge and kill it. The family needed meat. There was little game on the island and their own hunting grounds were overrun by the Rockhampton town and farms.

They'd rowed across to the mainland, a long way south of the town, with two young men of the Woppa-bura clan. Banggu wanted to show them that game could still be found in this heavily wooded, hilly area that he knew well, and their new friends were eager for the opportunity to hunt.

But then there were the soldiers.

Banggu, this much-travelled hunter, knew that they ought to get back to the canoe as quickly as possible, because there could be danger here now, but the thought of taking back a fat pig was too tempting. Everyone would be so happy, and his father would be proud that he and Gudala were making themselves useful. And the soldiers had gone. They'd gone. Why would they turn back? They'd tried to find the rock throwers last night but could not. And at daybreak they didn't even bother to search for them.

Nevertheless, his concern remained. 'Maybe we come back another time,' he said. 'When no soldiers here.'

'But the soldiers have gone,' Gudala cried, anguished. 'We can't go home empty-handed!'

The Woppa-bura men, their mouths watering at the thought of pig meat on their campfires, sided with Gudala.

'It won't take long,' they said. 'We'll kill the pig and throw it in the canoe; then we row back to the island quick time. They'll never think to look for us over there.'

Gudala was startled. Who would be looking for them? Would the soldiers come back? Excitement gave way to fear. How could he have thought they would not? They had killed a soldier! Of course there would be payback.

He raised a hand to restrain Banggu, to tell him that it might not be a good idea after all, but his brother was already moving swiftly through the bush.

'Come on,' he called. 'You have to keep up, Gudala.'

Constable Joe Tebb, the lone representative of the law for the district of Plenty, wanted to send the inspector and his party on their way.

'I'll handle this matter,' he said. 'I don't see much sense in sending blackfellers to catch blackfellers. They'd let these bastards get away.'

'I don't think you understand,' Marcus said. 'That is exactly what they're good at. These fellows are trained to flush out and apprehend dangerous wild blacks.'

'Maybe so, but you said yourself that this lot are raw recruits.'

Joe looked around him. Already villagers were converging on the police station, demanding to know what was going on. He knew there'd be uproar when they heard that a soldier had been killed at Finlay's Gorge by wild blacks, and when that happened he wanted to be the boss. He wasn't about to let this snotty-voiced officer take all the glory. And anyway, it served them right for setting up camp with their backs to a wall.

'Why didn't you go after them while you were there?' he asked.

'Not that I need to explain my actions,' Beresford said curtly, 'but I felt it my duty to bring in the sergeant's body — he's entitled to that much respect — then report the attack to you as well as the measures I intend to take. Mr Heselwood will remain here. I will take my troopers back to the gorge for a full-scale search, but we'll be travelling light, so I will leave most of our equipment in your care. We'll find those blackfellows! My men checked the area at dawn and they say there were only four of them . . .'

'Only four!' Joe was beside himself with excitement. 'Jeez, Inspector, I thought there must have been a band of twenty or more. But the point is, I'm responsible for police matters here. Native Police answer to me like anyone else. You have no orders for active duty in my back yard, so to speak, so why don't you just leave it to me?'

He turned and called to the crowd: 'Have I got any starters for a posse?'

A thrill ran through his audience like a beating of wings, and Joe obtained the response he needed. There hadn't been a good manhunt in this district for years. Volunteers shoved themselves forward, vowing to 'get the black bastards'. Others ran for their guns and their mounts to make certain of a place in the posse.

'See!' Joe said to the officer. 'I'll have a legal posse out there in no time. We know that area, we go pig hunting there. We'll bring in all four of them, no trouble at all. Leave it to us, Lieutenant.'

It suddenly occurred to him that Beresford hadn't been keen on the search all along. The inspector's arguments faded into a weary admission that Joe's men were eminently capable of capturing those fellows. And he was shortly heard to remark to the civilian with him that they should be able to make it to Rockhampton by nightfall.

Joe grinned. A couple of sassy-looking young blokes like that pair were probably more interested in chasing ladies than a quartet of stupid blacks.

'I mean,' he said to his wife, 'how stupid can these black raiders be to attack a unit of police troopers? They're lucky they've been given a start, but that adds to the fun.'

The pig was harder to pen than they'd imagined. They'd built makeshift barriers of rocks and branches to herd him into a small pen that they'd constructed at the mouth of the gorge, but for a heavy animal he was light on his feet, darting and dodging away just when they thought they had him.

Banggu had managed to wound him with his spear, but that only caused him to add squealing to the chaos he was causing, as he crashed in and out of the scrub.

He charged into Gudala, winding him, so the Woppa-bura men, who were becoming frustrated by this chase, shouted for him to stay out of the way. That suited Gudala, whose eyes were suffering from the dust the pig was kicking up. No matter how hard he rubbed, he couldn't see clearly at all. He climbed a tree, trying to work out from the shouts and snorts who was winning.

They worked so hard trying to corral that pig, but it got away on them every time, so they decided to call a rest for a while: cool down in the stream; hunt about for nuts and berries to quell the ache in their dispirited stomachs.

One more try, they decided, only this time forget about herding the pig; they'd just have to creep up on him when he was quiet and use the spears.

It was late in the day when they sighted him again, but he'd learned his lesson of the morning, his snout quivering as he smelled his stalkers. Banggu hurled his spear at him, but it glanced off the tough skin, and sent the pig hurtling back into the scrub.

They heard a shot. Saw the pig stumble, then fall. And lie still. They all stared! Gudala rubbed his eyes. Pus came on to his hand. He wiped it on his bare thigh.

'Run!' his brother shouted.

Gudala couldn't see where Banggu was, but he ran anyway, realising it had to be white men with guns. Pig hunters is all, he wanted to say, but he remembered he'd killed the soldier, so he ran wildly, tripping and charging off again until he was out in the open, able to move faster. As he ran, swifter than he'd ever run in his life, he heard a horse thundering after him, but he would not look, he couldn't spare a second.

Gudala thought it was strange that he actually heard that rope coming after him . . . a lasso, what they used to rope cattle, he told himself. He wondered if the cattle to be roped, or the calves, could hear the lasso coming too. He was jerked backwards, the rope pinning his arms, and hauled along the hard ground that banged and bumped him and tore at his skin.

The rider jumped down, dragged him to his feet, belted him across the face with the back of his hand and proceeded to lash his wrists together. When he climbed back on his horse, the man tied Gudala to his saddle and shouted. 'Hey, Joe! I got one. You owe me two bob.'

The man, Joe, was wearing the black uniform with silver buttons that made him a policeman. He rode over and said: 'Jeez! Look at his eyes. Make you sick.'

They sat him in the grass to question him, prodding him with their boots.

'Hey, blackfeller! You bin throw rocks at policemen, eh?'

'Where are your mates?'

'Where you come from?'

'You kill soldier with them rocks, did you?'

'Where are your mates? They still here with you, dummy?'

Gudala hid behind his almost blinded eyes. At first he wouldn't answer, then he replied in his own language, pretending he didn't know any English, which they accepted.

'Tie him to a tree,' Joe said, 'while we go after the rest.'

Gudala was shocked when about ten more horsemen gathered in the clearing and then began beating the bush as if they were on a kangaroo hunt. He hoped Banggu had made a dash for the canoe; it was the best way to escape from horsemen.

He heard another shot, and shook in fright.

He had to wait a long time tied to that tree before they dragged up the islander called Yuradi, who was weeping pitifully. He told Gudala that they had caught him at the beach and smashed the canoe. Then some of the men lay in wait for his friend, who saw it was a trap and ran for the sea.

'They shot him,' he wept. 'He was swimming. Getting away from them! They fired guns at him and he went under. He was washed back by the waves. Dead! They pulled his body out of the water.'

'What about Banggu! They haven't caught him, have they?'

'I don't know. Might be they shot him dead too.'

'Aaah!' Gudala wished he hadn't said that. Life seemed bleak and cold now. His eyes were streaming but he couldn't clear them; his hands were tied.

'How many men sitting behind us?' he asked.

'Two fellers. With guns.'

'Where are the others?'

'They be still hunting.'

'Then they have not found Banggu! He is clever, they won't catch him.'

'Might be he come back and get us!'

'I don't think so. Too many fellers.'

After a while one of the men came over to Gudala. 'You want some tucker?' But Gudala kept his head down, muttering in his own language. He was saying: 'Don't talk to them, don't talk to them,' but Yuradi couldn't have heard him. He was proud that he could say some English.

'Plis yes, tucker, mistah,' he said in his turn.

There was no tucker. Gudala listened as they dragged Yuradi away, tied his hands to a high branch and began flogging him, at the same time shouting questions about the rock throwing. He listened to Yuradi's screams and his own tears stung. In the end he heard the white men talking.

'We got them all right. This one is called Yuradi. He's from a mob called Wamai.'

'Never heard of them!'

'Neither have I, but they're all the same colour.'

At first Gudala thought poor Yuradi was mad with the pain, but then it dawned on him that his Keppel Island friend was deliberately drawing the white men away from his own people. There was no such clan as Wamai.

The policeman Joe was pleased they'd accounted for three out of four.

'We'll get the other fellow. It's only a matter of time. I'll put out a Wanted flyer on him when I take these two in.'

He ignored Yuradi, who curled up on the ground near the tree, his back torn and bloody, a feast for flies, and began to run out chains. Gudala flinched. He'd seen poor blackfellers being marched along in chains, and felt desperately sorry for Yuradi when he was first to have the iron collar clamped around his neck.

Their hands were still tied; the chain was run through rings on the collars, connecting them, and on to its base on Joe's saddle. Then their walk began.

When they were paraded through a village called Plenty, the murderers were abused and pelted with rotten eggs, which they licked at gratefully, turning the anger to amusement.

A few days later they marched again, headed for Rockhampton, but this time they were chained behind a black-draped wagon containing a coffin. The body of the soldier they'd killed at the gorge. As he trudged along, Gudala felt a bit sorry for that soldier.

Ladjipiri's wife tied his hair back and trimmed his long beard. She wept when she saw all the grey hair that was dimming the black, but he knew she wasn't weeping over a few grey hairs. She was frightened and afraid to speak the fear.

'You go and bring them back, those boys. They find pig hunting not so easy as they think. Pig skin not as soft as kangaroo even! You should have told them that.'

He nodded. He had, but they were all afire with this adventure. And they were men now.

'You tell them we don't need pig. We got plenty fish. You tell them come on back!'

They'd been gone three days.

'I will insist.'

Woppa-bura women stood near his gunyah, silent, anxious. They were shy people. Their language was different. They had lived on these islands for countless generations, and knew little of the mainland, except for trade. They lived in gunyahs made of saplings and tea-tree bark, with bases made of earth and stones. Ladjipiri recalled that his women had been very impressed with their new camps when he first brought them here.

Two men were waiting for him. As soon as he emerged from his camp they turned and began the run down to the point from where their sons had set off.

Ladjipiri fell in behind them, finding the pace steady but too slow. He was accustomed to fast cross-country running. These islanders had no distances to confront. Nevertheless, he was always aware that he and his family were guests in their land, so he patiently picked up their rhythm and remained in the rear.

A boat was waiting, bigger and faster than the small one their sons had taken, with a carved totem at its nose. It was not familiar to him. The other men laid their spears on the bottom of the boat. They were not hunting spears; they were shorter, needle-sharp. Ladjipiri sat behind them as they took up the oars, and in minutes these experienced oarsmen had the boat skimming swiftly across the bay, their passenger hoping against hope they'd find his sons enjoying an excursion with their mates.

But it wasn't to be. As they neared the shore, their keen eyes spotted the battered canoe washed up on the high-tide mark of a narrow beach, and they rowed towards it.

'Do you think it overturned, throwing them into the sea?' Ladjipiri asked nervously, as they walked up to examine it.

'No. This hull is smashed,' he was told.

Worried, they began to infiltrate the bush, but they hadn't gone far when the smell assailed them.

'Smells like a dead animal here somewhere,' Ladjipiri said, his heart pounding.

He held up a hand for the others to wait and raised his spear to defend himself as he moved forward. 'Might be a dingo feeding.'

Dingoes *had* been feeding! It was a body. He choked, reeling back as his friends pushed past him.

One man shrieked. His son was dead there in the rough sandy scrub, his head still recognisable.

While he stood by, tears flowing, asking them what he could tell his wife and aunties, Ladjipiri and the other man dug a grave for his son. They lined it with large flat leaves and then told the man to go down to the ocean and sing his passing, while they moved the remains into the grave.

It was then they saw the bullets!

'Whitefellers kill him,' Yuradi's father said fearfully.

The grave was closed with more leaves, and filled in. They topped it with stones to prevent dingoes digging into it, trying their best to show respect, while fear and rage surged within them.

From the very start their search was hopeless and they all knew it. Many horsemen had been here. Far too many. There was no chance of tracking anyone through this bush, so they wandered dizzily inland, coming upon evidence of even more horses.

Ladjipiri led his companions into the gorge, where they saw recent urine stains on the walls and the ashes of many campfires, and for a few minutes he thought his eyes were playing tricks on him.

'These horse riders were barefoot,' he said, confused.

'Is that bad?' Yuradi's father asked.

'White men wear boots. The soft soil in this cave says only two or three boot prints. All the rest barefoot. This is strange.'

'There is blood here, on the ground by the stream. Someone bled here long while. Then got dragged into the cave.'

Ladjipiri dropped to a squat to examine the ground more carefully, and nodded. 'Yes, blood.'

He remembered the other cave he'd experienced in the far country, and in his mind's eye he saw that Dreamtime bird again, but it was not a painting this time, it was in the gorge, hovering over the gently flowing waters, its yellow eyes still focused straight ahead. One of the Woppa-bura men walked right under it without looking up. Ladjipiri tried to call out to him, but instead heard himself say:

'A man was killed here. The spirits will have to send elders to cleanse this place.'

'Who? Who was killed here?' Both men ran towards him.

'A white man,' he replied.

The bird had gone.

'The knowledge was put in my head,' he added. 'This is a spirit place. We have to go. There is nothing more for us here.'

'What about the lads?'

'They are not here.'

'Where are they?'

'This I do not know, but I will find them.'

The islanders rowed him further up the coast, and at his request pulled ashore in the mangroves nearer to the town.

'From here I will make my way into the big town,' he said, 'so that I can ask after our lads. I believe they would come this way, to get back to the island. Banggu and Gudala know plenty of people here. You go on back with the sad news, my friends, and begin the mourning for your beloved young man. I am sorry, to my heart, for his death.'

It was low tide. The mangrove roots were exposed, allowing him to clamber through the vast muddy swamp without having to do battle with foul-smelling waters thick with mud.

An old hermit called the Planter lived in a hut on the outskirts of this swamp. Ladjipiri had known him for many years, and now he needed his help. Clothes. He needed a shirt and trousers to be able to enter the town.

No one had heard a word from any of the lads. Ladjipiri talked to the people who congregated under the big trees by the river; people who knew him and his boys. He went to camps on the outskirts of the town, and to the marketplace where giggling black girls sold baskets and shells and beads, but no one had seen them.

In desperation he went to the Chinawoman who sat on a big cane armchair outside her son's store and sold spells. He had no money, or time, for her spells, but she was a kind woman, she listened to him.

While he was talking to her, a funeral came by with plumed horses stepping to the mournful beat of a drum. The coffin, covered in a black cloth, was in a magnificent windowed wagon, and horsemen in uniform, carrying flags, followed.

Ladjipiri couldn't help but stare at this grand event.

'Someone die,' he told the woman, and she nodded. But her store of knowledge exceeded his.

'Soldier man die,' she said. 'Got killt. Bad joss that.'

He wasn't much concerned about the death of a soldier. He was too busy peering into the crowds gathered to watch the parade, in the hope of seeing his sons.

The China lady was miffed by his lack of interest in her news.

'Blackfellers killt him. Velly bad fellas. They in rockup over dere.'

She pointed to the forbidding watch-house across the road.

He felt a tug at his heart. 'What blackfellers?' As he said it, he felt stupid. His lads didn't go around killing policemen. Why would they? Who had shot the Woppa-bura lad, though? And why?

But she was a purveyor of news, and wouldn't be turned aside. She put down her tray of trinkets and spells, climbed out of her chair and waddled into the store, ignoring his pleas not to bother.

He stood at the door, peering in as she leaned across a counter, grabbed a thin newspaper and came back, her face creased with concern.

'These not your lost boys?'

'No,' he said, brushing the foolish writings aside.

'Pitchers,' she insisted. 'You lookee.'

She was waving the words at him, holding the paper up to his face, and he saw pictures pass by his eyes, two pictures, blurred, foolish things. Newspapers were mysteries to him, like so many things.

When he wouldn't look at the page, she stopped a passer-by. A white girl.

'Missee,' she called. 'You read writings, eh?'

'Yes.'

The Chinawoman cackled. 'Blackie no read. Chinee lady no read. You read, eh?'

The girl stopped. 'What do you want me to read?'

'Names. Names on them two blackies.'

'Oh yes. I see. They are unusual. Hard to say. But I will try. That one is Yu-ra-di. That one is Gu-da-la.'

She handed back the paper.

'Thankee, missee. You buy a love spell, eh?'

The girl shook her head, stepped around Ladjipiri, and went on her way.

The woman looked at his ashen face. 'Those your boys?'

He couldn't speak. He was rooted to the spot. Shocked that her spells were so strong that she could find the lads for him with a wave of her hand. He took that hand, pressed it in gratitude and shuffled away, suddenly old, to slink into the shadows of a narrow lane.

When he had recovered, as much as he would ever recover from a shock like that, he went back into the bush to think this through. He desperately wanted to go to the watch-house to see the lads, to be sure it was Gudala and Yuradi and ask the headful of questions that needed to be answered. Was this true? What had happened? Where was Banggu? Was he dead too? But he dared not until he could be sure they wouldn't lock him up as well.

By morning, everyone knew about the lads. The people asked him questions, all wanting to know had he seen the pictures? What happened? But Ladjipiri had no answers. He went in search of clan elders.

'This', the two old men told him, 'is a very serious matter. They are accused of killing a policeman. Though we know your sons to be good boys, it will be hard to prove they are innocent.'

'Even if the white men shot a lad whose name can't be mentioned now? He was a Woppa-bura lad. Only eighteen years old.'

'When did this happen?' They were truly surprised. 'Are you sure?'

'We buried him ourselves down near the gorge.'

And so the worrying discussions went on. For hours.

Two more elders joined them with the news that the police were looking for the third blackfellow who was with the murderers.

'Murderers?' Ladjipiri cried. 'Our boys are not murderers! The white men are the murderers! Would you accompany me to the police station so that I can demand to know who shot the Woppa-bura lad and left his body to rot in the bush?'

'That's not a good idea. You could get locked up. Remember they are looking for a third man, and one of the prisoners is your son.'

'Prisoners! Did they drag them here as prisoners?' Ladjipiri was in such a state, they called for some Pituri brew to calm him down.

Eventually a decision was made. This was a job for a white man. They had to ask a white man to go to the watch-house and find out all there was to know. But who?

When Ladjipiri awoke, they asked him if he knew the man from Oberon Station.

'Yes. Mister Paul. Me and some other Darambal men helped him search for the black men who killed his wife and the other lady. It took a long time but we got them.'

'We thought you were there. He's a good man. He wouldn't have forgotten you. He's still at Oberon. Would you speak to him of this terrible business?'

'Is there time?'

'Yes. It is said there will be accusations and judgments in the courthouse.'

'I will go immediately. In the meantime, will you try and find my son Banggu and see him safe?'

'That we will do.'

Paul it was who saw the tall, lean blackfellow loping up the track from the low hills at the base of the Berserker Range, and he nudged his horse forward to place himself between the newcomer and the homestead. But then he recognised his visitor and broke into a broad smile.

'Well! If it's not my friend Trader,' he said, dismounting to welcome Ladjipiri. 'I haven't seen you for years. Have you been travelling the long miles again?'

'Yes, Mister Paul, see plenty places, long ways out there.' He pointed west.

Paul was intrigued. 'How far inland did you go?'

He saw Trader trying to find a way to answer the question with no concept of distance marked in miles, so he tried again. 'Let's see, you know the town of Emerald?'

Trader grinned. 'Yes, know that feller.'

'Goodoh. Now show me here on the ground.' He squatted to smooth a patch of soil, then took a stick and jabbed it in the ground. 'Here Rockhampton, all right?'

Trader squatted beside him and nodded enthusiastically.

'Good. Now here's Emerald. Right? It's straight out there. West.'

His friend frowned. And laughed, thinking this a joke.

'Wait a minute. This is good. You see.' He handed Trader the stick. 'You show me how far you go out there. As far as from Rockhampton to Emerald?'

Trader studied the map. He drew a line from Rockhampton to Emerald.

'That's right,' Paul said. 'Man walking.'

'Ah!' The Aborigine trader measured the distance between the river town and Emerald, then measured the distance west. Then he smoothed the soil further on to jab a stick in the ground. 'This place,' he said. 'BullaBulla River.' He circled the area.

Paul was amazed that this man had covered such distances. It was roughly a hundred and fifty miles from Rockhampton to Emerald, and if Trader's map was right, he had travelled more than three hundred miles further on.

As he watched, though, Trader rubbed out the spot Paul had marked as Emerald and moved it just a smidgen south.

'This feller Emerald down a bit,' he commented.

Paul laughed. 'If you say so. Good country out there?'

'Yes. All good country; fellers bring mobs of cattle. Then go back.'

'They do? Why?'

Trader shrugged. 'Might be bad joss.'

Remembering that Trader was always fond of strong black tea boiled in the billy, Paul invited him to come on up to the men's quarters, where the kettle was always close to the boil.

As they tramped along the track, he would have liked to hear more of the outback, but Trader seemed to have lost interest.

'Is anything wrong?' he asked.

The black man looked at him, his forehead creased with worry, and nodded. Tears welled in his eyes. 'I need good man to do talking for me, Mister Paul.'

'Looks to me like you need that tea first. Plenty of sugar too, eh?'

Paul heard his story, or rather what Trader could make of events, and agreed that it would not be a good idea for him to be trying to talk to the lads just now. As a matter of fact, he added to himself, it would be a better idea for all black people to make themselves scarce right now, especially a relative of the accused. If a policeman had been murdered by blackfellows, there'd be a backlash among the townspeople. The anti-black faction was always ready to stir up trouble.

He hadn't seen a newspaper, but by the sounds of things, the future of the young men who'd been arrested, whoever they were, looked bleak. And like Trader, he wanted to know who'd shot the Woppa-bura lad, and why.

'I think I'd better come into town with you and see what I can find out,' he said. 'Do you reckon that's a good idea?'

'Reckon yes, Mister Paul, please.'

'Come on then, we'll get my wife.'

He saw Trader gasp.

'It's all right. I've got a new wife now. She'll come to town with us. She likes going to town. And we'll saddle up a horse for you. Come to think of it, why don't you ride a horse on those long journeys?'

'Horses got no kin here,' Trader shrugged.

Paul smiled. 'I don't suppose they have.' He was still trying to grasp the extent of the knowledge this man had, to be able to walk massive distances without apparent support of any kind. Except of course the support his beloved land gave him at every step.

Police Inspector Pennington wasn't in the best of moods to receive Paul MacNamara, but he supposed he'd have to get it over with sooner or later.

'If you've come to complain about the presence of Native Police in the town,' he said after offering him a seat, 'you're wasting your time. I didn't have a say in the matter. I also have not seen sight nor sound of the extra police the commissioner promised me; they're all talk, those blokes.'

'I didn't come about them,' MacNamara said.

Pennington didn't seem to hear him. 'And you can tell Langley Palliser the same thing,' he went on. 'They're complaining that there's no police presence out west, so, by God, they'll get the Native Police or none.'

'I think that's a good idea,' Paul grinned.

'You do?'

'Yes. Make sure they've got officers who can keep them under control, though. But I wanted to talk to you about another matter. I believe a soldier was killed at the gorge. Could you tell me what that was all about?'

'Read the paper.'

'I have, but the families of the lads in the lockup are confused; they don't know what's going on. I thought to get the correct story from you and calm them down.'

'You could start by telling them that the pair I've got here will swing.'

'Why?' Paul asked patiently.

'You're not a lawyer, are you?'

'No. I simply told the families that you are the big boss and a fair man, and that you'll give me the true facts.'

Pennington leaned back in his chair and frowned. 'Yes. Well, this is it in a nutshell. Three blacks attacked the Native Police in the Finlay Gorge by dropping heavy rocks on them. Sergeant Wiley was struck on the head by a rock and killed.'

'That would have been bad luck, wouldn't it? They couldn't aim from that height. They might have thought it a lark.'

Pennington scowled. 'You get a rock dropped on you from that height, you

225

wouldn't expect to brush it off either. Anyhow. They caught two of them and they're up for murder. We'll see if they think that's funny.'

'Names?'

'Can't you read?' He pulled a notebook towards him and gave the names. 'Yuradi and Gudala. The other one escaped.'

'Three blackfellows, kin of your prisoners, came across the body of one of those lads near the gorge. He'd been shot. Who shot him?'

For a minute there Pennington seemed mystified, then he shrugged. 'I don't know. Probably the Native Police.'

'Wouldn't it be on record?'

'Yes. It'll be on record.'

'It wasn't in the paper. They didn't mention that one of the group got shot. See what I mean about the papers? You only get bits of the story. Maybe the police shot that blackfellow first and his mates were retaliating by throwing rocks.'

'I don't know! I'll have to look into it,' Pennington said impatiently.

Paul didn't want to push his luck. He stood to leave. 'I'd appreciate it. Thanks for your time, Andy. The fathers of the two in custody, could they visit? Only for a few minutes.'

'If you come with them.'

'I rather think a lawyer might be better.'

'If you can get one for those mugs.'

The lawyer came. He tried desperately to convey to the jury that there was no intent to kill. He insisted that his clients had not thrown the rock that killed Sergeant Wiley; he claimed it was thrown by the third member of the group, who was now known as the Deceased, since according to Aboriginal law his name could not be mentioned.

Marcus de la Poer Beresford was called to give evidence at the trial. In discussion with Inspector Pennington, he insisted that troopers of the Native Police had informed him that there were four men in the gang attacking them. 'Where are the other two?' he asked.

'Your recruits were mistaken,' the inspector argued. 'The prisoners themselves are adamant that there were only three of them.'

'The prisoners are lying to protect the one who got away,' Beresford said angrily. 'And I want to place on record that my men did not shoot the third member of this gang. They are being blamed for that death, and it is quite unfair.'

'We have no proof that a member of this gang was shot! Only the word of the father of one of the prisoners.'

'So now this gang is reduced to two!' Beresford was smarting over jokes circulating in the town concerning the incident in the gorge. People were making snide remarks, in his presence, about the platoon of Native Police that couldn't defend themselves from stone throwers.

'I didn't say that.'

'Perhaps you simply can't add up. You caught two. The third one was shot; you could require Constable Joe Tebb of the town of Plenty to give an account of how that happened. And, as is bloody obvious, the fourth one is still at large.'

To prove his point, Beresford interviewed Ladjipiri, the father of one of the accused, who was acting as translator for the prisoners, who had little or no English.

'Is it true that one of these lads was shot?'

'Yes.'

'How do you know?'

'I found 'im. Buried 'im there.'

'And the fourth one. Fourth . . .' Marcus held up four fingers. 'He run off, eh?'

The black man shook his head. 'No four. Only three fellers. You tell the judge them good boys, eh? Sorry. Them very sorry, boss.'

'You're lying! And yet you want me to put in a good word for those bastards? I'll put the rope round their necks myself!'

His day didn't improve. When he entered the pub, he saw a cartoon on the noticeboard, and walked over to see what it was about.

The cartoonist had drawn blackface police crowding fearfully under a table, and in their midst was a terror-stricken white face . . . his! Some black kids with small bags marked STONES were dancing a jig on the table.

He ripped the cartoon from its centre spot and shoved it into his pocket.

But at least Ned was there to commiserate with him. They bought their drinks, and, following local custom, took them over to the open window, where they stood to enjoy the beer and watch the passers-by.

'What are your plans now?' Ned asked him.

'I'm waiting for a replacement for Sergeant Wiley.'

'What then?'

'I take the lads out on patrol of the outlying stations, sort of doing the rounds, to see and be seen. I have to shunt on any wild blacks that hang about, and then enjoy the best of station society. But what about you? Where did you say you were staying?'

'I'm at a boarding house; it'll do for the time being. I'll probably go down to Sydney in a few days.'

'A boarding house? If you're short of chips I can help, you know.'

'Thanks, Marcus, but I'm flush. One good thing about my old man, he's very generous with funds. I'd better write to the parents and let them know when I'll be home.'

'No need to dash off, then? We can't deprive the local gals of your company just yet.'

'Certainly not. Another pint?'

Marcus was distracted for the minute. He thought he saw someone he knew.

'Hang on a tick, I'll be back . . .'

He dashed out the door and called, 'Harry! I say! Harry!'

A tall fellow in workman's duds stopped and looked about him. Then he saw Beresford and threw his arms wide.

'Marcus, you old rascal!' he called as he dodged a cart to cross the road.

They came in together, and Ned was introduced to the gentleman, recently arrived back in Rockhampton from fields afar. That much he managed to ascertain as the two friends compared notes on their travels.

'I've got a little place here now,' Harry said. 'Not enough room to swing a cat, but a good base. My wife is here with me. Why don't you come and meet her? Come and have a meal with us. You too, Ned.'

After one more drink they were persuaded.

That was how Ned came to meet Harry Merriman.

When he retired to his boarding-house room, and opened the windows wide, he sat down to reflect on the evening.

Harry, he found, was only a stockman, but a likeable chap, and his wife, one hell of a good looker with a mass of gleaming red hair, was a truly nice woman. Charming in fact, when you stood back from her excitement at their first visitors. It was easily seen she adored her husband.

This was the poorest residence he'd ever encountered, outside of the thatched peasants' cottages back home in England, but neither of the Merrimans appeared embarrassed with their one-roomed cabin that sported a kitchen one end and a double bed at the other. Without even a screen between.

'He'd warned me,' Mrs Merriman said to Marcus, 'that the cabin wasn't much, and it's not. I consider myself lucky that he bought a stove. My mother used to say she cooked on a camp oven on the farm for the first year of their marriage.'

'Had I known that, I could have saved some money and bought you a camp oven instead,' her husband grinned.

'It wouldn't have mattered. I was too impressed with this marvellous garden,' she said, 'to be worried about the house. The garden is huge, isn't it? All the tropical trees and flowers are just gorgeous. I love it.'

'That reminds me,' Harry said. 'I knew the garden would be overgrown, but I couldn't get back any earlier. It was a surprise to arrive home and find someone had cleared the whole block for me. A pleasant surprise I can tell you, because I'm not keen on gardening.'

'Who cleared it?' Marcus asked.

'You'll never guess! Duke did! Remember him? We met him at the races. He was with Mrs Forrest and Lucy Mae.'

'Ah yes. You were staying at the same hotel! I recall him saying he was heading north.'

'All roads lead to Rockhampton these days,' Harry said.

He turned to Ned. 'Did you know the bigwigs here are campaigning to slice this huge colony in half, along the Tropic of Capricorn, which happens to be right here, and form another colony with Rockhampton the capital?'

'No, I didn't know that. But I'm finding it hugely interesting. This place has a real frontier feel about it.'

'Do you really think so?' Marcus asked.

'Oh yes, indeed.'

'Wait till you see the rest of the colony,' Harry said, and Marcus laughed.

'Our friend here's a real live frontiersman!'

Ned was intrigued, but he still felt very much out of place. He worried that he was imposing, and was a little put out that Marcus had dragged him in, unannounced.

Mrs Merriman sent the men outside to sit under the trees until dinner was ready, and Ned took the opportunity to speak to her.

'I don't want to intrude, Mrs Merriman. I think I'd better trot along.'

'Goodness me no, I wouldn't hear of it, Ned. You go and join the others out there.'

He followed them out to find Harry dispensing rum, and that made him feel a little more relaxed.

'What about Duke anyway?' Marcus was asking Harry. 'What's he doing here?'

'He owns a cattle station, no less. Called Mango Hill.'

'Don't know that one, but we'll find it, and go a-visiting.'

'We surely will. I have to thank him for all this hard work. He's a good chap.'

Dinner was early, good plain fare of beefsteaks and a pile of vegetables and a bread-and-butter custard. One of Ned's favourites.

Afterwards they sat outside looking down on the twinkling lights of the proposed capital of a new colony, and the talk ran to Harry's travels.

Ned was astonished that this fellow had also worked as a drover, forging hundreds of miles inland, and was curious to know what was out there. Had he got as far as the inland sea?

'No, I believe that's way out into the centre of the continent. But I'd love to see it. That'd be something, wouldn't it?'

'So what are you doing now?' Marcus asked. 'Are you going back to Cameo Downs?'

'No. Change of plans. I'll be taking my own herd of cattle west.'

'To sell?'

'No. To open my own run.'

'You already have land out west?' Ned asked.

'No again. I'll keep going until I find it.'

Marcus laughed. 'Does that surprise you?' he asked Ned.

'No, that's how my father got started. It just surprises me that it can still be done. In England it is understood that the good pastures have all been taken.'

'No fear,' Harry said. 'There are thousands of acres going begging.'

As Ned and Marcus walked back into town, Ned's curiosity was still at work.

'How does a stockman like Harry afford to buy all those cattle and equip such a long journey?'

'I don't know. He's single-minded, I can tell you that much. He doesn't gamble and has never been one for wine, women and song. Though he likes his rum. I suppose he saves every penny.'

'Even so, on a stockman's pay?'

'And keep. He could be socking it away.'

'Where does he come from?'

'I've no idea. His wife said something about a town called the Crossing at one stage, but that could be anywhere. Maybe he's got a rich papa too.'

'And he lives in a house like that? I doubt it. But I envy you fellows. Your lives aren't dull. I couldn't imagine staying at Montone Station nursing cattle for ever, which is what my old man expects me to do. It's a very boring life. Maybe I should have joined the army after all.'

'Too late for that, old son. If you can dig up some cash, there's nothing to stop you taking a team of your own and heading west. But for now – the pub up ahead has some pretty little barmaids. We ought to call in and bid them good cheer.'

Ned didn't stay long. He left Marcus with a woman called Goldie, who was more approachable than the sassy maids, and tramped the dark streets to his boarding house, thoroughly depressed.

What to do now?

He had begun a letter to his mother, hoping that she was well and that her leg was healing quickly. He told her that he had been exploring the countryside, had had quite a few adventures and was now in Rockhampton. He then went on to say that he would be coming down to Sydney shortly and was looking forward to seeing her and Father . . .

But was he? He wasn't looking forward to the inevitable confrontation with his father, which could only end amicably if he agreed to go back to Montone and get on with the job laid out for him. And if he rewrote the letter, taking out the bit about going to Sydney, where *was* he going?

From here on, travel got tough. Not the sort of place for a new chum to do his roaming alone, he reflected.

And that's what was really upsetting Ned. His uncle had told him that Jasin was almost broke when he set sail for the colonies with his wife.

'They were so poor, they travelled on a ship that was transporting a hold full of convicts. My mother was appalled that her daughter should sink to such a level, but Georgina was madly in love with Jasin, so there was no stopping her.'

And yet, Ned had been told, Jasin went after his ambitions like a bull at a gate. He'd hired convict stockmen and forged across the Blue Mountains after the great pasturelands, and then dashed further and further afield for more land conquests, to become a greatly admired pioneer in a very short time.

But he was a ruthless operator. No one got in his way. He ruled with an iron hand, and thought nothing of the double-cross, leaving in his wake enemies like the Forrests and the MacNamaras, and plenty more.

Ned knew he didn't have that sort of get up and go in him, and his father knew it too. That was why Jasin wanted him to run his station, a place already well managed by Clem: to appear to be more like him. The real truth was that he despised his son. Edward had felt that as soon as he stepped ashore from the ship. Even as his handsome, suntanned father had reached out to shake his hand with that broad welcoming smile.

He wrote the letter and gave his address in Rockhampton but made no mention of returning to either Montone or their Sydney home.

Even posting the letter the next morning depressed him. But then he met Marcus, who was in a great hurry. He had to appear in court to testify in the trial of the two blackfellows who had killed Sergeant Wiley, so Ned went along out of curiosity. He'd never been in a court before. He slipped into the back row of the crowded courtroom, peering between heads at the magistrate, a small man surrounded by a huge cedar desk and the inevitable witness box. Over to the right was the jury, the twelve men and true, mostly bearded gents in their Sunday best; bodies stiff, too intimidated to fidget, but their eyes flicked about furtively, needing respite.

For a while there Ned thought he might also be called to testify, but apparently they had no need of him.

Ladjipiri sat beside Mister Paul, his face grim with pain and terror.

When the lads were brought in, shoved forward for all to see, chains jangling, they looked so much younger to him. They were only boys, despite their anguished faces, and they hung their heads as they listened to the babble of voices. Hard, clipped voices that all told the same story: of the killing of a white man, and the reason for this meeting . . . to decide payback. But there was no mention that payback had already been enacted. That one of the blackfellows had been shot dead. Killed for that crime.

231

He shook his head, trying to understand.

Then Yuradi, who was weak from the beatings and suffering from fever, collapsed, pulling Gudala with him. As they both disappeared behind that waist–high wall, amid commotion, it seemed to Ladjipiri that he'd seen them fall through the trap, the hanging trap so often used by white men, and he now knew, for certain, the outcome of this meeting.

Both lads were dragged to their feet, Yuradi swaying, with Gudala trying to hold him up.

The judge banged a hammer. Shouted: 'Remove the prisoners!'

And in a flash of time they were gone from the stage, through a back door that closed with a small snap behind them.

Then the meeting recommenced.

Ladjipiri knew he need not hear any more. The judgment was made. He slipped down the side aisle and out into the street.

Paul MacNamara followed him. As he left, he thought he saw a familiar face in the back row, but shrugged it off. This was no time for socialising.

Poor Ladjipiri should never have come into the courtroom; it was too much for a father to bear, but he'd insisted, determined to stand by the lads as long as possible.

'They will die?' he said to Paul.

'I'm so very sorry, Trader. It looks like it.'

After the sentence was announced, the lawyer approached the judge and asked if the two Aboriginal fathers could be given the bodies for burial in accordance with their laws. The request was refused. They were buried without ceremony in an unmarked grave at the edge of Potter's Field.

Paul read about the unmarked grave in the papers, knowing that unmarked graves would not escape the eyes of black men. And so it was.

Ladjipiri, defiant in his grief, came to tell him goodbye.

'Got one son yet, Mister Paul. Still got one son. Banggu gone long ways from here. Now we take our young fellers home for proper burial.'

CHAPTER TEN

Georgina was delighted to receive a letter from Edward, but shocked to hear he'd left Montone. While there was no doubt Clem could manage the station, Jasin would be furious that his son had left his post without a word. And obviously soon after they'd departed. She supposed he was lonely. And she wouldn't blame him. All stations were isolated by their sheer size, but colonial country people were accustomed to that life and made the best of it. Unfortunately Montone had not been reopened long enough to gain social contact with the neighbours. It was hardly a hub of hospitality.

Her travail, as she liked to call it, was finally over. More or less. The operation had been a success. When the plaster was removed, she found the leg was thin and weak, but she could walk again, using a stick. Apart from being rather shaky, she had to learn to walk with a missing big toe, thanks to the gangrene, and she found that dreadfully embarrassing. To make matters worse, Jasin teased her about it, and that made her cross. They seemed to be going through a bad time lately, both of them out of sorts, with little to cheer their way.

They both missed Rosa's company. Georgina because she hated being deprived of the young woman's kindness and sense of fun. And talk! They had so much in common, they'd never run out of conversation!

Rosa had loved the elegant Sydney house, but she'd had to return to Brisbane on the first suitable ship so as not to upset her husband. She promised to return with Dr Palliser, for a longer visit, when time permitted.

Unfortunately Jasin missed her too. That was plain to see. He had been at his charming best in Mrs Palliser's company, and they'd spent quite a few hours together each day. Now he was quite rude to the special nurse who replaced her, as if the woman were a pest in his house. Georgina had been aware that he was a little too impressed by Mrs Palliser, and she'd deliberately taken a risk asking her to accompany them to Sydney, but she had no regrets. Rosa's delicacy and patience had been a godsend. Now she was in the hands of a stranger, her own patience strained by spartan treatment.

This was the state of affairs in the Heselwood household when Edward's news was delivered to them. Georgina considered not mentioning the letter, but she deemed it unfair to their son. When eventually Jasin did hear that Edward had left the station, he could rightly claim he was never advised.

As for the man himself, he'd been socialising quite a bit lately, enjoying the races and dining out whenever he pleased, adding to her loneliness, but she refused to complain, or even comment. She'd trusted Rosa, certain that nothing untoward had happened between them, so now she hoped his infatuation with her would simply up and fade away. Like the fifty magnificent roses he had surprised Rosa with when she'd entered her cabin for the return voyage.

She had written to let them know she'd enjoyed the voyage and was safely at home in Brisbane, and in the course of the letter thanked them for the roses. Roses that Georgina knew nothing about.

She sighed. Nothing one could do but press on. She had some dear friends coming for lunch, so she could forget about Jasin and his tantrums for a while.

He was livid! He hurled Edward's letter across the room, claiming that he'd made a bloody fool of his father! He'd given him a superb property to begin life in his home country, and what did he do? Threw it back in his face!

'What is this?' he shouted at Georgina. 'Adventure? Where the hell is the adventure in riding a horse a few hundred miles to Rockhampton? His business is cattle.'

'He probably found Montone lonely,' Georgina ventured, setting off another tirade.

'And who's this officer friend of his? Beresford? Never heard of him.'

'He says his uncle is a marquis, de la Poer Beresford.'

'And he believes him! Like you believed that frightful fraud of a doctor. You were both behind the door when they handed out common sense. You write to him and tell him to get himself down to Brisbane. I'll meet him there.'

Georgina was startled. 'I beg your pardon?'

'Tell him to meet me in Brisbane.'

'So now you're off to Brisbane.'

'What's wrong with that?'

'It's very convenient, isn't it? You can take roses to Mrs Palliser every day. Don't you think you're a bit old for her?'

He stopped charging up and down the long sun room, and glared at her.

'How dare you, madam! After her kindness to you!'

'Don't twist my words, Jasin. If you want to go to Brisbane, just go, but don't use Edward as an excuse. And by the way, what did you say to Rosa about her mother?'

'I don't know. Nothing! I just said we knew her. And we did. Why?'

'Because she was asking me about Delia. She seemed to think we'd come out on the same ship.'

'Ah,' Jasin said. 'Now wait a minute. I think I did say something like that.'

'Oh really, Jasin. Was that necessary?'

'What does it matter?'

'It matters a great deal. She was talking about Delia!'

He laughed. 'What did you say?'

'I let the remark about the ship pass, and brought it to her attention that Delia and Juan had actually visited Montone homestead when it was first built and thought it was quite beautiful.'

'So . . . Rivadavia never told her about his wicked ways?'

Georgina was fond of Juan Rivadavia; she hated to admit this. 'I don't think he has.'

'Was she upset? I didn't mean to upset her.'

'I don't know. It's rather worrying.'

Home again, Rosa was bored.

Charlie had missed her. He made a great fuss for the first few days: a romantic evening at the Royal Park Hotel and a jolly weekend with friends at the beautiful Belvedere Country Lodge, but then routine took over.

As it should, she told herself. He had his work, which he loved, and she had her place here, in this very comfortable house, with the best housekeeper in the world, but . . .

She wandered into the garden to cut some flowers, feeling angry with herself that she should be bored, remembering that one of the other doctors' wives had suggested that she should take upon herself some good works. She supposed she should.

Her housekeeper called to her that she had a visitor. Mrs Pilgrim.

Rosa was pleased. This was Lark's first visit since she'd taken up residence, once again, with Juan. She was probably calling to break the news to his daughter officially. Certainly Juan hadn't mentioned that he'd invited his ex-paramour to return to the fold. He would never do that. He wouldn't consider the matter anyone's business but his own. But . . . he would send Lark to tell her, once he'd decided that the arrangement was permanent. Well, more or less permanent, Rosa smiled, until he decided to marry again. He was still a very attractive man.

She ran up the steps to welcome Lark, who was always such fun. She'd missed her when Juan married Dolour, who was far more serious, and not in the least interested in fashion and gossip.

'*Ooh là là!*' Lark called when she walked into the sitting room. 'How beautiful you are, *ma chérie*! I swear you are wasted in this town! He should take you to live in Paris. Did you know I spent three years in Paris? I had a most charming residence on Rue Berton. But there, I talk too much, I am so excited to see you . . .'

'And you, Lark, you are looking very well,' Rosa said, guessing that her father had been generous to her when she was replaced. 'Would you stay for morning tea?'

'Coffee, dear, if you have it. I much prefer coffee. I hope you would not be offended, but I brought some little chocolate eclairs for you.'

'No, I'm delighted. Thank you.' She walked across the room and pulled the cord to summon the maid, and Lark clapped her small hands.

'Ah, it's so good to see you've kept your figure. You always had such a small waist. And you're not letting babies spoil it, like silly young brides do these days. They gallop off to see how many babies they can have, all copying that fat old queen.'

Rosa was laughing so much when the maid came, she was spluttering as she requested coffee, and plates for the eclairs.

'How have you been keeping?' she asked Lark.

'Extremely well. But *chérie*! How intriguing! What have you been up to?'

'Me? Oh, nothing much really.'

'But you went to Sydney. With Lord Heselwood! How *très chic*!'

'No. I went with Lord and Lady Heselwood. I accompanied Lady Heselwood really, to help her get by on the ship . . .'

'No need to make excuses to me. I saw your picture in the paper; no sign of the doctor and it said you were travelling with them! And I thought, she is so gorgeous, Lord Heselwood won't be able to take his eyes off her! And look at you! You naughty girl! You're blushing!'

'I am not, Lark. It was all perfectly proper.'

'So you say, of course,' Lark giggled.

'I thought you might have some news for me.'

'Ah, I do. Your poor father was devastated when Mrs MacNamara passed away . . .'

'Mrs Rivadavia,' Rosa corrected.

'Ah yes, of course. Silly me. Yes, your poor father. A lonely man now, you understand, and getting older. He's asked me to take up residence with him, and as a dear friend, how could I refuse? You wouldn't want me to leave him in the hands of housekeepers at his age, would you, *chérie*?'

Rosa kept a straight face. 'No, of course not, Lark. It's very nice for him to have company.'

'Ah, excellent! You are the sweetest of girls. You always were. I tell my friends you are such a lovely lady. Wasted here. Why don't we all take a trip to Buenos Aires? I know your father has a hankering to go back home . . .'

They chatted on for quite some time, but then as the lunch hour approached, Lark rose to leave. 'You must come to dine. Bring your husband. We shall have a special French menu. I think your papa will like that. You make it soon.'

'Lark, did my father see that picture in the paper?'

'No, no. I did not think he would be happy to see you with Lord Heselwood. He is not a friend, you know.'

'I was not with Lord Heselwood.'

Lark shrugged. 'Ah well.'

After she left, Rosa ate another delicious eclair. Thinking about the Heselwoods, she recalled that conversation with Jasin, when he'd said that they'd come out on the same ship as her mother.

Rosa had found that interesting. She hadn't known it before. And yet Georgina hadn't wished to discuss the ship. In fact a slight redness had appeared on her pale cheeks and she'd launched into the story of how Juan had brought Delia to Montone in its heyday. Before the Aborigines had burned the house down. The story she'd heard a dozen times from all of them, including Delia, who'd claimed that the colony was unsafe, a terrifying place! Juan had had a lovely home on Chelmsford Station, but even that didn't please Delia, who eventually won the argument. He gave in and purchased the house in London for Delia and Rosa, and they'd rarely seen him after that.

'Except for the day he walked in and collected me,' she smiled. 'Rescued me, I used to say.'

She remembered that she had a postcard somewhere. An old postcard of a ship that Delia had given her. She'd said she had voyaged to Australia in that ship with her grandfather, the late Lord Forster.

'There to meet and marry a handsome Argentinian,' Rosa murmured, as she went in search of a small camphor chest that contained a collection of souvenirs.

'Where did I put it?' she asked herself.

'Good God! It's you, Marcus!' Duke called as he ambled down to greet two horsemen at the gate to his homestead.

He turned to the other man, not realising who it was until he saw the white-blond hair. 'And you, Harry! What a surprise! Come on in, both of you, it's good to see you again. I think this calls for a dram or two, wouldn't you say?'

'The surprise was on me,' Harry said. 'It was neighbourly of you to clear my block for me. I've come to thank you.'

'Someone had to do it; you could have hidden an army in there. But what are *you* doing back here, Marcus?' Duke asked.

'Orders,' he shrugged. 'I brought up some new recruits. I had trouble on the way up. My sergeant was killed. I'm waiting for a replacement.'

'Then what?'

'Patrols, I believe. Cameo Downs. Out that way. Harry knows that territory; he worked at Cameo Downs.'

They sat on Duke's veranda for a yarn, and to deliver another surprise for Duke.

'Harry's married,' Marcus said. 'Brought a pretty wife back with him.'

'Congratulations,' Duke said. 'I'm looking forward to meeting the lady. So you'll be living in Rockhampton?'

Harry nodded. 'Sort of . . . I'm looking west.'

'How far west?' Duke asked.

As he listened to Harry's plans, Duke was fascinated. And more than a little envious.

'Jeez,' he said. 'I'd love to come with you. I've been itching to know what's out there.'

'I told you what's out there when we were in Brisbane. It's great country, spectacular and there's good pasture land, but you've got to learn to live with it, not just in it. I had a good teacher in a drover, Slim Collinson . . .'

'Are you saying it's dangerous?'

'Apart from blackfellows? Well, there are no marked routes and no doctors; the countryside can stay the same for a hundred miles before you get a change of scenery; and it's often a struggle to keep up on supplies and water.' He grinned and added: 'Nothing out of the ordinary.'

Marcus was full of enthusiasm for Harry's great trek. 'He has already started getting his equipment together,' he told Duke. 'His garden looks like an ironmonger's yard. And he's got everything labelled, from bridle bits to axe handles. By the way, I've been meaning to ask you, why did you buy a dozen axe handles, Harry? That seems a bit much.'

'Because I can't make them and I won't be able to replace them. That's the secret, Slim told me. I have to make sure I don't forget things like that. Buckets, for instance. They're easy to lose, hard to replace.'

The visitors were interested in the property, so they ambled about the immediate surrounds, and Marcus was surprised to see Duke had so many horses.

'Are any of them for sale?' he asked.

'Yes. I go after brumbies in my spare time. It's great sport and pays well.'

'You ought to contact the super. They're expecting a score of police to arrive in Rockhampton soon, and they'll need horses. These mounts look in good nick; you could name your price.'

'Thanks,' Duke said. 'I'll do that.' His mind was still on Harry's plans, though. 'How many cattle are you taking for a start?'

'Five hundred.'

'What if I matched you?'

'At what?' Harry said amiably.

'Cattle. What if I came along with five hundred cattle of my own? We could pool resources.'

Harry stopped, took off his hat, ran his hand through his hair and scratched the back of his neck.

'Well now, we could talk about it, Duke. Give it some thought maybe. Yeah, we could, but before another word is said, with respect, Duke, there can only be one boss on a drive, and that's me. I'm hiring drovers. No matter what resources you put up, you'd only be another drover. You think about that, mate. Give it plenty of good old-fashioned cogitation before you throw your hat into this ring.'

Marcus was surprised. 'Why would you want to go, Duke? You've got a honey of a place here, all running smoothly. Harry, you ought to buy something like this too. If you're so bent on going through life the hard way, you could take up flagellation, or wear a hair shirt.'

He laughed and turned to Duke. 'He probably already does!'

Harry simply smiled and walked on, but Duke called after him: 'It's not just cattle, is it, Harry?'

'I got the books, Duke. Remember?'

'What books?' Marcus asked, confused.

'Mineralogy,' Duke said. 'They say there are tons and tons of valuable minerals out where he's going.'

'So they say! They say there are tons and tons of gold around Rockhampton too! And who's seen any of that? I haven't.'

'But don't you see what Harry's doing? He's on a three-way bet. He's after land, hundreds of acres, which he'll own in no time. And he can run hundreds of cattle. And look for minerals. Isn't that right, Harry?'

'Whatever you say, gents,' he replied. 'But for me, I'm just going. I always wanted to go, far, far west, and I can't wait to get back out there.'

Before his visitors left, Duke told Harry he was serious about joining the cattle drive.

'Sleep on it awhile,' Harry said, 'and if you're still game, come into town and we'll see about it. And don't sell all your horses to the police yet. I'll need forty and I get first pick. Mate's choice.'

When word spread that newcomer Harry Merriman was planning an expedition inland along the Capricorn line, he had a rush of applications from interested parties. Most were poor settlers with little else than a horse and cart, who had to be turned away.

'I feel sorry for them,' Tottie said to him.

'Save your breath. You wouldn't try to cross the Pacific Ocean in a canoe, would you?'

'No.'

'Well their equipment amounts to the same thing.'

Next came the gentlemen who wanted to sell him necessities like household furniture, cure-all lotions and potions, a whisky still, half-priced pound notes, slightly smudged, a box of odd boots to trade with the blacks, and so on until Tottie placed herself at the gate to deter them.

One visitor surprised them. It was Beresford's friend Ned.

'Good to see you,' Harry said. 'What have you been up to?'

'I've been exploring the district. Been up in the ranges, and out to the coast. It's quite beautiful out there. I've been trying to decide whether to go back home or go on further. Then it occurred to me that you might let me travel with you if I paid my way. I really would like to see that country, Harry, and I could make myself useful. I was born on a cattle station in New South Wales, even though I've spent some years in the Old Country.'

'Were you now? I didn't know that!'

'Yes. And forgive me if I'm speaking out of turn, but I could perhaps help with your finances?'

'In what way?'

'Well, as I said, I would be happy to pay my keep, but obviously cash is no good to you out there. If you named a sum that you thought was fair to cover a tagalong . . .'

'Sorry, Ned. I wouldn't take tagalongs. Only workers.'

'That was the wrong word. Maybe I could come in as your offsider. I'd be willing to pay you, say . . . fifty pounds down, right away. For the privilege of being in on this expedition.'

'Fifty pounds! That's a lot of hay! What's at the end of the rainbow for you? Are you looking for land too?'

Ned leaned on the tray of the large German wagon that Harry was fitting with new wheels. 'I don't actually know. You've been out there, I haven't, so I couldn't say yea or nay to that. But I really would not want to miss this chance of actually getting to travel that far west.'

Harry nodded. 'I know what you mean. I've always had a need to push past boundaries just to see what's beyond. Tell you what, I'll think about it. But as I've said to a couple of other men, I'm the boss, the captain, and like on a ship, my word's the law. You come back and see me in two days, but before you do, remind yourself that this will be tough going.'

That evening he discussed Ned's offer with Tottie. 'Extra money would be handy,' he said, 'but I don't know about taking on a passenger.'

'I thought you said he would be prepared to work.'

'Yes, but at what? I need experienced men.'

'How much experience had you, when you joined Slim's outfit?'

'I was an experienced stockman. That's close enough.'

'Still,' she said, 'he's a nice type of fellow. A bit posh, but . . .'

'That's another worry. I don't know how he'd fit in with the other blokes.'

'And what about this Duke fellow?' she asked. 'He sounds a bit posh too, got his own station and all.'

'Ah no. He's different. He knows cattle. He's lived on a cattle station all his life. But I won't make a decision until you meet him.'

'And what about a guide, Harry? I'd feel so much better if you had one. You say yourself that Slim was uncanny: he could always locate water and find a way through the maze of hills when everyone else worried that he was lost.'

He put an arm around her shoulder, surveying the growing piles of equipment. 'Fear not, my love, I've been given a name. The publican tells me there's a blackfellow called Trader who has been back of beyond time and again.'

'Is he an actual trader?'

'So I believe. They say he treks from tribe to tribe, trading ornaments and boomerangs and things . . .'

'Like a gypsy?'

'I suppose so. But he's known to speak English and can make himself understood in other languages.'

'Don't all the blacks speak the same language in Queensland?'

'They've never heard of Queensland. They've got their own territories all marked out, and their own languages.'

'That's complicated.'

'No different from Europe, I suppose. But I've asked some of the old blackfellows if they can find him for me. I think they will.' He kissed her. 'I'm getting there, love. Day by day.'

'And you're looking more tired day by day. Come and get into a tub and I'll scrub your back for you.'

'I'd rather make love to you.'

Tottie giggled. 'Why don't we do both?'

'Splendid idea. Did I ever tell you how much I love you?'

'I think you did, but I don't believe you, because you're leaving me. You love the wilderness more than you love me.'

'Never,' he said, but there was a slight waver in his voice, as if the required conviction for such a response was lacking.

Tottie heard it. Tottie was so attuned to his every mood that she'd heard it like the dropping of a pin. She looked up at him, and the hurt in her eyes almost broke his heart.

'I do come second, don't I?' she whispered. 'That's why you're able to leave me for a year or more, and not care. I'm your wife, Harry,' she added, pulling away from him. 'Don't you know by this how much I love you? You're my life and yet you can walk away from me . . .'

'Come back to me, Tottie,' he said gently. 'This is the trouble. I have never been so happy in all my life as I have since we were married. I didn't know such love existed, such beautiful contentment. I want to be with you every minute.'

'Then take me with you.'

He folded her in his arms and murmured into her coppery hair: 'I can't leave you, my love. I couldn't ever leave you.'

Having made the decision, Harry was restless that night, until Tottie, curled up in his arms, told him to stop worrying.

'How can I stop? If anything happens to you out there, I'll never forgive myself.'

'Nothing will happen to me except I'll have the best time. I wouldn't have let you go without me, sweetheart, so think positive. Now you won't have to hire some mad cook.'

After further discussion, Harry agreed that Duke could join the party. He immediately arranged to inspect cattle from Duke's herds with a view to purchase.

'No favourites,' he said. 'I'll be hand-picking these cattle. I'm after the fittest herd I can find. If you can fill my bill, Duke, then we ought to muster both of our herds at Mango Hill. I'll need stockhorses too, and a couple of packhorses. When can I have a look at them?'

'What about tomorrow afternoon?'

'Good. But before you go, I want you to meet the camp cook.'

'Have you got one already?'

They walked up to the cabin and Tottie met them at the door. When Harry introduced them, she could hardly wait to find out what was happening. 'Is Duke coming with us?' she asked.

'Yes,' said Duke, and then he looked at Harry. 'Us?'

'I'm the cook,' Tottie said gleefully. 'Isn't that wonderful?'

'That is good news, Mrs Merriman. I'm delighted. I've come across some horrible camp cooks in my day, but now I'm saved that misery.'

'Thank you, Duke, I'll do my best. Now if you look here, I'm making up lists. We'll need flour, sugar, tea, rice, salt, curry . . .'

'All in good time, Tottie,' Harry said. 'We'll sit down with Duke in a couple of days and work it all out. Then you'll be in charge of provisions.'

'Who'll be running your station while you're away?' she asked Duke.

'My overseer can handle it. He's a good man.'

'That's fortunate. And would you mind if I asked you a personal question?'

'Not at all.'

'Why Duke? What's your real name?'

'My real name is Duke. A whim of my father's, that's all.'

'Good on him. Most men's names are so dull. I think Duke is a good name. Cheerful. Reliable.'

'Then I'll have to live up to it, won't I?'

The next morning Ned was on their doorstep, anxious to plead his case.

'I've thought it over carefully,' he said. 'I really hope you'll allow me to join you.'

'So have I,' Harry said, 'and I think you're just the man I need to help me keep the rig in working order. You'll also have definite duties, of course, because everyone has to take turns keeping watch. But I couldn't accept fifty pounds, Ned. Make it thirty and we'll call it square.'

Ned was thrilled. He shook hands with Harry. 'I'm happy to pay more for my passage. I wouldn't want to impose on you. Are you sure thirty is enough?'

'Yes, that's fair. Consider yourself on the team.'

Ned spun about and rushed over to Tottie. 'Did you hear that? I'm to join the trek. Isn't that marvellous?'

She laughed. 'I know just how you feel, Ned. I'm coming too!'

'Are you? Jolly good! It would have been awfully lonely for you to have to stay here on your own.'

He was so excited he hardly knew which way to turn. 'Well . . . I know you're busy. I'd better go back to town now. Unless there's something you want me to do?'

'Yes, you could put a notice on the board at the post office. Drovers wanted. Experienced. For a cattle drive. West. That'll do, won't it?'

'I believe so. Will I put your name and this address?'

'Yes. It's time I started getting drovers lined up.'

Ned almost ran down the path to where Saul was tethered. He rushed over to the horse with his great news.

'We're going west, old boy,' he chortled. 'Way out west. It'll be a huge adventure! I ought to take pen and paper and document a trek like this. And I might just do that.'

He was whistling happily as he rode into town, making for the bank. Ever since he'd arrived in this town he'd felt out of place, a stranger with no business here, but now he too had a part to play, so he was pleased with himself. As soon as he drew out the money to pay his way into Harry's enterprise, he would write to the parents and let them know that he was heading out on this trek. It was quite a coup on his part, he felt, being accepted by these men as a fellow traveller on the arduous journey that this promised to be.

His news would impress his father, he was sure. Jasin would now find out that he wasn't the only one in the family who had the courage, and the ability, to take on the Australian outback. He wondered if his father had ever been as deep into the wilderness as he was planning to go. Rather than quiz Harry too much, Ned had been asking fellows in the bar about distances, and the bushies were only too pleased to discuss the subject that was second only to horses. They figured that places like Cloncurry, where graziers and mineralogists were already putting down stakes, must be nigh on six hundred miles west of Rockhampton as the crow flies.

He rode down the main street, but when he passed the post and telegraph office he remembered the errand Harry had requested, so he dismounted, hitched Saul to a rail and walked back.

Telegram forms, along with scratch pens and drying ink, were available on the high counters under the open window, so he used the back of a form for his advertisement, printing it in bold letters.

There were so many scraps of paper pinned to the noticeboard that Ned could find no room for his important message, so he took it upon himself to restore order. He removed messages that he considered out of date or illegible and dropped them in a paper bin, then replaced others, leaving a neat square in the centre so that Harry Merriman would have pride of place.

The errand completed to his satisfaction, Ned marched off to the bank to draw out his fare, his passage to adventure.

The teller behind the grille looked up with a cheerful smile as Ned approached.

'Good day, your honour,' he called. 'Nice day, eh?'

'Yes, it is indeed.' Ned resisted informing him that he was not a judge, and passed over a slip with his signature, requesting thirty pounds. While he waited, the door swung open and Marcus Beresford strode in, wearing a deeply furrowed frown.

'What's up?' Ned asked his friend. 'You look as if you've swallowed a wasp.'

'That's what it feels like,' Marcus said. 'They've created new police districts out west, and I've been appointed officer-in-charge of the Cloncurry River District! I get to keep a European camp sergeant, thank God, but we have to take a squad of native troopers out there and set up headquarters! Without delay!'

'But that's where we're going! Maybe not that far, but I believe we'll be in your district! What a stroke of luck!'

'Luck nothing!' Marcus scowled. 'It's the end of the bloody earth! And what do you mean? Are you going with Harry's team?'

'Yes!'

'Excuse me, sir, your honour . . .' The teller was asking for Ned's attention.

'Just a minute!' Marcus barked at him. 'Are you mad?' he snapped at Ned. 'It's one thing to toddle up the coast with me, another to take on that country without military training. It's alive with wild blacks! Forget it! Go home!'

'God, no! I'm dying to go. It will be terrific.'

'Excuse me, sir, Mr Heselwood . . .' the clerk persisted, and Ned laughed as he turned back to the teller.

'Stop worrying, Marcus. I'll catch up with you later.'

'Mr Heselwood . . .' The teller leaned forward and spoke in a hushed voice. 'I'm very sorry, but you haven't got thirty pounds in the bank. You've only got nine pounds, two shillings and thrippence.'

'Rot! Have another look! You'll see that·I do have the funds available.'

'Perhaps . . . the manager?' the teller whispered.

'Yes. This minute! Where is he?'

Ned was quickly ushered through a swinging door to find the manager hastily pulling on his jacket.

'What's this?' he asked. 'I'm informed my account is low. But if you recall, I have a letter of credit signed by my father, whom I believe you know quite well, sir.'

'That I do, that I do, Mr Heselwood. A fine man. Unfortunately, it appears Lord Heselwood is making other arrangements for you. I have a telegram here . . .'

He handed it to Ned and stood back, hands anxiously clenched at his paunch as he awaited Ned's reaction.

'He's cancelled the letter of credit?' Ned was bewildered. 'Can he do that?'

'I'm so very sorry, Mr Heselwood. Yes.'

'And now I only have nine pounds in this account?' He tried to make it sound as if he had other accounts, to save face. 'Then could I have the nine pounds?' he said stiffly, not wanting to have to line up again.

'Certainly, Mr Heselwood.' The manager fled to the teller, dug him in the ribs and whispered his mission . . . his urgent, anxious, mission . . . standing impatiently while the teller counted the money again and stuffed it into a brown envelope. Then he galloped the few steps back to Ned and pushed the money into his hand as one would to a beggar.

'Thank you, sir,' Ned said graciously. 'You've been most helpful.'

Outside, the glare of raw sunlight seemed harsher than usual. He felt sick. Bilious! As if he'd had a sunstroke. Somehow he managed to ride across town to the boarding house and take refuge in his room to digest this low blow, this destroyer of the chance of a lifetime.

His landlady came to the door. 'Mr Heselwood. There's a telegram for you. Did someone die?'

'I'll see,' he said quietly. He opened the telegram with care and read the neat handwriting. 'No one died,' he said to her. 'I've got a job as a station manager.'

She beamed. 'Well, I say! That *is* something then, isn't it?'

He closed the door and stared at the telegram.

Return immediately to your duties at Montone Station and earn your keep. Father.

That afternoon Ned Heselwood failed to appear. Harry was worried, not about the money for Ned's passage, as he called it, but because it seemed out of character. The fellow was so excited to have joined the team that Harry would have bet a gold brick Ned would have been back within the hour.

But then he did have other people to see.

While he was working in the yard, Tottie called out to him that there was a blackfellow standing at the gate.

245

'Go down and see what he wants!'

'Righto.'

Tottie hurried down the path, startling a flock of galahs that were scrabbling about in the grass. The birds protested with a sudden flurry of pink and grey feathers but returned quickly to the business at hand, stomping around, head down, picking at seeds like little old ladies. Tottie laughed.

'Dropped your knitting, did you?' she said to them.

Ladjipiri heard the laughter and judged it a good omen.

When she came towards him with a smile of goodness, and hair the colour of the brilliant rocks out there in the far country, he knew she would lead him to his son. To Banggu.

As soon as his cousins came to tell him that a white feller was preparing to drive cattle out there, and needed a guide, his wife had insisted that he take the job.

'I lost one son to them. You have to go over those mountains again and search for my other son.'

'They're taking more of the cattle beasts. Why should I help them?'

'Because you can't stop them. No one can. If you don't go, others will take the job. You won't be missed. But with the white men you can listen to their talk, find out things. Watch for my son.'

'Our son, woman! Even if I find him, I can't bring him back. He's not safe here any more.'

She wept. 'Can't you hear what I'm asking? I have to know that he is still alive, not shot by a gun and thrown to the crows in the gorge like what happened on that terrible day . . . the day you found and buried his friend! What happened to Banggu? No one has seen him to this hour. Did he die there or is he safe with your friends? You must tell me.'

Ladjipiri took a deep breath and stood tall by the gate.

'I am looking for Mr Merry,' he said to the woman, and found himself grinning as the word suddenly translated itself in his mind.

'Mr Merry,' he said again, knowing that this woman would, of course, be Mrs Merry. They were indeed strange people, these white folk.

Tottie looked at the tall blackfellow with a plaited band holding back long greying hair, and a face like a rock that had sprouted a dark goatee. He was wearing ragged dungarees and a shirt, both too small for his large frame.

'Yes, Mr Merry is here,' she said, anxious to please. 'Are you Mr Trader?'

He nodded. 'Trader.'

'Good, come on in.'

The fence was of wire, strung between posts and the gate, Harry's invention of crossed saplings, hung on rawhide hinges. Trader stepped over it easily.

The two men sat crossed-legged on the ground beside a large covered wagon.

Mr Merry had blue eyes, not of the sky but of deep blue water on a sunny day. They were full of love for his woman. In the front of those eyes was a firmness, but in the depths, hurt. This man was still carrying crying that he'd never put down. He was a physically strong man, and that was all to the good, Ladjipiri thought when he heard where this boss wanted to take cattle.

'That country hard on white fellers, boss.'

'I know. I've been out there before. We drove cattle to the Thomson River, but the local Aborigines were unhappy, so we pulled back to Cameo Downs. You know Cameo Downs? Plenty black fella live there.'

Ladjipiri nodded, remembering the white woman the Irikandji men had killed, near the river that he had since learned was called 'Tom's son'. And that ocean of cattle. Was he looking at this man for a second time?

'I'm the boss this time,' Mr Merry was saying. 'I'm not taking so many cattle. But Trader, I want you to know that I don't wish black people any harm. I want to be friends. My wife too. She is a kind person. Would you tell people that? Can you tell them we come in peace?'

He nodded.

'Do you speak the same language as the black folk out there?'

'Some. All different.'

Mr Merry groaned. 'That's too bad. I had hoped to learn the language. Which one should I learn?'

Ladjipiri was astonished. He'd never heard of a white man talking proper black language. He scratched his head. Pitta Pitta people might talk with him. Then again, it might be safer for Mr Merry to learn Kalkadoon. He shuddered. He didn't wish these people any harm either. He wanted no part of the wars out there. He just wanted to find Banggu.

'Better maybe you learn some Kalkadoon words, like me.'

'Why? Are you Kalkadoon tribe?'

'No. I learn them. This man, this country Darambal. Out there Kalkadoon country, Pitta Pitta country. Depend where you walk.'

He saw that Mr Merry was startled. And even some fear showed.

'Allasame, you know,' he said.

'Yes, thank you, Trader. I'm a bit worried now that I am taking my wife.'

Ladjipiri had no opinion on that.

'So will you be our guide?' the boss asked.

'Can do.'

'Then what about we have something to eat? You like some tucker?'

Ladjipiri nodded. 'Plenty hungry.'

★ ★ ★

As they both stood, the conference over, Harry was surprised to see Ladjipiri turn and stride off towards the street.

Next thing he was back with a large plaited dilly bag, a tall spear, a boomerang and a hunting knife. These he placed on the ground under a black wattle tree.

'Are they for trading?' Harry asked.

'No plurry fear. These good hunting fellers. We eat now?'

Their guide had moved in, but their passage-paying friend was still in his boarding house, thanking the Lord that he had chosen cheap accommodation rather than one of the finer establishments on Quay Street.

'I'd be out on my ear by this,' he moaned. He'd long learned to beware of pricey hotels, not because of the daily rates but because of the amount of cash he could be inveigled to spend once caught in their clutches.

But that was small consolation now. He supposed he could send a telegram to Jasin, asking for his credit to be re-established.

'And waste the price of the telegram!' he muttered.

But what about Mother? Would she help? Not if her husband forbade it. It wasn't as if she could slip him a few pounds; she'd have to go to the bank and explain. Jasin would find out, and the last thing their son wanted to do was to cause ructions between them.

So. It seemed that all that was left was to go to Harry and explain that his funds were too low to be able to pay his way on the expedition after all. Make a clean breast of it. Wish them well and fade into the night. Unless . . .

Unless he applied for a job as a drover. He could do that. Just riding alongside a mob of cattle, day in and day out. Why hadn't he thought of that in the first place?

Then he remembered the notice that he had written and placed on the noticeboard at the post and telegraph office. It had specified that Harry needed experienced drovers. Ned would embarrass the man horribly by applying for a drover's job, forcing rejection.

So that's that, he told himself. I'll ride out to see Harry, apologise to him, and make myself scarce. But I'm damned if I'll go back to Montone with my tail between my legs after this insult. I'll simply have to find employment up here somewhere.

His horse was hitched to a rail in a shady spot under a spreading poinciana tree carpeted with fallen orange blossoms, and he looked quite splendid in those lovely surrounds.

'You look as if you're posing,' Ned said to him as he walked over and patted his flanks.

And then it occurred to Edward Heselwood that here was his answer.

He dismissed the idea out of hand. He couldn't do that! It would be a sacrilege. A terrible thing to do.

'Very well. Go back to Montone,' a voice said. 'Forget the grand expedition!'

He sat on the fence by that poinciana tree for more than an hour before he rode out to the sale yards and met a fellow called Chester Newitt, auctioneer.

'I want to buy a good stockhorse,' he said.

'Then I'm your man, sir. Ain't you Ned, friend of Officer Beresford?'

'That's correct.'

'Thought so. Well I'll look after you. I just happen to have a good strong feller here.'

'I want a horse that can handle a long journey.'

'You mean you want a packhorse?'

'No. I want a good horse that I can ride.'

'If you don't mind me saying, Ned, what about the one you're riding. He's bloody beautiful.'

'He's for sale.' Edward fought a gulp and the sting of a tear.

'What?'

'I'm going far west on a cattle drive. With drovers. Saul is far too good a horse to take out there.'

Newitt shook his head, disagreeing, but made no comment.

'I want two hundred pounds for him,' Edward said.

'Hey now, wait on, mate. That's a bit hot.'

'I've got his papers . . .'

'So you might, and it's easy seen he's top class, but we've got a lot of horse breeders up here, and a shortage of ready cash. Like half the world might want to own that beauty, but not this half. What's his name?'

'Red Shadow, but we call him Saul.'

'I tell you what. A horse like this deserves a good home.'

'Of course.'

'Then I'll take him off your hands myself, for a hundred, cash down. On the table.'

'I presume you're joking.'

'I'm making you a darn good offer, but I'll throw in one of our best stockhorses, a tough feller called Merlin. He's quick on his feet and smart as a tack. You wouldn't be going with Harry Merriman?'

'Yes.'

'Then believe me, Harry's a good judge of horses. He'd have my hide if I foisted a second-rate stockhorse on his mate.'

In the end, Chester Newitt bought Saul for one hundred and twenty-nine pounds, and Harry's mate Ned rode away on a black stockhorse called Merlin with a white flash on his forehead.

Proudly Chester galloped into town on Saul, showing off. Everyone was impressed, except his wife.

'Are you mad, paying that much money for a horse!'

'He's worth every penny.'

'But you don't need a horse like that, you fool of a man.'

'We'll see who's a fool when Harry Merriman's mob get on the road.'

'Why?'

'Because that's when I'll advertise Red Shadow far and wide, and have a special auction right here in town. Maybe even at the town hall.'

Harry's first question was: 'Where's Saul?' and Ned was taken aback.

He hadn't given a thought to a blunt enquiry like that, though he'd expected that someone would notice he was missing, sooner or later.

'Um . . . I sold him.'

'What the hell for?'

Ned was about to say that he had been offered a good price for him, as if it were a simple business deal, but he hesitated, and then blurted:

'My old man stopped the funds. I needed the money.'

'Ah, that's bad luck. Why did he pull the plug? Not happy about you coming on the drive?'

'More than that. He hasn't got a lot of time for me, to be honest. I seem to have a habit of letting him down.'

'That's not hard,' Harry growled. 'I could never do anything right for my old man. If you can't afford to pay now, you can fix me up another time.'

'No! I've got the passage money here now.' He handed Harry the cash and smiled. 'I say, that feels good. I'm really on my way now. Incidentally, did you receive any replies to the advertisement?'

'Yes. I've got a few starters, including two men who were on Slim Collinson's drive with me . . . Come up and meet them.'

Ned was introduced to drovers Matt Doolan and Ginger Magee, the latter a much older fellow, a typical bushman, who reminded him of his father's offsiders, Jack and Clem, now running Montone Station. And to Trader, Harry's Aborigine guide, a strange-looking fellow with long, skinny legs.

'Is your friend Duke coming too?' he asked.

'Oh yes, he's as keen as mustard. Bringing his own herd. We'll have about a thousand cattle.'

'That's interesting. Is there anything I can do to help?'

'Sure. Tottie would appreciate some help with collecting and packing provisions. She's being very particular, keeping a record of stores so that she knows what to buy at villages along the way, until that source dries up and we're on our own.'

'Right you are. I'll go up and see her now.' He hesitated, then . . . 'By the way, I've been meaning to ask you. I used to know a kid called Duke. It's an unusual name. What's his surname?'

'MacNamara. He's got a brother here too. Another cattleman. Is it the same fellow?'

Ned Heselwood forced himself to answer normally. 'It seems so. Yes.'

'Well whaddya know! It's a small world.'

Duke had everything under control. He was glad now that he'd retained Murphy's overseer Snowy Drummond, because he knew he could safely leave Snowy in charge of Mango Hill while he was away. So with that finalised, he had arranged to take Harry out to see Paul about picking up more cattle from him. He couldn't afford to decimate his own herds.

And now there was time to do the very thing he'd been putting off ever since he'd decided to join this cattle drive.

Write to Lucy Mae.

Though he knew they'd be sure to have all sorts of problems on this trek, he had managed to shake off thoughts of danger. There was danger right here, he'd told himself. Snakes, crocs, fever, stampedes, bad weather . . . all of these hazards were not confined to the back country, so there was no use worrying on that account. As for the Aborigines, well, as Harry had said, you simply made certain you were armed at all times.

Still, he reflected, he'd be away a long time. Months. So he should at least write to Lucy Mae. Keep in touch.

But his letter took on a life of its own.

He had started off hoping she was keeping well and that the Brisbane weather was kinder these days with the humidity of the wet season over. Then he announced that he was off on this cattle drive to the far west in a few days, describing the great distances they would be covering, and that caused him to become a little emotional, as if there were a chance he might never see her again, and so he was on to another page, telling her that he missed her and that he was truly sorry if he had offended her in any way. He didn't seem to notice, as Lucy Mae did when she read this letter, that his father's fate was weighing heavily upon him. Though he did not mention Pace, he seemed to think he might not return from this long journey. To Lucy Mae, it sounded like a premonition. And then it came. He told Lucy Mae that he truly loved her, again asking her to forgive him for his wrongful attitude, because of his own foolishness, and begging her in all sincerity to honour him by consenting to be his wife.

Lucy Mae wept when she received his letter. She was emotionally exhausted. Tears blotted the earnest words written by the father of the child she was carrying as she read it over and over. Then she hid it in the small pocket of her skirt. She couldn't bear to discuss it with anyone, least of all her mother, who, as yet, had not noticed that her first grandchild was stirring.

The maid announced there was a lady visitor. 'I put her in the sitting room.'

'Mother will see to her,' Lucy Mae called through her closed door, frantically pressing a damp handkerchief to her eyes.

'You mother is out, Lucy Mae.'

'Oh yes, I forgot. Who is it?'

'Mrs Palliser.'

'Who?'

'Dr Palliser's wife.'

'Rosa? Oh. All right. I won't be a minute.'

Rosa was disappointed that Milly wasn't home. 'I was just passing by and I thought how remiss I was not to have called on your mother for quite some time. But you're Lucy Mae, aren't you? I thought I saw you at the funeral.'

'Yes, Mrs Palliser, I am, and it's very nice to meet you. My mother will be sorry she missed you. Would you care for tea?'

'Oh, no thanks. But I'm still Rosa,' she smiled. 'I was wondering if you and your mother would care to come to tea one afternoon. Just ladies, the three of us. Perhaps Wednesday?'

Lucy Mae shook her head. 'I'm sorry, I don't think so. She hasn't been well. I mean, I'm not feeling well.'

At that she burst into tears.

Rosa gasped. 'Oh goodness! What's wrong, Lucy Mae?' She put an arm around her, trying to comfort her, but that seemed only to make matters worse. She sobbed as if her heart would break and Rosa felt so sorry for her. 'Can I help?' she asked gently.

'Would you please close the door!'

'Do you want me to go?'

'Oh no. I'm sorry. I just . . . the maids, I don't want them fussing.'

'Yes, of course. I see.' Rosa jumped up and closed the door.

'Can it be all that bad?' she asked.

'Oh yes. I'm sorry, Rosa. I'm such a fool.'

'No you're not. Now what is wrong? I insist you tell me. If it's a dark secret I promise I won't tell a soul.'

As her sobs began to subside, Lucy Mae looked at her visitor and saw a sweetness that surprised her. She'd always thought Rosa had grown into a very haughty person, who wore gorgeous clothes. Like today, she thought miserably, as she noticed Rosa's navy silk suit, the floor-length skirt weighted with a wide hem.

'I'm sorry to be so stupid, really I am. We'd love to have tea with you . . .'

Another storm of tears erupted and Rosa put her arms about her again. 'Come on now . . . has there been a death?'

'Oh no! Nothing like that.' Lucy Mae took a deep breath, fished out the letter and handed it to her new friend.

'Should I read this? Are you sure?' Rosa asked. Lucy Mae simply nodded. 'Why! It's from Duke!'

'Yes.'

Rosa seemed to take an interminable time to read the letter, and when she saw her turn a page Lucy Mae whispered: 'You won't tell anyone, will you?'

'No, of course not,' Rosa said absently. 'But why are you crying? He's proposing to you! This is marvellous, Lucy Mae. You should be happy, jumping with joy.'

'Oh no!' Lucy Mae took the letter quickly and slipped it back into her pocket. 'Here's my mother!'

'Don't you want her to know?'

'Definitely not. Please don't say a word.'

'All right.' Rosa opened her handbag and took out a small gold compact that contained white face powder. She fluffed some over Lucy Mae's cheeks and dabbed a little more around her eyes. 'There,' she said. 'That helps. Now let me smooth your hair back.'

Lucy Mae managed a smile. 'I've never worn face powder before.'

'Then you must get some! It's very handy.'

When Milly dashed in, she was all of a flutter. She gave Rosa a hug.

'For heaven's sake, I was wondering whose gig it was out there, and it's you, Rosa. How good of you to call. And you, Lucy Mae, what are you thinking of? Have you ordered tea or a cool drink for Rosa?'

'No, it's all right,' Rosa said, taking command. 'I was just passing when I realised that Lucy Mae and I are almost strangers, so I called by to ask her to tea on Wednesday, and she has kindly accepted. But I have to run along now. By the way, Milly, there was something I wanted to ask you. When you first came to Australia, what ship did you come in?'

'Oh. The *Emma Jane*, my dear. Dermott and I were so young. But why did you . . .'

Rosa lied: 'I'm just doing a little "life and times" card for Georgina Heselwood's birthday next month.'

'Very nice, very acceptable, those cards. How is Georgina? I believe you took on the role of nurse after the accident. What exactly happened to her?'

'It's a long story. I'll tell you another time. Now I really must go. Don't forget Wednesday, Lucy Mae. Pip-pip!'

'Extraordinary!' Milly said. 'Pip-pip? What's that? Argentinian for ta-ta? She might have extended an invitation to me. She's my friend.'

'I think she might be lonely for company her own age,' Lucy Mae ventured as she drifted out of the sitting room.

'What are you going to wear?'

'Oh Mother, I don't know.'

Lucy Mae was on her way to the kitchen, relieved to find no one about as she quietly fed Duke's letter into the hot coals of the stove. As she stood by to watch the pages curl at the edges and then flame, she had a small sense of relief that her mother would never get her hands on it. She just couldn't bear for her to read it.

And Rosa! 'I don't know what possessed me to show it to her,' she moaned as she slipped out the side door and walked quickly away from the house, 'but she was really kind. And very smart.'

Lucy Mae was amazed at the way Rosa had taken over. Obviously she had meant to continue the conversation . . . hopefully without any more blubbering, and had very neatly sidestepped having to include Milly.

'Takes practice, that,' she mused. Milly was always saying Rosa was a little minx, thoroughly spoiled by her father, but from Lucy Mae's point of view, the little minx was a very likeable person.

She was nervous about the invitation to tea and rather hoped Rosa would send a message with some excuse to cancel, because she didn't dare beg off. She'd never hear the end of it from her mother. It would be easier to go.

Lucy Mae had wandered around to the front gate and was walking along the leafy street before she realised that she wasn't wearing a hat, or gloves, but then, and suddenly, she found she didn't care. Not one whit! She kept going, thinking of Duke's letter, wondering if Rosa had noticed the date. It had been written three weeks ago.

Duke would have left on the cattle drive by this time.

Tottie was as meticulous as her husband in preparing for the drive. While he was making certain all of their equipment was in good repair, she was busy pickling vegetables and salting meat, and it occurred to Ned that these arrangements were not unlike preparations for a sea voyage.

He was a bit surprised to be detailed off to kitchen duty while other men were working at oiling and packing equipment, but he took it in good part when he saw she needed him to start loading heavy bags of provisions into the store wagon as she checked them off.

They got along remarkably well. She insisted he call her Tottie, otherwise she'd have to call him Mr Heselwood; she advised him to grow a beard to save having to shave, and get himself a sheepskin jacket because Harry had told her that the nights out west could be very cold.

When he'd done all he could to help her, for the time being, Ned dutifully reported to Harry that he had to go to see someone, but would be back early in the morning.

'Good. I'd like you here to keep an eye on things. I'm going out to Oberon Station to look over some more cattle. If any more drovers come asking about the job, have a talk to them, and if you think they'll be any good, tell them to come back in the morning. Just use your own judgement; get rid of the dross.'

The stockhorse, Merlin, was a feisty fellow, and Ned thought he'd enjoyed the ride out to Mango Hill Station as much as he did, although the horse, unlike his rider, wasn't carrying the burden of trepidation.

He tried to think of other things. Like his father's fury when he discovered that Saul had been sold. Correction, that he had sold the horse. And Jasin's teeth gnashing when he was informed that his son, his only son, had not reported for duty as ordered.

Anyone would think the old man had been in the military the way he carried on, ordering people about.

He considered writing to Jasin before he left for the wilds. But after that insulting telegram, forget it! Then again, he really should write to his mother.

Edward hadn't cared about being packed off to England at the age of seventeen. He'd found it exciting to voyage across the world alone and he'd had a jolly time aboard ship. He'd been looking forward to staying with his mother's family. They too were titled people and well off, and since he'd presented at the door with the family's fair good looks and manners, he'd expected to fit in easily. It hadn't occurred to him that he would not. That they would look down on him as a mere colonial, socially beyond the pale. That they would raise eyebrows at his accent, and give astonished visitors slyly apologetic glances when his voice surprised them.

His cousins called him a liar to his face when he told them, in answer to their questions, that his father ran thousands of cattle. That being the last straw, Edward began to fight. And that he could do, having grown up on a colonial cattle station. He was in so many fist fights, his uncle called him a thug, and insisted he learn to behave or leave his house.

'You have come to me with an unsavoury reputation,' he said. 'For your own good I would not besmirch the family name by ever allowing the reason for that reputation to pass my lips, but believe me, had either of my sons committed such a dastardly act, I would have horsewhipped them myself. It is therefore incumbent upon you to pray to God for forgiveness, and the ability to repent your actions.'

That night, for the first time since his drunken attack on Mrs MacNamara, Edward truly saw the enormity of his actions and experienced a sense of shame that had him feeling nauseous for weeks. It was as if his self-respect had been shattered beyond repair.

Gradually he began to pick up the pieces, acknowledging that he was no longer in a position to strut about as the boss's son; that he'd been demoted to something akin to the poor relation. Somehow he managed to settle down in this unpleasant environment, until he heard snide remarks about his reason for residing in England, and knew it had leaked out that he had been banished from his homeland.

He reflected on all this, admitting there wasn't much he could do about gossip but realising that he could fight back in other ways. He began to pay attention to sporting activities, beginning with cricket. He'd only played backyard games at home, on rough pitches, but now he really concentrated on the game and was soon a valued player.

Eventually there came a time when people stopped bothering him. He was even invited to join a hunt club, but he declined, simply because he found the concept too formal, thereby branding himself a misfit again. By then, as the years had passed, he had found his own interests and enjoyed the wonderful social life afforded single men about town – until his father advised it was time to come home.

Edward was surprised to find he'd arrived at the gates of Mango Hill so soon, and had to hurry himself into the present to face up to what could be a very awkward situation.

Dogs barked as he rode towards the small homestead, and as he had expected, there was a tremendous amount of activity taking place on this station. He bypassed the house and followed the raised dust down to the mustering yards, where horses were being branded.

'I'm looking for Duke,' he called to some stockmen.

'The blacksmith's,' one of the men answered with a jerk of his thumb.

Duke was in there, examining some ironmongery as the blacksmith hammered at a red-hot horseshoe on his anvil. He was bigger, heavier, but it was young Duke all right!

At first MacNamara didn't hear him speak, over the double clang of the hammer, but then he turned, squinting at the figure standing in the light.

'Could I have a word?' Edward called.

'Yeah,' Duke said easily.

As he approached, Edward smiled. 'You don't remember me?'

'I can't see you against the glare. Should I remember you?'

'Yes, I think so. I've joined Harry's drive. I'll be riding with you.'

'Ah well, good for you!' Duke was obviously perplexed, but he stuck out his hand. 'What did you say your name was?'

'Ned.'

'Ah. Right! Yes, Harry mentioned you. And by God! Now I look at you, aren't you the bloke I collected from muggers one rainy night in Brisbane? I stuck you in a cab with a cranky driver! Now I remember you!'

It was Ned's turn to be confused. 'Was it you? Then I must thank you. I don't remember much about that night, I have to say: rather too much imbibing at the Palace.'

Duke laughed. 'Me too! I shoved you off to the Royal Park Hotel.'

'There's something else I wanted to remind you about, Duke, and hope you won't hold it against me. I'd appreciate it if we could be friends.'

'Why wouldn't we be?'

'My name. It's Heselwood. Ned Heselwood.' He braced himself for an explosion.

'Heselwood?' Duke blinked, brushed dust from his right eye. 'Heselwood. Carlton Park? That Heselwood?'

'Yes. Our fathers didn't get on too well,' Ned said, praying with all his heart that Georgina was right, that Duke's mother had not told her family about that event.

'You're Lord Heselwood's son?'

'Yes. Edward, but I prefer Ned.'

'What are you doing taking on a cattle drive? Your old man's got enough cattle to feed England.'

'I just wanted to do something myself. Something different. Cut loose a bit, if you see what I mean,'

'Don't we all,' Duke said. 'Family reins can get bloody tight.'

'Exactly.'

'Especially yours, I bet,' Duke grinned. 'We were all a bit scared of your dad, and he and my dad didn't just not get on, they hated one another!'

'Too competitive, I think.'

'You could be right there. Anyway, I'm pleased to meet you. I heard you lived in England. What were you doing there?'

'Nothing much. Having a good time.'

'Nothing much? Jeez, Ned. Are you sure you know what you're doing? I mean, this trek won't be a ride in the park.'

'I'll be all right.'

Duke shook his head in doubt, then said: 'Listen, I've got a bit more to do here. You can have a look around. I'll meet you up at the house in an hour or so. Make yourself at home. There's rum in the kitchen.'

He turned back to talk to the blacksmith and Ned walked away, his nerves still on edge. He had rehearsed his speech of abject apology to have it ready if that old business with Mrs MacNamara was thrown up at him . . . probably delivered with a fist to the chin . . . and now he could breathe easily again. But the connection with Duke had to be made before they set off, and had this man vetoed his inclusion in the team, he would have had to pull out.

He found the rum bottle, poured a shot, tossed it down and walked out to the veranda. He looked over at two Aborigine women sitting under a mango tree plaiting strips of rawhide into ropes as they talked, dark fingers flying.

Everyone on this station seemed to be working at top speed to get the boss properly equipped for the drive; he'd seen saddlers and fettlers at work; canvas ground sheets, blankets and billy cans neatly laid out in a barn ready to be rolled into swags. He'd spoken to a veterinarian who was checking on the horses and asked him if he were coming along on the trek.

'No bloody fear!' was the swift response.

His talk with Duke soon got around to women. 'You married?' he asked.

'Not yet,' Duke said. 'I've got a girl in Brisbane. You might remember her. Lucy Mae Forrest.'

'The name's familiar, but I can't place her.'

'What about you? Did you bring a wife back with you from England?'

'Ah, that's rather a sore spot. I intended to. A young lady and I planned to marry, but her parents stepped in and refused permission.'

'Why?'

'They didn't consider me socially acceptable.'

'Why not? With your dad a lord and all that, I would have thought you'd be a shoo-in.'

'Oh, not at all. We're colonials, you know. Not quite the thing.'

'Well bugger them!'

Ned laughed. 'I'd better get going. I imagine we'll have plenty of time to talk soon.'

'Yes. Bring your best yarns.'

They were days away from departure.

Paul and Laura were in town. Paul had sold more than eighty head of cattle to Harry . . . no thanks to his brother for sending out the buyer, of course, Duke reflected crankily . . . and they'd stayed to witness the exodus, which was turning into quite an occasion.

As a result, Paul was marching about Mango Hill, making himself useful, as he told the station hands. He was busy checking every aspect of the drive to be sure his brother had everything under control, and it annoyed the hell out of Duke. Especially when Paul claimed that the branding had been slapdash and ordered a recheck of the herd he was taking. He seemed to be interfering all over the place, insisting that Duke should include a couple of packhorses with their own balanced saddles, for emergencies, even though they were taking two wagons, a cook-wagon, and the Merriman home on wheels.

Paul even knew Trader, who was now camped at Mango Hill with most of the other men, and made a great fuss of him.

'You couldn't do better than Trader,' he told Duke, and the guide stared at them, astonished.

'This your brudder?' he asked Paul.

'Surely is, my young brother!'

'I din know dat,' he said, and patted Duke on the shoulder. 'Why not you come too, Mister Paul? See all big different lands.'

'One day I'll have a look out there. You just keep an eye on my brother, eh?'

Trader nodded, looking suddenly sad, and wandered off.

'His son was one of the boys they hanged,' Paul said, but Duke wasn't interested.

'Yes. I heard. Someone said Moynihan is up at the house. What does he want?'

'I don't know. You'd better go and see.'

The police sergeant was yarning with a couple of the drovers at the water tank. He didn't seem in any hurry.

'What's up?' Duke asked him.

'I just arrested one of your men. Got him locked in the shed over there. Thought I'd better wait and give you the drum.'

'Who's been arrested? What for? We haven't had any bother out here.'

'No, but Murphy did. Remember? The horse thieves. Murphy's had someone keeping an eye on one of your neighbours; he had a stockman planted there. We've tracked down quite a few of the horses already.'

'Which neighbour?'

'Jimmy Kimber. Out on your west boundary. A lot of scrub country. Do you know him?'

'I only met him once. He seemed all right.'

'Maybe so, but he's been arrested, and he spilled the beans. He had a mate working here who set up the job for him. They did all right out of it too, except that Murphy was suspicious of Snowy Drummond all along.'

'Who?' Duke almost shouted. 'Snowy? My overseer!'

'Your ex-overseer, mate,' Moynihan grinned. 'I'm taking him in.'

Paul had come up at the tail-end of the conversation. 'Isn't Snowy the one you were leaving to manage the station?' he asked Duke, genuinely concerned about this sudden and very awkward setback.

'Reckon I came just in time,' Moynihan was highly amused now. 'You'd probably have got home to find your Mango Hill turned into Mother Hubbard's.'

'Snowy would have left you a steer or two, Duke,' one of the men laughed, as he took a dipper of water.

'Yeah. Or he could claim it wasn't his fault. Someone left the gate open.'

'That's right,' the first man hooted. 'While they were having a barn dance.'

'Bloody hell!' Duke spat, ignoring the humour. 'Get him out of here, Moynihan, before I throttle him myself.'

He stormed up to the house with Paul hard on his heels.

'Now what?' he asked Duke. 'Who's your next in line?'

'For what?'

'To manage the place.'

'I don't bloody know. Snowy was the only one with any go in him. The rest of the blokes here probably couldn't count to ten, let alone run a show like this.'

'Well you'll have to find someone quick.'

'Don't I bloody know that!'

Paul stirred up the stove and put the kettle on. Duke stood in the kitchen doorway staring out towards the Ironstone Mountain of the rear of his property.

Eventually he turned back to his brother. 'Have you got anyone? You could send over one of your blokes.'

'No fear. It has taken me a long time to get good men at Oberon. I wouldn't mind lending you one of them for a week or so, but you'll be away for the best part of three months. You'd better ride into town and ask around. I'll keep things moving here.'

'Ah yes, you're a big bloody help.'

'Are you sure there isn't anyone you could count on here?'

'I told you no!' Duke was taking three good stockmen with him, but there was no point in asking one of them to stay behind and run Mango Hill. Those men, he knew, would make good drovers but they were fancy-free characters who'd run a mile from the responsibility of a station and its workforce.

Paul made strong black tea and neither of them had much to say until Duke came up with an idea.

'What about you run this place? If your men are that good, you can leave someone in charge and manage Mango Hill for me.'

'Why the hell would I do that?'

'I'd pay you.'

'You couldn't pay me enough. You were underpaying Snowy, I noticed.'

'You could do me a favour; that wouldn't kill you.'

'Ah yes. Like you did. Grabbing this place from under my nose.'

'So now you're going to punish me? I might have known that would be coming sooner or later.'

'Jesus, you carry on, Duke! You go off half-cocked in every direction then expect people to fix your blunders. Like borrowing money on Kooramin.'

'I'll pay it back!'

'When? From what I hear, you're going backwards.'

'You would say that! You'll look stupid when I get home from the west with more land staked out than you've ever seen.'

'Righto. Let's see you do it. I'm going home.'

Paul strode from the house without a backward glance. Duke remembered his immediate problem, and felt trapped. He had twenty-four hours to locate an experienced station manager, and they were always hard to find. He'd had Chester Newitt trying to find him one for weeks before he finally settled on Snowy Drummond. The bastard!

He kicked a chair out of his way, left the house and headed for the stables. Paul was still there, ready to mount up.

'Tell you what,' Duke said. 'I'll lease Mango Hill to you.'

'Ah yes? For how long?'

'One year.'

'Don't waste my time. I wouldn't make a bean in a year. Your herd needs building up and you haven't made any improvements here since you bought this place, not a bloody thing. You haven't even fixed the wall of the barn, which looks as if it'll fall down any day.'

'Two years.'

'Didn't you hear what I said? You've let this place run down. Thought it was easy being the boss, didn't you? I wouldn't lease it. Find someone else.'

He banged his hat on to his head and mounted his horse. 'Then again,' he said, 'I could buy it from you.'

'The hell you will!'

'Righto, please yourself.'

Paul sent the horse trotting quickly across the courtyard and out of the open gateway, and before Duke could think of a reply, he'd taken off down the hill at a canter, to eventually emerge from a clump of trees, streaking across open country towards the road.

Even if he wanted to, Duke thought dully, he'd never be able to catch him now.

Mr and Mrs MacNamara dined in the hotel that night, and were interested to hear that Beresford had already been ordered to set up a police district in the far west.

'That's good news,' Paul said, but Laura was concerned.

'I thought they were sending more European police out there. I don't think it will help at all to be sending those Native Police. They will only aggravate problems.'

'I realise that,' Paul said. 'Which is why I keep arguing that they should be disbanded. But if they have to use them, I say take them someplace else.'

'Maybe with better training . . .' Laura began.

Her husband shook his head. 'Under Beresford? Don't be ridiculous!'

She flushed. 'You've been cranky all evening. Just because you're cross with Duke, don't take it out on me.'

He reached across the small table and took her hand. 'I'm sorry, love. But talk about aggravate! He's a prize aggravator.'

'Oh well, he's doing his best.'

'His best? Laura, he isn't a kid. He's plain lazy! And incompetent! And a double-crosser!'

She started to laugh. 'But otherwise he's all right?'

'Ah, forget about him. You can't help people who won't help themselves. I feel sorry for Harry Merriman, taking him on as a partner.'

'I think he'll cope. Don't forget we promised to go and meet Harry's wife in the morning.'

They took a stroll along Quay Street before retiring, but only to the corner and back, because it was Saturday night, with more than the usual number of revellers out and about since there were rumours of new gold strikes in the nearby hills.

Late that night, or rather in the quieter dark of the early hours, there was a banging on their bedroom door.

Paul was out of bed in an instant, fearing fire, this being a rambling two-storey wooden building; or at best, a drunk; but it was his brother, who fortunately was not drunk.

'What the hell do you want at this hour?' Paul hissed at him as shouts of 'Quiet!' reverberated along the passage.

'I've decided to sell.'

'Who to?'

'You.'

'How much?'

'Five hundred plus stock.'

'Oh grow up!'

'Four fifty?'

'Four. It's not even worth that now. Four hundred and that's more than I would have paid for it in the first place. Murphy saw you coming.'

'Do you want to buy the bloody place or stand here preaching?'

'Shut up!' a voice shouted at them.

'Four hundred plus stock,' Duke said.

'Oh all right. Now let me get some sleep.'

Laura was sitting up in the bed. 'What was that about?'

'I just bought Mango Hill.'

'Oh! Excellent! I thought you would. Sooner or later. I think we ought to extend that house and . . .'

'Laura. Can I go back to sleep now?'

On the Sunday afternoon, when they were all gathered at Mango Hill ready to begin their exodus the next morning, Harry Merriman, as their leader, called them together and stood on a box to say a few words. He spoke simply of their need to attend to their duties with an extra sense of responsibility, because 'on this trek there may be no second chances. There are eighteen of us in all, including our guide over there . . . Trader. Let's give him a hand, because we need to keep in his good books!'

When they cheered him, Ladjipiri looked up in surprise, and managed a grin.

'In case you're trying to figure out who's who, this gentleman here on my right is Duke MacNamara, who owns half the herd, and this feller is Ginger Magee. He'll be head drover. He was on the last drive out there and he knows a thing or two, believe me. On my left here is Ned Heselwood; he's agreed to be my right-hand man. Or my left-hand man,' he grinned, 'we'll work it out between us. Another feller who's already been out to the back country with us is young Matt Doolan there, and he's still keen to go back. So that's a good omen. The rest of you who've been helping with the mustering probably already know one another.

'I only have a couple more words to hand out, and that's to wish you all good luck and ask you to think of us as a team. We have to share everything from now on, the good and the bad, and take care of one another. And most of all try to respect the other bloke; that goes a long way towards us all having a good time.'

That raised a cheer, and Harry held up his hand.

'Mrs Merriman would like us to say a prayer with her for God speed.'

He jumped down from the box and stood beside Tottie, who began: 'Our Father . . .'

CHAPTER ELEVEN

Banggu knew he couldn't outrun the two horses. He felt like that pig dashing and dodging through the scrub, but this time the hunters rode huge animals and he could be trampled to death at any minute. Then he heard a gunshot and screamed as if a bullet had struck him, such was his fright, and when he looked over his shoulder he saw a man on a horse winding a lasso, unable to throw it yet because they were in the scrub! Banggu's brain was flashing images at him. Up ahead was the clearing, where the lasso could get him. Rope him in! Abruptly he turned, heading back into the scrub, but once again he was at the mercy of those pounding hooves.

Another image. This time the mangroves on the seafront, past the little sandy beach where they'd left their canoe. He changed course again and ran and ran, darting in and out of the trees, but now he knew where he was going and that gave him heart to run faster. He couldn't shake off the horses, he knew that, but he was drawing them into a world of sad and skinny trees that struggled to survive when the tide came in and left them waist-deep in salt water.

He sprinted over the sandy soil, feeling it give way to a fine ooze of mud, and then threw himself into the deep green tangle of mangroves. The mud was thick and deep but he was ready for it, easily pulling himself up on to slimy roots and swinging away to safety.

Behind him the horses plunged into the mud, squealing and snorting as they tried to back out, and the men were shouting in a panic for they all knew that mangrove mud could be evil.

Banggu hoped it had sucked them down but he didn't have time to think about that now; he had to find the others. He kept on through the mangroves until he reached dry ground again and turned back into the scrub, but suddenly the ground disappeared from under him. As he slid into the dry, crackling undergrowth, something jabbed into his leg, but he clenched his jaw tight to lock down a scream of pain.

Time passed. His thigh was impaled on a broken sapling that was sticking up from the ground. Only recently broken. Strong and sharp. He would have to lift himself off this fixed spear. He couldn't pull it out.

Time passed. It was still daylight. Flies buzzed. He hoped the other lads had dodged the white men and were looking for him, but he didn't dare call out. At least he was well hidden here in the undergrowth. But now that he came to think about it, all was quiet again. No sign of horses or their riders. Or of his brother and their two friends. Of anyone . . .

He was lying on his back. He could see the bloodied spike. It was holding his right leg up like a freshly caught fish, tilting him on his side.

A dingo came through the grass and stared at him. Banggu wasn't afraid of the old fellow; he tried to coax him closer so that he could grab hold and use him to drag himself off this trap. He had a kind face, that dingo, but he still had his wits about him, and no, he wasn't about to co-operate. He was company, though, as Banggu steeled himself for a desperate move.

He tried to throw himself up and over the stake that held him but failed, causing excruciating pain and no doubt worsening the wound.

After that he lay very still, waiting for the pain to subside, watching miserably as the dog slid away from him. Deserted him.

Finally he decided he would have to try to break the short sapling, or at least bend it, so that he could slide his leg free. The only way he could do that was to throw his whole body across it. Crush it.

Then again, a move like that might not work, and would hurt like fire. It could even make his situation worse.

Suddenly he threw himself to the right, across his impaled thigh, and as he did so he could feel the roots of the young tree dragging loose. Now that he had an advantage, he pushed forward along the hard ground, dragging at the stubborn roots, trying to dislodge them. Gradually the sapling began to slip. The bloodied green stick was giving him up!

For a few minutes he collapsed back into the earth, closing his eyes, shutting out the pain to get his breath back, but when he looked up, the dingo was back, and with him was an old blackfellow, who crouched down to examine his injuries.

Banggu was back in the gorge. He was in a cave under the watchful eye of an elder called Guringja who had come to cleanse the area after the death that had occurred here. Guringja had treated Banggu's wound with muddy potions, refusing to allow him to move and dislodge the dried casings, but Banggu was frantic.

'You don't understand!' he cried. 'I have to find my brother. And my friends. White men were here . . .'

'I know. So you must be quiet. Now drink this . . .'

Banggu slept. He saw the three of them in his dreams. He saw a very large bird-like creature hovering over the gorge, but it had no feathers and he flew with it over the coloured hills that his father had shown him. He also saw an eaglehawk that was his brother, who was named after the proud bird, and he wept when it wouldn't stay with him.

At times Guringja would sit cross-legged beside him as he lay in that cave, interpreting his dreams, telling him Dreamtime stories that required great reverence and concentration, and Banggu fought against this delay. He resented being kept there against his will while his brother was in danger.

Sometimes Guringja spoke of Banggu's father Ladjipiri, a man of goodness who was suffering, and in a roundabout way told Banggu that if he wanted to protect his father from further suffering he should have patience.

Banggu did not know how long he was in that cave with the dingo, the old man and his teachings, or how knowledge of certain things had come to him. But when he stepped from those cold surrounds, strong in limb and mind, he was aware that his brother and the two islanders no longer walked the earth, and that his father's hand was directing him to flee into the coloured hills of the three tribes.

They gave him a horse. Ladjipiri didn't want a horse. He didn't need a horse! Besides, these creatures, like the cows, had no totem and he felt uncomfortable with them. But when it was time to saddle up and ride with Mr Merry, he couldn't refuse. He got into a confusion trying to put the tangle of headgear on the horse, which kept pulling away from him and bouncing its head up and down, but then Ned came to his aid.

'Haven't you ridden a horse before?' he asked.

Ladjipiri nodded. 'Yeah, done that, but some other feller does this fixings.'

'Well never mind. I'll show you the fixings. You put these straps over his head and then you take this shiny bit and slip it into his mouth . . .'

As the lesson progressed, the owner of the beast stared in shock. He didn't fancy shoving even the palm of his hand anywhere near the animal's big teeth, but he would lose face if he dared not, so with Ned's patient tutoring and follow-up lessons over the next few days, he was soon as adept at the job as the next man.

Then a strange thing happened. The horse began to follow him whenever he forgot to leave it tethered, causing various men to roar at him to 'Hitch the bloody nag. Tie it to a tree or something!'

To make sure he wasn't imagining this phenomenon, he left the horse to graze one day, out of sight of the drovers, and walked away to hide in a clump of trees.

Sure enough, the horse watched him go, gave it some thought and then came trotting after him. It seemed to him that the animal regarded him as his companion, possibly even a friend, and he was humbled by the honour.

As the days went by, riding his horse beside the main herd, he tried to think of an appropriate totem for the horse, one that he would bestow, himself, in a secret ceremony, but it was difficult to find anything suitable.

When Ned asked him the name of his horse, he misunderstood. He thought Ned had wanted to know the Aborigine name for horse and he'd replied: 'Yarraman', a word only recently introduced to the blackfellow languages. And so the horse became known as Yarraman, which he found amusing but disappointing. He'd missed the chance of naming his own animal.

But Yarraman didn't seem to mind and he was happy to take Ladjipiri anywhere he wanted to go.

The difficulties began when they reached the hills. Being a guide for a multitude presented problems for a man who was accustomed to taking the first direct route in his travels. Now he was grateful for the horse, because he had to ride on ahead and seek out the safest routes, not only for the cattle but for those lumbering wagons. He deemed them the greatest nuisances and would have tossed them aside along with all the paraphernalia these white people thought was essential to their existence.

After a slow journey of twenty-three days, they rested at a village called Greenvale, which surprised them with huge yards for cattle sales from surrounding stations. Since their animals were in good health, offers of purchase were made to Duke.

Ladjipiri, the Trader, found their trading very interesting.

'I thought this was cattle country,' Ned said to Harry as they wandered about the village. 'Why are there so few cattle in those sale yards?'

'Because the stock routes out here have been impassable, thanks to floods, though I expect they'll start coming in any day now.'

'I thought the wet season was over.'

'So it is, but the monsoons bring massive rains to north Queensland, filling up the rivers, and that water causes widespread flooding. It happens every year,' he added. 'Some of the rivers can be miles wide at flood times. It's rough on the graziers, but they smile when they see their dusty plain turn into wide green pastures.'

Duke came up to them looking very pleased with himself. 'I've just been offered top price for my cattle. There's a bloke here who'll take the lot. He lost half his herd in a flood.'

Harry stared. 'Our herd's not for sale.'

'Your half, but I'm thinking about it. I'll still ride on with you, Harry. I'm still looking for land.'

'You don't have to look for land! It's there. Then you'd have to come back for cattle. Forget it, Duke, it's penny-wise.'

Duke thought it was rather high-handed of Harry to be so definite about this, without even discussing his plan. He stood to make forty pounds on this deal, money that he needed, having been just about cleaned out by Paul and his haggling. But then, back at the camp, drovers who had obviously got wind of the proposed sale were grumbling, and he realised he'd have to pay off half of them and that'd make a hole in his cash.

He decided to hang on for the time being. He could probably get a better price further out anyway.

Harry was pleased that a bridge had been built over the Comet River since he'd last been out this way, and as they headed out again, Tottie was relieved to be back in open country, because she'd found the going very hard.

'Thank God we're through with all those hills,' she said to Harry, but he shook his head.

'I'm sorry, love. We're not. We have to cross the big Dividing Range yet, then we're over the worst of it.'

That was too much for Tottie. She burst into tears. 'There's more? I can't, Harry. I can't. It's too dangerous. I had no idea it would be such a monstrous job to get the wagons over those hills, with all that heaving and pulling. And it's worse on the way down! You should have warned me! I'm tired and I'm sore and I'm sick of cooking over campfires.'

'All right,' he said quietly. 'It'll be all right. Don't worry. You get some rest.'

'And the driver of my cook-wagon is too hard on the horse!' she added. 'Please get someone else.'

He called for volunteers, and surprisingly, Ned stepped up. 'I'll drive it,' he said. 'Pleased to get out of the saddle for a while.'

'Mrs Merriman's a bit weary,' Harry announced to the men. 'I'll need a cook. Any starters?'

Matt, the young drover, offered to take over, but admitted he didn't know where to begin, so Harry handed the job to two drovers, excusing them from night-watch duty if they served up decent meals.

He insisted that Tottie rest in their home wagon for the next few days, only riding or walking when she felt like a change.

'I knew it would be too much for you,' he said, noticing for the first time that she'd lost weight, 'and I blame myself for this, Tottie.'

'You mustn't do that,' she said miserably. 'I pushed my way in! I'm such a fool. I thought it would be as easy as pie. I read in the papers about those pioneer women, cooking marvellous meals out of next to nothing, and driving their wagons as well as the men! I only lasted a few days as a wagon driver. I was hopeless! And you were so kind,' she added with a sob, 'and that made me feel worse.'

'Then I'll stop being kind,' he said. 'Tottie, you don't need to be doing so much. Stop worrying about it. There are enough men on this trek to get us to Darwin and back. I want you to enjoy yourself. Take more time to look about. Write your journal like Leichhardt did. He came this way and even named that river back there.'

She managed a smile. 'Maybe I'll get to name a river.'

'I'll see to it,' he grinned.

Tottie was embarrassed. She had been so proud when they'd left Rockhampton after giving the herd a few hours' start. Several neighbours and all the people from Duke's station had come out to wave them goodbye.

Harry had delegated one of the new men, called Kelly, to take turns with him driving the covered wagon that was to be the Merriman home for the months ahead, and she was driving the lighter cook-wagon, as they called it, though it was more of an open cart with supplies protected by oilskins.

It had been fun for a start, with Harry and Ned riding ahead to show her the way, and the first few nights she'd cooked good solid meals without mishap, even though her arms were aching. Then it rained overnight and the road was churned up by the cattle. Her wagon didn't spin along any more; it bumped and rattled all over the place, and became bogged as they tried to haul it across a creek.

To make matters worse, despite her careful lists and packaging, by the time they got to Greenvale, everything in the cart was in the most awful mess. She never seemed to have time to keep the supplies in order: she'd made a mistake and tipped curry powder into the flour bin; spilled sugar everywhere; found that opened tins of jam became ants' nests, and everything seemed to be covered in fat. Smaller items were constantly lost, and she either made too much damper bread or not enough. Every so often the men would butcher a bullock and bring her the meat carved into the cuts she required, but she preferred not to think about that any more. She wasted more than she used, to save time.

In the end she served only grilled beef or stew, along with salted beef for cold cuts. Vegetables went into a pot. No more trying to bake nice seasoned meals in the camp oven with hungry men sitting waiting nearby. And what upset her most of all was the absence of the blissful nights she'd been looking forward to, with just the pair of them sitting out under the stars and then retiring to their private wagon.

There was never time to sit under the stars. She was too tired. And every second night Harry was on watch, minding the cattle, which were always at least half a mile distant.

She felt a fool, a downright fool, but couldn't bear to be relegated to a back seat all day. She helped the cooks where she could, becoming chief baker; darned socks and washed clothes for the men; and did all sorts of odd jobs, but there was never any improvement in the 'pantry', as the men called the cook-wagon. They were worse than her at trying to make sense of the disorder.

In any event they battled on for weeks, through country that was now drying out, though there were still rivers to ford, causing bogs, detours and delays; and forced stops at remote station homesteads to bring in injured drovers and seek information on the road ahead. They were battered by high winds across the plains, and when the sun went down the nights were freezing; long nights for drovers out keeping watch.

When the ranges loomed up in the distance, Harry was permitted to rest his team and his herd on a station called Canterbury Downs.

The owner informed them that they were now three hundred miles from Rockhampton. He had a large family, and they were happy to receive company, so they organised a celebration in the barn. This situation reminded Duke of Murphy's barn dance, so he posted an extra watch on their horses, and warned the night watch to take special care of the herd.

That caused irritation amongst the men, who complained to Harry, but sure enough, just before midnight shots were heard. Everyone tumbled out of the barn to find out what was happening and Duke was first to grab his horse and his rifle and hurtle across the fields towards the horse paddock.

The men on watch there had also heard the shots, but they hadn't encountered any trouble. So Duke gave a shrill whistle to the riders following him, and they changed direction.

As he drew closer to the herd, there were more shots fired and men were shouting angrily.

'What's up?' Duke called.

'Bloody cattle duffers,' Ginger shouted at him as he rode headlong round the flanks of the herd. 'Up this way!'

Duke loaded his gun and took off after him, in time to see clouds of dust raised up against the night sky as a mob of cattle were split from the herd. In the distance he could see Matt and two other men trying to outrun the mob and head them off, and nearby Ginger was gaining on one of the rustlers between the herds, so Duke veered off to the left.

He had to put his horse to the gallop because the bellowing cattle were gaining speed, whipped along by a dark figure on a grey horse who seemed not to care that he was creating panic in the main herd just so long as he could cut this lot loose.

Duke raised his gun and shot him, saw him fall but raced past to slow the mass of cattle that was now responding to Matt's efforts. He heard a cheer and saw two men, obviously a couple of the would-be rustlers, galloping towards the forested end of the fields.

He returned to the fallen rider, who, thankfully, wasn't too badly hurt and was trying to stand.

'I never was much of a shot,' he said to the stranger. 'Where did I get you?'

'Winged me, you bastard.'

'Then you'd better start marching down to the homestead. The cattle are so excited by the efforts of you and your mates, they're likely to stampede any minute. So get going!'

Duke turned about and joined Harry's drovers, who were endeavouring to calm the restless main herd. Then they began rounding up confused strays, cursing that it would take hours to get them all under control again on such a cold night.

The winged rustler didn't hand himself in at the homestead, which was no surprise to Duke. His horse wasn't found either.

The owner of Canterbury Station was angry that bushrangers had attempted to steal cattle from his property, insisting that his men had had nothing to do with it.

'Another non-surprise to me,' Duke muttered to Ginger. He was convinced the raid was home-grown.

Harry decided they'd leave the next day, since the atmosphere between the stockmen on the station and the drovers in his mob had become frosty. But some good came out of it in the person of a cheerful little Irishman called Flint, who was the station cook but who had been persuaded by Harry's temporary cooks to quit Canterbury and join their rig.

Tactfully Harry appointed him assistant cook, but Tottie explained to Flint that she preferred to be his assistant, and that was agreed upon.

They were on the road again that afternoon, with everyone on alert in case of another attack.

'Were they bushrangers or stockmen?' Duke asked Flint.

'Well now, sir, I'd have to be saying a bit of both.' Flint smiled and would make no further comment.

Before they reached the ranges, several days later, they crossed paths with a swarm of locusts that Harry estimated must have been about a mile wide. Tottie was nearly hysterical at being caught by the sudden onslaught out in the open, but Ned found her and dragged her through the whirring throng to push her up into the wagon. He told her to crouch on the floor while he covered her with blankets, then did the same for himself.

'Will the horses be all right?' she called to him, her voice muffled by the noise and the blanket.

'I hope so.'

'This is just dreadful,' she wailed, wriggling to divest herself of infiltrating insects, 'I hate this place, this bloody awful country!'

'Haven't you seen a swarm before?' he asked.

'No.'

'Well you've been lucky. When I was a kid we had a station in New South Wales, and we had a grasshopper plague for days.'

'Days?' she screamed. 'Will this go on for days?'

'I don't think so. I think it's thinning out now. But we had another plague that was worse. Mice! They were into everything, running everywhere: the food, the beds . . .'

'Aaah!' she cried. 'Mice?'

'Yes,' he laughed. 'Now that was disgusting. And they leave poo everywhere.'

'Thank you for that, Ned,' she said, laughing too. 'Any more disgusting stories?'

'Ah yes, do you want to hear about the spiders?'

'No thank you. Can we get out of here now?'

'Yes, they're passing us by at last. Off to torment someone else, I suppose. I'll help you sweep out the ones they left behind. They're everywhere. I think the Aborigines eat them. Do you want to try one?'

'No.' She emerged from her blanket and saw hundreds of buzzing locusts all around her. 'Bloody hell! You know, I've noticed your voice is getting more countrified every day, while me, I'm learning to swear. My mother would be shocked.'

Dread of crossing those deeply forested ranges had Tottie so concerned that she was relieved to find that they were travelling well, first through the foothills and then up into the high country. There were spectacular views, and as Harry pointed out, they were now looking towards the end of their journey.

He had been worried about her, so he'd stayed with her over this section and his enthusiasm for the magnificent scenery laid out before them was infectious. These ranges seemed no different from forested areas in other places until they traversed open sections and came across waterfalls, fascinating rock structures and ancient caves. One of them had strange paintings on the walls, but when Ned went in to investigate further, Trader called to him.

'That feller no go,' he said. 'Bad joss.'

'Oh!' Ned said. 'Sorry. A sacred place, is it?'

Trader simply nodded, and Ned backed out, taking in the wall pictures that he could view as he retreated.

'Who painted them?' he asked.

'Blackfellers, long time ago. Dreamtime stories.'

Duke had been walking with them because he was on night shift. 'What sort of stories?' he asked.

'Jus' tings.' Trader looked uncomfortable. 'Blackfeller business.'

'Where?' Duke strode forward, ducking his head to cope with the low ceiling.

Ned called him back. 'Trader doesn't want us to go in there, Duke. I think it's sort of private.'

'Don't tell me what to do!' Duke said angrily.

Tottie tried to dissuade him. 'It's probably a sacred place. Like a church.'

'Then I'll bless myself first,' Duke laughed and continued in.

They saw him light a match, and looked back to Trader who seemed to be taken aback that anyone should go into that cave uninvited. He turned about and strode away.

'He's seen us go into other caves,' Tottie said to Ned. 'And he didn't seem to mind.'

'Did they have wall paintings in them?'

'No. Do you think that's why he was scared of this one?'

'He wasn't too happy, was he? I think you're right, it's probably a sacred place and only the initiated are allowed in.'

'Do you think Duke will be all right?' Tottie asked nervously, staring into the dark hollow.

'As long as he doesn't go too far, I suppose.'

'Well I'm not going in after him,' Tottie shuddered.

A few minutes later Duke emerged, brushing spider webs from his hair. 'There's nothing in there but a few old bones. It goes in about thirty yards then there's a dead end.'

'Were there any more paintings?' Tottie asked.

'Yes. Kids stuff. Stick men with moon heads. But they look fresh, so the would-be artist must live around here somewhere.' He laughed. 'He could do with a few lessons! And what are you looking so po-faced about, Ned? Did you think ghosties would get me?'

'No, of course not!'

'Then you go in!'

'I'd prefer not.'

He began to walk away, but Duke was on for a game. 'I dare you to go in and bring out one of those bones.'

'I don't fall for dares. Learned my lesson on that score the hard way. Come on, Tottie, we're getting left behind.'

'No, wait!' Duke insisted. 'I think you're too scared to go in there.'

'It's not that,' Tottie tried to explain. 'Ned doesn't want to hurt Trader's feelings, do you?'

'I think it would be best to keep out, yes.'

'And I think you're a bloody sook. Hiding behind Tottie's skirt.'

Tottie sighed: 'Oh no!' as Ned turned back to face Duke.

'I beg your pardon!'

'Oh dearie me,' Duke taunted. 'He begs my pardon for calling him a bloody sook. Which he is. You've spent too much time la-di-dahing in England, mate . . .'

Ned punched him. Hard!

Duke staggered back, clutching at a jagged rock to support himself, but the rock crumbled and he slipped down, tumbling over more rocks to end up sprawled at the mouth of the cave.

Blood was seeping from his bottom lip as he clambered unsteadily to his feet, shouting abuse at Ned, who had walked on. Tottie stepped in.

'Shush now,' she said. 'You've said enough for one day, Duke.' She took her handkerchief and dabbed it on his lip. 'You know Harry's rules. No fighting. So just calm down.'

'After he punched me! Didn't give me a chance!'

She laughed. 'You sound just like my brother. If I may say so, my dear, you were looking for it. Harry said it was inevitable there'd be fights when men got bored.'

'I'm not bored.' He rubbed his jaw and straightened up. 'And he's not getting away with that, Tottie.'

'All over a cave?' she said. 'For heaven's sake, Duke. Give over. Would you walk with me, please. The track is slippery going down.'

He took her arm to assist her, and Tottie deliberately slowed their progress, hoping he'd cool off before they reached the rest of the party following the wagon.

Fortunately Duke didn't retaliate and Harry brought Ned to task for striking him, and the incident seemed to be forgotten. But that night as Harry sat with Tottie to watch the fiery sunset across the western horizon, he worried that there was ill will under the surface with that pair.

'All over nothing too,' she said. 'They'll get over it.'

She was so enjoying the chance to spend more time with her husband these days that she wasn't particularly interested in the disagreement. Romance was on her agenda again, and she had her loving husband back. By the time they struck out into the grassy plains, she was beginning to regain her confidence, and with it her genial disposition.

Harry was very much aware that trouble was brewing all along the line, and he talked to Ginger about it.

'Yes,' his offsider agreed. 'Three of the drovers had a fight over a horse, and that's still festering. Matt's a slacker. Your mate Duke's a bloody handful; he likes to give orders, but he's not too keen on taking them. We've crossed swords a few times.'

'But these men, they're always bickering about something,' Harry said. 'I'm worried someone will start a real fight and then where'll we be? It beats me how Slim kept all his drovers so well behaved. He had twice as many men as I've got.'

Ginger laughed. 'You never got on the bad side of him by the sound of it. If anyone looked like trouble on his rigs, he'd give him a belting and then kick him out. No matter where we were. Your trouble is, Harry, you're too easy on them.'

'I'll have to try harder,' Harry sighed. 'But I just thought of a little plan. How far are we from Cameo Downs?'

'I reckon we'll be crossing Cameo country tomorrow morning.'

'Yes. I thought so. And I figure the homestead would be half a day's ride north-east. Right?'

'You're not about to detour?'

'No fear, we're forging straight on. But do you reckon we could spare Duke for a few days? He's been telling me his brother is a great mate of Palliser's. He wants to go for a visit and give Mr Palliser our respects, seeing as we're crossing his land.'

'I dunno about that,' Ginger said. 'He can go visit Palliser when the drive's over. You tell him to stick to the job.'

But Duke had his heart set on meeting Palliser. And finally Harry agreed.

'You can't go on your own, though,' he said. 'I'll talk to Ginger and see who we can spare.'

'We can't spare anyone,' Ginger snorted, 'but if it's only for two days, let him take Matt. Lately he's about as useful as a hat on a heifer.'

Had they not fallen out, Harry would have suggested to Ned that he might find it interesting to visit Cameo Downs homestead with Duke, since he was free to go where he pleased. Until the last minute he hoped that Duke would relent and invite Ned to join him instead of Matt, but it didn't happen.

Tottie put her foot in it, asking Ned why he didn't go too. 'I'd love to see the place myself,' she added.

'I think not,' Ned said. 'I'm really enjoying this trek, and the lads tell me my droving skills are improving. I wouldn't have missed this journey for the world.'

His father would not have agreed. Jasin received a telegram from Clem at Montone to tell him that he had seen an advertisement in a Queensland newspaper about the auction of a pedigreed horse, Red Shadow. Family name, Saul!

Jasin was ropable! He was convinced the horse had been stolen, if it was the same animal. Georgina on the other hand, panicked, certain that Edward had met with foul play. She insisted Jasin send a telegram to Edward at his boarding house immediately.

'On second thoughts,' she called to him as he was leaving the house, 'make it a reply-paid telegram.'

When the reply came, a day later, they were astonished. It read: *Ned not here no more. Landlady.*

'That's it, I'm going up there,' Jasin said.

'Where?'

'Rockhampton, of course. I know it well. I'll telegraph those auction people to postpone the sale. That horse could be stolen.'

'One would think you'd be more concerned about your son,' she snapped.

'Oh, I am. I'll want to know why he's selling one of the finest horses in the land. I never should have given him Saul in the first place! The horse was too good for him!'

CHAPTER TWELVE

At the request of the owners of the Boney Creek copper mine, Inspector Beresford left his men on the outskirts of the little mining town and rode in with Sergeant Krill.

His new offsider was a young fellow, eager for the job. His father had been head stockman on Montone Station when it was raided by blacks, and Krill never stopped talking about it. Marcus couldn't decide which was more important to Krill – the fact that his father not only worked for Lord Heselwood and was apparently held in high regard by the great man; or that he died a hero trying to fight off the savages. Whatever, Krill needed no further incentive to keep their squad of Native Mounted Police in order, mainly by random use of the whip, and he positively burst with energy when ordered to chase after recalcitrant blacks.

Thinking about that now, Marcus sighed. He missed Sergeant Wiley, who'd been much better company. Still, he shouldn't complain; it had been hard to find volunteers for this duty. Three other police sergeants had stepped back when it was mentioned. Too squeamish to do a job in defence of innocent white folk who were just trying to make a living in the bush.

As they rode along the wide treeless street that led straight to the mine, he saw blacks hanging about the front of a general store and skulking around the rear of the wooden buildings, obviously out to steal anything that wasn't nailed down.

He met with the manager, Jock MacAdam, leaving Krill outside to mind the horses, since the blacks in this district were known to be belligerent.

'What's the trouble?' he asked.

'The blacks have taken over the town. There's a brothel here; he's only got black women, no white women within a bull's roar, and the black men don't like it. They come into town causing fights, thieving, and smashing things. It's asking for trouble walking down the street without a gun.'

'Why don't you close the brothel?'

'I tried that. The miners threatened to quit.'

'How many workers have you got here?' he asked.

'About sixty.'

Marcus had been given the order to open a police district out at Cloncurry, but because of the shortage of police across the whole colony, his instructions were to attend to certain problems along the way, at the request of private citizens. He and his men were only about a hundred and fifty miles into their journey so far, and he was becoming irritated by these constant calls for his assistance.

'Why drag me all the way across here then? Surely you've enough men to sort them out yourselves?'

'Of course we have, but the miners won't take responsibility for a full-scale attack on the buggers. They say they're not here to start a war. You may have noticed there are a helluva lot of blacks in this colony.'

'And flies,' Marcus said wearily.

He stayed to lunch with MacAdam and enjoyed a few drams of his excellent Scotch whisky, but he had no wish to remain in this dusty outpost overnight. The mines manager had informed him that there was a reasonable station homestead about ten miles north of Boney Creek, so that would be his next stop.

In the meantime . . .

He walked out to Krill. 'Mount up, we've got work to do.'

'I'll say we do, Inspector. Here we are, in our uniforms, and these blacks don't give a damn. Look at them! They're swaggering around barely covered.'

'I don't suppose that would make much difference here, since there are no ladies to be seen.'

On their way out of town he gave Krill his instructions. 'This place is just a dot on the landscape. Not a fence in sight. I want you to post four riders on the outskirts of the town, with rifles. North, south, east, west. We're about to round up a mob of blackfellows. Tell them to fire into the air if any look like escaping from the town.'

'Will that stop them?'

'No, but it'll give them a fright!'

As he waited, he blew a whistle for the other black troopers to mount up.

'Line abreast!' he shouted, and then rode along the line inspecting their drab and dusty uniforms, as if it mattered, thinking that his own smart black uniform with its silver buttons could do with a good clean.

Krill came galloping back, his ruddy face aglow with excitement. 'All in place, sir!'

'Good. Send for the packhorse with the chains.'

'We haven't got enough chains for all of them, sir.'

'Krill, when I say jump, you jump! You don't ask questions. Now get going!'

Marcus now had twenty men before him, so he made an announcement. 'We are about to ride into this place where blackfellows are making a damn nuisance of themselves. Each one of you is to make an arrest. Each one grab a blackfellow, hey? You got that? I want twenty blackfellows. No women.'

They grinned and nodded their excitement.

'Grab him. Hold him. Put on the handcuffs. Right? And be sure he's only a blackfellow. Those white men in there will shoot you if you make a mistake.'

The inspector knew the exercise would be like throwing foxes into a chicken coop, but confusion was the point, so he took his men into Boney Creek and set them loose.

Several miners came out on to verandas to watch the troopers chasing blackfellows in all directions, and they cheered them on. They heard gunshots, and blacks who'd tried to run out of town came tearing back only to be grabbed by these police. For about twenty minutes they were entertained by an all-in brawl, with black men fighting, kicking, wrestling in the dust, as a police inspector sat his horse, calmly watching the affray.

They took bets on who would win, the black troopers or the local blacks.

Marcus didn't much care. His men had already handcuffed several local blacks; that would do, but they might as well keep on until the fight fizzled out.

As it did. The local blacks who managed to escape fled the town.

Krill lined up his battered prisoners. There were fourteen of them, their equally battered captors standing proudly by.

'We've only got ten chains,' he hissed.

The mines manager came over. 'What now?' he asked.

'I'm arresting ten of these fellows,' Marcus said. 'I'll free four of them to pass the message on that if they come into this town again, I'll be back.'

Which I won't, he mused. Never mind.

'I'm taking them with me. I'll hand them over to the boss of that station you were telling me about and he can hold them until they can be taken in to jail. That all right with you?'

'Yes. Surely.'

'If they start slipping back in here, grab a couple yourself and send them into jail. They're scared stiff of the lockup.'

For his troubles, Marcus earned a bottle of that Scotch whisky. Then he headed for the station homestead, his ten prisoners, linked together by chains attached to iron collars, dragging along behind the squad, guarded by Sergeant Krill.

The squatter welcomed the inspector and his bottle of whisky, and offered to put him up for the night. He would have his own men take the prisoners into Clermont, so there was no need for Marcus to bother about them.

He was an interesting fellow, and Marcus enjoyed hearing about the district, since Clermont was the first inland settlement in tropical Queensland. It was here that a gold commissioner had murdered his own escorts and stolen the gold bound for Rockhampton. He was hanged for his deeds. And another piece of local lore – only a few miles from where they were sitting a thirty-foot-high wall of copper had been found. Thirty feet high!

'All of this country on to the far west is a miner's dream,' the squatter told him, and Marcus made up his mind that once he had the police station set up out in Cloncurry, he'd have a serious look at making real money. 'They say there's gold around Rockhampton,' the squatter said. 'Is it true?'

'No, just a tale,' Marcus told him.

The next day, on the advice of the squatter they detoured south to avoid almost impassable high country ahead of them and eventually camped at the town of Emerald. Here the local policeman requested his assistance to track down some bushrangers who were stealing horses, but Marcus invented urgent duty further west and kept moving. He had no wish to take on bushrangers, who were usually armed and backed up not only by gangs, but by settlers who were paid for co-operation.

He had been ordered to investigate the disturbance at a teamsters' depot on the western side of the ranges, and eventually located the place known as Barleycorn's Retreat only to find windswept ruins. There was evidence that a fire had destroyed the store and several sheds months ago, but no one in the police department had bothered enlightening him.

Investigate what? he asked himself as he reread his notes. White folk didn't burn down their own stores, so obviously the blacks had committed this crime.

'Arson is the one weapon that blacks use successfully, and all settlers are vulnerable,' he told Krill. 'Which is why we have to crack down hard on this crime.'

'I know,' Krill said. 'They burned Montone Station homestead to the ground. They say there were . . .'

Marcus ignored Krill's favourite subject. 'We'll follow this road. By the looks of it, teamsters are still using it. Look out for a place called Mischief Creek.'

That wasn't hard to find. A fading sign beside a wide stone causeway proclaimed the turbulent waters that washed over it to be the creek in question.

The inspector rode down a track to the banks shaded by fragrant eucalypts, irritated that this area was also deserted and the detour he'd had to make was a complete waste of time.

Just as he'd decided to leave, he saw movement in the bush on the other side of the causeway, and yelled to Krill: 'Over there! Over there! Who's that?'

After a short chase they hauled up a tall blackfellow wearing only a possum skin at his waist. He was middle-aged, his leathery skin covered in cicatrices, denoting tribal markings.

'Another fella out there, boss,' one of the troopers called as he jammed their prisoner against a tree.

'Don't call me boss,' the inspector growled, and turned on the stranger. 'Who are you?'

'What you want?'

'At least he speaks English,' Marcus said to the troopers watching the interrogation. 'Name?'

'Jericho,' the man said angrily. 'What you want?'

Marcus tapped him on the face with his whip. 'What are you doing here?'

The black man stared at him. 'Get 'im wakari. Fishes.'

'Where's the nearest blackfellow camp?'

'No camp, boss.'

'You're lying. Where are your gins? Your women?'

Jericho looked at all the uniformed men around him and his eyes widened with fear. 'No gins,' he muttered. 'Allasame gone walkabout.'

The whip cut across his face. 'We'll see about that.'

Krill came up. 'The other fellow got away.'

'Bloody hell! You couldn't catch a fish in a net, Krill. Which way did he go?'

'I don't know. There's a lot of rough scrub. Maybe that way.' Krill pointed north-east.

Marcus turned to the prisoner again. 'Your camp that way, eh? Never mind, I'll find it. Now you listen to me. You know the store back there?'

Jericho seemed confused. He shook his head.

'Who set fire to it? Blackfellows?' Marcus insisted, making a show of this pointless interrogation in front of witnesses, for his records.

After a few more questions with predictable negative replies, he turned back to Krill: 'Get me some handcuffs.'

'Where are we taking him?'

Marcus scowled. 'To find his mates. We'll round up a few of them and see if they'll give up the arsonists, because they'll know who it was, you can bet on that.'

It happened so fast, Marcus didn't even see him go. Apparently the trooper who was supposed to be holding the prisoner relaxed his grip. He got the surprise of his life when Jericho suddenly dropped to the ground, slid into the undergrowth and dived down the sloping bank.

They searched for almost an hour before Krill spotted him racing up the other bank past the causeway. He kneed his horse forward, and took off over the causeway, wheeling off to the left in hot pursuit of the runaway, but it looked as if the blackfellow would win this race. The distance between them was widening.

Krill reined in his horse as if he were giving up, and raised his rifle. His troopers, watching the chase, yelled encouragement, drowning out the inspector's shout of 'No!'

★ ★ ★

They buried the body in the scrub.

There was no mention of this mishap in Inspector Beresford's journal. No need. Nothing could be done about it. It was just an accident. No one need know.

Unfortunately, someone did know.

Jericho's murder was witnessed from the top of a tree by his travelling companion.

That blackfellow, Jericho, from the same Darambal tribe as Banggu, son of Ladjipiri, had been on his way to visit his wife's family in the highlands to break the news to them that she had died.

'She was gored by a bull crossing a paddock,' he told Banggu, in his slow, distracted way. 'She was never afraid of the cattle, she liked them. She never minded the men cattle and she liked the big cows that gave milk and she used to laugh at the calves; she loved to mother them.'

'Do you work on a station?' Banggu asked.

'Yes. We had to go in, life got too hard. My wife worked for the missus. Me, I'm a stockman. Boss let me go to tell her mamma. His missus, she's minding my children until I get back. They were sad.' He managed a proud smile. 'They said to tell her mamma she was a good girl.'

'It is a fine thing they speak so well of your wife.'

Jericho nodded. 'Where are you going?'

'Out to Pitta Pitta country. My father was a trader. We have friends there.'

'Long ways from your own country. Why would a young man like you be going so far? Trouble at home?'

'What home?' Banggu said angrily. 'You said it yourself, life's hard now.'

'Do you speak the English?'

'Yes.'

'Then why run away? It's still your homeland; better to try to live in their world than to fall back in the shadows.'

Banggu couldn't bring himself to tell this man that he was on the run. When he'd met Jericho, eight days ago, when they'd shared that first campfire, Banggu had been unable to talk about what had happened at the gorge, but Jericho had sensed that he was troubled, and to ease his mind had told him ancient Dreamtime stories as they travelled on, stories of spirits who had left the earth before their time and come back to put things right.

His wife, he grieved, was one of these spirits. 'She will not rest until her mother hears this terrible thing and can sing her to her Dreaming in the correct manner. It's the same with warriors,' he explained. 'Many are unprepared when the blow falls. Not ready. Some have no one to perform the ceremonies for them, so they linger.'

Listening intently, Banggu found a little hope. He whispered: 'My father and my mother and my sisters and other families will see to proper mourning for my brother, won't they?'

Unsurprised by this odd question, Jericho nodded. 'So many hearts grieving and giving him the proper respect. He would be proud.'

Banggu sat by the shallow grave, weeping, his heart full of hate for the white policeman who had killed his friend. And for the other evil men who had stood by, uncaring, as they put him in the ground. Smoking. Talking. Filling their billycans with water.

'I don't know your wife's name,' Banggu wept, 'or I would find her mother and take your crying to her.'

Then he wondered if his friend was still here. Taken too soon. Was he fated to find his wife and walk hand in hand with her now? Both of them spirits, caught unprepared.

Somehow that soothed the young man desperately in need of comfort. It seemed romantic, a bittersweet Dreamtime story. Maybe his wife was waiting for her beloved husband? Not waiting for her mother to perform the mourning rituals at all.

That night he slept by the banks of Mischief Creek without fear of bad dreams. He slept soundly, as if he were in the company of friends, but awoke suddenly, startled into remembering the events of the previous day. Startled into rage.

He waited a few hours until he was in a proper state of calm to farewell his friend with reverence. He did not know much in the way of rituals, but he did manage some singing, believing the good man would know he'd done his best.

Then he set off to follow the squad of policemen west, sticking to the bush but keeping the road in sight. This direction was his chosen route anyway, so he didn't want to deviate unless absolutely necessary, in case he became lost.

Inspector Beresford found the boundaries hard to identify, despite maps understood only by God, graziers and surveyors, but he pressed on, knowing that in the long run, no one minded police patrolling their lands. No one, that was, to his knowledge, except that loudmouth Langley Palliser, who was always in the papers demanding that the Native Mounted Police be disbanded. It was pleasing to note that few graziers agreed with him. They understood that police protection from marauding blacks was essential in the outback, whether the police were European or Aborigine.

Two days after Krill's mishap, for which he had apologised, citing excitement and fear that the fellow would escape, Marcus sat at the folding table outside his tent and studied his maps.

Though he spoke as if he knew exactly where he was, in fact he had only a hazy idea. Cattle stations were marked on these maps by name, and depots servicing several stations – like Barleycorn's Retreat – soon evolved into villages. Being the next best thing, he supposed. That particular depot was marked on his map with a small star, and he'd been pleased to find it, if only the burned-out ruin, to know he was on the right track. Now, of course, he had to locate the new depot, which as yet had not made its way on to any charts. At his last stop, a timber cutters' camp, he was advised to follow a stock route due west from Mischief Creek until it veered left at a large forest.

'Horsemen can cut through the forest,' they explained. 'Vehicles and cattle have to detour. It covers a large area. It's quicker to go through. Just keep going straight ahead, and eventually you come out on to open pastures. You'll see a rocky outcrop shaped like a wedge. Can't miss it. That landmark points to the new depot, on by the river.'

According to his calculations, the inspector and his squad were travelling parallel with the boundary of Cameo Downs, which was about ten miles to his right, and that suited Marcus. He was happy to stay clear of Palliser territory.

Five hours later, when they emerged exhausted from that wretched, gloomy forest with its slimy undergrowth, Marcus was unaware that he had veered well on to Palliser's property. And that the homestead itself was only three miles away.

This was pastureland, as expected, but they could find no sign of any outcrop, nor were they anywhere near a river.

Disheartened, he decided to make camp. He was still on the lookout for blackfellows who would inform on the arsonists, but he also needed to locate the depot and interrogate teamsters. They could help him sort this whole thing out.

That afternoon he wrote out a list of questions for the teamsters to answer, and add their signatures to:

Name? Occupation?
Were you present at Barleycorn's Retreat on the night of this incident?
Did you witness the fire?
Can you identify the arsonists?
Were you present at the incident at Mischief Creek?
Was there a fight between white men and black men?
Why did the blacks attack?
Why did the white men retaliate?
Were any white men killed or injured?
If so, by whom?
Were any black men killed or injured?
If so, by whom?

He thought that would do for the time being. Possibly he would think of more questions during the night. This often happened. He could enlarge in the morning if need be.

There was still an hour or so to sunset. He sat back with a whisky and called to Krill: 'Get up two search parties and locate that depot and a blackfellow camp. At the same time bring in some game. Preferably birds, wild turkey. There were some big nests in the forest so they're around.'

It was peaceful to be alone here, looking towards the smoky blue hills. Marcus sighed. All was quiet. He seemed the lone occupant of all these wild acres. Not a soul to be seen in any direction. No movement on the low hills, so dreamily blue, so deeply ancient and introverted. The shadow of a small cloud froze an island of dark green on the lush grasses that hid rough untamed soil, the enemy of the plough. His horse, always hitched near his tent, stood quietly by a big ironbark tree, intent on its own memories.

Marcus wondered if he should bother interrogating any blackfellows. They'd only waste his time. Their names meant nothing and their crosses for signatures even less. He could invent a scenario of interviews that would do just as well. Besides, he was rather jumpy about the fellow they'd buried back there, and could do without the company of intense black men. He had enough of his own here. Always yapping. Slovenly bloody lot.

Marcus dozed. Too soon, Krill was back with several birds and the news that the troopers had failed in their other tasks.

Bloody hell.

Banggu kept on, though not knowing why. Because what could he do? Run in and arrest a policeman? Or kill one? Another one. His heart leapt in fright at that reminder. He just kept following them, like a stubborn dog that didn't know when to turn back. And it came to him, as he thought about those horsemen, that he ought to get himself a horse. How much faster he could get to Pitta Pitta country that way! Up ahead were those secret walkabout tracks through the old country that his father had shown his sons. They led from one waterhole to another; to places where nuts and berries could be gathered in certain seasons; to 'spectacle' sites where man could admire the grand scenery; and there were even sacred sites, most of them kind to travellers.

'If I had a horse,' he said, 'that would impress the elders and my beloved Nyandjara.' They would be surprised, and pleased, he hoped, to see him back. Though she was probably promised to someone now, or even married.

Those gloomy thoughts were at home in the steadily darkening forest, so he chased them away by thinking about the horse, and how he might come to own one. Eventually he slept among the sturdy roots of a massive fig tree and woke, scratching skin lacerations, to be confronted with one noisy thought. Steal.

He would have to steal a horse.

In the white world, that was akin to killing a man!

Banggu shuddered, but determination set in, so he continued his slow and painful journey through the cruel forest with new vigour.

Two stockmen from Cameo Downs were just leaving the new teamsters' depot when they heard that a big squad of police were in the area. The two lads, being Aborigine, were very excited. One of them turned to the storekeeper.

'Maybe they come to find out about that bad business at Mischief Creek, eh?'

'Yeah, probably,' the storekeeper said, not being particularly interested in any more yarns about Mischief Creek. As a newcomer to the area, he reckoned those tales had more holes in them than a leaky bucket.

On the way home the stockmen spotted campfires at the edge of the old rain forest, and knew them to be the long-awaited police, so they detoured over to the station blacks' camp to give the news to the elders.

By this time, the grieving relatives of the victims of that attack had given up hope of any justice, but their leaders had the word of Langley Palliser, so they prepared themselves for an all-important meeting. Six men, some of whom could speak English, dressed in their impressive finery of topknots, cockatoo feathers and ochre markings, and set off through the night carrying only their spears.

As a result, the native troopers rising with the sun were greeted by the sight of six blackfellows, standing in the golden light like a row of bronze statues.

One of the troopers swaggered over to them. He had woolly hair and a dark beard, and was wearing his uniform, but the jacket lay open untidily, unbuttoned, revealing his dark bare chest.

The delegates were Mitakoodi men. Their lands covered this area and continued far west. They were bordered on one side by the Kalkadoon and on the other by the Pitta Pitta tribe. Many of them chose to reside on Boss Palliser's station, though they didn't fully understand the concept of ownership by one man or his family. Some had learned enough English to get by with the whites, even work for them in return for a home place.

But this feller, this blackfeller who'd walked over to the Mitakoodi men, there was something strange about him!

Other blackfellers like him came over to stare at them. Two had guns!

'What you fellers want?' the first strange one asked them in lordly tones. He had never seen wild blacks in their getups before and couldn't tell whether they were wearing war paint or corroboree.

'Tell 'em to put them spears down!' muttered one with a gun.

'You want tucker, eh?' another one said. 'I reckon they're hungry.'

Finally the spokesman for the delegation cleared his throat of his astonishment and said: 'Where the police fellers?'

The first strange one laughed; he doubled up laughing and turned back to his mates to have them join the hilarity.

'Me,' he said. 'Me police feller, mate. Me Trooper Pompey Lee!' With that, he saluted them. 'All of us police fellers, mate. Now you tell us what you want, eh?'

'We come sit down talk about killen at Mischief Creek there,' the spokesman said, unable to keep the anger and frustration out of his voice.

Trooper Pompey Lee paled. As he stepped back he heard the word 'payback' emanate from the deep voices of these men. He knew that word well. The situation could be dangerous. There could be more of them in the forest.

Suddenly he lost his swagger. Suddenly he was one of them.

'Mischief Creek?' he whispered. 'That wasn't us! It was our sergeant. He shot him. Sergeant Krill.'

The Mitakoodi men from Cameo Downs began stamping their feet on the ground in unison as they pondered this vital piece of information. Men of authority themselves, they knew that this slovenly collection of rockheads would have a boss somewhere, and since they knew neither his name nor his title, they were summoning him in their own way.

Sure enough, a whitefeller emerged from a tent and his minions parted to make way for him. He buttoned his trousers, pulled on a shirt and hooked braces over his shoulders as he strode up, running a hand through thick hair the colour of grasses bleached in the sun.

This was a man of authority. The stamping stopped abruptly.

'Good day,' he said to them, but they weren't ready to respond to pleasantries right now. Their faces impassive, they saw another white man come hurrying out of the forest, a younger man, and did not fail to note the eyes of all the troopers swerving nervously towards him.

The spokesman jerked his head at the newcomer. 'Who he?' he asked sternly.

Bewildered, the boss man looked around him. 'What? What's going on? What do you mean, who's he? He is my sergeant. Now look here. Say we have sitdown talk, eh? Put the spears away and we have a good sit down.'

He turned back to Krill. 'I might as well see if they know anything about the incidents back at the depot, since they're here.'

'If they're local,' Krill said. 'They look a wild lot to me. Probably a hunting party.'

The delegates listened to that exchange, unmoved.

The boss man sent a trooper running back to his tent to return with his coat, a policeman's black coat with the silver buttons, and they watched approving as he pulled on his badge of office and buttoned it into place, even to the high collar. They were now being treated with respect. Their eyes lit up appreciatively.

The spokesman said: 'Mistah. That feller Krill? He your prisoner?'

'No. No, no! My sergeant. He's a good fellow. Now where do you come from? You live round here? What mob you?'

'This our country, mistah. Here! This Mitakoodi country.' The spear thumped the ground. 'That feller he kill blackfeller. Why he not prisoner?'

Another Mitakoodi man shouted: 'He kill blackfeller! We take 'im. Blackfeller law!'

Krill stood for a minute. Dumbfounded. He realised they knew he'd killed that black bloke, Jericho! The one who'd got away, Jericho's mate, he must have told them.

The sergeant turned and ran for his rifle. The troopers scattered.

Gun loaded, Krill took refuge in the trees on one knee, preparing to take aim in the long-established military manner, ignoring Beresford's desperate shouts of 'Stay there. You don't have to come out. But put the bloody gun down!'

Not one of those steely men with spears had moved. They could see that rifle trained on them but they didn't flinch.

Marcus had no choice. He strode out into no-man's-land facing the blackfellows, his back to Krill.

'Gentlemen,' he said quietly, 'we don't want any trouble. That fellow back there is upset. There's been a mistake here. I came here to arrest bad men and take them away. You leave it to me, eh?'

A wrinkled greybeard stepped out of line and gabbled at their spokesman, pointing at Krill. Pointing at the rifle very steady on the whitefeller's shoulder.

'Arrest that feller,' the spokesman grated, slamming his spear into the ground again.

Marcus felt faint. He felt that the old goat was practically inviting Krill to fire. He looked for his troopers; saw them watching the confrontation, eyes popping, from various vantage points well out of the line of fire. Some of them had rifles. He wondered if they would have the nous to fire without orders if he were menaced.

No matter what they claimed, true or not true, he couldn't hand Krill over. Impossible. So this was a bloody sticky situation.

'Bugger Krill!' he muttered to himself.

Endeavouring to appear calm, he called to the troopers to dress correctly and fall in, forming two lines behind him, between Krill and the vigilantes.

Then he walked back to his tent, and brought out his folding canvas chair. He couldn't think what else to do. Stalling seemed appropriate. The wild blacks might just go away.

But not right now, he mused, as he settled comfortably into his chair between the row of six blackfellows and the two rows of fourteen troopers, all of whom looked thoroughly confused.

The two stockmen had returned to the station having tipped off their friends, found some grub and taken themselves off to bed. But in the early morning, when they were lining up for breakfast, they remembered to mention that a band of policemen were camped over there by the old rain forest.

The news soon found its way up the ladder to the boss.

'A band of policemen?' he asked. 'Not military?'

'No, they said policemen, come to investigate the Mischief Creek murders.'

'Police don't travel in bands,' Langley said to his manager. 'You better get over there and take a look.'

'Unless it's the Native Police, of course. They travel in squads.'

'What? Those bastards are here? On my land?' He grabbed his boots. 'Wait for me!'

The stalemate had only lasted a half-hour or so when Marcus realised that the vengeance-seeking black men would probably stand there all day; for the rest of the year, for that matter, if that was what it took to wrest Sergeant Krill from his pack.

But he couldn't sit here indefinitely, watching grass grow, while he waited for them to give up and go away.

He glanced at his troopers and saw contempt for their tribal brothers. The fools were almost sniggering that they were in a position of power; silently boasting that six men had no chance against their guns.

Marcus was on his feet in an instant, startling them into straightening up, to stand at attention. The delegates did not flinch.

'Now,' he said to them, 'I have come here in the name of our great Queen to look for bad men in the teamsters' camp. You know that camp?'

Several men nodded.

'Which way is it?' he asked.

The spokesman turned and pointed, but as he did so, Marcus saw riders galloping towards them from the other direction. As they pulled in, he recognised Palliser, who shouted at him:

'What the hell are you lot doing on my land, Beresford?'

'We're not on your land, sir!'

'You bloody well are!' He looked at the strange scene. 'What's going on here anyway?'

Marcus had to think fast. He'd have to bluff for a start and see how to get out of this mess. He nodded at the six blacks, who still hadn't moved an inch.

'These chaps are upset. I've been trying to sort it out.'

Palliser swung down from his horse and strode over to them, and to the inspector's horror reached out and shook hands with the greybeard. He'd hoped Palliser would chase them away.

'What are you doing here, you old rascal?' he laughed. 'I thought you'd be back home with your new wife. She plenty woman, eh?'

The blackfellow cackled his pleasure but referred the boss to their spokesman, who gabbled something to him in English. Palliser shook his head, as if to say that whatever they were telling him didn't make sense, then, confused, turned back to Marcus.

'They say you've got one of the killers from the Mischief Creek massacres with you? Is that right? Have you arrested someone?'

'No, not exactly.'

'What do you mean, not exactly?'

Suddenly the greybeard broke ranks. He dashed towards the troopers and yanked one of them out of the line.

'Dis man,' he said. 'He tell you, boss.'

Behind him the spokesman called: 'Dat ri', boss. He tell you.'

'Tell me what?' Palliser growled.

Marcus sighed. The game was up. Better to explain now since Palliser, this local autocrat, wasn't about to turn away and mind his own business.

Carrying the chair with him, he beckoned the squatter back towards his tent, out of earshot of the others. 'I was sent to investigate that incident at Mischief Creek . . .'

'That massacre,' Palliser corrected.

'As you will! We saw where the store was burned down. No one about. Moved on to the creek. Found a blackfellow there, name of Jericho . . .'

'Ah yes, I know Jericho. His mother-in-law works for me.'

Marcus quaked. 'I asked him if he could give me any information, but he ran away. My men gave chase and unfortunately he was shot.'

'He was what?' Palliser flew into a rage. 'Shot? Was he wounded? What? Where is he?'

'I'm afraid he was killed.'

'Jesus! You stupid bastard!' Palliser lowered his voice. 'You shot Jericho! Another blackfellow killed! You come out here to investigate a massacre and kill another one? Are you mad? The blacks are up in arms over the massacre as it is! Do you realise you could cause a war with this tribe? They're not your quiet townies!'

'I'm well aware of the situation,' Marcus said stiffly, 'and I can do without your abuse.'

'I haven't started yet. Who shot him? Was it you?'

'No, of course not!'

'Then who did? Was it that bloke?' He pointed to the trooper that the greybeard was holding.

'No, not me, boss,' the trooper screamed. 'Krill shot him, I tell these blackfellers. They want take him.'

'Who the hell is Krill?' Palliser shouted.

'My sergeant,' Marcus said quietly. 'I was taking him in. There'll have to be an enquiry, but those six blacks got wind of it and they've been demanding I hand him over. Which is quite impossible. All I've been trying to do is to keep the peace.'

'Where's Krill now?'

'He's behind us, in the forest.'

'Then go get him!'

'Mr Palliser! Let me remind you that you are not the law here.' He called to the nearest trooper: 'Go and ask Sergeant Krill to join us.'

'Where did you put the body?' Palliser asked.

'We buried him in the bush by the creek.'

'You did, eh? And I suppose you placed a nice headstone over the grave?'

Marcus ignored that remark, turning his back on the squatter, who went over to talk to the blacks and then on to confer with his own men. Two of them remounted and rode away.

Krill had been watching proceedings. He was proud of the inspector, who had no intention of giving in to a half dozen black scarecrows. He hadn't wasted any time lining up the troopers to give his sergeant cover and a chance to slip away into the forest.

Krill wasn't worried. The inspector would get rid of the blacks one way or another. He wouldn't sit on that chair all day. He was being very fair, considerate really, allowing the blacks to let off steam, for they were seriously outnumbered. Any minute Mr Beresford would give the nod and bullets would have those flat black feet doing the shake-a-leg dance. They'd scatter pretty bloody fast then.

But Krill's expectations were shattered when riders came on the scene: a station boss and his stockmen. The boss immediately started throwing his weight about, interfering in government business, and it didn't take more than a few minutes for Krill to realise that this bloke was on the side of the savages, shouting at the inspector as if he were a mere lackey! Demanding that he, Krill, be got out into his presence. As if he were a criminal!

Krill, the son of a hero, slipped back into the forest. He had shot a blackfellow in the course of his duty, and that wasn't a crime. The inspector had known that but the squatter didn't seem to think so. There was a good chance he'd appease the blacks by taking matters into his own hands, this being lawless territory, and the sergeant had no intention of waiting around to find out. He hung on to his rifle, circled quickly around to his horse and then moved swiftly among the other horses, cutting them loose. As soon as he was mounted he fired a shot in the air, sending them into a panic.

Clear of the spooked horses, he wheeled his mount and tore deeper into the forest. Soon he heard several of the freed horses racing along behind him and laughed. That would throw them into enough confusion to give him a good start. He was a police sergeant; he'd worked hard to get to this rank, and would not easily let the likes of that squatter run the show. He had no supplies but that couldn't be helped; there was plenty of water about still. He could make it back to that last police station in about four days if he kept moving, and the two men there would back him up.

His horse and a couple of riderless hangers-on were hurtling through the forest as if it was race day at the track, but the others had dropped back. Krill thought he saw a lone figure standing on a tree stump as he tore past but had no time to dwell on it.

The person standing there saw that the killer of Jericho was on the run himself now. As it should be. He hoped the other police could catch him. But then right in front of him was a smart little pony, trailing broken reins. He had given up the mad race with the other horses to nose about in a sunny clearing for the sweet-smelling grass.

He didn't mind when Banggu swung into the saddle and picked up the reins; didn't mind at all. Together they left that busy track, moving quietly away from the noise and clamour of pursuit, the shouts of men trying to catch the runaways, trotting steadily, carefully, for a very long time, until they reached the outskirts of the forest.

Banggu dismounted to survey the area beyond the forest. It was open pasture, most of it cleared land, but there wasn't a soul in sight, just some emus grazing by a stand of bamboo. That was a good sign; they'd bolt if horsemen were about.

He led his horse out into the open, climbed aboard and let the sturdy little fellow have his head. He already knew, from Jericho, that he was in Mitakoodi country, so now he was racing for the coloured hills that his father had so loved.

The inspector stood calmly by as the troopers went after the horses. Some of their mounts had galloped into the forest; others had come bursting into the open, easily breaking up the stoic stance of the six black men.

'He's getting away!' Palliser yelled at him.

'Who is?'

'That bloody Krill, of course!'

'No he isn't. He's still on duty. He has nothing to run from. He'll be back.'

More likely, Marcus thought, my sergeant is busy getting the hell out of here. He would have heard Palliser throwing around orders as if he were the Police Commissioner, and known that I couldn't use force to prevent him being charged in a kangaroo court.

'Well done,' he murmured as he returned to pack up his tent.

'What are *you* doing?' Palliser snorted at him.

'We're moving out as soon as the troopers catch their horses.'

'What about Krill?'

'That's my business.'

'It's bloody obvious that he deliberately spooked the horses to give himself time to get away.'

Marcus shrugged. 'If that's your opinion, sir, you're welcome to it.'

'I've sent my men to retrieve Jericho's body. I don't trust you lot. I'd like to see for myself how he did die!'

'Don't forget to send in a report,' Marcus snapped.

He called to several troopers who were leading their horses back to camp: 'Start packing up now. Quick smart!'

The tribal blacks stood with Palliser's men, looking mystified as the troopers dashed busily about, eager to be on their way.

All the horses were eventually caught, except two, and that annoyed Marcus because he needed to leave this company right away. There was no time to search for them. He hoped he could find the teamsters' depot. Under no circumstances would he stoop to enquiring about exact directions from Palliser.

'Right then, double up!' he instructed four of the troopers, and strode over to his own mount.

As he rode away from the camp site at the head of his squad, he tipped his hat to Palliser, and nodded respectfully to the tribal blackfellows, happy to let the squatter deal with their gripes.

He found the depot a few hours later. It had already developed into a small village with a very wide street to accommodate turning bullock teams. There seemed to be no initiative as to names here, Marcus pondered as he passed a Teamsters' Store, a Teamsters' Billiard Parlour and a Teamsters' Inn, but unfortunately there was no Teamsters' Post and Telegraph Office as yet.

Police or not, no blacks were allowed in the village, so Marcus promoted Pompey to corporal and instructed him to set up camp somewhere down the way.

'See you keep them in order,' he instructed as he made for the inn. His men could hunt down their own tucker; he was looking forward to a kitchen-cooked meal for a change, and hoped that the inn could provide some decent fare.

There was a sudden quiet in the bar when the police inspector appeared in the doorway; tough bullockies, rangy stockmen and a burly blacksmith, still in his leather apron, turned their backs, dropped their voices and contemplated the rows of bottles behind the bar.

Marcus grinned. He was always amused by this attitude. Authority wasn't popular in the outback for any number of reasons. A bushranger would get a kinder welcome.

Unconcerned, he marched in, ordered a whisky, then another, and felt better than he had for days. Since it didn't appear that he intended to arrest anyone, talk resumed in the bar while he enquired after a meal and a bed. And . . . he'd almost forgotten, where he could buy two horses.

As for the innkeeper, who was also the barman, he was relieved to be able to inform his regulars that the copper and his 'blackies' were just passing through.

Marcus had decided to give himself a break. Someone else could investigate the incidents at the old depot. A lone copper would be off his head to try to interrogate teamsters in a backwoods haunt like this place. Anything could happen to him. It wasn't his job anyway. In the morning he'd write up a report blaming Palliser for creating difficulties and undermining his authority, and he'd also explain how the aggressive blackfellow brandishing a spear was killed while escaping from custody at Mischief Creek.

But for now . . . relax.

The meal was foul and his bed stank of mould, but the whisky was good. Marcus took a pint bottle upstairs and sat on the balcony in the dark, listening to the usual thuds and roars from the drinkers below, caring not one whit when a fight spilled out on to the road.

Two stockmen rode up to the inn. Always two, he pondered. Too many men had met with disaster going it alone. This was hard country, and Marcus found it exciting. He couldn't imagine himself as a farmer or cattle breeder relying on the vagaries of nature, with its weapons of flood and drought.

The stockmen took their mounts to a horse trough on the other side of the road, where the animals drank greedily. Then they hitched them to a rail and made for the inn, detouring to avoid the lash of stockwhips wielded by two warring drunks.

As they stepped on to the timber veranda beneath him, Marcus heard the larger man say: 'I knew there'd be an inn around here somewhere.'

The other man didn't bother to answer, or if he did Marcus missed his response. He was on his feet trying to peer at the first stockman, because the voice was familiar.

Then he gave a piercing whistle. The drunks stopped in their tracks, stumbling blearily about. The stockmen kept walking.

'I say, Duke,' Marcus called, 'what are you doing rambling about the bush at this hour?'

'God Almighty! It's you, Marcus,' his friend croaked. 'I could say the same of you. Come down to the bar.'

Duke and his offsider, Matt, were exhausted, and so thirsty they each swallowed two pints of beer before they could talk coherently. Marcus was amused by their sorry tale but kept a straight face as the pair laid the blame on each other, still arguing angrily, though their ordeal was over.

They'd got lost! Apparently they'd been riding around in circles for days, dangerously short of water.

'*He* said he knew how to get there!' Matt said.

'Get where?'

'The Cameo Downs homestead,' Duke told him. 'And we would have been there days ago if *he* hadn't insisted on following the river.'

'I did not, that was your idea. You said it led to the teamsters' depot, but there wasn't any sign of Barleycorn's Retreat anywhere.'

'Oh well, we're here now.'

'No you're not,' Marcus laughed. 'This isn't the old Barleycorn's Retreat; that's about sixty miles from here.'

'I told you so,' Matt shouted. 'If you'd listened to me we'd have been there days ago.'

'That wouldn't have been any use to you. It's derelict. You're lucky you stumbled on this place.'

They calmed down after a few more drinks' and ate cheese buns unhappily because the cook had retired for the night.

'That's the best thing on the menu,' Marcus grinned. 'Eat up and be grateful.'

He was genuinely pleased to have their company, but gave them an earful about Palliser.

'The man's a loud-mouthed bully!' he said, explaining the confrontation he'd had with the squatter. 'I'm the law, but it didn't mean a thing to him. I was on his land so all he could do was try to tell me my business. If you want to go on over there, you go by all means. But I'm staying put here for a few days. Then I'm making for Longreach. I figure Harry should be there with his cattle sooner than later. Anyway, I'll wait for him. But tell me, how's the drive been going?'

'It's going well,' Matt said. 'The cattle are holding up. Harry sees to it that they're not pushed too hard.'

Duke intervened. 'I'm starting to feel alive again. Any women round here?'

'I saw three women, definitely women, not girls, in the bar earlier,' Marcus told him, 'but they were well guarded.'

'In that case I'm going to bed. Point me to my room, someone.'

'You'll have to share the sleepout with your mate there,' the innkeeper told him. 'That's all I got now.'

In the morning Duke heard that some of the teamsters had planned a fishing expedition.

'Why don't you come along, and bring the inspector?' the landlord said. 'I've got a boat. Built it meself. There's some mighty good fish in our river. Barramundi they call 'em.'

Duke was all for joining them, but Matt wanted to press on to Cameo Downs.

'By the sound of things we'll have a better time here,' Duke said. 'Forget about Palliser. You heard what Marcus said. He sounds too bossy for me.'

But Matt was adamant. He wanted to visit Cameo Downs homestead. He found a teamster who was headed that way with a load of supplies and bedding, and joined up with him.

'I'm off,' he told Duke. 'I'll find my own way back to Harry's rig.'

'Please yourself,' Duke said. 'I'll be heading for Longreach with Marcus.' He laughed, adding: 'The inspector has his own cooks!'

'I think it's just as well for you two to split up,' Marcus said. 'You would end up killing each other at the rate you're going.'

'True. He's a lazy bastard. He'd eat grass if he could, rather than cook something.'

It was a great day on the river, Duke found: a men-only party with plenty of liquor and no shortage of sizeable fish, and that night they cooked the fish on a campfire. Much better fare than the landlord served at his table.

After another day's rest he set off with Marcus and his police squad, feeling pleased with himself to be travelling with them rather than on the cattle drive with that tiring bloody sentry duty every second night. He hoped Harry wouldn't mind that he was taking more time out on this trip than he'd planned. Only a couple of weeks, he mused. He won't miss me. Since he wasn't sure where exactly the town of Longreach was located, Duke told himself that they'd probably meet up with Harry on the road much earlier than Marcus expected because they were moving so much faster.

Anyway, he told himself, I'm one of the bosses on that drive. I'm not working for Harry. I can please myself what I do. The drovers know their job; they'll get on with it.

Ginger Magee, the head stockman, was struggling, An old back injury had reared up again, but there was no use complaining, they were in enough trouble as it was. Everything seemed to be going wrong. They were only about a hundred miles from the Thomson River, where Harry had planned to stay awhile so that he could explore the countryside. But folk along the way had warned him that there wasn't any land left around that area, unless a man bought from speculators, which Harry couldn't accept. It would defeat his purpose. Then he and Ginger were surprised to learn that the long reach of the river where they'd camped, and where Lena had died, was now a town called just that, Longreach. And there was another village even further out, known as Pelican Waters.

'We'll have to keep on past Longreach,' the boss informed the drovers, 'and set down instead at this Pelican Waters.'

The drovers were unimpressed. They were trail-weary, and short of spare mounts, having lost two in a particularly hazardous river crossing and another in a fall.

'Where the hell's this place?' one of the men growled.

Ginger hoped that Harry would crib a few miles off the distance, and shook his head when he told the truth.

'About a hundred miles north-west of Longreach,' he said without hesitation.

'Jesus! You mean we've still got a hundred miles to go? You're mad, Harry! It'll be desert.'

'No, if it wasn't good country there'd be no new towns. And I happen to know the government has ordered police stations to open as far nor'-west as the Cloncurry River. So they have faith.'

'Yeah,' Ginger grinned. 'The blacks know we're coming.'

'What about water?' another man asked.

'Trader says there's water. Underground water. Natural springs if we get too far from creeks. He's never let us down yet, has he?'

'That's true,' Ginger said, to back Harry up. 'We've had a good run thanks to Trader.'

'Don't give up too soon,' Harry said to them. 'We'll still refit at Longreach. Give us all a rest. Get some fresh horses and rigs. And each one of you can have a bullock to sell to a butcher or whoever.'

His generosity cheered them, and it was agreed they'd push on to Pelican Waters, but Ginger was curious.

'Jeez, Harry! Did you rob a bank after you quit Cameo Downs? You left there with a stockman's pay and came back a boss.'

'I had a farm down south. I sold it to pay for this drive.'

'A fair gamble, mate. I hope you make it.'

Only two days later Harry came down with food poisoning, or so they thought at first, but he was violently ill and developed a fever. Tottie nursed him in their wagon for days, insisting they keep going, hoping to find a doctor along the road, but not one could be found.

The stations were so big, homesteads sighted from the road were few and far between, but Ned saw one house and rode over for help. The squatter's wife, an Englishwoman, rode back with him to see the patient. She announced that Harry had what they called swamp fever.

She was a forceful woman. 'He's a very sick man, missus,' she said. 'Best you bring him and your wagon over to my place. He's got to be washed down to cool off the fever and rugged up when he shivers. And he needs invalid food that you can't give him on the road. So come along now.'

Tottie wasn't too sure what to do, but Ned was so worried about Harry, he advised her to take up the offer.

'You just stay on there with him until he gets better.'

'She seems a good woman,' Ginger told Tottie when she looked to him. 'And to be honest, I don't think you have any choice.'

'But Harry will be upset when he finds out we've left the drive.'

'That's not important now,' Ned said gently. 'Let's just get him well first. You stay here until he recovers, and when we get to Longreach I'll come back for you.'

Tottie hugged Ned and thanked him, then she climbed up into the driver's seat, fighting back tears as she followed Mrs Elsie Wise along a bush track towards a large house with a red roof; terrified for Harry, and terrified of being left behind with strangers in this lonely place.

She wept all the way to their door.

'Where the hell are that pair?' Ginger asked when Mrs Merriman had driven off with the station woman.

Ned knew who he meant. He'd been asking that question about Duke and Matt for days.

'I don't know. I'm worried about them. I know Harry was angry that they weren't back four days ago. Do you think we should raise the alarm? Inform someone they're missing?'

'Inform who out here? It's my bet them lazy coots are living it up at the Palliser household. Probably chasing his daughters round the barn. Harry's too soft, that's the trouble. From now on we kept a tight rein on everyone. No slacking. And that bloody pair can work the night shift when they deign to turn up.'

'We can hardly give Duke orders, I suppose. Half the cattle are his.'

'Don't you go soft on me too! Of course we can give Duke orders, or we can dump his cattle on the road. I'm sick of his bloody nonsense.'

Ned grinned. 'You're a hard man, Magee.' The two men walked away from the cook-wagon together. 'I was talking to some drovers returning from Longreach, and they said there's a lot of trouble on past there. Apparently some of the squatters setting up their stations are chasing the blacks off their land with guns. They're even hiring extra station hands to clean them out. That's the actual expression.'

Ginger shrugged. 'Nothing changes. Those characters spoil things for everyone. The real trouble is that they're in the majority.'

'I have a friend who's bringing out a squad of Native Mounted Police to keep the peace. That might help.'

'No it won't. There won't be any peace, only killings, for as long as it takes. Keep your rifle handy. And keep it clean,' he added as he strode over to a group of men hanging about the campfire, and shouted at them to get off their bums.

A new era, Ned mused, and decided he'd better get a move on too. He shoved his rifle into its holster, mounted his horse and rode out to take his place on the flanks of the mobs of cattle as they lumbered onwards, taking with him the warmth of Tottie Merriman's hug. At first she'd amused him and then he'd come to admire her, especially when she was struggling with the daily burdens of this harsh environment. He'd tried to help her then, to spend more time with her, but he realised this was not appropriate, and deliberately kept a reasonable distance. But he was so fond of her, he missed her company and ended up spending more time thinking about her than was appropriate. She was a married woman. His friend's wife!

To counter what he kept telling himself was an infatuation, he turned his mind to Jasin. His father could curdle any pleasurable emotions! Ned decided to write to his parents from Longreach, a place they'd probably never heard of. Further into the wilds than Jasin had ever been, if one counted forays in miles. A letter would probably take more than a month to reach their door.

All the better!

CHAPTER THIRTEEN

Before he left on Merriman's cattle drive, Duke rode into town to accept the cheque in payment for Mango Hill, by which time Paul was beginning to wonder if his brother had changed his mind about selling to him. In fact, knowing how fickle Duke was, he couldn't bring himself to tell anyone how excited he was to be buying the beautiful property he'd wanted for such a long time, in case something went wrong.

But here Duke was at last. The almost ex-owner of Mango Hill.

'Now go straight and bank the cheque,' Paul said to him. 'Get rid of that bloody loan.'

He'd struck a hard bargain, paying his brother only a bit more than the original purchase price, but he had no sympathy for him. Neither would John Pace and Eileen, though they would be relieved to learn that Duke's outrageous lien on Kooramin Station would now be lifted.

It meant they were all back where they started, but Paul was in a happier state of mind. He had decided it would be best to keep Kooramin in family hands, so Duke was outvoted. And he'd better not try to pull that trick again or they would take legal action. He'd already warned Duke about that.

'Don't think we won't,' he'd said. 'It'll cost you a heap more in legal fees to get out of it next time.'

Surprisingly, Duke took that pasting rather well. Too interested in his latest adventure.

Paul and Laura had gone to see him off. To see them all off. To her, Mango Hill seemed to be in chaos, but Paul could see that everyone was well equipped, and the stock was already moving out with the head stockman, Ginger Magee, an experienced drover. And there was Trader, to be the guide once out west . . .

'Your mate Harry seems to have thought of everything,' he said to Duke.

'Yes, he's been droving out there himself and has spent a year planning the drive.'

'Good for him.'

Just then Paul saw a neat fair-haired horseman ride past. 'Who's he?'

'Don't you know? I've been waiting for you to wake up.'

Paul stared after him. 'He looks familiar. I've seen him in town somewhere. Who is he?'

'He used to be our neighbour. At Kooramin.'

'Good God! It's Edward Heselwood!'

'None other!'

'What's he doing here?'

'I met him in Brisbane, then I came across him up here again. He calls himself Ned these days. Been living in England for years.'

'Yes, I remember now. How's his bloody father?'

Duke laughed. 'All right, it seems, but apparently he doesn't chuck his money around. Ned had to sell his Thoroughbred to get a berth on this trek. Harry said it was the finest horse he'd ever seen. Real bad luck.'

'Is that the one Chester Newitt bought?'

'I think so.'

Paul tucked that information away for the present, and stayed to farewell the teams, then he and Laura wandered about the station.

'The house in this setting, shaded by those lovely mango trees, will be beautiful when it's tidied up,' Laura said blissfully. 'It has a nice calm feeling to it.'

Paul didn't comment. He believed Laura was still rattled at having to live at Oberon in the shadow of those murders, so Mango Hill, to her, had extra and urgent appeal.

'I was thinking,' she added, 'we have to get rid of that smelly swamp. Instead of just clearing it, why don't we turn it into gardens when we get rid of the crocs?'

He nodded. 'I'm hearing now that no one has ever seen crocs in there. It was a tale to keep busybodies out.'

'Why would they do that?'

'To hide stolen horses,' Paul laughed. 'No one told Duke, of course, and he never bothered to take a good look at the place.'

'Neither would I,' Laura shuddered.

The next day while they were in town they called on Chester Newitt, and he took them to see the horse, stabled nearby with an armed guard.

'This is Red Shadow,' Chester said proudly. 'Isn't he a beauty, Paul! I never seen the like before.'

Paul stroked the sleek chestnut, and stood back in awe. 'Neither have I, Chester. I can't imagine why Heselwood would even consider selling him.'

'Strapped for cash, I'd say.'

'But they're bloody millionaires!'

Chester shrugged. 'Not the son. His old man tried to stop the sale. Sent the law round to tell me it was stolen.'

'That sounds like him. Calling his own son a thief.'

Paul patted the horse. 'I'd dearly love to own you, young feller, but I can't afford you. What are you asking, Chester?'

'Nothing under a hundred and sixty pounds. He's up for auction. What do you think, Laura?'

'I think he is beautiful!'

'If I hadn't just bought Mango Hill from Duke,' Paul said, 'I'd be making a bid. When's the auction?'

'Two weeks from today. Right here,' Chester said, rubbing his hands. 'Two weeks from today!'

Since he was reluctant to do business with Sam Pattison at the Queensland Commercial Bank, Paul engaged a solicitor to obtain papers relating to the release of the title deeds of Mango Hill and Valley of Lagoons now that Duke's debts were covered.

He explained that he had purchased Mango Hill from his brother and those deeds would now have to be registered in his name. The land at the Valley of Lagoons, though, was still owned by Duke.

But Paul was thinking about that horse, and in discussions with Laura he decided he would buy Red Shadow.

'It'll be your horse,' he said. 'A wedding anniversary present.'

Then he winked at her. 'You thought I didn't notice that the auction is on our third wedding anniversary.'

A week later they were in the front row of the auction, which had a large attendance but surprisingly few bidders.

'Money's short,' people were saying.

'Two ships have gone down on the Barrier Reef in just one year. This town will die if we don't get a railway line.'

'The government has been promising us a railway line, but where is it?'

Listening to the moans and groans, Paul took heart. Few bidders would keep the price down.

The auction started slowly, and in the end was a disappointment for the audience, but Paul MacNamara was wildly excited to find he'd bought Red Shadow for Laura at the very low figure of one hundred and forty pounds. They were standing happily showing off their pride and joy, accepting congratulations from all and sundry, when Sam Pattison approached Paul.

'Could I have a word, MacNamara?'

'If you must.'

'Yes, I must. I had a very confusing letter from Perry Mills, your solicitor. He asked me to hand over the deeds to Duke's property, Mango Hill.'

'And?'

'Why should I do that? That property is mortgaged. Duke made a payment recently to keep his obligations up to date, but there's still two hundred and two pounds owing. What's going on?'

'It's not hard to understand,' Paul said angrily. 'I bought Mango Hill from Duke. He banked more than enough to cover that loan, so he's square with you now. And Perry Mills needs to transfer the title deeds . . .'

'Excuse me, MacNamara. You paid your brother for the property?'

'Yes.'

'And you're claiming he banked all the money in my bank?'

'Yes.'

'I can assure you he hasn't paid back the balance of that loan, so the title deeds stay where they are. I don't know what tricks you and your brother are up to, but I warn you, they won't work with me. As far as I'm concerned, you don't own a blade of grass on Mango Hill. Kindly tell Mills to stop sending me letters.'

Pattison strode away and Paul stood staring after him. He was devastated.

Laura was still holding Red Shadow's reins and the enthusiasts were drifting away.

'Is anything wrong?' she asked Paul. 'You look as if you've seen a ghost.'

'I have,' he muttered.

There were three banks in Rockhampton, including the Queensland Commercial, managed by Pattison. Paul banked at the Commonwealth Bank. He hurried around there to learn that his cheque had been deposited, and cleared in the Bank of Australasia. The manager of his bank was able to learn from a colleague that Duke had withdrawn some funds from that account, but that the rest of the money was intact. And unassailable.

Paul was in such a rage Laura feared he'd have a heart attack. She brought him a whisky and insisted he sit quietly in their room at the hotel until he settled down. Then she accompanied him to the office of his solicitor, Perry Mills, who frowned at Paul.

'Is he mad, your brother? This is false pretences. But perhaps he decided at the last minute not to sell?'

'Ah no!' Paul said. 'I thought I'd taken every precaution with this purchase. He signed a contract of sale. Look, here it is! Witnessed by the owner of the Criterion and his wife. It's properly dated, and here is the paper Duke signed acknowledging receipt of the money I paid him.'

Perry clucked his annoyance. 'All very well, but it seems to me he did change his mind. He still owns that property. He's reneged on the contract. Not much you can do unless you take him to court.'

'I can go after him, that's what I can do!' Paul said wildly. 'They can't have gone far. I'll go after the rat and give him a decent hiding this time. I'll make him sign papers releasing that money in the Bank of Australasia to me. Or at least to the Commercial Bank . . . You draw up a foolproof letter for me, Perry. Any sort of a bloody letter, just see it's set in stone!'

Laura listened to Perry cautioning Paul about violence, which would only aggravate the situation. He advised legal action, explaining it would be simpler to proceed that way to enforce the contract.

'We can force him to pay?' Paul asked.

'I'm sure we can.'

'I'm not so sure; he's got more tricks than a tinker's monkey.'

'Excuse me, Paul,' Laura said. 'I'm really disappointed with Duke, but I don't want you getting into a fight with him. While you're inflicting pain on him, what will he be doing? He's not your little brother any more; he's a big man. I don't want either of you hurt.

'On the other hand, Paul's right, Mr Mills. Legally it could take time, and I'm sure Sam Pattison would be delighted to call in the loan if Duke reneges on him, and that means we've lost Mango Hill.'

'But what if . . .'

'No, Paul. No ifs. You've been talking about buying another property since . . . well, even before we were married. You said you would be leaving Oberon. Every time we look like moving, something happens and we stay on and on. You could have bought Mango Hill long before Duke got here, but you never seemed to have enough money. Then all of a sudden you do, when Duke needs help. I need help too. Am I family or not?'

'I'm sorry, Laura,' he said. 'I thought you were happy I was buying Mango Hill.'

'I was, regardless of your reasons. When do we move in?'

'Darling, we can't. You know that. Not until we sort out this mess.'

She stood up. 'We can, but you won't. How is it that you suddenly found the money to buy that property and you even had extra to buy Red Shadow?'

Paul scowled at her. 'What? Do you want to sell him now?'

'I want you to stop procrastinating. I am not going back to Oberon. You've been saying you want to buy Mango Hill, so damn well buy it,' she said bitterly. 'Pay off Duke's loan.

'With what?'

'With what your brother used. A loan from the bank! You can deal with Duke later.'

Perry turned to Laura. 'I'm sure we'll have this problem overcome soon, my dear.'

'Ah, but I've lost my patience, Perry. Would you explain to my husband that the banks lend money to people like him, who own good solid properties.'

Paul turned on her angrily. 'I'll get that money back from Duke. You know I hate the thought of owing money to anyone, especially these vultures of bank managers. I will not borrow to buy Mango Hill or anywhere else. We'll wait until I sell Oberon.'

The solicitor looked from one to the other, went to speak, but decided this was not the time.

'It is usual', she said, 'to let people know a property is for sale. I don't believe you ever intended to sell Oberon. You wanted both properties.'

'I've been trying to do the best for us, Laura.'

'Oh spare me! You could try to think past money. That would help. And try to keep your promises to me! Anyway, I'm moving in with my Aunt Grace. She'll let me have my old room back.'

'Please yourself!' he snapped. 'Don't forget to take the horse with you!'

'Oh I won't, believe me. Sorry if we've embarrassed you, Perry. I'll be going now.'

'I'll walk you back to the hotel,' Paul said, opening the door for her.

'Don't bother.'

'Women!' he said angrily, as his wife swept down the narrow corridor that led from the legal offices to the street, her trim shoes tapping firmly on the black-and-white floor tiles. 'As if I don't have enough to think about!'

'What do you have to think about,' Perry asked, reaching for his pipe, 'that's more important than your wife's well-being?'

En route to Rockhampton, Jasin's ship called in to Brisbane, where he was met with a telegram from Clem advising that his northward dash had been in vain. The horse had been sold.

He stormed into town, furious that the auctioneer had ignored his request to delay the sale, and made for the telegraph office, where he fired off a reply: *I will attend to this.*

His second telegram was to the Chief of Police, Rockhampton: *Sale of thoroughbred horse Red Shadow by auctioneer illegal. Fear stolen. Advise Lord Heselwood at Royal Park Hotel, Brisbane.*

Chester Newitt wasn't impressed when Chief Inspector Pennington himself came to his office, fussing over the sale of a stolen horse called Red Shadow. He figured that Pennington, a weak little rabbit, only came out of his burrow when someone with clout was badgering him.

'In the first place,' he said, 'the horse wasn't stolen. The papers were in order. And in the second place I don't fall for that old trick of holding up an auction to suit someone who might or might not buy.'

'But the complainant is Lord Heselwood!' Pennington wailed. 'He can cause a lot of trouble for you.'

Chester yawned. 'Heselwood spends a lot of time causing trouble for anyone who gets in his way. I can recall the night, before your time, when Rivadavia belted him one in the Criterion bar. What a night that was!'

'How do you know the papers weren't stolen along with the horse? Did you think of that, Chester?'

'It'd be a lucky thief who could grab the papers *and* the horse; they don't normally carry papers on them. However . . .'

Chester was looking forward to playing his ace card. 'However . . . this was no thief. This was Heselwood's son. Dead ringer for him too. I've got his signature in my journal.'

'Who bought the horse?'

'I bought it.'

'You did? Where is it now?'

'I sold it.'

'You're being obtuse, Chester. Who has the horse now? Lord Heselwood might wish to know.'

'Bully for him. I don't have to answer that. This isn't a police matter. It's private business.'

Lord Heselwood always refused to count the words in a telegram. He considered it beneath him to be totting up pennies, so he wrote: *To Chief Inspector Pennington, Rockhampton. Surely a police force with average faculties is able to detect the name of a person who purchased a certain horse at auction in your town stop advise immediately stop Heselwood.*

He handed it to the clerk, who adjusted his green-lined eyeshade and peered over his glasses at the sender.

'This is going to cost you a mint. I mean at sixpence a word it adds up. Now if you leave out . . . hmmm . . . actually, it's too many words. You'll have to do it again.'

'Send the bloody thing!'

'I can't. You've got too many words here. They don't fit.'

'Then break it in two and send two.'

'That'll cost you double.'

'Send them!' Jasin steamed.

'Do you want them reply paid?'

The sender threw a pound on the counter. 'I want you to get on with it!'

He stormed out of the office, almost running into an attractive lady who happened to be walking past.

'I'm so sorry, madam,' he said, reaching out to steady her. 'Do forgive me!'

She laughed. A lovely, light, musical laugh. 'Why, Lord Heselwood, you are in a hurry! Is the world coming to an end?'

Recognising her, his mannered smile broadened into genuine pleasure.

'Upon my word! Mrs Pilgrim! No, I think the world is doing quite well now that you've brightened the day.'

'Thank you. You're so sweet. I can always count on you to cheer me up, Jasin.'

'Why, what could be wrong?'

She pouted. 'I'm having a small soirée this evening. A sunset soirée in the rotunda. You know, in the Botanic Gardens. Just a few friends, and the musicians have let me down. It'll be boring now.'

'I'm sure it won't.' He loved her fancy new French accent. Lark Pilgrim was never boring.

'Come along.' He took her arm, and moved her further along the colonnade of the splendid new GPO. 'We're holding up the traffic. But do tell. I heard you'd moved back here?'

The question was a tactful way of saying that he'd heard she'd moved back under Rivadavia's wing. He'd been dying to learn more of that.

'Oh yes. Poor dear Juan, he cannot bear to be alone. Or so he says. But where has he gone now? To Singapore. Always business. So that is why . . . oh heavens, you don't want to hear of me. What brings you here?'

'Business,' he smiled. 'I'll be here for a few days, I suppose. Perhaps you could join me for luncheon at the Royal Park one day?'

'That would be *merveilleux*. We could talk of old times and interesting people, no? But wait. You must come to my music-less sunset soirée. Be my gallant knight to the rescue! You're still *très* handsome, you know. The ladies will swoon.'

'I'm not sure if I . . .'

'But you absolutely must, darling. You'll be my brilliant social coup!'

'I should be delighted then,' he said, raising his grey topper. 'Do you need an escort, with himself away?'

She giggled. 'Oh you are so naughty! Now run along and don't be late.'

Lark had to hurry now. She had to invite another guest, praying that she would be at home.

'My dear,' she said to Rosa, who *was* home and had walked out to the carriage, 'I'm glad I caught you. I'm in such a rush. Are you coming to my lovely soirée in the gardens this evening? You forgot to reply to my invitation,' she lied, since she hadn't sent an invitation to Dr and Mrs Palliser. She thought he was a bore. A despicable bore who'd cut her in the street last week. In front of a mutual friend. 'I'd dearly love for you to come,' she begged. 'You were to be my guest of honour. I've gone to so much trouble.'

'Oh goodness. I'm sorry, Lark. How rude of us. I don't remember seeing the invitation.'

'Not us, my sweet. Just you. It's only a little sunset soirée for ladies, with music. For just an hour or so. Do come, I need you to help me make it a success. Your father is away, so I'll be hostess alone. Shall I call for you? To save you ordering another carriage? Yes. I'll do that. I'll call for you at four thirty. Wear a pretty dress, it'll be a lovely warm evening . . .'

She'd hardly drawn a breath!

Rosa laughed. 'All right. Very well, I'll come. And yes, you can call for me. That's a good idea. Are you sure you wouldn't like to come in for a coffee?'

'No, darling, I haven't time. *Au'voir!*'

As Lark's carriage skimmed down the drive, Rosa turned back into the house. She wondered what had happened to the invitation. She'd had several arguments with Charlie about Lark. He disapproved of her, was unhappy about her coming to his home and strenuously objected to Rosa being seen with her in public.

'Even if I wanted to, I cannot snub my father's friend,' she'd said. 'He would be offended.'

'Friend? You mean his doxy. He has brought you up with no sense of propriety, Rosa. Where could you learn? He returns to the colonies with his young daughter on one arm and that Mrs Pilgrim on the other. For God's sake, can't you see what a scandal that was! And now he has installed her . . .'

'Charlie, enough, please. What my father does is none of your business.'

'It is when it involves me. I hope you're not considering inviting them to dine in my home?'

Rosa bristled. 'Do not threaten me, Charlie. My father is always welcome here, no matter who he chooses to accompany him. He is not interested in trivial society rules, especially in these backblocks.'

'Ah, but you're wrong. He is basically very conservative but he thinks his wealth can buy him the freedom to do as he pleases. Well it does not. Decent people won't tolerate the sort of behaviour we're discussing.'

'Oh stop pontificating. Just answer me this. Is my father welcome here?'

'Of course he is.'

'And can he bring his lady friend?'

'Definitely not.'

'Then I suggest you tell him that when they come to Sunday dinner.'

'You've invited them on Sunday, without discussing this with me?'

'Yes,' she said, triumphantly. 'I'd love to see you turn them away.'

'There's no need, I shall be unavoidably detained elsewhere.'

Rosa was convinced that her husband had disposed of Lark's invitation to prevent her attending the little gathering. It didn't sound very interesting and she might not have accepted, but since Charlie had begun to censor her engagements she certainly would.

'And I'll make sure he knows,' she vowed as she stood in her dressing room, trying to decide which of her many tea gowns she might wear this evening.

After a leisurely bath sprinkled with perfumed oils, Rosa read a fashion magazine while she filed and buffed her nails, then went back to the rack and selected a gown of cream Lyons silk embossed with tiny flowers. It had a fashionable boat neckline, a trim waist accentuated by a bustle, and its soft drapes were slightly longer at the back.

Her maid brushed her hair loosely around her face, then pinned it up at the back with pearl-encrusted combs.

'That'll do.' Rosa saw no need to fuss for this occasion. 'I'll just have the small pearl earrings.'

While she waited for Lark, she worried about Sunday dinner. Juan and Lark were already invited. Nothing she could do about that. But would Charlie really absent himself? Surely not. Juan would react very badly to a snub like that. From family! She quaked a little at the thought.

'It'll be a strange ending to a crazy week,' she told herself.

Early in the week they'd had a letter from Langley Palliser, who was concerned at the increase in attacks between the Aborigines and the European settlers. So much so that he was thinking of sending his wife and daughters down to Brisbane, out of harm's way.

Brisbane meant his brother's house, and Rosa didn't mind that. 'I'll put on an extra maid,' she said to Charlie.

'Why? With more women in the house, one would think you'd need fewer maids.'

'Because one doesn't ask guests to muck in, Charlie! And it's five extra at table; Cook will need some help. Don't be such a grouch.'

'The grouch is paying, remember?' he muttered from behind his paper, and Rosa made a mental note not to tell him about domestic arrangements in future. She could always pay extra staff herself.

Then Lucy Mae came to morning tea as arranged. Poor dear Lucy Mae, who could be quite amusing even amidst her woes. Which were startling, of course. She was pregnant! And dreading telling Milly.

'She'll have the smelling salts in one hand and a shotgun in the other,' Lucy Mae had sniffed through her tears. 'It'll be hell. Will you sit with me when I break the news to her?'

'Me? God, no!'

'Please? I shouldn't have burned Duke's letter. You can say you saw it. That he's my fiancé!'

'Is he? Did you write to him accepting?'

'No, because I'm not sure I want to accept.'

'Lucy Mae!' Her attitude amazed Rosa. 'Do you mean to say you won't marry the baby's father? I mean, you have to!'

'Who says I have to? I'm not sure I'd be happy with Duke.'

'Gosh!' Rosa was impressed. For sheer daring, this took the cake. She wished her husband could hear it. Juan's social infringements were as nothing compared to Lucy Mae's bold stance. She smiled, realising she might yet have another friend banned from her household.

'Why are you crying then?' she asked.

'Oh, I don't know. I think it's my condition, and I'm rather confused.'

'So am I,' Rosa grinned. 'What day do you want to break the happy news to your mama?'

'She'll be home Saturday morning. Would that be convenient?'

'All right. I'll come early, so we can get it over with.'

That was tomorrow morning, Rosa reminded herself nervously. Milly was a formidable woman. Scary.

'She's likely to take the strap to both of us,' she muttered, as Lark's carriage crunched in through the gate.

The Botanic Gardens were glowing in the waning sunlight. The heavy foliage on the trees was tinged with gold as they looked down on the rich green lawns and colourful garden beds that bordered the paths.

They walked towards the rotunda, and Lark seemed surprised. 'Oh my. Some ladies are here already, Rosa, and they've brought gentlemen with them! Oh well, I suppose it doesn't matter.'

'Where's the band?' Rosa asked.

'It wasn't a band. It was to be a quartet, playing Mozart, but at the last minute they let me down. It's too bad. The rotunda looks stupid empty!'

'Never mind. The tables and chairs set round it look lovely. I wasn't expecting to see such a pretty scene. Chinese lanterns and all.'

'Well, it gets dark so early in this glorious winter. Do you like the settings? I adore pink and white.'

Next thing, Lark swept into the gathering crowd, taking Rosa along with her.

'Ah, my dear Julia and Jonas! How kind of you to come along. And you, Alice . . . this is my friend Mrs Palliser. Where is your sister? I'm so sorry about the music, but do find a table. The waitresses are serving champagne, French of course, and the cakes are to die for.'

While Lark dashed about her duties as hostess, Rosa mingled with newcomers, most of whom she already knew, chatting happily, until suddenly she found herself face to face with Jasin Heselwood!

He was startled. 'Rosa! How wonderful to see you again. Lark didn't tell me you were coming.'

'It was a last-minute thing for me,' she said, blushing a little at the suspicion that Lark had set this up. 'I didn't know you were in town.'

'Ah yes, some business to attend to. How is the good doctor?'

'He's very well; he couldn't come this evening. How is Georgina?'

'Ah,' he sighed. Lied. 'Her leg's improving, but I think the whole business upset her more than I imagined. She's talking about returning to England. Really fed up with the climate. The summers can be trying . . .'

Lark appeared. 'Sorry to forsake you, Rosa dear, but I see you're in good hands. Now you both must come along, you're at my table.'

Jasin toasted his good fortune at seeing Rosa again and she drank her champagne giddily, delighted with his company, before other people joined the table, but they had little interest in the newcomers. Their hostess fluttered back and forth in her floaty pink and white muslin gown, making no attempt to interrupt them.

The lanterns had been lit for quite a while, and it seemed to Rosa that the soirée was over almost as soon as it had begun. Guests, much jollier now, were thanking Lark, praising her lovely party, making new arrangements, but then Rosa couldn't find her.

'She must have gone out to her carriage thinking I'd gone on ahead.'

'Shall I walk you there?' Jasin asked.

'If you wouldn't mind? It's just by the gates.'

She took his arm as they walked around the gravelled pathways. It seemed natural to do so, in this dim light.

'I had a lovely time,' Rosa said. 'I really did.'

The carriage was in place, nestled by a tall hedge, but there was no sign of Lark.

'I'll just have to wait then,' Rosa said.

'Shall I go back and search for her?'

'Oh no. She'll be along.'

Jasin helped her into the carriage, and stood at the door chatting to her for quite a few minutes before climbing in beside her. 'I have to tell you something.'

'What would that be?' she asked.

'You're the most beautiful woman I've ever met.'

'Oh!' was all Rosa could think to say to that, but then she was in his arms. And he was kissing her, and she was in a small heaven with this handsome, charming man.

They didn't hear Lark come up and tiptoe away. But shortly they did hear her call from the gates.

'Are you there, Rosa?'

Jasin slid out of the carriage door beside the hedge and replied: 'Yes, over here, waiting for you. Where have you been?'

'I had to rescue my silver centrepiece from the caterers, who would have walked off with it.'

Lark handed the parcel up to the driver as Jasin hurried around to open the other carriage door for her.

'Can we drop you at your hotel?' she asked.

'No thank you, my dear. It's just across the road. I've had a most enjoyable evening. Thank you for inviting me.'

He closed the door when Lark was settled in the carriage and bade both ladies a good evening.

'He is such lively company,' Lark sighed as the carriage moved off. 'There are far too many dreary people in this world. I daresay Juan Rivadavia and Jasin Heselwood are the two most sophisticated and attractive men in the country. Though Juan wins in my eyes,' she added with a giggle. 'He has such a sexy voice.'

'But then Juan is not a lord of the realm,' Rosa smiled.

The dreaded meeting with Milly Forrest was just as terrifying as Lucy Mae and Rosa had expected it to be.

They chatted over morning tea for a long time before Rosa kicked Lucy Mae under the table and her friend began to speak, with a brave attempt at joy.

'Mother, I have a pleasant surprise for you. You are to be a grandmother!'

Milly blinked. Put down her teacup. 'I was wondering when you'd deign to tell me. I didn't come down in the last shower. Obviously you've told Rosa, who is looking pleased about this. I gather she hasn't noticed that there's no husband in sight.'

'But there is,' Rosa said, defending herself. 'Tell your mother, Lucy Mae.'

'What?' Milly glared at her daughter. 'Don't tell me you've rushed off and married the grocer. Or our gardener.'

'There's no need to be sarcastic.'

'Oh? How should I be?'

'You should offer a little understanding. Duke is the father. And if I recall rightly, you were matchmaking there. You wanted him for a son-in-law. That's why you decided we should visit him.'

Milly stiffened. 'Did you hear that, Rosa? I'm to blame for her condition now.'

Rosa shook her head, numb.

'So where is your husband?' Milly continued. 'Last I saw of Duke MacNamara, he had another girl on his arm, the wretch!'

'Not actually a husband,' Rosa said. 'A fiancé; that's the real situation, Milly. You see, Duke wrote to Lucy Mae asking her to marry him.'

'What? When was this?'

'Only recently.'

Milly turned to Lucy Mae. 'And it wasn't worth a mention? To your own mother? Why not, I pray?'

'Because last time I saw him he had another girl on his arm.'

'Forget about that now. We are going straight back to Rockhampton and you two will be married right away.'

'We can't,' Lucy Mae said. 'He's not there. He's gone on an inland expedition. He'll be away for months.'

'Who's running his station?'

'An overseer, I suppose.'

'Oh my God. You stupid girl. You should have told him earlier. I don't know what I can do now. I'll have to think. First she marries a crook, and now this! You'll have to excuse me, Rosa, I can't bear her sordid situations. I'll have to take a rest.'

Milly staggered out of the sitting room and made for the stairs, calling to a maid to bring her fresh tea.

'She thinks I'm going to marry Duke,' Lucy Mae whispered. 'That will keep her quiet for a while.'

'You'll probably have to in the end.'

'Even if I don't love him?'

'It's hard. I don't know.' A picture of a ship on the wall in front of her caught Rosa's eye. She walked over to it and read the ship's name. *Emma Jane*.

'What's this?'

'It's the ship my mother and father came to Australia on,' Lucy Mae said dully. Then she looked up. 'And guess what? Duke's father Pace was on board. They were always good friends.'

'Oh yes. I think I remember that now.'

The sweet memories of the previous evening were too much for Rosa. She had to talk to someone.

'Can I tell you a secret, Lucy Mae?'

'Oh yes please. Mine could do with some company.'

Rosa leaned forward and whispered: 'I'm having an affair.'

'You are? Good Lord, who with?'

'That part is the secret.'

'Fair enough.' Lucy Mae twirled an emerald ring on her finger as she wandered over to the window.

'Duke treated me as if I were only having an affair with him, an affair that had to be kept secret, and I hated that. I had to put a stop to it. You should too.'

'Oh, but he's divine.'

'That's worse. You're sounding lovesick. Affairs should not be serious, otherwise you'll get hurt.'

'Don't worry about me.'

'I can't thank you enough for being here, Rosa. If you hadn't come along to keep me calm, I'd have ended up in a rage with Mother. I never win an argument with her, but I think I made progress today with your help.'

She was walking to the small front gate with Rosa when an upstairs window flew open and Milly stuck her head out.

'Lucy Mae!' she screeched. 'We're going to Rockhampton!'

'No we're not,' her daughter said to Rosa. 'We definitely are not!'

The telegram from Chief Inspector Pennington came at a convenient time for Jasin. It advised that the horse Red Shadow had been sold to Mrs Paul MacNamara of Oberon Station.

Jasin was well aware who these MacNamaras were and was even more furious with Edward that he would allow any of that bloody bog-Irish family to get their hands on Saul. He was truly fond of that horse. It had been a wrench to hand him over to Edward, but friends had persuaded him that it would be the perfect homecoming gift for his son.

To get the horse back now would require more tact than money. At first he'd thought of having a solicitor write to MacNamara offering to purchase the animal on behalf of a client, to disguise his part in the transaction, but then he remembered that the owner would have the papers. He couldn't fail to recognise the name Heselwood, and, Jasin foresaw, would refuse to sell from sheer spite.

Instead, he now began penning a letter to Mrs MacNamara, advising that the horse had sentimental value to his family, and so he wished to buy it back at Mrs MacNamara's asking price. He also wrote that he couldn't imagine what had possessed his son to sell it in the first place, except that Edward might have been in a nervous state of mind at the time.

In closing, he hoped that Mrs MacNamara could see her way clear to granting the Heselwood family this favour. Her kindness and generosity would be greatly appreciated.

Then he smiled. This meant he would have to stay here in Brisbane until he received a response. That was very convenient timing, given his fortunate meeting with Rosa.

If Mrs MacNamara wouldn't hand over the horse, or allow him to send someone to collect it, then he'd have to go to see her himself. Confront her and persuade her. He wanted that horse.

His mood darkened. He supposed he should write to Georgina, but not just now. Nor could he be worried about Edward. Wherever he'd got to, he could fend for himself.

He gave the letter to the concierge to mail, and set about his next problem. He was desperate to see Rosa again. But how to manage another meeting? He wouldn't embarrass her by sending one of those so-called discreet notes, or calling at the house uninvited.

Lark! He'd have to talk to Lark.

* * *

314

Juan Rivadavia escorted Lark to Sunday dinner at his daughter's home. The two women got along well, so it hadn't been too much of an upheaval to introduce Lark into his life again. In fact Lark had reported that Rosa had been delighted to have her call. Which was pleasing.

What was not so pleasing, though, was to be met by an apologetic daughter, who explained that her husband, the doctor, their host, had been called away on an emergency.

'I quite understand,' Juan said.

A little while later he excused himself from the ladies' company, walked quietly out to where his gig was waiting and sent his driver on an errand.

They had an excellent dinner, with both Rosa and Lark in fine form.

'I haven't enjoyed myself so much in a long while,' Juan told Rosa when he presented her with a silk sari he'd brought home from Singapore. 'It seems like old times again. Just the three of us.'

Rosa was relieved. She'd tried so hard to make the dinner a success, despite her shock that Charlie had carried out his threat, insulting both her father and Lark.

In seemingly mellow mood, the Argentinian strolled out to the gig while the ladies dawdled behind, gossiping as usual. He beamed on them – they made a pretty picture, the pair of them, in their fashionable, feminine afternoon gowns – and turned to speak to his driver.

He'd thought as much. The good doctor was not at the hospital. He was at his club, playing billiards.

Charlie Palliser had deliberately snubbed Lark in the street. His prerogative, Juan allowed. But when Rosa had issued the dinner invitation, that had given him cause to wonder at the reception Lark might receive from their host on this day.

Palliser's response had stunned him. For the man to absent himself from a private family gathering was so discourteous as to be outrageous!

For himself, he was not concerned by the snub. For Lark, not at all. She enjoyed life; such incidents were nothing new to her, and she dealt with them in her own way.

But Palliser had embarrassed Rosa. Forced her to lie to her father. And that hurt him. Angered him.

Several afternoons later, Rosa and Lark took tea together at the Royal Park Hotel.

After a while, as people began to drift away, the two ladies walked calmly from the tearooms into the lobby. They turned right and walked deeper into the hotel alongside the grand staircase and past several ground-floor guest suites. Then they turned around at the rear of the staircase and made for the lobby from the other side. Except this time there was only one lady.

Mrs Pilgrim strolled through the lobby and out into the street, casually opening her umbrella against the misty rain drifting from the dark storm-clouds gathering behind the lush trees in the gardens across the road.

Paul MacNamara took the plunge. At first he'd considered borrowing from John Pace, money he could return as soon as Oberon was sold, but John Pace and Eileen were so cranky and suspicious at present, they'd probably think it was a plot to throw Kooramin deeper in debt, thanks to Duke's shenanigans.

Even though he'd finally taken out a loan with the Commonwealth Bank, paid off Duke's debt to the Commercial Bank and was now the official registered owner of Mango Hill, he was still enraged by his brother's duplicity.

'When Duke gets home I'll have that money back,' he railed at Laura. 'Every bloody penny!'

She could sympathise with him on that – Duke was an absolute wretch – but she wished he'd cheer up. They were already in the process of moving stock to Mango Hill and it should be a happy time. Instead he was marching about snapping at everyone.

Then came a letter from Lord Heselwood, wanting to buy Red Shadow.

'What a bloody cheek!' Paul stormed. 'As if I'd sell to that mongrel.'

'Why is he a mongrel?' she asked.

'My father hated him. He used to say he wouldn't trust Heselwood as far as he could throw him.'

'But that's nothing to do with you. And I don't understand why it is a cheek for a man to want to recover an animal that he's obviously fond of.'

'It's a cheek to ask us to do him a favour.'

'He didn't ask us. He asked me.'

'Same thing,'

'No it's not. Somewhere along the line you seem to have forgotten that I had a life before I met you. I know Lord Heselwood. I met him several times. I think he's a charming man.'

'Where did you meet him?' Paul challenged.

'At home. My father was the Member of Parliament for Rockhampton, remember? He often had meetings with cattlemen at our house.'

'Each to his own.' Paul shrugged and pushed open the wire door to survey the back yard of their new home. 'As soon as we sell Oberon, I'm going to pull down those dirty old sheds and rebuild. We could turn this area into a shaded courtyard.'

'You'll leave the mango trees?'

'Of course I will. But if we had guest rooms out there as well as utility rooms, like the laundry and storerooms, we wouldn't have to do too much to the house. What do you think?'

'I think it's a good idea. I can't wait to see this place with a scrub and a paint.'

It took Laura several days to pluck up the courage to tell Paul that she intended to let Lord Heselwood have the horse.

'You know how much I love horses,' she said to him. 'I can't see myself holding on to an animal that really belongs to someone else. Someone who cares about it.'

'So much for my anniversary present.'

'I'm sorry, but it was spur of the minute, Paul. You know that. We both got carried away. He's a beautiful horse. I just don't feel he belongs here.'

A few days later, without any more prompting, Paul said: 'If you're unhappy about owning the horse, you can sell him to Heselwood. But get a good price! He can afford it.'

The strange thing was, Laura reflected when she made twenty-five pounds on the deal and they said their sad goodbyes to Red Shadow, their lives seemed brighter. They were both very busy organising their home. Paul cheered up; he could even laugh these days. And when Oberon was sold it was as if a great burden had been lifted from their souls.

There was no cemetery on Mango Hill, and secretly Laura vowed there never would be.

For days Rosa was wildly happy. She had never experienced such love making before; she had never known, or shared, such passion. She yearned for Jasin in a shocking, voluptuous way that she encouraged whenever privacy allowed. But guilt was also present, no matter how much she tried to sidestep the issue, to put it out of her mind with more entertaining reminiscences.

Guilt had her worrying about another rendezvous that Jasin had vowed to arrange as soon as possible. A rendezvous she ought not to keep. She would have to be very firm. She must not see him again. She couldn't.

Her husband solved that problem, rushing home to tell her that his father had suffered a serious heart attack at his country home, and they had to leave immediately.

Rosa had never seen Charlie so upset, and she felt sorry for him. Duncan Palliser was such a strong personality, so full of life, that it was difficult to think of him struck down. She hoped he'd recover quickly, but judging by Charlie's panicky reaction, the news didn't sound too hopeful.

'Has anyone notified Langley?' she asked him as she packed for the journey.

'I don't know,' he wailed. 'Do hurry, Rosa. Please hurry.'

His manservant loaded their luggage into the buggy as the housekeeper rushed to place a small hamper in the back, along with rugs and coats in case of cold weather. Charlie took his place in the driver's seat, still calling to Rosa to hurry.

When they were out on the road, it was Rosa who had to ask the doctor to calm down. 'I know you're worried,' she said, 'but if you intend to keep driving at this rate, you'll fatigue the horses before we get halfway. Now please settle down and drive sensibly.'

'I'm sorry,' Charlie said, taking her advice. 'But they said he's asking for me. I don't want to let him down. I let him down by taking on medicine instead of running the station, you know. I don't think he ever forgave me.'

'Of course he did. He's very proud of you, Charlie.'

'Is he? Do you really think so?'

'Yes. I believe so.'

Duncan was very ill with pneumonia, drifting in and out of consciousness, but Charlie was on hand to care for him and that was a great relief for everyone on the station.

'He couldn't be in better hands,' the housekeeper said proudly. 'What a great thing it is to have a doctor in the family!'

Then, late one night, Langley arrived, surprising everyone because they'd heard floods were rampant in the north and in many places impassable. Langley though, had detoured to the coast, adding days to the long ride south, but he was as cheerful as ever, making light of distance travel, as if spending days, even weeks, on horseback was normal, even enjoyable.

His father childed him for leaving his cattle station for so long, but it was obvious he enjoyed the company of his elder son.

The next night at dinner with Charlie and Rosa, Langley laughed.

'On the one hand Pa encourages me to set up out-stations fifty miles or more beyond my boundaries, and on the other he goes crook at me for leaving the head station in the hands of my overseer. Which reminds me, Rosa, I met Laura MacNamara on my way down, and she sent her regards.'

'Did she? Thank you. I must write to her. I'm very fond of Laura. Since Paul's my step-brother, she must be my step-sister, I think.'

'Yes, I suppose she would be. By the way, they've moved recently. Their new address is Mango Hill via Rockhampton.'

'About time,' Charlie sniffed. 'Paul should never have taken a new wife to live at Oberon, after the murders there. Quite wrong of him, and tell me, Langley, have you had any more trouble with the natives up your way? Are your wife and children safe, with you away?'

'To the first question, some aggravation, and to the second, my wife is in Rockhampton settling the kids into boarding school. She'll remain there until I return, and she says there's no hurry, she can entertain herself shopping.'

'Yes, I imagine she would, but tell me, where is your latest out-station anyway?'

'West. North-west.'

'That doesn't tell me much; exactly where west?'

'Hang on, I'll be back in a minute.'

Langley hurried out of the dining room to return with a bottle of Duncan's best port wine.

'The old man still keeps a good cellar,' he grinned as he yanked the cork from the dusty bottle. 'Will you have a glass, Rosa?'

Normally she enjoyed a glass of port, but she didn't feel like one this evening.

'Thank you, Langley, but no. I think I'll turn in. You two will have plenty to talk about I'm sure.'

'But he's not as good looking as you,' Langley countered. 'Are we really to be deprived of your company?'

'I'm afraid so,' Rosa smiled.

'Well then, dear sister-in-law,' he said, 'let me tell you you're looking beautiful. Positively glowing. Isn't she, Charlie?'

Her husband nodded. 'She is indeed. The country agrees with her.'

'Thank you, gentlemen,' she laughed, gathering up her skirts. 'I'll see you in the morning.'

Both men stood as she departed.

It had been a pleasant evening but Rosa wasn't feeling too well. She'd been slightly off centre, so to speak, all day. And as the days moved on she'd felt queasy in the mornings and she wondered if she could be pregnant.

Then the wondering gave way to a certainty that she was pregnant, and Jasin was the father. She talked it over with herself interminably, coming back to that certainty with a vow not to tell a soul the truth. Not Charlie. Good God, no! Not even Jasin. She blushed at the thought of that conversation. And not Lucy Mae either. Hers was an entirely different situation. And her father must never know!

They were all greatly cheered when Duncan began to make progress. Soon he was able to sit up and take light meals, but unfortunately he then became a difficult patient: restless and demanding. He insisted he didn't need a doctor any more, that Charlie should get back to work, but the doctor was cautious, worrying that his cranky patient would bring a relapse upon himself.

Duncan's overseer, Tom Berry, came into the line of fire for not reminding his boss that he had sent steers into the Brisbane saleyards.

'But you told me, a month ago, to get them steers ready for the Brisbane sales,' the overseer told him, 'and so I did. Two stockmen have taken them in. They'll be right. Don't worry about them.'

'I worry about the bloody price,' Duncan stormed. 'I won't have stockmen deciding what they'll go for!'

He called for Langley. 'Get yourself into the Brisbane yards. I've got two hundred bloody steers in there and they're likely to be sold for a song with no one to set a reserve.'

'Calm down, Pa,' Langley said. 'Your lads won't let them go that easily.'

'Don't tell me to calm down!' Duncan roared. 'Why is it so bloody hard to get anything done right around here? The sales are tomorrow.'

'Why can't Tom go?' Langley said.

'Because I asked you, that's why! And if you won't go then Charlie will have to go!'

'Not me,' Charlie said. 'Here, let me take your temperature, Pa.'

'Get that bloody thing away from me!' Duncan snapped, 'or I'll chew it up and spit it out.'

'Oh, stop fussing, for God's sake!' Charlie said. 'Langley will go.'

Rosa missed that tantrum but she was commandeered by Charlie to read to her father-in-law as a way of settling him down. Duncan's choice was *The Cattleman's Monthly*, which she thought was deadly boring. Deeply troubled by her own problems Rosa found it hard to concentrate and kept losing her place, irritating the old man, but he soon dozed off, so she was able to steal quietly away.

The next day, needing to unburden herself of some of this stress, Rosa told Charlie that she thought she was pregnant and was greeted with whoops of joy. He rushed off to tell Duncan, who hugged Rosa and claimed this was the best medicine of all. Soon the news spread and everyone from the station hands to the black women who worked in the laundry rushed forward to congratulate her, but somehow the happiness she'd provoked didn't help her. She felt bleak; as if disaster was waiting in the wings.

For weeks Jasin had been forced to cool his heels in Brisbane, waiting for Clem to bring Saul down to Brisbane. He was thrilled to be able to retrieve the horse with so little fuss and planned to take him on to Sydney himself, but heavy rains had caused wide-spread flooding, with the result that Clem and his charge had been held up, waiting for the waters to recede.

In the meantime Lord Heselwood was finding Brisbane a dreary place.

He'd been horribly disappointed to pick up the morning paper and read that Duncan Palliser was gravely ill, and that Dr and Mrs Charlie Palliser had left town on a mercy dash to his bedside. Rosa, he grumbled, could at least have left him a note letting him know how long she'd be away. Charlie was the doctor; there was no pressing need for her to stay on out there.

Lark was unavailable too; busy with some project of Rivadavia's that she didn't bother to explain.

Several so-called society types, discovering that he was staying at the hotel, had offered to put him up in their homes, but he'd fled their importunities.

'I'd rather bunk down in a chookhouse,' he muttered.

He lunched with friends at the Cattlemen's Club most days, occasionally returning of an evening, if the high stakes card school was in session. On a few occasions he looked in at the Palace but found it over-run by juveniles, and he'd even attended the theatre one evening, sitting manfully through a confusing musical until the first interval provided him with an escape route.

In the mornings though, he was usually ensconced in the front lounge of the Royal Park, within call of the concierge so that he could issue or receive messages. Here he liked to be served coffee as he read his paper, and viewed the street through the leaves of the genteel aspidistras by the window.

He saw Rivadavia stride past at one stage, and later Milly Forrest with her daughter, whose name he couldn't recall.

He was shocked to read that Harvey Bell, the well-known geologist, had been speared to death by blacks near a settlement known as Pelican Water Hole.

That was distressing. The news turned his stomach. A terrible way to go. He was a nice fellow, Harvey. Very interesting.

Jasin finished his coffee and found himself thinking about Duncan Palliser. That hoary old coot, he mused. They're wasting their time rushing to his bedside. He'll outlive the lot of them.

Turning to the middle page of his paper he saw that cattle sales were being held this very day and, to his astonishment, Aberdeen Angus cattle were being offered for sale. He swallowed his coffee and leapt up! He'd been planning to turn a section of Montone into an Angus stud farm, and had been learning all he could about the breed famous for its quality flesh and its high dressing percentage. He'd even managed to acquire a copy of the first *Polled Herdbook of Aberdeen Angus cattle*, published in Scotland only a few years ago.

'Now all I need are the cattle,' he laughed, as he took the lobby stairs two at a time, heading for his room. 'And one never knows what I'll find at these sales if I'm quick off the mark.'

At the hotel stables, he was irritated to find that the horse he'd been riding all week had been sold.

'Sorry, sir,' the groom told him. 'The boss's brother took a fancy to it. But I can hire you this bay. He's a good fellow, reliable.'

'I wouldn't ride that hack, you idiot. What do you take me for? It's only good for a baker's cart! What else have you got here?'

Jasin charged along the row of stalls. 'What about this horse?'

'He's privately owned. By Mr Swinburne in room three. Most folk staying in the hotel', he added, with a patronising whine, 'have their own mounts.'

Jasin rounded on him, almost ready to box his ears for his impertinence, when he noticed a good-looking horse out in a paddock.

'That horse there. The big fellow. Is he for hire?'

'I wouldn't reckon you'd want him, mister. He's only half broke.'

'I asked you if he's for hire.'

'Ah, well, sort of. Some of the young blokes take him on, but you'd be better served to ride the bay.'

'I'll be the judge of that. Let me have a look at him.'

The groom shrugged and called to a stablehand: 'Hey, Fred, bring in The Russian, will ya?' He turned to Jasin with a grin. 'They call him The Russian because he's always rushin' around. Get it?'

Unamused, Jasin strode away from him, watching impatiently as the lad, with a halter and a whip, tried to corner the horse that managed to dodge away from him at every advance.

The groom had followed him. He said, 'See. That feisty feller's a brumby. He's not ready to settle down yet.'

Jasin didn't bother to answer. What they had, he reflected, was a good-natured young horse that was enjoying playing a dodging game. Another brumby might have lashed out at the lad with the whip by this time and broken free.

Obviously the groom had the same opinion. He jumped the fence and strode towards the pair. As he approached he gave a shrill whistle, distracting the horse enough for the lad to slip the halter over his neck.

Taking no chances, the groom grabbed the halter and held it firmly as he patted The Russian's head, calming it, talking to it quietly, encouraging it to come along with him, rather than lead it over to the gate.

Soon the horse was ready, bridle and saddle slipped on him, but not without some initial prancing about.

'There you go,' the groom warned, 'he's flighty. He needs a firm hand, like any of the young 'uns, but he likes to know you're on his side, if you get what I mean.'

Jasin nodded, appreciating the fellow's wisdom. 'Then I might take him around the paddock and see if he approves of me.'

'Righto.'

As Jasin climbed on board the horse began backing away, but he held firm. Then it made a dive towards the closed gate.

'No, you don't,' Jasin said to it. 'We'll just have a little trot about here, and you have to behave yourself or neither of us will be let out.'

Ten minutes later Lord Heselwood rode the tall chestnut away from the stables and set off on an easy-paced journey to the sale yards.

On this sultry summer's day the place was all noise and bustle, with an auctioneer's voice bellowing over the plaintive mooing of penned stock and the shouts of the stockmen perched on the high fences.

Since the sales had already begun, Jasin hitched his horse to a nearby rail and hurried through the crowds to a large tent that was obviously the hub of the proceedings. Inside, he managed to procure a sales catalogue and was relieved to find that the Aberdeen Angus cattle were listed for early afternoon. That done, he made his way to the holding yards where he met several acquaint-ances, who were also interested in the Angus lot, if only to view the proud beasts.

Jasin wished he had his book with him, his precious book on the better attributes of these animals, because he wasn't inclined to believe auctioneers' spiel.

Some people, who had luncheon victuals in the back of their buggy, kindly invited him to join them in a light repast, which he did, finding their company quite pleasant, but he was in for a surprise. Just as they were packing away the picnic baskets Langley Palliser came by to pay his respects.

It seemed he had ridden south, post haste, on hearing of his father's illness so, of course, everyone had to know how Duncan was progressing.

'He's not the best,' Langley replied, 'but no sooner does the old man get a whiff of his surrounds again than he remembers what day it is, and that this sale is on.' He laughed. 'Then he starts bellyaching about the steers he sent here for sale and complaining that neither of his sons cared what price his stock were sold for, so here I am. On a mission to make certain those steers don't go cheap!'

His audience was highly amused, but one man was concerned. 'How long did it take you to get down here?'

Langley grinned. 'Five days in the saddle. But in my father's pack, a couple of hundred steers are worth more than my backside. It was easier to let Charlie stay bedside and get myself over here.'

'And did you get his price, Langley?' Jasin grinned.

'Ah yes. That's done!'

He strode over to Jasin, hand outstretched. 'Good to see you, Heselwood. How have you been keeping?'

'Extremely well, thank you.'

'I hear your lad's out on the western trails. A chip off the old block, eh?'

Taken aback, Jasin could only nod and mutter; 'Ah yes. Edward.'

'They tell me his head stockman, a young chap called Matt, visited Cameo Downs homestead to pay Edward's respects as they were passing through. I was away at the time.'

His head stockman? Edward's head stockmen?

Jasin improvised. 'Typical of young blokes,' he shrugged. 'Edward should have made the time to visit your station himself. Not sent a jolly messenger.'

'Oh no. The lad's got enough on his hands. I believe he and his mate Harry Merriman are moving more than a thousand head west. Good fellow, Merriman. Used to work for me, you know.'

'I didn't know that. But I'm pleased to hear they're still going strong. This is good news for me, Langley. I haven't heard a word since Edward left Rockhampton. I've been wondering where they'll end up.'

'Matt said they were planning to take up land near Longreach . . .'

'Where's that? On past Cameo Downs?'

'Sort of . . . I've extended my boundaries to Longreach. But word is that they were a bit late. They had to take their mob further out to be able to claim worthwhile land. Some of their drovers paid off at Longreach and came back via Cameo Downs. They said the Merriman mob was headed for Winton.'

'Good God!' As far as Jasin knew, these places were not yet on any maps.

'They'll do all right,' Langley said. 'It looks like Edward's following in your footsteps, pushing on into wild country beyond the boundaries. You must be proud of him.'

'I am indeed!' Jasin said, his voice firm as he fought off bewilderment. 'You know,' he added wistfully. 'I'd have loved to go on that drive with my son, but I wasn't asked.'

'Ah well, they have to be boss. I was the same, I had to show Duncan what I could do on my own. What are you after here anyway? The Angus?'

'I might be.'

'Good. Let's have a look at them.'

Eventually, with Palliser's enthusiastic encouragement, Jasin bought a prize bull, some breeders and later, a small herd of cheaper animals. Then his friend introduced him to a reliable drover and his team, who agreed to take the cattle up to Montone Station.

By the time the paperwork was completed, dark storm clouds were closing in from the west, offering relief from the sultry heat of the fetid, dust-clogged saleyards and the crowd was thinning out.

Though his efforts on this day had been successful, Jasin was too immersed in news of Edward to care. He was more than a little confused and anxious to get back into town so that he could make enquiries about that cattle drive, and the places Langley had mentioned. And find the answers to a million other questions gathering in his head.

Suddenly the heavens released a torrent of rain. Jasin hurried over to his horse, unrolled the wide oilskin coat that he always carried with him in this monsoonal weather, and pulled it on. Now, with his battered leather hat in place, the rain didn't bother him. It felt like old times, he told himself, as he mounted his horse and rode back to farewell his luncheon hosts.

'Are you going into town?' Langley called to him.

'Yes. Do you want me to wait for you?'

'No. You go on, I'll catch up.'

'Righto.'

Any other time, Jasin would have enjoyed young Palliser's company but right now he really preferred to be alone. It was awkward trying to contain the conversation about Edward and his friend Merriman, whoever he was, without making a total fool of himself.

Obviously his mount didn't appreciate teeming rain, Jasin reflected, as his skittish horse balked several times on the track down to the gate, preferring to seek shelter under overhanging trees, but Jasin was having none of it. He held the reins tight and urged him out on to the road.

'Now go, my lad,' he said, as distant thunder rolled. 'The sooner you get moving, the sooner you'll be home, safe and sound.'

A mile or more later, even though heavy rain persisted and the road was deteriorating, the horse had the measure of his task and was galloping steadily.

'I think you're enjoying yourself now,' Jasin said to him, taking care to avoid the overflow of a roadside ditch.

But then he was thinking of Edward again. Remembering Saul. It would be shocking to use a Thoroughbred like him as a stockhorse! Jasin felt almost faint thinking of the dangers that Saul would have to face, rounding up wild cattle. Then he laughed, accusing himself of worrying more about the horse than his son. But that was probably why Edward had sold the horse. And he'd found a good owner, had he not? In Laura MacNamara.

'And by God!' Jasin almost exploded. 'He must have bought cattle with the proceeds! Where else would he get the money to buy a herd of cattle?'

'His own cattle drive, eh?' Jasin was impressed, believing the information as it had filtered through to him from one of Edward's stockmen.

And a big herd too! Well, good for him! I knew he had it in him! He was game enough to buck me. Just marched away from Montone knowing I'd be ropable! Took a risk. I could have cut him off without a penny.

Jasin interrupted his deliberations to peer at the road ahead as the horse slowed. The rain was still pelting down, accompanied by intermittent growls of thunder, and water had carved a fast-flowing stream across the road. He halted the horse for a minute, preparing to make the jump, which a horse like this could take with ease, but being a careful man, decided against it. His mount could suffer an injury, he worried, if the bank on the other side crumbled.

With that he detoured around the cave-in, leaving the road to make his way through bordering trees.

In one instant he saw the flash and heard the deafening bang as lightning hit one of the trees. The horse screamed, reared, and bolted in a panic towards the trees, its youth and strength proving too powerful for its rider to regain control.

He was comfortable. Warm. In the shelter of the trees. The rain had stopped pounding. It was quiet now. A relief. He heard a distant bird call. He wondered if Georgina had heard from Edward. In a way, he hoped not. He wanted to be the one to tell her that Edward Heselwood was boss of a cattle drive out into the far west, and going well.

She'd be pleased. So pleased. Able to say 'I told you so' to his father. And by Jove he wouldn't mind. He'd even admit it had never entered his head to venture that far into the unknown. But what was this about Georgina returning to England? That can't be right. She knew he'd never leave her. He might flirt a bit but . . . no. They were happy in Sydney and she loved the house. And the grounds. He liked the way they smelled after the rain . . .

Jasin dozed.

'Whoa!' Langley shouted as a bolt of lightning struck somewhere nearby and his horse shrieked in fright. It took all his strength to prevent the big animal from bolting, and as he fought to hold it he smelled the burnt timber.

'That was close,' he told the horse, patting it now, soothing it. But just then a riderless horse trotted out of the forest on to the road, and stood there, shivering.

Langley dismounted quietly and began talking to it as he approached. 'What's up, young feller? You got a fright, eh? Settle down now. The storm's gone. You'll be all right. Where's your boss?'

The horse had lost its saddle but the bridle hung loose. Langley had expected to be able to catch it easily, but the fool of a thing kept leaping away from him. In the end, after a few minutes of this performance, he became more concerned for the rider, who hadn't appeared, so he left the strange horse to its own devices, and led his mount into the forest.

At that point, he stood back in awe at the sight of a huge tree split down the middle, its charred trunk swaying helplessly under the weight of bulky, collapsed branches.

His own horse was nervous, so he hitched it to a branch and stepped around the destruction. Langley was nervous himself. He had a bad feeling about this.

A few steps further on he pushed a branch aside and saw a man lying on the ground. He recognised him instantly as Jasin Heselwood!

'Jesus wept!' he cried, dropping to the ground beside him, wiping leaves and mud from his face.

'Jasin! Are you all right?' he cried, knowing that this man was not.

'If you could just help me up,' Heselwood whispered politely, as if he were asking to be raised from an armchair, but Langley knew better than to attempt to lift him.

'Yes,' he said. 'Yes, of course. You'll be just fine now, Jasin. I'll look after you. You'll be all right.'

Jasin nodded, whispered. 'Decent of you, Langley.'

A little while later, as Langley held his hands and prayed, Jasin, Lord Heselwood drifted from this life.

His young friend, who had admired this distinguished gentleman for the sheer audacity with which he'd conducted his business affairs as he acquired huge land holdings, shook his head and wept.

The approach of voices brought disappointment.

Langley felt it was too soon to disturb this quiet glade, but the very stillness of the forest subdued the newcomers, who clutched at their hats in sorrow at the passing of one of their own, be they station owners or lowly stockmen.

'Typical of Langley,' Charlie sniffed when his brother failed to return from the cattle sales as expected.

'It's a long ride, so he had to stay overnight in Brisbane. Why are you making such a fuss?'

'Which meant he should have been back here yesterday afternoon! I don't know where he's got to.'

'He probably called on friends. Goodness me, Charlie, he lives so far away he rarely gets a chance to get to town.'

'If he intended to do that he should have said so. Pa is waiting for him.'

'Oh, let him wait!' Rosa snapped. 'Langley's a grown man. He can do what he likes.'

'Now, now,' Charlie soothed. 'You mustn't upset yourself!'

Rosa sought refuge in Duncan's study, idly turning the pages of some old copies of *The Ladies' Home Journal* that she'd found stacked in a corner. She desperately wanted to go home now but the decision was not hers to make.

Then Langley was back, several days overdue, bringing the shocking news of the accident; of Jasin Heselwood killed by a fall from his horse in a storm, and how he'd followed after Jasin, hoping to catch up with him, and had found his body!

They were all stunned. It seemed the three men in this house could talk of little else, while Rosa reeled in shock, unable to accept that this could be possible.

'How could such a thing happen?' she cried, in a futile attempt at denial. 'He was an excellent rider! You know that, don't you, Charlie? You rode with him several times at Montone Station.'

But her husband shrugged. 'My dear, the cemetery is full of excellent riders. Caught off guard. And, as Langley says, in Lord Heselwood's case, it was lightning. These things happen.'

He reached out and took her arm. 'I think you should lie down; you're looking very pale. We're all upset, but in your condition you must take extra care. Perhaps when you're feeling better you could write a nice letter to Lady Heselwood expressing our condolences. She was very fond of you, and it will comfort her greatly to hear from you.'

As they made for the door, Charlie called back to his brother, 'Where's the funeral. In Brisbane? If so, we should attend.'

'I don't know. They have to wait for word from Lady Heselwood.'

'Who are "they"?'

'The Governor has an equerry in charge of the situation for the time being.'

'Oh well, I suppose that would follow,' Charlie said, ushering Rosa along the passageway. 'It just goes to show, you never know what's around the corner.'

He blinked in surprise to see tears streaming down her cheeks. 'Don't cry, dear. You mustn't upset yourself. Pregnant women can be over-emotional. I'll have the housekeeper bring you in a nice cup of tea and some biscuits. Or would you rather some cake? I'll see what's available.'

Rosa mourned Jasin's passing in her own way. When they returned to Brisbane she made a lone visit to St Stephens Cathedral and sat in the cool depths of the dim building for a very long time. Still confused, feeling genuine sorrow at his untimely death mired with guilt, she prayed for forgiveness. She was only too aware now that she had not only betrayed her husband and the child, but also her friend Georgina Heselwood and, repenting, she wept for them.

Rosa knew that heartache would never leave her, and all the reminders and reminiscences had to be borne in silence because, selfishly, and for their sakes, this child would be Charlie's. She would never revoke that decision.

As she closed the heavy cathedral door behind her, she smiled wanly at the bright sunny day, and reflected that this had to be the first of better days for Charlie and Rosa Palliser. She'd see to it, she determined. They'd have more children too, maybe four . . .

The air was filled with the perfume of the old frangipani tree. Rosa plucked a tiny white flower to savour its scent, and held it carefully in her hand as she walked away.

CHAPTER FOURTEEN

From the time he'd gained himself a horse, which he called Giddyap because he thought it was such a funny whitefeller word often used for horses, Banggu had seen many terrible things.

There were more herds of cattle now, some from the east, some coming directly from the south. He saw white men attacking each other in the bush for the right to claim trees, and hiding the bodies. He saw a gang of men stampede cattle into another mob, wrecking the drover's camp and stealing his cattle. He found a white man who said his name was Bell in the lonely bush with a spear in his chest. He lifted out the spear and caked the wound with mud, trying to stop the bleeding, but it was too late; the man died. Banggu piled rocks over his body so that it would not be disturbed by animals, and rode on into the coloured hills.

When he crossed through the hills, he expected to see open country with the usual knots of trees dotted out there as far as the eye could see, but below him on either side of the river great mobs of cattle were grazing. And from his vantage point he could see houses, miles apart but occupied, with smoke curling from their chimneys. It was as if he'd taken a wrong turn and was back in the outskirts of Rockhampton.

Confused, he sat down to try to work this out, because he wasn't as clear about tribal boundaries as his father had been. He thought he was probably still in Mitakoodi country but he wanted to get into the Kalkadoon lands, to ask about Nyandjara. She would be well married with babies by now, but it would be worth the detour to make sure.

Once out into the far lands he met many of the people; some living normal lives in their own territory, abiding by the laws and following the seasonal food routes. They seemed unconcerned about the white men, choosing to avoid them so that their life patterns were undisturbed, but he came across more and more people who told him fearsome stories of white men's brutality. These people were bewildered; too set in their ways to consider flight.

'How can we run to other tribal lands without permission to enter?' they wailed.

A woman asked how they would find water, food and shelter in strange lands without the knowledge handed down to people for generations.

'We wouldn't be able to read the signs,' she said. 'And we don't know their laws. It could be dangerous.'

'You will have to ask your elders to prepare the way for you,' Banggu said, but it was bleak advice; to most of them unthinkable.

He crossed the river at a set of waterfalls and then rode down on to the plains, keeping within striking distance of a creek because he'd learned that a horse needed a lot of water. What a shock that was! It caused him to debate the viability of an animal that couldn't just go where he wished. He never had to carry water for himself; now the horse was carrying its own, in discarded waterbags he'd found on the stock routes. Banggu reckoned his father would have a good laugh if he could see this arrangement.

So there he was, riding quietly along on Giddyap, when he saw horsemen herding a group of blacks ahead of them, whips cracking at them as if they were cattle.

They were a family mob. Harmless. Women with babies, children, old people and just a few young men. They were weeping, running and stumbling, dragging each other along, trying to stay clear of the horses' hooves. There must have been about forty of them!

Banggu could only gape at the scene as he dismounted, leaving Giddyap behind so he could creep closer to this terror. He hid in the bush and watched, helpless, as two women, cut by the long stockwhips, were made to run faster towards the creek. It had deep sides, that creek, and steep, witness to the force of waters that rushed through this watercourse in the wet season.

He saw people jumping, tumbling into the rocky creek and heard the shouts of stockmen telling them to get out and stay out.

'This here creek's our boundary,' a man shouted. 'You lot don't come back or guns will get you!'

With that he fired into the air, adding frightened screams to the confusion down in the water.

Now rid of those black people, the riders turned for home, and Banggu backed quietly away. But he backed into a stockman with a gun!

'Gotcha!' the man said, shoving a rifle into his back.

Banggu was already fired up with rage, having to watch the ill-treatment of those poor bush people. He didn't waste a second. Whirling around to grab the rifle by the barrel, he slammed it against the stockman's head. But the huge stockman came at him with a punch so hard that Banggu thought he had broken his head. He couldn't breathe. Strong hands were around his throat, slowly, painfully crushing the life out of him, and he realised he was dying here in this strange place, after he'd come all this way . . .

But then he felt the man jolt against him and the hands fall away, and

Banggu began to slip to the ground. The man stood very still for a few seconds before he began to crumple on top of him.

A hard-looking blackfellow, about forty, Banggu would have said, pulled his attacker aside, and muttered to Banggu to come with him. He was dragging him away from the inert stockman with a short spear in his back, but Banggu wanted to go back for his horse. He was trying to explain about the horse in his own language, but this man would have none of it. He was jabbering at Banggu, shaking his head, trying to haul him along with him.

It took a few seconds for the strange words to sink in. Whether he had managed to translate or his brain had come to the same conclusion, Banggu finally grasped the problem and began to run after his rescuer.

The horse would have to be abandoned. Horses left tracks. Any self-respecting black tracker could follow it. Would say there were two horses here, not just one. Two blackfellows here. Bare feet. Kill stockman. One run away to creek. Other gone, horse-riding.

Besides, he thought as he ran, this narrow stretch of bush along the creek was too thick for a horse to use for cover, and the other alternative would have been to take his chances riding it out in the open.

He crashed down the steep bank, splashed across the creek and began to climb up the other side, hoping the white men would take care of Giddyap. He was dizzy, his head ached and he felt faint. He scowled, thinking of the horse, and began falling back, slipping down the slope.

'Of course they'll look after the horse,' he muttered to the confused black faces above him as they pulled him up. 'They're kinder to horses than to our people.'

'Who are you?' the hard-faced man asked.

'I am the first son of the Trader. I am trying to get to the Kalkadoon people.'

'Us Kalkadoon.'

He ran with three men, ran all day it seemed to him, with the sun pounding on his head and his eyes on their feet in front of him as they went thud thud, thud thud, keeping the rhythm.

Banggu was in familiar territory again, camped with displaced families by a deep lake. He'd walked around this lake with his father and brother, never dreaming that one day he'd be back here alone and seeking refuge.

Determined to make himself useful, and by doing so, acceptable to these people, he went out with the hunters every day, adding his catch to the communal fires.

Then one day he saw a familiar face. It was Kapakupa, one of the Pitta Pitta elders! He ran over to greet him.

The old man was a good listener, for which Banggu was grateful. He'd been alone for months and was desperately in need of someone to care that he'd been set adrift. But first, in answer to a question, he was able to tell of his father: that he was in good health and living with the family back home.

'On an island,' he said. 'Learning to be a fisherman.'

'Ah, but I hear he is nearby, Banggu. Travelling with white men and a mob of cattle, and each time he meets people he asks for you. Why does he have to search for his son?'

'I didn't know he was looking for me. I'll have to go to him. Might be there is even more trouble. I'll have to seek him out myself. Where is he?'

Kapakupa ignored the question. 'What brings you here?'

'Trouble. Terrible trouble,' Banggu said.

He went on to speak of the disasters that had caused him to flee the white men, including the deaths of his brother and his friends. And the subsequent death of the black man he'd met at Mischief Creek.

'You talk a mix of our languages,' Kapakupa said. 'Some bit Kalkadoon, some bit Pitta Pitta. These people don't know what to make of you. They ask me to identify you.' His rheumy eyes fastened on Banggu. 'Where did you get the horse?'

Banggu was easily able to explain that. 'I stole it, from the blackfellow police,' he said proudly.

'Yes, it has a police brand on it. So did the saddle. People think you are one of them. The white men did too. They think you're a runaway policeman.'

'No! Not me.' Banggu was shocked. 'I didn't know about any brand.'

'Did you meet a white man called Bell?'

'Yes, he was dying. A spear. I tried to help him, but I couldn't. I buried him . . .'

'The cattlemen back there, they think you killed him.'

'Why me?' Banggu yelped. 'Why pick on me?'

'Because they found a shiny ornament in the saddle of that horse. It belonged to the man Bell. They are very angry.'

Banggu sighed. 'He asked me to give it to some white man. Anywhere. Because it had his name. I meant to. For his family. So they know he is dead.'

The old man shrugged. 'No wonder Trader looks for you. You're walking trouble.'

'Could I ask a question? About a girl. A Kalkadoon girl.'

'Who?'

'Her name is Nyandjara.'

'Aaah!' The tribal elder clapped his hands over his ears. 'Say not the name! She is dead. Shot by guns. Killed in a raid by whitefellers with her husband Uluyan, son of the clan leader.'

'Oh no! She can't be!' Banggu was embarrassed by the tears that welled from his eyes, but he couldn't control them. He held his head in his hands, shamed.

The old man patted him on the shoulder. 'You've had some bad times. You can stay here with these people, they will welcome you now. I will make sure Trader knows where you are.'

Banggu nodded his agreement. To embrace his father again, that would be a joy. Should have been a joy, had not this grief seared his soul. She was dead. Gone! The love that he'd stored in his heart was shattered. He wished he could turn to his dear brother and tell him about this terrible thing, but he too had gone into the Dreamtime.

He walked down to the lake and waded in. The water was freezing but it served to take his mind off the pain, render him numb for a while . . . for a long while, as the grief was gradually replaced by rage.

A young woman was watching the man Banggu as he emerged from the water; watching his strong, shining body when he shivered off the cold and crossed the pebbled shore.

She walked towards him, knowing her sleek body was a match for his, and stood before him.

'Is it cold?' she asked him.

'Yes.' His sad eyes took in her firm, full breasts, but they raised not a glimmer of interest.

'Ah. That's not good,' she sighed. 'I have walked far today. I would have liked to bathe.'

She lifted her thick hair up from the nape of her neck with both hands, knotting it into place, at the same time showing off the elegance of the female form.

'It's not that bad,' he told her.

She turned to look at the lake, and shivered.

'If I go in,' she asked him, 'will you warm me when I come out?'

'If you like,' he replied politely.

'Promise?'

'Yes.'

She ran down and dived in, and came up squealing and splashing. 'Oh! Oh! Oh! It is too cold.'

She was back on shore in seconds, jumping about and shaking her hands when he came to her, his arms wide as promised.

She took him into the forest, to her gunyah made of bark that was only a few long steps from the lake, and there he warmed her and she warmed his injured heart.

'What is your name?' he asked her.

'I am Wiradji.'

'I have not seen you before.'

'Kapakupa brought me here. He said you need a wife. But if you don't like me, he will get you someone else.'

Banggu needed her. He held her close. The way he felt right now, he didn't want to ever let her go. 'We'll tell him I don't want anyone else.'

All along the tracks, Ladjipiri had kept asking if anyone had seen his son, the Trader's son. His name was Banggu.

For a long time there was nothing; then he began hearing whispers of a lone young man who spoke the Darambal language. There was no name, but he was said to be in the Mitakoodi country, riding a horse.

That gave him doubts. Why would his son need a horse? It wasn't as if he'd ever worked as a stockman and become accustomed to being carried by the proud animals. And where would he have got one? Ladjipiri supposed he could have stolen it.

The lone travelling man they spoke of had only been seen in wild country, never in white settlements or on the stations, so it could be Banggu. And he had good reason not to give his name in case the police were looking for him. Then again, it could be anyone. At times Ladjipiri felt his search was hopeless; that the earth had swallowed his son, but strangely, the responsibilities of this long march had kept him so well occupied, he lacked the time for melancholia.

He was greatly relieved that Mr Merry had overcome his illness, but he looked thinner. Too thin. He and his good wife had caught up with them in the village of Longreach, before they all set their eyes in the direction of the Pelican watering place, which Ladjipiri knew well.

It was sad that Mr Merry had come back to trouble, but there it was. The drovers were refusing to push the cattle on without extra pay.

Trader understood the situation very well. He sat by the cook-wagon, swishing flies away with a leafy twig as he listened to their complaints. The original plan was to bring the cattle to this place, where they would be paid off. But now that many extra miles were needed, they wanted extra money. Ladjipiri nodded solemnly. That was fair.

Not that anyone asked his opinion.

Fortunately Mr Merry agreed to pay them on the spot and they settled on a new contract to take his cattle further out.

'What about Duke's cattle?' the other drovers asked.

'Nothing to do with me,' Mr Merry said, his eyes as hard as the clear blue stones found in the hills. He was angry that Duke was still missing. 'I don't even know if he wants to push on.'

'What about our pay?' they asked.

'Your contract for his cattle was with him. He has to pay you the same amount I paid you.'

'Where is he?'

Mr Merry shrugged. 'I've no idea.'

Ginger talked with the drovers. 'Looks like we've got two choices. We can take Duke's cattle on with Harry's mob and get paid out there.'

'No!' came the shout.

'Or we can push them into the local sale yards, and leave a couple of blokes to hold them until he turns up. With our pay.'

'There's a third,' another man shouted. 'We can sell 'em.'

'I don't think that's on the cards,' Ginger said casually. 'Not yet anyway. We've got his cattle, we'll get paid one way or another.'

While these discussions were under way and Mrs Merry was stocking up for the last section of the journey, Ladjipiri sought out some of his own people as usual.

His footsteps took him along a bush track to a small camp where two women were scaling fish on a flat rock. One of them looked up and smiled at him.

'He's here,' she called in the Pitta Pitta language, and a young man stepped forward. Sadly, his right arm hung loosely and his chest was badly scarred.

'You're the Trader!' he said, excitement in his voice. 'The old man said you would come. I am Pali. I am to tell you your son is well. He is with the Kalkadoon people and is to marry soon. He said there will be a corroboree at the same place again. If you like to go.'

'Pali, you are very kind to hold this message for me. I am thankful to you and pleased with your news. I was worried about my son. Now the clouds have lifted.'

As a courtesy, he remained to talk with the people for a while, hearing that they felt safer near this white community than out there where the wild white men roamed and anything could happen to them.

'Yes,' he said. 'Out there the battles rage. But you can't stay here. I have seen the way they spread their villages. Soon they will want to clear this scrub to grow food.'

'What can we do then?' Pali asked. 'What will become of our children?'

'Can you not return to your own land, where you must stay very quiet and keep together? And not antagonise them.'

'Not antagonise them?' Pali's wife said bitterly. 'We didn't even know about them until all these horse riders with guns came upon us and chased us away from our own place. Look at Pali's arm! Bullets did that. And see this . . .' She showed him the scars of burns around her own neck.

'Did they try to hang you?' Ladjipiri breathed, reminded of the death of his younger son.

'They dragged her along the ground by a rope,' Pali said. 'Her sister cut the rope and saved her but then she was killed. Trampled by horses.'

'Where can we go now?' a woman wept.

Ladjipiri shook his head; he supposed they could go back east, right into occupied lands where the fighting was over, but they were outback folk; the changes they would have to make very quickly would suffocate them. And they had no English.

Or they could hang about here, bereft of sustenance and respect.

'The old man told us you would help,' Pali said, his eyes shining with trust.

'I don't know how,' Ladjipiri said. 'What can I do? One man. My own homelands were overrun. My family takes refuge with another tribe.'

'All the tribes are being run over. The whites came too quick,' Pali said. 'Except for the Kalkadoon. Their warriors are making ready for war. Their message sticks speak of nothing else.'

The Trader sat down with Mr Merry.

'I must leave you now,' he said. 'I have fulfilled my duty.'

Mr Merry was disappointed. 'I know you agreed to bring us this far, but as you know, we have to move on. To Pelican Waters. Do you know that place?'

Trader nodded.

'Then couldn't you stay on until we reach there? It is only about a hundred miles from here.'

'I cannot. You can follow the wagon wheels to the Pelican Waters.'

'We will miss you, Trader. Are you sure you won't change your mind?'

Ladjipiri shook his head. 'That I cannot do. Why not you stay here?'

Mrs Merry came over to join them. She squatted on the grass beside her husband.

'Trader's leaving us,' he said.

'Oh no! It won't be the same without you, Trader. Who will find bush honey for me and laugh at me when I do my washing in the creeks? Are you going home now?'

'Soon,' he said, which meant after he'd seen his son.

Suddenly he was sad for them. 'Why you have to come so far to make a home?'

They were nonplussed by the question.

'Harry's looking for land,' Mrs Merry said, 'to run his cattle. Unoccupied land. Empty land.'

'But it's not empty. Many, many people live here.'

Mrs Merry's cheeks turned red and she looked at her husband, who said: 'It's a hard question, Trader. There has to be room for all.'

'People ask me where you white people come from.'

'From all over the world. Like the Chinese people you see also. You know? The Chinese?'

'Yes. More better if you all stay home, I reckon.'

Mr Merry smiled, a half sort of smile as if he thought it more better that they maybe talk about this another time.

Trader nodded, understanding. Then he made a suggestion. 'S'pose I say you don't go to Pelican Waters? What you think about that?'

'Where do we go instead?'

'Better place.' He picked up a twig. 'You here. Up there the Pelicans' place. Halfway, you branch off like this. You go out there.'

'No wagon wheels to follow out there. And no guide,' Mr Merry said. 'I don't think so.'

Trader was trying to keep them away from Kalkadoon territory.

'I give you guides,' he said. 'They doan have homes no more. They go with you. All family together. You mind them. They mind you.'

'Who are these people, Trader?'

'They friends of mine. Good people.'

It took a day for them to absorb the idea that their guides would be a family of black people who knew the country and who would take them there . . . on condition that they would be able to stay on the land with them when Mr Merry marked out his station.

'They don't call him Trader for nothing,' Harry said to Tottie. 'I think he's sold you on his plan.'

'Why not? Trader said we'd be safe from black attacks with them in tow, and we could protect them from the gun-happy white men we keep hearing about. Besides, we know nothing of the land out there, and they'd help us. Plenty of blacks work on stations; why not these people?'

'Ah fair go, Tottie. We can't have a family of ten blacks traipsing along with us. We'd be a laughing stock.'

'Twelve. You forgot the babies.'

'Just the same. I haven't even got a station yet.'

'So let them help you.'

'I don't think so. We're on a cattle drive, not a walkabout. I don't want to be worrying about them. They'll be in the way.'

Tottie stood her ground. 'There you go again. It's all your way. I'd feel a damn sight safer with ten black people on the march with us. I'd even appreciate their company. Especially the women. Did you ever stop to think I might miss the company of women?'

When Trader arrived with the shy family, Tottie realised they couldn't speak any English, a small matter she'd overlooked, but she had no intention of backing down. If Trader believed this was a good thing, then it was good enough for her.

Trader introduced them to Pali, the leader, who was about thirty and had a crippled arm, and who in turn called the names of two other men his age, two young lads and a very old man as they stepped forward. Next came the four young women, two of them carrying babies in slings around their necks. He seated them all in the shade of a stringy gum and offered to translate questions, but it was really only Tottie who needed answers; she was intrigued by the chance to actually get to know an Aborigine family, and learn about them.

In the end Harry interrupted proceedings. 'Tottie, you'll have plenty of time to find out who they are and how they live once we're out on the track.'

'Does that mean they're coming with us?'

'If they want to.'

Immediately there were smiles all round and Tottie was on her feet to fuss over the babies.

That afternoon she bought a new journal and an extra supply of pens and nibs. She was determined to keep a record of their progress this time, and no slacking. She was looking forward to the last leg of their long journey, but when she came to put her purchases into the wagon, she noticed a bulky parcel wrapped in hessian at the end of the bunk.

Guns! New guns, and pistols, and boxes of ammunition!

'What's this about?' she demanded of Harry. 'Are you getting ready to start a war out there?'

He hesitated, and then said: 'I won't lie to you, Tottie. It is time for us to be more careful. I taught you to use your rifle and keep it handy but you keep forgetting, and that won't do any more. I'll be angry if I see you riding without it again. The same goes for the men. They're getting too complacent.'

'All right. I'll remember. But what's happening now? I thought we were leaving in the morning.'

'No, we have to hold off for a day or so. We need more horses, I should have some by tomorrow. With luck.'

Proudly Tottie watched her husband stride away. He was always handsome, she recalled fondly, but now, with his steely blue eyes glinting from under a face almost hidden by a sandy beard and straw-like hair that still flopped over his forehead, he looked even more attractive. He had a place here, she reflected, tears welling. He was no longer just a stockman; he was a boss, highly regarded by his men, several of whom had offered to stay on and help him get started.

'With luck,' he'd said. More and more Tottie had come to realise they'd need a mountain of luck to face the hazards that were confronting them and find their Promised Land.

Though she was sitting on the wagon in the warmth of the sun, with not a breath of a breeze, she shivered.

'God help us.'

★ ★ ★

338

Marcus loved the scenery out this way. 'The sky is massive,' he enthused. 'You can see right around the horizon, it's so flat. And the colour, it's so blue! Not a mark on it, not even a dot of a cloud. It's flawless!'

'It's relentless,' Duke said, unimpressed. 'Day in and day out, all this bloody blue. When does it rain? And how far are we from Longreach?'

'Only about five miles.'

'Thank God for that. I hope Harry's there with the mob.'

'He's there. That wagon master said your mob has been there for days. I'm looking forward to taking a break, then I push on north-west.'

'That wagon master also said there's no more land up for grabs around here. Looks like Harry has miscalculated.'

'No one could have guessed it would go so fast. But there's plenty more.'

Marcus was looking forward to a few days' break in this frontier town. At the head of his troops, operating without a sergeant, he'd had hair-raising clashes with mobs of blacks, who didn't take kindly to being shunted off new cattle runs, while Duke dallied at station homesteads. Since he would outrank the Longreach constabulary, Marcus planned to commandeer one of their number to replace Krill so that he could continue as ordered. His instructions were to open a new police district, not to be hurtling about the countryside at the beck and call of whingeing squatters.

Duke was disappointed by the dry and dusty outpost of Longreach. It seemed to be no more than a shambles of huts and tents tacked on to huge holding yards of sheep and cattle, and populated mainly by stockmen and drovers.

'I just remembered,' Marcus said to him. 'The bushranger Redford stole two thousand head of cattle from this district. He drove them all the way to Adelaide and sold them for five thousand pounds.'

'That's some drive,' Duke said. 'Must be a thousand miles and all. But a lot of cattle out here must be fair game for thieves. How the hell can some of these squatters keep an eye on their stock? The size of their stations is insane!'

Marcus laughed. 'Isn't that what you're after? Endless land. Lord of all you survey?'

'Not on that scale. Fifty square miles will do me. But I'll still need someone to help me blaze out boundaries. Someone I can trust. Why don't you give up this policing business and come in as my partner? There's a fortune to be made. You can see that.'

Marcus rode back to confer with Trooper Pompey Lee for a few minutes, then, as the squad wheeled away, led by Pompey, he caught up with Duke again.

'I've sent them off to make camp somewhere and report at the police station in the morning.'

Some riders were coming towards them. 'Where's the police station?' Marcus called.

'Follow your nose,' came the response, so they rode on along what might be called the main street, though it was more like a marketplace, with people milling about examining dusty wares heaped on the trays of wheelbarrows and wagons. Women pored over baskets of boots and clothing, while children clambered around discarded crates and goats chewed at refuse strewn recklessly along the sidelines.

'Obviously this is the commercial centre,' Marcus laughed, as their horses picked their way past the dismal scene. 'And up ahead, as we were told, is our police station.'

Duke gaped as they rode into a stockade surrounded by a high fence made of split logs. They hitched their horses and marched across the wide apron of the stockade to the station house, which was built like a fortress, with loopholes in the walls to accommodate guns.

'Expecting trouble?' Duke asked with a grin when they walked into the long, cool building and met a craggy-faced constable.

'This office has seen its share of trouble, mister!' the man at the desk snapped, not appreciating the stranger's humour. Then he blinked at the other visitor's uniform.

'Jeez! You're Inspector Beresford! We got your sergeant here.'

'Sergeant Krill?'

'The very one. He says he rode like the dickens to get here afore you.'

'Good. Well done.'

'I'll send for him,' the constable offered. He disappeared through a rear door, and they heard him yell for someone to find Krill.

When he returned he said: 'He won't be long, Inspector. He's staying in our barracks out the back there. Will you be wanting to stay here too?'

'By the looks of things, yes. I should appreciate digs. There doesn't seem to be much out there.'

The constable nodded. 'Nothin' to recommend, sir.'

'What are the blacks like out this way?' Duke asked him.

'Numerous and nasty. Hostiles, our sergeant calls them. You're gonna be kept busy, Inspector. You got the black troopers with you?'

'I have. But the blacks we saw were easy to handle. Too scared to put up any arguments.'

'Is that right? Did they have many bucks with them?'

'Bucks?'

'Young men.'

Marcus was taken aback. 'I suppose they did. I don't know. Why?'

'It's being said the smart ones are pulling back into Kalkadoon territory.'

'What good will that do them?' Duke asked.

'Safety in numbers,' the constable growled. 'Our boss, Sergeant Hannah, will be pleased to see you. He was called out to an attack on the road to Pelican Waters. That's the beginning of your district now, Inspector. A blackfellow was shot for spearing a bullock. Then came payback. Two stockmen murdered by blacks. Sergeant Hannah had to investigate. He'll be back in a day or so.'

'I'll wait for him then.'

'Goodoh. We were saying to Krill that them blackfellow troopers had better watch their backs. The wild blacks have got spies everywhere. They will know they're coming.'

'They'll cope,' Marcus said stiffly. 'They're well trained.'

Duke soon found Harry's camp, and was surprised to hear that Matt Doolan hadn't returned.

'What do you mean, you split up with him?' Harry said angrily.

'He went on to Cameo Downs. I met a mate of mine and had a look around the countryside with him.'

'You didn't think you were seeing enough of the countryside travelling with your cattle?'

'I just took a break, that's all. I don't know why you're getting hot under the collar, Harry. I'm here. Everything's under control.'

'Is it now? Half the drovers are waiting to be paid. They're entitled to a break too, but they've been sitting here without any money, having to rely on their mates to shout them a drink. And I'm moving on tomorrow.'

Duke shrugged. 'All right. I'll find them and I'll pay them. And we move on tomorrow. Have you got anything else to complain about?'

'No. I said I'm going. You'd better go and find your cattle.'

'Find them?'

'Yes. Your drovers have quit. They bunged your cattle in the sale yards. You'll have to pay to get them out. And pay the drovers or likely you'll be in more trouble.'

'I'm disappointed in you,' Duke said. 'I didn't think you'd get so cranky just because I took a few days off. But I'll sort it out. I'll pay the drovers, and the blokes at the sale yards, and go you halves in whatever supplies you've bought here . . .'

'No you won't. You're out, Duke. You're on your own. You find your own drovers and rig, while I go to the police station and report a missing stockman, by name of Matt Doolan.'

'Ah well, whatever you say, Harry. I think you're being tough on me, but we only agreed to get as far as here anyway. So no hard feelings.'

Harry was astonished at Duke's cheek, but he took the proffered hand, relieved that they were parting on good terms.

'Where are Tottie and Ned?' Duke asked. 'I'd better say goodbye to them.'

'Just a minute. Where did you leave Matt?'

'Near the Cameo Downs homestead. He went over there with a teamster pushing bullocks.'

'And who was the mate you met?'

'Inspector Beresford. He's travelling with a squad of native police to open a new police district north of here.'

'Duke, the native police aren't too popular with a lot of folk.'

'Try telling that to the squatters. They welcomed them with open arms. So might you, Harry, so don't be too keen to judge.'

Ginger Magee was spokesman for the drovers who were camped at the stockyards. As soon as he saw Duke he stormed over to him. 'About bloody time you turned up, MacNamara!'

'What's it got to do with you? You're on Harry's team. I'm here to pay my drovers.'

'And I'm here to see they get their fair share. They're waiting for you by the fence there.'

Duke turned and saw them: six men leaning sullenly against the railings, backed by a crush of cattle being fed through the yards. Despite the dust raised by the cattle and the shouts of the stockmen mustering them, the men made no move towards Duke, making him come to them.

'Better late than never,' he said. 'Now I reckon I owe you two pounds ten each. Right?' He stared aggressively at Ginger, knowing the figure was two shillings more than was actually due to each man. 'Right?' he challenged.

Ginger ignored him.

The grim-faced men took their pay with barely a nod, and began to walk away. 'Hang on,' Duke called. 'Who wants to sign on for the next leg? On to Pelican Waters. Same money?'

Ginger tipped his hat back on his head and hitched up his trousers. 'You'll never get a drover for them cattle of yours now. You're too bloody unreliable.'

'Ah, get out of my way!' Duke snarled, giving Ginger a shove. 'And mind your own bloody business.'

Taken unawares, Ginger almost lost his balance, but he still managed to throw a punch at Duke's jaw. Fortunately for Duke, it didn't quite connect.

Instantly, stockmen came running. A fight!

It didn't last long. Duke came back at Ginger, fists flying, until Ginger's hard knuckles collided with his ribs. He buckled to his knees as Ginger strode away, and the small crowd melted into the groups of passers-by, anxious to get this day's work over before the sun slipped down. Were they interested, they would have noticed that the sun was now a huge golden ball in a wash of red that coloured both the massive expanse of sky and its underling, earth, without favour.

Duke saw the sunset and groaned. He'd have to pay for his cattle in the sale yards for yet another day. And his ribs hurt like hell.

The next day it was Duke, living in a flea-ridden timber shanty, who had work to do, while Marcus relaxed in the sparse barracks.

There were no drovers to be found. Despite his aching ribs and bruised face, Duke rode from end to end of the rough settlement, searching for men to move his cattle, even offering more pay, but he couldn't find drovers or stockmen to work for him. They either had work or had completed their contracts and were headed back to civilisation.

'Ah what the hell!' he said to Marcus. 'I ought to sell the bloody cattle and go home. I can make more than two pounds a head for them out here. That's real cash.'

Marcus took him into the deserted barracks common room and poured two whiskies.

'You know your trouble?' he said. 'You haven't been bitten by the land bug. It's as bad as gold fever. You're happy to toddle along while the rest of these characters out here are going full steam.'

'No I'm not. I can't take the cattle out there on my own.'

'I don't think you ever wanted to open a run out there.'

'Where'd you get that idea?' Irritated, Duke downed his whisky in a gulp.

'You keep talking about selling your cattle,' Marcus said. 'Now take your mate, Harry. Selling wouldn't enter his head. From what you tell me, he's out to get a huge whack of land, run his cattle, build a house, live there, call it home.'

'That's right, and so am I.'

Marcus laughed. 'You wouldn't last ten minutes out there. You'd get bored. Face it, Duke. You're no pioneer.'

'It's different for Harry. He's got a wife.'

'That's only an excuse. Few of these land grabbers have women with them; they're too obsessed with the job at hand.'

'So am I. I just have to get some drovers.'

Marcus poured him another drink. 'Do you mind if I give you some advice?'

'You never stop giving me advice!'

'All right. Then here it is. Sell the cattle, then saddle up and go after your land. Race for it. Isn't that what your father did? Get the land and worry about stocking it later.'

'But I wanted to get the land and stock it in one hit.'

Marcus threw up his hands. 'It was only a suggestion. You make up your own mind. I have to find some workmen to take with me when we head out into the wilder wilds. Obviously I'll need a stockade just like this. My troopers can help them, but they'll have enough to do cutting down hostiles who still think the spear can beat the gun, and the authorities can't expect me to set to with an axe.'

A fierce wind raged through the night, and Duke was grateful that he'd chosen to stay in this rooming house at the rear of a tavern. It was built of mud and twigs and provided a fairly reliable shelter, but it could not shut out the scream of the wind as it hurtled across the plains, unnerving him.

All night he worried the problem. He even thought of approaching Harry and asking him what he thought of the plan Marcus had suggested. Asking him, maybe, to come in with him and make a dash for land. With good horses they could cover long distances in a few days, put in a couple of days blazing boundaries and then get the hell out. He'd noticed a Lands Office had opened here in Longreach, so the claim could be registered and the licence approved! Hurrah!

But who'd have thought the natives out here would be as savage as those fiends up north? He'd been under the impression, as most people were, that there were few blacks living way out here. It was commonly accepted that the vast inland of this colony was empty.

Then again, he reminded himself, Ned was a free agent. He should ask him.

He climbed off his bunk in the morning nursing a bout of the miseries. His mouth was as dry as a bone and everything he touched was covered in fine dust that had infiltrated the ill-fitting doors and windows.

Outside, mounds of red sand added to the litter tossed about by the storm, giving it a permanent air, and the old blue sky was only just throwing off that reddish shawl.

Duke made for the water tank, a rusty-looking former ship's tank, but took one look at the sand-filled mug attached to a chain and headed for the tavern.

A sweeper at work in the bar nodded as he reached for a bottle of beer and swigged down half of it before giving a sigh of satisfaction. Never before had beer tasted that good. He finished the bottle, put a coin on the counter and strode out the door, his mind made up.

Two of the black women from the family Harry had acquired were batting dust off the wagon, and another one was inside rearranging it with a large cloth. Obviously new to the tasks, they were enjoying themselves immensely until Ned walked over.

They were suddenly solemn and he felt a spoilsport, so he smiled and waved his arms for them to continue.

'Where's the missus?' he asked.

They looked one to the other to translate the question, then one of the women said: 'Missus!'

As one, they pointed to the nearby cook-wagon sheltering under a straggling gum. With no horses in place, and a mantle of red dust over the canvas, it seemed abandoned, but Tottie was around the other side, washing tin plates and pans in a bucket and setting them out to dry on a check tablecloth spread over a patch of wiry grass.

'I see you've acquired staff,' Ned smiled.

Her back to him, Tottie nodded, concentrating on the task.

'What a nuisance that dust is,' he said. 'It must be maddening trying to do that in cold water. Do you want me to boil a billy for you?'

'Not yet. You could grate some soap, though,' she said, her voice tight.

He looked down at her and saw that her eyes were wet with tears.

'That jolly storm,' he said. 'I thought we'd had our share of sandstorms. Where's Flint, your cook? He should be doing this.'

'He's gone to the doctor to get a tooth out.'

Ned picked up a bar of soap from her work table. 'Where's the grater then? I'll be chief soap grater.'

She stopped sloshing the plates about. 'I don't know where I put it. I really don't know,' she sobbed. With that she dried her hands and dabbed at her eyes with the apron. 'To be honest, Ned,' she gulped, 'I don't know what I'm doing lately.'

'Aren't you feeling well?'

'Oh yes. I'm feeling well. Very well, in fact. That's the problem. I haven't got any excuse . . .'

He wished he could take her in his arms and console her. Instead he said: 'For being upset? All that damned dust is enough to drive anyone to drink.'

'It's not that. It's nothing really.'

'It has to be something, hasn't it? Or do ladies just need a weep now and again? I'd better boil that billy and make you some tea.'

She was quiet, standing back by the wagon while he stirred up the campfire. He ladled water from a cask into a billy, sloshed away lingering dust, ladled more water into it and was hanging it over the fire when she said: 'Ned, I don't want to go.'

He set the billycan in place and turned back to her. 'Go where, Tottie?'

'Out there.' She pointed down the road that led out of town. The road that led west.

'Ah, I see.'

Tottie studied the hem of her dress. One section had come undone and was trailing in the dirt. She kicked at it angrily.

'Don't you want to know why?' she asked without looking up.

'Only if you want to tell me.'

'You're always so polite, aren't you, Ned? Well I *shall* tell you.' She took a deep breath and the words came out in a rush. 'I'm scared, Ned. I am so frightened I can't think straight. All anyone talks about is the savages, people getting speared. Camps attacked. Why are we doing this? I thought we were to be settlers, not frontier fighters. I had no idea it would be this bad.'

This time he did reach out to her. He put an arm round her shoulder.

'What does Harry say?'

'Harry's too busy getting us moving. He's champing at the bit over delays. He's bought more guns. That's his answer.'

'You haven't told him you're frightened, have you?'

She shook her head. 'No. What good would that do? He didn't want me to come. He warned me. But I was too stupid to listen. Too much in love with him.'

He stood there with her, trying to think what he could say without causing conflict.

The water in the billy was bubbling, so he found some tea and threw it in, along with some sugar.

'You take it off now and let it draw,' she sniffed.

'Righto.'

Ned placed the billy on the ground to draw, and stood staring down at it.

'You'll have to tell Harry,' he said.

'And what can he do?'

'He's entitled to know you're worried.'

'No he's not. It's too late.' She dabbed at her eyes and sighed. 'I'm sorry, Ned. I shouldn't bother you with my woes. Please don't tell Harry. Promise you won't.'

'All right. I promise. Is this tea ready yet? Aren't you supposed to swing it around first? I never got the hang of that.'

She smiled. 'I never do, I think it's a myth.'

They sat on the bench by the wagon and drank the tea.

'Where are you going from here?' she asked him.

'I'll be travelling on with you. I have to see where you settle down.'

'Harry thought you'd turn back once we reached this place. That was the plan. He didn't expect to have to push on, so you don't have to stick with us. The drovers are staying on.'

'I've come this far, I'll see it out.' He smiled. 'That's if you'll have me.'

'Of course we will.' She kissed him on the cheek. 'You're a good friend, Ned. Would you do me another favour?'

'Yes.'

'See if you can get some sense out of Duke. We don't know what he's doing and Harry gets so cross with him.'

CHAPTER FIFTEEN

Georgina was in a daze. She couldn't accept that Jasin was dead. Killed! She was mildly irritated by the hushed and kindly tones surrounding her that whispered of his passing over, his meeting with his Maker and all the other euphemisms that shuffled around the fact that he was dead. She was in an agony that she could not express. Even to him. Even to Jasin. The man was such a cynic he'd have trouble accepting that she was in terrible pain. Broken-hearted! She could barely face the word herself for fear of his disdain. His amusement.

'You're what? Really? And what brought that on?' she could hear him saying.

And what did bring it on? she asked herself.

Thirty years married to a man she adored might be a good place to start. Thirty years married to an ambitious man who could be an absolute wretch but was also debonair, witty, elegant and a gentleman. Life with Jasin had never been dull. He abhorred dull people. At times their relationship had been fiery, but mostly they got along very well. Georgina had to admit that her husband wasn't given to romantic endearments, which hadn't mattered to her anyway; she found them rather puerile. She was more comfortable . . . no, happier, she corrected, when he called her 'old girl'. That was Jasin's endearment. The best he could offer.

She was sitting on the veranda watching stormclouds gather, and thinking about that, how she loved being called 'old girl', when the priest, who had rushed to her side on hearing the sad news, invited her to join him in prayers for the departed.

In the midst of her misery, from the gloom, she could hear Jasin's derision.

'Departed? How dare that upstart refer to me as the departed! Show him out, Georgina. I shall be in the study.'

She was waiting for news of Edward, desperate to find him now, and had issued instructions to the maids that she could not receive any more callers. No exceptions. She needed time to herself. It seemed the Premier had been informed of Jasin's sudden death by the Brisbane authorities; he'd contacted the bishop of this Anglican diocese, who had sent the parish priest to bring the news that Georgina couldn't accept. And then came a surge of friends and acquaintances offering condolences and advice.

'How do they know it's Jasin?' she'd argued. 'This could be a mistake. I'll have to go to Brisbane myself. If only I could find Edward! No, I can't just sit and wait here, not knowing what's going on! What have they done with him? Is he in a hospital?'

She remembered he had a lawyer in Brisbane, so she began rifling through his desk, tossing papers aside in a search for the name, but she wasn't absorbing a word on any of the pages; it was just something to do.

And then a maid brought her the telegram. 'Who is this from?' she asked, half expecting it would be an apology. From someone. For this horrible mistake . . .

'Mr Rivadavia, ma'am.'

'Who?'

'The name is hard to pronounce, ma'am.'

'Give it to me!'

My dear Lady Heselwood. May I extend my heartfelt sympathy to you upon the death of your dear husband Lord Heselwood. Forgive my intrusion, but if you need someone in Brisbane to look after matters I am at your service. Respectfully, Juan Rivadavia.

'Oh thank God,' she said. 'I'd forgotten he lives in Brisbane these days.'

She sat at Jasin's desk, in his custom-made leather chair and reflected on all the years that had passed since they'd first met Juan.

Her husband had never liked him much. He used to call him 'the Spaniard'. Only jealousy, of course, since the young and handsome Rivadavia had arrived from Argentina a wealthy man, sent out to expand his family's cattle interests, whereas everyone else was struggling.

She sighed. Jasin never knew that when their fortunes were at their lowest ebb, and they were faced with ruin, it was Juan who had come to the rescue. He had quietly shown Georgina a way out of the impasse with the banks and lent his good name to a sealed guarantee. He had always been the kindest and most reliable of men, and here he was ready to help when she was most in need.

'Thank God,' she said again, aware now that Jasin really had died. Rivadavia would never make such a mistake. She put her head in her hands and wept, but then realised that she'd better answer Juan's telegram before some stranger became involved.

She replied thanking him for coming to her aid. She asked him should she come to Brisbane? He wrote back suggesting it would be more suitable for her to remain in their home town among many friends. Wording telegrams was difficult under the circumstances, but Juan, with his old-world delicacy, managed. He took charge of matters and offered to accompany Lord Heselwood home.

Lady Heselwood accepted his extremely kind offer, and then had to attend to the arrangements for the funeral, refusing to allow anyone else to assist with decisions.

'You will have a decent funeral, I promise you,' she said to Jasin as she sat at his desk, where she seemed to be most of the time these days. 'Exactly as you would expect. But no reception. No wake. I couldn't bear it. A funeral would be bad enough with all its cloying condolences, and even worse if Edward can't be found in time.

And then, while she was worrying about her son, a letter arrived from Paul MacNamara, who now lived in Rockhampton. He too offered condolences, but more importantly he wanted her to know that he'd seen Edward some months back. As she probably already knew . . .

'Which I did not,' she murmured. 'Not a word since the reply-paid telegram from his landlady. I have no idea where he is.'

Paul advised that he had joined a droving expedition to the far west, along with Duke MacNamara, who, she might recall, was Paul's younger brother. They were still away, and Paul was concerned that Edward would not have heard of his father's death. Their destination was too far west for a telegram, so Paul had taken it upon himself to write to Edward and have the letter placed in a designated mail bag for the far-western settlement of Longreach.

Georgina was devastated by Paul's news, knowing it could be months before Edward made it back to Sydney, if indeed the letter even found him.

'Just when I need you the most,' she wept, hoping she didn't sound like his father.

She'd seen so many women, newly widowed, much comforted, even greatly cheered, by the presence of friends and relatives in their homes, and wondered at their ability to socialise so smoothly at such a time. As if playing the hostess had to remain high on the agenda.

'This widow', she sighed, 'can't do that; doesn't want to see anyone but her son. Is that too much to ask?'

She found that Jasin's office had become cold and restricting, so she moved outside to the warmth of the small summerhouse with the view of the harbour framed in the doorway. It became her daily retreat, a buffer against the shock of his death, where she sometimes just sat and gazed, and other times drifted into contemplation of many things. Many things.

She remembered Paul's letter . . . Edward going west. With Duke. Duke MacNamara! The name startled her. Frightened her. She could understand Paul MacNamara's kindness in attempting to contact Edward for her, despite the family differences. Any gentleman would do that. But there was Edward's situation! Good God in heaven, what was he doing associating with any of the MacNamaras? With his background!

Unless, she reflected, unless their mother had kept that business to herself. Had told no one. No one, that is, except the local police sergeant who had filed her formal complaint against Edward.

Unfortunately the sergeant, a kindly man, had let the matter slip to Milly Forrest, in a vain attempt to persuade Dolour to relent. Milly'd had no more luck than Georgina herself.

Dolour MacNamara was a hard, uncompromising woman. In the end it wasn't Edward she was striking at, it was the system. Georgina would never forget the words of someone who of that time was wealthy and well respected, but was still bitter about her convict past.

In begging her not to force her son into exile, Georgina had said: 'But this is his home. He was born in Australia. In Sydney.'

She could still see the woman's dark, impassive eyes as she murmured, 'I was born in Ireland and I was forcibly taken out of my country, and I hurt no one.'

'I think you're being very hard, Mrs MacNamara.'

'Convict ships make you hard.'

And smart, Georgina nodded. Dolour would have known the reaction of the men in her family had they learned that Heselwood's son, their neighbour, had assaulted her. So she'd kept it from them. Her case would have been lost had Pace and his sons been up for assault too if they'd taken revenge on Edward.

She shook her head, relieved. All these years I've been worrying about this and now I have Paul reaching out to help Edward, and Duke travelling with him. I needn't have worried; she never told them. No doubt Edward is aware of that too.

'I wish you'd come home,' she said.

She'd found Jasin's will in the desk, dated and signed three years ago. Witnessed by his lawyer. Everything was in order. His beloved wife and son were the sole beneficiaries of his substantial fortune in shares and property, estimated, in his own hand, to be worth more than a million pounds.

Georgina smiled. She remembered teasing Jasin that his hobby was sitting in his counting house, counting out his money.

'You can laugh,' he'd said. 'One day you may need to know so that you don't underestimate the situation.'

'Oh no,' she said, as she heard a carriage coming up the drive. But she wasn't thinking of the visitor, whoever it was; she was still thinking of Jasin. 'Oh no, my dear,' she smiled, 'it never occurred to me to underestimate you or your situation.'

The only visitor she was expecting was standing quietly in the parlour, hat in hand.

Georgina wrapped a cashmere shawl about her shoulders and went in to greet Juan Rivadavia.

The letter addressed to Edward Heselwood arrived at the general store at Longreach several weeks after the funeral service for the late Lord Heselwood had taken place at St Andrew's Cathedral in Sydney.

People lined the streets to watch the cortège travel the short distance to Sandhill Cemetery and peer at the widow, who was accompanied in the lead carriage by an old friend, Lady Rowan-Smith.

When the ladies had passed by, there were cheers or jeers, as the case might be, for the top-hatted politicians who had turned out en masse to show their respects.

Several people were miffed that they'd not been invited to attend a reception after the service, but others who took a chance and headed for the Heselwood harbourside mansion found the gates securely locked.

Georgina still could not face such an ordeal, but was comforted, in the absence of her son, by her friend, Vicki Rowan-Smith, and Juan Rivadavia.

A week later she received a letter from Clem Batterson, the manager of Montone, who was obviously very upset to hear of Jasin's death, but who wanted Lady Heselwood to know that he had the horse, Saul, safely back at the station. Apparently, as far as he could make out, Edward had sold the horse to Mrs Paul MacNamara and Lord Heselwood had bought it from her.

Georgina nodded. 'Of course.'

Jasin had said he'd find the horse. And he had.

But how on earth did that come about? she wondered. Then she supposed all would be explained when Edward came home.

'Had I known that Juan Rivadavia was taking Jasin's coffin down to Sydney,' Milly Forrest wailed, 'I'd have been on the same ship. By the time I found out it was too late. I thought it would have been the other way around. That Georgina would have come to Brisbane and buried him up here. It would have been quite a gathering.'

'Why would you want to go to his funeral?' Lucy Mae asked her. 'You never liked him.'

'That's not the point. I always liked Georgina. She's a great lady, you know. A fine woman.'

'But she's not really a friend.'

'Of course she's a friend. Good Lord, I've known her longer than anyone in the colony. We came out on the same ship.'

Not *that* again, Lucy Mae thought, trying to bury herself in the pages of the latest *Ladies'* Journal.

Milly looked up from her embroidery. 'I should have gone to that funeral. I could have got there in time. It would have been a feather in my cap to have been there among the Who's Who of the whole country!'

'You didn't have an invitation.'

'Oh bosh! *I* wouldn't need an invitation! Why are you being so snippy? See how you feel when all of your friends start dying off on you.' Milly sighed, a long, sad sigh, and flicked a tear from her eye. 'Do you realise Georgina and I are the only ones left of the paying passengers on the *Emma Jane*?'

'What other sort of passengers are there?' Lucy Mae laughed.

'Convicts! We were shocked. But your dear father said: "Now we know why the passage was so cheap." '

'Lord and Lady Heselwood were on a convict ship?'

'Jasin wasn't a lord then, though I can tell you, he was fit to be tied when they started bringing chained prisoners aboard. But he'd paid his fare like the rest of us, and there was nothing to be done about it except to turn around and quit the ship. It was so hard to obtain passages in those days, none of us felt inclined to risk it.'

'Weren't you frightened, with convicts on the ship?'

'No,' Milly said hurriedly. 'They were chained down below. They did make quite a bit of noise, but I don't want to talk about that. There was one funny thing, though. Dr Brooks and Adelaide, his wife, were on board with us, and the captain asked Brooks to come down and see to sick convicts. But Brooks informed him that he was a doctor of astronomy not a doctor of medicine! The captain was furious, but it wasn't Dr Brooks' fault.'

'That's rare, a doctor of astronomy. What became of him? You never speak of him.'

'Oh, poor old Brooks. He fell ill not long after we landed, and died. That long voyage was too much for him. His death devastated Adelaide; she was much younger than him and felt stranded in a strange country. But she was a good-looking woman, very elegant. She had some hard times for a while, until she met Rivadavia.'

Milly laid out her handiwork. 'The work on this tablecloth is taking an age to finish. It's too big. I'm sorry I started.'

'I'll finish it if you like. It's a lovely piece to work on.'

'No, I'll have to keep going. Your work isn't up to standard; it would show. I'll leave it for a while and write to Georgina.'

'You've already sent our condolences.'

'In times of trial,' Milly huffed, 'people should do their very best for others. Now I want you to go into town and find out if there are any ships sailing for Sydney in the next two days. After that it will be too late.'

Milly folded the unfinished tablecloth into its tissue-lined box and carried it to the linen press, then made her way to the large ornate secretaire in her sitting room, to attend to her accounts. At least, she pottered with them until Lucy Mae left the house.

She sniffed, irritated, as she picked up a pen to write a second letter to Duke.

He hadn't replied to the first one she'd written, inviting him to visit so they might discuss his gallant proposal. As far as she knew, Lucy Mae, the stupid girl, had only acknowledged his letter, his proposal of marriage! As good manners decreed. But she hadn't given him a yea or nay.

Milly was terrified she'd turn him down. Or that Lucy Mae's lack of an enthusiastic response had caused Duke to look elsewhere for a bride.

This time she wrote an equally sweet letter to the dear boy, making no mention of his failure to reply to her previous epistle. She apologised for her daughter's tardiness in replying to him, but pointed out that Lucy Mae had a delicate matter to discuss with him, along with his well-received proposal, and had been expecting him to visit as requested.

Since months had passed, Milly wrote sadly, it was therefore incumbent upon her to be more specific: *To have you know that a certain person is carrying your child.*

In closing, she made it plain that Duke's company at her home, as soon as possible, would be most appreciated.

The letter, sender's name inscribed on the outside, arrived at Mango Hill. It was the second letter to Duke from Milly Forrest.

'What do you think she wants?' Paul asked Laura. 'I mean, two letters!'

'Perhaps she's just concerned about him. As I am. There hasn't been a word from him! I thought he'd be back by now.'

'Duke can look after himself. Maybe he's not coming back. For all I know he could have sold those cattle and gone off somewhere else. I should have warned Harry Merriman that he's as reliable as a rundown clock.'

'Do you want me to write to Milly and tell her he sold us Mango Hill and . . .'

'And left us all his bloody bills,' Paul growled. Then he laughed. 'But he didn't count on any money coming his way, did he?'

John Pace had kept his promise and sent them a profit-and-loss statement on Kooramin, covering the time since their mother's death. After taking his salary and a small wage for his wife as bookkeeper, he was able to inform his partners that the cattle station had returned a substantial profit, to be shared by all three owners, and had forwarded two cheques to Mango Hill.

Paul had banked his share and told John Pace that he was holding Duke's cheque against the money he was owed. Both brothers agreed that was fair enough.

'Ah dammit. I'm going to see what Milly wants,' he said now, and reached for the second letter.

'You can't read Duke's mail!' Laura protested.

'I can't what? He sells me a property still under mortgage and you say I can't read his bloody mail. Just watch me! I hope he hasn't borrowed any money from her,' he added as he opened the letter and scanned the page.

'Oh Christ,' he said. 'Why did you let me read his damn mail?'

She grinned. 'Don't go blaming me! Why, what's he done now?'

'Bloody hell!'

'What?'

'Lucy Mae's pregnant!'

'Duke?'

'That's our boy.'

'Oh God. How is she?'

'That isn't considered. I think his future mother-in-law is too busy trying to bring Duke to heel.' He laughed. 'He won't get the better of old Milly.'

'Let me see.' Laura reached for the letter. 'Poor Lucy Mae. What a spot to be in! I wish you hadn't made such a mess of that envelope. We can't let on we know about this. I'll get another and re-address it to him.'

'With no stamp on it?'

'I'll put a stamp on and dirty it up a bit.'

'My, aren't you the devious one!'

'You should never have opened the damn thing!'

'Any word of Duke?' Rosa asked Lucy Mae as they strolled along the riverbank.

'No. Nothing.'

'Are you very upset? I mean you don't look it. You look so well.'

'Rosa, I'm really happy to be having a baby. I am. Somehow I can't make myself take all the rest of it too seriously . . . no husband, Mother marching around with the great "what-will-people-think" question plastered on her face . . . that's small fry compared to having a child of my very own.'

'What about Duke? He'll want to know.'

'I told you, I haven't heard from him.' Lucy Mae shrugged.

'But he proposed to you!'

'I think he's still away. He was going bush on a cattle drive. It's my guess he's still out there, but try and tell my mother that!'

'What will you say when he does turn up?'

'I don't know.' Lucy Mae smiled. 'I'll see. Anyway, what's happening with your affair?' She whispered the question as if the birds pecking at the lawns might hear and tell someone.

Rosa had been waiting for it. She forced a giggle. And lied: 'I couldn't go

354

through with it. I got cold feet. I met him for tea a couple of times, but when it came to keeping an assignation I stayed home. Hid. I'm such a coward.'

'No you're not. You did the right thing,' Lucy Mae said. 'You'd hate to be involved in an affair, really you would. Have you seen him since? I mean socially.'

Rosa shook her head. Shrugged. 'No.'

Although her doctor husband had confirmed that she was pregnant, Rosa was not able to mention her condition to Lucy Mae.

'Have you thought of any names for the baby yet?' she asked.

On her way home Rosa decided to call on her father, only to find he was still away and Mrs Pilgrim was not receiving.

'She's still abed, Mrs Palliser,' the maid said, with a disapproving sniff.

'Is she ill?'

'More put out, I'd say.'

'What about? Oh, never mind, I'll go and see. Which room?'

Rosa knocked on the bedroom door and called to Lark: 'It's Rosa. May I come in?'

A small whimper came from the other side of the door and Rosa took it to be affirmative.

Lark was sitting up in the four-poster bed in a very revealing nightdress, surrounded by the paraphernalia of her day. A Persian cat was curled serenely on the large pink and white satin eiderdown amid jars of cosmetics, fashion catalogues, discarded plates, a jar of toffees, hairbrushes and combs, other odds and ends and a veiled straw hat.

She burst into tears when Rosa walked in. 'Ah! Someone cares if I live or die. Come in, *ma chérie*. Sit by me.'

Lark tried to shove the cat aside but it spat at her, so Rosa pulled up a chair.

'What's the matter, Lark? Are you ill?'

'Ill? Of course I'm ill. I'm ill with despair!' She searched under the bedclothes, located a hand mirror and stared into it.

'Look at me! I'm a wreck! He has done this! He is a cruel, heartless man. Pass me the hairbrush. There's no life in my hair now, do you notice? It shows in your hair when your health is receding.'

'Who is this cruel, heartless person? My father?'

'Of course your father! He has left me. I am deserted!' Her voice had an edge of hysteria. 'He invited me to come here. To this house. I didn't invite myself, *chérie*. And now he's gone off without a word of when he'll be back . . .'

'But he is in Sydney. Why are you so upset?'

'Because he's in Sydney! He didn't have to go. Not this time. I have my intuition. I know what he's about. He's after that woman!'

355

She suddenly grabbed Rosa's hands and sobbed: 'Oh my darling, how terrible of me to be burdening you with my sadness when you have suffered as well.'

'Me?'

'Heselwood, darling,' she whispered. 'He passed away.'

'Oh yes, Lark, it was a dreadful shock for everyone. Just too sad. My husband and I were out at his father's station at the time.'

'*Mon dieu!* What a shock for you, darling! But you are strong! And young. You mustn't look back. You promise?'

'Yes, I promise. But Lark, why are you so upset with Juan?'

'Why would I not be? Heselwood died! It was none of your father's business. But no, what does he do? Step forward, playing Sir Lancelot to the lady.'

'What lady?'

'His wife. The widow. Lady Heselwood. Your father is so kind,' she sneered. 'Heselwood died here in Brisbane. The lady lives in Sydney. So what to do about a funeral? No trouble. Juan steps forward and offers to escort the coffin home.'

'You can't be angry with him over that. They've known each other for years!'

'So what does that prove? Nothing! They never got along. It was the talk of the town when Juan punched Jasin right in the face. You don't think Jasin would forget something like that? No, he never did, you can believe me.'

This was the second time Rosa had found herself in this argument. Charlie had made the same comment: 'Why would your father suddenly become pall-bearer for Lord Heselwood if they didn't get on. As you yourself said?' he'd asked.

'My father', she said, this time to Lark, 'would always help where he could. He and Lord Heselwood had their differences, but Georgina had no argument with Juan. They greatly respected each other.'

'Is that what they call it?' Lark asked nastily, reaching for a powder puff.

'Call what?' Her tone irritated Rosa. 'What my father did was not only a very gracious act, but also sensible. It was typical of him to come up with the answer to a problem that must have seemed almost insurmountable to Georgina at the time. I mean, what do you do when your husband is killed in another city so far away?'

'You ask your son to attend you. A relative, not an acquaintance! Jasin said their grown-up son had come back to live here. Why not have him look after their private business?'

Rosa was startled. 'Oh yes! Edward.' Then she added, lamely: 'He must be away somewhere.'

'You would say that! Any excuse will do to hide the truth from me!'

'Oh Lark, don't be ridiculous! He did Lady Heselwood a favour. That's all. He'd have stayed in Sydney for the funeral and . . .'

Lark hurled a silver-embossed hairbrush across the room. 'How dare you call me ridiculous!' she shrieked. 'Of course he'd stay there with his friend the widow! The high and mighty titled lady! He'll stay there at his charming best and she'll encourage him because she's so lonely. Poor little rich widow!'

'That's enough, Lark. Please. I really have to be going.'

'You're so naive, Rosa. You don't know your father as well as I do. You love him and so do I, but I see a pattern happening all over again.' She dabbed at tears spilling down her powdered cheeks. 'He was happy with me until his great friend Mrs MacNamara was widowed. Next thing, poof! Lark is sent away and he marries her.'

'Oh please don't take on so. You're overreacting. This isn't the same at all.'

'You don't think so, eh?' Lark said angrily. 'Of course to you Señor Rivadavia can do no wrong! Well there is a pattern to it, let me tell you!' She grinned slyly at Rosa from under lowered lids. 'What about his first mistress, the one he had in Sydney before Delia came along. The Honourable Delia Forster. She told me about that mistress herself.'

'I don't know anything about that,' Rosa said coolly, 'and what's more, it's of no interest to me.' She picked up her gloves. 'I really must go now.'

'Her name was Adelaide,' Lark continued in the same sly tone. 'Adelaide Brooks. She came out on the same ship as the Heselwoods. The *Emma Jane*. Poor Jasin told me about her.'

Rosa was feeling unsettled. A small bell rang in her head. She recalled the comment Jasin had made that he'd met her mother on board the ship, which she now knew to be the *Emma Jane*. But he'd been wrong. Delia had come out on a different ship with her uncle Lord Forster.

Lark continued, her voice oily: 'He dropped Adelaide for Delia and now he'll drop me a second time for this Sydney woman. I don't think he should get away with it again. Do you, Rosa?'

'I'm sorry. I don't know anything about all that. I'm going, Lark. You look after yourself now. Get a good sleep.'

'Well go then!' Lark shouted. 'Leave me stuck here on my own! You ought to ask him about Adelaide! He called her Dell. You of all people ought to ask him! But maybe you turn your head away like he does. Closing doors behind you. Just as you have with poor Jasin. He was your friend! An intimate friend, one could say,' she added, 'yet you have forgotten him already! You care not a whit that his life was snatched away! You're as selfish as your father!'

Rosa managed to retain enough composure to close the door quietly and call the maid to let her know she was leaving the house.

Her driver handed her into the gig, and as soon as it was on its way she slid into a corner, a bundle of nerves, pulling her shawl tightly about her, trying to hide from the malice that still lingered, along with Lark's overpowering perfume.

Rosa had been grappling with guilt ever since that first afternoon with Jasin, but the shock of his sudden death and her pregnancy had all but overwhelmed her. She was so depressed she felt as if walls were closing in on her and she was losing her way to the light. She'd visited Lucy Mae in an effort to appear as if all was well in her world, and having achieved a reasonable calm couple of hours she'd stopped in to see Lark for the same reason.

Now she was in a state of panic. Was she really so selfish? And worse. Was she bad? What exactly constituted a bad person?

'Liar? Adulterer?' a dark voice asked.

Rosa wept. How could she ever face Georgina again? And Edward? And what about Charlie? Poor Charlie, who was so happy. What had she done to him?

'Oh dear God!' she cried as the gig turned into her street. She wished it could keep going and never turn back. Never.

Juan was back from Sydney. He called in for tea one Sunday afternoon, and Charlie greeted him with the wondrous news that he was to be a grandfather, insisting that all three of them take a glass of champagne to celebrate.

Juan was so excited at the thought of a grandchild that he returned the next morning with a gift for the baby.

Rosa managed a smile. 'May I unwrap it now?' she asked. 'I can't wait for months to see what it is. The box is quite heavy.'

'You may,' he beamed, and Rosa unwound the wrappings and opened the box.

'Oh Daddy!' she cried, bursting into tears. 'You shouldn't have. I don't deserve anything so beautiful!'

He looked down at the jewel-encrusted cross that had once belonged to his grandmother, and took his daughter in his arms.

'I'm giving it to the child, not you,' he chided gently, 'and it's an early gift because I needed an excuse to come back. What's wrong?'

Rosa took a handkerchief and turned away to blow her nose. 'I'm sorry,' she sniffed. 'I know it's for the baby, Daddy, but it's so beautiful. Are you sure you can part with it?'

'It's staying in the family, Rosa. My grandmama will be smiling down from heaven, so don't fret about that. Now you come over here to the sofa with me and tell me why you look so miserable. You have black shadows under your eyes.'

'I'm not miserable,' she said. 'Pregnant women, especially dark-haired people like me, often get shadows under their eyes.'

He shook his head. 'You looked bleak yesterday, even with the champagne. And you don't look much better today. Are you ailing?'

'No, I'm not. You heard Charlie say I'm in the pink. Nothing to worry about.'

'Ah yes. The Irish poet. *The pink of perfection!* But your father sees a woman troubled about something. Is it so bad you can't tell him? Look at me, I have broad shoulders.'

Rosa shook her head. 'Please, Daddy, I'm all right. How's Lark?'

'Ah! That woman! I returned on a tinpot ship that was thrown about like a top once we left Sydney harbour. I couldn't touch the disgusting food they served and I was so much looking forward to the comfort of my own home. But what was my welcome? A mad woman! Drunk. Screaming. Throwing things at me. She smashed the glazed urn in the lobby!'

'You always thought that was a fake anyway.'

'Which is not the point. The point is that I was vastly upset. I sent her to her room, but the haranguing continued.' He sighed. 'But we won't discuss this any further. She is gone.'

'Oh Lord!'

'Heselwood's funeral,' he said, 'was well attended on a fine sunny day. All the right people as they say, even a couple of dukes. But sadly Edward wasn't there. Lady Heselwood was distraught, hoping until the very last minute that he'd appear. But alas no. Are you hot in here? Your face is red. Let me open a window.'

He opened both windows, inviting a dust-filled breeze to harass the curtains, and continued his story.

'I believe he has gone exploring inland and Paul is helping to locate him.'

'Paul who?'

'Your stepbrother, my dear. Paul MacNamara. It is possible that even now Edward Heselwood has no idea that his father has died.'

'How awful!'

Juan talked a little longer about Sydney and the new hotel that had accommodated him exceedingly well.

'Would you like to stay for lunch?' she asked.

'Thank you, no, I am not able. I have a business fellow to see at the club. I will probably lunch there. And tomorrow I'm going up to the horse stud. We have some new colts. I can't wait to meet them.'

Rosa was suddenly concerned for him. His stud farm was in the Brisbane Valley. It was a long ride at his age.

'You be careful,' she said. 'You're not going alone, are you?'

'No. I'm taking Carlos.'

'He'll be happy.' Carlos was Juan's manservant-cum-driver, but he loved to ride.

'I wish I could make my girl as happy,' her father said wistfully, and quoted: 'He cast off his friends, as a huntsman his pack, For he knew when he pleas'd he could whistle them back.'

Rosa sighed. 'Oh Daddy, please. I'm not like that.' She threw her arms about him. 'I do love you, best in all the world. And thank you for your lovely gift. Charlie won't believe we have it. He'll want to put it in the bank.'

'Never mind about that. You get rid of those shadows, my precious. They're unbecoming.'

After he left, she remembered she should have asked him about Adelaide while he was in such a caring mood. But maybe not. Why would she want to pry into his past loves? 'You of all people!' Lark had said. But then Lark had been talking a lot of rot. And provoked Juan into doing just what she'd dreaded would happen.

For some reason Rosa was crying again.

CHAPTER SIXTEEN

He found them at the Twin Waters, far into Kalkadoon country. When the big wet in the north sent raging waters down to flush out the rivers in the middle earth, these waters were submerged into a small shimmering sea, alive with myriad birds and game. Then as the land dried out, the waters receded and left two lakes at either end of a wide plain of renewed pastureland, much loved by kangaroos and wallabies and all the smaller creatures that inhabited the area.

Because of the abundance of food, this plain was often chosen for corroborees, but Ladjipiri knew as he approached that this huge gathering was no everyday event. He could feel the tension and the suppressed excitement as he made his way through groups of men and women, all of them too intent on their activities to offer him a glance. And it was these activities that caused his heart to sit heavily in his chest. He recognised many of the artisans at work: the makers of tall spears and shorter shafts; the experts who could produce the large boomerangs, so sharp and so true that they could course across the sky in a shining arc and bring down a big red kangaroo. He saw women decorating tall war shields and waddies, and skilled hands sharpening spearheads on worn flints, and noted there were few children running about. An ominous sign.

But then he saw Banggu amid a crowd of young people by the water's edge. He was standing proudly with several other warriors as women applied the ochre war paint to his body. His hair was piled into a topknot, his face, already painted, was barely recognisable and he wore the traditional headband and cockatoo feathers of the fearsome Kalkadoon tribe. This must have come at some cost, his father reflected. The Kalkadoons did not lightly accept strangers in their midst, and as he circled closer to the group he was able to make out fresh initiation scars on Banggu's torso.

'Ah yes,' he muttered bitterly. 'My son has earned the right to get himself killed.'

It was too late for Banggu to withdraw now, even if Ladjipiri could persuade him to do so. Tribal law dealt harshly with deserters.

Ladjipiri blamed himself for not finding his son sooner, but this was an immense land occupied by thousands of people. He would have to explain to his wife that he'd been fortunate to find him at all. He watched the woman with him, a strong, handsome woman, and saw their love. They would have fine children; how proud that would make his mother, who had lost her other son to the white men.

Suddenly Banggu recognised him, face agape with surprise and joy, and raised his fist in defiance. As if in a dream, Ladjipiri was made aware that Banggu knew what had happened to the three lads, including his brother, and in the manner of payback had stepped forward and joined the fight against the white men. His destiny had passed into the hands of the great spirits.

Sadly Ladjipiri waited until one of the elders had performed a short ceremony of protection for the readied warriors, and then he walked towards his son.

Banggu broke loose from the ranks, grabbed the woman and raced over to him. He greeted his father with open arms and little regard for his finery, while his wife stood back, eyes sparkling with happiness.

'This is Wiradji,' Banggu was saying. 'My wife.'

And to her, over his shoulder: 'My father! This is my father. The famous Trader! Ladjipiri! But why are you here? It is too dangerous out here now. They would kill you in a stroke and throw you in a creek, a blackfellow alone. I saw that myself with my own eyes.'

Ladjipiri held up his hand. 'We needed to know where you were. Your mother couldn't rest not knowing if you were alive or dead.'

'This one is very much alive,' Banggu said fiercely.

They had little time to talk as all the warriors, armed with spears and boomerangs, soon left the assembled groups, heading south, Ladjipiri noticed.

'Does he not look magnificent?' Wiradji breathed, her eyes following her departing husband.

Ladjipiri smiled. 'He has grown taller and hardier. And braver, with such a beautiful wife to defend. I am sorry I had no gifts for you. I shall have to look about. It is not proper for a father-in-law to be so forgetful.'

'Don't worry, my husband has a gift for me,' she smiled. 'He has promised me that when the trouble here is all over, he will take me across the great trading route and show me the wondrous ocean. He told me that is where I will meet you and his mother and sisters, but here you are already! Come, I'll take you to my family. Their campfires are over there by that stand of coolibah trees.'

She stopped, suddenly shy. 'That is if you wish to meet them.'

'I would be honoured, Wiradji, for I will not be staying long. I have had a slow trek out here and must be home before the coastal rains make the rivers and forests impassable. My wife', he added, 'is impatient for news.'

* * *

Inspector Beresford left Krill to ready his troops for departure from Longreach while he went in search of his friends. He was in time to see Harry's wagons pulling out, in the wake of the diminished herd, and was astonished by the additions to the company.

'Are they mad letting that mob of blacks trail along with them?' he asked Duke as they watched the Merriman wagons depart Longreach.

'Why? We had the Trader for a guide; why shouldn't they have a few blacks to give them a hand?'

'Because you can't trust any of them. Harry will wake up dead one morning.'

'Ah come on, Marcus. You're getting spooked. Harry's got his drovers to back him up. He's no fool, he'll take it quietly. He has the same maps we have, and he plans to move his cattle from one land claim to another. Each squatter can give him the drum on the next claim until he runs down unclaimed territory.'

But Marcus wasn't listening. 'What happened to that blackfeller you call Trader anyway?'

'I don't know. He was only used to get us to Longreach. I don't know where he got to after that. Probably hoofed it back home.'

'That's where you're wrong. My people tell me he went north-west. Now why would he do that? Why didn't he stick with Harry if they're heading in the same direction? I say he's a spy; the blacks have got spies everywhere, and an English-speaking joker would come in bloody handy for them. I tell you, Duke, if I come across him he'll get a bullet in his belly.'

'You can't shoot Trader! He's no spy!'

'One less blackfellow to worry about,' muttered Marcus.

Duke pretended not to hear him. He was becoming irritated by his friend's trigger-happy attitude to his job. But he was too busy to worry about him right now. He had a lot to do before he set off. He'd sold his cattle for a stupendous four pounds a head and banked a heap of money. Then, after some debate, he'd managed to talk Ned into making the dash with him . . . a wild ride to the very edge of civilisation to stake their claims and get the hell out.

It was Harry who had persuaded Ned to go for it.

'What's the point in trailing with us?' he'd asked. 'Tottie and I are putting down stakes. So are two of the drovers. They're staying on to work for us; they're not interested in cattle runs of their own. Neither are Ginger and the other blokes. They're drovers, they like what they do. They'll be taking their pay and heading home. They'll probably pick up jobs on the way.' He lit his pipe. 'That accounts for everyone but you, Ned. I know you started off just wanting to look at the countryside, but you've travelled hundreds of miles and worked hard. You've got to have something to show for it, man!'

'You don't want to settle down out here, do you?' Duke asked him.

'God no! I take my hat off to Harry and Tottie for their determination, but I'm no pioneer.'

'Neither am I, as it turns out,' Duke grinned. 'But I sure want a bite of the cake now that I'm here. Listen, we get the best fast horses we can find and we ride like hell! The blacks won't bother us; they'll be too busy scowling at the wagons and the herds rolling into their back yards. Anyway, I figure we could be in and out, ten days at the most. Come back, register our claims, have a rest, then take an easy ride home with packhorses.'

'It would take more than a few days to blaze out the boundaries of our runs,' Ned warned. 'We'd be vulnerable to attack then.'

'We'll be well armed. And besides, one of our boundaries will be in common. That will save time.'

Ned had been surprised that Duke would even want him as a partner in this enterprise, given their minor differences on the trek out here, but then, he supposed, better the devil you know . . . What really astonished him, though, was Duke's passion to make this ride. And his refusal to accept the possibility of danger.

'Duke seems to have forgotten that his father died on a similar mission. Killed by blacks,' he confided to Harry. 'And I don't like to mention it.'

'He wouldn't have forgotten,' Harry said. 'This isn't as tough an assignment as his father took on. He and his friend rode into very dangerous country looking for a specific valley. They already knew it was prime land, thanks to the explorer Leichhardt. There were no neighbours, no settlers anywhere up there. They were alone. This trek is different. There are settlers out there already. We're simply leapfrogging from one claim to the next. Sometimes I think Tottie is more worried than she should be about this leg of our journey . . .'

Ned was relieved that Harry had some idea of Tottie's concerns.

'Then keep her with you as much as possible,' he said. 'She'll need that reassurance. Any woman would.'

'I guess you're right. We'll miss you, Ned. After a few years, once we get settled here, we'll be sitting out the wet season on the coast like all the great and grand squatters do. That's why I'm keeping my little block in Rockhampton. You'll always know where to find us.'

'Are you sure you want to go with Duke?' Tottie asked him.

'Oh yes. I might as well. He's a madcap, but he means no harm. Besides, I sort of feel responsible for him.'

'Why, for heaven's sake? He's big enough and silly enough to look after himself.'

'Oh, family stuff, you know.' Ned was embarrassed. He wished he hadn't said that. But he'd suddenly had a vision of Duke's mother, that fiery Irishwoman, standing hands on hips, challenging him. 'We were neighbours after all,' he added lamely.

Ned and Duke were both there to farewell them. Tottie wept and smiled and promised to write. Harry kissed her, a long, passionate kiss that drew cheers and whistles from onlookers, and lifted her into their wagon, then he walked round to the other side and took the reins. Their Aborigine friends paced alongside, shouting gleefully as they passed other tribal folk. It seemed to Ned that the Aborigine numbers had increased significantly, but Harry and Tottie appeared not to mind.

Their departure left Ned feeling rather depressed. He was glad, though, that he had chosen to team up with Duke rather than spend any more time mooning like a spotty schoolboy over a happily married woman.

'You'll have to sharpen up now,' he told himself. 'This next journey won't be the picnic that Duke envisages.'

He took the time then to write to his parents and found the grace to apologise to his father for his irresponsible behaviour. He had learned a great deal on this long trek, living and working with drovers: mainly that he should look about him and stop seeing only himself and his problems. There were times when he'd been so exhausted, not just for a few hours but for days on end, that he'd considered quitting at the next village and turning back. Fortunately, though, he'd begun to notice that the other men were just as weary in the saddle as he was. More so, with the added workloads.

He watched them come into the camps and squat down to eat in silence, almost too exhausted to swallow a meal, though they knew they must. He saw them take all manner of injuries in their stride, as they pushed on through the rugged bush with their temperamental charges, patching one another up as best they could. Eucalyptus seemed to be the cure for such ailments as back sprains, coughs and splinted broken fingers; bush honey for infections and rum for whatever else ailed you.

Now, at the end of the journey, he had a great affection for men whom he'd originally thought to be rather tedious, and hoped they thought well of him. Certainly each one had sought him out to shake his hand in farewell or clout his ear to tell him he was 'all right', and that made Ned singularly proud.

'Give you a job any time!' Ginger Magee had said.

Ned was in the main street searching through a pile of leather goods for a saddlepack, since his was worn thin by this time, when Duke caught up with him again.

'I just met Matt Doolan down the road,' he said.

'Who?'

'Matt. The missing drover.'

'Oh yes. Where's he been?'

'He's whingeing because he joined another droving team and the boss gave him a belting for falling asleep on watch. He was all for riding after Harry and his mob and wanted to know if Harry would take him back, but I told him to bugger off.'

Ned laughed, remembering that neither Duke nor Matt was Harry's favourite drover.

'Where are you going now?' he asked.

'I have to post a letter.'

'Good. Would you post this one for me? Then I'll meet you at the pub. I want to have another look at the maps.'

'Righto.' Duke turned Ned's letter over. 'That's a good boy. Writing to your parents. Did you tell your old man we're going after big claims tomorrow? That'll impress him.'

'No, actually. In case we don't make it.'

'Jesus, Ned! Give it a go! Of course we'll make it! See you later!'

Duke had written to Lucy Mae to tell her he'd be on his way home as soon as he registered his new claim and so he hoped to see her within a couple of months. He even added that he missed her dearly.

As he walked up to the counter of the post office store, the owner's wife called: 'Letter for you, Duke! And there's one here for your mate, the English gent Mr Heselwood.'

Duke took the two letters, then bought stamps for his letter to Lucy Mae and Ned's letter to his parents, and handed them over.

Duke was certain that his letter, which was addressed to Mango Hill and had been sent on by Paul, was from Lucy Mae. In his excitement he jammed Ned's letter in the back pocket of his dungarees and scurried away to a quiet corner so that he could read Lucy Mae's response to his proposal in private.

But it was from Milly. His disappointment brought a muttered 'Bloody hell! What does she want?'

A man standing nearby grinned. 'The missus, eh?'

'Yeah.' Duke shrugged and turned away to concentrate on Milly's spidery hand.

'God Almighty!' he said in sudden surprise and bolted out of the crowded shop to reread Milly's instructions, for that was the content. The gist of it told him that Lucy Mae was pregnant with his child and he had to get home immediately to marry her!

'All right, I'll do that,' he said to the pages. 'Haven't I already asked her?'

He wondered if he'd done the wrong thing writing to Lucy Mae. Proposing to her directly when maybe he should have spoken to her parents first. But Lucy Mae's father was dead. He had died years ago.

So did Milly believe she should have been the one to approach?

'She would,' he muttered crossly. 'I can believe that, the old battleaxe.' He shrugged. 'Anyway, it doesn't matter now. I've been given the go-ahead. But

Lucy Mae should at least have written to me herself. I'd have liked that. It's a real let-down only hearing from her mother.'

Duke fronted the counter again. 'Are you sure there are no more letters for me? I was expecting another one.'

The woman shuffled through the dusty pile of mail again. 'No, Duke. Sorry. That's it for this month.'

He wandered out of the store, disconsolate, reminding himself that, according to Milly, he was to be a father, but that didn't seem to be real at all. None of it seemed real, for some reason, not even that he was to marry Lucy Mae. He felt he should be madly happy at this prospect. Instead he was really down in the dumps with the big ride ahead of him. Not the time to be feeling out of sorts.

When it came time for Ladjipiri to leave, Banggu begged him to stay a few more days.

'We need private time to talk. Father and son,' he said.

Ladjipiri was warmed by the request. This son had been given the time his brother had been denied to develop into a strong and confident man, and yet he still needed to defer to his father. He looked about him for a suitable setting for this important family discussion, and chose a high bank at the edge of a forest overlooking the quiet waters. From that point he could imagine the torrents that must roar through here in the summer, greening the parched land again. He mused that it would be a sight to see, but by that time of the year he'd well away.

When his son joined him, they spoke of this great gift of water sent from the north. They spoke of the family back home, and Banggu admitted that he sorely missed them. Then for the first time they talked about the tragedy that had begun at the gorge.

'We brought that on ourselves,' Banggu said, holding up his hand to ward off Ladjipiri's protestations. 'No, let me speak. We threw rocks at the soldiers . . .'

'Not soldiers, policemen.'

'Same thing. We thought it was fun. We were stupid; proud that we'd killed one of them. Too stupid to see that we had stirred up a hornets' nest and there would be terrible payback. There was, Father,' he continued. 'So for that stupidity, ending in the deaths of my brother and our friends, I seek forgiveness.'

Ladjipiri tried to brush aside the apology as unnecessary but Banggu insisted.

'I want you to speak up now. Say the words that you forgive me, for it has been weighing heavily upon me. I beg you to grant me this before I can bring other important matters before you.'

Ladjipiri took hold of his son's strong arms and gripped them firmly as he gave his forgiveness, a salve for the grief they both bore.

'Now,' Banggu said, 'there is something else I want you to do for me.'

'You only have to ask.'

'I know that. You have been in this country long enough to know it has become very dangerous. I have promised Wiradji that I will take her to see the ocean one day. It has become more urgent now as it is safer back there. I am no longer afraid of the police arresting me. I will change my looks and my name and take her to live with our people.'

Ladjipiri's heart lifted. Could it be that his son was coming home?

'But I cannot leave until this fight is over, so I want you to take Wiradji on ahead with you.'

Disappointment showed in his father's face, but Banggu continued.

'There is no safe place here for any of us, Father. There is to be a war . . .'

'But surely . . .'

'No. I am not speaking of raids and small attacks; I mean outright war, to rid Kalkadoon country of the white men, and I must do my duty.'

'But this is not possible!'

'You do not know that,' Banggu said quietly and firmly.

'Neither do you!'

'I do not argue these matters. I am a warrior now. But my wife is not, and there is no law against sending her away. I will join her as soon as I have fulfilled my obligations here.'

Ladjipiri couldn't bear this any longer. 'Let us all go,' he burst out. 'This is not your fight.'

'These people gave me refuge. Now I am needed.'

'Ah, son, I beg you. Come with me!'

'You know I can't. You have a horse. I will find another one for Wiradji, and you are to take the northern routes away from here as quickly as you can.'

'What if she won't go without you?'

'She must. She is with child. She cannot endanger my child. You will take them to safety.' His voice softened. 'I hope the sight of her grandchild will be some comfort to my mother and make up for the sadness she has suffered.'

'But Banggu! A war?'

'Maybe it's just wild talk. Who knows?'

Ladjipiri was not reassured.

CHAPTER SEVENTEEN

They were two days out, riding swiftly across treeless plains towards rocky red hills, and already they'd bypassed the last of the pioneering settlers on this particular route. Duke was confident they were making good time.

Ned was enjoying himself. Though they'd agreed not to ask too much of the horses for a start, it was too great a temptation for the pair to stick to a steady, sedate routine, so they threw caution to the winds and raced away into the wild trackless country.

Once again Ned marvelled at the wide vistas opening up before them. The horizon seemed to have been lowered to accommodate the vastness of a peerless blue sky, unhindered by even a glimpse of cloud. From a distance they occasionally saw groups of Aborigines trekking across open country, usually in single file, which intrigued Ned, and where they saw a massive flock of gaudy parrots wheeling above some trees, they guessed that the patch of forest could hide a waterhole.

Without giving it much thought, beyond the necessity to keep their waterbags filled, they headed in that direction and rode straight into the forest; clumsily, Ned realised, as they barged into an Aborigine camp.

A woman screamed and ran, dogs yapped at them, men and women moved quickly out of their way, as if to allow the horsemen to pass through to the waterhole that glinted silver through the shady glen, but both men dismounted quickly, offering apologies in hand signals for the intrusion.

The dark faces that surrounded them were clearly nervous, their eyes more intent on the guns slung by the saddles than on the strangers.

Ned saw little children peering at them from the safety of the trees, and desperate to please, he grabbed a tin of golden syrup from a saddlebag. They both loved this syrup. It tasted like strong treacle and was a favourite in the bush because it could sweeten tea and give a little cheer to the most miserable of stale food.

He opened the tin, took some syrup on his finger and licked it, savouring it in a charade for the benefit of the children. Then he walked towards them, offering the open tin.

A bold little boy, about ten years old, ran forward to taste the wonder, but a woman, obviously his mother, jerked him back by the arm and grabbed the tin herself. Everyone watched as she tasted it gingerly, her face a cloud of suspicion, and Ned recalled that in his younger days he'd heard of squatters poisoning whole families of Aborigines to rid them from their land.

But the woman was grinning. She dug her fingers into the tin for another taste, and the children herded about her, calling for a share.

After that, Ned and Duke were permitted to take their horses through to the waterhole to slake their thirsts on this very hot day, but when they brought down their waterbags, an elderly man ran over to them, waving his hands in protest.

'What's wrong?' Ned asked.

'Put down the waterbags,' Duke called to him. 'I think it's taboo to take water from this place.'

He turned to the protester. 'Drink yes? Bag no?'

The old man nodded. Pleased.

'We go now,' Duke continued, smiling and chatting easily as if the black man could understand everything he said. 'It's been nice to meet you. We'll take our empty waterbags, though. We tipped the last of our water into your billabong so's to get a fresh refill, so thanks very much.'

He reached out and shook hands with the elder, and motioned to Ned to do likewise.

Quietly they mounted their horses, and waved to everyone as they took leave of them.

'Now we're right out of water,' he growled at Ned. 'Whose idea was it to stop there?'

'At least the horses are well watered. They'll have to earn their keep today.'

An hour or so later they saw a mob of red kangaroos racing ahead of them, appearing to be in flight, barely touching the ground, and tried to catch them to test the pace of these animals, but the mob suddenly veered off in another direction. Emus, it seemed, were different. Two of them were on for a race against the horses. Encouraged by the horsemen, they raced along at a great speed, their huge strides a real challenge, until they lost interest and dropped away.

Nearing sunset, the riders searched unsuccessfully for a lagoon marked on the map, and were forced to camp overnight without water. Rum and dried bread made an odd meal.

'We have to go through these hills tomorrow, don't we?' Duke asked.

'Yes. After we find that lagoon.'

'If we do we'll have plenty of company. Look up there.'

The hills directly above them were dotted with the lights of campfires.

'I don't think there are that many whitefellers in the whole district,' Duke added. 'I reckon we ought to rethink.'

Ned moved to douse their campfire with dirt, but Duke objected: 'Don't do that. We'll freeze in this frost. They know we're here. Looks like we'll have to stay awake, though, so load your rifle.'

They were not bothered by the blacks that night, but they were on their way well before dawn, sticking to the flats until they found a little water in a muddy creek. Then they took another route through the hills a considerable distance away from their original plan.

The view from the highest point revealed a vast area lightly forested by grey-green trees, and not much else except for the usual rocky outcrops here and there, but as they descended the steep slopes, leading their horses, they saw smoke curling from the trees, and were soon able to make out dwellings of some sort.

'Time to call on the neighbours,' Duke said. 'I'm not sure where we are, to be honest.'

The dwellings turned out to be a timber cottage with a shingle roof and several outbuildings set in a large clearing. The residence of squatters Claude and Martha Gubbins and their twenty-year-old son Bert. They hailed from Yorkshire in England, and as Martha explained to the welcome visitors, they had not yet become accustomed to their situation at Gubbins Station.

'We can boast that we're lords of thirty square miles or thereabouts, all our very own land,' she said. 'But it ain't natural not having neighbours. Real neighbours, I mean. Not them blackies.'

'Have you had any trouble with them?'

Bert laughed. 'I caught one only yesterday, buck naked he was, making off with a bag of flour, so I peppered his bum with pellets and he dropped the flour and bolted.'

'Aw, they snoop about,' his father added. 'But they know we got guns and they mostly keep clear.'

Claude studied their map and pointed out that Inspector Beresford and his blackie troopers had come this way only a few days back, and that they were heading for Pelican Waters, about seventy miles further out. He took Ned's pencil and marked a route. 'You go down this valley, then nor'-west again to this place, Blackwater Creek, a crossing much used by prospectors and their drays. Try and stick to the low country, even if you have to make a few detours. You can easily make that spot by tomorrow afternoon, lads. Not much to hold you up. From then on you should be able to find yourselves some decent pastureland.'

Typically, straight out of the settlers' handbook, Ned reflected, Martha insisted they stay for a meal. They enjoyed it but were anxious to be on their way, and by midday they were riding west again, their waterbags filled and their high spirits revived thanks to Claude's volatile homebrew.

Once they cleared the forest they rode along a wide valley hampered by high, sun-bleached grass.

'I think we're being followed,' Duke said. 'Every time I turn my head I see movement in the grass back there behind us.'

'You're sure it's not just a breeze?'

'Breezes don't carry very tall spears.'

'Then we ought to get out of here fast.'

'Right! Now!' Duke shouted, digging in his spurs, and as both horses surged forward, spears lobbed behind them. Looking back, Ned saw a half-dozen black men beginning the chase, but the two horses, recently rested, had taken fright and were racing across that deceptively even land as if it were a prepared track.

Soon their stalkers were far behind, but when they left that valley they kept the horses at a canter until they came to a sign nailed to a tree that announced: *Blackwater Creek*.

They stared at it in amazement!

'That's the first sign we've seen out here.' Duke laughed. 'We've come hundreds of bloody miles without even an arrow to mark directions, and we finally find one way out here in the middle of nowhere. All right, Blackwater Creek will do us. We can ford here and camp on the other side.'

'Why don't we give the horses a spell here for half an hour and then we can ride on to the Pelican place.'

'Fair enough. I'm so hot I think I'll sit in their Blackwater Creek. This is supposed to be winter. Do you reckon it only ever gets cold at night?'

'Seems like it.' Ned grinned.

When they rode into the lonely village set on a plain so flat that Ned had to squint to even find the distant horizon, all was quiet.

The waterhole wasn't immediately evident, nor were the pelicans, but Pelican Waters did sport a hotel, a well-established store, and boiling artesian bores, which, given the daytime temperatures, didn't attract either Ned or Duke.

They were disappointed to hear that Beresford and his troopers had passed through the village several days ago, making directly for Cloncurry, which was approximately one hundred and fifty miles further out.

'Always further out,' Ned groaned, wondering how he'd allowed himself to be talked into this back-breaking adventure.

After a few ales and the hottest curry they'd ever encountered, compliments of the Afghan cook, a retired camel driver, they sank some more cooling ales with the publican. He advised them to rest awhile and join a party of twenty stockmen who would be riding towards Cloncurry after dark, taking advantage of the presently clear, moonlit nights, and, of course, the much cooler temperatures.

From then on the journey was easier. Their companions knew the country, helped them swim the horses across several rivers, led them through the hills and provided plenty of information about the properties they traversed – the size of the claims and the herds, often sheep and cattle, and the residents, especially the women. They also had lurid stories about the confrontations between the blackfellows and white men, a reminder to the newcomers to remain alert.

Inspector Beresford's first duty was to supervise the work on his proposed police station at Cloncurry. He found that this village, by the Cloncurry River, which had been named by the ill-fated explorers Burke and Wills, was a mecca for prospectors as well as a centre for sheep and cattle stations. Before he left Longreach he'd received orders from the Police Commissioner to crack down heavily on lawbreakers, because the area was rich in copper, with several mines already in production. *The Colony*, he had written, *is desperately in need of the revenue that could emanate from mining in that district, and the Premier does not want investors turned away by rumours of lawlessness.*

Rumours? Marcus fumed. It had taken only a few days to discover that law itself was only a rumour. What with blacks and bushrangers, town shootouts, fights over mining claims and all the rest, he needed an army to maintain law and order in this wild frontier town, a thousand miles from the comfortable seat of government in Brisbane.

He'd replied from Cloncurry that he would do his best, though seriously understaffed, and would assure the residents of Cloncurry that the government would be sending reinforcements of regular police at the earliest opportunity.

'That', he said smugly, 'puts the ball back in your corner, sir.'

He was pleased that he'd had the foresight to bring carpenters with him. They were already pacing out the plans for the site, while native troopers were being pressed into service as axemen in nearby woods.

Marcus found that his reputation as an officer who gave no quarter to recalcitrant blacks had preceded him, and he was happy about that. As he explained to a local publican, 'The only way to keep the blacks under control is to put the fear of God into them. And the only way to do that is to strike first. I intend to do that, so that this area can flourish.'

The publican, a former merchant from Liverpool, England, agreed with him heartily. But he was confused to be surrounded by huge properties called stations.

'I mean, Inspector,' he complained, 'we got police stations and railway stations. Why are they calling their farms stations too?'

'Because the original settlers in this country were the military . . . officers stationed with their men in various districts. They continued to say they were stationed on land they'd been granted. Hence stations.'

'Well how about that? And how long are you staying here?'

'I'll be here for quite a while. A sub-inspector and more police will be joining me soon, and eventually we'll have the whole area under control.'

'Not before time, sir. Not before time. A lot of pastoralists are getting very nervous, threatening to quit the district.'

'They'll be safe enough now. In a couple of days I'll take my men out to begin sweeps of the immediate area, and gradually we'll widen the scope until we can send out patrols where required.'

He and Krill explored the area around the town as if they were about to begin a military operation, noting landmarks and station boundaries as well as the camps of the ever-present prospectors. When they returned, they found the builders complaining that their native troopers, working as timber-getters, were falling down on the job.

'As soon as you turned your back, they downed tools and headed for the river,' the boss said angrily. 'If we have to get out there and cut our own timber, it'll take twice the time to build your compound!'

'Hey, Inspector,' one of the builders called to him later that afternoon. 'You got visitors!'

'Who?' he called, irritated by the interruption.

'Your latest residents, his lordship Duke MacNamara and the Honourable Ned Heselwood themselves,' a familiar voice boomed.

'Good God, it's you, Duke!' Marcus laughed. 'You actually made it!'

'Unscathed,' his friend confirmed.

Marcus was genuinely delighted to see them, and took them to one of the quieter pubs for a meal.

'If you need a roof tonight, this pub's the best of a bad lot. You'd be wise to grab a room here before the miners come into town and mayhem sets in.'

'That's a great recommendation,' Ned sighed. 'We'll take it. Are there mattresses on the beds? That's my priority, and the sooner the better.'

'Some,' Marcus allowed. 'Horsehair if you're lucky. Then there's chaff or canvas. But I can't stay talking, lads. I've heard that a certain bushranger, Dinny Dwyer, has been living in a hut upriver, and I'm hoping to nab him tonight. Bushrangers have been holding up miners out here for months. If I can grab this chappie it'll be a feather in my cap and I might get a bit more co-operation from the miners.'

He finished his whisky and prepared to leave. 'We'll discuss your plans tomorrow. I might be able to help you get started.'

'When are you going on the bushranger hunt?' Duke asked him.

'At sunset. Why?'

'Can I join you? It sounds an interesting bit of action.'

'If you like. I'm taking Sergeant Krill and a half-dozen troopers. Do you want to join us too, Ned?'

'No fear. I've had enough of night riding. I just want to sleep.'

'Righto then. Come over to my camp at sunset, Duke. I'll have a fresh horse for you.'

Duke could hardly wait for sunset, but with time to kill he unrolled his swag and took out his other pair of dungarees. They were stiff with dust but a little more presentable than the battered pair he'd been wearing since they left Longreach. He ought to discard that pair, he reflected, since they'd been ravaged by an encounter with a forest of prickly pear trees.

'But they're comfortable,' he told himself, 'and the rips let in the air.'

He put them aside, hoping to find a Chinese laundry to wash them, along with his smalls and his other shirt. He wasn't much of a washerman, and Ned was worse.

As he hauled on the trousers he felt something light in the small back pocket.

'Oh Gawd!' he muttered as he pulled out Ned's letter, now crumpled and brown with sweat. He'd forgotten all about it. 'He'll be furious with me!'

His first instinct was to rush down and wake Ned, who was sleeping only a few yards away from him. There were no rooms as such in this pub, as it turned out, just a long veranda with beds furnished with thin horsehair mattresses. But Ned had dropped off to sleep in minutes.

Duke looked at him. He was out cold, clad only in his corduroy trousers . . . 'posh', Duke called them, to tease him. The rest of his gear was slung under the bed.

I'll give it to him later, he decided. He won't be in the best of moods if I wake him up so soon, and this won't help.

It crossed Duke's mind that it might be wiser to burn the letter. Simply forget about it. But he couldn't bring himself to do that. He dared not pocket it again, so he rolled it in his swag and left it on his bed for later. Then he filled in more time cleaning his rifle before he donned his sheepskin jacket, a box of bullets snug in the pocket, and set off, walking up the road to the police base even though the sun was still a yellow glare in the west.

Marcus was full of complaints about the builders, but Duke envied him the large and comfortable tent containing a clean bunk piled with warm rugs, a folding table and chair, even a mat! The envy intensified when Marcus opened a picnic hamper that proudly displayed cutlery and glasses and invited Duke to join him for a few fine whiskies to warm them for the job ahead.

★ ★ ★

As sunset darkened the deep red soil of the outback track, the police column led by Inspector Beresford rode quietly out of the town of Cloncurry.

Duke was riding with Krill, and eight native troopers were bringing up the rear.

'I thought we were heading for the river,' Duke said.

Krill shook his head. 'We don't want anyone tipping Dwyer off. He's cunning; if he's in this area there'd be a reason. The inspector thinks he could be planning to hold up Rosslyn Station, so that's where we go first. It's only about seven miles from here.'

'This bushranger, Dwyer. Would he hold up a homestead on his own?'

'No, he'd have a couple of mates with him. We'll just look in on the station folk to see if all's quiet, then instead of going back to town we'll swing over to the scrub bordering the river and see if we can locate his hideout.'

Rosslyn homestead was a sandstone house with tall, slim windows and dark shutters. Very grand, Duke thought, for this remote neighbourhood, and a clear indication that the owner, one Jack Tully, was looking to permanence.

Tully had not heard that Dinny Dwyer was in the vicinity and was most appreciative that the inspector had taken the trouble to deliver the warning himself. Apparently another bushranger, masquerading as a servant, had robbed the Tully family of a large sum of money the day they moved into this house, so they were naturally very jumpy about these predatory bushmen.

Marcus introduced Duke to him and they were invited to partake of the squatter's Jamaican rum while Krill and the troopers inspected the outbuildings and their surrounds.

'Mr MacNamara has just arrived, along with his friend the Honourable Edward Heselwood,' Marcus said blandly. 'Son of Lord Heselwood, the cattle baron. Do you know him?'

'I've heard of him!' Tully said enthusiastically.

'They're looking to find land and establish two substantial runs out this way,' Marcus told him. 'Do you have any suggestions about where they might seek some decent pastures?'

'You've come to the right place, Mr MacNamara,' Tully said. 'We'd be honoured to have you and your friend take up residence in our humble district. Why not bring him out here in the morning so that we can discuss what's available?'

'Thank you,' Duke said. 'We'd be most grateful for your advice.'

As they remounted, he murmured to Marcus, 'Do you really think Dwyer will have a go at robbing this place?'

'No. It just seemed like a simple way to ease you into the know, as they call it here.'

'What's the know?'

'The difference between claiming large spreads of land that would be more trouble than they're worth, and getting it right the first time. As you can see, men like Tully also look for the right neighbours as well.' He grinned. 'And, I'm told, freeze out the wrong 'uns. Nothing wrong with that,' he shrugged, 'and bloody convenient for you two.'

'I wondered why you were hanging on there like a toff in a top hat. I suppose you've already made sure they know you're the goods, as well as Ned.'

'Of course,' Marcus laughed.

They searched for Dwyer's hideout for hours. The tangled scrub bordering the river was hard on the horses, so a trooper was left to guard them while the rest of the company went in on foot.

The intent was to work their way quietly towards Dwyer's hut and catch him by surprise, but after they had searched upriver for more than a mile, Duke noticed that several of the troopers were beating the bush noisily as if the prey were foxes and needed to be flushed out.

'I reckon Dwyer would have to hear us coming,' he remarked to Krill, who was ahead of him, hacking through matted vines with a tomahawk.

'It doesn't matter now. If he makes a run for it we'll get him.'

'How will you find him in this maze if you can't even find his hut?'

'There are ways,' Krill said loftily.

'Is that right?' Duke wondered what these mysterious ways could be as he tramped along behind the sergeant, wishing he hadn't volunteered to join this party. He'd imagined a gung-ho chase across the plains, or something in that order, not this business of stumbling about in a dark maze where a man could hardly see a hand in front of him. He'd be willing to bet that Dwyer, if he'd been in the vicinity at all, would have been long gone by this time. Even the birds were squawking at the disturbance.

Then there was a shout. Duke followed Krill for quite a distance until they came upon two excited troopers who showed them dim lamplight emanating from a hut almost hidden among the trees. Krill sent one to fetch the inspector, and turned to the other man.

'Take up a position at the rear, and if anyone comes out, shoot!'

'Are you sure it's Dwyer?' Duke asked nervously.

'It has to be.'

Krill moved forward, stealthily now, to keep the hut under surveillance, his rifle aimed at the door. Since Duke wasn't keen on shooting the first person to emerge from the hut, he kept his distance from the sergeant and that loaded gun, nervously watching smoke curl up from the chimney into the frosty night.

'Is he in there?' the inspector hissed from behind him.

'I wouldn't think so,' Duke whispered.

'Someone is,' Krill said. 'Look at the smoke.'

'Righto!' Marcus sent the other troopers to take up positions around the hut, then he shouted: 'Police here. Lay down your arms and come out. You're surrounded. I say again, come out, hands up.'

That brought quiet. An ominous stillness. Duke wondered why he'd forgotten to ask if Dwyer was dangerous. He was a robber, but had he actually harmed anyone? Shot anyone?

Krill fired his rifle towards the hut. 'That'll wake them up,' he said.

Still no reaction.

The dark form of a bird flapped overhead, and another one screeched from afar.

'I'll give you until the count of ten to come out,' the inspector shouted. 'We're not about to stand here all night.'

He began the countdown, and the number one came and went without result.

'All right, Krill, go in. Take two of the boys. Be careful.'

The advance party kept under cover as far as they could and then made a dash for the timber door. As they bashed it open, Duke heard screams and shouts. Marcus dived away from him, racing over to the hut, a revolver in his hand, but then Krill emerged and Marcus began shouting.

'What?' he yelled at Krill. 'What canoe? Where?'

The answer obviously wasn't much help, since Marcus shoved Krill aside and stormed into the hut. Duke could hear the inspector's raised voice, and a woman sobbing.

'What's happening?' he asked a trooper who was walking towards him.

'I go bring up de horses, boss.'

'No. Inside there. Is Dwyer there?'

'No.' The trooper sounded disgusted. 'No bad feller. Only woman and kid.'

As far as Duke was concerned, the worst was over, and all he could do was wait to be summoned. He propped his gun against a tree and lit a cheroot, a habit he'd learned from Ned, who hated pipes, and eventually other troopers gathered outside the hut.

Marcus seemed to have forgotten Duke was there. He came out of the hut, issued orders to Krill and set off with one of the troopers around the side of the hut, heading for the river.

A few minutes later Duke heard the woman shriek, a terrible cry of fear and pain, and a child started screaming. For a few seconds he froze. Then he began to run towards the hut, and as he ran he shouted: 'What's going on there?'

The screaming stopped. Abruptly.

Krill stood in his way. 'The inspector has gone down to look for Dwyer's canoe. Down there.' He pointed. 'Round the back.'

Duke pushed past him as a couple of troopers emerged from the hut, then another one followed. They made no attempt to prevent him from rushing inside.

The first thing he saw was an old bush lantern on a tin shelf nailed to the far wall. It gave only dim light to the room, but it was enough for him to see an Aborigine woman in a cotton shift sitting at a small table, sprawled across it as if she had fallen asleep at a meal, perhaps.

But the all-too-familiar smell of blood forced him to reassess, and he realised she was dead, blood dripping from her head. He turned swiftly to the low bed and looked for the child.

A small boy, about six years old, was lying face down on a blanket. The black stain spreading across the blanket was blood, Duke knew that, but he felt for a pulse, desperately hoping to find signs of life. But he was too late. He pulled the rest of the blanket over to cover the child, as if he were cold, and then turned to the woman, but he could do nothing for her either.

The couple of troopers left outside turned and stared as he charged after Krill.

'They're dead!' he shouted. 'Someone killed them. Who did this?'

'They fought like tigers,' Krill told him. 'If they'd been good, they wouldn't have got hurt.'

'You bloody liar!' Duke could only see the neat little hut with the lamp still steady on its fragile stand as he grabbed Krill, shaking him. 'They've been murdered.'

He turned on the troopers. 'Who did this? Answer me, you bastards. That's a young woman, and a little boy. Your own people! Tell me who did it!'

They shrugged. No remorse. No pity.

'You better buzz off,' Krill said. 'This is police business.'

'You can bet your bloody life it is. I'll see to that.'

The voice behind him was firm. Restrained. 'You'd better come with me, Duke.'

'Where to?'

Marcus replied: 'Back to town. Dwyer escaped in a canoe. It's over the other side of the river.'

'Bugger Dwyer! A woman and a little boy in there have been killed.'

'She was his woman.'

'What?' Duke was incredulous. In his mind's eye he recalled his brother's long-running objection to the very existence of the Native Mounted Police. Paul always claimed that they were being trained for no more than the obliteration of Aborigines. He had even kicked up a fuss that they were back in Rockhampton, but since their officer-in-charge was a friend, and a gentleman, Duke had kept out of the argument.

Now he was shaken to the core. Shocked that Marcus could be so callous.

'So what? She was no threat. And the child? Are you mad?'

379

Duke saw Marcus turn and nod his head to Krill, and thought he was being threatened. He picked up his gun and levelled it at Marcus.

'You'll have to answer for this!'

But then there was a blast of heat and the hut was on fire.

'Oh you bastards!' Duke cried. They all stood back, unmoved, from the funeral pyre that the little hut had become. Everyone, that was, except Beresford, who was already striding away towards the horses in answer to a shrill whistle from their keeper.

Duke had no alternative but to follow the police party as they rode back towards Cloncurry. He knew that when he reported these murders, no one would do a thing about it, even if he were believed.

Two people would have believed him. Two Kalkadoon men who had seen the police arrive but could do no more about it than the white man who'd screamed his objection at the big police boss. The boss wore a black uniform with silver buttons and his name was Beresford. They knew his name all right. Their mate Dinny had warned them about him, and his evil black policemen.

The next morning other people came to search through the ashes for the remains of their kinswoman and her son, so that they could be given a proper burial. They were guarded by four armed Kalkadoon warriors in full mourning paint, who waited patiently while the women sang their crying songs and scattered white flowers over the blackened patch in the once pristine bush.

Banggu was the leader of the band of Kalkadoons. They wanted immediate payback, insisting that they should raid Rosslyn Station that very night. Burn it down!

'No,' he said. 'Their turn will come when the war begins. We know who the leader of this pack was, and we know where he lives.'

'But he is protected by many guns.'

'So is that big house at Rosslyn Station. First we have to let the elders know that it was Beresford and his policemen who did this. He is a big man among the white people. It is not up to us to decide what to do about him.'

They left the area immediately, travelling swiftly south-west towards the meeting place, noting ever-widening tracks made by wagons and drays coming from the direction of Pelican Waters, which Banggu knew had a different name now. It was called Winton.

Ned was stiff when he climbed off the narrow bed in the morning. As he stretched and flexed some muscles he noticed that the other three beds, including Duke's, hadn't been slept in. Obviously, he mused, they were the only customers in this outback Ritz.

He marched down the steps into the yard on a mission to find towels and a bathroom, and there was Duke, sitting on a bench under a pepper tree.

'What are you doing there?' he called. 'You look terrible. Have you been on the booze all night?'

'No. I couldn't sleep. I'm sick. I feel bloody sick.'

'What did you eat?'

'Nothing, come to think of it. No, I'm just sick to my stomach. Those bastards murdered a woman and a kid last night.'

'Who did? The bushrangers?'

'Oh no. Our law-abiding policemen. They murdered Dwyer's woman and a small boy. In cold blood. I saw the bodies! I thought I'd throw up there and then.'

'Did you tell Marcus?'

'Tell Marcus, that's a good one! He knew! He didn't give a damn. He left the bodies in Dwyer's hut and had his men set fire to it.'

'Surely not.'

'That's right,' Duke said angrily. 'You don't believe me.'

'Hang on. Yes I do. But Marcus . . . He must have his reasons. Did you give him a chance to explain?'

'Don't you understand! There's nothing to explain. I've been such an idiot. When I was travelling with him I waited at the homesteads when he went out on patrol; attending to trouble spots, as they called it. When he came in, and even when we moved on, he never spoke of what they'd been up to except to say they'd had to send a few renegade blacks on their way, or that they'd chased a few off station property.'

'So?'

'I heard a few remarks that I ignored, having faith in Marcus as a gentleman, but now I really believe that there was more to those patrols. I believe they did use force, and worse, clearing Aborigines from the stations.'

'If the blacks put up a fight?'

'Like that woman last night? And the little kid? Surrounded by terrifying men with guns and bowie knives?'

'I don't know, Duke. Let's get something to eat. You'll feel better.'

'How?'

'We'll talk it through again.'

Their talk didn't help, except to remind Duke that they had an appointment today to be shown available land by a settler called Tully.

'That's marvellous. How did you swing that?'

'Marcus has his ways. I just remembered that the last thing he said to me last night was that he'd collect us and take us out to Rosslyn Station in the morning. As if nothing had happened.'

'Doesn't sound like the remark of a guilty man.'

Duke thumped the table. 'Will you stop defending him! He *is* bloody guilty. He allowed and condoned two murders!'

The hotel's only public room overlooked the street. It featured a bar which was already open to a couple of burly characters, and a few tables and chairs set by the windows where their breakfast of steak and eggs was served.

Ned looked out of the window. 'Well he hasn't forgotten. Here he is now. The devil himself.'

He stood politely as Marcus came in, but Duke remained resolutely in his chair.

'Are you two ready to go?' Marcus asked. 'I said I'd take you out to Rosslyn Station this morning.'

'I'd like to know what you've got to say about last night,' Duke growled.

'Ah yes. Last night.' Marcus nodded to the drinkers at the bar. 'Dwyer slipped through the net. But we'll get him. It's only a matter of time.'

'I meant about the woman in the hut. And the boy.'

'Unfortunately, they got caught in the fire.'

'Like hell they did!'

Marcus placed a polished boot on the lower rung of a nearby chair, and leant towards Duke. 'I'd prefer it if you minded your own business and let me mind mine.'

'I bet you would. But it's not going to happen. I'll report you as soon as we get back to Longreach.'

The inspector sighed. 'Please yourself. I had no idea you were so naive, Duke. But anyway, looks as if you've had a good breakfast. Are you ready to go?'

'No. I wouldn't cross the road with you, you bastard!'

'What about you, Ned? Tully is looking forward to meeting you.'

Ned looked from one to the other uncertainly, and then said: 'I'll have to talk with Duke first.'

'You're passing up a great opportunity.'

'We'll see.'

Unperturbed, Marcus shrugged. 'Suits me. I've a lot to do today anyway. I'll see you later.'

Ned watched him ride away. 'What now?' he asked Duke.

'I don't know. I'm fed up with the whole situation.'

'That won't do. We're partners. You can't go on strike because he's upset you. We've got work to do.'

Duke drained some cold tea from the pot and stared at it. 'I think I'd rather have a whisky.'

'I'll get you one. Two if you'll wake up and get moving!'

'All right, but wait on . . . I just remembered something. I'll be back in a minute.'

The something was Ned's letter. Duke realised there would be no right time to give it to him, so it might as well be now.

When he returned, he drank half the whisky for moral support, and made a little speech. 'Ned, I'm sorry about this. I've got something belonging to you. I forgot I had it. I can only say I'm really sorry. And I'm sorry it's a bit of a mess,' he added as he handed over the letter.

'What's this?'

'It's for you. They gave it to me at Longreach and I put it in my pocket and . . .'

'How did anyone know I was in Longreach?' Ned asked as he slit it open with a table knife. 'It's from your brother. Paul. Why would he . . .'

'From Paul? What's he doing writing to you?'

Suddenly Ned was on his feet, staring at the letter in horror. Then he pushed his chair aside and rushed out of the bar.

Duke finished the rest of his whisky and went after him, finding him in the back yard of the hotel, standing facing the pepper tree where their day had begun.

'What's up?' he asked. When Ned didn't reply, he asked again: 'Is anything wrong? I never meant to hold on to your letter, Ned. It was in my pocket all the time.'

He realised then that Ned was weeping. Not knowing what to say to his friend, he retreated, lit a cheroot and planted himself on the back steps to wait out the storm. Not long after that he saw Ned read his letter again and sink awkwardly on to the bench under the tree, as if his legs were giving way. He sat there for a long time, his head in his hands.

Duke finished the cheroot. He wondered if he should offer one to Ned. Or get him a whisky. He hoped he wasn't to blame for Ned's misery. In the end he did nothing. Not wanting to intrude.

The yardman went by, pushing a wheelbarrow, intent on his duties. A huge flock of galahs flew overhead in a rush of pink and grey, casting a shadow over the hotel for a short space of time, then the sunlight seemed harsher.

'My father's dead.' Ned's voice was flat. Full of pain. 'He was killed. Fall from a horse.'

'Oh Jesus, no!' Duke called to him. 'Oh no. I'm so sorry.'

Guilt welled up in him. He'd been carrying that awful news about with him for more than a week. It seemed like a year. He castigated himself for being such an idiot. Tried to think what he could do to help.

'Can I get you a brandy, mate?'

'Yes. Perhaps . . . yes please, Duke.'

After a while, Duke asked him what he wanted to do.

'I mean, would you like to go back? Now? Today? It'll be all right. We'll both go. We could make good time. Head straight for Rockhampton. You can get a ship to Sydney from there. To be with your mother.'

Ned was still so shocked, he could barely speak. 'Yes. I suppose that's best,' he murmured. 'But I'm not feeling very well. Do you mind if I lie down for a while?'

Duke could only imagine what poor Ned was going through, finding himself so far from his mother at a time like this. So out of touch too. Had he been in England, they'd have been able to telegraph him. But out here, no such luck. And that letter. Had he given it to him when he should have done, Ned would have turned back right then. He wouldn't be stuck out here, unable to communicate with anyone. Duke felt responsible for Ned's situation now and was determined to make it up to him. They could head home today.

He found the bathroom, had a shower, and washed his torn pants by stomping on them in the shower. Then he went out and attended to the horses, giving them a good hose down, rubbing them with a borrowed currycomb, and brushing their manes and tails until they shone. Spoiling them was a comfort as he filled in nervous hours waiting for Ned to come up for air.

When finally he did sneak up on to the veranda, he found Ned lying on his bed, wide awake.

'I've been thinking,' he said. 'We have to finish the job.'

'What job?' Duke asked.

'The one we came out here to do. Lay claim to land that's going for free.' He sat up. 'If I were to walk away now, my father, had he lived, would have called me a damned idiot. And I do believe Pace MacNamara would have too. Nowhere else in the world could a man get a prize like this unless he struck gold.'

'Forgive me for saying this, but the Heselwoods aren't exactly poor. And you only came for the ride anyway.'

'That's true, because I was at a loose end. But if I'd stumbled on gold, would I have left it there? Would you? And why don't you just forget about your land in the Valley of Lagoons?'

'Because it'll make a great cattle station one day.'

'I rest my case.'

Duke sat on the bed and pondered this. 'I'm really sorry about your dad. Are you sure you're all right? You've had a bad shock.'

'I'm as all right as I can be. It's hard to believe that he's gone; he always seemed invincible to me. And I'm hurt that we weren't on the best of terms when he died.'

'He should have waited a bit longer,' Duke said. 'You'd have come home with a great hunk of Cloncurry prairie to add to his collection. That would have evened things up.'

Ned smiled. 'I just remembered, maybe things were all right. I did apologise to him in my last letter. I hope he got it.'

'Your mother would have it. That would make her feel better.'

'I hope so. But how are you after your expedition with the police? You had a shock too.'

Duke nodded. 'I never want to see anything like that again. It'll take a while to wipe that scene from my mind. And I'll still report it, but I think you're right. We ought to get out to see Mr Tully first thing.'

Ned agreed. 'I have another idea,' he said. 'Why don't we stake out just one big property. That will save days. We can subdivide later on.'

'Suits me. What will we call it?'

'We can argue about that on the way home.'

That night the two men held a private wake for Jasin Heselwood and talked about many things. Duke even produced the letter he'd received from Milly Forrest.

'Your lady friend's having your baby?' Ned was astounded! 'And you're not there to hold her hand? Poor girl, I feel sorry for her,' he muttered unsteadily. 'You'll have to buy her the biggest diamond ring in the world to get over that, old chap. I think I might go to sleep now,' he added, and slid under the table.

The publican came over to them. 'You mate's as drunk as a lord. Do you want a hand with him?'

'Yes.' Duke nodded. 'We'd better put him to bed.'

Marcus soon learned that Ned and Duke were working to the north of Rosslyn, blazing boundaries for a new station, ably assisted by Tully and several of his stockmen. There was even talk among the women of the town that young Lord Heselwood and his friend were staying at the Rosslyn homestead.

'The young lord!' he sneered. 'Where did they get that from? He's no lord. His father is.'

'It's close enough,' a girl giggled. 'We're taking a picnic basket out to them tomorrow.'

'In that case, I might join you,' the inspector teased.

'The more the merrier,' her mother rejoined.

I might just do that, Marcus reflected as he rode away. Duke will have to grow up if he wants to live out here. But I imagine he'll be over his sulk by this. He put Ned in a difficult position, making him choose between us. Yes, he said to himself. I ought to be able to get out there tomorrow.

But that was not to be. A rider from a station at the base of the McKinley Ranges galloped into the police base to report that Kalkadoon natives had killed a man called Britcher. By this time Marcus was aware of the escalating number of attacks on miners and stockmen by Kalkadoon men, so he took immediate action.

'I'm going after this mob myself before they disappear,' he said to Krill. 'Get my horse saddled up. I want four troopers. Make certain there's a tracker among them. Give them good fast horses and see they're well armed, with saddle packs of emergency supplies so I don't have to waste time foraging. Have them ready and waiting within a half-hour.'

He hurried back to his tent, changed into a clean uniform, checked his rifle and revolver, and took a swig of whisky from his silver flask, before refilling it. Then he entered his proposed course of action into his daily log, put on his cap and walked out on to the cleared grounds, pleased to see the building was at last taking shape. Too many local folk were complaining that the Kalkadoon tribe was already out of hand, so a good solid police stockade would help to restore confidence.

Before he left, he gave further instructions. 'I'll be back in a couple of days. I'll get those bastards, dead or alive. In the mean time, keep this area under guard at all times, and maintain constant patrols on the outskirts of town.'

Two days after the inspector left, a guard was speared and most of the police horses were stolen. It was said that Dwyer had joined forces with some of the natives, and those horses were now in the hands of bushrangers.

At first Banggu's wife Wiradji was terrified of the horses, but with her husband and his father insisting she ride the animal Banggu had chosen for her, she hid her fear and reached out to touch the massive head.

The horse nodded gently, and she took that as permission to stroke its neck. Horses, she decided, were definitely far superior animals to cattle, and perhaps even to camels. She would have to think about that.

Suddenly Banggu swept her up and dumped her upon the horse's back. She screamed, expecting the horse to throw her off, but it didn't seem to mind.

'Put your feet in these irons,' Ladjipiri said. 'They'll keep you steady. And hold on to these reins for telling him where you want to go.'

For days her father-in-law led the horse around while she sat on its back, waving to her gaping friends, but then he made the horse go faster, leaving her to bump about on its back and work out the riding business for herself. Then suddenly she gained the rhythm and was charmed! She loved riding the horse! But when Wiradji gathered family and friends together to watch her triumph – to see how she'd mastered this pursuit by galloping the horse across the plains as far as the row of giant anthills and back, her dark hair flying in the wind as the horse's hooves flew over the earth – the life she knew came to a halt.

Everyone was thrilled when she brought the horse to a standstill and cheered her when she dismounted, uninjured. Some even asked to be taken for a ride, but Banggu couldn't allow that. Instead he hurried her over to a grove of trees, where her parents and Ladjipiri were waiting.

'My wife is ready,' he said quietly. 'They will leave in the morning.'

Wiradji was shocked. 'No!' she cried. 'Not yet. I won't go! You tell them, Mother! You can't send me away yet.'

Despite her pleas, the decision was final.

'You must obey your husband,' her father told her. 'We will grieve to lose you, but if he wants you to join his kin, this is as it should be.'

'But he is not accompanying me,' she argued. 'This is not what it should be. I won't go. I want to stay by my husband.'

'Go you must. This is the law.'

Her mother hugged her. 'Your husband is a wise man. He thinks only of your protection and for this I shall be forever grateful.'

She clung to Banggu through the night, begging to be allowed to remain with him, but he was adamant. Their parting was sheer anguish for both of them.

Wiradji was hoping that Banggu could at least travel some of the way with them, but when Ladjipiri came to their camp with the horses, she realised this would be impossible. Men on foot could not keep up with horses.

Since she could no longer refuse the wishes of her husband and her parents, Wiradji looked upon the journey from this troubled land as a personal challenge.

She submitted to being dressed in the same white-man garb that Ladjipiri was now wearing, stood proudly as a Kalkadoon woman should, and said: 'Be assured I will see your father safely home, dear husband.'

Banggu did not register surprise or amusement at that statement. Instead he nodded gravely and kissed her farewell.

CHAPTER EIGHTEEN

The two young gentlemen who had laid claim to seventy-four square miles of land out along the Cloncurry River were farewelled royally by the Tully family, who promised to organise a race meeting on their return.

Anxious now to be on their way, the pair rode into town to pick up supplies, but first Ned wanted to call on Marcus.

'Not me,' Duke said. 'I told you I intend to report him. I can't shake his hand one day and blow the whistle on him the next. But you go if you must.'

'I think I should. It seems rather rude to just leave without a word.'

Ned left Duke at the store and rode down to the police station, surprised to see the carpenters already working on the roof.

Sergeant Krill came out to meet him. 'The inspector's not here, Ned. A party of blacks raided a station somewhere near the McKinleys; a white man was killed. The inspector's gone after the savages involved. They'll get what-ho when he gets his hands on them.'

'Yes, I'm sure,' Ned muttered. 'We're heading back east now. We've staked out land along the river. Will you tell him I'm sorry we missed him, and wish him all the best for us?'

'I'll tell him. Sure you can't stay on? He should be back in a day or so.'

'No, I'm sorry, we can't. I've urgent business back home.'

'Well, all right,' the sergeant said. 'I'll tell him. And you see you keep your guns handy out there. If I could spare some men I'd give you an escort to Winton, but we're still waiting on reinforcements.'

As they left Cloncurry they passed several heavily burdened bullock wagons travelling together for safety. They thanked the drivers for their offer to travel with them, but declined, determined to stick to their plan for a fast ride back to Rockhampton, which would include a change of horses at Winton and Longreach.

When they crossed Blackwater Creek and headed into that long valley, Duke remembered that this was where belligerent blacks with spears had surprised them, though now all was quiet. They were nearly through when a mob of blacks appeared about half a mile ahead of them, standing defiantly in their path, waving spears and shouting, as if daring them to try to pass.

Immediately the two men veered away, racing the horses for the shelter of the hills.

'I'm not certain this is a good idea,' Ned called to Duke as they rode along the rocky slopes. 'Remember all the campfires we saw in these hills on the way out?'

'That was on the other side of the valley.'

'Which doesn't mean they won't live on this side as well. I have a feeling those fellows down there have sent us into a trap.'

Duke reined in his horse. 'Do you want to turn back?'

'No. Not yet anyway. If we can find our way through here, we could make a run for Claude's station.'

'Fair enough.' Duke loaded his rifle and fired two shots into the air. They echoed all along the valley.

'What's that for?'

'To confuse them. They'll be wondering who we're firing at. It also lets the buggers know what they're in for if they come too close. We've got plenty of ammo; we'll fire off a few shots every so often.'

Ned loaded his own rifle, though he wasn't comfortable trying to guide the horse along ever-steeper tracks, and avoid shooting himself at the same time.

'We can't go too high,' Duke warned. 'The hilltops in this country are bloody bald. There's no cover.'

Ned dismounted. 'Then we'd better lead the horses until we find a way through.'

'Look down there,' Duke said, pointing to the valley below.

'God help us, we almost rode into that,' Ned gasped, looking down at a huge Aborigine camp nestled across the end of the valley. Light was fading and campfires were beginning to dot the scene. 'Maybe they were just warning us off,' he added. 'They've got women and children there. And a lot of huts. It could be a meeting place.'

'All the more reason for us to get out of here. This track looks well worn; we'll have to try it.'

Eventually they found that the rocky track was descending, and they both breathed a sigh of relief when they reached forested low lands.

'Which way now?' Ned asked.

'South-east I'd say; look for cattle so we know we're on someone's land.'

As he spoke, a spear seemed to come from nowhere, thudding into a nearby tree.

'Come on!' Duke screamed. 'Ride!'

His horse, a stockhorse, bolted in fright, dodging expertly through the trees, but when Duke looked back he saw Ned's horse rearing, trying to escape from two tribesmen who were intent on dragging him down. He turned and raced back, causing one of the black men to turn away from Ned and run at him, head on, spear raised for direct aim, but Duke already had him in his sights.

He fired. The spear dropped. The tribesman cried out in pain, clutching his bloodied bare chest, but to Duke's amazement refused to give way. Instead he strode boldly into the path of Duke's horse, forcing it to swerve away, before he collapsed on the ground. Duke saw that Ned was still managing to stay on his badly spooked horse, but was grappling with his attacker for possession of a nasty-looking tomahawk.

This time Duke fired in the air and the tribesman released his hold on the weapon to dive behind the horse's hind legs, risking life and limb there before sprinting into the forest, shouting for help. Ned jumped down from his horse to retrieve the rifle he'd lost in the fight before he'd had a chance to use it, while Duke steadied his horse, and then they were both galloping away.

The two horses raced as one until they reached open country and could breathe easily again.

'Are you all right?' Duke said, eyeing the blood on Ned's shirt. 'Yours or his?'

'Mine, dammit! That one came at me from behind with his bloody axe! If this horse hadn't been so spooked, leaping about in circles, the bugger would have taken my arm off.'

Duke insisted on examining the wound on Ned's upper arm. 'Only a graze,' he said. 'More bruised than broken. You were bloody lucky.'

'I was very lucky. Thank you for coming back for me.'

'I didn't go back for you, I went back for the horse,' Duke laughed.

He didn't mention that he was feeling queasy. He had never shot a man before. He could still see the fine, strong features of the young man who'd confronted him before he fell, with nothing left to fight with but sheer determination.

Duke's heart welled with pity. And admiration.

Travelling on, with the setting sun at their backs, they followed a dried-up watercourse until at last it dropped down into a series of billabongs, stranded until the monsoonal weather sent rain aplenty to restore them to their river status.

But the ploughed-up banks of the billabongs were evidently waterholes for cattle, so they looked about for what could be a stock route and followed it, even as darkness set in on them, hoping they were going in the right direction. Soon they came upon a few cattle settling quietly for the night by the odd tree, so they kept going until they saw a large herd ahead of them.

'Who goes there?' a voice demanded from the shadows.

'MacNamara from Cloncurry!' Duke shouted.

'What the bloody hell are you two doing out here?' the voice responded, and Ginger Magee rode towards them.

Ginger told them the story as he escorted them on to the homestead.

'This is our herd. We were going well when we were attacked by a large mob of blacks. They burned the cook-wagon and stampeded the herd, so it was nasty for a while. Harry got a spear in his leg . . .'

'Good God! Is he all right?' Ned asked. 'And Tottie? What about her?'

'She's fine. So is Harry. Poor old Paddy Flint suffered bad burns when the wagon burned; he's being looked after up at the homestead.'

'What homestead?' Duke asked.

'Didn't you know? You're on Gubbins Station. Claude said you visited on your way west.'

'So we did! We've been trying to find the place.'

'Well you've made it. We took shelter here while we rounded up the cattle. That's our herd back there. You can see the lights of the homestead over there,' he pointed, 'to your right. I have to stay on watch; the cattle are still spooked. Why don't you go on ahead?' Ginger laughed. 'You're in for a surprise.'

The cook-wagon had been burned to the ground, along with their supplies and, to Tottie's annoyance, all her carefully collected utensils and cutlery, suitable for life on the road. Because of that, it took a little while for their situation to sink in.

Harry was still laid up in the wagon when she burst in on him. 'We haven't any food. What shall we do?'

'There's food, love, don't worry. Ginger has already sent some men out to find game. We'll probably be eating turkey or wallaby tonight.' Adding, to tease her: 'Without salt.'

'There's no tea either, remember?' she said, knowing how much Harry loved his hot black tea with plenty of sugar.

'That's a disaster! But if my calculations are correct, we're crossing a station owned by people called Gubbins. We should be able to buy stores there.'

'I hope so,' Tottie said grimly.

Later, Ginger brought the good news that they were indeed crossing Gubbins Station and the homestead was only a few miles up ahead. Tottie was so relieved, she asked one of the stockmen to drive the wagon carrying her husband and Paddy Flint, so that she could ride the rest of the way. She needed to be on her own; to get her breath back, to recover from the shock of that raid. The attack that had come on the mildest of starry nights. It was all over in minutes, but amid the screams and shouts and banging of guns, and her heart pounding like a bass drum, it had seemed like hours.

Even now, when she could ride quietly, looking about her as she liked to do, listening to the birds, smelling the various scents of the bush that she was learning to identify, that heart of hers, she knew, was poised, ready to start its awful pounding again at the slightest whiff of trouble.

She needed this time to herself to calm down.

It had all happened so fast, she recalled. At first they'd thought the cook-wagon had caught fire only a hundred yards from their wagon, and Harry was racing towards it when he was struck by a spear. Tottie herself had been right behind him and had dragged him under cover of their own wagon, too afraid to climb up and get their guns. And then the shooting had started and she could see black figures reflected in the light of the fire! There were men above them in the wagon, and Tottie shrieked in fright, but it was their own men firing at the blacks.

At the same time the blacks had thrown firesticks at the cattle, sending them berserk and causing a stampede. The men were still trying to round up strays.

'It's over!' Tottie chastised herself. 'Stop dwelling on it! That was almost two days ago. Calm down. Forget about it. Here you have another cattle station, another place of interest to people of your ilk! Pay attention!'

Tottie had her first view of Gubbins Station as she rode past a smooth cliff face of colour-streaked rock and emerged on high ground overlooking open prairie with the shimmer of a river in the distance.

She called to Ginger, who was leading the way: 'What river is that?'

'It's Blessington Creek, according to my map. But it'd do me for a river by the looks of it.' He pointed. 'The track to the homestead goes down there through the tall grass.'

'Where's the herd?'

'They detoured around this patch of hills, heading for that creek. I'm going down to see the station owner. Do you want to come on with me?'

'Yes, I'd like to.'

She looked back. The wagon was following at a steady pace.

They were stunned to find the owners of this station packing their belongings on to a large dray.

'Those savages,' Martha Gubbins wept, 'they killed our lovely son, Bert. Killed him dead. And all over a bag of flour.'

'It wasn't a raid?' Tottie asked, confused.

'No. Our stockmen found him dead at the back of the stables with a flour bag over his head.'

'No point in us staying here any more,' Claude Gubbins told them. 'Not without our son. It was to be Bert's land to give to his children. And their children.' The poor man was weeping too. 'It's a dream gone bust, that's what it is. My Martha wants to go back to where she's got neighbours again, and that's the least I can do for her.'

'I'm so sorry,' Tottie said. 'So very sorry. Is there anything we can do?'

'Just say a prayer for him, missus, that's all. You and your husband, put him in your prayers tonight.'

'Oh! This isn't my husband,' Tottie said. 'Ginger's our head stockman. My husband's back there in our wagon. He's been hurt. We have another patient too . . .'

'What happened to them?' Martha asked.

Tottie looked to Ginger, thinking that mentioning the attack might further upset this poor couple, but Ginger explained about the raid, and the next minute Martha had taken charge. She cleaned and stitched Harry's wound, and tore up a good sheet to give Paddy a supply of fresh bandages after she'd attended to his burns. Then, when they were all sitting around her kitchen table, she frowned at Tottie.

'If you have any sense, you'll go back, missus. This is no place for a woman.'

Tottie blushed. Martha was voicing her own fears.

'Are you simply walking off this property?' Harry asked Claude.

'Yes, sir. We wouldn't be the first. Plenty of folk walking off the land out here. Can't make a go of it, or too scared of the blacks. You've got a black family travelling with you. Where were they when you were attacked?'

'They were frightened. They hid in the bush.'

'They didn't fight?' Claude was suspicious of all blackfellows now, and with good reason, Harry admitted.

'They don't carry arms,' he said. 'There was nothing they could do, but they were able to say that our attackers were a well-known warlike tribe called Kalkadoon.'

'They're all warlike,' Claude gritted. 'Listen now, you folk can stay as long as you like. We're leaving tomorrow.'

'What about your cattle?'

'We'll drive them back to Longreach. They'll fetch a good price; well fed they are.'

'Yes, I noticed that on the way in. It's fine land, Claude.'

Harry had a quiet talk with Claude about this huge property.

'What are you asking for it?'

'Asking? I'm not asking a thing. I couldn't give it away right now.'

'I'd take it.'

'Then it's yours if you're mad enough to want it. But you'll have to do all the paperwork. Bert was going to do that but he never got time to finish the claim forms. They're tricky, those forms, I tell you.'

After more discussion, they came to an agreement. Claude had a well-stocked storeroom and he was pleased to be able to sell his cattle to Harry rather than face a slow plod back to Longreach, but he wouldn't accept even a small payment for the land.

'I don't take charity, Mr Merriman. And it's easily seen you don't have money to burn or you wouldn't be here. But there's one thing I ask. Will you leave the name as Gubbins Station in memory of Bert?'

'We'd be honoured, Mr Gubbins.'

Harry had a quick word with Ginger, then the time came to tell his wife what he'd done.

'There wasn't time to consult you,' he apologised. 'I had to make up my mind quickly. But this is a beautiful property, Tottie.'

She sat facing him, tight-lipped. 'I see.'

'No you don't. I've decided we're going back to town. I'm offering you a compromise. I've spoken to Ginger. He likes this country. He'd like to stay on with us as overseer, but he's aware that trouble is brewing with the blacks.'

'How does he know that?'

'Our Pitta people told him. They said the attackers were Kalkadoon warriors and they're planning a war. So . . .' He heaved a sigh. 'You and I are heading back east for a while.'

'No we're not!'

'What?'

'Harry, I haven't come this far to turn tail and drag all the way back. You're right. This is lovely country, from what I've seen of it, and it's our home. Think about it. We're here. Home! I don't think that's sunk in with you yet, or you wouldn't even consider leaving. I'm really excited and I can't understand why you're not!'

He blinked. 'I think it's all too sudden for me. But I'm still worried about you. Would you consider going back to Longreach for a while?'

'We'll see. We'll talk to Ginger about that.'

It was sad, parting with the grieving parents of the young man buried beneath the small fenced garden of coloured stones scattered with wild flowers. They held a farewell service by the grave and then went on their way, accompanied by their two stockmen, leaving the new owners feeling lonely and depressed.

To throw off the mournful mood, Harry decided that he and Tottie should ride down to have a look at the river.

'We can't,' she cried. 'You're not well enough and I've got too much to do.'

'We can, Tottie. I can ride and we've got the rest of our lives for chores. Let's just go down there, sit by the river, our river, and let the world go by while we talk to God.'

'What about?'

'I want to thank him for delivering us to this our new home, and for giving me such a darling wife. Do you want to add anything?'

'Yes. I want to tell him how happy I am, and how much I love my husband, who is almost always right.'

'Almost?'

'Yes, except when it comes to the name of our property. I can't say I'm thrilled that it's to remain Gubbins Station.'

Harry smiled. 'Yes. Sorry. I didn't have the heart to say him nay.'

She kissed him. 'You're forgiven. Are you sure you feel like going out?'

Harry moved over to make room for her on the bed. 'On second thoughts, maybe tomorrow.'

That night, two riders approaching the outbuildings were intercepted by stockmen, who recognised them and gleefully led them over to the cottage to bang on the boss's door. For a minute Tottie took fright, but then she stood back amazed as Ned and Duke walked in.

There was much to talk about. They all had good news to share and compare, not only the newly acquired Gubbins Station, but the success of the new partners in staking their own claims out near Cloncurry.

'How marvellous!' Tottie said. 'You made it! What are you calling the property?'

Duke shrugged. 'We still can't decide. We'll think of something by the time we get to Longreach.'

'I hope you'll stay with us awhile,' Harry said. 'We can all explore this property together.'

'Oh yes,' Tottie said. 'There's no rush now. You've all the time in the world. We'd love to have you stay. We'll build a bonfire and have a big celebration . . .'

Duke shook his head. 'I'm really sorry. We can't stay, we'll be pushing on in the morning.'

Harry was disappointed. 'Are you sure? You're welcome to rest up here for as long as you like.'

'We have to go,' Duke said sadly. 'Ned's father passed away. He only just learned the bad news. He has to get back . . .'

'Yes,' Ned added. 'My mother . . . she'll be needing me. I have to get to Sydney as soon as possible.'

No matter how they tried to remain cheerful after that, their evening drifted into a sad realisation that this was, suddenly, a parting of the ways.

Duke made an effort to brighten the scene as they were leaving.

'Hey, Ned,' he called. 'We've got some fine springs on that land out there. Why don't we call the property Tottie's Springs?'

'Good idea. But couldn't we do better for this lady and call it Antonia Springs?'

Tottie was thrilled. 'That's so nice of you, Ned, and you, Duke. I'm really honoured. I'll be up there with Alice Springs and Julia Creek. It's really exciting.'

Harry winked at Duke. 'Thanks, mate,' he said quietly.

That afternoon as they rode over to inspect the river, Tottie turned to Harry. 'It's sad about Ned's father, isn't it?'

'Yes. A nasty shock for him. Is he the only son?'

'I think so. He never mentioned any brothers or sisters. But I was thinking . . . deaths go in threes. There was Bert Gubbins, then Mr Heselwood. Who's next?'

'Ah Tottie, that's an old wives' tale. Between you and me, I think Bert was looking for trouble, shooting that fellow over a bag of flour.'

'But he didn't really mean to hurt him, just teach him a lesson. He probably thought it was a joke, peppering a bare backside with shot.'

'A dangerous joke,' Harry growled. 'No one likes to be shot at, least of all these native people who are already easily spooked by white men. Their payback was a grim joke too, one might say. There's a problem here that I have to sort out quickly.'

'What if we leave a bag of flour out near Bert's grave tonight?' Tottie asked. 'Like a peace offering.'

'Good idea, it'd be worth a try. Make a start at least.'

The next morning Tottie ran out to check, pleased to find the flour had gone, and in its place was a necklace of shells. She was so thrilled she stood and called 'thank you' to the bush people over and over, waving the necklace in sheer delight. No one appeared but she knew they would have heard her.

Later, Harry called on the elder of the Aborigine friends who had travelled with them from Longreach. His name was Mungga and though his wiry hair was thick, he had a scarred bald patch above one ear, which somehow made him look lopsided.

'The flour has gone,' Harry said to Mungga, 'so the people who killed the white man are still here? You know them?'

Mungga nodded.

'Who are they?'

The old man seemed surprised. 'Dem PittaPitta.'

'Will they hurt us?'

'Your fellers not shoot dem no more?'

'No. All good people here. Black people. White people.'

'Den orright.'

'You bring them to my corroboree next big moon? I want to meet their head men. Make peace.'

Mungga cackled. 'White feller corroboree?'

'Yes,' Harry laughed with him. 'We make good corroboree, first sit-down talks then plenty tucker. Good eh?'

The old man licked his lips and nodded.

★ ★ ★

As a result of his talks with the Pitta Pitta leaders, Harry found that the coloured cliffs that marked the entrance to this property were also the northern boundary of their tribal land, which was interesting because he knew they could forbid Kalkadoons entry if they saw fit. He took long and tiring walks with them, marking out areas that were sacred to these people, as well as learning as much as he could about their way of life, so as not to offend.

He found all their information fascinating and related it to Tottie of an evening so that she could enter it into her journals, along with sketches and the Pitta Pitta words she was learning from the women.

When his herds increased and he employed more staff Harry introduced station rules equally as tough as those issued by Langley Palliser at Cameo Downs. The Aborigine people on this station were to be treated with respect, and there was to be no fraternising with their women.

Sergeant Hannah came by one day with the news that this area had been declared peaceful now.

'There are still plenty of attacks but they're further away these days,' he said. 'More out in the Cloncurry area. How are you getting on here?'

'No problems,' Harry said. 'I'm training some of the black lads to work as stockmen.'

'You might as well,' the sergeant said, as he took a brown envelope from his pack. 'The blokes at the Lands Office asked me to give these papers to you. They're the title deeds to your station. They said they're sorry it's taken so long.' He looked about him appreciatively. 'Congratulations! You've got a good-looking spread here, Harry.'

'*We* have,' Harry corrected, beckoning to Tottie. 'Come and see what the sergeant has brought us! We might persuade him to stay tonight and we'll have a bang-up celebration.'

'Count me in,' the sergeant grinned. 'And I just happen to have a bottle of my wife's best apple cider for you, Mrs Merriman, to mark the occasion.'

CHAPTER NINETEEN

After a week of torrential rains, the Brisbane River was hurtling out to sea carrying hapless palms and branches of trees foolish enough to seek residence on its low banks, while the townsfolk breathed a sigh of relief. A glimmer of sunlight could be seen in the leaden skies, bringing new hope that the town would be saved from the threat of floods.

Milly stood on the riverside balcony of her house, looking down on the inundated first level of her terraced garden.

'Another day of that and we'd have been flooded,' she told Lucy Mae. 'I've never seen such rain. And look! Oh my Lord! The boathouse next door has gone! It has been completely swept away! It must have happened during the night. I tell you, Lucy Mae, I should sell this house while I can. Get one higher up.'

She glanced at her daughter, who was sitting quietly in a cane armchair with a light blanket over her knees.

'Are you listening to me?'

'Yes, Mother.'

'I was mad to buy here in the first place. One only has to look at these high banks to know what heights this river must have reached in the past. Your father would never have made a mistake like this, but then you know me. I thought the house was so handsome, with the view and all its lovely big rooms, I forgot about the possibility of floods.'

She swung about and peered at Lucy Mae. 'Are you crying?'

'No,' Lucy Mae said, turning her head away.

'You are so! Now this has to stop. You're not the only person who has had a miscarriage; why, I know women who have had several. They don't sit about feeling sorry for themselves. You just have to buck up. You're not sick. The weather should clear by tomorrow. I'll arrange for us to go for a drive up to that star place. What do they call it?'

'The planetarium.'

'Yes, there. The driver will know where to find it.'

'I'd rather not.'

Milly frowned. 'I beg your pardon?'

'I said I'd rather not.'

'Did you indeed? You're the one who got yourself pregnant! Regardless of the scandal! I'm the one who had to worry about you, and send for a doctor in the dead of night. I'm the one who called in a nurse to look after you, and now you sit there pretending to be an invalid when I would like a little cheer in my life.'

'Mother, I wanted that baby!' Lucy Mae sobbed. 'I really did.'

'Then take it out on God, not me. If we have nice weather tomorrow we are going for a drive. So you get up in the morning, do your hair and be ready by eleven!'

Lucy Mae supposed her mother was right. She was being selfish. But she'd had such dreams of having a child to love and care for; dreams that had extended way past babyhood into a beautiful future for that beloved child, and it was so hard to give them up; to stop crying for her lost little one.

She did cry, once more, when she told Rosa, who cried with her, and she felt so much better.

This was an even worse time to announce that she was with child, Rosa told herself, when she came to visit and Lucy Mae sobbed her bad news. She did her best to comfort her friend, while trying not to notice Milly's 'it's-for-the-best' attitude.

But then there was her own situation. And she used it to change the subject.

'That picture,' she said to Milly, 'of the *Emma Jane*. Were Georgina and Jasin Heselwood on board too?'

'Indeed they were,' Milly said. 'It was quite a select little group of passengers when one looks back on the voyage. Georgina was perfectly charming, of course, but Jasin, God rest his soul, he was always very picky.'

'And was that where Dolour met Pace MacNamara?'

'Oh no. Goodness me, no. Pace was travelling alone. He met Dolour quite a while after we landed.'

'So there were only five of you?'

'No, seven.'

'And the convicts!' Lucy Mae added.

'We were not discussing the below-decks people,' her mother said icily.

'Who were the other two?' Rosa persisted.

'Dr and Mrs Brooks,' Milly said dismissively, with a frown for her daughter.

There was the name that Lark had thrown at her for some malicious reason. Yet why had Jasin said that he'd met her mother on this ship? Delia wasn't on the passenger list! How could he have made a mistake like that? And why had Georgina brushed aside her question?

At least she was getting some sense out of Milly.

'You were lucky to have had a doctor on board,' she commented in an endeavour to prolong the conversation.

'But he died, didn't he?' Lucy Mae said.

'Who?' her mother snapped.

'Dr Brooks.'

'Oh yes! That was later. Much later.' Milly flicked her fan at Lucy Mae as if to shut her up, and Rosa saw her friend blush. The little episode was akin to Milly kicking Lucy Mae under the table.

'It is so humid,' Milly complained. 'You'd think rain would cool the house; instead it imprisons us with the heat. Oh for a nice breeze. Ring for tea, Lucy Mae. You will stay, won't you, Rosa?'

'If I may.'

Later she piled her friend with more questions. 'Getting back to Dr and Mrs Brooks. I'm curious. What happened to her after he died? Why didn't your mother want to talk about her?'

Lucy Mae shook her head. 'I don't know.'

'Yes you do. So tell me.'

'Why are you making such a fuss about them? Mother did say to me that when Dr Brooks died Adelaide Brooks fell on hard times. They probably lost touch then.'

Rosa was suddenly intimidated, recalling Lark's anger. Adelaide Brooks? Known as Dell?

'Then why be so secretive?' she asked. 'It's not a rare scenario.'

'Rosa, I've no idea. Except perhaps Mother didn't approve of your father helping Mrs Brooks out of her difficulties.'

'My father did?'

'I believe so.'

'That's hardly a crime!' Rosa sniffed.

'Of course it's not. Mr Rivadavia has a reputation for being extremely generous.'

The weather was determined to remain damp, replacing the torrents with a curtain of misty rain, so her driver tucked Rosa into the gig and closed the leather flaps over the windows.

'We won't be long home, missus,' he called, but she had changed her plans.

'Thank you, but I'd like to go by my father's place first.'

She laughed as she sat back. Adelaide Brooks – Dell – was a widow. Juan was a wealthy young man. And handsome. And she was his mistress. So what? Who was Lark to throw stones, for heaven's sake?

She found him in his study and, as usual, delighted to see her. He jumped up and hugged her. 'How lovely of you to call on me. I haven't seen you for ages.'

'For six days,' she laughed. Then she saw the new pictures on his wall. 'Are these the colts? They're just beautiful. They're only babies, though. Isn't it a bit soon . . .'

'I just like looking at them,' he smiled. 'I will replace the pictures as they grow.'

'What are their names?'

'So far that is Beau and that is Belle. I am waiting to study their ancestors. Now we shall have coffee and you can tell me what you've been up to. No need to ask how you are; you're looking most beautiful today.'

Over coffee, father and daughter talked of this and that, until Rosa found the right time.

'May I ask you a question?'

'Of course you can. What is it you wish to know?'

'I heard of a lady called Adelaide Brooks,' she said, a giggle in her voice. 'Was she your mistress when you were young?'

Given her father's well-known relationship with Lark, she was surprised by his response.

'So you know about Dell?' he said sadly. 'Who have you been talking to? Milly Forrest?'

'Oh no, not really. I was just talking to her about the people who came out on the ship with her and her husband, like Pace MacNamara and the Heselwoods. I mean, what a collection!'

'And she happened to tell you that Dell was my mistress?'

'Oh no, Daddy! Please. You must not think that of Milly. She certainly didn't say any such thing. It was Lark. She was just being catty. I'm really sorry if I've offended you. We'll forget all about it.'

'Well,' he said slowly, 'I don't think we should forget all about it, now that you've asked me. I met Dell in Sydney. A truly beautiful woman, a widow, and we had an affair. Then, when I bought Chelmsford Station, I persuaded her to come with me. Dell was my mistress, I suppose it could be said, but she did not see it that way. She was so much the lady, she was embarrassed to be living with me.'

'Living in sin?' Rosa said.

'Yes. It really worried her, but I loved her. I didn't want her to leave me. I wanted her to marry me, but she kept making excuses, like she was older than me, and so on . . .'

Rosa was reminded of Lucy Mae's excuses for not marrying Duke.

'Didn't she love you?'

'Oh yes, or she never would have left Sydney with me.'

'Two people in love and you couldn't work it out?'

'We did in our own way. She liked to pretend we'd been married all along and leave it at that. Especially when she became pregnant. She simply couldn't imagine walking up the aisle pregnant.' He sighed. 'So there you are, that was Dell.'

'No it's not, Daddy,' Rosa said quietly. 'What became of her?'

He walked over to a cabinet, slid open a drawer and drew out a cream vellum folder.

'This is very difficult for me, Rosa. I hope you will bear with me.'

There was a photograph inside, carefully wrapped in tissue paper, and he handed it to her.

'Is this Dell?' Rosa said as she removed the paper.

Juan nodded.

'Oh, she's beautiful!' Rosa cried, admiring the delicate features of this lovely woman. 'So elegant! And what a gorgeous gown she's wearing!'

He sat down heavily on the leather couch by the cabinet. 'I was very young. Only twenty-two. I blamed myself when she died. In childbirth. 'Strangely,' he added, his voice distant, almost inaudible, 'Pace MacNamara was there at the time. He'd come to visit her.' He sighed. 'I couldn't believe she was dead. I was in shock. I had never met Pace before then, but he took over. Arranged everything. You see, Rosa, that lady was your mother . . .'

'What? She couldn't be! Delia was my mother!'

'No. Delia came to visit me some time later, with her uncle, Lord Forster. It was almost an arranged marriage. I needed a wife and a mother for my baby and Forster wanted Delia to marry well, so to speak. Marry wealth, I think that meant at the time.'

Rosa was barely listening. She kept staring at the photograph. Looking for herself.

'Why did you deceive me all these years?' she asked bitterly.

'Delia insisted that you be known as her child. I discovered later that you were a great convenience for her, since she never wanted children of her own.'

'But when she died? You should have told me then. We went to visit her grave. Why not then?'

He opened his hands wide to her. 'Why then? We were paying our respects to a woman who had always treated you as her daughter. She was rather shallow but she was kind to you in her way, and she never, ever admitted you were not hers. Can you understand that?'

'I suppose so. But when were you planning to tell me all this?'

'With your own baby coming I was thinking that would be a good time, but I was rather nervous of the reaction one might expect from your husband.'

Rosa's head was in a whirl. Charlie was predictable. He would not be impressed at all. He would consider he should have been informed much earlier. While she pondered this, Rosa realised she was the daughter not of the Honourable Delia, but of Adelaide Brooks. And Jasin Heselwood had known this.

I knew your mother! We came out on the same ship.

That meant Georgina knew. And Milly Forrest too, no doubt.

'Are you very upset?' Juan asked her. 'I am sorry, my dear, if I've caused you pain. You know I wouldn't do that for the world. But all your questions about that ship! The *Emma Jane*. I felt in my heart you were becoming closer to your mother. That she might have been reaching out to you.'

'Maybe she was,' Rosa said sadly. 'You know, Daddy, I think she was. But I'm really not upset. Only confused. There's a lot to think about. Could I come back another day so that we can talk this over?'

'I would like that. Though this is disturbing for you, I can only feel immense relief. You come and dine with me as soon as you are able. We'll have much to discuss.'

'Do you have any more photos?'

'No. I only managed to salvage this one.'

'Don't tell me,' Rosa smiled. 'Delia disposed of them.'

'I'm afraid so.'

One could say, Rosa thought, that Delia was predictable too.

That night at dinner, while Charlie marvelled at the discovery of huge deposits of gold near Rockhampton, Rosa studied him and decided to leave well alone. She was beginning to accept that Delia was not her mother, and had found a new respect for the woman who had adopted her. She could see no point in telling Charlie. This was her own business. She didn't need to share it with him.

As for her baby, the little soul she was carrying, that was another story. 'Like Father like Daughter', it might be called, she said to herself. Except this daughter was a mite cannier. No one would ever know that Jasin was the father. Not even Juan Rivadavia, who would find no fault with her; who might even find such information amusing, since he was still prickly over Charlie's snubs.

'My stepbrothers, the MacNamaras, have properties in the Rockhampton area,' she said gaily. 'They're probably picking up gold nuggets as we speak.'

'Yes. You ought to write to them and enquire about the viability of investment in mines up there.'

'I think it would be better if you wrote,' she sighed.

Charlie reached for the evening paper. 'Yes, of course. Quite right.'

One of the MacNamaras rode into Longreach with his partner, Ned Heselwood, but he was unaware that Ironstone Mountain, near his former station, Mango Hill, only twenty-five miles from Rockhampton, was becoming famous.

Both men were weary but they watered their horses, cooled off in a bar for the time it took to down two pints, then made for the Lands Office. There they lodged their claim for pastoral land to be known as Antonia Springs with the assistance of a surveyor, who took careful note of their reckonings in relation to the river, their blazed boundaries, and various landmarks. He, in turn, entered these details on the current maps of that area, and allowed the ownership to be registered to these squatters: men who squatted on land, taking possession until such time as the government sent out surveyors to create official maps of the districts. Sometimes this process took years.

Once Antonia Springs was registered, they produced the papers and maps required to lodge the claim for Gubbins Station by the signatories Harold and Antonia Merriman. There was some confusion over the names, but the patient surveyor managed to grasp the story and took detailed notes of this claim with the same painstaking care, despite Mr MacNamara's obvious impatience.

'This is taking hours,' Duke complained to Ned in a whisper. 'Can't you make him get a move on!'

'He has to get it right,' Ned shrugged. 'Why don't you go back to the pub and I'll be along when this is finished?'

'Righto!' Duke was gone in an instant.

As he walked into the pub, he saw the local police sergeant at the bar and remembered he had to report Beresford's crime to that gentleman – Sergeant Hannah, if he remembered rightly – before he left Longreach. But it would probably be more appropriate to make a formal complaint at the police station.

Which he would do, he told himself sternly, without bloody fail!

But then Hannah was coming towards him. 'MacNamara, isn't it?' he said. 'You and Ned. Mates of Inspector Beresford?'

'Sort of,' Duke said. 'As a matter of fact, I wanted a word with you about him. We've just come in from Cloncurry.'

'Ah. Then you've heard?' The sergeant looked to the door. 'Here comes Ned now. I gather you've heard about the inspector?' he said, this time to Ned.

'Heard what?'

Hannah pushed his wide hat back on his head in surprise. 'You haven't? Well . . .'

They stared as he took off the hat. A sign of respect, it seemed. 'A stockman brought the news this morning. Beresford's been killed. The blacks got him. Kalkadoons. They set up an ambush, and killed him and three of his black troopers.'

'Where was this?' Ned was shocked.

'Somewhere in the McKinley Ranges. One of the troopers was wounded, but he escaped, managed to get to a station to raise the alarm. I know you were mates of his. I'm sorry, lads.'

Duke was speechless with astonishment. Ned managed to ask if Marcus' body had been found.

'No, not yet, as far as I know. But the station people could have found it by now. A couple of my men have gone out to investigate. That only leaves a weak force at Cloncurry under Sergeant Krill. We'll have to get reinforcements. The situation is out of hand. I have to go, lads. I'm sorry . . .'

'But it's definite. He has been killed?' Ned asked.

'Ah yes. The trooper said those blacks knew who he was. They called him by name. Taunted him, the bastards.'

As Hannah left the bar, Duke gulped. Said not a word. For once in my life, he reflected, I'd better take a step back and let someone else do the talking.

Ned ordered a drink, then turned to Duke. 'He wasn't a bad fellow, you know. He just believed that what he was doing was right. It's strange to think that so many normal everyday English and European folk can suddenly think nothing of killing human beings of a different skin colour for their land, or for sport. I mean, Marcus was a gentleman . . .'

Duke shrugged. Noncommittal.

'I hope he didn't suffer,' Ned added sadly.

Little hope of that, Duke mused.

'You know,' Ned reflected, 'I hate the suddenness of these deaths. It's so unfair. I was such a disappointment to my father. It's too awful that I never had a chance to redeem myself.'

'Yes you have,' Duke told him. 'Your dad had cattle properties all over New South Wales and Queensland. You'll have your hands full keeping a tight rein on them, but you're not a new chum any more. Harry gave you a good schooling on that drive. I reckon you'll do well, Ned. And,' he laughed, 'if you mess up, you can always call on me.'

'Kind of you . . . What will you be doing?'

'I've decided I'm off to catch brumbies when I get home. There are thousands of wild horses roaming this countryside. You've seen them yourself! Real beauties they are. Money for jam. I'll break them in myself, sort the wheat from the chaff and sell them at auction.'

'What about Lucy Mae?'

'Lucy Mae? I'll bring her and the baby up to Rockhampton.'

'Didn't you forget something?'

'Like what?'

'Like a wedding.'

'That's the women's department.'

Ned picked up the folder of precious papers that held the record of their claim to Antonia Springs. 'I just remembered something myself. We're heading back into civilisation. There could be some mail here for us!'

They were out of luck this time. No mail for either of them, but as they pushed out into the crowded street, Duke took Ned's arm. 'Listen, mate, I just wanted to say. About Marcus. I am sorry. I wouldn't have wished that on anyone.'

Ned hitched his pack on his shoulder. 'Yes, I know. It's a terrible thing to happen. And his death will trigger even more violence.'

'Yeah. All the more reason for us to get out of there.'

His partner shook his head. 'God help us, MacNamara, you're all heart!'

CHAPTER TWENTY

Long before they reached the town of Rockhampton, the two men were astonished to find the road to the east busier than ever.

'What's going on?' Ned asked, and was met by an astonished stare.

'Where have you been, mister? On the moon?'

'Why?'

'There's a gold strike. In Rockhampton.'

Overhearing this, Duke was sceptical. He asked some stockmen: 'How can there be a gold strike in Rockhampton? Where in Rockhampton?'

'Not quite in the town,' he was told. 'Out a bit. Do you know of Ironstone Mountain?'

'I ought to,' he laughed. 'I've got a property in the shadow of that hulking old heap.'

'You had,' Ned reminded him.

'Oh well. It's the same thing. Family. Was this strike somewhere near there?' he asked the stockman.

'Not near there, mate. There. That old heap, as you call it, isn't iron, it's a mountain of gold.'

'Oh, is that right?' Duke laughed. He turned back to Ned. 'Did you hear that? I reckon these blokes are off their heads with gold fever. They're bloody mad.'

Ned was confused. 'Where are they all going if there's no gold?'

'You only have to say the word and it starts a rush,' Duke explained. 'There have been strikes out there, bits and pieces, even some copper they say, and every so often someone comes to town shouting they've found gold at Ironstone, but it turns out to be rubbish, mostly yellow iron pyrites.'

The traffic on the road became heavier, and the closer they came to the town the more that tale of a mountain of gold was being tossed around. In the end, Duke was nervous, almost convinced it was true. He insisted that they had to get to Rockhampton with all haste.

'Why?'

'Don't ask so many questions! Come on, we'll ride cross-country.'

He raced away and Ned had trouble keeping him in sight. This wasn't open plains like the western lands; the coastal strip was lush cleared pastures dotted with palms and huge shady trees, and often enough a tangle of jungle that Duke managed to avoid in his mad dash for the town.

Soon they skirted the Fitzroy River and pounded around the busy streets until Duke pulled up his horse, threw the reins to Ned and disappeared into a shopfront that bore the title of Lands Department.

A clerk recognised him. 'Hey, Duke! Haven't seen you for ages. What have you been up to?'

Duke rushed over and took him aside. 'One question, Casey. What's the story about Ironstone Mountain? Is it true about the gold find?'

'Sure is, Duke.'

'But is it big?'

'They say so. Fred Morgan's been fossicking there and he and his brothers are claiming the whole mountain!'

'Would it be worth staking out a mining claim on Mango Hill?'

'Bloody oath it would, but you have to get in fast before someone else grabs it. Get over to the Mines Department. Slip in the back door; you'll never get past the mob at the front. My brother Syd's working there now; give him the nod, he'll look after you.'

Ned waited in the street with the horses, watching people come and go from the Lands Office, but there was no sign of Duke.

Eventually he came striding down from the other direction, brandishing miner's rights to Mango Hill.

'What will your brother say about this?'

'I don't know. I have to call in at the bank. Will you see if there's any mail, and I'll meet you at the Criterion Hotel.'

Duke was careful now. He had some sums to do. He still had money in the bank from the sale of Mango Hill. Money he'd 'forgotten' to use to pay off the loan. And he had a fortune in his money belt from the sale of his cattle.

He breezed into the Commercial Bank to have a talk with Sam Pattison, who stared at the dusty figure at his door.

'Jeez, it's you, MacNamara!' he said. 'I didn't recognise you. I thought you were some bearded old bushie. You just get in?'

'Yes.'

'You might like to know I had your brother in here some time back, threatening to throttle me.'

'You mean Paul?'

'Of course Paul.'

'Don't worry about him, he's all right.'

'You sold him Mango Hill, you rogue, but you didn't pay off your loan! You had the money; why the hell did you do that?'

'I was going out west, I thought I might need some cash. So what happened? Did he pay it out?'

'What choice did he have?'

'So it's clear?'

'Yes. No thanks to you.'

'That's good. I knew he had the money. He's such a tightwad. So tell me, exactly how much do I owe him?'

Pattison dug out a file. 'Two hundred and two pounds. And I'd pay up before he spots you, Junior, or learn to duck. So how did the drive go?'

'It was great. Merriman's settled. He took up a grand spread near Winton, and Ned Heselwood and I now own a huge property on the Cloncurry River.'

'Sounds interesting.'

'And I sold my cattle, a few short of five hundred, for a goodly sum, so who's Junior now, my friend?'

Pattison whistled appreciatively and reached for his hat. 'Why don't we go next door for a drink so that you can tell me all about the wild west?'

'I can't, I haven't got the time right now. I'll catch up with you soon. In the mean time, reopen my account.' He dumped a wad of notes on Pattison's desk.

'Do you want me to pay off your brother with this cash?' the bank manager asked.

'No! Put it in my account. I've got the sale money stashed somewhere else.'

'I know that. You left it in the Australasian Bank.'

'So? Give me a pencil, Sam. What was that figure again?'

'Two hundred and two pounds.'

Duke wrote it on a slip of paper. 'I'll transfer it into Paul's account now, so he can't yell at me.'

'Don't bank on it. But your other brother, John Pace, seems more civil. He sent you a half-yearly cheque for three hundred pounds for your share in Kooramin Station.'

'Jesus! Three hundred pounds! That's a bit of all right.'

'For doing nothing it is! Here's the statement. But Paul's holding the cheque,' he laughed, 'since John Pace didn't know your address.'

Duke read the statement, and laughed. 'Half-yearly! How about that! What with one thing and another, I'll be a rich man one of these days, my man, so I require respect.'

'Good, you can shout the first drink. By the way, did you hear about Marcus Beresford?'

'Yes.'

'It must be grim out there, eh?'

Duke nodded. 'If you look for trouble.'

★ ★ ★

Dutifully, feeling ever so virtuous, Duke MacNamara deposited the exact amount owing into his brother's account, and walked away with a spring in his step, tipping his hat to two young ladies who were walking towards him. He was taken aback when they stuck their noses in the air and swept up their skirts to hurry on past.

He found Ned in the Criterion bar, where staff and patrons were less particular about a man's appearance.

'Righto,' he said. 'All's done. We can go out to Mango Hill to report to Paul and Laura. They'll put us up.'

'If you don't mind, Duke, I'd rather not. I received a letter from my mother . . .'

'Did you? Were there any letters for me?'

'No. I'm sorry. Anyway, I telegraphed her that I'll be back in Sydney on the next available ship. Which turns out to be the *Jindalee*, a new coastal steamer, fortunately. So we're in luck. It departs Rockhampton in three days, and calls in to Brisbane en route, so I booked a berth for you as well. Does that suit you?'

'Sure it does. I'll telegraph Lucy Mae that we're back in the land of the living.'

'Well then,' Ned sighed wearily, 'I'm off. I'll go to my digs near the stables. They're clean and quiet.'

'Why don't you stay here at the Criterion? If you're short of cash, I'll back you. We're partners after all.'

'Thank you, Duke, but my mother has telegraphed funds to the bank.' He smiled bleakly. 'I've been reinstated. My father wouldn't be impressed, would he?'

'I don't think he'd care now,' Duke said bluntly. 'How is your mother? Is she all right?'

'Coping, I gather. It seems your stepfather escorted Jasin's body from Brisbane to Sydney, which was a great help to her . . .'

Duke frowned. 'My stepfather? Oh yes, Rivadavia! Did he? Wonders will never cease!'

'Yes, I thought that was strange. I guess I'll hear all about it when I get home.'

'Are you sure you don't want to come out to Mango Hill with me?'

'Thank you, no. Not yet anyway. I just want to sleep. I don't think I'll ever catch up on all the sleep I've lost since I landed back in this country.'

Ned's first priority was to bathe and shave, and dump every item of the battered clothing he'd been wearing for months, joyfully replacing them with sweet-smelling new apparel, but not so Duke. He intended to play the part of the intrepid explorer and successful squatter to the hilt.

'They don't think I know what Dolour was up to, throwing away Dad's legacy,' he mused as his horse trotted amiably along a road packed with prospectors. 'Paul and John Pace think I'm too stupid to have worked that out,' he muttered to himself. 'But I don't care what they think. The main thing now is I've outsmarted Mum. I've helped to put Dad's dream back on the map. What with Kooramin, Mango Hill, Antonia Springs and Valley of Lagoons, his sons now own more land than Pace did, and we've only just got started. I wouldn't be surprised either,' he added, 'if Paul still owns Oberon Station. It's in the blood to hang on to land.'

He was right. Paul had not sold Oberon Station; he had only leased it.

This information was forthcoming after Paul had shouted at him, ordered him out of the Mango Hill homestead, accepted the bank receipt for full payment of Duke's debt with disbelief, and demanded to know how much he had fleeced from his friends in his travels.

'When can I expect a bailiff to come knocking?' he asked bitterly.

In the mean time Laura was full of questions about the cattle drive as she prepared dinner in the gleaming kitchen that featured a new stove, lace-curtained windows and polished flooring. But it was the exterior that had stunned Duke as he rode past the mango trees. He was even a little envious, thinking he'd made a mistake selling, because the house looked so grand now, painted white, and enclosed by a veranda on three sides.

Someone had mentioned to him that he should put a veranda on that stark unpainted house, for shade, but he hadn't bothered. To Duke a veranda was just that: an addition to a building, plain and purposeful. This one widened to bays at each corner to break the monotony; the railings, posts and fretwork above were also painted white, and the woodwork on the railings, he'd noticed as he walked up the slate steps, was polished beech.

'Bloody hell!' he'd muttered to himself in admiration.

After that, the inside, to Duke, bore no resemblance to his former residence.

'What do you think of it?' Laura had asked.

'It's all right,' he admitted, looking about him, stunned by the transformation.

'What would he know?' Paul growled.

Duke said not a word about Antonia Springs, because he knew Paul was busting to ask if he'd managed to claim land. Busting to hear that he'd failed.

'Did you hear about Marcus Beresford?' he asked as they sat down to dinner.

'We did. He got his just deserts,' Paul snapped. 'Friend of yours, was he?'

'Yes, he was.'

'Where's Edward Heselwood?'

'He came back with me. He's in town.'

'He took his time about getting back!'

'We didn't hear the news until we came back to Longreach,' Duke said, bending the truth somewhat rather than explain. He hated having to explain himself to anyone.

'Why didn't you bring him out here with you?' Laura asked.

'He's still in shock over his dad. He's arranging to go home.'

'And where's home for you, might I ask?' his brother enquired.

'I haven't decided.'

'Not even with a child on the way?'

'That's my business!'

'Is it? Milly Forrest has been making it my business too.'

'Ah yes,' Duke grinned. 'I thought you would have opened that letter you sent on.' He saw Laura flush. 'Don't worry, sis, I'd have done the same.'

'Have you heard from Lucy Mae?' she asked him.

'Dear girl, we've been so far afield we haven't heard from anyone. There's no telegraph, and mail is monthly if we're lucky. That's at Winton . . . where we were is even further out than that.'

'Where's Merriman now?' Paul asked.

'He took the herd on to a property this side of Winton, and he and his wife Tottie decided that was far enough. They've taken up thirty square miles.'

'Good Lord,' Laura said. 'That's a lot of country.'

'Some families have taken up more. One fellow marked out a hundred square miles, then woke up to the fact that it was too big to run and walked off.'

'Mad!' Paul grumbled.

'Your mate Langley Palliser isn't doing too badly. He keeps adding outstations to his properties.'

'And what did you do with your cattle? Lose them somewhere?'

'No. But several station owners out there have. They lost a lot of cattle in the floods, and I sold my herd to them. Did bloody well out of it too.'

'And after all that travelling, you come home with as much cash as you'd have earned if you'd taken a job for three months. Well done!'

Laura was becoming tired of the sniping. 'Paul, do you think we could have a civil conversation here. Duke has been out to country that few people have seen; I'm interested if you're not.'

'I am civil. It's like pulling teeth trying to find out what it was all about. Did you get any land at all, Duke, or did you just sell your cattle and take a holiday?'

'It was no holiday,' Duke said. 'Ned and I were attacked by blacks on two occasions . . .'

'No!' Laura cried. 'What happened?'

'We fought them off. And rode for our lives, that's what!' Duke said, happy to exaggerate. 'But since you ask, Ned and I have claimed and registered a spread we call Antonia Springs on the Cloncurry River.'

'Who's Antonia?' Laura asked.

'Harry's wife.'

'What size?' Paul asked.

'His wife?'

'No, you idiot. Your block.'

'Somewhere about seventy square miles, I'd say. We didn't want to hang about that country, it was getting scary . . .'

But Paul had jumped up from the table to return with a map of the colony of Queensland, his temper cooled by this exciting news.

'Seventy square miles!' he shouted, vastly impressed. 'This is tremendous!' He shoved plates and cutlery aside. 'Show me where these places are.'

'Right,' Duke said. 'Now here's a place that used to be called Pelican Waters . . .'

Paul stared. 'God Almighty, how the hell did you get all the way out there?'

'The hard way,' his brother said smugly. 'On bony stockhorses.'

Milly Forrest read the telegram addressed to Lucy Mae, because her daughter was out shopping and telegrams, being urgent messages, should not be left idle: *Dear Lucy Mae, Heselwood and I arriving in Brisbane on Jindalee in a few days hoping you are well and looking forward to seeing you stop Duke.*

'Where is it from?' she asked the telegraph boy.

'That one? Rockhampton, missus.'

Milly stared, rushed inside and slammed the door. 'My God!' she breathed. 'Heselwood! There's only one Heselwood . . . Edward. Oh my heavens, he's with Edward! Lord Heselwood!'

She turned and shouted: 'Lucy Mae, come here this minute!'

Alice, the maid, looked up from her dusting. 'She's out, Mrs Forrest.'

'Oh yes. I forgot. That girl's never around when I need her. Oh my goodness. Young Lord Heselwood! I shall insist they stay here. It's the least I can do. Lady Georgina would expect that of me. I wonder how he came to be in the company of Edward? Not that it matters now. Alice, I want the two spare bedrooms aired and made up with the best linen, right away. Do it now!'

When Alice scampered away, Milly bewailed the fact that Edward would be accompanied by Duke. What a damn nuisance, she frowned. There's no child. Lucy Mae never actually accepted Duke's proposal. She is free to pursue her own interests now. She shook her head. It was too late to tell Duke there was no necessity to come to Brisbane now. Dammit!

She fretted and paced the front parlour until Lucy Mae finally put in an appearance, loaded with garment boxes, which Milly made a note to inspect before they went into her daughter's wardrobe. It was imperative that she look her very best for the visitor. Visitors.

'I want you to go to the post and telegraph office and answer this telegram from Duke, and hurry, it's nearly closing time.'

'What telegram?'

Milly ignored her angry response. 'Tell him you insist they stay here with us.'

'I will not. I don't want Duke staying here. I need to speak with him privately.'

'Oh for heaven's sake. Forget Duke. Don't you understand. Edward Heselwood is coming with him. He's Lord Heselwood now. Isn't that amazing?'

'What's amazing? You always said he was rather unpleasant.'

'As a lad. Not any more. He's grown up now. Give him a chance, Lucy Mae. He's the best catch in the country, for God's sake. Go and send that telegram to Duke or I'll have to send Alice.'

'She'll never make it in time. I'll attend to it tomorrow.'

'Attend? What does that mean? Attend?'

'Oh leave it, Mother. You told Duke I was having a child. Did you ever rectify that appalling message? Tell him I'd miscarried? Of course not! So the poor man is coming down . . . Really, Mother, you are the end, now trying to push me on to Duke's friend.'

'I don't know how they came to be friends,' Milly began, but Lucy Mae had fled the room. Mortified.

While Milly had the maids working on a spring clean, and Cook replenishing the pantry with dishes that would please the palate of a young gentleman or two, Lucy Mae set off in the gig for the town centre.

Her first call was at the shipping office, where she ascertained that *Jindalee* was expected to leave Rockhampton on Wednesday and berth in the port of Brisbane at eight a.m. on Saturday. Then she hurried around to the fashionable Regency Hotel, where she reserved a room for Mr Duke MacNamara on the Saturday.

This being Monday, there was time for a telegram to reach him, so it was duly sent to Mango Hill Station via Rockhampton.

Lucy Mae had spent hours, the night before, trying to compose a telegram to fit this occasion, but it was extremely difficult, since the occasion itself was fraught with confusion. It wasn't until she was confronted by the telegram form that she finally made a decision; not one that pleased her, rather the best she could offer under the circumstances: *Accommodation reserved for you Regency Hotel Saturday stop LucyMae.* The name, she claimed, was one word and should be charged as such, and 'No,' she told the clerk firmly. 'I do not require a reply.'

In no hurry to return home, she wandered into the Linden Coffee Shoppe in Queen Street, disconcerted to find there were no spare tables, until someone called to her.

It was Rosa, who had a table by the window.

'I'm so pleased to see you,' Lucy Mae said as she joined her friend. 'Are you expecting anyone?'

'No, just filling in time. Charlie is taking me to view the new section of the museum at eleven.'

'What's happening there?'

'I don't know, dinosaurs' toenails or something. He's on the board and has to make a presentation. What are you up to?'

'Oh, everything's happening! Duke telegraphed that he's coming down from Rockhampton. He arrives on Saturday. What am I going to do?'

'Just tell him you don't want to marry him. That's easy.'

'But he thinks I'm having a baby, Rosa.'

'Let him off the hook. Tell him you're not now.'

'I will, of course. But he'll probably be upset. I feel really sorry for him. But I couldn't actually tell him not to come, could I?'

Rosa called a waitress and ordered more coffee, then she looked squarely at Lucy Mae.

'What's this I'm hearing? Are you having second thoughts? Might you marry him after all?'

'Oh heavens, no. Anyway, Rosa, he could have changed his mind. How would I know after all this time? And to make matters worse, Edward Heselwood is with him!'

'Edward!' Rosa was astonished.

'Yes, they'll both be here Saturday. Mother of course is ecstatic! Edward is Lord Heselwood now and she's floating on air. She's already sent Duke to the bottom of the class and is hell bent on achieving the perfect match: Edward and her daughter. She'll have him to the house by hook or by crook! You'll have to come too. You and Charlie. You can rescue me. Be a buffer . . .'

Suddenly Rosa was gathering up her gloves and pushing back her chair, even as the waitress approached with the coffee.

'I'm sorry,' she cried. 'I've just realised I'm late. I really have to rush. Forgive me, Lucy Mae.'

She was digging frantically in her small velvet clutch bag for coins when Lucy Mae reached over to her. 'Don't worry. I'll pay. But are you all right, Rosa? You're not looking at all well.'

'I'm all right, I am. I just have to go. Thank you, Lucy Mae, it was so good to see you. I'm sorry . . .'

She hurried to the door and within seconds had disappeared.

As Lucy Mae stared after her, the waitress put down the tray. 'Do you still want a full pot of coffee, madam?'

'Oh, yes, I suppose so,' Lucy Mae said vaguely, still bewildered by Rosa's sudden exit.

'Your friend will be fine,' the waitress said. 'Happens often.'

'What does?'

'Ladies get attacks of morning sickness in here on hot days.'

'Morning sickness?' Lucy Mae echoed.

'Oh yes. That's plain to see.'

'Is it? Oh! Goodness me!'

Lucy Mae felt a little better then. She'd been concerned that she had offended Rosa somehow. But now she smiled. Rosa was to have a baby! How wonderful for her!

Tears welled up but she brushed them away. She wouldn't allow herself to dwell on that heartbreak any longer.

'Just be happy for someone else, and it will go away,' an inner voice whispered to her.

The coffee was delicious.

Paul was angry again. 'Where's Duke? I can't turn my back on him for a minute!'

His wife looked up at him from her table in the Criterion dining room. 'Kindly keep your voice down. He'll be along shortly. And what's the matter this time?'

'He's taken out mining rights on Mango Hill!'

'Where on Mango Hill?'

'Where do you think? In the foothills beyond the swamp!'

'At the base of Ironstone Mountain? Oh well done! Why didn't we think of that?'

'Because there's no bloody gold there!'

Laura laughed. 'That's what they said about Ironstone.'

'That's not the point! The thing is, it's our property, not his . . .'

'Darling,' she smiled, 'not underground, according to mining law, or so I hear. If someone wants to prospect there, they can.'

'I know that, but he should have consulted me first. At least let me know what he's doing. But that's typical of him, isn't it? Bloody typical! He goes off doing what suits Duke, no matter what cost to others. Where is he now anyway?'

'He'll be here for lunch. He had to go up and check on Harry Merriman's place,' he said. 'He promised Harry he'd keep the block cleared.'

'All right, but he'd better get here soon, or we won't get served. I've never seen this place so busy.'

'Everywhere in town is busy. It's chaos!' She noticed a tall, well-dressed young gentleman making his way through the crowds, and whispered to her husband: 'Is that Edward Heselwood?'

Paul turned, realised that Edward was making for their table, and climbed quickly to his feet.

'I hope I haven't kept you waiting, Mr and Mrs MacNamara,' the newcomer said, 'but I was to meet Duke first and I appear to have lost him.'

Realising that Duke must have invited his friend to join them for lunch . . . without bothering to tell them . . . Paul managed a laugh.

'So have we. But do be seated, Edward. We've been looking forward to meeting you. I'm Paul, and this is my wife Laura.'

'Delighted,' Edward said with a slight bow, and Paul was astonished at how much he resembled his father, now that he had discarded his stockman's gear for the latest fashion, in true Jasin Heselwood style.

'Edward,' Paul said, 'I'm glad you could join us. Laura and I want to extend our most sincere sympathy to you on the sudden loss of your dear father.'

'Thank you. It was a shock, and it must have been a dreadful time for my mother. I'm hoping to make it up to her.'

For a while, he and Paul talked about their young days on neighbouring cattle stations, keeping Laura amused, and then she turned their attention to Edward's more recent activities.

'It seems you and Duke had quite a few adventures along the road.'

'We did indeed, Mrs MacNamara. It was a long, long trek, much harder than I imagined it would be. I had no idea this colony was so huge.'

'Sorry to interrupt,' Paul said to them, 'but don't you think we should order? Lunch goes off here at two.'

'I think we should,' Laura said.

'Oh yes, I would,' Edward grinned. 'Your brother can be a mite tardy at times.'

The lunch party had been Duke's idea, and he had certainly intended to be punctual, but circumstances had delayed him.

He had taken a labourer up to Harry and Tottie's block, checked the cabin to find it still in good order and then given the man instructions to weed and tidy the large garden. But as he was preparing to leave the gardener to his job, he saw his friend Chester Newitt ride up to the house next door.

He gave Chester a whistle and tramped over to the fence.

'What are you up to, you old rascal?' he called.

Chester reined in his horse and dismounted. 'Stone the bloody crows if it ain't you, Duke! I thought you were out west playing boss drover with Harry. When did you get back?'

'A day or so ago.'

'Did you have much trouble with your cattle?'

'No, we got them there eventually. On past Longreach.'

'There's a few miles under your belt then. But what about the blacks? I believe they're hostile out that way.'

'Too right. With good reason, I suppose.'

Chester pushed his hat back on his head and stared. 'Cripes! I never thought I'd hear you give them a fair go. You ailing or somethin'?'

'No,' Duke laughed. 'Just older. I reckon I aged ten years on that bloody trek. It's good to be home.'

'Then come on, I'll buy you a drink and you can tell me the latest.'

'I can't, I have to meet my brother. But what are you doing here?'

Chester held up a For Sale sign. 'Didn't you know? Old Miss Delaney died.'

'I didn't know. I'm sorry to hear that. You're selling the house for them?'

'That's a fact. Jack Delaney's her brother, you know. He wants thirty-five pounds for it. Asking too much, I reckon, but he can afford to wait.'

'I'll take it,' Duke said. 'I love this house; she showed me around a few months back.'

'What do you want it for?'

'I have to have somewhere to live. Paul bought Mango Hill.'

'That's right, so he did. All right, get your horse and we'll go back to my office and do the deal before you change your mind. No time like the present, mate.'

By the time Duke arrived at the Criterion, lunch was over, but all three were chatting amiably in the almost deserted dining room. He apologised, explaining that it had taken longer than he expected to find someone to tidy up Harry and Tottie's garden, but made no mention of his latest acquisition.

To his surprise, Paul didn't seem to mind that he had failed to keep the appointment. In fact he was quite affable; even asking the publican if the cook could rustle up some cold meat and leftovers for his brother. Duke was unaware that when they'd finished lunch, and his brother had still not put in an appearance, Paul had become so annoyed, he'd apologised to Edward.

'It's typical of him,' he complained. 'He's damned unreliable. Always has been!'

'I can't agree with you on that,' Edward said quietly. 'He's reliable when the chips are down. I'm sure Duke won't mention this, so I shall tell you. At one stage, he and I were ambushed by some Aborigines, and I was attacked by two of them. I couldn't shake them off, and to be truthful I was in a panic. Duke had taken off ahead of me. He was safely out of it, probably thinking I was hard on his heels, but when he realised I was not, he came back for me.'

Edward looked squarely at Paul. 'He rode back into the fray, firing his rifle, grabbed the reins of my horse, and dragged me out of there. He didn't have to come back for me and he brushed aside my thanks, and the incident, as if it were too trivial to even mention, but I will always be grateful to him.'

When Duke's meal was brought to the table, he tucked into it with vigour.

'What time does our ship sail tomorrow?' he asked Edward.

'Ten in the morning, on the dot.'

'Why don't we stay over and see them off?' Laura suggested to her husband.

'Good idea,' Paul said, and Duke blinked.

'Righto then. If you like. But now if you two will excuse us, Ned and I have some shopping to do.'

'We do? Since when?' Ned asked.

'Since I came in and saw you all dressed up. I need city clothes too. And a few other things. You can pick them out for me.'

When they'd left, Paul was in a genial mood. 'I enjoyed lunch, Laura, I really did. And it was kind of Edward to tell us that story about Duke. It made me proud, I have to say.'

'Yes. You should write and tell John Pace.'

'I will, I'll do that. Do you know, I think Duke is turning over a new leaf. Has he said anything to you about Lucy Mae? And the baby?'

'No. Except for when he got the telegram from Lucy Mae about his accommodation in Brisbane. He nodded and said, "Good." Taking it for granted.'

'It didn't mention accommodation for Edward?'

'I presume he'll stay on the ship. He's travelling on to Sydney to be with his mother. All the time we were talking to him I wanted to tell him about the horse, but I thought it might embarrass him.'

'He'll find out soon enough. Chester Newitt said Jasin's men took it back to Montone Station. My only worry is for Lucy Mae. I hope Duke does the right thing by her.'

'I'm sure he will. It'll be exciting. I love weddings.'

She didn't add that she hoped the wedding would be in Brisbane, so that she could get about and enjoy herself this time. And she would make sure they weren't staying at the same hotel as the other MacNamaras. She liked John Pace, but couldn't abide his wife.

To white men, these mountains were known as the Great Dividing Range, but in the black man's mindset they were the spine that gripped the eastern coastline right up to the northern tip.

It was when they were travelling through these heavily forested mountains that Wiradji called to her father-in-law that her time had come.

'What can I do to help you?' he cried.

'Kalkadoon women have only kin with them at births,' she smiled, 'and never male kin. So you may take the horses and rest somewhere for a few days. It will be good for you, Father. There is shelter here in that little cave, but I would like the horse blankets for warmth.'

Ladjipiri obeyed her instructions, his heart swelling with excitement. From here, in Darambal country, they were safe. Soon they would begin the last leg of their journey and his beloved wife would cry out in delight when they presented her with Banggu's baby. A gift of homecoming, along with her son's wife and the news that, as soon as he had fulfilled his obligations with her people, he would be returning to his family.

He took the horses that had carried them so far across the vast country, and began dropping down the eastern side of the range until his keen eyesight picked out a small green valley. There, he knew, was good food for the loyal animals and easy pickings for an old man.

With the sun high in the sky, he released the horses, confident that these two, in his care, would never require cruel hobbles. He took the worn saddles and bridles and deposited them under some trees, and searched about the forest for nuts and berries, which he found to be plentiful. He also noted a stream that would provide him with fish later, but now all he wanted to do was to stretch out in the warmth of that sun and sleep awhile.

Though his body was warm, his dreams were cold and frightening. He saw skies in turmoil, and desert winds thick with dust raging across the land, flogging animals that were screaming as they fled. And he was running too, but something was holding him back. He realised his feet were hobbled, and when he fell he saw a warrior leap from the rocks above, his spear raised ready for flight. Then the warrior, his face a fearsome sight, flecked with feathers and white paint, his body dressed in full war paint of white and yellow ochre, seemed to be suspended there against the deep blue sky.

He looked down at his father, as if surprised to see him. But he didn't fall. He remained there until the skies enveloped him and Ladjipiri awoke weeping.

How could he tell the girl, now delivering a child to the earth, that Banggu had gone to his Dreaming?

A choir of birds, all manner of birds, were singing their songs when she took the boy out to see his first dawn, and amid all the joyful clamour, Wiradji stood back and gasped in amazement.

At first the horizon was just a thin arc of light, no hills to disfigure the line. That in itself was a magical sight, but then fire flamed and flared all along the horizon and she clutched the baby to her heart in fear. Never had she seen such a terrifying sight! But soon dawn extinguished those flames and the sun began to rise, a golden sun that threw shafts of light across the flattest country she had ever seen.

She held the boy up to see the sun, and watched as the sky and the earth came into view, sparkling with colour. But that flat country on the far horizon was now blue!

Wiradji rubbed her eyes. How could that be?

All at once the answer came to her. It must be the ocean! Father had said it was mostly blue but could turn grey in storms. She was so entranced with this discovery, that she couldn't bring herself to turn away. Instead she sat on the high ledge to feed her son as she composed little songs to this most important of sunrises, and to her first glimpse of the ocean.

Two days later Ladjipiri was raised from his gloom by her call, a two-note whistle that resembled that of a whip-bird and was known to carry over long distances.

She was ready to move on.

And she had a grandchild for him. That hastened his steps. He took the bridles and headed out over the pasture, whistling to the horses. As they ambled towards him, two horsemen rode out of the forest.

They stopped, squinting at him in the early sunlight, and then galloped at him. The first rider felled him with a lash of his stockwhip.

Both men dismounted.

'Whose horses are they?' he was asked.

Over the years, the Trader had become a past master at dealing with bullying white men, but he had already prepared his answers in the event of a confrontation like this. Blackfellows had no right to own horses.

He cringed. 'Them fellers belonga Mr Merry.'

'Where's he?'

'Camp longa next valley.'

'What are you doing with them?'

'They get loose. This feller track 'em, take 'em allasame back to Mr Merry.'

'He's stealing them, more like it,' the younger of the two men snarled.

'We'll see about that,' the other fellow said. He pulled Ladjipiri to his feet. 'What are their names, Grandpa? If you are rounding them up for Mr Merry, you ought to know their names.'

Ladjipiri was relieved. He had a way out of this trouble.

He turned to the horses. 'That feller, he Yarriman. This feller, him name General.'

The older man frowned. He called to the horses: 'Hey, Yarriman!' and sure enough Trader's horse lifted his head.

Ladjipiri grinned. 'See, Mr Merry's horses.'

'Think you're bloody smart, don't you?' the young fellow snapped, and without warning he drew his pistol and shot Ladjipiri in the leg.

Ladjipiri felt the bone snap and sank to the ground with a sigh.

'What did you do that for?' the other man said. 'Sound carries in these hills. Grab the horses and let's get outa here.'

The four horses galloping away sounded like thunder to him as he lay on the ground, afraid to move, but when all was quiet again, he made the whip-bird call several times, to alert her, and then at intervals directing the girl into the valley.

By late afternoon she had located him, and was almost speechless with shock.

Gently she laid his grandson in his arms while she examined his leg, then she took the baby, wrapped it in a horse blanket, and used the other one as a pillow for the man she called Father.

She was no stranger to gunshot wounds, but this time the bullet had gone through the knee, too complicated a wound for her hands. A different and frightening problem. She ran all the way down to the stream with the billycan that Banggu had given them and brought him back water for his parched mouth. Then, on Father's instructions, she tried to set his leg straight. She cut strips of leather from the saddles which were still under the tree, and used them to bind splints in place.

'I only need to rest for a day or so,' he told her, 'and then I'll be able to walk with the aid of a sturdy stick. So don't worry. It's as well for us to stop a while anyway, for the little one to get used to the world. He surely is a beautiful boy.'

She called him Pintyamu in deference to the sun that rises from the sea, and together they marvelled at the strength in his little hands.

But Ladjipiri was not gaining enough strength to remain upstanding for more than a few minutes without her help, so Wiradji took him on her back closer to the stream, where she set up camp. She was an efficient hunter and kept them well provided with food, and she also brought home a certain clay to pack around the knee in place of the splints.

'I won't be able to walk with that load on my leg,' he complained.

'You're not expected to. It is to keep your leg quiet so the bones can heal. Then in maybe five and five days you will be able to walk.'

He was worried that his knee would take a long time to recover, if at all, but still hoped he would be able to manage to walk somehow. They couldn't stay in these hills for too long. It was dangerous country for a black woman without protection of family.

Even *with* family, he corrected himself. White gunmen had no pity for women and children left defenceless.

Grief at the death of Banggu had him in its clutches for five long days, but then fear for her and for the baby began to emerge as a much stronger emotion. It was time he made a decision.

'You have to go on without me,' he said. 'I will tell you how to get to a safe place.'

Wiradji laughed. 'That ocean is so far away. How can you do that? There is no hurry. We will go on soon enough.'

Ladjipiri was in no doubt that his attackers had been bushrangers, which meant these trails were known to men seeking easy access through the hills. Sitting about here, instead of keeping on the move, Wiradji was vulnerable.

Sooner or later someone would see the smoke of their campfire and come to investigate.

He couldn't protect her, so when that happened there could be only two results. Decent white folk would assist them, or at worst ignore their presence. As for the others? He shook his head.

The woman refused to leave. She was fierce in her determination to remain with him.

'I am a Kalkadoon woman! I can fight! I will stay and watch over you until you are better! What will Banggu say when he hears that I abandoned his father to save my own skin?'

The argument raged for days, until Ladjipiri was becoming so desperate that he almost told her his son had died in battle. But though he had seen it with his own eyes, it would take much to convince her under these circumstances.

In her absences he began summoning the spirits, seeking their advice, willing himself back to that cave again, a place of knowledge, until he was there, sitting awkwardly at the entrance, under the ancient bird with the long beak.

He felt no surprise to be there, looking out from the ledge over the brilliant hill country again. He saw clouds scudding across the massive skies, heard the screeches of black cockatoos before a wave of them passed over, flashing their cherished scarlet plumage, and smelled a whiff of smoke from a bushfire somewhere nearby.

A man emerged from the cave and they talked awhile.

When Wiradji returned to the camp with the baby in a sling over her back, and a dilly bag full of tuber roots and other delicacies, she was surprised to see they had a visitor.

He was a friend of Father's. But much older. And he insisted that Pintyamu was the handsomest baby he'd ever seen.

'There is no need for you to delay any longer,' Ladjipiri told her. 'My friend will stay with me until my leg is strong again. You have a duty to protect this boy. You must take him down to his father's people. You leave tomorrow.'

Wiradji was worried about facing a long, lonely trek over strange lands, but she could not admit fear; according to these two men, she had no alternative. She wished now that she'd refused to leave Banggu. She was sorry she'd listened to him. She missed him so much and she missed the great joy of living with her own proud people.

On her first day travelling through the hills, she took comfort in grumbling; revelling in it; telling the baby what a fool of a woman she had been to let them send her off into this wilderness, and what she would say to Banggu when he came following after her! She was so cross, she covered boulder-strewn slopes as surely and swiftly as the little rock wallabies that danced about her, not giving a fig to the possibility of falling. She kept on until a mist hid her path and she was forced to shelter in the trunk of a big old tree, listening to dingoes howling.

The muffled sounds of animals out there in the darkness unnerved her, and she clung to the baby, afraid to sleep.

But sleep she did, plunged into nightmares that monsters were trying to kill her baby, to snatch him from her. Screaming, she fought them off, over and over again, until they pushed her back and she was falling. But then came the morning light and a hand reached out to her . . .

Banggu was there. He'd caught up with her. She stepped out into the warm sunlight with the baby in her arms, and smiled at her husband. He was so beautiful, so tall and manly, he almost took her breath away.

She could no longer see the great blue ocean, but they began their walk to the east through the strangest forest she had ever seen . . . so lush and green, and full of life. Tiny birds flitted through streams of sunlight and she held the baby up to them, glorying in the warmth of this forest as it took her little family to its heart.

Lucy Mae was in the foyer of the Regency Hotel when Duke walked in. Fortunately, she thanked her stars, he was not accompanied by Edward Heselwood.

As soon as he saw her, he gave a gasp of surprise: 'Lucy Mae!' then plunged across the room to lift her off her feet in a big boisterous hug. 'Look at you!' he cried. 'You're prettier than ever! Truly the best looker in town.'

Lucy Mae was blushing. 'Put me down. People are staring.'

'Sure they are,' he laughed. 'Not every day they see a lady as lovely as you. But how are you? I mean, are you all right?'

Realising she would need privacy, and not the privacy of a bedroom, Lucy Mae had reconnoitred the ground floor of the hotel as soon as she arrived. Now she took him through to a quiet corner of the hotel garden, where Duke immediately moved to kiss her.

'No,' she protested. 'Please. We have to talk.'

'We can talk later,' he murmured.

'No we can't,' she said firmly. 'Now sit down, Duke.'

'The baby,' he whispered, though there was no one within earshot. 'Are you all right with that? I mean, we can get married . . .'

She sighed. 'Duke, listen to me. I'm really sorry. More than sorry. I was extremely upset. I lost the baby. I had a miscarriage.'

'Ah, did you now? What a shame. You'd have been a darling mother.'

He sat by her then, looking nonplussed. Awkward. Clutching a smart panama straw hat that she thought really didn't suit such a big man.

Eventually he found something to say: 'Hard on you, was it, Lucy Mae?'

'Yes.'

'I'm real sorry about losing the baby, but I wouldn't have you upset for the world. Are you feeling better now?'

'Yes thank you.' She shrugged. 'So you see, you don't have to marry me now.'

He blinked. His eyes seemed a much darker blue than she recalled, fringed by those incredibly long dark eyelashes that she'd envied.

'Didn't I ask you to marry me before any talk of a baby? I wanted to marry you, Lucy Mae, baby or no baby. Didn't you know that?'

'Not really. A letter is just words; you could have been having a fit of the lonelies before you went bush. We didn't part on the best of terms, because it was quite evident that you wanted to keep our little affair quiet . . .'

'No I didn't.'

'Duke, it's no use going over that again. No matter what you felt, I felt humiliated. And it was horrible! Thank you for your proposal, I am flattered, but no, I couldn't marry you.'

Having said her piece, Lucy Mae stood. She needed to break away from him now. There was nothing more to be said.

Duke stood too. 'Would it help if I told you I love you? That's not dry old words on paper, Lucy Mae. That's real.'

Lucy Mae's eyes clouded. She had rehearsed this conversation so carefully, and now he was ruining everything. She shook her head.

'Not even if I beg you to forgive me for being such an idiot?'

She studied the grass beneath her feet. Buffalo grass they called it. Good for lawns. Shook her head again.

'Well then at least we can talk,' he said. 'We've got a lot to talk about. Don't you want to hear about my travels? And did you know I sold Mango Hill to Paul?'

She shrugged. 'I have to go.'

'Righto then. I'll walk you out. Have you got the gig?'

'There's no need to walk me to the gig, I have shopping to do first.'

'I'll see you later then.'

'I beg your pardon?'

'At dinner! Your place!'

'What?'

'Your mother sent an invitation to the ship for Ned and me to have dinner at your place tonight.' He laughed. 'You'd better brush up on your piano pieces.'

'So I should,' she retorted. 'My mother thinks he's a better catch than you, Duke MacNamara!'

'She's right. He is at that! But I'll take my chances.'

Lucy Mae walked away, but then something struck her. She looked back at him. 'Ned?'

'That's right!'

As she rounded the corner she found herself laughing. She hadn't laughed in a long while.

When the pair of well-dressed young gentlemen with heavily tanned faces came in the door, Milly had her excitement under control. This dinner party was too important to be spoiled by the slightest hitch. She'd considered inviting several important Brisbanites to witness her social coup, but decided against it. There was no time to waste.

'As soon as they arrive,' she told Lucy Mae, 'you are to take Duke aside and tell him about the miscarriage.'

'I've already told him. I met him in town. The boat was early.'

'Oh well, thank God for that. And did you tell him marriage was out of the question?'

'Yes.'

'Oh. Excellent! That was a stroke of luck.' She looked at Lucy Mae suspiciously. 'Or a scheme of yours? No matter. It's done.'

Edward, who had shocked her by recommending she call him Ned, had brought her a small gift of an unusual china teapot. Nothing from Duke, of course, who, she sniffed, would know no better.

She and Lucy Mae extended their condolences to Edward over the sad loss of his father, and he accepted gracefully. She was glad when that part was over and they could chat in the drawing room, where she was proud to show Edward pictures of Forrest Station on the Darling Downs.

Duke asked Lucy Mae to play the piano, which was a help. She could hardly refuse, and she played well this time, thank God.

In all it was a very pleasant evening. She had seated Lucy Mae in the best light, across from Edward, and they'd had plenty to talk about; his observations of the people and landscape in the far west were most interesting. Duke had his bit to say, about having sold Mango Hill to Paul and bought a house in Rockhampton, which was of no interest to anyone.

Edward was quite impressed by the decor and comfort of the public rooms aboard the new steamship, and invited Lucy Mae to view them on the morrow. An invitation which her daughter accepted! She seemed to find it amusing, for some reason.

But at least she's going, Milly sighed to herself as they rose to take coffee on the veranda.

'The dinner was superb, Mrs Forrest,' her aristocratic guest said. 'I must congratulate you.'

'Especially since we've been living on beef and spuds for months,' Duke had to add, which she thought was quite unnecessary.

When they left, she flopped into her favourite armchair. 'Lucy Mae, bring me a brandy! I'm exhausted!'

Milly's delight at Edward's invitation was so evident that Lucy Mae didn't even try to explain that it was sheer mischief. She was in no doubt that it was a ploy engineered by Duke, and sure enough when Edward came to call for her in a hired open carriage, Duke was driving.

'What's he doing there?' Milly asked angrily, peering at them through a window.

'Driving, I suppose,' Lucy Mae said as she opened the door to Edward.

As he handed her up to the carriage she turned to him with a smile. 'Who invited him?'

'My dear, I couldn't get another driver.' Edward's face broke into a broad grin. 'It's hard to find decent help these days.'

He tapped Duke on the shoulder. 'To the wharves, my good fellow. I thought we might take morning tea on the boat, if that's all right with you, Lucy Mae. My driver wanted to have a word with you. Might I tell him he may join us?'

'If he must, but,' she sighed, dabbing a handkerchief at nonexistent tears, 'I'm horribly disappointed, Edward. I feel quite let down.'

'My apologies, dear lady, but I promise I'll make it up to you when next you come to Sydney. We'll have a grand old time.'

They sat back as Duke drove out of the gate. 'Tell me,' she said in a normal cheerful voice. 'What's this about him buying a house in Rockhampton?'

'I don't know. He's rather inclined to keep his cards close to his chest. What house did you buy in Rockhampton, driver?'

'The white one next to Harry's place,' came the reply.

'Oh, I say! Very nice.'

'Is it really?' Lucy Mae asked.

'A delight,' said Ned. 'I haven't been inside, but it looks very large and airy.'

'With a view?'

'Of course, a view,' he grinned.

'Why would he want a house in Rockhampton?' she asked.

'To live in, one imagines. A sort of headquarters for his business interests.'

'What business interests?' she laughed.

They teased the driver all the way to the ship, and no sooner were all three aboard than the captain came to greet them and assure Lord Heselwood that tea was ready to be served on the rear deck under canvas.

'Pays to have important friends,' Duke grinned as they were escorted to the elegant table.

'It's only set for two,' Lucy Mae observed. 'What a shame, you'll have to go, Duke.'

Edward held up his hand. 'Oh no. I'm so sorry, Lucy Mae, I just remembered I have letters to write. But my driver will take care of you.'

He hurried away and Duke stood looking down at her. 'Blue suits you, Lucy Mae. Am I allowed to sit down?'

'You might as well.'

'Thank you. I just wanted to tell you something. I'd do anything for love of you, Lucy Mae. I really would. So I dearly need you to forgive me. Give me another chance. Could you do that?'

'Maybe.' How could she admit now that she'd lain awake all night thinking about him? Meeting him again yesterday had been an unexpected shock; he was far more attractive than she'd remembered. Their lovemaking had come drifting back to her . . .

'Did you say maybe?' he cried. 'I'm not hearing things, am I?'

'No. I'd better pour. The tea will get cold.'

They talked, honestly, openly, about every little thing, and ate all the sandwiches and cakes on the silver stand. They were still talking when Edward appeared.

'No fisticuffs?'

'No,' Duke said proudly. 'I'm not sure, but I think this beautiful lady might agree to marry me, if I'm lucky.'

Edward bent down and kissed her on the cheek. 'If she does, you will be very fortunate. He's a fine fellow when you get to know him, Lucy Mae. You just have to keep him on a tight rein.'

On the way home, just the two of them this time, with a real driver, Duke suggested they elope, and Lucy Mae gave that some serious thought for a few minutes.

'I couldn't do that, Duke, much as I would like to avoid the fuss. My mother loves weddings, she'd want to organise everything. I have to let her do this. I'm all she's got. She'd be so disappointed if she were left out. Besides, I haven't had time to think yet. Marriage is too important to be decided upon over morning tea. Let's just put it to one side for a little while.'

Duke's heart slumped, but he had remembered Ned's advice, and while they were in Rockhampton they'd gone in search of one of the mineralogists they'd met in Longreach to examine his collection of specimen stones, with a view to purchasing gifts for both Lucy Mae and Lady Heselwood.

Now he took out a small box containing a ring.

'This is for you, Lucy Mae,' he said shyly, fearing rejection was looming.

'Is this an engagement ring, Duke?'

'I'm hoping so. It's a memento of the far west country.'

She looked at the single pink stone in its platinum setting. 'It's lovely, Duke. Thank you. I'll treasure it.'

Milly saw Duke MacNamara kissing her daughter by the front door that afternoon and shrugged, disappointed.

'I might have known.'

The ring did little to raise her spirits. 'What is it?' she asked.

'It's a diamond. The colour is very clear.'

'I've never heard of a pink diamond. It looks like a bit of glass to me!'

Duke sat morosely in his hotel room, trying to solve this impasse with Lucy Mae. He'd always made decisions on the run; he couldn't abide waiting about for Lucy Mae to make up her mind. They had to get on with their lives. He had things to do. He had definitely decided that he'd rather live in town than on a station, and he was sure Lucy Mae would too. From there he could pursue a variety of interests as they came up . . . There was a fortune to be made catching and breaking the wild horses that roamed the bush in their thousands. Then there was his right to prospect for gold on Mango Hill. His exciting treasure hunt. His own gold mine!

Also he had to follow up on the short talk he'd had with Chester Newitt, who was of a mind to bring in a partner. His business as an auctioneer and stock and station agent was growing at a pace, and Duke thought it should be expanded to include residential land sales, which were ready to boom in Rockhampton.

Duke nodded to himself. He rather liked the idea of being a businessman with an office in town. He was daydreaming about coming home after work to his lovely wife in the lovely white house when he was reminded that Chester could easily find himself another partner if he didn't get back to Rockhampton soon.

But he couldn't leave Lucy Mae at this crucial time either.

Maybe he could talk her into coming back with him?

Not a chance!

He pondered the problem, suddenly remembering the family story about his parents, who'd had a real bust-up at one stage. Apparently, according to his mother, Pace had said he would do anything for love of her.

Duke coloured a little at that thought. His father's words had come to him suddenly, when he was courting Lucy Mae down there in the garden, and he'd quoted them.

'I'd do anything for the love of you,' Pace had said.

Dolour had called him on it. 'What would you do for love of me?'

She had always been homesick for Ireland, and she'd been stunned by his answer: 'I'll take you back,' he'd said. 'We'll go back and live in Ireland.'

This from a man who had come to the colonies on the run from the British during the ongoing Troubles, and was still a wanted man in his home country.

That answer won the day! Dolour forgave him whatever it was that had upset her. And they stayed in Australia.

'I can't match that,' Duke shrugged. 'I've no idea what I could do for her, short of jumping off a cliff, which isn't in my nature.'

The morning, though, brought relief. An idea. It shocked him! He had to force himself to take the papers down to the government office building in George Street. He had to be resolute as he stood at the counter and gave the clerk instructions. Paying another six shillings, which he thought was outrageous. He winced as the parchment page was duly signed and stamped.

It was done. No turning back. He took the page and had it framed, choosing a neat gilt frame that looked very smart. Then he had it wrapped.

Lucy Mae was happy to see him. He didn't fail to notice the look of pleasant surprise on her face as she opened the door.

'Am I intruding?' he asked.

'Not at all,' she smiled. 'Come on in.'

'This is for you, Lucy Mae,' he said in a rush, in case he changed his mind.

'What is it?'

'Open it and see.'

Lucy Mae read the careful print several times. 'Mining rights? What does it mean? They're in my name.'

He grinned. 'Exactly what it says. You own the mining rights to a section of Mango Hill over towards Ironstone, which is now overflowing with gold.'

'But what can I do with it?'

'Start digging!' he laughed. 'No, you can employ prospectors. Or me!'

'But do you think there's gold on Mango Hill?'

'There could be. Who knows?'

'Oh Duke,' she said. 'I couldn't accept this. It's too much.'

'Or too little, Lucy Mae. It's yours and it'll be enormous fun finding out what your mines hold.'

'It will be. What a marvellous gift! But you should have registered it in your name. I'll have to change it.'

He was startled. 'To what?' he asked uneasily.

'To both names. Mrs Lucy Mae and Mr Duke MacNamara. How does that sound?'

When Milly came into the parlour, they were kissing again.

On this morning, Sydney Harbour was at its sparkling best. Blue skies and blue seas welcomed the SS *Jindalee* as she sailed proudly through the harbour between deep green shores and secluded bays, sure of her place in the sun.

Edward had kept to himself on this voyage, needing solitude to prepare for the emotional times ahead, but as he stood alone at the ship's rail, the familiar scenery brought waves of nostalgia, and with them hot tears that had to be kept from sight as he stumbled down to his cabin. He felt that he was coming home at last, but too late. He wept for the mistakes of his youth that had kept

430

him from his homeland for so many years, and for a father who was no longer here; who would never know how proud his son had been of him and how desperately sorry he was that he hadn't measured up to Jasin Heselwood's expectations.

As the ship neared Circular Quay, he dabbed water on his face to hide unmanly reddened eyes and stood looking out of the porthole until the wharf neared. He could see his mother, an elegant figure in black, standing quietly behind a small crowd of people who were waiting impatiently for the ship to berth.

Edward checked his black suit, stiff collar and soft black tie in the mirror, took a deep breath, picked up his top hat and made for the upper deck.

When he stepped off the gangway he waved, and hurried towards his mother. That was when Georgina's emotions gave way. She ran towards him and threw herself into his arms in a torrent of tears.

'I'm so sorry, Mother,' he said, his own tears returning, but she managed a smile.

'Oh Edward, darling, you're home. You're home! I'm so happy to see you.'

She was about nineteen years old, a lean, muscular woman with wiry black hair drawn back from a strong, angular face, and she had a baby in a sling across her back. She wore a ragged shirt, dusty dungarees and a fringed shawl, but no boots, the usual mismatch foisted on Aborigine women thrust into the white world.

Despite her odd appearance, she carried herself well, striding steadily towards the three horsemen with a confidence that startled them, though her voice was gentle.

She addressed Paul. 'You maybe boss man here, eh?'

He stared at her, astonished at the serenity in her dark eyes, feeling as if he'd suddenly come upon a benign force.

'What do you want?' he stammered.

'Come find uncle in that place.' She pointed in the direction of the blacks' camp, located near the western boundary of Mango Hill Station. 'Him old fella, allasame call Guringja.'

'Hey! Look out, boss!' called Sam, reaching for his rifle. 'Look over there!'

'Jesus wept!' blurted Noah, the other stockman.

Not more than thirty yards away from them, a huge Aborigine warrior in full ceremonial dress was standing on an elevated rocky ledge. His hair was piled high and decorated with plumes of cockatoo feathers. His coal-black face, with a bone through the nose, was striped with white paint, and tufts of black hair jutted from his jaw. His powerful body was daubed with paint as if outlining the bone structure, and he wore ankle bands of white feathers.

'Steady,' murmured Paul, looking warily at the tall spear the black man had jammed firmly in front of him as if he were throwing down a challenge. He turned to the woman. 'Who's he?'

'That my husbin,' she said proudly, her eyes glistening. 'He brung me here. For safe.'

Paul frowned. None of the blacks on this property were hostile, and they certainly did not march about got up like this fellow. Their war days were long gone.

'You go,' he said to her. 'I don't want either of you here. You don't belong with our mob. Go back to your own mob and take him with you.' He jerked his head at the husband.

The woman drew an arc in the dust with her toe, and studied it for a few minutes as if deciding what to do.

Sam patted his rifle. 'Do you want me to show the big feller the gate, boss?'

The woman looked at Paul. 'My husbin he go way now. He bring me long walk.'

'Good. You go with him. You can't stay here.'

She seemed not to have heard him. She hitched the baby higher and began to walk up the track towards the homestead.

Paul gazed uncertainly at the husband, who was watching them, and then back at the woman.

'Whoa!' he called. 'Come back here. I told you. You don't belong here. What mob are you?'

'Kalkadoon!' she said, head high.

'Never heard of them!'

'Yes you have,' Noah reminded him. 'They're the mob Duke talked about. They hail from the back country. Plenty trouble too. Do you reckon they're coming this way now?

'What? An army of two? Turn it up!' Paul called after the woman: 'You come back now. You and your husband, out! Do you hear me?'

She turned back and looked up at him, tears welling on to her grimy cheeks. 'He gone, boss.'

Her grief confused Paul. His horse reared suddenly, spooking the other mounts and causing them to back away, bumping into one another. As he dragged at the reins to keep his horse in check, he saw old Guringja wobbling down the track with the aid of a stout stick and his two wives.

'The big bloke's disappeared,' Sam said, pulling his mount into line. 'I'd better go and round him up.'

'He gone,' the woman insisted.

She ran towards Guringja, babbling in her own language.

'What's she saying, Sadie?' Paul asked one of Guringja's wives.

Sadie shrugged. 'Doan know that talk.'

Eventually Guringja explained. 'She Kalkadoon. Her name Wiradji. My mamma Kalkadoon so she kin of me. Big trouble where she comen from so she come here for safe with babba.'

'What about her husband?' Paul asked. 'I'm not having him here.'

Guringja's eyes seemed to flatten. 'No husbin, boss.'

'Don't give me that! He's lurking over there somewhere. She knows he's here.'

'Ah! Dat no one, boss. No one.'

'She said he was her husband,' Sam growled at him. 'I heard her.'

Paul turned to Sadie. 'You saw him when you were walking down here, didn't you? You must have . . .'

She shook her head and trudged over to the woman. 'Where your husbin?'

'He gone,' Wiradji replied sadly.

'Gone where?' Paul demanded, but Guringja grabbed Sadie's arm. He whispered something to her and the men saw her dark face blanch.

'Mr Paul,' she said quietly, 'better we take her longa camp, eh?'

'Not until I know where her husband's got to! I won't have him hanging about.'

Sadie sighed and walked over to Paul. She patted his horse gently and spoke so softly he had to lean down to hear her.

'No husbin here. Him fight big war. Got killt dead. She still makin' crying time.'

'What? Bloody rubbish! He was here! We saw him!'

Sadie lowered her eyes and scratched the back of her neck, obviously anxious not to discuss this any further.

Inadvertently Paul scratched the back of his own neck, maybe for the same reason. The hairs there felt like needles, and a shudder ran through him. For a minute he was at a complete loss to decide what to do.

Noah sifted uneasily in his saddle. 'Are they trying to tell us that blackfeller wasn't there?'

'No,' Paul said. 'It's just their usual double talk.'

'Where has he gone anyway?'

'I don't know!' Paul said crankily. 'He's just gone. Let me know if you spot him again.'

He nodded to the little group of Aborigines. 'Go on then. Take her up to your camp. She looks as if she needs a good feed.'

As the three horsemen rode away, Sam laughed. 'If Noah ever sights that husband feller again, you won't see him for dust!'

'What about you?' Paul asked.

Sam shrugged. 'Me? I never saw no one.'

Later that afternoon, Guringja and the strange black woman came up to the stables looking for the boss.

'What do you want now?' Paul asked.

'Dis woman here,' the old man said, 'she want help. Me, I tell her I too old, but this big boss, he help.'

'Help to do what?'

Guringja jerked his head at Paul, to indicate a private meeting was required, so Paul marched over to him. 'I said she could stay. Now what does she want?'

The old man lifted a gnarled finger and pointed at her. 'Her husbin, he son of Ladjipiri!'

'What? The warrior fellow who was here?'

'Son of Ladjipiri,' Guringja repeated.

Astonished, Paul stared at her. 'Who? Banggu? She is the wife of Banggu?'

The woman pulled her shawl over her head and hid her face as the old man tapped Paul on the shoulder, shaking his head, finger to his lips. 'No say name, boss. No say name. Bad joss.'

Paul's head was reeling as he tried to grasp the situation. The sun seemed to blind him at the same time. He pulled his hat down hard over his eyes. He had seen the man! Three of them had seen him. Was it Banggu? You wouldn't know behind all that war paint.

The general consensus had been that Banggu had headed far west to escape the police because he had visited that country previously with his father. So it could be that he'd gone out there and married this Kalkadoon woman. And now he was bringing her and the child home to his kin.

But if the name could not be spoken, that meant he was dead.

'Jesus!'

'She want us help Banggu's daddy,' Guringja whispered.

'Now it's us. She wants *you* to help him.'

'Boss, her daddy by marriage, he Ladjipiri your own fren'. She say Ladjipiri die soon.'

Paul strode over to her. 'Ladjipiri sick?'

She nodded. Pointed to her leg. 'Broke.'

'Where is he?'

She pointed west. 'Big hills. You git him, eh?'

He took them both up to the kitchen. Laura gave them tea while he struggled to get this woman, who was nervous of pencil and paper, to show him where the Trader was located.

'Bad fella take Yarramin,' she announced at one stage.

'That was Ladjipiri's horse,' Laura cried. 'Did you and Ladjipiri have horses?'

It was eventually established that they had been riding towards the coast when Trader was shot and their horses stolen.

'That solves your problem,' Laura said to Paul. 'She can ride. Give her a horse and let her lead you to him.'

'She know,' Guringja said, obviously relieved that this burden was about to be lifted from his ancient shoulders.

The next day Paul and Sam set off with the Kalkadoon woman, who insisted on bringing her baby along, and a spare horse. They eventually found Ladjipiri after a three-day ride, which was not the most pleasant, given that they were certain she had no idea where to find her father-in-law. But find him she did, and the journey home was a triumph for all concerned.

Word spread through the Aborigine community that Ladjipiri, his daughter-in-law, a Kalkadoon woman, and his grandson were lodged at Mango Hill Station while he recovered from his injuries. Soon a line of relatives and friends were trooping across Mango Hill to visit the man who had many new stories to add to family lore. Some folk claimed they saw Banggu standing guard on the hillside at sunset the night his father was brought in, and so he entered the Dreamtime as a warrior spirit who had come to rest at this place.

END NOTES

Brisbane Courier, 13 July 1882
Gold was found in the Mt Morgan (Ironstone Mountain) area and a claim was pegged out.
Four years later the Mount Morgan Gold Mining Company was formed with the issue of one million shares of £1 each. By 1889, the mine was paying dividends of £100,000 a month.

Brisbane Courier, 24 January 1883
Aborigines ambushed and murdered Marcus de la Poer Beresford, officer in charge of the native police at Cloncurry, and four of his policemen.
Battles between European and Aborigines continued for more than a year. Finally two hundred Kalkadoon tribesmen took a stand. They issued a challenge to the white men, police, pastoralists and miners, to come out to the hills and fight.

Brisbane Courier, September 1884
At Prospector's Creek, north-west of Cloncurry, a contingent of police and native police commanded by Sub-Inspector F.C. Urquahart made a punitive attack against the Kalkadoon Aborigines. Most of the Kalkadoon tribesmen were killed.
The area has since become known as Battle Mountain, where Stone Age weapons took on guns.
The last known Kalkadoon survivor died in Cloncurry in 1930.